**AGAINST THE BACKDROP OF THIS EPIC PANORAMA,** YOU'LL MEET A GALAXY OF MEMORABLE CHARACTERS...

## THE CAPTAINS

*Miles Parbury*, blinded in the Civil War, designer of a vessel he can know, but never see...

*Hosea Drew*, accused by some of treachery, yet fiercely loyal to a dead man's memory...

*Cato Woodley*, young and headstrong; he bought his title and thinks he can only earn it by racing to victory...

## THE WOMEN

*Dorcas Archer*, expelled by her God-fearing family, who, for Fernand's sake prefers to be a "scarlet woman"...

*Josephine Var*, in public a trained nurse, in secret the priestess of a dark religion...

*Louise Moyne Gattry*, thinking to escape insensitive parents, she fell victim to an even crueller husband...

*Eulalie Lamenthe*, heir to powers considered magical— powers that might lead to the sacrificing of her son...

...AND MORE

## THE OWNERS

*Langston Barber*, the upstart gambler who was hiding a guilty secret...

*Hamish Gordon*, mystery financier, risking other people's money on his grandest speculation...

*Matthew Rust*, his secretary, innocent and virginal at nineteen, yet capable of plotting blackmail...


## THE PILOTS

*Ketch Tyburn*, fat, bald, and wheezy, determined nonetheless to break some records before he quits the river...

*Dermot Hogan*, brilliant but superstitious, afraid to travel with a gray mare, a preacher, or a pregnant woman...

*Fernand Lamenthe*, the Creole, cast out by his relations, making his way in the world against all odds...

~~~~~~

## THE PASSENGERS

*Joel Siskin*, failed "gentleman of letters," desperate to make his mark at least as a reporter...

*Denis Cherouen*, the "Electric Doctor," bigoted, drunken, greedy for fame...

*Gaston d'Aurade*, would-be composer, staking everything on his flight from an artistic wasteland...

## AND, THE ONE MAN ON WHOM EVERYONE'S DESTINY DEPENDED...

*Caesar Predulac*, the ex-slave who can't even call his name his own...

# THE GREAT STEAMBOAT RACE

# THE GREAT STEAMBOAT RACE

## JOHN BRUNNER

BALLANTINE BOOKS · NEW YORK

John Brown's Body by Stephen Vincent Benét
From: THE SELECTED WORKS OF STEPHEN VINCENT BENÉT
Holt, Rinehart & Winston, Inc.
Copyright renewed 1955, 1956 by Rosemary Carr Benét
Reprinted by permission of Brandt & Brandt Literary Agents, Inc.

Library of Congress Catalog Card Number: 82-90222
ISBN: 0-345-25853-3

Manufactured in the United States of America

First Edition: February 1983
10 9 8 7 6 5 4 3 2 1

TO MALCOLM REISS
1905–1975
an admirable editor
an outstanding agent
and the person I most hoped
would enjoy this book

# AUTHOR'S PREFACE

*Late in June 1870 the following advertisement appeared repeatedly in the New Orleans press:*

A CARD TO THE PUBLIC

Being satisfied that the Steamer Natchez has a reputation of being fast, I take this method of informing the public that the report that the Natchez, leaving here next Thursday, 30th inst. intended racing, is not true. All passengers and shippers can rest assured that the Natchez will not race with any boat that may leave here on the same day with her. All business intrusted to my care, either in freight or passengers, will have the best attention.

T. P. Leathers
Master, Steamer Natchez

*And did it?*

*Did it, hell!*

—J. K. H. B.

# CONTENTS

*Concerning*
*Str.* ATCHAFALAYA,
*fifth of her name,*
*built 1866 at New Albany, Indiana,*
*and jointly owned by Hosea Drew and Langston Barber*

Length: 285′5″          Breadth: 48′
Chimney height: 95′     Draft under load: appx. 9′
Boilers: 8              Engines: 2
Cylinder diameter: 3′4″  Wheel diameter: 38′
Stroke: 10′             Buckets: 16′9″ x 2′2″
Steam pressure: 110 psi  Freight capacity: 1420 tons

Master          Captain Hosea DREW
Pilots          William TYBURN,
                Fernand LAMENTHE
Clerks          Euclid MOTLEY, Roger WILLS,
                David GRANT
Engineers       Hendrik FONCK, Patrick O'DOWD
                James EALING, Walter PRESSLIE
Carpenter       Josh DIAMOND
Mates           Thomas CHALKER, Jack SEXTON
Watchman        Eli GROSS
Caterer         Ernest VEHM
Steward         Lewis AMBOY

Cabin crew (including waiters, servants and cooks): 25
Deck crew (including firemen): 65

*Making all told a complement of 106*

*Concerning*
*Str. NONPAREIL,*
*third of her name,*
*built 1869 — 70 at Cincinnati, Ohio,*
*to the design of Miles Parbury but at the charge of Hamish Gordon*

---

Length: 303′        Breadth: 42′6″

Chimney height: 97′6″    Draft under load: appx. 9′6″

Boilers: 8        Engines: 2

Cylinder diameter: 2′10″    Wheel diameter: 42′11″

Stroke: 10′        Buckets: 15′8″ x 2′2″

Steam pressure: 160 psi    Freight capacity: 1510 tons


Master            Captain Cato WOODLEY

Pilots            Dermot HOGAN, Colin TRUMBULL,
                 Zeke BARFOOT, Joe SMITH, Tom TACY

Clerks            Ian McNAB, Sam ILIFF

"Mud clerk"        Anthony CROSSALL

Engineers         Peter CORKRAN, Brian ROY, Victor
                 STEEPLES, Caesar PREDULAC

Carpenter         Hiram BURGE

Mates            Solomon UNDERWOOD, Harry WHITWORTH

Caterer           Hans KATZMANN

Steward           Mortality BATES

Bandmaster        Manuel CAMPOS


Cabin crew (including waiters, servants and cooks): 26

Deck crew (including firemen): 69

*Making all told a complement of 114*

# THE
# GREAT
# STEAMBOAT
# RACE

## 18TH JUNE 1870

# THAT SETTLES IT

"It so happened that twenty-six years before . . . a boat named the *J.M. White* had broken all previous records in a fast run to St. Louis, making the trip in three days, twenty-three hours and nine minutes."

—Roy L. Barkhau,
*The Great Steamboat Race Between the Natchez and the Rob't E. Lee*

 Around the headland that is called Algiers the Mississippi describes the majestic curve that gave to New Orleans its ekename of The Crescent City. Doubtless the Sieur de Bienville chose the site so that unfriendly ships approaching from the ocean would be forced to put about in range of defending guns.

Into this sweeping bend on 18th June of 1870 there stormed the crack Atlantic liner *Franche-Comté*, out of Cherbourg on her normal route but with her best time bettered on this voyage by seven hours. And with her steam-siren howling at full blast, she scattered lesser traffic regardless of rule and custom: ferryboats and lighters and tugboats, paddlewheelers in the coasting trades doomed by this encounter to be overdue at Mobile or Brashear City, and excursion boats whose Sunday sightseers were thrilled to have this dividend of excitement declared on their invested nickels.

A lean smart keen-prowed launch was standing to, steam up but idling, abreast the wharf at the foot of Congress Street. The *Franche-Comté* was still at English Turn when her screams became audible to the launch's crew. Immediately they jumped to stations and she hurried off downriver at high speed. Seeing this, knowledgeable onlookers confided, "That French ship is surely due for trouble! There goes the Harbor Guard set to arrest her!"

Instead, the launch confounded them and rode postilion for the liner, clearing her path with government approval and adding a shriller whistle to the siren's row.

The noise attracted more and ever more people to the levees, to the hurricane decks of moored steamers, to the windows of riverside warehouses. Questions were hurled that even men who had worked on the river all their lives were forced to parry. Perplexed, observers by the thousand struggled to make sense of what they saw.

The heat was dreadful, and the air so humid that one could envisage taking a handful of it and twisting it until it shed water as plentifully as a dishcloth.

Not muffled, for it kept its loudness, but diffused in the dense hot air like a light viewed through a misted pane, the sound of the liner's onrush became detectable beyond Algiers, along the levee by the foot of Market Street.

There a boat lay moored that had no business to be in New Orleans. Literally. She had been advertised for Louisville on Thursday last, and her clerks had been put to improbable shifts by the cancellation of her scheduled trip. Not only were many of her intending passengers incensed at having to make alternative arrangements; urgent cargo had had to be transferred, in several cases at a loss.

3

Had she been a more ordinary vessel, simple explanations would have sprung to mind: the captain might be in dispute with his partners, or neglect of maintenance might have rendered her boilers so dangerous that the Cincinnati Board of Underwriters had refused the risk.

But this was the sidewheeler *Atchafalaya*, fifth of her name, the standard against which since 1866 other Mississippi steamboats must be measured. Grudgingly it had become the accepted view that here was the great steamer of her day. Some of her rivals were faster, but they were not so reliable; some were larger, but they were also slower; some were more luxurious, but they carried far less freight. One day the *Atchafalaya* would surely be outdone. For the moment—

For the moment she looked as though a hurricane had hit her. Since her return from Louisville on Tuesday, carpenters had attacked her like an army of termites. Every bit of superstructure not essential to her running had been dismantled; even the glazing had been ripped from her cabin so that the wind might whistle past the fretted ornaments, over the bright expensive Brussels carpet. Glass had been left only where it was indispensable, in the pilothouse. As much of the housings that covered her huge wheels had been removed as was consistent with protecting the main deck from splash and spray. And out of sight below they had sawn through some of her stanchions; it was held that a limber boat was a faster boat.

Additionally she had taken on pine knots by the ton load: resinous, hot-burning, and expensive.

Surely she must be being prepared for a race!

But against which other steamer? Candidate after candidate was considered and rejected. And when the field was narrowed down to one, the *Nonpareil*, there remained two baffling problems.

Quite possibly the *Nonpareil* was capable of running out the older boat. She had already set several records in the lower Mississippi. But according to this morning's telegraph messages she was at Cairo, southbound with a cargo from St. Louis.

And what was worse, the captain of the *Atchafalaya* was "Old Poetical" Hosea Drew. A man who never, never raced his boats.

Though he could handle them. Oh, yes! Not a few of his colleagues harbored resentment against him, a legacy of the war, but even his sworn enemies would not deny that Hosea Drew could match the best.

Then the *Franche-Comté* came bellowing upriver, and there was no more need for guesswork.

The liner was here too soon. Sooner than most people had been willing to bet. A few morbid souls had thought to make a sweepstakes on her time, but none had guessed that she would cut her own record by such a giant margin.

Taken by surprise, yet prompt upon the siren's signal—which had been agreed by transatlantic cable—the *Atchafalaya* cast loose in a grand flurry of shorebound roustabouts and workmen struggling to retrieve their tools. Her smokestacks uttered local thunderclouds.

Every eye was upon her as she stood out from shore . . . and headed in the wrong direction. Downriver. Downtown. Meanwhile frantic deckhands slung hawsers on her larboard side and to them tied thick fenders of hemp and coconut-fiber.

This was an unheard-of way to start a race. What in creation could Hosea Drew be at?

In the short Gretna reach she swung about with an easy grace and for a minute or two hovered bow-on to the current, wheels turning just enough to counteract it. Some watchers who had never been uptown farther than Canal enjoyed their first sight of this famous steamer named for a bay and river to the west of their city. On a dead slow bell she waited for the *Franche-Comté*.

Which came, tailing the launch, headlong around the Gouldsborough Bend.

The *Atchafalaya* went slow astern and aligned herself on the same course as the liner, then switched to half-ahead.

At this, the whistling from the launch took on a note of panic. Her commander was a mere lieutenant, and very young.

But since Head of Passes the *Franche-Comté* had been in the charge of a Louisiana pilot, the most experienced who could be found. He sensed what Drew intended, and exploited the steam-siren to utter such a vocabulary of wordless insult that the launch herself appeared to get the drift, and took it, sliding to larboard as the liner and the steamer closed. It was reported subsequently that the lieutenant had the decency to blush when he saw what he had come so near to preventing: a feat that rivermen were to talk of for a generation.

A great silence was falling along the banks and on the decks of all the ships in sight of this meeting. To any but the most informed observer it seemed certain there must be a collision.

Yet there was not.

The *Atchafalaya* took a sheer from the bow wave of the liner. In the same second Drew gave orders: full ahead! He could just be discerned in his pilot-house, wearing—as ever—a coat of defiant blue. His hair and beard had turned to gray the year the war broke out, and there were those who said that was only fair compensation.

Meantime, inappropriately clad in a thick frieze jacket, black trousers, heavy laced boots and a tall hat, a plump man emerged on the liner's deck clutching a leather bag attached to his right wrist by a chain. He was followed by a muscular sailor who carried a weighty portmanteau. Almost in step they advanced toward the starboard rail.

The vessels slid together and briefly touched. Some paint was scraped despite the fenders; some creaking was heard from the paddlewheeler's guards. And then they drew apart.

The plump man was aboard the *Atchafalaya*, supported by the arms of two strong blacks; a third caught the portmanteau. And the *Atchafalaya* was running as had the *Franche-Comté*, her whistle blasting likewise.

(Before the day was out eyewitnesses were already recounting in awed tones, "He did it without making fast a line!")

Admittedly the tall hat blew overside . . . but no matter. The important passenger was on his way to St. Louis, with his precious bag intact.

The liner, like an exhausted greyhound, lay back into the care of tugs to moor
at her normal landing. Her passengers and deckhands were uttering cheers. Unaware that there was a better reason to applaud than to express thanks for a
memorable spectacle, the many onlookers joined in.

Among them a handful knew the identity of the important passenger. One was
a young reporter who enjoyed access to certain information transmitted by the
oceanic cable. He had watched the drama with one hand upholding an old-fashioned brass-cased telescope, the other scribbling notes.

Beside him, wielding expensive new binocular field glasses, stood his cousin,
two years his junior but, since childhood, his best friend, who had returned the
year before from France . . . as it happened, aboard the *Franche-Comté* on her
maiden voyage. Now he said, "You think the physic will arrive in time?"

For the plump man was Dr. Émile Larzenac, colleague and rival of Pasteur,
and at St. Louis there lay abed two children with a wasting sickness, son and
daughter of the man reputed richest in the city. Speaking of their mother, the
reporter answered, "Well, Mrs. Grammont would rather trust in Drew than
railroads."

"So that implies she's bound to beat the *White!*"

His mind more preoccupied by the late conflict between the blue and the gray,
the reporter looked blank for a moment, then made connection with the legendary steamer whose time from New Orleans to St. Louis had stood unsurpassed for
a quarter of a century.

Sighing, he said, "I guess you're right. She'll take the horns."

"Don't look so glum about it," said his cousin. "It's all news, *n'est-ce pas?* You
must be grateful for whatever sells more copies of your paper."

By now the *Atchafalaya* was approaching the Jackson Avenue ferry and very
shortly would be out of sight. It was a fine beginning to a high-speed run. Yet, as
he followed the boat with his field glasses, his face fell.

"As to glum," said the reporter, "you should be cheerfuller yourself. You must
have won the sweepstakes on the liner because no one else expected her to be
more than three hours under her best time."

"But if I did, I've backed the *Atchafalaya* with my winnings."

"Oh! Have you now? To do what—break the record to St. Louis?"

"Naturally."

Looking lugubrious, the reporter chided, "One day you'll find a better use to
put your money too. . . . But we just agreed, or I thought we did, that here again
you're on a won bet. So long as she doesn't burst her boilers, she—"

"Did you hear a gun yet? I didn't!"

"Ah!" said the reporter with a nod. It was customary to fire a shot and mark the
official instant from which the beginning of a run could be timed. So far, none had
rung out from the ornamental brass cannon on the stem of the *Atchafalaya*.

"Is Drew going to spoil it all?" said his cousin pettishly. "Wouldn't that be like
him, *just?*" Lowering his glasses, he drew a watch from his fob pocket. Gold-

cased, it was made by one of the finest Parisian horologists and kept near-chronometer time. Consulting it, he went on, "I'll never understand how a man like him who simply doesn't groove came to be partners with a sport like Langston Barber—"

*Bang.*

He almost dropped his watch in the act of snatching up the binoculars again. A puff of smoke was still visible in the air above the steamer's foredeck when he got them focused, but a moment later it was dispersed in the raging draught of her eight vast boilers.

"Square abreast St. Mary's Market!" he cried, marveling. "The perfect place! That must be Barber's doing—can't be Drew's! I'll take the time off all the clocks in sight. Write it down, will you? There's always argument about how right a watch is, even one as good as mine."

Forbearing to comment, the reporter obediently listed half a dozen times that coincided to within a couple of minutes.

"That settles it," his cousin said with glee. "There's bound to be a race. And such a race, *mon vieux*, as never yet enlivened the monotony of what you're pleased to call the Father of Waters. The *Atchafalaya* is off to collect the horns of the *White*, so she will also acquire the *Princess*'s and the *Shotwell*'s. What force on earth or in heaven will stop Miles Parbury from coveting a bunch of trophies like that? *And* Drew's trespassing in his regular trade!"

"I can think of one thing that might stand in his way," said the reporter dryly.

"Oh!" —with a dismissive wave. "You know whose tune Cato Woodley dances to—who better? So does our mysterious Hamish Gordon, for all he conjured up the funds to build the new boat. She is very fast, you know: the *Nonpareil*."

"Yes, very fast," said the reporter, and slapped his telescope shut with a plunging noise before returning it to the tubular leather case that hung at his belt. The *Atchafalaya* was already into Greenville Bend.

# 30TH APRIL 1863

# THE DEATH OF
# THE *NONPAREIL*

~~~~~~

"To a white officer who counseled
magnanimity toward the rebels, one
Negro soldier explained:

"'O lieutenant! its very well for you
to talk; you can afford to: you haven't
got anything partic'lar against them
folks. Your back ain't cut up as mine
is. You ain't heard screamin' wimmin,
and seen the blood run out at every
lick, just 'cause a woman wouldn't
leave her husband and sleep with the
overseer. They never done you such
things; but I could kill 'em easy,—
children, wimmin, and all.'"

—John W. Blassingame,
*Black New Orleans*

 This amazing Mississippi!—huge, brown-green, sluggish yet fretful, more akin to organism and process than to a mere feature in landscape, not just because of its length and its width and its changeability, but because of its power over people . . .

Gazing at it, Captain Miles Parbury often found hovering in his mind a heathen sense of sympathy for savages who worshiped trees and storms. This river of rivers (and in his mind the *of* struck echoes: Song of Songs, King of Kings!), this colossal snake like the one which—so said Lyceum lecturers—the ancient Norse had pictured as engirdling the world, exhibited caprice. It was infinitely easy to mistake that for malice. Seeing a town stranded when the river took a notion to create a cutoff—a town that perhaps you yourself had godfathered by carrying its citizens-to-be upstream and bringing the saws and axes, the planes and hammers and nails they needed to erect their home, amputated suddenly from the commerce it relied on and becoming gangrened—or meeting it when it drifted toward you piece by piece, here scraps of flotsam which could be fended off by deckhands wielding poles, there an entire cabin which obliged oncoming steamers to run aground until the danger was past and the channel clear . . . that was what made the river's intolerance of humans credible.

And who should sense it more keenly than Miles Joseph Parbury?

His family had been better off than their neighbors. Without being rich, they were "comfortable." They had their own landing stage where steamers called with provisions like tea and coffee and necessaries such as cloth and gunpowder, while their frame house boasted a second storey that was more than just an attic. Additionally they could afford a hired hand.

But not a slave. Too risky an investment.

With such advantages, it was natural they should talk in terms of sending their youngest son Miles away to school, instead of being educated by his parents and the circuit minister.

From infancy, however, the boy stammered—a sign that his gifts were not preacherly. He grew tall and beanpole-lean. At twelve he overtopped his father, and though there was little muscle on his frame he had skills enough to help in the building of a barn designed to hold a full year's crops.

And at fourteen he had awakened from dismal exhausted slumber following a night of storms and watched it, containing all they had contrived to store, float off in an unfamiliar waste, disgustingly flat, with the repulsive sheen of a new-flayed hide. They were luckier than some nearby families; their house was on ground just high enough not to wash away. Nonetheless much hunger followed the flooding, and his father took to drink and blasphemy.

Therefore at fifteen Miles ran away and rode a timber raft to New Orleans, head full of adolescent dreams about his (middle) namesake. Success proved elu-

11

sive; however, he was intelligent, and the fact that his beard was growing early enabled him to pass for older than his age. He found jobs along the waterfront, and lived frugally, and after a couple of years went home with riches in his poke— a hundred dollars scrimped by nickels at a time.

Only on his return there was no sign of the wooden stage he had so often helped to mend after high water, nor of the house beyond. Nothing was to be found but level mud and the river following a different course, and he could get no word of his kin from the neighbors, save a grudging rumor that most likely they had drowned.

He cursed awhile, and when he ran out of objurgations he set his lantern jaw and went to sign on as a pilot's cub, for of all the people he had met or heard of none but the steamboat pilots tamed the Mississippi. It was precarious, like taming lions; still, it was the best there was.

Since then he had weathered countless setbacks while working his way up to sole ownership of one of the finest boats on the river. Yet he had never felt such a sense of menace as today.

The water posed no extraordinary threat. It was normal that the swollen current should undercut the banks and turn loose trees to sink or swim. If they swam they could smash the buckets off a steamer's wheel; if they sank they became snags or sawyers, according to whether they lay up- or downstream, and could open a hull like a knife spilling the guts of a butchered hog. True, they were more numerous this year than he had ever known them, but that was because since the outbreak of war snagboats had been treated as military targets. Those that had not been sent to the bottom had been withdrawn.

Having become a master pilot before achieving captaincy of his own boat, Parbury was skilled enough to read the ripple written on the surface by a shoal or a bar or the embryo of a towhead, yet not too proud to learn what had been forced on him the past couple of years, new inscriptions due to sunken barges which towboats had abandoned.

Not to mention casualties of war. Their traces were likewise novel.

Until now, however, he had never realized how much he owed to "Uncle Sam's toothpullers," which had been drawing the worst of the river's fangs since long before he set foot in a pilothouse.

Silently he offered thanks for the eyesight which had remained keen enough to let him locate the deep channel in all this waste of water without spectacles, even. Most of his friends and colleagues, including many younger than himself, were obliged to resort constantly to telescopes.

Friends . . . ?

His mind wandered, in a fashion he would never tolerate were a steamboat to act that way. Among those he had called friends were several he would not see again until the war was over, and among those there were a handful he would not wish to meet, whichever way the Lord decreed that victory should smile, for they had taken the opposing side.

Or, worst of all, as though they could usurp the status reserved by the Creator for natural, impersonal forces—like this river: neither side.

Creeping up on him unbidden, that thought focused the bitter truth about the special nature of this voyage. It was foolish to imagine that the river might be an enemy. He had succumbed to that idea for a while, forgivably; years of experience had taught him better. *Enemy* was a way of saying *human*.

Only another person could make plans to kill you.

The Mississippi, then—so Miles Parbury had concluded after countless hours alone in pilothouses like this one, standing a routine watch with the leather bench behind him innocent of pilots "looking at the river," his knowledge of the world confined to what could be discerned through smeared glass, his communication with it limited to the speaking tube on the breastboard, his control over events shrunk to his grip on a wheel so huge it was half concealed even from himself and the curt signals he could issue by tugging the brass knobs on the bell ropes—this river was a *risk* but not a *menace*.

On the other hand . . .

Repulsed four times in his attempt to capture Vicksburg, the Northern general Ulysses Grant had been reported as abandoning his Memphis base and moving down the west bank. Whether he had been instructed to select another target, or whether he planned to cut back and tackle the city from a different direction, was unclear. Either way, Vicksburg needed reinforcements and supplies.

Some of each were carried by the *Nonpareil*, reduced to a shabby parody of her former self. Cotton bales were stacked along her guards and decks: so had often been the case before, but this trip they were not for sale at journey's end. Instead, they were on board because those dense masses of fiber offered cheap and light protection against bullets. The main burden under which her engines labored despite being—to quote her chief engineer Hiram Burge, whom the repetition of this phrase seemed to afford private satisfaction—"overdue" pause "for overhaul," consisted in men wearing gray uniforms, a few with Sharps and most with Springfield rifles, plus their ammunition and a batch of rations. Sacks of cornmeal and rice, sides of bacon, jugs of whiskey and rum reserved (so claimed the manifest) for medicinal use, lay higgledy-piggledy among sealed cartons containing paper money that assured the bearer of specie when the bills were presented at the Bank of the Confederate States of America.

Additionally her sides were hung with the flimsy armor, thanks to which she and other conscript Mississippi steamers had been baptized "tinclads."

There was little in the life of Miles Parbury that he could love. True, he had married—but he came to the wedding naked of relations, while his wife boasted a family large enough to fill the bride-side of the church. A few of his colleagues from the river had to trim the list. True, also, he now had a son, but it would be years yet before there was anything for him to share with young James comparable to what he had shared with his father and brothers.

And sometimes he could not quite work out what had brought him to marry his wife, or her to accept him.

His boat, though: this marvelous creation that could outwit the river-serpent! He had designed this *Nonpareil*—and her predecessor too, but she had not belonged to him; not until she was three years old had she paid off the loans that financed her.

This one, by contrast . . . ! She was *all his*, exclusively and absolutely. Devised by him, invented, made real, and set afloat without a debt to weigh her down. Until . . .

This puzzled him. Often he lay restless into the small hours trying to make sense of that one key decision: to put her at the disposal of the Confederate forces. His attachment to the Southern cause was founded on no love of slavery, for he shared the opinion held by most steamboaters, to the effect that freemen made more economic deckcrew because when they fell sick they could be discharged at no great cost, whereas a slave had to be paid for. No more had any abstract principle of states' rights persuaded him. In strictest truth he did not have a reason, for to him this war was elemental, like the river's abolition of a city. He would as soon have known how to defy such process as a thunderstorm. To be told it was the sum and consequence of countless human choices signified nothing. Reason did not touch Miles Parbury on that level; it had not done so when he was in his teens, nor did it now. He had grown competent enough with words, though he still stammered occasionally, but speech was of secondary importance to him. Mainly, he sensed phenomena. Once, shortly before the war, an acquaintance had invited him to try a newfangled device imported from France, called a velocipede, and bet him a dollar he could not balance on it at his first attempt. He was puzzled that anyone should be so eager to lose money, for to him it was by no means half as difficult as what he took for granted every day of his working life. He could feel a boat's rudder respond to increasing density of silt; that fractional extra resistance sufficed to warn him of changes in the river's flow which other pilots had to learn of by reading the reports posted in their association's "parlor."

Perhaps there were ways of perceiving the world that transcended sight? Often as a boy he had heard the complaints of poultry and barnyard animals when a storm was approaching. Cooped and penned, they could not *see* the darkling sky.

By whatever means, he could tell that even for wartime this was a bad day. There was mist that threatened to grow up and be fog. There was a certain color, a certain drift to the water . . .

A shiver ran down Captain Parbury's spine.

The date was 30th April. The year was 1863. And the *Nonpareil* was laboring upstream at Petit Gulf with a record-breaking load of men and munitions and necessities of war. She had just left astern, to larboard, Waterproof Landing, and to starboard, Zachary Taylor's Old Farm. The next island would be Number 111; the next town, Rodney; while beyond that and a single bend away was Bruinsburg.

A bad day.

Caesar struck—

No. He had more than one name now. He had been forced to adapt the second when he enlisted. Curt, the recruiting sergeant had said that most niggers took the name of the owners they had formerly belonged to. He would not; his memories were too bitter.

Puzzled by the ways of these strangers, the first white men he had met who promised to pay him a wage instead of buying and selling him, but anxious to comply with their demands, he had cast around and eventually said, "How 'bout de place whe' I was bo'ned?"

Hearing even as he spoke how his carefully-articulated English was lapsing back toward his childhood dialect, as always when he was under pressure. But it made small odds. Those who surrounded him were northerners, and one variant of southern speech must sound pretty much like another to their ears.

With relief he heard the supervising officer give his verdict.

"Oh, why not? My family is called after some town in England, I believe! Mark him down the way he wants and let's continue."

There were dozens of other recruits behind Caesar, and a good few of them were black also; this was a time when any manpower was precious.

Pen poised, stifling a sigh, the sergeant said, "Where was it, then?"

Abruptly Caesar was embarrassed all over again, this time in advance of the question he knew to be inevitable.

"At Pré du Lac Plantation—suh."

And, as surely as night after day:

"How in tarnation d'you spell that?"

Caesar had to swallow. "I—uh—I never was to't to write it! But I rec'lec' it's French! Mist'ess wan'ed make it over, call it Lakefield, only mas'er said it wrong to change a name wen' back befo' de Purchase!"

The officer heard him out with a grin half-amused, half-annoyed. Now he repeated, "Lakefield? That settles it. I was about to ask whether the accent was acute or grave! But had it been Près-du-Lac it would have gone over into Lakeside! Write it this way, then!"

He filled out the next line of the roll with careful capitals.

"That's done," the sergeant snapped. "Move on!"

But Caesar lingered.

"May I not see," he ventured, "how it's written?" The crisis past, all of a sudden he spoke the way the lady of the Great House had tried to inculcate.

The officer gave a harsh laugh that turned into a cough. He said, "The simplest way, of course! This is the age when grace and style and all of what they called aristocratic is being washed away, drowned like those clapboard towns they keep founding along the Mississippi and naming after heroes and great cities! And for this catastrophe, this calamity, this disaster, I am to sacrifice my life without an enemy I can hate as much as you hate yours!"

The laugh tried to begin again, failed, had to be stifled in a handkerchief. When it was withdrawn, it showed red.

During that brief time the ex-slave Caesar had the chance to look on a white man as just another human being victimized—like so many people he had known in childhood—by consumption.

Also he memorized his surname and how to write it. Therefore . . .

Caesar Predulac, wearing that name with as much discomfort albeit as much pride as his stained and torn blue uniform, struck blow after weary axe-blow at a fallen tree, chopping kindling wood because he had been ordered to. His personal opinion was that it was too wet to burn; however, he had early learned that in the army too one obeyed superiors without questioning their judgment.

His aim was untidy because he was indescribably tired. His weariness was so extreme, he could have believed that his spirit was about to separate from his body: not to die, but to retreat temporarily elsewhere.

He wanted not to think about that, though. To leave the body? That notion harked back too far in his childhood, all the way to the stinking sheds on the edge of the plantation where he had been taken by his mother, watched her don *bram-bram sonnettes* and close her eyes and stamp around a packed-earth floor while black hands beat on drums made from old barrels . . .

Exhaustion suddenly obliged him to let the axe drop and lean on it a moment. His mother . . . she was dead. He had been twelve when she succumbed to childbed sickness bearing what would have been her fifth daughter, her eighth child, but died likewise. Children . . . he had been married, and had two of his own, probably still alive. He had been seventeen then; now, as near as he had been able to tell the recruiting sergeant, he was twenty-one. Of course, his wedding had been over the broomsticks, but at least it had been a Big Marriage and not a little one, even though it bore no resemblance to weddings at the Great House, with a hundred guests and forty carriages and—

"Chaw?"

The question, a single upturned word, brought him from past to present. He stood among willows on the west bank of the Mississippi. Behind and around were the rest of the gun battery which had accepted him because at the siege of Vicksburg they had suffered terrible losses and—for the moment at least—cared as little about the color of this man named Caesar as about the color of the horses they had commandeered on the way south.

Although he had noticed, with burgeoning anger, that it was always he who had the most menial task. Here he was chopping wood. The rest of the men were about the business of making a bivouac. Two were lighting a fire with the first batch of wood he had delivered; others were searching for anything that might serve as fishing line, in the hope of supplementing their rations with a catfish. Some had suggested going after wild turkey, but Captain Folbert had forbidden it. That would cost powder and shot, and both were reserved for killing people.

His decision proved unpopular, though there was no gainsaying it. They were all at the limit of their resources. They had hastened south along the river bank under orders to act as a kind of tripwire; they had started out as a sketch for a full battery—having the minimum complement of four twelve-pounders—and lost one when a wheel broke which they could not repair, so they had to spike the gun and abandon it, retaining the limber because it held precious ammunition. Tomorrow they would carry on to their designated station at Coles Creek Point. But now darkness was falling, and mist was closing in, so Folbert had made camp and posted sentries.

Free for a little from their traces, the horses moved fitfully within the radius of their tethers, grazing off what grass contrived to find lodging on this impermanent ground. Even they, Caesar told himself silently, are given more chance to rest than I am!

But the word that had disturbed him still hung in the air like the smoke from a gun glaced at when its noise arrives over long distance.

With a start he gathered himself. Extended toward him was a rich-scented plug of tobacco. The hand holding it was white. Long ago and far away white hands had offered him a brown bribe; that had been molasses taffy and the price of acceptance an order to take down his breeches. Nor was that the sole recollection from his childhood which often made him wish he had been assigned to a regiment of the Louisiana Native Guards—officered though they were for the most part by free persons of color who had not scrupled to own slaves themselves. These his companions were, as he had been assured he was also, American citizens. But they could as well have been inhabitants of the moon. They were more alien to the world he had grown up in than the folks at the Great House to the slave families of Pré du Lac Plantation . . .

But that was then and this was now and the person making the offer was Sergeant Tennice, who was rebelling against some strict religious sect Caesar had never heard of that banned liquor and tobacco and even coffee, yet took seriously other principles of the kind about which this war was being fought—to the extent of being courteous to a black recruit.

Muttering reflex thanks, he trimmed a small chaw from the plug with his left-side teeth. Those on the right were in poor shape. Last time the battery was in a settled camp the regimental surgeon had drawn one of them, but now another was starting to ache.

Having given back the tobacco, he waited to savor the first juice, then made to raise the axe again.

Tennice checked him with a gesture.

"Rest a while longer," he advised. "So far they didn't burn the wood you gave them already . . . Say, tell me something, soldier!"

Compared to some of the names he had been called, that title was such an honorific Caesar almost sprang to attention.

"Surely, Sergeant, if I can."

"More than any people of color I so far met, you talk like an educated person. I bet you must have been a house nigger—right?"

"No sir."

"But you can read and cipher!"

"Yes sir."

"Then how come?"

There was a taint of smoke in the air. It had arrived this moment. Caesar had snuffed it, drawn a conclusion, decided the conclusion was mistaken and dismissed it: that, in the space of a dozen heartbeats.

"I was set to work in the sugar mill," he muttered. "They had all kinds of machinery. The overseer was mostly drunk, but someone was 'bliged to keep it going . . . There was books sent with the machines. I figured 'em out. 'Fore that, of course I did have schoolin'. Mist'ess liked to give us Bible lessons, bein' min'ful of the souls of nigger chil'en."

Especially those who shared blood with her own!

That almost slipped under Caesar's guard. Nervous, before he could stop himself he found he was offering Tennice the ingratiating smile which in plantation days would have been necessary to escape a whipping, even though he had privately sworn that when he donned blue army garb he was exchanging it for the last of all such cringing grins.

The sergeant, however, having lost his bet with himself, was paying half a mind to something else.

"Ah, smells like they got the fire to burn at last. On with your axe-work, soldier! Tonight we shall enjoy hot victuals, praise the Lord!"

He was moving away when Caesar caught his arm.

"That smoke—it's not from our cookfire! And *listen!*"

Tennice cocked his head. His mouth grew round. A second later he was striding toward the captain's tent, shouting, while men who had lain down in the hope of a few hours' rest sat up, uttering groans.

Shortly he was back with Captain Folbert, bringing a telescope which the latter seized as he rushed up the one tiny hillock to be found at this spot and swung in the direction of what was by now incontestably the chuffing-popping of a steamboat under load. The wind, such as it was, blew from the south; across the intervening neck of land it carried not only the sound but also the smoky scent which Caesar had been first to recognize.

It wafted the mist this way, too, and in patches that was so dense as to deserve the name of fog.

The telescope still on his eye, Folbert said, "Sergeant, did we not post a sentry on the downriver side?"

"We did, sir," Tennice answered.

"And he hasn't given warning?"

"Not so far, Captain."

"In that case"—lowering the telescope—"next time we pitch camp we'd better hand him an axe and put the colored boy on sentry-go. Advance the guns! Wait on my order, for there's a chance that boat may be one of ours, but if not she'll be a sitting target as she breasts the point!"

 His eyes red-rimmed for lack of sleep, his gray coat open to reveal a dirty flannel undershirt, and his cheeks dark with grime and the need of a shave, Colonel Carradine said, "Shall we be able to run through the night, or shall we be obliged to tie up? It would be a pity now we're so close to Vicksburg."

Captain Parbury started. It had been long and long since, in the pilothouse of a steamer, he had found himself subservient to the orders of another—indeed, not since he ceased to be a cub and proudly accepted responsibility for a thirty-thousand-dollar boat. Almost defensively he kept overlooking that on this voyage he was compelled to share command. Ordinarily the pilot on watch was a supreme authority; even the boat's owners were not entitled to dispute his judgment. Here once again was the sensation that war, like the river, could wash away what one had taken to be fixed.

Resentful of the obligation to put into words what he understood perfectly without them, angry because his stammer—which confidence in his captain's status had almost erased—was apt to come back any moment without warning, he said, "All depends on what the fog does, Colonel."

"It doesn't look too serious right now."

"It surely don't," Parbury agreed with forced patience. "But we have torch-baskets that will lead us through simple darkness. When it comes to fog, though, all you can trust is your wits and your leadsmen."

He glanced at a stanchion beside him. There hung a present from his wife last Christmas: a combined thermometer and barometer on a polished wooden frame. He had thought it frippery at first, having run so many boats up and down the river without such help, but experience had shown it to be useful. He had made a point of saying so. Adèle had been overjoyed. It was the first contribution she had been able to make to that half of his life where she might never enter, only observe.

Carradine mopped his forehead—and small wonder, Parbury thought, for the thermometer was showing eighty-one degrees. The very wheel in his hands seemed to be sweating.

"Is no season on this river free of fog?"

For the moment Parbury had used up his command of words; his last speech had been uncharacteristically long. He contented himself with a headshake, and need not even have made that gesture, for Carradine had leapt to his feet, snatching up field glasses.

"Look there!" he barked, pointing to the headland they were approaching.

For a moment Parbury saw nothing remarkable; then he detected movement, and with an oath reached for his own—seldom-used—binoculars. Through them he made out the silhouette of a field gun being wheeled about, then its horses being backed to slack the traces. Men in crouched attitudes hurried to chock the carriage against recoil.

Automatically his hand sought the rope for the backing bell.

"Not astern!" Carradine snapped, thereby betraying the close attention he had paid to the operation of the boat. "Full ahead! Our best chance is to round the point before those guns are rammed and laid!"

"Guns? I saw one gun, but—"

"Guns! That was a twelve-pounder, and they run in batteries of four at least!" Carradine tensed as a breeze cut a clear line through the mist. "There's number two, but by a miracle she's bogged a wheel. The way her muzzle's canted she'll be there some time. But here comes at least one other, and her limber too— Sergeant! *Sergeant!*"

Rushing to the pilothouse door, he bellowed in a voice to overcome the roar of the chimney-draught and the heave-and-sigh of the engines and the swish of the wheels and the thumping of the pitmans which made life aboard any steamer like the *Nonpareil* a small eternity of throbbing and rocking.

"Sergeant, all sharpshooters to the foredeck except Mears and Locket, and I want them on the pilothouse roof! Jump to it—*jump!*"

Within, as it seemed, the blink of an eye, the rows of cotton bales were infested by men leveling rifles. The two whom Carradine had singled out by name, stripped to shirts and breeches and not even taking time to don the boots they had put off when they lay down to rest, scrambled up as directed over Parbury's head. Alarming creaks answered the imposition of their weight.

The mist came and went. Now the boat was in a clear spot, but the shore was veiled; now everything was wiped from view by a gray-bright cloud; now, without warning, there was a gap that showed the guns being readied for attack. Parbury concentrated mechanically on ensuring that the steamer followed the most distant safe line around the point. But the deep-scoured channel was, of course, close to the inside of the bend. There would be a cutoff here soon . . .

All that, though, belonged on a plane which did not call for words. He devoted his chief attention to framing what he planned to say the moment Carradine returned.

The pilothouse door swung wide. Promptly: "Colonel!"

"Yes?"

"You mean to run this point right now?" His stammer was threatening; any second, a crucial word might hit a snag. So he rushed on without waiting for a reply. "We have supplies aboard destined for Vicksburg—not the bottom mud!"

To his astonishment he even scraped over the shoal of that last phrase. But mere seconds later he felt his jaw lock into the trembling static mode which would ensure he could say nothing for the next minute, and he was totally unable to interrupt Carradine's retort: quietly-spoken, yet as blistering as an escape of high-pressure steam.

"What's your alternative? Think you can outdo the *Carondelet* and *Pittsburgh* in a tinclad?" He was referring to the Union gunboats which, a year ago, had run past Island Number 10 by night defying its Confederate garrison, and earned the admiration of both friends and foes. "Hah! If you go astray in the fog, you'll wind up sitting on a sandbank, a fixed target and the easiest thing to range on. And before you claim you're too good a pilot to drive us aground—which I believe, sir, for I've watched you closely and with respect!—think how little cover darkness offers to a steamer, fog or no fog. Did you never notice what a fountain of sparks your chimneys vomit, a hundred feet above the water? Did you never hear the rumble of your engines, that would show a blind man where to aim his guns? Why, the very ripples making a drowned log bob about would be enough to suit some gunlayers I know!"

Parbury, still tongue-tied, felt his cheeks grow as hot as a callow boy's. That was not uncommon. All the accomplishments lying to his credit, all the skills he had acquired as an adult, his marriage, his status as a father, had not sufficed to alter the personality of the gangling youth who had gone home to find his home had gone.

"Now me!" Carradine, a man who breathed confidence at every word, was scanning the shore again. "Me, I have experience of a battery like that one. While it's true they *could* lay their guns by sound alone, I doubt they *will*. Ammunition has grown precious in this war and they won't risk wasting it until they must. This implies that so long as the fog is less than solid they will wait until they have a clear view. But when they can see us, we can see them. And under my command, Captain, I have marksmen who will take the eye out of a squirrel so as not to spoil the skin. Given that, would you prefer to face three cannon . . . or three-score rifles?"

Parbury wanted desperately to say that something was amiss with Carradine's reasoning. He sensed the fact much as he could detect the changing current of the river. But for him words had always been treacherous, apt to collapse under the weight of his intended meaning.

The tightness in his jaw spread; he felt tension in his bowels now, which he was used to because it occurred whenever he had to steer a steamer across a bend new-made since last fall. The familiarity of the sensation entrained resignation. He was acquainted with the river. War, like the river, altered things. He was ignorant of war but there were men who had trained for it. One was here.

Dry-mouthed he said, "Aye, Colonel. At your orders."

With that he surrendered all judgment, all control. Passive, he awaited the outcome of events. The mist grew denser here, and thinner there; random gusts—some due to the steamer's furnaces—opened and shut the view like a picturebook's leaves turning under casual fingers. The engines' thumping mingled with the hull's complaints. The sky leaned down and darkened. He could feel its intolerable load.

 The manner in which the bone-weary artillerymen reharnessed their horses was not drill to satisfy a parade-sergeant. Nonetheless, it resulted in the rapid arrival of guns one and three at a spot where they could be brought to bear on the approaching steamer.

Number two failed to make it. A tree trunk, partly rotted, lay sunk in the dirt, invisible under moss and lichens. One of the gun carriage's wheels chanced to run lengthwise over its weakest part. It cracked open. The wheel fell into its hollow center and jammed at the point where punk wood changed to sound.

Fuming, Folbert shouted for Caesar to bring his axe and chop the wheel loose, while he himself took command of number one gun with Tennice in charge of number three, and ordered the spare limber belonging to the missing fourth gun to stand by under the direction of a fat and nervous private named Hall, who clung to his horse's halter like a lifeline.

Feeling mutinous, Caesar reluctantly complied. Why should he be, again, the man who undertook the dullest hardest job, when what he wanted most was to let fly at the enemy? There might not be a chance for long; the mist was thickening by the minute . . .

Still, if all else failed one could aim at the noise. He was well acquainted with small steamboats, for the Pré du Lac Plantation had a navigable connection with Bayou Lafourche, but this was the first time he had been in earshot of a two-hundred-foot Mississippi sidewheeler under full power, and he was amazed at how deafening she was.

So, if he did break this gun free, he might at least claim the right to fire a shot with it. Who deserved to do so better than a former slave?

Anger lent muscle to his blows. He had served in the Union Army four months; he had seen action during two attacks on Vicksburg. But he had been confined to commissariat duties. This was the first time he had been in confrontation with his former masters. He thought of all the rebels as detestable because some of them bought and sold other human beings. Never, since he learned to talk, had Caesar believed he was a mere object to be traded back and forth like an ox or a bedstead. This conviction had sustained him when he dodged the patterollers who policed the plantation's boundary, mounted on horseback and accompanied by hounds. Evading pursuit by swimming the bayou, he made his way north despite hunger and thirst and not infrequently despair, until he met soldiers wearing blue and begged to be enlisted on their side.

And found he was one of hundreds, and felt proud of his own people for the first time ever.

Of course it should not have been—*chunk* went the axe and chips and splinters flew—*not* have been a war that made it happen!

And likewise, since it had turned out that way, instead of swinging this axe—*thunk!*—he ought to be behind a gun loaded and laid to sink the steamer! Obviously it took practice to handle a field gun. But Sergeant Tennice, last time he put his black recruit through a drill, had told him he was doing well. *Thunk!* So—

"Fire!"

Folbert's command rang out, and twin explosions followed prompt. Caesar could no more resist the temptation to see what effect the guns had had than anybody else.

The captain had chosen a moment at which the mist was lifting. Down a gray-walled alley in the air loomed the bulk of the steamboat in her ugly wartime garb, her paint dull and peeling, her sides hung with boiler plate.

Of which one sheet was uttering a boom like a giant gong. The better shot had landed fair and square.

But the other, as a drift of spray revealed, had fallen short. Folbert had been overeager.

Struggling against the current, however, the steamer was making poor headway. Moreover the gap in the mist was increasing. There would be plenty more chances! Seeing his companions rush to reload, afraid he might be too late to help fire this extra gun, Caesar once more addressed the dead tree.

And suddenly, horribly, there was a sound like the crackle of wildfire in dry underbrush and all his expectations fell apart.

He knew, while it was happening, what was going on. But his mind so totally revolted against accepting it as real that he could only later reconstruct the sequence of events.

Which he did, waking and in nightmare, for years after.


Most of the shots fired from the steamer went whistling to waste. But one did harm enough to outweigh the rest.

The horse to which the limber of number four gun had been left harnessed was a nervous chestnut filly, still considerably gun-shy, commandeered on the way here to replace a well-trained gray.

The lucky shot hit the chestnut in her flank.

Private Hall was taken by surprise when she reared up screaming, and her fore hooves cut open the heads of two men who rushed to catch her. They fell bloody while she fled across the campsite. Dropping his axe, Caesar was about to help restrain her when he realized with preternatural clarity what impended.

The fire which had been lighted with such difficulty flamed in the horse's path. She was bound to shy from it.

She did.

The limber tipped. One of its doors was unlatched. Out spilled the powder charges it contained.

Caesar tumbled forward on his face, and there was thunder.

 So unexpected and so violent was the explosion, Parbury came close to swerving the *Nonpareil* out of the channel. He was following a line perilously close to its far side.

The cannon shot had done little harm, though its impact on an iron plate had made everybody's ears ring. And the crackle of rifle-fire which, a moment later, answered Carradine's order had been reassuringly purposive.

But this—! Why, it was as loud as though a boiler had blown up!

"What in tarnation was *that?*" he barked. Such had been the force of the blast, its updraught had sucked in strands of fog opaque enough to blot out what just now had been a clear view.

From the men on deck came ragged cheers.

Lowering his glasses in frustration, Carradine said, "Only one thing it could have been. A ball must have struck one of the limbers. Maybe hit the store of friction tubes. At all events it set off a load of powder . . . Well, Captain!" He briskened. "Luck is on our side today, it seems. We need expect no further trouble from *that* source. Let's make haste to Vicksburg."

But Parbury's hand was already on the rope that would sound the bell for half speed.

Out of the corner of his mouth he said, "I defer to you in military matters, sir. Now you trust me in a matter of navigation. I'll run as long as I can. I shan't tie up unless the fog obliges me. But I must put out men with poles to fend off floating logs. And if the fog grows any thicker I must send out leadsmen in the yawl."

That emerged beautifully, free from any trace of stammer. He concluded, "Do I have permission?"

The last with irony he meant to be, and was, scathing.

 Caesar's nose was full of smoke and his ears of screaming, and some of the screams were not human. His feet were trapped under a soft heavy object; also he was aware of wetness, mud as foul as dung, and an overriding sense of shock.

When at last he was able to open his eyes he saw scattered on the ground near him several bright brown rods, like a forgotten game of jackstraws.

With vast effort he worked out what they were, and simultaneously realized that the steamboat was chugging on her way unhindered, her engine noise slower but not less regular. The mist reduced her to a grayish hulk devoid of detail.

Here on dry ground, though, he could see all too clearly. The explosion had cut through the soldiers like a scythe across a patch of wheat. By number one gun lay Captain Folbert, wide-eyed, open-mouthed, motionless. By number three he saw Sergeant Tennice doubled over clutching at a wound in his belly. There a horse was streaming with blood from a hundred cuts and one vast gash; there a man was rocking back and forth and moaning as he tried in vain to staunch the leak from where his right leg had been . . .

And what pinioned Caesar's feet was a torso, armless and headless: a dead weight.

He cried out for rage and nausea and dragged free and scrambled upright. Stupidly he shook his fist at the steamer—and checked in mid-gesture as it dawned on him that even though one limber had blown up, the rest survived.

Also the steamer was not, as he had at first thought, going away; she still had to breast and round the point. So for another few minutes she would be drawing nearer, a larger and easier target.

While right here before him were . . .

Caesar stooped and caught up the brown rods, giving silent thanks. It was not the sort of blessing preachers usually taught their flocks to pray for, he reflected grimly, but in the circumstances it would do.

They were the friction tubes which fired the guns.

Glancing around, debating what chance he had of getting off even one shot single-handed, he was startled to hear a thin voice calling him.

"Number three, soldier—number three! It's charged with powder! Wad and load! Don't waste time trying to fuze a shell—use solid ball!"

It was Tennice, somehow mastering his pain long enough to utter comprehensible instructions . . . but the final word terminated in a groan and he slumped forward, face whiter than paper.

He was right anyway. Behind its dead horse the limber of number three gun had slanted and spilled, but that made it all the handier. Caesar snatched up a wad, and a twelve-pound ball, and cast about for a ramrod. Telling himself not to be overhasty, to remember all the drills he had been led through, he completed the task of loading and took station behind the gun to try and lay it.

And to his incredulous relief found he need not alter the alignment, only the elevation, for the steamer was coming up broadside to where he stood.

He made three wild guesses about whether to aim high or low, thrust a friction tube into the vent, stepped to the side and jerked the lanyard. The gun boomed.

Looking again at the shadowy bulk of the steamer, he was at first convinced he must have missed, and was wondering whether a second try would be worthwhile when he detected an alteration in the vessel's noise. Instead of a rhythmical thumping, she was emitting a sort of crunch-and-grind.

For a long moment he stared, mouth ajar in disbelief; then with abrupt frantic energy he set about swabbing the barrel.

"You do any damage?" Tennice whispered.

"I guess so, Sergeant," Caesar said. "I guess *somehow* . . ."

And thrust a fresh bag of powder down the hot muzzle.

"You ran aground!" Carradine gasped. The shock had sent him sprawling on the floor of the pilothouse.

It was a forgivable assumption. For a moment Parbury had made the same mistake. But a heartbeat later he could feel what had happened almost as though he had taken a wound in his own flesh.

A cannonball had struck the larboard paddlebox and broken a bucket as it rose. Turning over top center it had twisted down and back so that the buckets following jammed against the halves of it and in their turn broke. Also damage had occurred in the engine room in consequence, but he had no time to waste on figuring out its precise nature, any more than he had breath to answer Carradine.

Quickly but without haste he put in hand the necessary actions: stop larboard engine, turn rudder to compensate, back starboard engine . . . and even as he gave the orders knew they were not enough. The *Nonpareil* had been standing too far to the east of the channel and the verge staff at her bow was indexing, like a compass being swung, the degrees of her progress toward a stern-first encounter with the nearest shoal.

"Man, what are you doing?" Carradine raged.

"What I can!" Parbury snapped back, and the colonel had the tact at last to leave him to his own problems. Once more he scanned the shore with his field glasses as the whim of the wind parted the mist.

From overhead came shouted oaths, and one of the men on the roof called, "Colonel, do you see what I see?"

At that moment the *Nonpareil* did go aground.

It was a gentle impact. The starboard after portion of her hull slid up the soft gradient of a sandbar so yielding that it did not even warp her rudder, merely absorbed it. But she was carrying a thousand tons on a draught of less than eight feet, and when she groaned to rest she was securely stuck, bows-on to the head-land from which the deadly shot had flown.

As unprepared for this as for that, Carradine at least managed not to fall, though his dignity suffered. As soon as he could he rushed out, ordering his men to fire at any fair target.

Parbury was more concerned with the report from his chief engineer. Hiram Burge had worked with him for a long while; they were used to one another, and it took few words to fill out the picture. By jamming the buckets, the cannonball had sprung a crack in the larboard pitman—the tapered wooden bar linking the engine-piston to the paddlewheel crank—and it must be strapped with a metal band.

There came a crackle of shots from the foredeck. Loudly and obscenely Mears and Locket commented that the men below were wasting powder. One of them called to Parbury—he recognized Mears, for this was one of the few soldiers he had spoken with during the voyage—"Captain, do you have a field glass?"

He handed up his own, and they took turns.

Just as Burge was departing Carradine came back, demanding how long it would take to repair and refloat the vessel. Captain and engineer looked at one another.

"Two hours," said Burge.

"Make it one!" Parbury countered, and Burge flinched, but after a moment shrugged and made to leave.

"No better than that?" said Carradine in dismay.

"No!" Burge spat tobacco juice into the boxful of sawdust which served as a cuspidor. "*That's* taking it for granted you stop 'em shooting their tarnation guns at us!"

Carradine sighed resignedly and turned away.

Again from the roof: "Colonel!" A shriller voice—Locket's. "Colonel, seems like there ain't but one man on his feet over there—"

*Crash*.

The verge staff flew in splinters and bales of cotton joined scraps of dislodged armor plate in creating a chaos of men crying at the tops of their voices, some in agony, some trying to issue orders. The blow had come out of fog. Once more the breeze was drawing its curtain across the river.

Loud from the pilothouse roof, in the tone of someone not prepared to let a minor interruption distract him:

"—and that's a gawdamn' *nigger!*"

Mears chimed in. "Yeah! An' what chance do we got of knockin' down a black man *in* fog *at* twilight?"

Carradine said harshly, "One man on his feet? Just the one, and him black? And you're worried about him?"

Leaning over the edge of the roof, Mears gazed into the colonel's upturned face.

"Given what he just done, *sah,* I would surely feel less worried if this here steamboat were on the move 'stead of stuck like a peg to pitch hoss-shoes at."

A crack from his companion's rifle, and a curse. "Din' get him. Tho't I had him spotted clear, but . . . Save breath an' look over yo' sights!"

 Caesar had launched his second shot into mist, trusting to what his ears told him: that the steamer's two-hundred-foot length was no longer being driven upstream. He was almost too deafened by the report to catch what followed, but sound carried clearly across the water and he detected screams and moans. Chuckling, he set about a third firing.

And was hit in the leg.

At first he didn't understand what had happened. He thought he had tripped. But the fog was not yet so thick as to make him stumble.

Then pain came, and wetness mingled with it. Blood was streaming from a hole the size of his thumbnail in the front of his thigh. And there was another behind. The ball had passed straight through without, miraculously, touching bone.

For a while he was so distraught by agony he could do no more than shut his eyes and sway back and forth. He realized after a little that he was cursing, and he should rather have been praying.

No! Neither was right. He ought to be staunching that blood!

Feverishly he sought something to make a bandage, and found part of some-one's coat. From it he contrived to rip a piece of cloth long enough to bind his leg.

Whereupon he felt master of his fate again. Those damned rebels weren't going to get the better of Caesar, proudly called Predulac, who was carrying away from the plantation more than its owners would enjoy after the Union's victory. They would be denied even the right to use its name . . . so everybody kept promising.

But his exhilaration was brief. He had lost enough blood to weaken him. With abrupt and fearful clarity he knew he must seize this chance to shoot at the steamer, for there would not be another. He gathered all his forces and began to recite aloud the ritual of the gun drill, as though he were not only himself but Tennice also.

He had dropped the bag of powder he had been about to load. It was incredible how much heavier it had grown in these past few minutes, while as for the twelve-pound ball . . .

Somehow, though, he got it wadded and rammed, and then staggered around the gun, fumbling for the necessary friction tube . . . in his pocket, he thought . . . but the *other* pocket . . . and here was one and there it was ready in the vent, and . . .

It was like being very drunk indeed. Sick-giddy drunk. He detested the sensation from the uttermost depths of his being.

With swimming gaze he looked up and found that fog now hid the steamer altogether. But he had sunk his total resources into loading the gun. He must at least fire it. He tugged the lanyard. At the shock of the explosion his injury betrayed him and he collapsed sidelong on the wet ground.

When he raised his head for the last time before he slumped unconscious, he saw that the fog—like his uniform, and his dead comrades'—was dyed red.

 Men with crowbars and mallets forced clear the splintered boarding of the paddlebox. Others with hatchets smashed the broken buckets into fragments and dropped them overside. On the main and boiler decks resounded the cries of those injured by the latest shot.

At least there had not yet been another. Carradine reported that Mears was cautiously prepared to revise his former opinion. Perhaps he had hit the black artilleryman after all.

But Parbury was concerned only to get his beloved vessel under way again.

Fortunately the frame of the wheel was not so badly out of round as to jam, and there were enough spare buckets aboard to replace the damaged ones. As soon as that had been attended to, backwash could be used to erode the bar. That would take time and patience but little skill; even towboat pilots understood the trick of it.

What was going to take longest was making a strap for the pitman, but Burge's portable forge had been set up and a deckhand was frantically pumping its bellows, while Burge himself was donning the cowhide gauntlets he always wore for any job that involved hot metal.

Parbury saw with relief that, satisfied with the temperature of the coals, he was signaling for bar-iron to be laid on them. So, if within the next hour the fog did not grow impenetrable . . .

He glanced anxiously upward to see whether it yet veiled the tops of the chimneys, which a whim had led him to have cut in the shape of coronets, and his heart sank like a leadsman's plumb.

The towering chimneys that reared up ahead of the pilothouse were identical tubes of sheet iron supported by cross-bracing. Each served four boilers, whose furnaces enjoyed a forced draft created by venting spent steam into the base of the chimneys . . . though now, of course, the fires were being damped down and the relief valves on the boilers set to their lowest. If steam were not regularly bled off there was the danger that a badly packed joint might spring a leak, or even that a boiler might explode. The boats which ran this river were very fragile.

This second *Nonpareil* was no exception, for all her speed, her elegance, her ability to carry enormous cargoes on negligible draft, and her tacked-on armor plate. Struck like a skittle by a bowling ball, her larboard chimney broke from its base and fell slantways with a sullen boom and a great crunching of the upperworks. The portion of the deck where Burge was working canted at a sudden crazy angle, opening a gap to the hold. Through it the coals from the forge tumbled in a searing cascade. They fell on wood, and bales of cotton, and stacks of rations that included fat bacon and other greasy meat, and—and . . .

And boxes of ammunition piled all anyhow.

During the first few seconds before the flames roared up some of the deckhands rushed to try and smother the fire. They found themselves driven back by soldiers. Screaming and yelling, green recruits jumped overboard, abandoning their injured comrades, hoping to make good their own escape in the shallows by the stern. Carradine struggled to delay them, yelling orders that could not outdo the crackle of burning.

Half-choked with fumes, yet still refusing to believe in the doom of his darling, Parbury turned to see what shred of hope remained. If the powder could be dumped before the blaze ignited it—

Too late. It smote him with a red-hot fist.

# 28TH APRIL 1865

# THE SHOCK OF INDIVIDUAL DISASTER

~~~~~~

"The cumulative figures of steamboat
losses were not generally available,
and the data on the comparative risks
of stagecoach, sloop and steamboat,
even if accurately determined and
widely published, would not have ma-
terially affected the issue. What
aroused public opinion and moved
legislative bodies was less the cold
calculation of total losses and relative
risks than the shock of individual disasters which did not occur at an exotic
distance, but frequently at one's very
doorstep. Many were inclined to accept the view of the mid-century observer who declared: 'The history
of steam navigation on the Western
rivers is a history of wholesale murder
and unintentional suicide.'"
—Louis C. Hunter,
*Steamboats on the Western Rivers*

The *Atchafalaya*—fourth boat to wear that name—gentled in at a New Orleans wharf she had last visited in April 1861. The river was close on bank-full and she had made fast time from Cairo, so she was arriving when people were more concerned with breakfast than the day's work. But that was not why she was able to moor straight away. The years of bloodshed and destruction had left their traces in every corner of the nation. Fortunate though New Orleans was, in the accepted view, to have fallen to Union troops as early as April 1862, this city had not escaped unscathed. In the old days its port had been so crowded that incoming steamers were obliged to stand off, impatiently sounding their whistles, until a place could be contrived for them. Now there was room and to spare. So many of the famous vessels that used to call here lay like corpses in the upriver shallows, their hulls to rot and their boilers and engines to make fossils for the future.

But the *Atchafalaya* too was famous, and her reappearance was bound to create a sensation, particularly because it had been harbingered by telegraph messages hinting at a coup on the part of her captain that was exciting among his colleagues at best envy, at worst fury. It had always been customary for Mississippi steamers to work in whatever trade proved profitable and to lay up when none was paying well. But only the most devoted friend of someone who had laid up during the entire war, then reemerged to snatch the most sought-after contract going, would presume to defend his course of action.

And the captain of the *Atchafalaya* was Hosea Drew, a man who seemed dedicated to managing without friends altogether.

From a distance the steamer shaped up every bit as splendid as "befohdewoh." Not until she drew alongside did onlookers enjoy the melancholy satisfaction of observing the rust that almost exceeded in area the red paint on her chimneys and the hasty patches applied where rot had attacked her decks and guards.

And, since most of those on board were released Confederate prisoners of war as eager to see their homes again as the authorities in Washington were to be shut of them, not until her cabin passengers filed on to the levee did word get around concerning mildew staining the carpets, fungi that made several staterooms too disgusting to be slept in, hellish noises announcing steam leaks at all hours, and the cries her timbers uttered when the slightest cross-current was encountered. Then accusations spread like fire taking hold of a steamer's fretwork finery in a windstorm. Among the passengers were some who had a special cause to feel aggrieved; these were southerners trapped by the war in the squalid feverish marsh of "Egypt"—meaning Illinois in the vicinity of Cairo—who had been unwilling to return home until the fighting was over and even then were reluctant to patronize a northern steamer. For this special reason they had been delighted to

33

hear of the *Atchafalaya*, with her solid Louisiana name, and were appalled to find her captain wearing blue.

Worst of all, he himself had spent the journey in the highest of spirits. The most vigorous representations concerning the condition of his boat and the suffering of those who had been foolish enough to take passage with him were brushed aside.

It had consequently been resolved that something must be done to make amends. Something. Anything! Before he was out of reach.

"Captain!" And more insistently: "We demand to speak with the captain!"

The cries grew to a chorus as the most infuriated of the cabin passengers clustered at the foot of the steps leading to the hurricane deck. Accustomed to priority, they had been balked in their attempt to be first ashore by freed prisoners who showed no concern for baggage, since they had none, nor indeed for anything except haste.

The *Atchafalaya* being secure now, she might be left in the care of her clerks and mates. Here came Drew from the pilothouse, humming. Not all captains were qualified pilots, nor did all pilots aspire to captaincy. Many of the former owed their commands to nothing more than having scraped together the price of a boat. Earned, borrowed, inherited, won at the gaming tables—even, in a few notorious cases, stolen—money was money, and enough of it could purchase a steamer.

But without pilots that vessel remained worthless. There were captains who paid themselves three hundred dollars a month out of their takings and were glad to pay two pilots five hundred each. They were the princes of the river, sporting kid gloves and silk hats and diamond rings, and even when serving with a captain who was himself a pilot they reigned supreme during their allotted watches.

To look at Hosea Drew without knowing more than that he owned a steamer would lead people superficially acquainted with the river to assume he must have made his way up the ladder as a mate: a commoner course formerly than now, when a clerk stood a better chance since he was in a position to buy part shares in a promising cargo while it was still on shore, but colorable enough because Drew seemed older than his actual age.

Nobody judging wholly by appearances would have guessed that for twenty years he had been as good a pilot as the oldest rivermen could recall. One simply did not picture a pilot turned captain in these terms: greasy ancient cap askew on his head, gray beard untrimmed and marked with traces of the chewing tobacco that was his sole indulgence, gray hair hanging untidy over the collar of a coat that had been uniform blue but was now greatly faded, clutching both a much-mended carpetbag and a knobbly staff that, rumor claimed, served not only to discipline his crew but also to impress his authority on passengers.

And, at just about the moment Drew appeared, the pilot who had served alternate watches with him this trip—portly, balding William Tyburn, who was never addressed as Bill or Willy but some of whose close associates knew the complicated and indirect reasons why they might call him Ketch, not meaning any sort

THE SHOCK OF INDIVIDUAL DISASTER

of boat—was following one of the black deckhands, the porter of his portmanteau, down the forward stage of the levee.

A red-faced man stepped into Drew's path, expression menacing.

"Captain, another trip aboard this steamer would be enough to—!"

But Drew clapped his shoulder with his free right hand, beaming.

"My agents are at Thirty Tchoupitoulas! Call there, and Mr. Caudle will see you right!"

After which, somehow, the stumpy figure had passed on.

To be confronted by a positive gorgon of a woman in black with bottle-green relief at neck and cuffs, leveling a parasol like a gun.

"Captain!" she rasped in a voice which displayed all the sweetness of a shaft bearing with sand in its oilbox. "The sustenance provided during this voyage has been—!"

"Yet another casualty of war, ma'am," came the response with the slickness and free movement of a perfectly aligned piston. "Thanks to the hostilities, I long ago lost my regular caterer, with whose provisions no one ever used to find fault! Good day!"

Still another passenger accosted him. "Mr. Drew! Your rates for freight, as well as passage whether on deck or in the cabin, can only be described as—"

"My rates?" echoed Drew. "See the chief clerk, please—Mr. Hopper. But bear in mind that while we're completing our government contract there will be great pressure on the space available. Good morning!"

By this point he was through the thick of those who had paid their own way here and well among those who had been delivered at the charge of a relieved government. Not only were the latter grateful to be home; they were fresh from military prison camps and anyone rating the rank of captain sparked reflexes in their minds. Not many actually thanked Drew, but a good few made way for him and ensured that others did too.

He was therefore able to shout at Tyburn while still in earshot. Albeit with a deep sigh, the fat pilot told the deckhand to wait until Drew caught up.

Frustrated, several of the cabin passengers were nonetheless sufficiently annoyed to follow Drew's parting injunction. In ordinary circumstances it would have been a normal enough procedure. Under the master, and pilot or pilots, three officers on a riverboat exercised significant authority: the first mate, who oversaw the crew; the chief engineer; and the senior clerk, who attended to matters touching money. Because they included the taking-on of cargo and the letting of cabin and deck space, it was the latter's name that customarily appeared with the captain's in advertisements.

Mr. Hopper, though, rebuffed the complainants in tones of frigid formality.

"Sir—ma'am—I signed on specifically to attend to commercial matters. I am unfamiliar with Mr. Drew's practice in other departments of steamboat operation because this is the first trip I ever made in his employ!"

Resigned, the passengers gave up and went away. Only a handful lingered long enough to hear him add, under his breath, this entirely and absolutely unprofessional qualification:

"God willing, it shall also be the last!"

 Negotiating the maze of merchandise that littered the wharf, Drew caught up with Tyburn. Automatically the black man carrying the latter's bag reached for the former's also.

And looked abruptly puzzled, for he could heft it on one finger. "Cap'n!" he exclaimed. "Are yo' sho' dishyear bag—?"

"Yes, it's the one I meant to bring," Drew interrupted, still obviously in the high good humor he had enjoyed throughout the trip. "It may be empty right now, but I'm on my way to fill it. Mr. Tyburn!"

He was not among those privileged to say "Ketch."

Tyburn dressed and acted in a style more suggestive of a pilot's station in life than Drew did; during the voyage he had frequently been addressed as "Captain" by passengers who imagined the boat's owner to be a hireling. Moreover he was of peculiarly striking appearance. He affected side-whiskers, but he was ash-blond, while his skin was tanned and leathery from much exposure to weather; consequently he gave the curious impression of being reversed, like a photographic negative.

In response to Drew he cocked an eyebrow.

"Are you bound for the parlor?"

That was the meetingplace of the Pilots' Guild to which they both necessarily belonged, the room where all newly arrived members were obliged to post their latest findings about the condition of the river.

"It's expected," Tyburn murmured.

"Then let us walk along together."

"Walk?"—in a gentle but quizzical tone.

"Why, it's less'n a mile from here to Gravier Street, unless the river drifted this bit and that of the city farther apart since last I called here!"

"Far's I know," Tyburn said, "Gravier is where it was. But you, sir, draw a deal less water for'ard than do I!" He patted his comfortable paunch. "Walk if you prefer it. I'm about to call a landau."

For an instant Drew's notorious meanness could be seen struggling with the courtesy due a colleague. It was a standing joke up and down the river—or it had been in the days "befohdewoh"—that if he could avoid spending a single cent Drew would so so . . . despite having run two of the most popular of Mississippi steamboats. Some of his competitors had amassed fortunes despite the war by taking risks. One in particular had cleared a quarter-million dollars from a single trip in 1863, because cotton was selling at four cents a pound in Louisiana, where the growers were desperate to clear their warehouses, and at forty cents in the

North, which had been cotton-starved since the war broke out. But it would have been foreign to Drew to gamble so much capital on one load.

Of course, it was possible he had changed since moving north; this was a time of changes. He might equally have decided to quit New Orleans for St. Louis even without a premonition of the war. Rightly or wrongly, though, his acquaintances down here were unanimous in assuming he must be worth a hundred thousand as he stood.

It didn't show. He hadn't built a mansion; he hadn't launched a new and spectacular boat, but had spent the war meekly serving as a hired pilot in short upper-river trades. What could he have done with his savings, this bachelor who begrudged himself any luxury beyond a chaw of tobacco?

Who was even sorry to part with the cost of a cab ride!

This time at least he yielded, and the black man ran to find a landau. In it the rivermen rolled away from the waterfront, speaking little. Drew was preoccupied with the look of the city, which he had not lately visited, and Tyburn with the state-of-the-river form he, like Drew, was obliged to fill out.

At only one point did he address his companion directly. Tucking his now finalized report into his pocket, he suggested, "You had yours ready before we tied up, I guess."

"What?" Drew had been lost in thought. "Oh, my report? Yes, I care better for first impressions than those recollected in tranquillity. Distance lends—*disenchantment* to the view."

During their trip Tyburn had been half-smothered with the captain's sometimes misremembered poetical allusions. He had settled on the safest course, which was to let them pass like floating garbage and concentrate on the main channel of conversation.

"There's one thing I would like to say," he began. Drew rounded on him.

"Bad news? Complaints?"

"The very opposite!"

"Amazing. You sounded as solemn as a doctor telling his patient to get measured for a coffin."

Tyburn gave a dutiful smile. "I only set out to say I was impressed by the way you tackled the lower river. There have been a lot of changes. I was making bets with myself that one would catch you. I lost them all."

For once it seemed Drew might respond in kind to a kind word. His look was that of a man so unaccustomed to compliments that he had steeled himself against the eventuality.

But the landau got under way again before he thawed. All he uttered was the admission that he was tolerably content with what he'd done.

Wonderingly Tyburn shook his head, but he forbore to press his point.

They halted outside the large and handsome building, let as offices at street level, whose second floor contained the premises of the Pilots' Guild. Tyburn paid the driver, without offering to divide the fare with his companion, and turned to enter.

And checked in mid-stride.

Drew was staring up the street, whose west side by now enjoyed the morning sunlight.

Approaching along the same sidewalk on which he and Tyburn stood, but as yet out of earshot thanks to the constant noise of the city—shouting, grinding of cart and carriage wheels, clanging bells on streetcars, and above all the racket of new construction, for the end of the war had triggered a wave of development—came a woman of middle age clad in whole mourning.

Walking half beside, half behind her, his left hand resting lightly on her shoulder and his right grasping a cane, was a lank and bony man in equally somber garb. He went with a hesitant gait that caused his guide much difficulty. A tall hat cast shadow over his face, but as the distance reduced it became possible to discern that his eyes were barred with a black cloth band.

"I could swear—!" Drew exclaimed suddenly. "But surely it can't be!"

With transient malice Tyburn simply waited.

"Parbury?" Drew breathed at last.

"Yes."

"Is that his wife?"

"She has to lead him about now. Or someone must. Most days she's well enough to walk abroad. Now and again she takes sick, so their servant does it, but often then he can't leave home because she needs constant attention."

"What happened?" Drew seemed almost to be choking.

"You didn't hear he was blinded when a Union battery sank his last boat?"

"I . . ." Drew swallowed hard. "I was told he lost the *Nonpareil* in some such manner. But that was all."

He swung to face Tyburn. "You said 'their servant'?"

"Yes, a nigra woman used to nurse their boy before he died. Stayed on 'cause she had no place else to go."

"*One* servant?" Drew emphasized.

Tyburn shrugged. "All they can afford, I guess."

"And their son is dead . . . ? Mr. Tyburn, here's my report!" Feverishly he drew the folded paper from his pocket. "Convey it to the officers of the Guild— they'll find it done in regulation style! But as for me . . . Well, I realize the business I must attend to next is more pressing than I allowed for! Tell 'em that!"

By this stage he was almost gabbling. Incapable, it seemed, of further speech, he spun on his heel and marched away. Tyburn watched him go in frank astonishment.

Ten minutes later, having exchanged civilities with Parbury—and his wife, whom he as ever turned back with a mutter of insincere thanks—and having tried to help him up the tricky narrow stairs, to no avail because the blind captain was as neat at dodging the heavy picture frames that shoaled the walls as formerly in eluding traps set by the Father of Waters, Tyburn was able to pin on the bulletin board his pilot's report.

To which, having unfolded it, he added Drew's.

"Drew?"

The monosyllable multiplied. A hush had fallen in the comfortably furnished parlor, as ever when reports were being posted.

"*Hosea* Drew?"—at last, in a tone bordering disbelief.

"We never voted to disbar him!"

That croaking comment came from Parbury, now settled in his regular seat, surrounded by his regular entourage. Some were themselves pilots; to a man, these felt that the war had cheated them by interfering with their careers. Additionally, on the fringe of the group, there were half a dozen steersmen in training who had detected that Miles Parbury possessed a talent their own mentors lacked, and often appealed to him, an eyeless man, to arbitrate disputes between two whose sight was whole. These were they whom some wit had baptized "Parbury pirates." In the old days such "cubs" had not been allowed the run of the Guild's premises. The war, though, had thinned the ranks of the profession, and Parbury had been insistent about the need to bring youngsters into the company of experts as soon as might be. His opinion, as always, had been heeded.

On being offered an eye-opener, Tyburn had accepted with alacrity, for if they hoped to stay in the profession pilots did not drink while working, and his latest trip had been difficult as well as dry.

To him Parbury directed a harsh question, his blind gaze perfectly aligned.

"What do you think of Drew?"

Tyburn sipped, and thought, and sipped again. Silence returned by degrees. At length he deemed it appropriate to deliver the verdict with which he had been pregnant most of the way since Cairo.

"Captain Drew—now he's a daisy pilot! I'd trust him at midnight in fog and shoal water, 'spite of the rotting tub he calls a steamer, and I wouldn't so much as breathe if he told me not to. But that don't imply I have to *like* him."

To emphasize, to underline this oracular pronouncement, the heavens wept. Warm summer rain began asperging New Orleans.

 On this corner had stood Bonaventure's Coffee House and Slave Exchange. Now it was a burnt-out shell. The rain gathered on charred timbers and dripped dirty to the ground. The banquettes, the wood-plank sidewalks of the Vieux Carré, were interrupted here with such contempt that no one had troubled to sling a warning rope across from what was left of the wall to what was left of the poles that formerly had upheld a handsome balcony ornamented with wrought iron. Incautious by night, a passerby might have stridden into a puddle caltrapped with rusty nails.

Coming on this, Drew was briefly disoriented. His sight of Parbury had so shaken him that he had nearly not arrived here in one piece. Descending from a streetcar on Canal—as much a boundary between the "American" and the "French" zones of this improbable city as though even now its English-speaking population constituted a besieging army—he had stepped off the "neutral ground" and almost been run down by a young man in a cut-under buggy who seemed to think he was Jehu reincarnate.

And who, on noticing Drew's blue coat, lashed out with his whip. He missed by scarcely an inch.

These two encounters sufficed to evaporate the good spirits the captain had been enjoying. Distracted as he was, he briefly suspected he had missed his way. But, looking about him, he found that everything else was much as it had been when last he saw it. And if a slave exchange had been burnt down, surely that was the fair inverse of a Roman holiday . . .

Not, judging by the Negro beggars who whined after alms with one eye fearfully cocked for patrolling soldiers under orders to round them up and put them to work, that freedom had brought signal benefits to the colored Orleanians. The devil with them, though! Just let Marocain be at his office! When today was over, please the Lord, Hosea Drew would have time to spare for strangers' troubles.

 Obliged during this and every other sort of weather to maintain himself in a condition impeccable from his starched cravat to the high-sided boots on which his uncle, and employer, did not tolerate the slightest grain of dust, and moreover bored because so far today all the customers had been claimed by his cousins and senior fellow clerks Eugene and Richard—who were legitimate, and lost no chance of rubbing in that fact—Fernand Lamenthe was already on the verge of eruption when, through the glass door on which gold letters announced that here were the premises of E. Marocain, Goldsmith and Silversmith, Jeweller, Pawnbroker and Banker to Distinguished Families, he espied a shabby figure carrying a battered carpetbag.

Surely that could be no customer of Marocain's!

However, having surveyed the vicinity—the shop faced not the street but a courtyard large enough to turn a carriage with four in hand—he set his hand to the door and thrust it wide.

At once, bristling, Fernand was at his side, hoping all he needed was directions to some place else. Four other clients were present, regular and valued patrons: Mrs. Imelda Moyne, who had come with her slim and pretty daughter Louisette to select a watch as a present to her husband Andrew on their twentieth anniversary; Major Hugo Spring of the Union Army, who wanted to choose a ring for the young lady he had it in mind to propose to; and his intended groomsman Arthur Gattry, who thanks to sleekly classical good looks had wider experience of women and had been pressured into offering his advice. All of them looked on the intruder with distaste and dismay.

So did Eugene and Richard, whose expressions were not devoid of glee that the lot of tackling this unsavory personage had fallen to their cousin.

Terrifyingly conscious of being watched, but determined to brave it out, Fernand said, "May I assist you—sir?"

And wished for once that his octoroon complexion, heightened by contrast with the fashionable beard and moustache he sported in imitation of Emperor Louis Napoleon, were dark enough to hide the violence of his blushing. He was nineteen, tall, lean, and—so he had been assured more than once—rather good-looking.

But he was not enjoying his career. His mother never tired of assuring him that his prospects were marvelous, which was probably true, and that his uncle had been very generous, which was beyond dispute. Even so . . .

"You owe me twelve thousand dollars," said the man in shabby blue. He let fall his carpetbag. "Pack it in there, quick as you can. Gold, or Union bills—don't make no odds, just so long as I get every cent."

There was a moment of total silence. Then:

"Obviously crazy?" said Major Spring to his companion, who nodded. They rose and approached. Eugene, with a muttered apology to the Moynes, and Richard rounded the ends of their respective counters. Neither was as tall as Fernand but both were heavier-set.

It would have been pardonable for Fernand to stand aside. But the idea felt amiss. He could not have defined his reasons; they reached back to the first time he had come here, clad in hasty black for his father's funeral. The Cathedral of St. Louis, redolent of incense, had that day become intermingled· in his awareness with this temple to the rival deity Mammon, and there were certain acts he regarded on a less than conscious level as unbefitting to the shop.

Offering violence to a stranger was one of them.

Like steam in a boiler finding its proper outlet to the engine, his potentially explosive rage transmuted to decision. Stepping square in front of the newcomer, he said, "Do I take it you have funds deposited with us?"

"Damn' right I do! Money I've sweated blood and eaten dirt to earn! And I want it now!"

This with a glare calculated to melt the younger man like a wax image over a candle flame.

Feeling the blood in his cheeks as hot as that image on the verge of flaring, Fernand said stubbornly, "Sir, I do not recollect that I saw you here before."

"Hmm!"—after a pause. "No, I guess you wouldn't remember me, at that. I last walked through Ed's door in March of '61. Here, send my card to him. *He* knows me."

He proffered a slip of pasteboard. It identified Hosea Drew, Master, Str. *Atchafalaya*.

Fernand almost dropped it in astonishment. This—this vagabond was the man who had brought off so barefaced a coup that the city, nay the state, nay the river community clear to St. Louis was gossiping about it! His *Atchafalaya* was being paid from public funds to transport prisoners of war to the river port nearest where they hailed from. Many were doing the same on an informal basis, but he was the only steamboat owner to have thought of applying for government money instead of negotiating with the prisoners and their families. A single telegraph message, rumor said, had assured him of six profitable trips and maybe eight.

Yet to look at him one might assume he was so poor he could not take his boots to the cobbler.

During one diabolically tempting instant Fernand considered letting Eugene and Richard make fools of themselves. He needed only walk out in the direction of the countinghouse as though to see whether Mr. Marocain was there. Having little to do, he had been watching the courtyard and knew his uncle had hobbled back to his bureau, which was connected to the shop by a speaking tube installed since his illness. He was virtually certain the others had been too busy to register the fact.

So by the time he came back to apologize for taking so long . . .

No. His cousins were bound to rebuke him anyhow, for being right. There was no point in making matters worse. So he said loudly, "Ah, Captain Drew! I shall advise my uncle of your presence right away. Forgive my apparent discourtesy, but the *Atchafalaya* must have made capital time. I was expecting you tomorrow."

"Expecting me, were you?" Drew said as the other clerks exchanged horrified glances.

"One tries to keep a finger on the pulse of business, you know." Fernand gave a genteel wave, copied from his father. "Be so kind as to take a seat!"

Suddenly Drew's mask of gruffness was displaced by a crooked grin that said as plain as words he had seen through Fernand's pretense and didn't give a damn. Richard came rushing to place a chair at Drew's disposal while Eugene culled his repertoire of doubletalk to explain to the other clients why the steamboater had not been summarily ejected.

Filling his lungs before applying his lips to the speaking tube—it required a deal of wind to sound the whistle at its distant end—Fernand had to struggle not to laugh. Ever since childhood he had been fond of the phrase "poetic justice." He relished this, the first occasion he had found it applicable to the real world.

*Real . . . ?*

Guiding Drew toward the bureau, Fernand tried to revise some of what he had not until recently thought of as his illusions. Having repeatedly been told—chiefly by his mother—that it was time to discard vain ambitions about becoming an explorer or a deep-sea mariner, and being dutiful and because steamboat piloting was one of the careers he had vaguely dreamed of, he concentrated on the fact that the man beside him was ill-dressed and ill-mannered, and right now was scratching without shame.

But what did it spare you to be "respectable"? Certainly it could not save you from the Angel of Death! Perhaps avoiding liquor and low company might prolong life in this world, but priests were forever uttering warnings against attachment to

the treasures of Earth. Sometimes it seemed that only a handsomer tomb rewarded those who sacrificed their lives to stuffy dull convention . . .

He had not quite completed that thought when he rounded on Drew.

"Say, Captain!"

"Yes, boy?"

Fernand almost bridled, but was glad he managed not to.

"Captain, you may need to prepare yourself for my uncle's condition."

"Don't be so cryptic!"

"Well, last year he had rheumatic fever. Left him very stiff and weak, and as for
his heart . . . Well, he's not in his first youth."

"To every thing there is a time," Drew said sententiously. "Thanks for the
warning, though." And before Fernand could knock on the bureau door he added
a further one-word question.

"Uncle?"

His face a sudden mask, Fernand forbore to answer.

But once again Drew deciphered his expression. He said softly, "Don't get me
wrong, boy—*youngster*. I have all possible respect for people who honor family
obligations."

Shabby and prematurely gray this man might be; incontestably his wits were
razor-keen. He seemed to have analyzed Fernand's position in the world within a
couple of minutes . . . not that it was so rare as to make the feat truly astonishing.
His mother, one of the prettiest quadroons of her generation, had lived *en
plaçage;* in other words she had been the acknowledged mistress of a wealthy
white man. That man was dead: Alphonse Marocain, Edouard's younger brother,
carried off by yellow fever. The relationship had been as close and nearly as formal as a marriage, but their son was called Lamenthe, a common New Orleans
patronym: her name, not his. Fernand, at least, they had agreed on . . .

He was an only child—now. There had been twin girls before him, but they
were sickly from birth and both were dead by the time he learned to walk. No
more had followed.

Many people thought of origins like his as romantic, invoking terms like "lovechild" and the attendant superstitions that made bastards somehow special. He
disagreed. Nothing in his heredity had saved him from the future he must endure. For him a path had been mapped through a monotone world of bookkeeping. Adding endless columns of figures was not how he had hoped to spend his
life. However, since he was now his mother's sole support apart from his uncle's
allowance to her—

The idea flashed into Fernand's mind that Drew might have taken "uncle" for a
euphemism. Well, that was a pardonable error, and were it to prove true he
would not be altogether disappointed . . .

He rapped on the bureau door.

 For a while after replacing the speaking tube on its hook, Edouard Marocain sat thinking how he had altered since he and Drew last met, and how much he would have preferred to see his visitor tomorrow, at all events later. Word had reached him that the *Atchafalaya* was making exceptional time, but that was a small surprise; the river was being kind to its navigators this spring. Even so, what was Drew about? He could not possibly have supervised the disembarkation of passengers and the unloading of baggage and freight, *and* complied with the unwritten law of the Pilots' Guild that obliged him to report at their parlor before proceeding about other business. What had driven him to come straight here? A cold shoulder from his colleagues? The Drew he had known in the old days would certainly have brazened matters out, defying everyone to divert him from his solitary course. Admittedly, stress and sickness might work improbable transformations . . .

"Who should know that better than I?" whispered Marocain to the still air of his darkened office. Its windows were tightly shut against the miasma that might bring renewal of his fever; heavy drapes obscured them not so much to exclude the sun on this cloudy and intermittently rainy morning as to disguise from visitors the scrawniness of his hands, the parchment tautness of his cheeks, the shivers that racked him and occasionally peaked in fits of coughing. Against these, a device like an incense burner rested atop his English roll-front desk, uttering pungent fumes: not that he could have sworn to their doing him any good.

And if they were, to what end? What was he going to leave behind? The riches of this world, of course, to the best of his ability—and none could say he had not made painstaking provision for his heirs . . . but if Richard were to marry that girl so much like—so much *too* like—the gaudy frivolous butterfly Eugene was tethered to . . .

Maybe, in spite of all, the sound strain of the Marocain family had passed via Alphonse's loins? No, that was pitching it too strong. Likelier there had been excessive interbreeding among the old French families of the city, and some sort of outcrossing—even to the stock of their former slaves—was essential to renew the vigor of the line. At all events Fernand . . . poor Alphonse's only . . . Fernand . . .

Adrift, his thoughts were rammed by a loud knock. He gathered his wits. On the desk lay a mound of confidential papers. Effortfully, for every time he raised his arm above shoulder height he suffered twinges, he drew down the roll front. He turned his chair, which was modern and mounted on a swivel, so he was facing the door. At least his voice had survived his illness; except when coughing interfered, it was as mellow and resonant as ever. Therefore he declaimed his greeting as soon as the door swung wide.

"Captain, welcome back to New Orleans! Fernand, dispose a chair for our visitor. Call for oysters and a decanter of the Muscadet that arrived by the last liner. And bring the captain's ledger of account. You've posted the telegraphic credits, I feel sure."

"At your service, Mr. Marocain," said Fernand with the formality which the old banker insisted on even his sons displaying when a client was in his presence.

"That nephew of yours," said Drew, "was shook by my looks."

"And so are you by mine," said Marocain.

Disconcerted by such directness, Drew surveryed the room. New and fashionable European paper decorated its walls; a cut-glass chandelier depended from its ceiling; the carpet was resplendent with the latest chemical dyes. He said at length, "Don't look like you let it interfere with business."

"In spite of everything one continues to make ends meet. Now there's a chance of trade reverting to normal, one looks forward to a brighter future. Doubtless your beautiful steamer will contribute to the renewal of our prosperity. The fact that you're here sooner than expected suggests that she suffered no harm while she was laid up."

"There's damn' all traffic on the river," Drew said curtly. "That's how I got here ahead of schedule. The boat? Hah! You can't scarcely take ten steps along her deck without the planking threatens to give way!"

Marocain raised his eyebrows. But before he could speak again Fernand returned bearing a leather-bound book on whose spine was stamped in gold *DREW Capt. H.* He set it on Marocain's desk, open to the current folio, and would have withdrawn but that a black maidservant appeared with a tray on which reposed oysters in cracked ice, a bowl of hot sauce, a barrel of small crackers, the wine Marocain had specified, and the requisite forks, glasses and napkins. Fernand helped arrange these on a table between his uncle and the visitor. Then once more he turned to leave, but Marocain checked him.

"Captain, you'll not object to Fernand staying? I move now only with difficulty; even using the speaking tube calls for vast effort."

Drew doused an oyster liberally with sauce. "Makes no odds to me," he grunted, and gulped it down, then helped himself to crackers with black-nailed fingers. Puzzled, for his uncle did not ordinarily welcome company when interviewing clients, Fernand took station by the door and maintained an expression of courteous alertness.

"That there book," said Drew after swallowing noisily, "should show you hold twelve thousand dollars of my money."

"Including the credit you left at the beginning of the war," Marocain murmured, not even glancing at the ledger, "the total comes to twelve thousand eighty-three. And six cents."

"I want it," Drew said, taking another oyster. "All of it. Now."

To cover his surprise Marocain sipped his wine. It was good, of course; it had been long since he had been obliged to put up with inferior provisions. But the certainty gave him little pleasure, for he could not truly enjoy it. Not only did the fumes from the burner on his desk ruin his sense of smell—the mere act of reaching out his arm sent pangs like splinters of glass through his back and shoulder.

He needed time, though. Time to reason out, with this strange exasperating slowness the disease had murrained on him, Drew's purpose in making this demand. And believed he had hit on it for long enough to put the idea into words.

"Ah! Will your new steamer also be called *Atchafalaya?* Fernand, prepare a sight draft, please."

Drew downed his second oyster and interrupted.

"New steamer?" he echoed with contempt. "Hell, *what* new steamer? I got to get along as best I can for as long as I can with the wreck I presently have. Makes things easier, I guess, there being so few top boats at work this season, but I wouldn't lay two cents on her paying her way next year. . . What's it to you, anyhow? You don't hold any paper on her! You don't write steamboat insurance!"

Marocain countered placatingly, "You must admit that it was reasonable to assume you planned to commission another."

Drew drained his wine with a grimace. "If ever I can, I shall," he muttered. "I have in mind a boat that will . . . But next year. At the soonest, next year."

By now Fernand had opened up the hinged shelf where he had been trained to take dictation like his cousins before him. Marocain believed in his staff learning all branches of the business; he expected them to switch at a moment's notice from the shop to the countinghouse, from calculating the discount on a bill to appraising jewelry.

On it Fernand set an inkwell and penwiper, a stack of forms printed with the firm's name and an engraving that purported to show the Vieux Carré in 1803, and a pen with a brand-new nib . . . which he caught himself sucking, to get rid of grease. His lips moved in a silent curse; what was tolerable in the countinghouse was a gaffe in the bureau.

To the captain Marocain was saying evenly, "If the draft is not to be in favor of a boatbuilder, should it bear your own name? If so, where shall I cause it to be payable?"

"Cash!" Drew barked.

"I beg your pardon, sir?"

"I said cash! I'd as soon take Jeff Davis dollars as one of your scraps of paper! I want *real money* even though I must rent a handcart to carry it away in!"

Marocain thought that over for a while. The stimulus of this confrontation was making his mind active again. He answered after due consideration, "Then you will have to wait until Monday. Possibly Tuesday."

"You refuse to pay?"

"Refuse?" Marocain signaled with his eyes to Fernand, for what he was about to do was risky, given the captain's notorious temper. Luckily this young man had twice the insight of his own sons . . . or so, in the dismal grip of insomnia, he had often suspected. A restless, discontented streak had cropped out in Fernand, and the old banker found it made him think again of his own beginnings. There should be an element of rebellion in young people, a determination to improve on what had gone before. Whereas Eugene and Richard had always done as they were told, taken their generous allowances, said thank you for being accepted into the firm . . . Dull, both of them! Reliable, but boring!

That was what he was thinking. Aloud, he was saying, "Did you lead a very sheltered existence during the war, Captain?"

Drew's head jerked as though he had been slapped. "What the devil d'you mean by that?" he rasped.

Marocain said nothing. But his sharp eyes, between lids that had the tint and consistency of suet, were fixed unwinkingly on the steamboater.

"I did nothing I'm ashamed of," Drew said at last, and hefted his wineglass meaningly. A twitch of Marocain's eyebrow gave Fernand permission to refill it.

And then, with a grinding tone like pebbles in a spring spate: "I did the best I could in my position."

As though the last couple of sentences had never been uttered, Marocain said, "It goes against my grain to disappoint you, but we hold smaller quantities of bills and coin than in the old days. Indeed, if there's any place in the city where twelve thousand dollars cash can be found right now, it's likely the safe of an army paymaster. But there's an excellent chance of getting it by Monday. With the speed of modern railroads . . ."

He let the words tail away. Just as he had hoped, reference to railroads was enough to make Drew think again. Gulping wine, the captain said, "Your draft—well, of course I know it will be honored! But even so . . ."

"If I may put in a word," Fernand ventured, "many people nowadays prefer them. There's danger in carrying money through the streets."

"So I've heard," Drew grunted. "That's why I chose my oldest bag to pack it in. And—!" He patted a significant bulge under his coat.

"Granted, Captain," said Fernand. "But apart from the question of whether your bag will stand the weight of gold or the bulk of bills, there are some so poor that even a shabby bag is desirable, and many of them are armed, too."

Once more his uncle's eyebrow twitched. This time what it signaled was approval.

At last Drew heaved a monstrous sigh.

"I'd so looked forward to tossing it in the devil's face! All the way from Cairo I've been thinking of how he'd drool and scrabble about on hands and knees to make sure not one penny escaped. . . But I'd rather buy him off my back than wait until this week is out. Write one of your damn' papers. It'll have to do."

Fernand seized his pen. "For how much, sir?"

"Twelve thousand level. If he hopes for interest he may go whistle. It's bad enough that I've been forced to—"

Drew broke off, as though suddenly he had heard what he was saying, and drowned the rest of the remark with wine.

"In whose favor should I make it payable?" Fernand prompted.

"A son of a bitch who too long has gone by the name of Langston Barber. *May he rot!*"

With convulsive violence the captain flung his glass to shatter in the fireplace.

Fernand was glad of Drew's outburst. It permitted him to ascribe to startlement the great black streak his pen spilled across the page, obliging him to make a fair copy.

But it was not the noise of breaking glass that had shaken him. And he suspected his uncle had realized.

However, the old banker remained impassive while authenticating the draft with his now crabbed signature. Then to Fernand as he applied the blotting paper he said, "Show the captain out. Then come back. I have other matters to discuss."

Aware that something was amiss yet unsure what, Drew scrutinized the document, found it in order, pocketed it, and awkwardly took his leave.

Fernand was by no means sorry.

Marocain sat statue-still. But his mind was livelier than at any time since illness struck him down. He was reviewing all he knew about Hosea Drew: rumors, hints, allegations, libels . . . And thinking also about his older half-brother Jacob, who had married a St. Louis girl. Hosea had been his mud-clerk—no, his mate. That had been aboard the first *Atchafalaya*, and the present one was the fourth, so it had all been a long time ago, before (so the story went) his celebrated meanness drove Hosea to train as a pilot in order not to have to pay anybody more than himself.

The old man's ruminations led to a conclusion. Were it true, then Hosea Drew must be just about the most dogged man who ever navigated on the Mississippi.

And quite possibly one of the silliest, too.

The door opened again. He roused himself.

"Sit down, young man. Take some wine. Finish the oysters. And relax. I'm not about to roast you for wasting ink."

Fernand gave a sheepish grin and perched obediently on the edge of the chair Drew had vacated. Having poured barely enough wine to wet his lips, but making no move to touch it or the food, he awaited his uncle's pleasure.

Staring into nowhere, the latter said, "I have the impression you do not relish the prospect of dedicating your life to loans and pledges and rates of interest."

In a properly horrified tone Fernand replied, "Sir! I assure you I'm most sensible of your patronage and do all I can to deserve it."

Marocain made a dismissive gesture—only it wrenched his arm, and for a second he had to close his eyes and grit his teeth.

"Uncle! May I bring you medicine? Or call your doctor?"

Mastering his pain, Marocain snorted. "To perdition with doctors! My last one gave me pills made of opium. My mind was so foggy, I was spending half my time in wonderland. I'd rather suffer honestly than be consigned to a cotton-candy jail. But . . ."

This with a deep slow sigh.

"But may it be long before you find out what it is to be trapped inside an aching head, balanced on a neck that's usually stiff with pain, and when it isn't fills your ears with grinding noises as it turns, and all *that* on a body which betrays you every time you let your attention wander . . ."

He gave a harsh laugh, more like a croak.

"Even so, I remember what it was like to be your age. In those days I hadn't yet learned that the flow of money through the world is as much a force as the current of the Mississippi. Its workings are more subtle than spectacular, but they are real . . . Why did you spill ink on hearing mention of Langston Barber?"

Biting his lip, Fernand stared at the carpet. But his uncle's patience threatened to last indefinitely. He was compelled to make a go of it.

"It would be unfeeling for someone in my position, sir, to disown his non-European ancestry. Repression and ignorance fetter the colored citizens of this nation. Given the chance, though, free persons of color have proved they can lead lives as respectable as anyone's."

"One heard some such argument during the war," Marocain said with gentle irony. And made haste to add, "Don't misunderstand me. Knowing how attached your father was to your mother—caring somewhat for her myself—could I disagree? But what does this have to do with Barber?"

Emboldened, Fernand said, "Contrariwise, some people who boast of all-white descent are capable of barbaric actions!"

"And he is one of them?"

"Yes!"

"Curious, then, that he should be regarded by many swells of your generation as a model to be emulated, inasmuch as he began with nothing but a shack and now owns one of the largest hotels in the city."

"Hotel? It's a gambling hell and house of assignation! And knowing how he acquired the funds to buy it—"

"*Do* you know? Am I to take it that you speak with authority because you frequent the Limousin?"

It was on Fernand's tongue-tip to say, "How could I, on what you pay me?" In the nick of time he substituted a meeker answer.

"No, sir. But I'm acquainted with one or two men who do."

"Yes, I've been informed you spend your spare time in what is known as river company. Is that the case?"

Fernand swallowed hard. "Well, while it's true that some rivermen are not even rough diamonds, the majority—"

Marocain contrived to raise his hand.

"I've been serving the banking needs of rivermen since before you were born. There's no need to defend them to me. Which is why I'm so amazed at Captain Drew! Can you think of any reason for him to make over his entire credit to this Barber whom you believe guilty of crimes beyond description? Pour more wine and eat those oysters before they grow a mold."

Fernand reached hurriedly for the decanter.

"One would imagine," he ventured, "a gambling debt."

"But we are talking of Hosea, are we not?" Marocain cradled his glass in claw-thin hands. "Hosea, so little of a gambler that he let his steamer rot rather than risk losing her in action! Had it been his half-brother who marched in demanding all his funds in cash, I'd have had my explanation ready-made: he must have passed a bad night at the tables and needed to pay off his IOUs and finance the *Atchafalaya*'s next trip. Not the present boat, naturally; the first or second. By the time the third was afloat he was in the grip of the malady which was to prove his doom."

"What was that, sir?"

"Jacob, the older of the captains Drew, was a drunkard and a lecher as well as a gambler, and years before it killed him the pox drove him insane."

Looking like a boy who has just discovered that his father too is capable of lusting after a pretty girl, Fernand sat so long without speaking that Marocain finally probed, "Do they not talk about the Drews in your circle?"

"Oh, no! Since I've been old enough to seek company of my own choice rather than people Mother thinks it advisable to cultivate, Captain Drew has not been much approved of."

"Because his sympathies lay with the North?"

"I think more because he declined to share the common burden which the war imposed . . . Uncle, it isn't like you to talk this way about a client!"

"It isn't like my clients to behave this way!" riposted the banker with acerbity. "The older one grows, the more one wants the world to carry on in its accustomed fashion, the less attractive one finds novelty! How *is* it that you talk so glibly about the source of Barber's money?"

Fernand at last took a healthy swig from his glass.

"The whole city was abuzz concerning a charge laid by Mr. Hanks, superintendent of the Bureau of Free Labor. Am I to disbelieve him of all people?"

"Of course not. I applauded his appointment as a welcome change from the repressive policy of the Union forces—a betrayal, or so it appeared to someone like myself who can recall my grandfather proudly displaying his copy of the Decree of Sixteenth Pluviose, Year Two of the Republic, which was to have abolished slavery throughout France and her possessions. He acquired it while Louisiana was still under Spanish rule. Had he been caught, he'd have been executed for sedition. . . You're looking vacant, boy, and I'm appalled. Never tell me you're ashamed of your respectable revolutionary heritage!"

"I don't recall father mentioning much about it," Fernand muttered.

"When war broke out you were—let me see—fifteen . . . Oh, perhaps Alphonse felt you weren't ready for the footnotes to our family history. Though when Eugene and Richard turned fifteen I'd already made it a point to enlighten them concerning what knowledge I could foresee them needing in later life. Which did not include"—with sudden force—"the affairs of Langston Barber! You seem better informed about him than about our family!"

"That's because what we've done hasn't been made into the small change of every scandal sheet in New Orleans!"

The rain had moved north. Sunshine was shafting through the one window that was less than completely curtained. On the hearth where Drew had smashed his glass it glinted in bright points as sharp as pepper.

"I trust," his uncle said heavily and at length, "that you aren't implying you feel excluded from the family?"

"Sir, you have treated me with every kindness!"

"Thank you for that," Marocain said dryly, sipping his wine; he seemed to be moving more freely than before. "What you were alluding to," he resumed, "must, I think, have been Mr. Hanks's assertion that he was offered five thousand dollars by a planter to return what the man was pleased to call 'my' Negroes. Being who he is, Mr. Hanks naturally refused."

"Being who he is, Barber didn't!"

"But do you know that for certain, young fellow? It's true that a gang of ruffians, armed, paid, and plied with whiskey by somebody with a lot of money, did make away at pistol point with a hundred men from an army labor camp."

"Who are now as much enslaved as ever!" Fernand burst out.

"Granted, and it's a slur on the military administration of this city that those responsible have never been brought to book. The fact stands, however: neither you nor anybody else has proof that Barber was behind it."

"Where did he get the money to buy the Limousin, then?"

Marocain sighed. "You've been very properly raised to disapprove of gambling. No one who has charge of money belonging to other people should indulge in it. However, Barber has always claimed that he made enough out of the marks who came to his hovel near the Fair Ground, and you mustn't let your detestation of gambling blind you to the fact that he could well have done so, particularly since the builder of the Limousin was on the verge of bankruptcy when he returned to France. So I counsel you to keep your suspicions to yourself. Barber has contrived to be admitted to society, or at least its raffish fringes. His friends may be no more moral than those he left behind in his old hut, but they wield enormous influence. Such people can be very dangerous."

Silence fell, except for the sudden distracting grind of iron-tired wheels as a carriage was backed and turned in the courtyard. Fernand waited for his uncle to speak further, and finally rose.

"If you have no more need of me I should return to the shop."

Marocain started. "I'm sorry! My mind went wool-gathering . . . Sit down again. You're about to learn a salutary lesson concerning the force money exerts as it works its way through the world. Name one of your river friends who patronizes the Limousin."

"More acquaintances than friends, sir. Their company is faster than I care for."

"Never mind! Name one who has a mouth too large for his own good, who can easily be persuaded to talk about other people's business, and who is in the city at the moment."

After a moment's cogitation Fernand offered, "What about Mr. Cato Woodley?"

"Excellent. I'm told he's an associate of Captain Parbury; that means he spends time with men of the older generation. Where do you meet him?"

"At Griswold's, sir. That's a billiard hall where steamboaters go more to talk than to play. It's handy for the Pilots' Guild parlor and the agents Mr. Parbury used to employ before the war—the same, of course, that Mr. Woodley is with now."

"Mr. Woodley is not himself a pilot, I seem to recall."

With frank admiration Fernand said, "That's right, sir. A legacy enabled him to buy a boat when they were cheap at the outbreak of war. But he had served time on the river—as a mate, I believe."

"Is he the youngest captain presently? I make him at most twenty-six."

"Uncle, your memory amazes me! I didn't know you'd more than heard his name!"

Marocain chuckled. "Tell me, Mas' In'erlocutor, what do dem dah fireflies do fo' a livin'?"

Today he was full of surprises. Fernand had never expected to hear him shift from his normal tone to the classic exaggerated style of the end man on a minstrel line. Summoning the answer as best he could, he responded with, "Ah can't rightly say, Massa Bones, but fo' sho' it pay dem well!"

"Whaffo' yo' b'lieve it pay dem well?" said Marocain, and supplied the rest, this time in his usual voice. "Because they're an awful flash crowd. And by now you should have come up with a better explanation for the fate of Drew's twelve thousand dollars."

"Well, he could be paying off a debt incurred by his half-brother."

"That," Marocain said with mild irony, "fits what facts we have. Confirm our guess!"

Rising uncertainly, Fernand said, "Do you mean at once, or when I finish work?"

"At once! This *is* work! Don't dare forget it!"

So sharp was the banker's tone, Fernand was halfway to the door when—

"I'm sorry, boy. That's the impatience due to age. So little time remains. . . If Richard or Eugene should challenge you I can be contacted by tube. I prefer, though, not to be disturbed for the time being."

Fernand felt a grin spread over his face. He knew exactly what the old man meant: he was to take the far exit from the courtyard so as to avoid being noticed from the shop. It had begun to dawn on him that this stiff-limbed, stiff-mannered partriarch was far more like his scapegrace brother Alphonse than was generally believed, and therefore the stories told about his younger days might actually be true.

"And—here!" Marocain concluded, forcing up the front of his desk. "You'll need this." He produced a roll of silver dollars in brown paper. "Account to me for it afterwards, but make no written record. This is what, when I was your age, we used to call 'trouble-entry bookkeeping.'"

"Yes, sir," said Fernand, and then with even greater feeling: "Yes, *sir!*"

 There are certain buildings where, it seems, the hand of doom was laid before the foundation stone.

The Hotel Limousin was one of them.

It was large; it was handsome in a florid but much-admired style; it was ornamented with gilt and marble and countless mirrors, and—grand extravagance—it incorporated a bathing establishment. Located within a few minutes' walk of Tivoli Circle, it might have been expected to prove attractive to visitors having business almost anywhere in New Orleans.

But from the start things failed to work out. Advertised at competitive, and then at dirt-cheap, rates, half its rooms stood always empty. Daily, most of the cutlery and glassware in its spacious diningroom had to be removed for dusting, not washing. At a time when balls were being held even on the premises of the United States Mint, a string band hired at vast expense played to so few patrons that couples were embarrassed to take the floor.

Then, just as it seemed the tide of fortune might be turning, came the war, and the hotel suffered a disastrous blow when it was commandeered to serve as a barracks. Heartbroken, the proprietor was glad to dispose of his white elephant for scarcely more than his fare home to the province of France after which he had sentimentally named it.

The name remained. And, if not exactly in the manner first foreseen, the hotel was now flourishing. Hordes of wealthy young men ascended its broad front steps to seek diversion. Craps could be played here, and report held that the games were more than averagely honest. Roulette was offered on European wheels with a single zero, and a dozen card games. The bars offered a remarkable range of drinks, particularly cocktails; in the kitchen reigned a tolerable chef—though most of his time was misapplied to sandwiches and other snacks for gamblers too impatient to leave their places.

Also there was a ladies' entrance. This had been patterned after the one at the world-famous St. Charles Hotel and was similarly meant to attract prosperous women traveling without their husbands who were not content with boarding-houses.

It had rarely been used in the old days. Now the door swung constantly to and fro. It bore, as it always had, the minatory legend "Ladies Only" . . . but while those who came and went by it were indubitably female, to term them ladies in the strictest sense would stretch a point.

Descending from the streetcar that had brought him here, gingerly avoiding the pools of water which, as ever after a fall of rain, turned St. Charles Avenue into a quagmire, Drew stared at the Hotel Limousin. Over the past several years he had had little consolation save in solitude; nonetheless consolation was what he had found, though his few friends and many enemies would have been surprised to hear to what event he traced it back: the discovery, long before the war, of a volume of poetry forgotten by some passenger, which he had opened solely to pass the time.

Books he had naturally known: *the* Book, which he had been raised to because his mother, his father's second wife, had been devout; later, functional books of blank or plain lined paper to be hand-posted and grow into ledgers, journals, diaries; on the margin of his awareness, printed volumes ranging from abstruse sermons that he had no time for, clear to the lightest and most frivolous of novels, which he equally despised. Too much reality was inscribed on the Mississippi to let him share the popular addictions to hellfire and make-believe. When he met a preacher or a novel-reader he was . . . courteous.

But poetry seized him. Once, tackling a tricky cutoff during the first long-trade run after the spring rise, he had astonished the company of unemployed pilots who had begged a free trip of him. Drew looked on them as chickenhearted parasites.

So, savagely, he recited as he spun the wheel and played considerable carillons on his bell ropes:

> "Straight into the river Kwasind
> Plunged as if he were an otter,
> Dove as if he were a beaver,
> Stood up to his waist in water,
> Swam and shouted in the river,
> Tugged at sunken logs and branches,
> With his hands he scooped the sand-bars,
> With his feet the ooze and tangle . . .
> Show yourself now that we need you!
> Where the devil are you, Kwasind?"

Blank looks greeted him on all sides. No one could even detect the tag he'd added. It had been in his mind to crack a joke; thus far life had offered him few occasions for humor. Resigned, he made no attempt to explain the point.

In secret, nonetheless, poetry continued to claim his soul. It lit his gloomy passage through the world with scraps of philosophy he had small difficulty in adapting to his own experience. From what he read he culled a succession of memorabilia and for a week or a month or—rarely—half a year resorted to each as his temporary motto. Duty had been taught him before he was old enough to shave. The notion that pleasure might be found in compliance with duty was something his mother had neglected to explain, perhaps because her stepchild was pleasure-loving and undutiful, and the paradox surpassed her skill to resolve.

To her, his duty had been discharged by death . . . but fate had laid another on him, and—

No matter; this duty would end too, and very soon. He set his shoulders, grasped his staff, and as he advanced on his destination repeated the quotation that, more than any other, had lately been sustaining him:

> "Dauntless the slughorn to my lips I set
> And blew. Childe Roland to the dark tower came."

 Sleekly affluent now, Langston Barber moved through the public rooms of the Limousin on his daily tour of inspection, pausing now and then to exchange fashionable gossip with early-arriving patrons, wondering along with them whether the revived Metairie racecourse would prove a success, whether the true assassin of President Lincoln had been found or whether a megalomaniacal actor had been executed to disguise another's crime.

Silent in his wake followed his most trusted servants: one white, Jones; one black, Cuffy. Both had been with him since his days out by the Fair Ground. They were not as completely transformed as he, who now sent to London for his shirts, Paris for his cravats, but liveried in dark blue with gold facings they scarcely resembled the pair of pugilists who once had jointly boasted that either could have beaten up Mike Fink.

Today things were going well. It was not until he reached the front lobby— which it was his custom to check more than once a day, because its marble floor and walls made it cool, hence attractive to passers-by who were not patronizing the hotel's more profitable facilities—that anything disturbed his even progress.

Standing just inside the main door was a stumpy figure bearing a staff and a carpetbag.

A great weight should have been lifted off the heart of Hosea Drew by this confrontation. It marked the culmination of years of struggle.

But what he chiefly remembered afterward was how quickly it was over.

"Captain Drew!" And the imagined villain was an affable man of middle height, extremely well-dressed, his face and hands a trifle swarter than average and ever so slightly shiny. "Be so kind as to accompany me to my sanctum."

Horribly aware that he had arrived in a different world from his pilothouse or even the *Atchafalaya*'s once-splendid cabin, Drew complied. In a room paneled with Caribbean woods he sat on a velvet chair positioned by Jones while Cuffy relieved him of his staff and bag. He was offered a cigar—refused. And a choice of liquor—refused. But these did not smack of bribery; they were offhand, a normal courtesy.

And brightly Barber was inviting him to explain his business.

"I think I know your errand," he added. "But there really was no need, sir."

"Need?"

The single syllable escaped Drew against his will. He had wanted to pitch a bagful of money at Barber and—

But he had been cheated by the Fates. And this man dared to speak of need!

"It is customary to regard a debt of honor as dissolved by death," said Barber delicately. "And since your brother Jacob quit this vale of tears some time ago . . ." A wave of his right hand; elegantly manicured, it displayed a ring set with possibly real diamonds.

"So how did you guess what brings me here?" Drew rasped, reeling under the implications of what had just been said. Throughout his adult life the urge imposed on him by duty had been like hunger, like thirst, like what little he permitted himself to know of lust. Far worse than finding himself armed with a flimsy paper rather than a load of metal was this smooth—this impervious—this waterproof calmness Barber displayed.

"It was not only to me," the latter said, "that Jacob owed huge sums. Even as early as the time he had to be committed— Excuse me, but it has never been a secret, has it?"

Drew dumbly shook his head.

"Even at that stage, like all my colleagues and associates, I'd have renounced my claims against him. But you, sir, declined the easy option. The manner in which you have rectified the blemish your half-brother left on your family's good name is famous now. Famous!"

Drew was laying the Marocain draft on Barber's desk. He blurted, "Are you telling me you *don't* hold Jacob's IOU?"

Barber looked at the draft. Sphinxlike, his face betrayed no reaction. Slowly he said, "It's in my safe, tagged as a bad debt."

In tones of triumph Drew retorted, "But it ain't one!"

And with a grave inclination of his head Barber signified agreement, exchanged the draft for Jacob's note-of-hand, and personally and cordially escorted his visitor back to the entrance.

All the drama Drew had hoped for from this showdown, all the satisfaction and relief, would have been leached away but for a chance encounter as he and Barber were approaching the exit.

Turning away from the reception desk, a thin black boy in a multibuttoned uniform collided with him, shouting, "Paging Mars' Woodley! Paging Mars' Woodley!"

So there was a delay while Barber reprimanded the bell captain. And during it Drew had the chance to notice that the person paying most attention to the page's progress was a man trying elaborately not to be recognized.

It was the helpful clerk from Marocain's, Fernand.

 Ensconced in an armchair in the smoking room behind the Limousin's main bar, Cato Woodley awaited the sazerac he had ordered by way of a phlegm-cutter. He was scowling. So far as he was concerned, today had scarcely begun and already it was going badly. And most days were the same.

Apart from a bet or two that looked less promising by sunshine than by candle-light, none of his worries was financial. He had been liberated by the bequest from his father that enabled him to acquire a nearly new steamer and rename her after the author of his good fortune: the *Hezekiah Woodley*. While she was by no means a crack boat, she was earning her keep, and his.

But he had hoped for more.

What kind of "more" he could hardly define, even to himself. But it had much to do with the concept of a magic barrier to be crossed only by people possessing a certain status, or secret insight, or membership in orders like the Masons of the Scottish Rite.

That notion had been printed in his mind when he was a child by the grand difference between any ordinary day and a special one—a birthday, or above all Christmas. When he was three or four it had seemed a genuine miracle that transformed his home into a treasure cave of presents tied with gaudy ribbon, scented with nutmeg and cinnamon uttered at stentorian volume by great bowls of punch, cross-connected with sounds like the chorus of his sisters around the piano that once a year was put in tune so his mother might display her rusting talents. He was her youngest child and only son.

True to his childhood beliefs, he had imagined that ownership of a Mississippi steamer and the honorific Captain would constitute the golden key.

But it wasn't so much, really. At twenty-six he was the same age as the governor of Louisiana . . . Besides, within the closed world of the river there were other intangible barriers. His few years as a mate had informed him that even a boat's master must defer to her pilot; nothing, though, had prepared him for the real-life bitterness of accepting orders aboard his own steamer.

And so he felt shut out. Here, where he spent much of his free time in New Orleans, he had companionship enough; the fact that he owned a steamer while still in his mid-twenties made him an object of curiosity for many young men who could afford the Limousin's prices thanks only to their families' wealth, not to what they had earned themselves. But their patronizing tolerance was too much like what he experienced when visiting his sisters. All of them, and their husbands, believed with religious fervor that he had wasted his inheritance because the day of the steamboat was over and he should have invested in the flourishing Baton Rouge & Opelousas Railroad. Visiting with any of them was therefore like being on the mourners' bench!

How could he possibly explain to anyone he knew why he wanted above all to be a steamer captain? His motives at bottom were merely sentimental; he knew no grander sight than that of a score of steamers darkening the sky of a summer evening, one by one backing from the wharf and turning into line. So it had dismayed him to discover what dirty, repetitive, boring—and sometimes dangerous—work went into making possible that daily spectacle.

Now he visited the Limousin, or similar establishments up and down the river, searching for that lost glamour in the company of men born to riches, who had "style"—whatever that might be—and drank his health in liquor he had paid for and advised him about racehorses and the newest whores to arrive in the sporting houses.

But what he wanted most was what he could never have. He wanted admission to the select company of pilots.

Among the other places he frequented in New Orleans was Griswold's. There it was a popular pastime to watch Captain Parbury playing billiards by sound alone; he always had to be persuaded, but he always gave in, and he always amazed the onlookers, for the sense of position and timing that had made him a master pilot allowed him to judge how hard his cue must strike, at what angle, and for what result, after merely touching the three balls with feather-light fingertips. The spectators wagered on his chance of bringing off such-and-such a stroke; it was, in Woodley's experience, safer to back Parbury than bet against him. Indeed, on one occasion he had won so much from a stranger and a doubter that he insisted on sharing his good luck with the old captain, and had been vastly surprised to find the offer accepted with touching gratitude. Up to that point he had been timid in Parbury's presence; with astonishment he thereupon learned that a shy, affection-starved personality was concealed behind the gruff guise of this living legend. He had heard over and over the story of the loss of the *Nonpareil,* for Parbury never tired of telling it. But each time Woodley expressed his sympathy his sentiments were unfeigned. Along with all his family and most of his friends he had enthusiastically supported the Southern cause. It had been that which led him, on his way here today, to lash out at a blue coat. He had at once regretted the impulse. Not only was it futile to make such gestures now; every time he did that sort of thing, he was betraying his lack of the qualities he admired in pilots: their calmness, their power to analyze faint clues that others missed, to transcend reason and logic and come up with answers making sense . . .

"Paging Mars' Woodley!"

The black page had spotted him and was advancing smartly. Relieved at the distraction, he fumbled a quarter from his pocket and, standing up, made as though to offer it.

And checked, just before the boy's white-gloved hand could close on it.

Anxious, the page said, "Suh, dey a man at de fron' desk askin' fo'—"

"You want this?" Curtly, rolling the coin between finger and thumb.

The boy dropped his eyes. He said, "I get mah pay, suh. I don't got no right to—"

"It's yours anyhow! On one condition! Next time you page me, remember it's not *Mister* Woodley—it's *Captain* Woodley!"

He tossed the coin at the boy and stalked away.

In the moment before Barber returned from reproving the bell captain, Drew saw a fair man in his twenties, overdressed, with a long jaw and protuberant eyes, appear in response to the page's summons, and hesitate on realizing that by the front desk stood *two* men he recognized, one a mere clerk—and of mixed blood into the bargain—and the other an unknown whom he had come close to whipping a few hours ago. Visibly he was torn three ways, suspecting, as it were, a challenge to a duel, the serving of a process, and the yet worse prospect of being doubly ignored.

It was a sight to be relished, and Drew made the most of it. He turned his leave-taking into a ceremony and marched out making the greatest possible racket with his staff. Best of all, he recollected before he was over the threshold a quotation apt for Langston Barber, who had given him so improbably warm a welcome.

"A man," he told the air, "may smile! And smile, and be a villain!"

The rightness of the phrase restored his spirits. Perhaps, he reasoned, the disappointment he had felt might be due to the novelty of freedom. Perhaps a slave, told without warning he was no longer owned, might find himself at a similar loss?

But the crucial truth was that when he returned to St. Louis he would be able to confront Susannah and her children and tell them their lives were no longer clouded by a legacy of disgrace. He wanted desperately to be forgiven for his apparent selfishness during the locust-eaten years of wartime, when sometimes even she had reproached him for giving no more than the house they sheltered in and the food his money daily brought to table. But surely, when all the facts were laid before her, she'd relent!

Suddenly he realized he was hungry. Before reaching his agents' office he stepped into an oyster bar and enjoyed a gravy-dripping po'-boy and, by way of celebration, a beer or two.

Or three, or maybe half a dozen.

 At twenty-eight a disappointed man, ex-prodigy Gaston d'Aurade defied superstition and peered through a chink in the stage curtain at the audience assembling for this afternoon's performance in the Grand Philharmonic Hall.

Which was not grand in the least. Its décor had been shamelessly copied from the French Opera House, which was one of the showplaces of New Orleans, but everything had been scratched and scuffed and spoiled by careless customers. And as to philharmonic—why, the Muses must be weeping on Olympus!

At any rate, that was Gaston's opinion.

Not that he was in the habit of voicing it. He had few friends and no intimates this side of the Atlantic. Five years earlier he had been beside himself with excitement at the invitation extended to him by his mother's second cousin, who had built the Hotel Limousin:

> "What we need to enliven the patrons of our ballroom is someone like your Gaston, who was sent to the Conservatoire on a scholarship, was he not? With his collaboration, I feel certain we could draw a capacity crowd, not only because he played so well, but because of his talent as a composer."

That talent had not made so great an impression on the professors of the Conservatoire. Consequently his parents were disillusioned; they were dropping hints about the law, or the church, or commerce. Directing a ballroom orchestra, besides, had not been what he originally envisaged. His tastes tended more toward the symphony ensemble with twenty first and a dozen second violins. At least, though, he defiantly declared, he would be making a living at music if he emigrated to America!

Where (but he did not mention this point aloud) the competition would be less intense. His visions were of an artistic desert. Eighty years after the foundation of their country, with so much aid from France, what had Americans produced by way of music? A handful of pretty songs suitable for refined drawing rooms; the barbarities of Gottschalk; and the nigger minstrel show!

Surely his refined skills would automatically make an impact on so bleak a musical scene!

Except they didn't.

Convinced he was headed for fame and fortune, he had engineered a change in his name while crossing the Atlantic. *Daurade* in French designated a humble fish. As early as fourteen he had dreamed of a lost apostrophe that would transform it by the honorific *de*, and thereby create an ancient dukedom: Aurade! According to what he read, the so-called "democratic" Americans were just as vulnerable to hints of old nobility as his compatriots under the Second Empire. Steeling himself for argument, he had explained to the customs inspector that there had been a minor error, doubtless due to jealousy on the part of some plebeian bureaucrat . . . and found his well-rehearsed story wasted on a man used to transcribing unspeakable names from Sicily and Armenia and the Lord knew where. Indeed he had said outright, "Makes no odds how you spell it, long as you always spell it the same!"

Likewise his name-change had done nothing to draw dancers to the Hotel Limousin when printed on countless posters to advertise its luxurious appointments. No more had his physical appearance, of which he was almost as proud as of his musical gift. More than one portrait artist had desired the privilege of fixing his features on canvas. . . back in France. The "artist" assigned to capture his likeness for publicity in New Orleans worked with glass plates and foul chemicals, and a sitting amounted to agonizing minutes rather than leisured hours.

What a land this was for rush and hurry, and how little substance underlay the surface! It was like its money—the paper that had financed the late war and was now to be redeemed, so rumor went, at a cent on the dollar if you were lucky. Before the bankruptcy of the Limousin both he and its owner had been naïve enough to take anything that bore a dollar sign. Half of the bills he had accepted were now fit for nothing but—well, blowing your nose.

Ultimately he had been cast ashore here, like a survivor from a steamer wreck. On first hearing its name he had assumed this hall to be a serious establishment dedicated to the great composers. In fact it was a vaudeville theatre, where the audience came less to listen than to marvel at scene changes made by steam machinery. The band under his direction was generally composed of incompetents, and as for the shows themselves, he could barely endure to watch them once; the tenth or twentieth time was torment. Yet people parted with good money to watch these clumsy tumblers, these cork-blackened coon singers, these crude melodramas interrupted halfway through so that some shrill soprano or booming bass could intone a sentimental ballad. . .

It was time to start the overture. Turning away, he wondered whether fortune would ever smile on him again.

 "Oh, I do so hope this is a good show!" sighed Louisette Moyne as she and her friend Anna Parks crossed the foyer of the Grand Philharmonic Hall. The plan had been for them to enjoy a picnic by Lake Pontchartrain; thanks to the rain they had canceled the project in favor of the French Opera House, only to find there were no tickets left. This place was a raffish second best, and neither of their mothers would approve their being here.

"Do I take it," said Anna perceptively, "that today went wrong even before we called off the picnic?"

"Oh, we spent ages and ages at Marocain's ordering a watch for Papa. Mama can't keep her mind made up two minutes together!"

"She seems to have kept it made up for twenty years."

"You know what I mean! But—oh!"—clasping her hands as they followed an usher to their seats—"I must tell you! I saw someone at Marocain's who is apparently *notorious!*"

"How thrilling," Anna said with a noticeable lack of emphasis.

"Almost too thrilling!" Louisette insisted. "When he marched in demanding twelve thousand dollars to put in a horrible old bag he'd brought, I thought he must be a robber! At all events he didn't get what he came for."

"Was he thrown out?"

"No, no! But you must have noticed that a full bag makes a person carrying it walk differently from an empty one? It always annoys me at the theatre when they don't put a rock in the property baggage to make it convincing."

"How observant you are!"—with gentle mockery. "But you haven't told me who this notorious person was."

"Oh! The steamboater, Captain Drew!"

Wincing as he discovered how loudly his chair was going to creak throughout this afternoon's performance, Arthur Gattry took a surreptitious swig of whiskey from the silver flask he always carried, glancing around in search of acquaintances and pretty girls. Then he had to conceal it hastily as his companions took their places: his sister Violet, and her husband Morton Farmiloe, who dealt in sugar, molasses and tobacco now that slaves were no longer to be bought and sold, and disapproved of the fast life of a sporting man like Arthur.

At random, thinking to ingratiate himself, he said, "You know Marocain the jeweler and banker?"

"Of course. I have funds out at interest with him," said Farmiloe. "Why?"

"A repulsive man came into his shop this morning while I was helping Hugo to select a ring. Frankly we thought he was demanding money with menaces, and I was all set to pitch him back on the street when it turned out he was this Captain Drew who's making a fortune out of repatriating prisoners of war."

"He must be raking it in by easier means than theft!" said Violet. "What gave you such an idea, anyway?"

Arthur explained. Partway through, he stiffened in his seat, staring at two girls—one fair, one dark, both attractive—gossiping in the front stalls. Surely the blonde . . . ?

But the light was poor and he could not be certain.

Hurriedly, because the overture was drawing to a close, he concluded, "But Marocain can't have given Drew what he was after. I swear he left without a penny of it!"

Violet failed to repress a giggle.

"You find that funny?" Arthur demanded. "Why?"

"Not you, not you!"—veiling her amusement with a lacy fan. "The conductor! He just gave you such a murderous look for talking while the music's going on!"

"Ssh!" said several people within earshot. The curtain had begun to rise.

But Arthur paid more attention to the girls, and his flask, than what was happening on stage.

 The offices of T. Caudle & Co., shipping agents, were businesslike to the pitch of austerity, particularly compared with Marocain's: a long dark wooden counter marred by the knives of errand-boys who had carved their initials or whittled its edge; china inkwells chipped and cracked; gaslights without benefit of globes. . .

At the moment Drew walked in, Mr. Theobald Caudle himself was putting his head around the plain deal door of the room where he held confidential discussions.

"Captain Drew!" he exclaimed. "Where in heaven's name have you been?"

Drew blinked incomprehension.

"We've been searching the city high and low—thought you must have been taken ill or . . . Never mind! This way, please, and hurry!"

Present already in Caudle's bureau were three other men: two plainly dressed, each carrying a thick memorandum book and a sheaf of pencils, and a third in army major's uniform.

"Major Arbrey!" Caudle said breathlessly as he resumed his chair beside a desk that had seen better days. "And Mr. Sweet and Mr. Vanaday, who are—"

"Government inspectors of steamboats," Vanaday said in a rumbling voice. "I don't believe we ever met before, Captain, and I'm sorry we should meet now under such circumstances."

For Drew the world seemed to be grinding to a halt. He said, putting his boldest face on matters, "What d'you mean?"

"You," the major declared, "have executed a fraudulent contract!"

"When he signed up," Sweet put in, "Captain Drew may not have known about the defects which—"

"Defects?" Drew barked.

"Very well," Vanaday muttered. "If that's the way you prefer it. . . Captain Drew, it is my duty to bring to your attention this list of defects in the steamboat *Atchafalaya* which render her unfit for navigation."

He held out a document which Drew numbly disregarded.

Tossing it on the desk corner nearest him, Vanaday said, "This doesn't have to be served like a regular process. You can't refuse it. Man!"—with sudden force. "What possessed you to sign up for a government contract with a boat in that state? It's a miracle she didn't go the way of the *Sultana!*"

Drew jerked forward on his chair. "What about the *Sultana?*"

"You didn't hear?" Amazement spread over Sweet's face. "Surely at the Guild parlor—"

"Haven't been there yet," Drew cut in gruffly.

The others exchanged glances. "We presumed that was where we'd find you," Caudle said at length. "One of my clerks has been waiting there half the day. Had you followed the normal professional routine, I assure you the *Sultana's* fate would not be news."

"There *are* other agents in this city!" Drew flared.

"What makes you think they'll take your business after this?" demanded Arbrey. "Even if you have a boat to do business with!"

"I do have a boat, damn you! Spend a couple of thousand on her, and she'll . . ."

But his words tailed away. All of them knew that, in the condition the *Atchafalaya* had now reached, money for repairs would be wasted.

"Well, what about the *Sultana*, anyhow?" Drew snapped, as though desperately seeking to elude his predicament. "I saw her on a long whistle just a couple of days ago, out of Vicksburg for St. Louis as I recall, in the same trade as me except she was carrying prisoners from a Confederate camp. She—"

"She made it to just beyond Memphis," cut in Vanaday. "She was licensed to carry three hundred and seventy-six people, and the captain took on board above two thousand. And she blew up. They say she rained dead bodies on either bank."

After that, silence obtained for a while. At last Drew managed to grind out, "Are you going to take away my license?"

"Can't," said Sweet succinctly. "Won't neither. Any man could run a wreck like yours in record time from Cairo to New Orleans just has to be a lightning pilot. But if you wish to be a master again, sir, it got to be aboard a sounder boat."

 Night had fallen when Drew returned to the levee with slumped shoulders and dragging feet. He paused for a while and stared at the silhouette of the doomed *Atchafalaya*. To be so repaid for all his efforts! It was monstrously unjust!

And then, of a sudden:

"Suh, ain't you Cap'n Drew?"

Coming out of darkness, the words made him raise his staff in alarm. Then a light was struck and dispelled the murk enough for him to identify those waylaying him: Fernand and Cuffy.

"Thank heaven we found you!" Fernand exclaimed.

"Think I've been in hiding?" Drew countered sourly. "Let me by."

"But we have a message for you—an important message!"

"To blazes with it and you! I said let me by!"

"This *is* important, sir!"

"And even if it is, why should I listen?" Drew planted his staff firmly on the ground and clasped both hands around it, glaring. "I can guess who it's from. I know this nigra—saw him earlier today. *And* you! Not just at Marocain's but at the Limousin too, paging a son of a bitch who'd tried to run me down with his buggy!"

"I went to the Limousin, Captain," said Fernand in a tight voice, "not because I take special pleasure in the company of Mr. Woodley, but because my uncle so directed me. I came here to relay Mr. Barber's message for the same reason. As soon as he heard about your boat being condemned—"

"He learned that so quickly?" Drew interrupted. "Well, it figures. 'For evil news rides post while good news baits!'"

"Today's news may not be wholly evil for you, sir. That's the point. Mr. Barber has sent a carriage. Will you go with Cuffy?"

"Oh, hell," Drew said wearily. "Maybe he wants to help me find a job. It's certain I don't have one now. 'Othello's occupation's gone!' And so"—realizing with a start—"is my bag . . . but never mind. I guess one of those folk you were talking about, so poor even an old bag is precious— Boy, I reckon I'm drunk. Am I?"

"Well, to be blunt, sir, I would not care to be aboard a boat you were taking round Plum Point in your present condition. If you'll excuse me."

"Hah? What?" Blinking ferociously. "Have you put in river time?"

"As a passenger, that's all. But I surely would like—" Fernand broke off. "Well, sir? What about Mr. Barber?"

"I hoped I'd never hear that name again," Drew sighed. "But I don't have any choice, do I?"

 Dining with his brother officers, Major Hugo Spring said, "Name of Drew mean anything to you—Hosea Drew?"

"Steamboat captain," the man opposite said promptly. "Went north, but laid up his boat instead of putting it at our disposal. We could have found a use for it, believe me!"

"That's the one. Well, he marched into Marocain's today demanding twelve thousand dollars he'd left on deposit. Wanted it packed in an old carpetbag!"

That provoked mild interest. Another of his comrades said, "I have money with Marocain, too. What happened?"

"I saw him leave. And I swear his bag was no heavier than when he brought it in."

Imelda Moyne and her husband were dining alone tonight . . . alone, that is, but for the black servants who silently attended them as though the war had never happened. Between them stretched an immaculately polished mahogany table on which silver and lace and cut crystal betokened affluence that permitted their sons to be at college in Europe and status that befitted membership in the Mistick Krewe of Comus and had caused their daughter to be cited as a potential Queen of the Mardi Gras.

Silence reigned for most of the meal. Andrew Moyne was much preoccupied at present with what had come close to being a financial disaster for them. Seeking sound investments when most American currency was turning into paper as valuable as autumn leaves, he had poured money into a Scottish firm that planned to supply wood for the new "safety" matches invented in Sweden and now being mass-produced in Britain. Long-range inquiries indicated that the Mr. Donald Macrae who had launched the enterprise was regarded as a business wizard. Unfortunately he had expropriated all the liquid assets of the venture the day before it was announced that the trees which he intended to exploit did not belong to him, but to the Dukedom of Buccleuch. Keeping up until the last a fog of prevarication and excuses, he vanished thereafter from the ken of mankind.

Moyne was not the least eager among countless persons who looked forward to finding Macrae and flaying him alive.

However gloomy his reflections, though, he conquered them long enough to inquire how the day had gone for his wife.

She explained. And added thoughtfully, "I feel inclined to withdraw our custom from Marocain."

"Why?" Her husband blinked in surprise.

"One has the impression he caters to a less select clientele than formerly. At all events a man stormed in this morning wearing such foul clothes that Louisette was positively shaken. Foul-mouthed, too, and for all I can tell flea-ridden! He insisted that they owed him twelve thousand dollars and wanted it in cash. Not that he got it. He'd brought a horrible greasy bag to put the money in, and when he left it was as light as before."

At mention of so large a sum her husband's full attention had come to bear. He said cautiously, "Did you find out who this person was?"

"They called him Captain." She frowned. "Not an officer. I mean, not an army officer. One of those was present and courteously assured our safety. But the clerks addressed him as—I have it! Captain Drew!"

Moyne started. "Master of a steamboat, was he?"

"I imagine he might be."

"Hah!" Draining his wineglass, he rose. "Thank you for warning me!"

"What about, dear?"—in a puzzled tone.

"I'd heard that Drew was back. And he's an astute businessman. If he's withdrawing his credit from Marocain's, there's bound to be an excellent reason!"

Fueled by such rumours, a run on the Marocain Bank began next day.

In an alcove secluded by screens from the Limousin's main dining room, Langston Barber was preparing to attack a dish of pompano with *sauce aux crevettes*. Fridays detracted little from the luxury enjoyed by those among his customers who, like himself, insisted on the strict observances. And they were many. In New Orleans, perhaps more

than any other city of North America, superstition held the worshipers of Lady
Luck in bondage; they slid from rarefied Catholicism to the use of brutal slave-
taught charms without noticing a hiatus in their thinking.

Knife poised, he was interrupted by a rasping voice.

"So this is what a stately pleasure dome looks like! If I'm addressing Kubla
Khan, what happened to the ice?"

Into the chair facing him slumped Drew, manner and tone alike hostile. It was
stuffily hot in this room despite its high ceiling and marble walls, not only because
the night was warm and humid but because of the many gaslights. Barber summoned the nearest waiter.

"Bring my guest a drink! Captain, what would you like?"

"To be anywhere except here! Oh . . . Same as you, I guess. *I* don't understand
liquor. I went without for so many years, and it and I don't get along."

"In that case, sir, I won't commend the champagne I'm drinking. Particularly
because, if we are to discuss the matter I mean to broach, I would not wish to put
you at any disadvantage."

"Hah?" Drew's head jerked up. "Discuss what? I thought you must have had
me haled in here so you could gloat!"

"Captain!"—with an expression of distress—"I assure you the proposal I have in
mind is perfectly valid!"

"Then break it on my bows," sighed Drew. And, seizing a clean glass from the
array in front of Barber, he waved it in the direction of the waiter. "Ah, fill it up
with whatever's going!"

Receiving a nod from his employer, the waiter lifted the champagne bottle and
poured to the two-thirds mark. Drew drank that at a gulp and signaled for more.

"There's no justice in this damned world," he said suddenly. Barber flinched,
afraid he was to be shouted at; however, Drew's tone was rather of resignation
than of fury.

"Why do you say so?" Barber parried. And, in passing: "May I offer you anything to eat?"

"Not hungry."

"In that case . . ." Replacing his cutlery, Barber let the waiter remove his dish,
saying, "Tell the cook to keep it warm, if he can without it spoiling. Otherwise
send it to another table. It's untouched."

"All manners, aren't you just?" Drew said with contempt. "Show and shine and
finery! Like the cabin of my boat—like it *was*. . . And did you earn it the way
they taught me, by slaving and sweating and struggling till I was like to die? The
hell! You got it by gambling!"

He looked for a place to spit and located an engraved brass cuspidor. But when
he pursed his lips to let go, he realized there was no chaw to generate juice. He
felt in his pocket and found no sign of his plug tobacco. Under his breath he
began to curse.

And thereupon the ice jam broke that he had constructed within his head for
two decades. Out came the secrets he had planned to reserve for Susannah and
her children. Out came the resentment that festered in his mind because he saw
his rivals enjoying the advantages of wealth for far less effort than he had to in-

vest, while every cent he earned was already pledged: so much to pay off crazy Jacob's debts; so much to support Susannah in a house with at least a couple of servants; so much to provide for Elphin, and Dorothy, and Eustace, and Jerome who woke every night screaming because he always dreamed he was about to suffocate; and last of all a residue that was again subdivided, chiefly to keep the steamer running, ultimately to keep her master's body together with his soul.

As the minutes ticked by, the torrent of words eroded the mask of the strict steamer captain. Revealed like a mussel in a broken shell was the naked heart of the teen-age boy within, the boy who had so idolized his half-brother that he would hear of no other career but one where they could work together; who had quarreled with his mother and insulted his father and come close to losing his family completely; who had carried his admiration for Jacob to the point of falling in love with the same girl . . . and then, slowly and horribly, discovered that his parents had been right after all, for the man he thought godlike, wonderful, fell victim first to drink and then to disease, and bet away at the gaming tables what was not his to lose, at last making so conspicuous a spectacle of himself that his few remaining friends felt obliged to commit him to an asylum, where he wore away his final years in a delirium of fanciful projects that would make him millions and restore all he had pilfered from his relatives, from his wife, from what should have been the portion of his children. It was not the least of the matters on his conscience that he had infected Susannah with the syphilis that was killing him. Miraculously, it appeared that the children had escaped.

Though it was impossible not to wonder about poor Jerome.

Abruptly it dawned on Drew what he was saying . . . and also that tears were leaking down his cheeks. As ashamed as though he had wet his pants, he stared at the man opposite. What magic had been worked to make him open his secret thoughts to someone he detested beyond measure?

And why was this fiend incarnate shaking his head with a sympathetic look and flourishing Marocain's draft?

With infinite effort he composed his mind and readied himself for Barber's reaction like a cub awaiting a senior pilot's verdict on the way he had steered through the last bend.

But the words he heard were gentle and made sense.

"Mr. Drew, who better than a gambler should understand misfortune? Did I not tell you I was not expecting you to honor your brother's debts? To take advantage of a sick man—why, I'm appalled that you thought I'd do such a thing!"

He leaned forward, displaying the draft much as a lady would wave a fan.

"What will you do now, Mr. Drew?"

Drew shrugged, remotely aware that his glass had been filled again, and also that Jones had turned up at his employer's right. He tried and failed to recollect what had become of Fernand. His presence would have been welcome, like a second's at a duel.

"They were magnanimous enough not to take away my license," he said eventually. "I guess I'll get a job that pays—sufficient."

He drained his glass for the latest of too many times.

"But you stand no chance of repairing the *Atchafalaya*?" Barber pressed. "Or selling her for enough to commission a new steamer?"

"Hell, no. The inspectors are right, damn them! My fault, I guess, for specifying cheap wood, cheap piping, cheap everything, to save money. But if I'd had the chance . . . !"

"To do what?" Barber encouraged.

"I have such a boat in mind as would put the nose of any rival out of joint. Think I'm crazy? Maybe so. But I *know* I could design the finest steamer ever on the Mississippi if I had a fraction of her cost. If I had, let's say, ten thousand dollars."

"And you don't, after all your effort?"

"Oh, hell! You know how much Jacob owed when he was locked away? A hundred thousand! And I've paid it back! All of it! Yours was the last!"

There was a pause. Eventually Barber said, "Mr. Drew, when impulse made me send my servants to seek you out, I hoped and expected I was to make the acquaintance—the proper acquaintance, not a brief encounter like this morning's—of an honorable man, a gentleman. My expectations have been outrun by events. It would be contemptible were I to complete our negotiations under present circumstances. Allow me to put a room at your disposal. In the morning—"

"What's all this?" Drew rasped, eyes sparking.

"Captain, I merely wish to emphasize that, while I'm of course delighted that you find my wine so palatable, its effect on you has been—"

"*What negotiations?*" The final *s* blurred into *sh*. "Talk straight, damn you!"

"I was going to say: enjoy a night's repose here, and tomorrow—"

"Come to the point!"

Barber took a deep breath.

"Very well, if that's how you want it. You say you would like to build the finest steamer ever on the Mississippi, and you could if you had ten thousand dollars. I believe you. I am prepared to endorse this draft in favor of any boatbuilder you care to name, on account of her construction. I am further prepared to offer, whenever you are in the city, a room at the Limousin—no, make that a suite—and as many meals as you care to take, at no extra charge. I would regard this as an investment to be set against a half-share in the profits of this boat you claim you can design."

"Claim?"—belligerently. "I'll goddamn' well show you! You and everybody else. All the shit-kicking bastards who . . . It's a deal! Drunk or sober, I know when I'm on to a good thing!"

"I hoped that would be your answer," came the grave response. "I have derived the most favorable impression of your capability and integrity. Name the boatyard."

"I'd go straight to Hupp & Tonks at Louisville!"

"Done, sir! Shake hands on it! Jones, pen and ink!"

## 30TH JUNE 1870

# A NEW DREAM
# THAT YET WAS OLD

~~~~~

"He had been standing on the shadowy deck
Of a black formless boat that moved away
From a dim bank, into wide, gushing waters—
River or sea, but huge—and as he stood,
The boat rushed into darkness like an arrow,
Gathering speed—and as it rushed, he woke."
—Stephen Vincent Benét,
*John Brown's Body*

Miles Parbury woke to utter darkness and the sound of a woman praying, and for a moment thought—*knew*—they were burying him alive. The air was hot and heavy, oppressive enough to be a shroud, and though it was drier than of late and smelled of dust, that only added to the horrible illusion. Here in New Orleans corpses were not consigned to the clay from whence they came, but were ensepulchered in tombs above the ground: dry places, dusty places.

Moreover an instant earlier he had assisted at the sinking of the *Nonpareil*.

The spasm of fearful certainty receded as he realized that the steamboat he had just seen blown up was not the vessel he had brought for sacrifice to the altar of war. As time went by it was growing harder for him to visualize places and objects, even those he had been familiar with since childhood—Dr. Malone said this was common among blinded people—but the new, the most magnificent, *Nonpareil* was based on a model he had carved from oddments because words did not suffice him and he could not see to make a drawing of her. He was acquainted with every inch of her lean lovely lines. And the proportions of the boat in his nightmare were those of his new triumphant masterpiece.

A dream, then. Only a dream. Followed by startled rediscovery of the daytime world. That voice he could hear belonged to his wife Adèle. Every morning she begged the Virgin to grant repose to the soul of their only child. He did not understand how she could go on deceiving herself. For his part, it had been the loss of the boy which decided him once for all that the instruction the priests had drilled him through prior to their marriage was no more than mumbo-jumbo emptier than the charms and hexes black folk believed in.

He and Adèle slept apart now, their rooms separated by a sliding screen, for that and other reasons. She was half-crippled by rheumatism. So she had had to abandon her self-imposed duty of guiding him around the city, dense with traffic of all kinds from streetcars on their unforgiving tracks down to scorching velocipedists treading away the miles as though the public roads were private raceways. Other people thought of this as one more undeserved calamity heaped on his head; Parbury, though, could have wished the distance between them greater, particularly when she prayed, because of late she had given the constant impression that she was reproaching him, as though in the private world she shared with the Mother of God the death of her son also had been a deliberate act, and his father's blindness a self-inflicted protection against knowledge of his own cruelty . . .

However, this house he had been reduced to when the war wrecked his fortunes was a poky camelback shotgun, flimsily built and intolerably cramped. On the increasingly rare occasions when his wife's relatives deigned to pay a visit,

71

they could be heard sniffing their contempt of the place. And why should they not? Compared with what he had formerly been accustomed to it was a hovel. Compared to the luxury Drew wallowed in, earned by deceit and cowardice, crowned now by the illicit acquisition of gilded horns rightfully belonging to a steamer that worked regularly in the St. Louis trade—!

The rage crested in his head like a breaking wave. Over the past seven years he had been forced to accept that rage was his normal state of mind.

Abruptly, though, it gave way to a surge of excitement, an emotion so rare in his drab existence that sometimes he feared he might have forgotten what it felt like.

But today was *the* day. The day of the showdown. The day when Hosea Drew would learn to laugh with the other side of his face!

Rising on his pillows, chuckling, he groped for his repeater watch on its bedside stand.

And checked before he touched it.

That dream . . . Could it have been an omen? Oh, no! He mustn't believe that, mustn't even think it!

Yet the possibility was so appalling, he remained awhile immobilized, scarcely aware that the praying in the next room had reached its conclusion.

He had talked much recently about matters of life and death, but not (as though to spite Adèle) with a priest or minister—instead, with someone he regarded as his peer, a practical man using his hands as much as his tongue to get ahead in the world. He had made something of a confidant of Dr. Malone, who had taken care of his and Adèle's routine treatment since the death of old Dr. Halley.

Adèle did not care for him. On hearing his name for the first time she had assumed that anyone called Malone would of course be Catholic. If he was, he must be less than devout; certainly he was undogmatic as few of his profession were, regardless of religion. Now she fretted because he would not imitate Halley and promise that her back would soon be restored to youthful suppleness. She kept whining for her husband to call in the new, the celebrated, the fast-rising Dr. Cherouen, who used electricity and ozone and must be marvelous.

But Parbury liked Malone. Halley had reminded him of one of the pilots who had trained him as a cub: not deaf to reason, but gruff and quick to anger when his judgment was even mildly questioned. In this new physician he detected a concern for process akin to what had eventually made him a better pilot than any he had learned under. There was something the tides and shifts of a living body had in common with the seasons and the currents, and he had the same whatever-it-was in common with the doctor.

That was a revelation and a consolation. And not the only one. He heard the partition separating the rooms opening; here in a rustle of starched linen came another blessing he owed to Malone.

"Good morning, Dorcas my dear," he said briskly.

"Good morning, Captain," she returned, her voice sweetly inflected. "Shall I send in your coffee and beignets?"

It was a euphemism; she would not send but bring, for they could not afford—nor in any case would the house have accommodated—the establishment of servants they had been used to before the war. Still, things were improving. For years they had been reduced to one servant. Now they had two.

And this girl—no, this young lady—whom Dr. Malone had recommended as a companion for Adèle was better than a dozen unwilling slaves. She was gentle, dutiful, sympathetic, even generous. Had she not saved and scrimped from her exiguous pay to make him a present, and a valued one? In place of the coarse bandage that had formerly veiled his eyesockets, she had given him a bandanna of soft and supple silk.

Oh, she was worth her weight in gold!

Remaining in bed, as usual, for fear he might cut a ridiculous figure in bare feet and nightshirt, he replied to her question.

"Please do. Then lay out my clothing for a trip and pack my usual bag."

"Yes, Captain." A brief hesitation. Then, in a changed tone: "Sir, excuse me, but . . ."

"What is it?"

"Is there really going to be a race between the *Atchafalaya* and the *Nonpareil*? I don't know what I should believe!"

Drawing fast the sliding door, she came to perch shyly on the side of the bed.

"In the newspapers I see advertisements from Mr. Gordon and Captain Woodley, and Captain Drew as well, saying no one has the least intention of racing. Yet everybody keeps insisting that's a bluff, and so many people have bet such a lot of money there will have to be one now."

"Who's this 'everybody'—*hmm?*"

"Well, sir, when I bring you to the Guild parlor, there are by now certain gentlemen who recognize me, with whom courtesy obliges me to pass the time of day, and without exception they maintain a race is inevitable."

*So interested in my affairs!*

The idea filled Parbury with enormous satisfaction. It showed in his tone when he said, "What if it is?"

"Oh, sir! Surely even in peacetime the river is a dangerous place enough, with its snags and its sawyers and its shoals!"

Parbury started. Ever since she started guiding him to the Pilots' Guild, he had naturally talked about river matters on the way, but he had had no idea until this moment that she had so absorbed what he was telling her. She was continuing, moreover, and with such intensity that she was trembling; he could feel the vibration through the bedstead.

"Must one add other perils to what are there already? Suppose a boiler were to burst! Suppose—!"

"My dearest Dorcas!" he exclaimed, reaching for her hand and clasping it in both of his. "I'm touched, I'm deeply touched by your concern!" Her pulse was pounding under his fingertips; he tried to stroke her anxiety away.

"But I assure you, your alarm is needless! At no time is a steamboater more alert than when he's racing. The pilot musters total concentration; the engineers survey their gauges constantly; even the lowliest deckhands dedicate themselves entirely to success. After all, to win, you must arrive intact! You needn't worry. In spite of all, I hope to live out my time."

For, to his amazement, he had early discovered there could be compensations even for blindness. Soon after his return home, at about the time he became able to leave the house, it had dawned on him that he no longer stammered. And this, though it was hardly a level exchange for the keen vision he had reveled in, was at least worth having.

All the more so, it suddenly occurred to him, because . . . Well! How, for example—no: how *above all* would Dorcas have reacted to a blind man older than her father who was also tongue-tied? Not, surely, with frank expressions of concern for his safety, the outward show of what must be, what could only be, affection?

His heart pounded as violently as hers now he realized the full implications.

True, she had once been frail enough to bestow her affection unwisely. In that, however, she was not alone, and there were circumstances when—as even Adèle had conceded after a discussion with her confessor—such an act might proceed from no worse flaw than excessive generosity of spirit.

It had been balm to his soul to realize he was still capable of inspiring respect. The fact that the new *Nonpareil* had been built to his design and given the name he wanted was proof of it. Now here was evidence he might be loved as well! For Dorcas was still talking, her apprehension unallayed.

"You mean there *is* going to be a race?"

"I agree with those who say it's bound to happen, and it may very likely start this evening. All being well."

She had not let go his hand. Now she clutched it to her bosom.

"You approve?" she whispered. "Never tell me you are among the people who have laid bets!"

Sourly he said, "What with? I have no fortune any more! I have a part share in the *Nonpareil*, but that's only thanks to Mr. Gordon, and she's too new to have returned more than a pittance on what he's invested. No, but if she wins—*when* she wins—she'll have run out her major rival. From that day forward she will carry the choicest cargoes and the choosiest passengers."

"But she doesn't have to race to achieve that! Let her simply prove herself! Does she not already enjoy the reputation of being fast?"

"Oh, yes! As soon as she made her first trip, that was assured!"

"Then—"

"Dear girl!" Groping, he drew her to him and stroked the smooth hair which she wore in a tight knot. "I could no more . . . "

For a second his voice failed him. Without warning his mind was diverted off course toward a sensation recollected from his recent bad dream. He had felt a sort of resignation when Carradine insisted that the steamer round the point where they were loading enemy guns. He had known something was sure to go wrong, but he had been unable to convey his feelings.

Now he experienced the same, but in a mirror. He knew all would go well. If there were such a thing as weather in human affairs, then it was set fair for victory.

He remembered what he had not thought about for years: the thermometer-barometer, Adèle's gift, which had hung in the pilothouse of the old boat.

\*       \*       \*

Recovering, rising to her feet, Dorcas said, "Sir, you were going to say . . . ?"

"I was going to say I could no more stop this race than I could stop a war."

"Yes, Captain," she said after a pause. "I fully understand."

And hastily left the room, for she was afraid a sob might break into her voice.

She had done her utmost to dissuade Mr. Parbury from supporting the race. She had failed. But she had failed before, often enough to be no longer overwhelmed by the experience.

Resignedly, therefore, she went about her ordinary business in the kitchen.

And abruptly said to the air, "Why, of course! The old fool must think it's because of *him* I don't want there to be a race!"

A moment later she was struggling not to laugh.

**29TH JUNE 1870**

# THE HOLDER OF
# THE HORNS

~~~~~~

"As with all transport, speed was foremost concerning river steamboats. Records were kept of the best times between principal river cities, and to the fastest went the honor of 'holding the horns.' These were a gilded pair of deer antlers, a symbol of the speed king, mounted on the pilothouse. The horns were passed to the fastest boat, and since fast boats attracted business, the holder of the horns was in a unique position to profit from his distinction."

—Norbury L. Wayman,
*Life on the River*

 "But," said Captain Drew with a sigh, "even after my agree-
ment with Barber was signed and sealed, all was not even
then to be plain sailing. 'The best-laid schemes . . .'!"

"'Gang aft agley,'" automatically completed the reporter, scarcely daring to
believe his luck as his pencil flew across page after page of his notebook. Most
people who tried to interview the celebrated Hosea Drew had to go away content
with a few brusque comments about the unchallengeable superiority of his
steamer. Now it had been proved, he was in an amazingly expansive mood.

And the right note to make him open up still further had just been struck.
Drew was beaming: eyes sparkling, cheeks chubby and red above his neat gray
beard. For the summer heat, his regular coat of blue had been laid aside and he
was in vest and shirt-sleeves.

"Why, you're acquainted with the Bard of Scotland, Mr.—ah—Siskin?"

"That's right, sir: Joel Siskin!" It was only the fourth time he had talked with
Drew, and now his name was being remembered. Progress! "Yes, I've admired
Burns's poetry since my boyhood."

"Then you're a man of taste . . . ! But now is not the time to indulge my
hobbyhorses."

"You were referring," Joel hinted, "to obstacles which delayed the building of
the new *Atchafalaya*."

"So I was. We applied at once to Hupp & Tonks, of course. But their yard had
been severely damaged in the war. Next on my list would have been D. & J.
Howard, who had lately built the *Ruth* for Captain Pegram."

Joel knew all about the *Ruth*. The New Orleans *Intelligencer*, for which he
mostly wrote, had published a grandiose puff for her about the time he sold his
first article to the paper, five years before. But he wanted to know about the
*Atchafalaya*.

"Couldn't Howard's take your business either?"

"Oh, they had contracts to occupy them the next eighteen months. Besides,
there was a shortage of iron. The boilers alone would call for forty tons of it, and
when you figure in the main engines, the doctor engine, the freight hoister, and
everything else, I was bound to need at least another hundred. So for a while I
was again obliged to make ends meet in casual employment."

"Would your partner not have saved you from such makeshifts?"

Abruptly Drew's tone grew harsh. "Oh, I guess so! But being holed up here in
lonely luxury . . . Not to my taste at all! Besides, this river of ours—she's a cunning old bitch!" He glanced through the pilothouse window at the broad brown
flow aswarm with boats. "So I felt an obligation to make all the trips I could and
keep my hand in. Once that habit's in your blood you can never break it. Captain
Parbury, you know, goes tripping in spite of being blind."

Here was another fantastic stroke of luck. Joel had been hunting for a chance to mention the gray eminence behind the new *Nonpareil*. Hamish Gordon might have financed her; Cato Woodley might officially be her master; but the man who had created her was Parbury. And there she lay two berths distant!

Before he could phrase a fresh question, however, Drew was back on his former course.

"In the upshot, eight months wore away before a yard was found to take on such a grand project. When news was brought that a Mr. Cleech had tendered from New Albany, that rang none of my bells. Still, New Albany was where they built the great *Eclipse,* so at the next opportunity I visited his yard, and what I saw of the work he was doing on smaller boats decided me at once. Mention Wenceslas Cleech in your report, Mr. Siskin! He deserves it. The *Atchafalaya* has passed her fourth anniversary. Many steamers are worn out by that age, but this boat of mine was built to such a standard, she will serve as long again. You'll note that workmen have restored all the fittings which were removed for the run I was obliged to make to St. Louis the other day"—his eyes strayed almost guiltily to the golden horns swinging between the tall red chimneys; others, for shorter sections of the journey, adorned the pilothouse—"and deduce that were she not extremely sound I'd never have felt that worth the outlay. But I did, and you may assure your readers she is now as fine as ever she was, or maybe better."

"If proof were needed," Joel said in a professional tone which hovered on the edge of fawning, "that fast run would have supplied it. Has any other steamer achieved so long a run without touching shore?"

"None that I have heard of," said Drew with complacency. "It was a matter of—well, let's say of particular foresight."

"On the same tack," Joel pursued, "you went to some trouble to rehire the only pilot you ever trained personally. Was this with a record run in mind?"

This provoked a frown. Notoriously Drew's employment of a colored pilot on his high-speed trip was creating ill feeling among his colleagues. But it was far from the first time he had offended them.

"Mr. Lamenthe," Drew said at last, "qualified for his license under my supervision. Subsequently he has handled many other vessels and earned the approbation of their masters. Finding myself obliged to hire a co-pilot for the 1870 season, I judged it best to recruit one perfectly acquainted with the *Atchafalaya*. Any money I was obliged to lay out to release him from existing obligations seemed petty, for the lives of children were at stake. Bear that in mind!"

Maybe, Joel reflected sadly, this was how a man grew rich. Maybe he had to be hypocritical as well as clever. What he had seen in the case of his own father, who had bought and sold human beings like shares in a speculative flotation, and of the Moynes, who had treated their only daughter as though she were collateral for a long-term deal, indicated that might well be the dismal truth.

One naturally agreed that nothing was too much to save a child's life. But what could that possibly have to do with Drew rehiring his former cub—?

As though hauling on the reins of a runaway horse, Joel checked the headlong impetus of his thoughts.

There were other children at St. Louis: Drew's half-nephews and half-niece.

Perhaps he had not just been beating a retreat in face of the impending war. Perhaps he had been genuinely concerned about his closest relatives. Were they all the family he had? Joel's memory whirled like turbulence in the wake of a steamer's wheels.

But journalistic reflexes framed his next inquiry.

"Ah, I was about to ask whether you have news of the Grammont children."

"There have been telegraph messages. Seemingly they are as well as can be expected."

Obdurate, Joel probed further. "I've seen those messages, sir. Most are from Mrs. Grammont, not Mr. Grammont, and hint at the need for other treatment than the physic Dr. Larzenac brought from France."

"In medical matters," Drew said with frosty reproof, "I have the sense to rely on those qualified to judge. But should I be required to make another fast run to St. Louis, I shall do so. No one is better qualified to undertake *that*."

"Are there not certain parties who believe they are?"

"For instance?"

"Well, persons operating more frequently in the St. Louis trade, one of whom, according to report, once struck at you in public with a buggy whip."

For an instant Joel feared he had gone too far, because Drew took a long while in answering. Apparently against his will, his gaze strayed to the window through which the *Nonpareil* could be seen.

"We are enjoined," he said eventually, "to do good to those who hate us! If that disappoints you, then—too bad! You've been on this wild-goose chase since Mardi Gras, if memory serves. Long enough to learn better! I regard a high-speed run as normal practice, sir. Because I own a steamer in first-rate condition, I am accustomed to rapidity of transit. So are my passengers and those who entrust freight to my care. At no price, however, would I exchange a victory over anybody for the security of property or human life."

"Suppose, though, Mr. Parbury—excuse me: Mr. Woodley—"

"You *are* well-informed!" Drew interrupted with a humorless grin.

Joel gave a less than bashful shrug. And resumed: "The *Nonpareil* lies within sight of where we stand, and although she and the *Atchafalaya* are advertised for different destinations, the route both must traverse is common as far as Cairo. What if the *Nonpareil* attempted to pass the *Atchafalaya* under way?"

"Why, then, Mr. Parbury—*excuse me:* Mr. Woodley—would come to believe that the *Atchafalaya* was a hundred miles long! Now, Mr. Siskin, you must forgive me, but I have many urgent duties to attend to!"

## 19TH JUNE 1867

# CANDLES IN THE MIDDLE OF THE DAY

~~~~~~

"I entered upon the small enterprise of 'learning' twelve or thirteen hundred miles of the great Mississippi River with the easy confidence of my time of life. If I had really known what I was about to require of my faculties, I should not have had the courage to begin. I supposed that all a pilot had to do was to keep his boat in the river, and I did not consider that that could be much of a trick, since it was so wide."

—Mark Twain,
*Life on the Mississippi*

 Candles in the middle of the day . . .

Always, for as long as he could remember, Fernand Lamenthe had felt there was something false about that aspect of the religious practice he had been raised to. What merit lay in driving away a darkness that people had themselves created by erecting a roof between themselves and the sky where from dawn to dusk the Lord lit his own lamp?

As for the darkness of the grave—!

He shivered as he climbed into the carriage which had been hired to convey him and his mother away from the Cathedral of St. Louis after requiem mass for his uncle Edouard. The two Lamenthe had taken insincere leave of Eugene and Richard (Marocain!) and their wives who made even whole mourning into the excuse for another round of the game they played so obsessively: "who's in style?"

Eugene's Marie had a son. Richard's Hélène had recently brought forth a daughter. During the service Hélène had made it obvious that she thought her outfit, sent from Paris in advance of Edouard's death, evened the score.

Therefore Fernand went on shivering as the carriage clattered over the rough paving of Chartres Street toward Toulouse . . . and also because bit by bit the remembered odor of wax mingled with incense gave way to the charnel stench of the vehicle's black leather seating. Logically it was the heat that caused its dead-animal smell to be so perceptible, but for a moment he was prepared to believe he was inhaling the postmortem vapors of those who had starred at similar events of long ago. At home—at what he now forced himself to refer to as *his mother's* home, for he was determined to declare his independence as soon as might be— there was a set of bound volumes of the defunct magazine *Southern Literary Messenger,* and of all the contributors thereto a man called Poe had made the most powerful impact on the teen-age Fernand.

Whose present day successor forced himself to gather his wits and think about his mother on the seat opposite.

Past forty, she was still beautiful. Dressed entirely in black with jet and agate for her only jewelry, she was even more striking because her superb cheekbones were thrown into high relief. If only those dark limpid eyes weren't fixed on nowhere; those slim fingers telling a rosary of dull black beads; those broad lovely lips moving as she recited something which was plainly not an Ave Maria or any other prayer permissible to the devout . . .

Could an evil spirit be taking Eulalie Lamenthe in charge? Or was it just that in the grief she felt at losing first her own man, then his brother whom she had loved next of all, she was temporarily disturbed . . . ?

Fernand licked his lips. There had been other times in his life when he had asked direct questions. Why not now? With seeming irrelevance it came back to him how Hosea Drew had condensed a whole world of implications into the single word: "Uncle?"

Very well, then. He leaned forward and inquired: "Is this for the repose of—?"

Which was the point where, he later thought, he was made adult.

For years he had striven to think of his mother as a person with her own concerns, her own problems, her own failings—the last being the hardest for him to grasp, as for any child. He had fought to disabuse himself of the notion that his older relatives lived on a plane he could never attain to, because they were informed, capable, possessed of money and knowing how to generate more. On the day of his father's funeral he had sensed for the first time a link between the cathedral and the offices of Marocain's, bankers and pawnbrokers to . . . et cetera. Perhaps the word *office* itself constituted a clue?

And just as he was thinking: *have the money-changers taken over my life's temple?*—

"Not for the repose of anybody," said his mother in a tone like poison masked by honey. "That *they* may not sleep!"

"Who?"

"Eugene," his mother replied, telling another bead on her rosary, which was none of the usual kind, for at one end it terminated in crossed bones, at the other in a miniature skull. "And Richard. And their women!"

"Oh, *maman* . . . !" But Fernand's voice expired. For from the moment when Edouard had begun to show interest in his nephew rather than his sons—which could be dated precisely by Hosea Drew's return to New Orleans—Eugene and Richard had treated him and his mother with blatant hostility. Eulalie was convinced they had been complicit in the near-failure of the family bank. Within a day of Drew's visit the firm's biggest depositor, Andrew Moyne, had called in his credit; a dozen had followed his example. Eulalie swore the brothers were behind the scare. But that wasn't rational. Apart from the absurdity of imagining that such a greedy pair would risk their inheritance, neither in Fernand's view was competent to manipulate a money market even on so small a scale. (But it was politic to keep such opinions to himself.)

No, it made better sense to believe that the story of Drew's unsatisfied demand for cash had been magnified into a panicky rumor about insolvency. After all, Mrs. Moyne had been present at the time.

At all events the crisis had been weathered. Not comfortably. Drew's draft might have been presented at exactly the wrong moment. Miraculously, however, one shipyard after another declined to tender for the new *Atchafalaya*. When a contractor was at long last found, the bank was again on an even keel.

More than once, closeted with his uncle to examine the day's mail and hoping against hope that that bill would not be among it for honoring, Fernand had said wonderingly, "I never dreamed I might one day feel grateful to Langston Barber!"

"I advise you not to talk harshly about gamblers," the old banker would say. "You're not required to approve of them, but you should not despise them either. Why, I recall how . . ."

And business would be forgotten for the next ten minutes while he recounted an episode from his youth. The more stories he heard, the more Fernand chafed at having to pass his life in subservience to his cousins, denied all chance of rising higher than some nominal status such as senior clerk.

But he had breathed no word of dissatisfaction to his uncle. The strain was telling on Edouard by this time, and in the end he was obliged to retire, leaving the firm's direction to his sons . . . and nephew, jointly. That was his specific wish. He was repeating it on his deathbed and must by then have believed that his instructions had been implemented. But he had neglected to have them incorporated in his will.

Fernand said nothing about the petty slights Eugene in particular was visiting on him, nor about the way his mother's allowance and his own salary—both reduced at the time when the bank was in danger of failing—had been left at the new, lower figures, though his cousins were being extremely generous to themselves. He dared not speak up, partly for fear of making the old man's last days miserable, but far more because of a threat blandly uttered by Eugene: that if he insisted on his rights the world would get to hear about ceremonies his mother was conducting in the company of a one-eyed man who claimed he had been trained as a witch doctor.

And that way lay appalling risk of scandal. Half the folk of the city either practiced or at any rate believed in the magic which ran like a psychological undertow through all levels of society. For the most part it was harmless enough, providing an outlet for ill temper that might otherwise be expressed with gun or knife. Every now and then, however, there were hints of something deeper, something darker. Only a dozen years before, a grand exposé had rocked the city: ladies of good family who first applied to Dr. John or Marie Laveau for nothing more than a luck-charm had wound up making sacrifice to Damballah the snake god on St. John's Eve, and dancing naked along with his blackest devotees. Fernand well recalled how his mother had tried to keep newspaper accounts of the affair away from him, because a cousin of theirs was involved, Athalie Lamenthe whom he had never met.

The carriage was trundling up Toulouse now, toward Rampart. At the far end of this street lay Congo Square. Come Sunday next, as every Sunday, a great crowd of former slaves would gather there to sing, beat drums, and dance.

Innocent enough on the surface. But if some force connected with it could drive his mother to cast spells and recite curses . . .

Abruptly the carriage pulled to a halt and the driver scrambled down to open the door.

Startled, Fernand realized they had been brought only as far as the first stop on the streetcar line that served their district.

"Were you not given the right address?" he demanded of the driver. "We live at—"

"This is as far as I was told to carry you, sir," the man interrupted.

"Who told you?" Erupting from his seat in fury, Fernand almost knocked off his tall hat; but for that, he would have struck the driver.

The latter stepped back in alarm. "Why, my boss, sir! We have another funeral directly."

"I bet it was Eugene!" Fernand raged. "Is there no end to his petty insults?"

"Calm yourself," his mother said. "This is nothing compared to what they will try now your uncle is out of the way. But I am fighting to protect us, and we are in the right. Tip the driver; it is not his fault."

Standing among the dense noontide crowds, the sun unbearable on his mourning black, Fernand felt his resolution harden. As the car they were waiting for hove in sight he turned to his mother.

"*Maman*, I'm afraid I must ask you to return unescorted. I have business to attend to."

"Business?" She was instantly suspicious. "But the shop is closed today."

"A different kind of business," Fernand said grimly. "If all goes well, I need never see that damned shop again."

"You're going to do something foolish!"

"No, something very sensible. Something I should have done long ago."

"What, then?"

"I'm not sure whether I can bring it off. But if I do, I swear you shall be the first to hear."

"You're going to throw away a safe career on the chance of some vain—?"

"How long will Eugene and Richard let me survive in the firm? To the end of the year? I shall be lucky, then! No, I'd rather quit than give them the pleasure of driving me out."

"Fernand, I just told you I am working to protect us!"

"Mother!" This time he said it formally, instead of using the intimate French term he had been brought up to. "Mother, I am of age. I am twenty-one. And in my view, if what I am intending is foolish, then what you are doing is crazy!"

Between them there was a long chill silence. In the world outside everything else continued, and the streetcar arrived with a grind of iron on iron.

At last she said, "I hear your father's voice again in yours. He forbade me to dispute his judgment. He is dead and so is his brother. You are my last comfort."

"I swear it is better my way—*maman!*"

"I hope so," she said, climbing on the car. "I surely do!"

It distressed Fernand to offend his mother, but no matter how hard she tried she would never persuade him that her spells were a substitute for positive action such as Edouard would have approved! Consequently, as he strode along North Rampart toward Canal, his spirits lightened.

But his thoughts ran abruptly aground.

Ahead of him on the banquette was walking a petite dark girl wearing a plain brown dress and a hat in the style of three years ago. She was carrying a reticule and a hessian bag; the latter was so obviously too heavy for her that every few paces she was accosted by some lounger asking to help with it. She refused, not curtly. Very likely she could not afford a tip. Certainly she had the air of a stranger, for she earnestly scrutinized each building number and street name. Possibly, then, she suspected the bag would be stolen if she let an idler take it.

But she might accept assistance from someone more respectably dressed, such as himself. And really she needed it. Why, she was swaying as though about to faint!

And faint she did at the corner of Bienville. Fernand darted forward and was first at her side. Stooping on one knee, he experienced a violent shock.

This was the most beautiful girl he had ever seen. Her hair a raven black, gathered in a knot on her neck—her hat had slipped aside, being held by a single pin. Her complexion had the olive flush of a quadroon, though her cheeks were pallid. Long, very dark lashes rested on those cheeks, fluttering as though she was aware her lids were closed but lacked control to raise them. He caught up her left hand—slim, with perfectly formed nails—and chafed it, feeling suddenly foolish, for he had really very little notion what to do when someone fell unconscious, and by now he was surrounded by a crowd of passersby who assumed him knowledgeable because of his promptness. But at that point he was saved.

Descending from a smart imported sociable, a well-dressed man sporting red sidewhiskers called out, "Do you need help? I'm a doctor!"

Infinitely thankful, Fernand beckoned him. He strode over, his coachman—after securing the carriage—following with a black leather bag.

Briskly he felt the girl's cheek, then her pulse; then he made to roll back one of her eyelids, but at that she flinched and looked up, licking her lips.

"What happened?" she said in a husky voice that sent a thrill like electricity through Fernand.

"You fainted," the doctor said matter-of-factly. "And I'm prepared to guess why. When did you last eat a square meal?"

"Y-yesterday."

"Hmph!" Magisterially the doctor twirled his left sidewhisker. "Are you sure you don't mean last week? Who are you, anyway?"

"My name is Dorcas, sir—Dorcas Archer. I'm a stranger here."

"What are you doing—seeking lodgings?"

"No, sir. I'm looking for work."

"Then my advice is to find a place in someone's kitchen, where you can enjoy a decent diet!" He made to rise.

And stopped dead in mid-movement. Following his gaze. Fernand saw, on the frayed cotton petticoat that her fall allowed to show under her skirt, a patch of red.

"I've misdiagnosed your condition, haven't I, Dorcas?" the doctor said. "You need immediate treatment."

"But I have no money, sir!" she moaned.

"We'll worry about that later. You!"—to Fernand. "You're a well-set-up young fellow. Think you can carry her as far as Hamel's drugstore? It's at the end of this block."

"I think so," Fernand said, astonished.

"Good. My coachman can bring her bag. Don't try to bear your own weight, Dorcas—let the gentleman lift you."

But he rebuked Fernand for his awkward posture.

"Lord, when are they going to start teaching anatomy in the schools which charge such fees and discharge such ignoramuses? Not with your legs apart! Feet together! Use your thighs!"

And in fact it was amazing how easily he raised her.

"Now follow me," the doctor said, and set off at half a run.

The drugstore was a dim place whose walls were lined with labeled wooden drawers and, on high shelves, glass and china jars bearing the arcane abbreviations of the pharmacist's profession. Behind a long dark counter two young men were busy, one rolling pills on a marble slab, the other sealing small white packages with red wax which he warmed at a blue gas flame.

Starting, the pill-roller exclaimed, "Why, Dr. Malone! What's the matter? Has she been assaulted?"

"She's hemorrhaging violently," Malone said. "She may be miscarrying. Call Mrs. Hamel right away."

Turning to Dorcas, whose head was lolling on Fernand's shoulder, he assured her, "You're in safe hands now, my dear. Mrs. Hamel is a midwife."

Her only response was a whimper.

Shortly Mr. Hamel appeared from an inner room, a dry man of late middle age with gold-rimmed pince-nez. Behind him followed his wife, wiping her hands on a huckaback towel.

Grasping the situation, Hamel told Fernand to carry his burden around the counter and into the living room, where his wife spread an old blanket over a horsehair sofa. Fernand set the girl down with a sense of absurd reluctance. He was suddenly wondering whether he would ever see her again.

"Thanks for your help," Malone said, doffing his coat. "But there's no need to detain you longer. Be so kind as to tell my coachman to call on my next patient and say I shall be late, then return and pick me up."

"Of course," Fernand said, but lingered still.

"Pretty, isn't she?" Malone murmured. "But what's going to happen now won't be. On your way!"

Shaken not by the reproof but by the impact this unknown girl had made on him, Fernand obeyed. And found it necessary to stop at a bar before continuing to his original destination.

That was the levee beyond Poydras.

He was an avid reader of the river column in any newspaper that came to hand. From the *Intelligencer* he had lately learned that the *Atchafalaya* was at New Orleans on schedule and loading for a trip to Louisville, to start tomorrow. That made it ninety per cent sure Drew would be on board. It was no secret that he used the suite Barber had provided at the Limousin as rarely as possible.

And that same article had reminded Fernand of a law enacted only last year, drafted by the Board of Supervising Inspectors of Steamboats.

For whom Drew doubtless had little affection. But it was a law, and it did have teeth.

Of course, there was always the chance he might not have to mention it . . .

"Captain, a Mr. Lamenthe wants to see you. Says it's important. Says to mention the name of Marocain."

Drew glanced up from bills of lading compiled by his senior clerks, Motley and Wills. The clerks' office was the commercial heart of the *Atchafalaya*, as of any river steamer. The only place on board where Drew spent more waking time was in the pilothouse; even during a trip, when the passengers expected him to socialize, he was as likely as not to pass an off-watch hour here.

Diffident in the doorway was the bringer of the message, junior clerk David Grant, who was eighteen and timid . . . especially when obliged to confront the captain, from whom he usually shied away like a light boat taking a sheer from a reef in shallow water. But the reason for his boldness became plain as he added, "Mr. Chalker sent me!"

Tom Chalker was the first mate. Of him it had been said that he could put the fear of God into a bloom of pig iron, for it had been through hellfire already and knew what he was talking about.

Objurgation was a knack young David was never likely to acquire. Still, he was conscientious and clever with figures. Drew straightened with a mutter of thanks to Wills and Motley. These days he looked more spruce than formerly; also he had become less gruff. The security of possessing his own boat still eluded him, but he could have hit on a worse partner than Barber, for the Hotel Limousin and the interactions of the gambling set were far more attractive to him than the vagaries of the river. So long as he could be left to his own devices, Drew was nearly happy. As nearly as it lay in his nature to be, perhaps.

If only Susannah . . . But that was not his fault.

By the same token, however, the recognition was gradually growing in him that had he not sacrificed everything else to the rehabilitation of his brother, he might by now have been the father of a boy like Elphin, talented and studious and dedicated to the Baptist ministry—to the delight of his mother, naturally. She had feared the "taint in the blood" of which so many people spoke so freely without evidence.

Every time he thought about children, however, the same image came unbidden to Drew's mind. He saw again the gaunt figure of Parbury leaning on his wife for guidance and heard Tyburn's voice utter the sickening news that their only child had died in his father's absence.

Nonetheless the notion of passing on what he knew was growing by degrees more appealing. His head was stocked with such a mass of information about this river!

Such thoughts were novel enough to be discomfortable. He repulsed them with great effort and found his voice.

"Lamenthe from Marocain's? I remember him! Where is he, then?"

And retrieved his staff, propped in the corner by the door.

"Why, you're in mourning! Never tell me it's for your uncle!"

Reflexively doffing his hat, Fernand ventured, "You recall our meeting, sir?"

"Indeed I do," Drew answered, his expression grave. "Am I right in assuming . . . ?"

"Yes, unfortunately." Fernand crossed himself. "We celebrated a requiem mass for him this morning."

"I'm sure I should have heard the tragic news in due course. But I thank you for coming to inform me personally. I've had dealings with the firm of E. Marocain for many years. Many years." He was gazing along the busy wharves, but seemed to be looking into another time. "I trust the business will continue?"

"Oh—oh yes!" Fernand licked his lips. Now that the moment was on him, he was finding it terribly difficult to deliver the crucial statement with which he had primed his tongue.

"And no doubt it was to assure me of the fact that you took the trouble to call," Drew said dryly. "Very well—one understands that the world must go on in spite of those who take their leave of it. Would you care to be shown over the *Atchafalaya*, so you may report at first hand on her appointments?"

"A circuit of such a vessel under the guidance of her master would be a privilege!"

"Very well, then. Come this way. You will see that space on the main deck and the guards is available for cargo of a light but bulky nature, such as cotton or tobacco. Your eyes will inform you concerning the magnificent provision which the design of this boat makes for such a burden. Strangely enough, the boilers are not on the boiler *deck*, which is the next deck above—"

"Not so strange, Captain!" Fernand blurted before he could bridle the impulse. Drew bent a frosty gaze on him, but maintained at least the superficies of politeness.

"Is that so?"

"Why, yes—sir. The word 'deck' originally meant to cover, nothing more. You hear the same sound in 'décor' and 'decorate' . . ."

"Hah! At least you agree with the preacher I took to Vicksburg last year, who said exactly the same." Drew sought for and found the clew of his discourse.

"Above that again is the hurricane deck, so called because it gives protection against storms, and uppermost of all, bar the pilothouse, is the texas. No doubt you know how that got its name?" This with sarcasm.

Fernand had to swallow hard.

"Some say it's because it was lately annexed, sir. But it appears to me to be a regular Spanish word, in which language *techar* means 'to roof'. I believe there to be some connection with 'textile', meaning woven, and I'd hazard a guess the first texas was a canvas awning."

Drew thought awhile before replying. Then he abandoned his prepared speech.

"I'd be wasting breath to say what I intended now I've found you so educated! Let's go down to the hold. Which is called the *hold* because it *holds* the heavy freight!"

And he strode off ahead of Fernand.

Despite Drew's sharpness, though, the latter's determination was undiminished. What defiance of his mother had begun, his tour of the *Atchafalaya* completed.

For this boat was no mere dream, but a reality.

\*     \*     \*

What happened next was like becoming Jonah in the belly of the great fish. Fernand gasped. On the few occasions when he had traveled by steamer, he had explored every corner the crew would permit; this, though, was the only time he had seen the full volume of a boat's hold, for during a trip the view was always blocked by cargo.

Here, now, the process of freighting-up had scarcely begun. A stack of boxes fifty feet away did nothing to detract from the sight of this monstrously long and almost completely dark cavern of a place, threaded as by some gargantuan spider with a web of iron bars: the lengthwise hog chains, which lent her hull stem-to-stern rigidity, and the cross chains that transmitted to the keelson via wooden Sampson posts the enormous burden of her wheels and paddleboxes. Had timber been used to make her equally strong, she would have been three hundred tons heavier.

But a penalty must be paid for the advantage. Part of it was out of sight on the upper decks—those bars created problems at the peak of their ascending curves—and part was right here, proof of the time it took after every trip and often during one to make sure nothing had slackened to the danger point.

Walking along the echoing vault, they saw in the distance (its void was large enough to make one think in such terms) a wan and eerie light. Drawing near, they found a gang of men testing some of the iron struts by a glimmering oil lamp. Their leader was portly and almost bald; Drew named him as Josh Diamond, the boat's carpenter, but carried formality no further and at once set about interrogating him concerning the condition of the hull and upperworks. Satisfied, he remembered Fernand and led him onward to where barrel after barrel of salt pork was being transported from daylight to darkness by the freight hoister, an endless chain with angled slabs of thick wood attached to it. Its own small steam engine, chuffing away for all the world like a tired mule not quite ready to launch a kick at his boss, rolled the chain around and around and around. . .

Ill-advisedly, one of the hands stowing the barrels glanced up at their approach and came within a half-inch of dropping the next one on his foot. Drew barked at him. At once a long-faced man peered down from the hatch the hoister ran through.

"Cap'n! Didn't know you was there!" he exclaimed.

"You tell these men to act always as if I'm here, Mr. Sexton! Because if I'm not, I'm apt to be shortly! Understand?"

Without waiting for an answer, Drew moved on, confiding to Fernand as to an old friend, "He's a good man, is Jack Sexton, or I'd not have made him my second mate. But he gets taken by surprise a mite too easy. You just saw! And now let's go upstairs."

Leaving the hold was a relief. After her scant year in service the *Atchafalaya*'s timbers were already impregnated with the stench of her foulest cargoes: poorly cured hides, for example, or tung oil, or any of the countless substances that could turn rancid on a summer's day . . . particularly when nature's heat was augmented by the boilers on the deck above. Wiping his face with a black-edged handkerchief he had been given at the time of his father's funeral, carefully preserved by his mother and produced again now that such a symbol was once more appropriate, Fernand felt glad that today all but the one needed for the freight hoister were cold, and impressed, indeed awed, by their solidity in repose. The only steamboat boilers he had seen before had been aroar with coal and wood. Their red maws had fascinated him, fixing his gaze so fast he scarcely noticed whether the stokers who kept them fed were black men, or white but coated with soot and dust. It came as a shock to realize that they were framed in brick as substantial as any onshore. Through a high wall of it gaped eight furnace doors greedy for the fuel that was being stacked within reach against tomorrow's departure.

From one of the doors protruded the feet of a man lying belly-down in the confined space beneath the thin iron shell that separated fire from water. Another man stood by offering tools and advice neither of which—to judge by the answering blast of oaths—were suited to the task.

Drew forgot all about Fernand and marched over, voicing a flood of profanity almost poetical in its inventiveness.

Come to think of it, was this not a likelier reason for Drew to have acquired his nickname than the one generally proposed?

As if galvanized, the man inside the firebox emerged with a single improbable twist of his torso and in a blink was on his feet, raising a lead-headed mallet to strike down whoever had insulted him. Recognizing the captain, however, he at once lowered it and spoke in fluent technical terms.

"It's the trouble I told you about as we rounded Arnauld's Point, Cap'n! Steam showing in the firebed and the water low in number four. Must be a leak on the branch feed to the mud drum."

Drew craned to look into the firedoor's mouth. After a mere glance he appeared satisfied. Imitating him, Fernand found he could make out almost no detail in the ash-encrusted grate. He understood in principle what was being discussed. Steamers of this type drew their water from the river by way of a pump called "the doctor," which possessed its own engine so that the level in the boilers would be kept up when steam was being generated but the main engines were idling: for instance, at a landing. But river water was foul with silt and weed and sometimes worse. The function of the mud drum was to receive impurities and let them settle out. It was located underneath the deck the boilers rested on; consequently the pipes to it had to pass through the tiled floor of the furnace. But it must take an expert eye to distinguish the mud drum feed from . . .

Fernand realized abruptly that he had gone on staring so long, he was now in turn being stared at. Sheepish, he put on an embarrassed smile.

But Drew was obviously in a better-than-average mood. He identified his visitor and introduced him to—

"This here's Dutch! Dutch Fonck! And that's Irish!"

"Pat O'Dowd," said the man who had emerged from the furnace.

"Where's Ealing?" Drew went on.

"Aft by the starboard pitman with his new striker."

"What do you think of him?"

"Walt, you mean?" O'Dowd shrugged. "Jim says he's shaping up."

"He's young yet," Fonck supplemented. "I guess he'll grow into the work."

Listening, Fernand felt a pang of envy at the patent camaraderie between these men. He would never have imagined from his previous encounters with the captain that his crew could chat so casually with him. He had expected a sort of military discipline to be in force, and all conversation to be full of "Yes, sir!" and "No, sir!" and "Cap'n, if you please!"

How utterly different all this was from the atmosphere of the so-called "family" business he was used to, with its undercurrent of cutthroat rivalry. . .

Following the same route along the main deck as the steam pipes, Drew next led Fernand to the midships section, where the weight of the *Atchafalaya's* monstrous engines was concentrated, and gave a crisp summary of their characteristics, using his staff like a lecturer's pointer: forty-inch pistons, ten-foot stroke, a Pittsburgh cam designed to his own specification controlling the valves that admitted to the cylinders steam at 110 pounds per square inch.

Wisely forbearing to mention that, like anybody who religiously followed the river-news columns, he too could have recited these figures, Fernand looked at the back of his hand and mentally outlined there a square one inch by one, then tried to load it with 110 pounds. He failed.

A shiver ran down his spine. He thought of what it must be like to take deck passage up the Mississippi in foul weather, particularly if you were too poor to afford the regular fare and had to turn out at all hours to earn your keep by loading wood and coal from a shore landing slippery with mud or a barge that rocked insanely at every wake and ripple.

Nonetheless, in spite of all hardships, there was glamor about the notion of a steamer. Ever since the first voyage of the *New Orleans* in January 1812 the mere mention of the term conjured up visions of long voyages undertaken in amazingly little time. The world had been transformed from the days of wind and tide, towing and portage.

*Steamer* was the word that summarized the change.

Passing the huge tapered beam of the pitman, they came on the remaining engineer, Jim Ealing, short but thickset and obviously very strong, together with his striker Walt Presslie, a slight youth of about sixteen with a shock of hair that would have been tow-colored but for grease and smuts. They had carried out a minute inspection of the starboard wheel; it was so large, they could clamber about in it like monkeys in a treetop.

Having fired half a dozen questions at Ealing and received reassuring answers, Drew led the way toward the stairs that gave access to the deck above, the boiler deck. Fernand followed with more than one backward glance. Noticing, Drew asked the reason.

Sufficiently startled to reply with candor, Fernand said, "I was wondering how that boy copes when you're in a stretch of crooked river. Your camrods must weigh all of fifty pounds."

He was thinking of the laborious process involved in reversing, when the heavy metal bar governing the poppet valves had to be unhooked and reconnected three feet higher. He had watched it being done only once, on a trip with his father before the war, but he vividly recalled how exhausted the engineers had been after the boat had dodged her way through a score of reefs and bars with the bells coming faster than they could be answered. And he had just observed that no significant improvement over the old system had been incorporated in the design of this *Atchafalaya*.

A pace ahead of him Drew halted and spun around, staring. He spent the next several seconds looking Fernand over from head to foot. And then he said in a tone of disbelief, "His hands are clerk-soft! His cravat was tied by his mother! His shoes are shined for him every morning and the heaviest load he ever has to tote is a bag of money! So how come he knows such an all-fired *deal* about steam-boating?"

Unendurably embarrassed, as though this were his uncle lashing him with reprimands for carelessness, Fernand shifted from foot to foot. That a display of knowledge by an outsider could provoke such a blast of sarcasm went a long way towards making clear why few people called themselves friends of Hosea Drew.

At length he muttered, "I'm kind of interested."

"*Are* you now? Well, I guess that makes you one in a thousand! And the love of knowledge is the beginning of wisdom. Ain't it?"

Hastily: "Yes, Captain!"

"I'm glad you agree. But I figure you'll be more at home in the cabin than down here." He turned toward the stairs again. Smarting, Fernand followed. It looked as though to get his way he might after all have to invoke the law, and all of a sudden the idea of getting his way was a lot less attractive than it had been.

But he found himself gasping again when he entered the main cabin.

Well over two hundred feet long, it was ornamented with complex fretwork painted bright white and highlighted in gold. Neither the décor nor the equally impressive carpet betrayed the fact that this boat had already been in service over a year. Tables as solid and well-carved as any in a smart New Orleans drawing room were ranged in echelon down the cabin's enormous length. Halfway along stood a piano cased in maplewood; at the after end, two head-high mirrors of first-quality plate glass adorned the wall.

Years ago there had grown up an unwritten custom that family groups and single ladies should enjoy undisturbed the amenities of the cabin's midships section; single gentlemen were advised to move as far forward as possible in search of male company and male pastimes. Aboard the *Atchafalaya* the frontier was symbolized by that indispensable appurtenance of the Mississippi steamer, the water cooler. This one was taller than Fernand, silver-plated, strung about with silver-plated cups on silver-plated chains. It was located about two-thirds of the way toward the bow.

Beyond lay the area where the influence of Drew's unlikely co-owner was apparent. Not only was there a bar on the starboard side, at which men might purchase their own liquor instead of having it fetched by a waiter; there too were seen card presses, chuck-a-luck cups, a keno goose, and—at present being polished by one of the half-dozen tenders, all black, who were readying the boat for her departure tomorrow—a faro spread.

From which Drew was at pains to distract Fernand's attention. He pointed out instead another and more moral feature. Making the best of structural necessity, rows of pillars on either side of the main area created a sort of promenade dividing it from the staterooms, every one of whose doors was resplendent with a painting that depicted some aspect of American history.

Of these the captain was inordinately proud. Fernand did his dutiful best to admire them, wondering when he would pluck up the courage to speak out concerning the decision that had brought him here. Against his will he remained tongue-tied, or perhaps overwhelmed, while Drew showed off more of the boat's facilities: the nursery, the servants' rooms, the washrooms and bathrooms, the laundry room . . .

Gradually, however, the determination he had conceived at the requiem mass, while listening to ethereal, awe-inspiring music, revived and renewed his resolve.

Looking over the texas where the officers occupied the staterooms ahead of the mockingly named "freedmen's bureau"—so called after the department that had dealt with ex-slaves in New Orleans during the war, and reserved for black people paying cabin rates—his envy returned. Yes! Yes! He wanted this kind of life! *Not* one—his uncle's phrase came back to him— "circumscribed by loans and pledges and rates of interest"!

That made his nape hairs prickle as though he had heard a voice from beyond the grave.

But the fact stood. He wanted, one day, to be proud of Fernand Lamenthe. It could not possibly be done by second hand.

At which point he found his thoughts being disturbed by more introductions. It was dizzying to think how numerous were the personnel of a steamer this size; he was glad there would be no test, of the kind his uncle would have contrived, to establish how many of these strangers he could put a name to at second meeting.

He met one Ernest Vehm, boat's caterer, who could have stood in for the maître d'hotel of any restaurant in the city . . . and his cousin Peter, to whom he let the bar concession . . . and slow-spoken, elderly Lewis Amboy, steward in charge of the waiters and servants, who gave the impression of being vague yet was addressed by Drew with great politeness.

"I almost lost Lewis," the captain said as he prepared to climb the stairs to the last level: the pilothouse, whose exterior was gorgeous with fretted carvings that made it much resemble a wedding cake. That, Fernand suspected, once more betrayed the influence of Barber; it could scarcely match Drew's soberer taste.

"Lost, sir? Uh—overboard?"

"Rich!" Drew exclaimed. "That is *rich!* I'll remember it! But—no! He used to be my regular caterer in the old days. I lost touch with him during the war. He can't cope any more with the demands of provisioning for upwards of a thousand passengers and crew. Still, I'd not have him languish, nor anyone who stood by me in hard times. Let him work out his span!"

And on that note they arrived in the pilothouse.

In contrast with its outward guise, its interior was functional to the point of starkness, and Fernand—his nerves tuned to a raw pitch—observed how here, of all the departments of the vessel, Drew exuded contentment. It was like watching someone come home after a long absence. Below, in the cabin or when passing the boilers and engines and even when trudging the length of the hold, Drew had exhibited a sort of pride: *this belongs to me!*

Now there was a shift of emphasis. The mode became: *this is where I belong.*

It grievously excited Fernand's envy to learn that there could be such a place for such a person.

Only one man was in the pilothouse when they entered. Lean, of middle height, with keen blue eyes and a drooping brown moustache, he was checking off equipment on a neatly written list. He was dressed in somewhat old-fashioned style, with a string tie and a long-skirted coat . . . and under it, on his right hip, was the bulge of a revolver.

"Our watchman, Harry Whitworth," Drew said. Fernand extended his hand. The other made no move to shake it.

Vehm had; Amboy had, if a trifle absent mindedly; and if the engineers had not, it was because their hands were dirty. Fernand felt the blood rush to his head. But with considerable effort he mastered the impulse to ball a fist and apply it where it would hurt. Instead he commented in the calmest tones he could muster on the excellent view here afforded of both ends of the boat.

"Is all well?" Drew demanded, not addressing Fernand.

"I guess so." The watchman tucked his lists under his arm and his pencil behind his ear, then produced a coarse black cigar. One of his lower front teeth was missing; it made convenient lodging.

Fernand himself did not smoke, but since many of his friends did, he had taken to carrying matches. With a mutter of thanks Whitworth turned to the proffered flame.

A second later realization of what he had done appeared on his face; it seemed almost cruel. Clearly this was the role he expected "persons of color" to fulfill. Equally clearly he felt he had been caught out in some manner he could not wholly grasp.

"All's in order here, Cap'n," he said after a tense moment, and strode toward the stairs.

"Now, Mr. Lamenthe!" Producing a commonplace watch, Drew compared it with the clocks visible on land. "Is there any other matter you want to discuss, or may I have you escorted ashore?"

"Yes, Captain. There is something else."

Fernand turned his back to the broad forward window, equipped with shades that could be slid to block the sun; they divided it into patterns of irregular light and dark, and that seemed an appropriate setting.

"Well?" Drew cocked one gray eyebrow.

"I want to be a Mississippi pilot."

The world outside continued as before; to the noise of the engine driving the freight hoister was added another out of rhythm—a donkey engine powering one of the cranes lately introduced by a consortium from the victorious North, determined to modernize the port in spite of cheap black labor. Always there were shouts and banging sounds and the buzz of insects.

But here was an interval.

At last Drew said, compressing into the syllable a universe of incredulity: "*Why?*"

So Fernand explained. Chewing meditatively on a wad of dark tobacco, Drew heard him out with apparent sympathy. And eventually:

"If what you want is a career on the river, son, there are simpler answers. Any boat in this port now would sign you for a clerk's post with your background. And clerks can do well for themselves."

"I don't want that!" Fernand answered fiercely. "I want *this!*" And laid his hand on a spoke of the huge wheel.

Drew chomped solemnly awhile longer, then glanced around for the nearest box of sawdust and let fly; chomped again, and spat again. Fearing a rebuff, Fernand summoned his words of last resort.

"Captain, I'm informed it's now a legal obligation—"

And broke off, aware of having made a terrible mistake. For Drew's brow had clouded with the threat of storms.

When he next spoke, his voice was like the grinding of icefloes.

"You are correct, *boy*. The members of the Pilots' Guild are not happy about the law, but it was enacted and we must concede there does have to be a next generation of pilots, despite the railroads. Therefore someone in my position is compelled to take on any cub who rolls over at a skilled man's feet and whines with his paws in the air!" His voice passed from savage to caressing. "Still, needs must when the devil drives!

"For that reason and for that reason only you may present yourself aboard tomorrow at noon. Bring no more than one bag with you: plain comfortable clothing and what minimum of other gear will keep you fit for company on a summer trip. And the price of your education will be a thousand dollars. Mr. Motley can draw up an agreement. Come to the office."

He started for the stairs, and in mid-stride glanced back.

"You do have a thousand dollars, do you?"

Fernand tried to hide his dismay. He had been informed that the regular rate was more like five hundred. However, he put a brave face on matters.

"My uncle's bequest will be adequate," he declared.

"Then it's a deal . . . bar one more thing!"

"What?" Fernand's voice quavered.

"That you never tell anyone you threatened me, you fool! I was all set to say okay, and then . . . For that, I'll give you the toughest time of your young life, and you can put up with it or be damned!"

Within the half-hour Motley—with some advice from his colleague Wills—drafted a document binding both parties in a style that would not have shamed the best lawyers in the city. While the work was going on, word spread, and before he was invited to set his fist to the bottom line Fernand found himself surrounded by members of the crew: not only the officers, like Fonck and Ealing and O'Dowd, Chalker and Sexton—and Whitworth—but also Diamond, Amboy and Vehm, Presslie and the junior clerk David Grant who hovered at the door, torn between the need to get on with his asigned task and this press of his superiors who stood in his way.

Fernand almost identified with him while preparing to sign. Which he did with exaggerated legibility and a final flourish.

"See you at noon tomorrow, then," Drew said in a neutral voice, adding his own brisk scrawl to the paper.

Fernand turned to go.

By this time Whitworth's cigar had expired. With the tip of his tongue he carefully extracted it from between his teeth; rolled it a quarter-inch toward the center of his mouth; aligned it; and spat it—*pteugh!*—not at a cuspidor but through the open window of the office and clear over the side of the boat.

 There was a ceremonial quality about Whitworth's action that made Fernand abruptly understand the implications of casting a spell.

He intended to whistle the first cab he saw and ride home in triumph, to face his mother with the news that he had devised a new profession free from the toils of the Marocains. All that evaporated. The world of the riverboats was not different in essence from the one he was accustomed to; it also was populated by human beings capable of greed and generosity, friendship and hatred, and perhaps for no better reason than the common run.

And yet—! And yet—!

There was *something* about river people which not only tempted him but downright convinced him that he must cast his lot with them. Whatever it was, it had generated a feeling he wanted to participate in.

The term that sprang to mind was *communion*.

Counter to that, Whitworth had issued a warning, crude but fair. For a second his will had wavered; he had reconsidered Drew's proposal about a clerk's post . . . then scrapped it once for all. Fernand Lamenthe had the opportunity of becoming a pilot, and he was going to seize it with both hands.

Yet the all-too-patent shortcomings of the people he was committed to spend time among, contrasted with the miraculous transformation he had been promising himself, prevented him from rushing home. Instead of hailing a cab, he walked, and took by no means the shortest route.

Owing to reflex rather than conscious choice, he strayed along Bienville after walking almost too far east and turning north at hazard. And—amazed, in a way, that the sky was still light, for he felt as though enough had been crammed into one day already—he checked and turned back on spotting from the corner of his eye the sign of Hamel's Drugstore.

"No, for the last time, I will not make up 'magnetic salves'! Let Cherouen do his own quack cookery!"

Hamel barked the words as Fernand entered, and thereby frightened a thin yellow servant girl into snatching back a paper she had laid on the counter and taking to her heels. Fernand just had time to step aside.

"Good riddance!" Hamel exclaimed, and in the same breath returned to his normal polite tones. "Sir, what may I—? Ah! You came here earlier with Dr. Malone!"

Flattered at being recognized, Fernand agreed.

"I'm sorry about what you just saw," Hamel said, passing his fingers through already unruly hair. "But some people would rather believe in magnetism and miracles than medicine per se!"

A lecture was obviously on the brew; Fernand said hastily, "I was passing by chance, and thought to inquire after the . . ."

He had been about to say "the young lady I carried here this morning." But when he thought back he was scarcely able to credit that he had held in his arms a girl so beautiful. He would have been regretful but resigned had it turned out at this moment that she had never existed except in his dreams. To have one dream come true in one day was plenty for any reasonable person.

She certainly had been real, though, for Hamel finished the sentence.

"Oh, the girl? We made arrangements for her. With the Ursulines."

Fernand's heart sank. Their convent was a few blocks distant, a place of iron grilles and strict enclosure. He ventured, "Is she Catholic, then?"

"It seems not. But the Sisters are charitable, and—well, where else can you send someone in her condition?"

"Condition? Was she—?"

"Yes! She miscarried an infant fifteen or sixteen weeks gone. Dead, of course. She's half-dead herself, from inanition."

"I suppose," said Fernand from a dry throat, "her family ordered her out?"

On the slim hand he had chafed—her left—there had been no wedding band, nor even the trace that a ring leaves on the skin.

Hamel shrugged. "Who knows? She was too weak to talk. But Dr. Malone is a kind and generous man, and said that when she recovers he'll arrange a post for her. That's a better reward than some might say she deserves. And now, if you'll excuse me, I have work to do."

"Might I not at least—?"

"Were you previously acquainted with her?"

"Well, no! But—"

"Then take my advice. Leave well alone. Good evening, *sir!*"

For a brief instant the notion of invading the convent crossed Fernand's mind. All his upbringing rebelled. He sighed and resumed his homeward journey.

 The house where Alphonse Marocain had installed his beautiful Eulalie lay a little *apart* from everywhere else: from the bustle of muddy St. Charles Avenue; from the French Quarter where so much of life was public, literally on the streets; from all the districts where people were respectable . . . and also those where living was fun.

Fernand, still laboring under the dismal impact of being told that the lovely

Miss Archer had gone where he might not follow, was ripe to suffer pangs of nostalgia-to-be when he gazed at it for this, the last time when he would count it as home.

For there was about to be a showdown.

As he thrust his latchkey into the lock his resolution hardened. Abruptly he was again eager to impart news of his future career. His subconscious was equipping him with arguments to defeat his mother's opposition. How could anyone be a more rigorous instructor than Uncle Edouard? If he had been satisfied with his nephew's talents, why should Drew not be? And so forth.

But the moment he crossed the threshold he was assailed with waves of incense, and at the same time heard noises such as he had heard often and often, since about a year after his father's death. A drum was being beaten and someone was chanting in a language he did not recognize as English, nor even as the patois in which his nurse had taught him to sing concerning such waifs and strays as Pauv' P'tit' Lolotte.

When the drum fell silent there would be gasps, and cries, and moans . . .

For a second Fernand thrilled with rage. There had been a time when, because he loved and trusted his mother, he had been able to believe she was celebrating a protective magic rite. Little by little he had grown to think in other terms— above all, lust. But why in heaven's name, if she must take a lover (and he saw no reason why she shouldn't, healthy and beautiful as she still was), could she not choose someone worthy of Alphonse's memory? Why this gaunt and very black man Cudjo, finely enough dressed to be sure, but vulgar in every expression and gesture, who stole in furtive as a thief and only after dark, carrying a bagful of God knew what—John the Conqueror root and chicken feathers and goofer dust and other disgusting substances, no doubt?

The door swung shut behind him; its lock clicked like a telegraph key: ! His rage gave way to weary resignation. He had once tried to interrupt one of his mother's "ceremonies," but they took place behind a well-bolted door, and all his efforts earned him was a volley of curses. It was not to his taste to hear his mother curse him. In spite of everything, he suspected in his heart of hearts she might perhaps wield some sort of supernatural power . . .

So he wandered up and down in empty rooms, looking at the furniture and pictures and thinking how dark and durable they were in contrast to the water-borne world he had committed himself to.

During the war men's lives had been sold at a discount. Standing by himself in the fine salon of the home where his father would have wished to offer congratulations on his coming of age—but listening to his mother moan in ecstasy and thinking of the beautiful girl he had carried to Hamel's and making a web of connections he was terrified by—Fernand realized his existence too was not indispensable to the universe.

Climaxing into chaos, those images and memories and sensations combined to crown his day of growing up.

## 24TH SEPTEMBER 1869

# FORMED BY THE UNION

~~~~~~~

"Even when they passed the mouth of the great muddy Pekitanoui, they considered that to be only a tributary, not stopping to think that it might be longer than the branch called Mississippi, and in some other ways too a greater river. So, because the explorers first voyaged *down* the river, the northern name spread along it clear to the mouth. But if the explorers had come from the south, they would naturally have called the river by some southern name. When they reached the forking . . . the lower stream and each of the upper branches might have been known and named separately . . . and men would have said that the lower river was 'formed by the union' of the two upper branches."

—George R. Stewart,
*Names on the Land*

 Everywhere else today was Friday. But in the house where Caesar had found lodging, the saying went that any day was Juba day: Monday. Because here there was never any food but red beans and rice, flavored with a scrap of seasonin' meat. It was best not to inquire closely into what sort of meat that was.

He woke cold and with his body folded clockspring-tight. Even his jaw muscles were tense . . . and that was bad, because since his discharge from the army his teeth had given him more and more trouble. Also there was the inescapable ache from his leg wound. But time enough had dragged by for him to grow used to limping.

The crowded room smelled much of humanity and more of bedbugs. Two or three had bitten him in the night. As usual.

Cursing—silently, because none of the men who were still asleep would take kindly to being roused before they must—he forced himself to stand up. He slept in his flannel shirt. Over it he drew on old greasy breeches, last legacy of his wartime uniform, supported by leather galluses. From under the end of his straw pallet he retrieved his boots, which doubled as a pillow and as a safe place to store his few valuable possessions, including the money he had scrimped. Carrying them until he was outdoors, he stole away to face another dawn.

This was not exactly the freedom Caesar had believed himself to be fighting for. Except in dreams, though, his memories of the war were so distant and so strange that what he was recalling might as well have happened to a different person.

Yet he had finally struck lucky. After countless casual jobs he now had steady employment. There were very few steam cranes along the New Orleans levee, although they were common in the North and Europe; however, the machinery of the ones which had recently been installed did not differ greatly from the engine powering the sugar mill at Pré du Lac. After much persuasion Caesar had convinced a white man who was paid a fat wage as a crane driver that he could handle this job by himself—whereupon the white man agreed to part with a quarter of his pay so that Caesar could do the work and he could pass his time drinking and chasing women.

Caesar had been assured that just such a chance would come his way. He could still scarcely credit that the promise had proved true, far less the means which had brought it about.

Unconsciously he touched a small hard object hidden under his shirt, which hung around his neck night and day. He was never to take it off until its leather thong rotted naturally. He had inspected it as best he could without removing it; it consisted of two squares of black felt sewn together, with a feather intertwined among the stitches, and inside there was a lump that might be the last tooth he had lost, which had been required of him, and some dust or dirt, and a herb that had had a powerful stink, now faded.

A trickenbag. And moreover one prepared by Mam'zelle Josephine in person.

He shook his head. Until recently he had thought of all such magics as laughable; also they evoked nightmarish childhood memories. But even if it had been mere despair that led him to spend his minute savings on this charm, he could not deny he had been well repaid.

As usual, he shelved the mystery and hurried on his way.

 At the wheel of the steamer *Henry Clay Work* Fernand was concluding his dawn watch and struggling with all his might to keep from yawning.

And to exclude from his mind a nagging thought which kept recurring against his will. Was it possible that in sacrificing two years of his life to train as a pilot he had made a terrible mistake?

It was not the quality of his tuition that had soured his dream. Gruff Hosea Drew might be, but he responded honestly to good work well done, and eventually he had pronounced himself satisfied with his cub, reported the fact to the Pilots' Guild, and arranged the issue of his license.

But there was no welcome for Fernand at the Guild's parlor. He was qualified; therefore he was allowed to enter. But once inside, nobody sought his company. He would post his report and exchange a few frigid civilities with those of his colleagues who did not cut him dead. Were he in a defiant mood, he might purchase a cocktail before leaving—but only for himself. His offers to buy for others were routinely declined.

Some of this was due to having been Drew's cub. The treatment Drew received was identical. The grudges of the war were dying hard, and Parbury—who ruled unchallenged at the Guild—was among the unforgiving.

More, though, was due to the same cause that had led to him quitting the *Atchafalaya* at the end of his training. He had gone out of his way to display unfailing courtesy toward Whitworth. But the watchman was unimpressed. So far as he was concerned, people with "a touch of the tarbrush" were irremediably inferior to all white men, and the notion of one being trained as a pilot infuriated him beyond measure. He had complained countless times about the futility of trying to educate Fernand in such a skilled job, and when, one day, he addressed the younger man as "Rastus" and ordered him to bring coffee as though he were the texas tender, they nearly came to blows. Fortunately he made the mistake of doing it within hearing of another pilot, an experienced man called Ezekiel Barfoot, who had seen enough of Fernand's ability to throw the insult back in Whitworth's remaining teeth.

But his existence became progressively more miserable, and as soon as he qualified he took what jobs he could find on other boats. Most were black-owned, running in short or way-business trades, for a shadow of the prejudice Whitworth exhibited fell across all too many owners and officers.

Nonetheless there was magic in the name *Atchafalaya;* as he had realized with something of a shock, Fernand was the only cub so far trained on any of that splendid series of vessels. Though he was likely to be in charge of sugar and tobacco and the casual workers who had harvested them, rather than the genteel society that now patronized Drew, with their servants and their leather baggage monogrammed in gold, he had not so far found himself at a loss for employment. His proudest moment had come when by chance he found himself serving alternate watches with fat and wheezy William Tyburn. He had ascended to the pilot-house with tread as quiet as a great cat's and stood behind Fernand while he was cutting off a bend, new this season, all its reefs prickly with snags, without having bothered to send out leadsmen.

Fernand was halfway across a bar that came to within inches of the hull when he realized he was no longer alone. Sweating and almost shaking, somehow he completed the crossing. Dead silent until they were again in the channel, Tyburn said at last, "So Drew's a teacher too."

That held out hope—hope that in time he would no longer suffer slights at the Guild parlor.

One day, Fernand swore to himself, he would be back in charge of a great and famous riverboat. One day he would be able to escort his mother on board and install her in the finest of the staterooms for a voyage that would go down in history. And at his side there would be . . . a girl . . . The vision blurred. It always had to take second place to his steersmanship. But he knew what face he wished the girl to wear.

 Her tobacco-colored gown protected by a starched white apron, Dorcas Archer kneaded dough for bread. There was something magical about the transformation of powder and water into food, and it helped her to face the rest of the day. Just as the earliest yeasts had settled unbidden from the air to leaven loaves and ferment wine, so the spirit which infused eternal life—

She checked the thought. That image was popish, offered by one of the priests who had comforted her at the Ursuline convent, or possibly another who had called here to console Mrs. Parbury but paused long enough to interrogate the servants: to wit, herself and Fibby, the fat black woman who had been dead James's nurse and stayed on as cook-housekeeper. . . It frightened Dorcas to reflect that, in spite of her wrinkles and sunken cheeks, Fibby could be at most twice her age.

Was hers to be a similar future? Sometimes she feared so. Sometimes she regarded her situation—lucky though she was to have employment with a respectable family—as just another trap like the one she had been born into. The only daughter of a couple who both blamed her for not being a boy, she had been raised in a house ruled by spinsters: four of her mother's sisters and one of her father's. They were accustomed to think of themselves as wise virgins, and when they were not reading the Bible or at prayer meetings, they searched for signs of sin in others like buzzards quartering the air for the reek of carrion.

Not, as she constantly swore to the Lord when she was alone, from lust or concupiscence (whatever that might be; she had not yet plucked up the courage to ask anybody) but purely because there was no loving-kindness in her home, Dorcas had—she had . . .

Well, yes, she had! But what name to put to her deed she could not tell. The boy with whom she had done it had said something, blush-faced—he was fair, his eyes were like chips of sky—but she had not heard correctly, being distracted by waves of an unprecedented sensation. And there was about as much chance of seeing him again as there was of returning home. Her father and mother and aunts had been explicit: were she to show her face in town once more, they would run her out on a rail.

Vaguely she had dreamed, aboard the steamer that her last half-dollar paid her fare on, of making a new life in New Orleans. But the other new life growing within her had rendered that impossible. Her shame had been made public, on a public street. Had it proved a boy, she would have called him Jonas after his father; a girl she would have named . . .

*Stop*. As things stood, the Lord had been merciful. She was granted a roof over her head, enough food, clothing plain but serviceable, duties she was fit to bear, lying no more heavy on her than her body in the arms of the boy who— *Stop*. Down that path danger lay.

Her slender olive hands divided the dough into four equal loaves and laid them to prove under a damp cloth.

She tried to prevent herself from awarding each a name.

A bell jangled on the wall. She greeted the signal with relief, although her next daily obligation was one that ran counter to her conscience, for it was to assist Mrs. Parbury at her devotions before the shrine in memoriam of James. The notion of such idolatry made Dorcas flinch. On the other hand, nobody could say the nuns had not been kind in her hour of greatest need, and if one allowed for the suffering she had undergone, so too had Mrs. Parbury.

At least the captain hadn't awaked first, which was a minor mercy. Mornings when he did were apt to become intolerable. Quickly she rinsed her hands and hastened to respond.

But Mrs. Parbury barely suppressed a groan while being helped to her commode, and another escaped her when she bent to her *prie-dieu*. Worried, Dorcas hovered near the door . . . and then had to lift her mistress to her feet when her orisons were over. Today the pain from her rheumatism was so acute, she could not endure the prospect of being dressed, and returned to bed.

"Shall I send for Dr. Malone?" Dorcas offered. She liked and trusted that blunt-spoken man; it had after all been he who recommended her to the Parburys.

"Malone does me no good!" came the querulous answer. "I want to see the new doctor—Cherouen! And I mean to, and my husband may go to the devil!"

Dorcas clasped her hands in dismay.

"He's going to the Guild parlor today," Mrs. Parbury went on. "There's no question of my leading him. You must do it. And on your way back you will call at Dr. Cherouen's house and say I want him urgently. Tell him to bring the electrical machines I've read about in his advertisements."

More perturbed than ever, not just because since her arrival she had scarcely gone half a mile from this house, but also because she knew the captain's attitude toward doctors who issued dodgers and hand cards, Dorcas ventured, "Ma'am, Mr. Parbury did say—"

"I know what he said!"—in a weak but venomous whisper. "But he doesn't live in this wreck of a body!"

Noises came from the adjacent room: a cough, followed by the chiming of the captain's watch. It was too late to argue. With a sigh Dorcas turned away.

"Very well, ma'am," she muttered.

But it wasn't well in any sense at all.

 When the steward knocked at the door of his first-class cabin, Auberon Moyne was already drawing on his clothes. What had roused him was the changing note of the *Franche-Comté*'s engines as she nosed into the treacherous passages of the Mississippi delta.

But he was on edge anyhow. He was coming home for the first time since the war. Determined to give their sons the best possible education, his parents had dispatched him to the Sorbonne in Paris, and his younger brother Gabriel to Heidelberg. During vacations, and now since the end of the last academic year, they had been instructed to visit museums, art galleries, and archeological remains. Having made a few dutiful attempts to comply, Auberon had discovered that such places bored him. Of late he had compromised by buying guidebooks and souvenir photos at his official destination, then taking the next train for Deauville or Menton, or some other popular resort, in search of agreeable society. Being tall, with crisp brown hair, gray eyes, and an intriguingly broken nose—the result of a boxing match that went too far—and moreover since he was that alien curiosity, an American, he had little difficulty in finding jolly companions with whom to squander his not ungenerous allowance. He had been introduced to all the dissipations proper to a young Frenchman of aristocratic background: race meetings, gambling clubs, cabarets, restaurants with private rooms where a lady might discreetly make rendezvous with an admirer, and—inevitably—brothels.

Oh, yes: Europe had afforded him a liberal education, albeit in subjects his parents would not have approved. Consequently he intended to make sure they never found out. He had toyed with the notion of telling the truth in a letter to his sister Louisette; sport though she was, however, he feared she might tattle. So the only person here at home who knew what he had actually been up to was his cousin and lifelong confidant, Joel.

Putting final touches to his appearance before the mirror, Auberon wondered whether the two of them would still be on intimate terms in future. Emancipation had ruined the Siskin family. Convinced of a Confederate victory, Joel's father had bought slaves when everybody else was selling them. Thanks to that, Joel had had to abandon hope of a college education and the career he dreamed of as an author and poet, and take what jobs he could with ephemeral local newspapers.

Some of the new tastes he had acquired, Auberon felt, might be out of Joel's reach now . . .

He briskened. At all events his cousin had relieved the dismal prospect of returning home by describing the new amenities Langston Barber had made available at the Limousin.

He planned to sample them at the earliest opportunity.

Because—he tried and failed to suppress a cough, and spat red into his washbasin—there might not be very much time.

 A musical chinking of silver and porcelain announced delivery of breakfast to the suite occupied by Mr. Hamish Gordon at the St. Charles Hotel. As on all mornings since their arrival, it was prompt to time. Gordon's amanuensis Matthew Rust made a note of the fact in the journal he was instructed to keep during this trip, before emerging to inspect what the floor waiters had brought.

The coffee was hot; the toast was crisp; the grilled steak was oozing a suitably reddish ichor. The local newspapers had been brought, plus two New York papers forwarded by railroad express and four telegraphic messages concerning a deal in borax which was currently interesting Gordon. All this Matthew verified with forced unhurriedness, aware of how the waiters must feel when confronted by this slim blond boy who gave the impression of being at least three years younger than his chronological age of eighteen.

But if there was one thing he understood, it was how to please the clients of a hotel. Orphaned at thirteen, he had been adopted by his mother's brother, proprietor of a celebrated resort hotel in the village of Catskill, New York, and apprenticed to his uncle's trade. Beginning last summer, he had been delegated more and more responsibility. Gordon, taking refuge from exhaustion due to overwork, had been impressed by his competence and approached him when his two-month stay had a week to run. There could have been no negative answer to the question he posed: "Matthew, how would you like to see the world before you sink your roots? If you'd care to work for me, you shall."

And he had been as good as his word.

Of course, if the financier decided to purchase a property and settle down, as he often said he might, things would be very different. Matthew hoped fervently that by then he would have been taken to enough fascinating places to supply a fund of precocious reminiscence. To be world-weary and cosmopolitan before coming of age seemed like an enviable condition.

Sometimes, though, he felt that the strain of putting up with his employer's moods had already brought him halfway to being old.

Unable to repress a sigh, he poured a cup of coffee so that it would be at drinking temperature when Gordon sipped it, and went to tap on the door of the other bedroom.

Last night Gordon had stayed out late. However, he enjoyed a resilient constitution. Three cups of coffee and the steak restored his usual spirits. Mopping his spade-shaped black beard, he boomed at Matthew, "Well, boy, when do we set off on our excursion?"

"At eleven, sir," Matthew replied. "The boat is called the *Isaiah Plott*, and she is to return about six in the evening."

"Are you looking forward to today?"

Gordon had not so far mentioned how long he had been away from his native Scotland, but now and then the burr in his voice grew so strong, Matthew failed to discern his meaning. Wishing not to admit that that had just happened to him again, the boy put on a reflexive smile and half shook his head.

"Hah! Well, you'll have to stomach it at all events! I'm coming to tak' a gey interest in the boats that ply their muckle river!"

"So do I, sir!" Matthew insisted, realizing belatedly that there had been another misunderstanding.

Under bushy eyebrows Gordon regarded him. At length he shrugged his massive shoulders.

"Then it must be this town that disagrees with you—or city, as you Americans will have it. Aye, it is sweltering, but scarcely more so than Washington, and out on the water we may expect a refreshing breeze." He uttered an unashamed burp. "Eleven o'clock, you said? We'll be there ahead of time because I want to look at the boat's engineroom. Lay out my clothes, and be sure you select a silk shirt."

 Worried, aware how out-of-place his much-worn garb made him seem among the other people who had come to welcome first-class passengers off the *Franche-Comté*—and there were many of them, for this was her maiden voyage and she had broken the record for the Cherbourg–New Orleans run—Joel Siskin scanned the vast echoing volume of the customs hall.

He should not have been here. He had, in fact, strict orders to be somewhere else, and he expected to lose his job in consequence. But there was an overriding reason—

"Auberon!"

The shout burst from him unintended. A heartbeat after spotting four matched steamer trunks painted with the name MOYNE, he had recognized his cousin approaching to confront the customs inspectors: that, despite a newly grown moustache, a suit of the latest Parisian cut set off by a resplendent mauve cravat and a gold stickpin, and an expression on his face which betrayed amazement at the all-pervading stench, compounded by steamer smoke, goods of myriad kinds from tobacco to tarred rope exposed on nearby wharves to bake in the sun, and sewage and ordure discharged casually into the river.

Could he have forgotten the odor of his native city?

That reflection offered the first check to Joel's enthusiasm, and the second followed a moment later. He was not alone in coming to greet Auberon, naturally. There, the other side of the wooden barrier which he had circumvented by putting two bits in the proper hand, stood the rest of the Moyne family—bar, of course, Gabriel. There was Uncle Andrew, as Joel had been raised to call him; there was Aunt Imelda; and between them Louisette, fair, slender, sparkling-eyed . . .

Time was when, as a callow adolescent, he had dreamed about her in such images as made him glad he was not Catholic and required to make confession. She had been the despair of her family's servants because she was forever doing mad ungirlish things—exploiting her lesser weight to scramble higher in a tree than him or Auberon, or swimming longer underwater, or on one memorable occasion drinking most from a stolen jug of corn liquor and keeping it down while the boys' bravado led to vomiting and repentance.

For a while he had imagined they might marry, but that was before the disaster that overtook his family's fortunes. Now he preferred not to think about her.

Today, however, it was too late to hide. She had caught sight of him. He could not hear her, for there was such a racket, but the way she brandished her ribbon-decked parasol unmistakably signaled *come and join us!* Reluctant, yet expectant, Joel complied.

And was obliged to stand by, a pace and a half apart from the others, as Auberon airily tossed coins at the porters who were taking his trunks in charge, doffed hat and gloves with perfectly schooled movements, and in turn kissed his mother's cheek, clasped his father's hand with demonstrative warmth, embraced Louisette . . . and turned to Joel and said affably, "How decent of you to turn out, old fellow! Or are you just reporting the new liner for your paper?"

Since the war the Moynes had omitted to invite the Siskins to any of their grand affairs; similarly they had found excuses to decline invitations going the other way. In that moment Joel was far less than regretful about it.

But to be snubbed here by his oldest friend was intolerable. He advanced beaming, making no mention of the fact that he was supposed to be at the St. Charles Hotel investigating mysterious Hamish Gordon; that his editor had been displeased with his last half-dozen pieces and warned that, if this time he didn't bring in something rival papers would envy, he would surely be dismissed; that he had run the risk simply to greet Auberon on arrival and fix a date to talk over his experiences abroad. Instead—

"Great to see you!" he exclaimed. "Let me know as soon as you're settled, and I'll tell you about the changes the old burg has undergone since you left for Europe! A newspaperman, you know, has *all sorts* of contacts . . . !"

Appending a monstrous wink, he tipped his hat and marched away, seething.

\*     \*     \*

"How strangely Joel acts these days!" murmured Louisette as he departed. "Almost as though he doesn't like us anymore . . . But that's up to him, I guess."

Turning to her brother, she embraced him a second time with equal fervor. "I'll see you at home tonight!" she exclaimed.

Auberon blinked at her. "You mean you're not devoting today to the Prodigal Returned? But I have so much to tell you, Loose!"

"I'm sure you do, Obe!"—invoking another of the nicknames they had shared since childhood. (Joel had been Jewel. Gabriel had always been Gabriel; they had forgotten why.) "But—well, your little sister is growing up!"

"I can see that," Auberon said slowly. "What do you mean, though?"

Indulgently their mother intervened.

"She is pledged to make a river trip today with a gentleman called Arthur Gattry. He's the best friend—indeed he was groomsman at the wedding—of Major Hugo Spring, who has now resigned from the army and . . . Oh, Auberon, there is so much to tell you! Infinitely more than could be packed into a letter! Andrew, I think Louisette is in a hurry—what's the time? Oh, see the watch I gave him the year you went to Europe!"

"It keeps," her husband grunted, "less than railroad time. If Marocain weren't beyond reach, I'd tell him so."

Imelda threw her hands in the air. "Isn't that just like your father?" she appealed to Auberon. "The trouble we went to, trying to pick a suitable gift! And, come to think of it, that was a blessing in disguise, for it was at Marocain's that we first saw the gentleman who has invited Louisette today, along with his friend Major Spring who is now, as I set out to say, *married*. And it's his wife, a charming lady of very old family, who has agreed to chaperone them aboard the excursion boat—not that in these enlightened days one feels forced to adhere to the strictest of the old-fashioned conventions . . ."

Life at home had apparently changed little in four years. Auberon concealed a sigh, gave Louisette another peck on the cheek—which passed for forgiveness although inwardly he was fuming—and braced himself to endure his homecoming.

He was already regretting his disdain of Joel.

 Depressed beyond measure by Auberon's coolness, Joel now recalled with agonizing clarity the strictness of his editor's orders. Could he have thrown away a precious job on a pointless sentimental errand?

How could his absence have changed Auberon so radically? Or was it some sort of European affectation? Who could say?

At this time of morning the wharves and quays were swarming with people: not only passengers from the lately arrived ships, along with crewmen just paid off and looking forward to a spree, but also porters, roustabouts, shoeshine boys, customs officers, peddlers offering snack food and cold drinks.

Through this maze of humanity Joel somehow made his way, moving like an automaton, half thinking he might salvage his situation by going at once to the St. Charles and perhaps bearding Gordon in the lobby, for it was definite that no indirect approach would succeed. The hotel staff must have been well bribed.

Why such mystery? The effect had only been to increase public curiosity. Nobody as visibly rich as Gordon could fail to excite interest in New Orleans, where gossip was a thriving industry. He would surely have done better to give one dull interview to the first reporter he chanced across, whereupon competing papers would have admitted they'd been scooped and let the matter rest.

Could it be that he was hoping not to avoid attention, but attract it?

Yet, intrigued as he was by this puzzling financier, and worried as he was about his job, Joel found himself unable to transform intention into action. Not so much against his will as devoid of it, he simply wandered—uptown, upriver, for no better reason than that he happened to be facing that direction when he started.

"Hey! *Look out!*"

The shout so startled Joel that he lost his footing on a patch of spilled oil and went sprawling. Not only the hand with which he tried to break his fall, but his best pants that he had put on to go meet Auberon, were smutched on the instant.

But it was the lesser of two evils.

His random course had brought him to that section of the levee devoted to river traffic. Like a metallic forest the chimneys of side- and sternwheelers ranked by the score along the waterfront, while here and there a ray of sunlight gleamed on a brass bell or the tilted glass of a pilothouse window. A steam crane was hoisting bulky freight on to wagons, and its current load—hogsheads of tobacco in a rope net—was being swung across his path. Another step, and he would have been knocked over like a tenpin.

Two men nearby hastened to help him up. From the crane's cab an anxious black face looked out, and the same voice that had warned him in the nick of time inquired concernedly, "Boss, is you all right?"

"I'm fine, thanks," Joel answered dispiritedly, brushing his pants as best he could and retrieving his hat, now wet and dirty also. The two who had run to help him looked expectant.

Of course. A tip . . .

He found nothing in his change pocket bar a couple of dimes. This was not what they had been hoping for. Sullen-faced, they moved away, and Joel was about to do the same when a chord of memory resonated. He called to the crane driver.

"Jes' a minute, boss!" came the reply. "Las' one of the load. . . *Thar* she goes!"

And the barrels of tobacco completed their interrupted journey to the back of a nearby dray.

His immediate task over, the crane driver clambered to the ground, moving awkwardly because he had to favor his right leg. That made Joel certain of his identification.

"Suh, I sho' am sorry fo'—"

Joel cut him short. "Oh, I wasn't looking where I was going! But I think I know you. Didn't you advertise, just after the war, to find your wife and children?"

The driver froze in mid-movement. When he spoke again, it was in the accent of an educated man.

"I did, sir. We had been separated when I ran off to join the Union forces, and all other means of tracing them had failed." With a grimace he appended, "So did the advertisements."

"I'm sorry," Joel said lamely.

The other shrugged: that was the past! But his curiosity had been piqued. "How is it you recollect me, sir?"

"I was in the *Intelligencer*'s office when you came to place an advertisement. In fact I thought of trying to make a story out of your experience."

"Story?"—with a sour smile. "Only too real, sir."

"I mean a moralizing article. You were a soldier, of course. Weren't you wounded in action?"

A dismissive gesture was the main answer. It was supplemented with: "But I've been luckier than some. I do have regular work."

"Hah! Then that 'some' includes me, I guess. I was sent out today to bring in a particular story, and— Oh, no matter. But in the hope of rescuing something from the wreck I've made of my day: is there anything going on around here that might make news?"

He uttered that in the tone of one clutching at straws.

"Well, I heard tell that the crew of the *Dolores Day* planned to jump ship. Captain Grigg promised a raise in pay and broke his word, so they ain't going to let her leave till he shows the color of his money."

Joel shook his head. "Not much use to me, probably. It'll have been covered by our regular river correspondent. Still, I'll check it out. Is she moored far from here?"

"I guess about ten minutes' walk. Just before you get to the excursion steamers like the *Isaiah Plott* and the *Judah Rigby*."

"Thanks very much. Ah . . ." Joel's hand had started toward his pocket again before he recalled that he had no change left, only a five-dollar bill he could not afford to break. But in any case the black man stopped him with one amazingly pale palm upraised.

"No charge, boss. Just figure I'm glad your headline ain't going to read: 'Our correspondent brained by steam crane. *Necktie party held on waterfront!*'"

With sudden violence he spat on the ground, swung around, and reascended the ladder to his cab.

 Last night the audience at the Grand Philharmonic Hall had been unbearable: catcalling, booing, even throwing rotten fruit.

And yet in his heart Gaston d'Aurade could not blame them. Did they not have grounds when two of the performers were a juggler who kept dropping his knives and balls, and a singer whose voice would have shamed a crow? To make matters worse, some of the pit musicians had reported drunk.

After the show Gaston had had a stand-up row with his employer, and returned to his dismal lodgings so overwrought he could scarcely sleep. Waking at dawn, he had gone to early mass at the cathedral in search of spiritual calm.

But even the music he had heard there had done little to ease his mind, for every note brought back the collapse of his youthful ambitions. Why was he arranging for a theatre band of such dismal quality that he had to simplify even the plainest harmonies for fear of losing his musicians partway through a number? Why was he not devising beautiful brilliant anthems for the cathedral choir?

Silently he swore that if he was still in the same plight at the end of the year, at any cost he would break free. It was reported that since the war many cities scattered across the newly opened territories had become rich enough to afford a taste of culture. Indeed, one rumor claimed that a wealthy tycoon somewhere in the Midwest (but the names of his family and city varied from one version to the next) had invited an entire European orchestra to emigrate at his expense. Surely if even half, even a *tenth* of such stories were to be credited, there must be a better post for Gaston d'Aurade on this continent!

After mass he had breakfasted on coffee and beignets, then walked to the river and followed its levees westward. Watching the majestic flow of those broad waters often restored his peace of mind. Once he had planned to voyage from mouth to source and back and compose *en route* a tone poem which would capture all the Mississippi's moods. Now he feared that that too was doomed to become one more among countless empty dreams.

At least he had found a deputy for today's matinee performance, so he could spare time for a trip on an excursion boat; they were not expensive, and often one ate better on board than at his lodgings. Creole cuisine was not among the things Gaston had learned to approve since his arrival. Sometimes he wondered whether he had any real reason to remain in Louisiana, or whether he had stayed solely because of the shame he would feel were he to retreat to France poor and defeated, like his cousin who had turned the Hotel Limousin first into a laughingstock and then into a tragedy. . .

Suddenly he detected the faint sound of a marching band. At once his mood lightened. As a child he had heard the band of the *Garde Royale* parading through Paris. Ever since, music of that type had retained the power to thrill him. Maybe it could turn the trick again today.

But what lured him turned out to be nothing like the smart, well-rehearsed ensemble he had envisaged. Such bands did exist, for although few of the long-trade steamboats carried musicians—and aboard those that did one rarely found more than a string trio, its members black as often as not and required to double as waiters or barbers—most excursion boats and, of course, all showboats boasted orchestras equipped with ex-military instruments pawned by their former players at the end of the war. A few such, by their decorum and polished phrasing, had impressed Gaston.

This one at first sight—and again at second sight—did not. It was a gang of ill-clad men and boys aged from fifteen to fifty, about a dozen mulattos and half as many whites, under the direction of a short swarthy man with dark eyes, a bushy black moustache, and a manner as excitable as a fractious horse's. He was conducting his motley bunch of instrumentalists with frantic waves of a wide Mexican hat. If one could call it conducting! He was practically dancing, his gestures were so vigorous. Accustomed to formal concerts and regimental march-pasts, Gaston was shocked.

Yet the sound was potent, and not to be denied. He found himself on the verge of turning away, and at the same time prey to wistful jealousy. This was scarcely to be dignified with the name of music *proprement dite* . . . but yonder a clarinetist was evoking a fierce rich tone from an instrument overdue for the rubbish dump, whereas his opposite number at the Grand Philharmonic Hall customarily produced from a brand-new Boehm squeaks reminiscent of a door on badly oiled hinges.

Correct in pitch, granted, for the most part. Which was supremely important according to his teachers back home. So Gaston straightened, resolving to continue in the direction of the excursion boats—and abruptly recognized the tune the band was playing. He had often conducted it when it was popular five years ago. He had been glad when the audience ceased to shout requests for it, owing to its banal simplicity, yet . . .

Oh, could he really have failed to recognize "Wake Nicodemus"?

Incredible. And nonetheless that was the tune emerging from a chaotic complex of variations. Much against his will he found himself beating time. With an effort he canceled the impulse. Such peasant stuff appealed to the lower, to the animal side of human nature! Possibly the barbarizing influence of the late war . . . ?

But something was happening that fixed not only his but many other people's attention. Drawing abreast of a steamer called the *Jas. P. Tew*, the band formed a rough circle. Two or three of the twenty men who had been following it—along with a string of children of all possible colors—ran up her stage.

It dawned on Gaston what he was watching. There must be some dispute between the crew and captain of this vessel. Possibly Governor Warmoth's new police, the Metropolitans, would be obliged to take a hand. Gaston had never seen them in action, except against drunks, tramps and stray niggers, but he was flattered by the choice of their quasi-French name and found himself rationalizing yet one more delay *en route* to his intended destination on the grounds that this was as diverting as, and naturally cheaper than, a steamer ride.

 The little parade had already halted alongside other boats to drum up support for the strike against the *Dolores Day*. None had been forthcoming. So it was no surprise to Manuel Campos when the captain of the *Jas. P. Tew* appeared brandishing a pistol and yelling insults, accompanied by deckhands wielding clubs.

But what did startle Manuel almost to the point of dropping his hat was recognizing a man in an impeccable gray coat with matching silk hat, leaning on a walking cane and nodding in time to the rough-and-ready rhythms of his picked-up performers. It was the conductor he had seen at the Grand Philharmonic Hall. To inhabit such a world was Manuel's chief ambition. His esteem knew no bounds for the Frenchman who, with casual aplomb, directed a score of real musicians all capable of reading the dots-and-lines . . . which Manuel was not.

His heart thumped madly. Let this be the point where the parade broke up! Let this be his chance to make the acquaintance of that august personage! He badly needed a patron, for he was in the States without intention or resources. He had been supercargo of a boat which attempted to run the Union blockade and ran foul not of patrols but of a storm that wrecked her in western Louisiana, where the the people called themselves Acadians and spoke a language that Manuel could puzzle out by, as he put it, twisting his ears, and had no love for the Yanquis. Thanks to the fact that he could coax almost any musical instrument to emit a recognizable tune, he had reached the anonymity of this big city, thinking it easier there to obtain passage back to Mexico.

He had failed completely on that score. But now he was no longer eager to return home. He came from a fishing village with a sideline in smuggling: a boring place, as he had learned to describe it in English. New Orleans, by contrast, was full of endless variety. And no one had questioned his right to employment on the steamers that plied the Mississippi. So long as he was capable of doing the work . . .

But he was obliged to wait on table for his living, when he would rather be a full-time musician. Moreover there was none of the loyalty he had been used to among his family and friends. For the duration of a voyage, the crew of a steamer became a mutually supporting unit. It didn't last. At trip's end the group split up. And there was no solidarity between one boat's crew and another's. Today was an example. The master of the *Dolores Day* had thrice broken his pledged word to give his men better wages, but even those who customarily blackguarded Grigg for a thief and a cheat had driven the protesters away. Further struggle was obviously useless.

And he was not alone in so believing. At this latest rebuff the band lowered their instruments. More attracted by the music than the principle involved, the "second line" made that an excuse to drift away.

Realizing that now he must seek another job, Manuel sighed philosophically and replaced his hat on his head prior to making toward the elegant Frenchman. As he walked he drew from his pocket a pair of hand-rolled panatelas, preparing to offer one and request the share of a match flame.

But at that moment a number of excursion boats announced their impending departure by a variety of voices, loudest among them the steam calliope of the *Isaiah Plott*. Galvanized, Gaston headed in that direction with rangy strides.

Not to be balked, Manuel stepped into his path, uncovering, set to deliver a flattering little speech in his best English.

Gaston tossed a coin into his hat and marched on, leaving Manuel shaking with bewilderment that little by little grew into rage.

 True to his word, as soon as he set foot aboard the *Plott* Gordon insisted on being taken to her engineroom, which reeked even worse than the kitchen of the hotel where he had recruited Matthew.

Who had hoped his employer might be treated to a cursory tour of inspection and then ushered away with some colorable excuse. The advertised departure time had long been upon them; the bellowing pipes of the calliope had reached the fourth or fifth inexpert rendition of "Rosin the Beau." But Gordon began to display such expert knowledge, and ask such keen questions, that the engineers were at once disarmed. To compound the problem, one of them turned out to be Scottish, and much extra time was wasted in commiserating about their homeland, now being pillaged to benefit English landlords.

It struck Matthew that this was the first time he had seen his employer excited. Angry, yes: he could fly into a temper over the most trivial failing on the part of a servant or a clerk in a store. But here was a subject dear to his heart, and he waxed eloquent.

Some minutes after eleven he was at last persuaded to quit the engineroom. Matthew was almost faint with relief.

Gordon too, he judged, was not unhappy to lean on the rail and breathe purer air while watching the stages being raised, particularly since the calliope had progressed from wrong notes to squawks and then to blessed silence.

But as usual the financier grew restive after a while. Matthew tensed. Any minute he was apt to receive some unpredictable order, which Gordon would later justify as a test of his fitness to continue in his post, but which in fact amounted to no more than a discharge of accumulated mental energy. This was a man who could not, seemingly, enjoy the privileges his skill and industry had reaped; it was typical that his first concern should not be with the bar and amusements of this boat, but with her mechanism and her hull.

However, Matthew was doing his best not to feel resentful. Thanks to a rare access of confidentiality on the train to Cincinnati, he had learned that it was his own efforts, not an inheritance, which had made Gordon's fortune. All his life Matthew had been raised to admire the self-made man, and his uncle had often admonished him that the foibles such people exhibited must be speedily forgiven; they were a price paid for achievement on a plane the ordinary person might not aspire to. His uncle was an admirer of Andrew Jackson Davis of Poughkeepsie, and frequently larded his conversation with technical spiritualist terms like "plane."

Thankful that whatever eruption was brewing had not yet reached culmination, he suddenly recalled that on the way here they had passed a lively band. Optimistic for even a few seconds' diversion, he scanned the levee, and was disappointed. He could see men wandering about with brass instruments, but it was clear that while the calliope was playing the band must have given up. Would the day come when no human instrumentalist could match machinery? Already the toughest-lunged trumpeter could be outblasted; would unemployment follow for fiddlers, be their fingers never so nimble? There were stories of a machine that could play chess. . .

Abruptly he was distracted. Down on the quayside a young man had caught sight of Gordon and reacted explosively. He rushed for the stage—and *just* made it.

 Arthur Gattry had resigned himself to getting married. He hated the idea. Being an only son, he knew that sooner or later he must yield for duty's sake, but he had been enjoying single blessedness too long to abandon his style of living altogether. What he wanted was a *modern* marriage.

But until recently he would not have backed his chances of achieving one.

Meeting Louisette Moyne had changed all that.

A chance introduction led to him recognizing the girl who long ago at the Grand Philharmonic Hall had impressed him by her elegance and beauty. He had never dreamed that she would prove to be the well-educated daughter of a respected businessman. Girls like that simply were not supposed to visit such raffish places!

It followed that she was a sport. He investigated; he learned that she was as progressive as she was lovely, accustomed to pour scorn on the staid ways of the past. That suited Arthur to perfection. He resolved to lay siege to her.

Clearly she was having—like him—too much fun at present to think of accepting his or anyone's proposal, but he was in no great hurry. He was thirty-two; if necessary, he was prepared to wait until thirty-five before taking a bride. In the meantime he was cultivating her acquaintance: calling once or twice a week, making an occasional gift, arranging outings for her and her mother . . .

Today marked a breakthrough. It was the first time Louisette had consented to make an excursion with him on her own. When he suggested the idea, he had been unaware that her favorite brother was due back from Europe. On being told, he had expected to have to change the date. On the contrary: Louisette was thrilled by the prospect of a river trip and demonstrated the fact by arriving ahead of time despite having gone to welcome Auberon.

It was chiefly habit which had led Arthur to extend the invitation. He had often found that the romantic views afforded by the river had a gratifyingly aphrodisiac impact . . .

But now he was asking himself what in the world had led him to imagine that what amused and seduced a girl chance-met in a run-down ward of the city would have a similar effect on his intended wife. The moment she set foot on deck a cloud had crossed her brow, due to the seediness of this all-too-popular vessel. No doubt pressure of work accounted for the conspicuously full cuspidors and the used mugs and glasses on every ledge, but they made a poor initial impression. So too did the boat's late departure and the breakdown of its calliope, which in any case was deafeningly loud and alarmingly off-key.

All these setbacks were doubly infuriating because in other respects the outing had begun extremely well. Conspiratorial whispers had passed between Louisette and Hugo's wife Stella, who had thereafter swept her husband away with the plain intention of abandoning her task of chaperonage. That should have been the signal for Arthur to unmask all his batteries: to be charming, to be fascinating, to be altogether delightful, and to be rewarded with a lingering delicious kiss, at least. It would be far from Louisette's first, so Stella had confided, and despite his range of worldly experience he looked forward to finding out how well she had been taught.

So he should definitely not have been leaning on the rail, as tongue-tied as any fourteen-year-old at a party.

Glancing around in search of some diversion to offer, he muttered a low exclamation.

"What is it?" Louisette inquired. And, following his gaze, saw a heavily built man with a full dark beard, doffing his hat. Politeness obliged Arthur to acknowledge the gesture, though he would rather have ignored it.

"Who's that?" Louisette persisted. "Someone you know?"

Arthur reluctantly gave ground.

"That's Mr. Hamish Gordon."

"Really? The financier? How did you meet him? *Have* you met him?"

Arthur hesitated, but no doubt Louisette already knew about his favorite pastimes.

"We were playing cards together last night."

"Oh! Where was that?"

"At the—uh—the Hotel Limousin."

"Oh, you go there, do you?" Excitedly Louisette clasped her hands. "I've heard of it! Won't you take me sometime?"

Taken aback, Arthur prevaricated. "Well, my dear, I'm not sure it's the sort of place where—"

"Oh, stuff and nonsense!" she cut in with a stamp of one small foot. "People are always telling me that, and then when I finally manage to get to this sink of iniquity, this den of vice, it turns out to be tamer than a children's nursery! Anyway, I insist on being introduced to Mr. Gordon. I would adore the chance to meet him—and so would Father! As soon as he heard Mr. Gordon was from Scotland, he started wondering whether he has any information about the matchstick swindle, which I'm sure you remember— I say! What's going on down there?"

Birdwise, her attention had been distracted back to the wharf. A young man had rushed on to the landing stage just before it was withdrawn, and was now engaged in furious argument with one of the boat's officers.

"But that's Joel!" Louisette exclaimed.

"Who?"

"My cousin Joel Siskin! Oh—you wouldn't have met him, I guess. He doesn't come to our house any more. And he behaved awfully oddly when he came to welcome Auberon. . . I do hope he's all right! Will you go and see, please?"

Glad of the chance to make a good impression, but much put out on learning of this cousin, Arthur was on the point of complying when the disagreement was resolved. Money changed hands; the officer let Joel by; and to the relief of her impatient passengers the *Isaiah Plott* finally began her voyage.

Owing to the chill welcome he invariably received, Fernand had few qualms about being late in posting his report at the Guild parlor. Today an excellent breakfast and a chance encounter with a friend had used up most of the morning. He was in an optimistic mood when he did eventually make his way thither, and could almost have convinced himself that today was the day when one of his colleagues might offer civil greetings and accept a drink at his expense.

No such luck. Captain Parbury was ensconced already in his high-backed chair—not strictly his, but it had been donated by a pilot killed in the war, and other members were shamed to dispute possession of it.

Little by little, Parbury was taking over the affairs of the Guild, using his handicap as leverage. Whatever factions might form, it was doom to their success if they made so bold as to defy his rigid views . . . expressed, moreover, in impressive terms these days. More than once, while making his half-secretive entry and exit, Fernand had heard Parbury holding forth about how loss of sight had transformed him from a doer to a thinker; he claimed that when he could see he suffered from a stutter, whereas now he could unfold long oratorical passages with the best of them. Certainly nothing hampered his tongue when he described the unrealized glories of the third *Nonpareil,* a model of which resided on a shelf behind the bar, glass-cased like a collection of wax fruit or a record catfish.

And yet . . . and yet . . . that model did represent an ideal! Her lines were so pure and elegant that most members of the Guild had been tempted to contribute suggestions for her fitting-out, and someone who was not a member—Cato Woodley—had been so taken with the notion that he had given half a won bet on Parbury's skill at billiards to purchase dolls' furniture and equip the miniature cabin. An alternative version of the story had it that Woodley did no more than offer to share his luck, and it was Parbury who decided how to spend the money. Either way, some such event had created an improbable pair of cronies out of those two: at least as unbelievable as the association between Hosea Drew and Langston Barber . . . but for one key factor. There was an age difference between Parbury and Woodley which made people suggest that the blind captain had found a substitute for his dead son.

That, Fernand well understood. Occasionally during his schooling aboard the *Atchafalaya,* when Drew was finding fault apparently for the sake of being able to complain, he had had the impression that the grudge the older man was venting was unconnected with his pupil—that it had more to do with the ill luck that led to him standing *in loco parentis* to Jacob's children, so ultimately to his inability to find a wife and start a family of his own.

Inability? It was Drew's own word. In what sense must it be taken?

On separating from the *Atchafalaya* Fernand had devised a whole series of resentful explanations. More mature reflection had led him to a different conclusion. Drew had expended, on paying his half-brother's debts, all the emotional capital he had to spare. So he felt cut off from normal society. Having bought a home in St. Louis for Susannah and her children, and lived there because he was trapped by the war, he now preferred to spend his time in the Louisville trade, avoiding his relatives. Similarly the duty of circulating among his passengers often represented such a strain that he had to take refuge in the office, or even the engineroom, for a few minutes before continuing. So far as Fernand was concerned, this reaction was incomprehensible. After long hours at the wheel, he was hungry for the trivial commerce of his fellow human beings.

At least, of those prepared to converse with a person of color . . .

Still, he had by now met not a few people caught up in the routine of the river, resigned to finding work only when the level of the water permitted long trips with profitable cargoes, or eking out a miserable existence when flood or storm or ice made departure impossible, and all had demanded why he had quit a safe and well-paid occupation in favor of a chancy job where even when he was asleep he risked being drowned, or stranded, or blown halfway to the moon.

And because he respected Drew regardless of his dislike, he had tried to answer. Tried like blazes! Yet never quite conveyed the special lure of this career.

And likewise because Parbury spared no pains to make it clear that he loathed Drew and had no time for any of his associates. . .

Well, it was a fact that had to be endured, and the detestation never reached bedrock. At Griswold's Parbury had once, after a coup at the billiard table, permitted Fernand to guide him back to his seat.

Perhaps he had not realized who was offering help.

Thus reminded of Whitworth, Fernand was struck unhappy by a shaft of memory. Quitting the Guild, he found himself at a loss. Did he really want to go on to Griswold's, as usual?

Not much. But he did want to postpone calling on his mother. Eulalie seemed unable to accept that he was a man, in control of his own destiny. On the contrary, she imagined him to be menaced by every conceivable kind of disaster. At various times he had gathered that, according to her prescience, he was at risk from flood, storm, lightning, thieves, some crewman with a grudge, and a total stranger determined to find the excuse to fight a duel. Visiting her had become an ordeal of card readings, ink-pool scrying, and sometimes disgusting processes involving the decapitation of a chicken and inspection of its guts.

All this was owing to her cousin Athalie, who was tubercular and dying before her time. For years, since the decline of Marie Laveau, she had been a power in the psychic underworld of the city. Just as she began to weaken and spit blood, a newcomer—an upstart—made her presence known, and shortly even her most faithful clients were referring with awe to the skills of Mam'zelle Josephine, who lived somewhere in a rich district of the city and never dealt with anybody except through trusted intermediaries and at the highest price.

Appealing to family loyalties, Athalie turned to her cousin, who had somewhat commenced her studies, and set out to impart the whole corpus of her knowledge before death claimed her. Traditionally a widow was best fitted to become a wise woman; Athalie had buried three husbands, which her customers regarded as endowing her with peculiar potency. But she held the view that what counted was to have made sacrifice. Eulalie's man was dead; two of her children had failed to survive infancy; she was an ideal candidate.

Accordingly she was taught divination by the fall of wax from a candle, and how to read ashes mixed with urine and cast on a sand-strewn floor, and other things. Many more. Now she could no longer take tea without swirling the dregs around her cup and making some dire prediction from their pattern.

At first Fernand had been impressed against his will. He had taken the charms she forced on him, intending to throw them away, then found himself as incapable of doing so as of spitting on a crucifix; then, when threat after promised threat failed to eventuate, mere politeness prevented him from refusing them point-blank. Now he was at the stage of delaying, as long as possible, his dutiful visits to her.

Maybe one day he would achieve his ambition of inviting her aboard a boat he was piloting. Maybe, faced with incontrovertible facts, she would accept his new status in life.

Until that day dawned, however, he was happy to take the long way round to his former home. There were so many places in the city where he was assured of a livelier welcome. And since Griswold's was handy, and since it was there that he had enjoyed his only pleasant encounter with Parbury . . .

The weather was hot and humid. His clothing clutched at his skin. There were ceiling fans at Griswold's that could cope with the exudations of a hundred players and spectators. Also there was an excellent ice machine. Very well: that was where he'd go. As usual.

 Escorting her employer to the Pilots' Guild was less of an ordeal than Dorcas had feared, although it proved a strange experience. Not only was she publicly arm-in-arm with a man for the first time in her young life; despite the stick he carried in his free hand, he kept touching her in exploratory fashion, as though to establish in what manner she differed from his wife, and some of the touches were on areas more intimate than hand or arm.

At first she suffered him, thinking a sightless person no doubt needed such contact for reassurance. Then it dawned on her that he knew the route they were following and was giving her advice: watch for the kerbstone here; listen for streetcars at the next intersection; here is a favorite straight run for scorching cyclists. . . His memory seemed keener than her observation.

Therefore, when the sidewalk grew sufficiently crowded to justify his walking more behind than beside her, she pointedly placed his hand on her shoulder, having often seen him thus with his wife. He made no objection, and so continued the rest of the way.

But at the entrance to the Guild parlor he dismissed her with a brusque word of thanks, and that was when she started to feel truly apprehensive. She had no idea how to find Dr. Cherouen's house. Naturally she had not dared inquire directions of the captain, and as for Mrs. Parbury, she had snappishly instructed her to look up the address in Gardner's Directory.

But Dorcas had never seen a copy in the house, and Fibby assured her there had not been since the war. Small wonder. With the master blind and the mistress a near-cripple, what use were maps that showed the city entire?

As a child she had rarely been allowed out alone, and then only to visit places where she had been taken by her mother: her grandmother's home, a cousin's store, the nearby clapboard chapel. So far as her parents—and more to the point, her five aunts—were concerned, the need for her to be thus strictly controlled had been well proved . . .

With the consequence that she had never had to find her way across a busy city before, apart from the day of her arrival in New Orleans—and then she had been wandering haphazardly.

But she was older now, and more confident. On top of that she had been shown how strangers could be kind and generous. Though she had been half-unconscious, she treasured a vivid recollection of the young man who made haste to help her when she fell down, while Dr. Malone and the Ursulines had displayed true charity.

Therefore, not wishing to seem at a loss, she walked away from the Guild with affected briskness, assuring herself that having rounded a corner and got out of sight she would easily find someone to advise her.

But the weather, the noise, and the stench of the city were alike oppressive, and in a different sense so were the people. Their sheer numbers were overwhelming, to start with. On top of that, half of them seemed to be so busy, hurrying on mysterious errands, that they brushed past without registering her presence, while the other half were so much at leisure that they did notice her and made their reactions all too plain. The latter were the worse, whether they were neatly uniformed coachmen waiting for their employers to return, or loiterers not quite reduced to such ragged garb as would ensure their expulsion to a less prosperous quarter but keeping one eye lifted for the advent of a Metropolitan, or even—and this disturbed Dorcas greatly—women in tawdry finery, wearing blatant rouge on their cheeks and monstrous rings on most of their fingers. Where their gazes rested she felt as though flies were touching down on her body.

It made no difference whether their stares were real or imaginary, for already when she left home she had begun to feel conspicuous. Holding a man's arm had something to do with it; very shortly, though, she had realized that many couples were doing the same, and a great proportion of them were neither related nor married but unashamed lovers. Twice she had found herself blushing: one girl had kissed her young man's ear, tilting his hat brim to do so; another had brazenly urged a boy into a shadowed doorway . . .

Much had been said at the church her family attended concerning the wickedness of cities. She was perfectly aware that what she was witnessing must be what the preachers had in mind. But it was exciting. It stirred feelings she had striven to forget.

Besides, though Fibby had assured her that she looked "up to the minute," she had grown aware that her dress and hat were behind the style. The notion struck her that she might look in a few store windows and find out the price of hats, and perhaps other things too, and next time the captain told her to bring him here . . .

Though if Dr. Cherouen were as smart as his advertising claimed, that might never happen.


By now she had gone farther than she had intended. Abrupt recollection of the reason why she was not returning straight home brought a chill to her spine.

She glanced around. Had it been from the left or the right that she entered this street? Was it at the last but one intersection or the last but two?

Suddenly she seemed to see everything around her with preternatural clarity: the fronts of the buildings, the huge sales slogans they bore, the professional names and titles of businesses that stood out in gilt letters on blue or green or red, the awnings and marquees that flapped lackadaisically in today's halfhearted breeze. And none of it made sense! It was like being cast away in a foreign country!

For the space of a shuddering breath she was very frightened.

And then she did see clearly and was grateful. Like a beacon in a storm she recognized a name: Griswold's.

There were occasions when Captain Parbury came home chuckling, escorted by a pilot's cub who felt privileged to pay cab fare for the journey, and without exception it turned out that he had spent his evening at a place called Griswold's. Games were played there that Dorcas had no knowledge of. But for certain the company was agreeable. Many were pilots, finely dressed, sporting ebony walking sticks with silver knobs, diamond breastpins thrust into silk cravats, gold finger rings, and high silk hats.

Hearing about them from the captain in expansive mood, Dorcas had been reluctant to credit such people's existence, for they smacked too much of the prince in a fairy tale . . . especially since Parbury himself wore old clothes, shiny at knees and elbows, and boots with run-down heels. Possibly such heroes might be found in New York, or Paris, or other fine and distant cities. But the chance of meeting them in humdrum New Orleans, where life drifted on from day to day in an unchanging manner—although admittedly this district was different from the one she was accustomed to . . .

No matter! By the door to Griswold's stood three gentlemen, one plump, one of middle build, and one quite thin, and two of them matched Captain Parbury's description in every particular, while the third, the lean one, wore an old-fashioned long-skirted coat and had the general air of a minister on circuit. She mustered all her courage and approached them, drawing from her reticule (not hers, but loaned by her mistress) the letter she was to deliver to Cherouen.

 Although they had tripped together many times, Ketch Tyburn had small love for Harry Whitworth. However, he was newly recovered from a fever that had enforced bed rest and a slow convalescence. Encountering Whitworth by chance, he had been so pleased to meet a fellow riverman that he had hailed him.

And was not wholly sorry to have done so, for it turned out that Whitworth had spent the summer in upper-river trades of which Tyburn had little recent knowledge, and any pilot was always interested in adding to his stock of information.

Better still, when Whitworth started complaining about the master he had been serving under, Tyburn realized he had a grudge against the same man, who was given to issuing orders in the firmest terms, then canceling them an hour later with equal vehemence. By the time they had swapped stories about his maddening behavior, they were conversing very affably.

"Ketch! I heard you were sick! Good to see you back on your legs!"

Tyburn started and glanced round. Advancing in full fig, swinging his cane and beaming, here came one of the other people he would rather not have met at this juncture. Cato Woodley, so the rumor ran, cared more nowadays for the sporting life than the duties of a steamboat captain. As a result he had been unable to replace the *Hezekiah Woodley* at the stage when a prudent owner would have judged her uneconomic to repair. Now he was struggling both to keep up appearances and to make ends meet.

But with the rising challenge of the railroads it behooved a pilot who hoped to retire in his profession to be courteous to any owner of a working boat, even if he usurped a nickname you wanted to reserve to your best friends.

Some minutes elapsed, and threads of tension wove across the friendly gossip. Whitworth, plainly, was hoping that either the pilot or—better—the steamboat owner would invite him into Griswold's; neither liked him enough to make the move. While each was groping for a phrase that would settle matters, Tyburn abruptly noticed that Woodley's gaze was fixed behind his shoulder. He glanced around, and at the same moment Whitworth let go a shrill whistle.

Coming hesitantly toward them was a quadroon girl of heart-stopping loveliness: slender, graceful, with huge limpid dark eyes and a mouth that made one think instantly of ripe peaches, timidly proffering an envelope with an address on it as though herself unable to read.

"I saw her first," Woodley murmured, and with a great flourish of his hat strode to greet her. Whitworth took a step in his wake, and with a sigh—because now he was the father of a grown family, and his daughters might well wander into a situation like this—Tyburn prepared to argue with them. One glance had informed him that this was no common streetwalker, and a second had indicated that telling the others so would be a waste of breath.

Briefly he was tempted to make himself scarce. Conscience pricked him into remaining. Unfortunately it did not also make plain what he could achieve by that.

He watched.

\*     \*     \*

"Sir, if you please . . ."—addressing somewhat more the one with the long-skirted coat.

But the words Dorcas had rehearsed in her head failed her. There was little room for misunderstanding in the way these men looked at her.

"I please very much, and easily too," said the younger one with the silk hat, and extracted Mrs. Parbury's letter from her nervous fingers.

"I'm trying to find my way to that doctor's house," Dorcas said with what firmness she could muster. "An errand for my mistress!"

"Oh, we've heard of *this* doctor!" was the reply. "I bet most of his patients say they are bound to him in behalf of others. Whitworth, I guess the name Cherouen rings your bells?"

Drawing a thin black cigar from his pocket, Whitworth said, "It surely does. I reckon I heard of not a few young—ladies—who had to visit him kind of in a hurry."

He smiled at Dorcas, exposing the gap in his teeth.

"But he was a lucky man who made your case so urgent!"

Uncomprehending, growing dizzy, Dorcas reached for the letter; Woodley withdrew it just beyond her reach.

"Please! Can't you tell me how to get there?" Dorcas implored.

"I don't have the least idea," Whitworth said. "You, Mr. Woodley?"

Reading the superscription with exaggerated pantomime, Woodley shook his head. "But I guess it will be easy to find out. Come inside and take a refreshment, and I'll locate someone to set you on the proper course."

Beaming, he offered his arm but made no move to give back the letter.

She snatched at it; once again he was too quick for her.

Whitworth put his arm around Dorcas's shoulders, muttering, "There, there, my dear!" And added more loudly, "Captain Woodley, I think you should restore this young lady's property!"

Unruffled, Woodley said, "You wouldn't have her going the rounds of Griswold's, would you, as though she were on some improper mission? No, my dear, you just leave it all to me. Come along!"

There was a pause. Then Dorcas knocked aside Whitworth's arm with all her force.

"Give back that letter," she said between clenched teeth.

"My dear, as I keep saying—"

"Are you Captain Cato Woodley?"

"I—ah . . . I own that I am"—blinking with surprise.

"Then your manners are a disgrace to your profession and I shall so inform Captain Parbury, whom I just had the honor of leading to the Pilots' Guild!"

"You know Parbury?" Woodley demanded incredulously. "How come?"

"My guess would be because she works for him. Am I correct, *Miss Archer*?"

Another voice cut in. Dorcas, sensing a savior, turned, expecting him to be the third man who had been conversing with Whitworth and Woodley. But the portly pilot was still hovering in the background. Instead, here came a much younger man of somewhat dusky complexion, neatly attired in a smart dark coat with velvet lapels, matching narrow pants, boots that glistened like mirrors, and a fine silk

hat. He sported a moustache and an imperial beard and carried a black cane with
a carved ivory handle.

"That letter," he said to Woodley, "belongs to Miss Archer. Give it back!"

"I . . ."

But Woodley's automatic defiance collapsed because of something he read in
the newcomer's eyes. Silently he surrendered the envelope.

"Next time you will remember that a lady of color is still a lady! For if you
forget, then I swear on my father's grave that I will drag you to the Oaks and fill
your lousy hide as full of holes as a pepperpot! I thought you and Parbury were
like *that*"—holding up two fingers tightly crossed. "How come you don't recognize Miss Archer, *hm?*"

"Probably, Fernand, because Parbury never invites anyone to visit him at
home," Tyburn said, advancing at last to join the group. "I hear he's ashamed of
his house, compared with what he owned before the war."

"I see." During the previous exchange Fernand had held his cane ready for use
as a weapon if need arose. Now he let its tip drop to the sidewalk with a rapping
sound. "But he will know her in future, I'm sure. And I trust he will also know
how to treat her. Miss"—turning to Dorcas—"I gather you need directions."

This time she eagerly showed the envelope.

"Oh, yes, I know the district well. In fact I'm headed that way. If you would
care to accompany me . . . ?"

"Thank you, sir," Dorcas said with a curtsey copied unconsciously from Fibby,
and when Fernand offered his arm she had no least hesitation in taking it.


"Now how come you let a coon talk to you that way?" Whitworth demanded as
Dorcas and Fernand moved away.

"Watch your mouth, Harry!" Tyburn snapped. "We all heard how Lamenthe
put your nose out of joint! Zeke Barfoot told me, and I believe him! And some of
us know—us *pilots* at any rate!—that he's damn' good at his work!"

Woodley flared, "He's still a nigger when all's said and done!"

"You look no deeper than a man's skin," said Tyburn in a tone that was suddenly grave, "you're in the same trouble as a pilot who can't look beyond the
surface of the river. What am I saying? Nobody who can't look past the surface
could *become* a pilot!"

Taking a pace back, he gazed squarely at Woodley.

"Why do you pay your pilots more than you pay yourself, if it ain't because they
look deeper than what shows? Think about it, *Captain!*"

And, having contrived to make the title sound like a mortal insult, he stumped
ponderously away.


As soon as they were out of sight, Fernand halted and seized
both of Dorcas's hands in both of his.

"My dear Miss Archer, I have hoped—I have *prayed* that we
might meet again! I applied to Dr. Malone, and the nuns, and Mr. Hamel the

druggist, and all refused point-blank to say what had become of you, save that you had found employment. The slightest clue would have brought me to Parbury's house within the hour!"

As he spoke she could only stare at him, lips parted, eyes wide. Surely there was just one person in the world that this could be! But she remembered her rescuer as vastly tall and incredibly strong, while this man was of ordinary height and build. Of course, at the time she had been weak from lack of food, and in childhood she had found out that hunger can play tricks on the mind . . .

Nonetheless she was on the point of responding with enthusiasm to match his, when she was struck by a fearful realization.

He knew—he *must* know—about her shame.

She had learned no other term to apply to her lost lovechild, or at any rate none that made the experience more tolerable even in the privacy of her head. Even Fibby, who spoke with incredible matter-of-factness on subjects that at home Dorcas would have been punished for thinking about, let alone discussing aloud, had no vocabulary to offer bar the crudest.

But memory certified that, however foul and agonizing her miscarriage might have been, what caused it had been precious.

On the other hand it was common knowledge—save among the lowest class of people, to whom shame was meaningless—that a gentleman would have nothing to do with a fallen woman. According to the precepts she had been raised to, according to the sensational novels that were among her few recreations, there must necessarily be a sinister motive in this man's mind.

Yet meeting him again had been a dream so vivid for so long that—perhaps because minutes earlier she had been betrayed by a vision of another sort—she found the idea of it bursting, bubble fashion, more than she could stand.

Besides, his delight seemed so unfeigned!

In a trice she hit on a compromise. With an apologetic smile she murmured something about delay, to which he reacted at once.

"How selfish of me! Show me that address again . . . We could make it quicker by streetcar, I guess. Do you have to be there at some special time?"—drawing from his fob pocket a gold watch he had recently acquired, a repeater like Tyburn's because he often needed to consult it in darkness.

"No, sir," Dorcas said after the slightest possible pause. "And since I'm now in your debt twice over—"

"You do remember me!" Fernand flashed. "For a moment I was afraid . . ."

"I'd just made use of you to get away from those unpleasant men? Oh, I did! But I promise you, I well recall how kind you were on my first day in New Orleans. So were other people, of course. I was amazed, to tell the truth. I'd always been warned that in big cities . . ."

Immediately they were chatting as though since their first encounter each had kept an image of the other constantly in mind, and both were so accurate that they had thus become well acquainted. Besides, each had much to say and no one to say it to. On Fernand's part, the pressure had built up because Eulalie showed no interest in his achievement as a pilot. At best she approved in offhand fashion, whereas what he desired was warm—fervent—praise.

In Fibby, Dorcas did at least have a confidante, but the older woman was resigned to the small world created for her by the Parburys, occasionally reminiscing with repugnance about life in plantation days or when she was seeking work for the first and only time. She had once had a husband; he had wanted children and she could not conceive, so he abandoned her and she found refuge tending James, who died so tragically. The first time Dorcas heard her tale, she was shaken to learn that a woman could be thrown out of her home for not having a child, as well as for having one . . .

Alarmed, she found herself on the verge of saying so, and bit back the words for fear there might be limits to this miraculous young man's tolerance, that he might take offense at too frank an allusion to her past.

So far he had shown no sign. Instead, he was making disclosures of his own, as though it were the most natural thing in the world for two virtual strangers to exchange intimate secrets on a busy street. To be born of a mother *en plaçage*, lacking a legitimate claim on his father's estate; to have jealous cousins and no means of countering their vicious but legal depredations—it was a trap that left no alternative but flight.

He had made good his escape, however. And one day he looked forward (how this escaped him, he dared not guess, for he had never before breathed a hint of it) to depositing the profits of a steamboat of his own at the Marocain bank, confident that neither of his cousins would be making as much as he was.

Here for Dorcas was the image of the Mississippi pilot as Prince Charming that she had been encouraged to believe in by Parbury.

Here for Fernand was the image he had clung to ever since the day he had looked on Dorcas's face and known it for the loveliest in his personal world.

Yet neither could find the perfect words to match the perfect occasion. They chanced on a streetcar going in a convenient direction and telescoped their journey to a minimum. The rate at which time flowed away grew frantic. Essential things remained to be said: remained unsaid.

To have overruled captains aboard their own steamers, yet not to be able to find a proper opening or a proper phrase—! It galled Fernand. Because he had seen Dorcas's eyes light up on recognizing him, he wanted the world of now to be absolutely other.

It declined to oblige. And what he wound up saying when they were walking along the very street, new-built, lined with handsome houses among lavish gardens, where he must take leave of her, was no more than this:

"Why Cherouen? What's wrong with Malone, who has been so kind to you? Isn't he a first-class doctor?"

"I like him very much!" declared Dorcas. "But, you see, Mrs. Parbury . . ." And she explained how her mistress's condition grew worse by the week and Malone would not promise what she craved: a miraculous recovery.

Fernand thought for a while; then, as they drew abreast of their destination, he said, "Miracles do happen. One happened to us today, didn't it? Perhaps Mrs. Parbury is right. Perhaps electricity and ozone will cure her. . . May I wait until you've seen Dr. Cherouen?"

She shook her head, smiling. "You're very kind! But please don't. I have no idea whether he's at home, and if he isn't I shall be obliged to stay indefinitely."

"Then may I call on you at the Parburys'? Do say yes! You're so beautiful I can hardly believe it!"

For a long moment Dorcas wondered whether, like the heroines of so many novels, she ought to refuse before there was any chance of Fernand being disappointed in her. Let him cherish for life a vision of her as flawless, wonderful; let her recall him as her gallant rescuer and let time restore her picture of him as a giant in strength instead of an ordinary man with—well, with a charming manner and a cajoling voice . . .

It was no use. She was not cast in the mold of heroines. She heard herself say in breathless tones, "That would make me very happy, sir!"

"Then I'll try and make you as happy as you just made me!" Fernand exclaimed, doffing his hat and making as though to bow. But he canceled the movement and instead risked an embrace, aiming to kiss her on both cheeks.

He forgot his cane, which he had tucked under one arm.

Which fell to the ground with a clatter.

So interrupted, they found themselves gazing into each other's eyes from a distance of three inches. And neither could help laughing and hugging hard.

There was a while during which the rest of the world seemed muted and dim and far away.

Suddenly Dorcas said, "Thank you for being real after all."

And broke loose and headed up Cherouen's driveway in a rush. It was almost as undignified as the hop-and-skip with which Fernand made his way back to the streetcar stop.

 For at least five people aboard the *Isaiah Plott* it was also turning out to be a lovely day.

Arthur Gattry had been prepared for the opposite, even before Joel came scrambling on deck to the accompaniment of Louisette's cries of welcome. But her rapid introduction set Arthur's mind at rest immediately. While her cousin's career might strike Louisette as romantic, in actuality it sounded more like a struggle to make ends meet. When making inquiries about the Moyne family, he had heard reference to Siskins fallen on hard times. Finding that Arthur was acquainted with Gordon, Joel was in seventh heaven. Sheer luck had ensured that he would now save his job.

Enlisting Louisette's support, he persuaded Arthur to present them, and let go with a barrage of questions which Gordon answered readily. Yes, he had naturally heard of the Macrae affair; no, he was unacquainted with the details because he had been fortunate enough to resist the scoundrel's blandishments; he was in the States because, thanks to the depredations of the Sassenachs . . .

Arthur seized the chance to slip the steward a dollar, whereupon three black tenders cleaned up this section of the deck so rapidly that when Louisette next glanced around she blinked in disbelief.

"This Gordon is the man nobody can get to talk about himself?" Arthur murmured in her ear.

"You heard Joel say so," she whispered back.

"Then none of those who tried before can have possessed your charm—or your inside information, for that matter. I'm most impressed!"

Eyes sparkling at the compliment, she returned, still in a soft tone, "Oh, Father believes girls should be educated in financial matters for fear they might marry men who want to cheat them of their fortune."

"Very wise! Ah . . . was your father badly hit by the collapse of Scottish Timber?"

"He got off lightly, compared to some. Even so, if he could lay hands on that crook Macrae, I think there might be murder done!" She gave an exaggerated shudder.

"Well, we can leave this interrogation to your cousin—he's an expert, I'm sure. Let's go view the liners. Two are on maiden voyages, and the papers say they're most impressive."

"Oh, they are! My brother came in today on the *Franche-Comté*!" She offered her hand for him to help her to her feet, and he retained it for longer than was needful, but she raised no whit of an objection.

Walking along the deck, she said thoughtfully, "You must meet Auberon. You'd get on well. In fact you sometimes remind me of him."

"You like him a lot, I guess?" Arthur ventured.

"Oh, sure! He's much more fun than most of the boys I know."

Distant in time Arthur felt he could hear wedding bells. But it was too soon to mention them. He contented himself by saying, "If I remind you of someone you like, I'm overjoyed . . . Oh, look! There's the *Franche-Comté*!"

He had remembered to slip a pair of opera glasses into his pocket. Handing them to Louisette reinforced her view of him as a man of intelligence and forethought. All was going splendidly after all.

Especially because, while she was studying the liners, he was able to take a surreptitious swig from his flask of whiskey.

Hamish Gordon was in his element. One hand brandishing a fat cigar, the other with its thumb hooked in the armhole of his vest, he was holding forth in response to Joel's prompting about international trade in the post bellum context, with particular stress on the perfidy of the English. Already more than a dozen other passengers had gathered with the frank intention of eavesdropping.

Meantime the *Plott* was leisurely picking her way between the wharves of downtown New Orleans. Excursions of this sort began with a circuit of the ocean port, where some of the finest ships in the world lay at anchor.

By the time the *Plott* turned back, the passengers would be thinking about the midday meal—and what better point at which to slot it into the schedule than while returning past sights already seen? The afternoon would be devoted to a slow struggle against the current, affording an opportunity to view the changes that recent development had brought about in Jefferson and Carrollton on ground that until lately had been no-man's-land.

At evening there would be a fast return to base.

The arrangement met, Gordon declared, with his full approval, and so did the steamers plying this great river. What a difference a few score vessels of the Mississippi type—modified for local conditions, since they would have to venture into open water—would have made to the Highlands and islands whence he hailed! What trade they could have opened up! What markets there were in the south for Scottish produce! All this and more he expounded to Joel, whose flying shorthand covered page after page, to the visible envy of Matthew, who stood by with his own notebook but made no attempt to imitate him.

"Are there no steamers among the Scotch islands, then, sir?" Joel asked.

"Certainly there are a few. But the lairds treat them as private conveyances. Since the crofters are being evicted from their lands, the only use the ordinary person makes of them is when they carry him away for the last time!" Snorting, Gordon discovered his cigar was out; he tossed it aside and produced another, and half a dozen bystanders offered him a light.

"Mr. Gordon, as you doubtless know, few businessmen any longer show interest in the prospects of the steamboat. I gather you're an exception."

Amid a cloud of dense smoke Gordon was seen to nod.

"Because you plan to have some constructed and relieve the plight of your fellow countrymen?"

Gordon sighed heavily. "Out of the question, to my muckle regret. I've decided to abandon my homeland for ever. Such is the rapacity of the English, even a man in my position can be driven away like a humble fisherman and forced to seek a new life beyond the ocean."

There were listeners with Scottish ancestry; that remark was greeted with a rumble of approval.

"Sir, this year has seen the liquidation of the great Atlantic and Mississippi Steamship Company," Joel persisted. "Why then your optimism about steamers?"

With a wave of dismissal Gordon said, "From my study of the case, the directors had only their poor judgment to blame."

"Yes, sir, perhaps that may be so, but does not the railroad have unsurpassable advantages? It's faster, it can follow more direct routes, a train of more or fewer cars can be assembled according to need, it's more nearly independent of weather apart from heavy snow—"

"All of what you say is true," Gordon interrupted. "But these are not the only factors. I set out westward from New York aboard one of your country's finest railway trains. Within a short time I found it cramped, unstable, and unreliable. I had the good sense to leave the railway at Cincinnati and thereafter enjoyed a progress in luxury down the Ohio and Mississippi all the way to New Orleans.

"From the viewpoint of a passenger, I can assert that steamers are superior. A great factor in their favor, too, is that so many American cities have grown up on rivers precisely because of the existence of steamers, and when Nature has furnished a highway free of toll and open to all, it cannot but be unprofitable to prefer a mode of conveyance which calls for a road to be laboriously made out of expensive iron. And one thing more, which for me outweighs the rest."

He leaned forward to tap Joel on the knee, as though they were closeted in private instead of being the cynosure of forty fascinated excursionists. "Throughout this century the progress of invention has assured more and more of the inhabitants of this globe of an easier life. The chores which, as I recall from my own humble childhood, made the daily round a misery—from churning butter to doing the family wash—have one by one benefited from those who have devised machinery to lighten the load.

"What shall it profit us if we neglect the blessing our extra leisure has bestowed? Are we now to make our lives more burdensome than before by insisting that we adjust to the pace made possible by modern machines? Are we to fit ourselves to their Procrustean measure, so that what we have thus far gained will be lost again? While it's fine and wonderful to cross the ocean in high style, independent of the wind, it's the reverse to travel from one handsome city to another in cars more suitable for freight or cattle than for humans. Compare the discomfort of eating on the railway, having to balance a hamper on your knees if the other places are taken, with the convenience of dining in the cabin of a steamer. One is like an old stage coach; the other like a drawing room. Coming from a lowly background as I do, I greatly fear that, instead of our liberation from drudgery being allowed to continue until it affects the class on whose efforts all our fortunes must ultimately depend, it will be at some point cut short, and instead of their lives being rendered insupportable by sweeping and scrubbing and the cost of bread, our descendants will be made miserable by machines that govern every instant of their time, demanding that it be filled!"

Obviously impressed, Joel flipped to the next page.

"So the Mississippi steamboat is in the class of machine you would approve of?"

"On the basis of my acquaintance with such vessels, yes. It's an astonishing feat to carry such huge cargoes on a draft which in Europe would be considered adequate for a rowboat!"

"There's a saying among river people," Joel ventured, "that you must always keep a barrel of beer on board."

Gordon blinked at him. "I understand most large steamers boast a well-stocked bar, and—"

"No, sir. It's so that when the river's low you can float her on the foam. They tell of a pilot who made seven miles on a gallon keg."

Gordon broke into peals of laughter. He rounded on Matthew. "That's capital—capital! Boy, note it down!"

"Mr. Gordon," Joel said thoughtfully when the financier had recovered from his mirth, "I believe this to be the first interview you've granted since reaching New Orleans. May I ask why?"

"Isn't the answer obvious? Wouldn't a man be foolish to go on record in a foreign city before he'd taken time to look it over?"

Joel narrowly avoided clapping himself on the forehead.

*Obvious!*

\*      \*      \*

The steam whistle let go an echoing blast and the pilot put over the helm. The *Plott* had reached the downstream end of her trip. Waiters with little gongs appeared to announce that meals would shortly be served in the cabin.

Heaving himself to his feet, Gordon said, "Do me the honor of joining me for luncheon. And perhaps you'd also invite the charming young lady who was with you before—your cousin, did you say?"

"Yes, Miss Moyne. But . . ." Joel hesitated.

"But Mr. Gattry would not care to be separated from her? Then bring 'em both along. Make up a party. I'm sure we'll pass a most agreeable time together."

 Her encounter with Fernand had so affected Dorcas that until she had rung the bell at its front door she scarcely registered the contrast between the house she had come to and the home of her employer.

Then, chillingly, the magnitude of the property impinged on her: a broad driveway where two carriages were waiting; a pillared portico with marble steps; a sudden alarming transformation at top-storey level where a gallery from the French Quarter, complete with elaborate ironwork, seemed to have been elevated as by a gigantic flood to heights where it did not properly belong; a conservatory to which fat steam pipes led . . .

Dorcas trembled. This felt less like one house than several.

Still, she comforted herself, if Cherouen could afford such a palace, he might be as clever as he claimed. She hoped so. In the grip of pain Mrs. Parbury sometimes grew unbearable, finding fault with everything and visiting revenge on everybody around her for imagined slights.

"Yes?"

Dorcas started. The door had opened. Before her stood a striking mulatto woman with strong facial bones and large capable hands. She wore a costume Dorcas had never seen the like of: a blue cotton dress, long-sleeved but short-skirted, not touching her ankles; black stockings and black square-toed shoes; a wide apron, a collar, cuffs, and a square cap, all of white linen starched until one could imagine it breaking like china.

"Yes?" she said again with a touch of impatience.

"Is the doctor at home?" Dorcas forced out.

"I am Miss Var, Dr. Cherouen's principal nurse. You may explain your business to me."

Silenced, Dorcas handed over the letter she carried. Having read it, Nurse Var stood back.

"Come in and wait. The doctor is very busy, but there is some chance, I guess, he could attend your mistress. I'll inquire as soon as he is free."

\*     \*     \*

Dorcas was left sitting on an uncomfortable antique bench in a hallway floored with marble, hung with red-and-green velvet drapes, oil paintings in heavy gilt frames on every available wall. A pendulum clock ticked away half an hour.

Suddenly a door was flung open and a very young yellow girl, dressed like Nurse Var, hurried toward the back of the house. While the door stood wide, Dorcas caught a glimpse of the room beyond. On its walls hung medical and scientific engravings: a dissected heart stuck with more arrows than St. Sebastian, an arm showing the muscles separated and named, a head with the phrenological zones in a riot of contrasting colors . . .

Dorcas shuddered.

The yellow girl returned carrying a device of straps and buckles. The door slammed shut. Another ten minutes passed. It reopened, and Dorcas saw a tall man emerge, ruddy-cheeked, with a bushy black moustache and black hair swept back from a high forehead, wearing a long-skirted black coat and black pants, a white shirt, and a thin black necktie, the sole relief from this chiaroscuro being a gold watch chain.

He was ushering along a lady who had doubtless been very pretty in youth but was now obliged to keep up the color in her cheeks by artificial means. She was muttering querulous complaints. Behind followed a lady's maid, looking anxious. Dorcas overheard only snippets of what was being said, but she garnered the impression that the woman's treatment was taking longer than promised, and that the man was Dr. Cherouen in a hurry for his next appointment.

At length he got rid of her, and carriage wheels were heard on the driveway. Turning back, the doctor wiped his forehead in unashamed relief. And caught sight of Dorcas.

A purr entered his voice.

"Who may you be, my dear?" he inquired.

Rising awkwardly, Dorcas tried to explain, but was forestalled by the reappearance of Miss Var with the letter.

"Hmm!" Cherouen said. "The wife of a steamer captain with such a dreadful affliction—a tragedy, a tragedy! I'm sure my methods will afford her much relief!"

But the nurse drew him aside and whispered something. He pondered awhile, frowned, and at last turned back to Dorcas, sounding regretful.

"I'm advised that, owing to pressure of work, I'm unable to take on extra patients. Should her—should *her circumstances alter*, she's at liberty to contact me again. For the moment I'm reminded that I'm overdue for a housecall some distance away, and my carriage has been waiting for an hour."

He hesitated, looking at Dorcas anew, this time with a broad smile.

"I hope to see *you* again, in any case!"

Nurse Var handed him a silk hat, lightweight coat, and walking-cane; the yellow girl reappeared carrying a black leather bag. Dorcas stood by in frozen horror until the carriage wheels were out of earshot. Then she meekly obeyed the nurse's order to depart, and found herself back in a world from which she seemed to have been rejected—worse: spewed out.

Buoyed up by her meeting with Fernand, she had briefly been a perfect optimist. Now she wanted to cry for help—and there was no one to listen.

With grim satisfaction Josephine Var closed the front door. The worst part of the day was over. Only during the morning did patients visit the house. In the afternoon Cherouen attended those too unwell to venture abroad. So until his return at about five o'clock she could become what she was: mistress of this mansion. She was entitled to that. After all, she had been the making of its master.

By now half of the people who counted in New Orleans must have heard of Denis Cherouen, and many of the wealthiest had consulted him.

But scarcely any knew the story behind the doctor's meteoric rise. And, she sincerely hoped, none at all knew the truth behind her own ascent to fame in a slightly—but only slightly—different field.

Graduating from medical school, Cherouen had volunteered as an army surgeon with the Confederate forces. His regiment had been shattered before Atlanta, when his loyalty to the Southern cause had already been eroded by the reality of war. On being captured, he had been invited to give his parole and continue helping the wounded. He had consented, but his cynicism grew ever deeper.

Save in one respect. He talked obsessively of panaceas: marvelous cures still secret in the womb of time that would render obsolete today's messy improvisations like laxatives and bandages, the scalpel and the cautery. The mysterious forces of electricity and magnetism; new substances as wonderful as chloroform and nitrous oxide, such as in particular ozone which European researchers had found abundant at just those seaside resorts where for generations they had been accustomed to send their convalescent patients—surely there if anywhere must be sought the key to perfect health!

At about the time his assertions began to earn him a reputation as a fanatic, he ran across Josephine Var.

Nominally she was a "free person of color." That is to say, when she was born her mother was not officially the property of someone else.

Her father was a rich white man, too respectable to admit his responsibility other than by making clandestine gifts, which grew fewer after he married a girl approved by his family, and eventually ceased. Then came the war, and her mother died of a fever reportedly brought by Admiral Farragut's sailors. Desperate as a result of the monetary crisis following the occupation, she had taken to prostitution rather than let her daughter suffer such a fate. On her deathbed she claimed her fatal sickness was caught from one of her customers.

Orphaned, Josephine obtained work tending wounded soldiers. An officer on Farragut's staff had been impressed by the work of Florence Nightingale, in the Crimean War, and Henri Dunant, founder of the Red Cross, and aspired to create an American corps of army nurses.

To a degree he succeeded. But to a greater extent he destroyed his own plan. He made available within reach of soldiers, most of whom were away from the control of parents and ministers for the first time, a supply of women who were not camp followers—women to be raped because they would not yield.

They court-martialed the man who stole Josephine's maidenhead. But that was too late to prevent her winding up in the care of Cherouen, who cleansed her, dressed her injuries, and held her hand while she wept away the worst of her agony.

Therefore she grew interested in this doctor, whom she had known only from a distance, an issuer of orders who was forever in a hurry.

And finding in her a listener, Cherouen talked.

For lack of anything better, he was plying her with heroic doses of the tincture of cannabis used to relieve women of periodic and labor pains. The raw ache in her loins receded; her body became almost unreal, while the words and images floating through her mind took on the aura of transcendental truth. Abruptly she had an insight. Her mother had been tutored by Marie Laveau. She had been raised under the protection of chants, charms, and symbols; she understood the power of faith. That was what could cure. For all his talk of gases and machines, there was small difference between this educated doctor and his counterpart in the black community with his goofer dust and High John de Conquer' root.

But when she struggled to tell him what she had realized, he soothed her like a nurse calming a feverish child.

Growing angry, she sought another way of convincing him. Shortly she found one, when he spoke of the money he needed to prove his theories. What fortune could a man in his predicament look forward to, reduced by the war to a sawbones and stitcher-up of sword-cuts and, moreover, working for the wrong side? This was toward the end of hostilities, when everybody who had rashly abandoned plans for the future fell prey to sudden doubts and fears.

Recovering, Josephine had been able to nurse the wounded again, and he came to rely on her, even take her advice. Therefore he was prepared to listen when she proposed a means of raising the money for his research. She contrived to make him jealous of old ugly men in stinking huts who received incredible payments in cash or in the form of jewels and other gifts. What was their secret? It was no secret at all.

They were simply *believed in* by the proper people.

Who were the proper people to be told about a young doctor with brilliant radical ideas?

The rich, of course. Ideally the very rich and somewhat ill, fidgeting under the notion that their money could not purchase them immunity from bodily afflictions, obscurely convinced that it should be possible for them to cheat death, even if nobody else did.

Now that peace had opened up opportunities in the South for those who had done well out of the war, there was no lack of people newly drunk on affluence. They would be ready to credit that some breakthrough in medical research could stave off the Grim Reaper—for a lucky few.

And, as Josephine persuasively argued, what counted most was for someone other than herself to believe in him, for she was poor, unknown, and—worst of all colored.

Recently, so it was claimed, scientific means had been devised to minimize this last handicap. She had sent to New York for a preparation fashionable there, designed to lighten the complexion—without informing Cherouen, for it contained arsenic, one of the minerals he invariably condemned, although mercury, antimony, and such substances formed the mainstay of the pharmacopoeia. Possibly in this instance he was right; so far Josephine had observed no benefit from her expensive investment.

Accordingly they set about making sure that Cherouen and his ideas were heard of. The social climate was perfect. Two years saw them installed here, in a house built by a now bankrupt slave dealer for his eldest son. Attired in a uniform based on the one evolved by the famous Miss Nightingale, and overseeing a staff of half a dozen girls—colored, because almost all their patients were white women used to undressing in front of slaves as though there were no one else in the room— Josephine Var was the *éminence grise* . . .

No: the *éminence noire* of the whole operation.

All was not without flaw. There was another reason why all the girls working here were colored and very young. Cherouen had preferences. She had seen how his eyes lit up at sight of Dorcas, and that was typical; she was glad that her research among the *nouveaux riches* of New Orleans had enabled her to warn him that the Parburys were down on their luck. But finding girls at once bright enough to carry out their duties, and docile enough to endure Cherouen's more personal demands, was growing ever harder.

Yet it had better be done. So far he had only made advances to Josephine twice. The first time had been before the end of the war, and she had rebuffed him easily because he knew how fresh her horrible experience remained in memory. But the second had been quite recently, in a fit of drunken depression that made him so violent she scarcely managed to divert his attention to one of the young nurses, whom afterwards she had to dismiss with a fat bribe.

There must not be a third time. Her sexual favors were reserved for ceremonies where white folks had no part, and if she ever bore a child it must be at the behest of her dark lord. Accordingly she set about conjurations in which her mother had carefully rehearsed her. Today was a most propitious day, the date of the autumn equinox. What human beings devised in the way of machinery and gases was doubtless all very well after its crude fashion. But what had been created by the lord who sometimes answered to the name Damballah was far more ancient, and since people too had been created by him . . .

It followed logically, and she stood convinced.

Why otherwise should there always be more and more money paid secretly and in darkness, in exchange for luck charms to be worn by people she had never come into closer contact with than receipt of a lock of hair, a nail clipping, or—in the frequent case of a man worried about his virility—semen caught on a scrap of rag?

Sometimes she felt that those who patronized her services regarded her as having occupied commanding heights in enemy territory. What enemy? The churches? White folks' medicine?

Sometimes she felt guilty of an obscure betrayal, for those who could afford her prices could not be the worst afflicted by fate. But when a story caught her attention, she would slave for days to perfect a single trickenbag. Her best ever had gone to a man who sent a rotten tooth. She had suffered face ache far too often;

into that one charm she had sunk a week's effort, though all he could pay was a pittance.

And sometimes she felt as though people who ought to be her allies were marshaling against her.

When today's necessary rituals were finished, she decided, she would gut a rooster and try to learn their identity from its entrails.

 By four o'clock Hamish Gordon was presiding avuncularly over a game of cards in the *Plott's* cabin, calling constantly for wine and whiskey to keep his companions' glasses full. After a few hands of *bezique*, they had settled on *vingt-et-un*. There was little money on the table, and Stella and Louisette won suspiciously often when Gordon was the dealer, but the bank was changing hands with unusual rapidity and considerable tension was being generated.

This being an excursion boat, there was no strict division of the cabin into fore and aft areas, with ladies confined to the latter; even so, the presence of the girls attracted more and more attention as more and more passengers retreated from the deck to escape the sun. Some of the onlookers were hostile, making sour faces and whispering behind their hands, or urging the children away from this device of Satan. Far more, however, grew as involved as any bystanders at the Limousin, and when at last a match for serious stakes developed between Gordon, Arthur, and Hugo Spring—who had rejoined the group with Stella after luncheon—a few young sports were sufficiently caught up in the excitement to begin laying side bets.

Gaston, standing nearby, felt his face growing longer and longer. Maybe he should have given up this idea of an excursion; during an attack of melancholia he was rendered not less but more depressed by the sight of others enjoying themselves.

Nonetheless he had forced himself to come aboard, trusting that the pleasant weather, the views, and the majesty of the river would work their normal magic on him.

On the contrary, he had been cast down by the sight of so much commercial busy-ness at the ocean port, for where was there a fane for the Muses among these temples of Pluto, these forges of Hephaestus?

Wandering into the cabin, thinking he might find genteel company, he had discovered instead that everyone was obsessed with the card party: either fascinated by it, or horrified. Two distinct factions had formed, but all was decorous so far. One of the boat's officers, glancing in, decided there was no cause for worry and went out again.

Matthew was rocking on his heels a short distance from the card table. The heat and the gentle lulling motion were conspiring to make him doze off. Therefore, glad of distraction, he answered in detail when Gaston requested information concerning the players.

Gaston's heart leaped. A financier! Maybe a millionaire! Had chance brought him into contact with the person who could rescue him from his plight? Eagerly he asked whether Monsieur Gordon was a patron of the arts—looking, perhaps, for a conductor who could recruit and direct an orchestra? A small one to commence with, *bien sûr*, a mere chamber group, but conceived with a view to expansion. It would be a most generous gesture for someone in his position, and an enduring memorial into the bargain!

For a few seconds Matthew pondered, anxious neither to disappoint this polite stranger nor to decry his master. Finally he said, "Well, he never talked to me about music. But I guess he may like it, for as we came aboard we heard the calliope, and I saw he tapped his foot in time to it."

Gaston's face froze. His hopes dashed, he bowed and turned to stare out the window. It was not just— It was not reasonable—it was not *right* for this great nation to be so heedless of the culture which was all that tipped the scale between a civilized community and barbarian tribes!

First to lose interest in the cards, about the time the steamer reached the end of her upriver journey, was Stella. With a sigh Hugo escorted her back on deck, even though swarming flies made it pleasanter to be inside. One of the bystanders received license to play in Hugo's stead.

That came as a grateful respite to Joel. He had borrowed some money from Louisette, bet cautiously and lost only six dollars, but he could ill afford even so small a sum, whereas Arthur and Gordon were already staking in twenties.

But there were two or three other watchers debating whether to buy in, so his departure would not spoil the game.

Muttering a feigned excuse, he headed for a quiet corner near the stern where he could organize the data he had collected about Gordon into a coherent article. It wouldn't be easy. The financier remained as mysterious as ever. It was as though he used a screen of verbiage to protect his inner self.

His—?

A crucial insight hovered on the brink of awareness, and was quashed before it could take on words. Louisette had come to join him. She dropped into a chair and gave him a dazzling smile.

"Dear Jewel!" she said. "How much more like your old self you've been today! Why have you been avoiding me? Why didn't you come to my last birthday ball?"

Joel hesitated, then said gruffly, "Was I invited?"

"Of course you—!" She broke off, tensing. "Jewel, Mama said you had declined. But, come to think of it, I never saw your reply."

"There wasn't one." A waiter was approaching; Joel caught his eye and looked at Louisette; she shook her head and he waved the man away.

Meditatively Louisette said, "Joel, what do you think of Mr. Gattry?"

"I can scarcely judge on such a short acquaintance, can I?"

"Of course not." All the sparkle had suddenly gone out of her. Producing a phial of eau de cologne, she dabbed her wrists and forehead.

"Excuse me, I think I've had too much wine . . . Oh, Joel! I wish I didn't hate my parents so much!"

"Now that's pretty strong language! What makes you say that?"

"Because sometimes I think I ought to get married, and then the next day I get frightened about how long a married life can be!"

"Married? Who to?"

"Why, Arthur, of course. When he asks me."

"But—!" Joel was half out of his chair with dismay. "But how well do you know him?"

"Oh, hardly at all! But he's handsome, and amusing, and—"

"That's not enough to found a marriage on!"

Unintentionally Joel had raised his voice; seeing people all around turning their heads, he leaned closer to Louisette, laying his hand on her arm.

"Loose, you can't be serious!"

"What else am I to do? I can't stand my parents any more—I mean that! I thought, even this morning, that you'd turned against me, that you'd refused to come to my ball. But now I believe they never sent your invitation, or Uncle Howard's either. And it's all because he lost so much money, isn't it?"

"If it is, then as of today I can safely say that Auberon is taking after his father," Joel muttered. And was instantly horrified to hear himself utter the words . . . then relieved to see her nod agreement.

"Yes, I was amazed at the way he snubbed you!"

"On the other hand," Joel said, beginning to smart under the impact of her threat to marry a stranger, "you were less than adoring, yourself!"

"Running off for this steamer ride, you mean? Oh, that's different, I swear. I've been trying to do things Mama wouldn't like for ages now. Do you know where Arthur first took notice of me? At the Grand Philharmonic Hall with Anna Parks! The trouble we've been to, hiding that from Mama and Papa, who'd have conniptions if they heard!"

"Do you mean he picked you up?" Joel grated.

"Oh, goodness, no! But he remembered when we were finally introduced, and really it's become quite a storybook courtship. I think he thinks I haven't realized what he's about, but I promise I caught on very early, and the more I think about becoming Mrs. Gattry, the more I like it. If only I liked it because of what he is"—growing abruptly bitter—"and not because I want to get away from Papa and Mama!"

"But what for?"

She made to stamp her foot. "Because they treat me more like an investment than a human being! My value has gone down because I didn't make Queen of the Mardi Gras. If I had, I'd have been married off already to someone they chose, not I. But they're still planning to sell me to the highest bidder."

"Then how come—?"

"How come I'm here with Arthur? As far as I can make out, they're hoping that in his company I'll run across a suitor more to their taste! Joel, the way they've treated you and Uncle Howard is just typical! They're such *hypocrites!*"

Overwhelmed by her vehemence, Joel forbore to reply. After a pause she resumed in calmer tones.

"That's why I'm here instead of oohing and aahing over Obe's adventures. Though frankly I'm not sure I wanted to spend today with Obe anyhow."

"But he's your brother, and after so long away—"

She brushed his interruption aside. "Did he write you from Europe?"

"Yes, several times."

"What about?"

"Oh, this and that." Joel felt his cheeks grow hot. He had never been able to lie to Louisette as a child; as an adult it seemed even harder. But he did his best. "Much like what he wrote you, I guess."

"I don't believe it. His letters were chiefly interesting because of what they didn't say. Let me guess." She fixed him with her clear blue gaze. "Did he boast about what he was really doing when he was supposed to be imbibing culture?"

In passing, Joel reflected that it was as well he now stood no chance of marrying his cousin. If she displayed such insight into masculine wiles, she would be unbearable as a wife.

Finding no way to evade her question, he gave in. "Yes, you could put it that way."

"I *thought* so! I don't want to ask what he chose to keep secret from me. I hope it's the sort of thing you wouldn't talk to me about. You're right: Auberon is taking after Papa. Do you know what I found out the other day?"

She bent confidentially close.

"All my life he and Mama have been telling me to behave myself, act like a lady, be 'moral' and 'decent' and the rest. But for years Papa kept a mistress in the Quarter, a *colored* woman, and Mama knew and married him in spite of it!"

"And the woman's name was Var," Joel sighed, "and she had a house at the north end of Bienville, and she was carried off by a fever during the war, and do you have any more revelations for me today?"

For a long moment she simply stared at him, her mouth working to form words that would not emerge. At last she seized her parasol and reticule and rose to her feet. When he also stood up she rounded on him in fury.

"Leave me alone! You—you *beast*! I never want to speak to you again!"

 Amazing. The wharf was clear of cargo and it was barely five o'clock. Caesar exhaled with violent relief. It had been a long week, but tomorrow was payday.

When the white man he deputized for would turn up, more or less sober, to collect wages he had not earned. He would of course keep his promise to share on the basis agreed. In the dead cold eyes of the black man he had hired, he had read without words the consequence of trying to cheat.

But it was not, Caesar thought as he cleaned what must be cleaned about the steam crane and locked with padlocks what must be locked—it was not a proper way for man to live with his fellow man.

Distantly he could hear whistles and guns. The upriver steamers were pulling out. He could see in his mind's eye the people on the levee waving their kerchiefs while twenty boats jockeyed for a favorable position. Sometimes when, as today, all the cargo he had to deliver was safely stowed, he had energy left to walk that way and watch the free show.

But right now he could not rid his memory of how he had come within inches of braining a white man. Touching his charm, he shivered. Soon, the sooner the better, he must get a safer job. But so far work had not been found even for all the discharged soldiers and returned prisoners of war. The odds against him were colossal.

Maybe not impossible, though. After all, this morning he had been recognized by a white man. And not the way a slave owner would have done it, which was no different from how he told his horses or his hounds, but person to person, by someone who talked of making his experience—his, Caesar's!—into a newspaper article.

For a second he thought of tracing the reporter and begging him to write the piece. Perhaps that, if nothing else, might lead him to his wife and children.

But he was too cynical now to dream as he had once done. Tandy must long ago have found another man. Probably she had other children. Certainly if he met his own again, they would not remember him as their father.

As he limped back to his lodgings, he wondered whether he would ever be able to start a new life with the same security as folks had relied on in plantation days. Was it preferable—the fearful notion crossed his mind—to have a good master and the assurance of a full belly and a sound roof?

Just so long as you could guarantee your master was good! And none but the Lord could ensure that. So in the upshot things were better this way, spite of all . . .

 Leaning on the *Plott*'s after rail, struggling to discipline his mutinous thoughts, Joel grew aware of a wave of excitement passing along the deck. A crowd of people headed for the bow. Copying them, he found that the steamer was about to meet her sisters setting out in the long-distance trades. Most were small, a couple were of medium tonnage, and only one was of the premier class.

But that one was the *Atchafalaya*.

Sounding an occasional blast on her whistle, she advanced through the lesser craft like a buffalo striding among a herd of calves. Vast arcs of spray leaped up behind her wheels; her wake made boats and barges rock clear to either bank. Her decks were a mass of people waving to those aboard less luxurious vessels.

If only, Joel thought, if only I could buy passage on a boat like her and travel until I found a spot to suit my fancy, forget the ties which hold me here and start a new life—

A hand fell on his shoulder. Startled, he found Gordon at his side. "What boat is that?" he demanded. "Can you make her out? My damned boy has wandered off and I don't know what he's done with my field glasses."

Joel told him. He looked briefly blank; on the name being repeated, light dawned.

"Ah! Yon's a steamer I read about lately in a newspaper. But I took her name to be Atcher-fer-layer. Wait! Did I not also see it in a poem by your Mr. Longfellow?"

Impressed, Joel nodded. *"Evangeline,"* he said. "And he stressed it wrongly, never having visited the Cajun country."

"Let me hear you say it again!"

With exaggerated care Joel pronounced, "A-chuffer-liar."

Gordon echoed him, and continued, "Is there some special reason for everyone to gaup at her? I grant she's a handsome spectacle, but . . ."

"She's generally considered the finest steamer on the Mississippi."

"Is she truly so impressive? How long is she?"

"About two hundred eighty-five feet."

"And broad?"

"Forty-eight."

"And how much cargo can she carry?"

"Over fourteen hundred tons."

"I take it that would be when the river is at its deepest?"

"No, sir. At most times of year. She only draws one and a half fathoms fully loaded."

Gordon blinked rapidly. "If this is another of your Yankee tall stories—" he began.

"Sir, it isn't politic to address anybody in the South as a Yankee!"

Gordon hesitated. Producing a large white handkerchief, he mopped his forehead. "Aye, I'd overlooked that. From the far side of an ocean, any nation appears all of a piece, ye ken. My slip was on all fours with your countrymen's error in calling me English. But you'll forgive me?"

"I took no offense," Joel said. "But there are a million who might."

"I'll remember that." Gordon tucked the handkerchief back in his pocket. "I wish yon boy of mine were half as well informed as you, anyway. Doubtless you can tell me even more about the *Atchafalaya*? Her working pressure, for example?"

"A hundred and ten pounds," Joel answered promptly.

"That strikes me as low for such a large vessel. What's the diameter of her cylinders? What's the stroke?"

"Forty inches," Joel said. "Ten feet."

"Does she have two cylinders—engines, as you say over here—disposed in the usual fashion, one either side?"

"That's correct. And if you'll pardon my saying so, it's my turn to call you well informed. You didn't learn all you know by visiting the *Plott*'s engineroom this morning!"

Gordon smiled, proffering a cigar case stocked with aromatic Havanas.

"As well as being knowledgeable, you're perceptive. You have penetrated my mask. I already referred to my lowly origins, but— Well, let's see if your intuition can take you further. What was I twenty years ago?"

Joel's heart raced. To spend a while in the financier's company had been his ambition for today; to be welcomed into his confidence was the most amazing lagniappe.

"You were acquainted with steam engines early in life," he hazarded.

Gordon crowed with laughter. "Right you are! I left school at twelve and entered the service of the North British Railway, and all my fortune has been founded on just those iron roads which I now compare with steamboats to their detriment. Sincerely, I assure you! I'm a restless man, Mr. Siskin, but now and then I'm forced into contemplation. Lately, on doctor's orders, I've been obliged to spend some weeks in idleness at the resort where I recruited young Rust— unlicked cub that he is, but I'll see him right in the long run. Where was I? Oh, yes!

"Chance brought to my hands, while I was there, a magazine which included an article by the celebrated Mr. Twain, and at once I was convinced that, of all modes of travel on this continent, the riverboat offered most scope. And, truly, if the finest steamer of the day is working to so low a pressure as a hundred and ten pounds, there must be ample room for improvement!"

Privately Joel wondered whether Gordon had considered hot-air balloons, which would better match his effusive talk, but honesty forced him to concede the point.

"You're not alone in that view, sir. I know one man who believes he could build a steamer to run out the *Atchafalaya*, and he wants his boat to operate at far higher pressure, a hundred and fifty at least."

"You interest me strangely," Gordon said. "Who is this person? Is there any chance that I might meet him?"

 Mouse-quiet despite her bulk, Fibby stole along the rear landing of the Parbury house toward Dorcas's room, a mere compartment partitioned off above the kitchen. She carried a bowl of soup, a spoon, and a candle to dispel the darkness.

At the door she whispered, "Dorcas honey, is you okay?"

Hearing no answer, she peered in. Eyes swollen with crying, Dorcas was raising herself from the bed. She contrived a smile and Fibby entered quickly.

"Drink some of dishyear broth, yo' soon feel better," she urged. "An' don' you take on so! Miz' Parb'ry, she always ac' dis way when Mars' Jim wuz alive—shout at him one minute, fo'get it all de nex'. She don' mean de ha'f wh'at she say!"

Accepting the soup, Dorcas countered, "But I meant what *I* said! I did exactly what she told me, and Dr. Cherouen said he couldn't come because he already had too many patients. So she called me a liar and a traitor and—and a scarlet woman! Didn't she? You heard her! She shouted loud enough for the whole street to hear!"

Her own voice had risen unconsciously. Realizing of a sudden how late it was, she reverted to a more normal tone.

"Where is she? What's she doing? And is the captain still abroad?"

At the back of her mind: vague threats of telling Parbury about the orders his wife had given her.

"She done sat quiet in de parlor dis hour or more," Fibby said. "Befo' dat she groan' a long whiles, and den she pray some—"

"I know what she wasn't praying for," Dorcas interrupted. "To be forgiven for bearing false witness against me!"

"Now hesh yo' mout'!" Fibby said, appalled.

"Why?" Dorcas snapped. "Tomorrow she'll call for a priest and tell him her side of the story, and he'll give her permission to slander me all over again!"

"Dey say misery love company," Fibby muttered. "But it jes' natcherly ain' true." And she turned ponderously toward the door.

"No, wait!" Dorcas cried, almost upsetting the soup. "Please come back! It doesn't matter if the captain has come home or not. She can't make him do anything to me, can she? She won't dare say she sent me to Dr. Cherouen, so . . . Fibby, what's wrong?"

The round black face had grown solemn in the light of the guttering candle.

"Dey was a ge'man call to see you. 'Bout six o'clock. Leastways I'd a-call' him a ge'man. A fine high-yaller man wea'in' a silk hat an' carryin' a cane."

Very slowly, as though afraid the trembling of her hands would betray her, Dorcas set the bowl on her bedside table.

"And he asked after me?"

"He sho' did! Came an' rang de bell an' I went answer an' he ast fo' you." Fibby paused impressively.

"Why didn't you tell me?"

"Well, honey, it wen' dis way. I as' him ter wait, an' Miz' Parb'ry call out an' as' who dere, and I sez jes' same's I sez ter you, 'Dey a ge'man come see Miss Dorcas.' An' Miz' Parb'ry she say, 'Ain' no ge'man come callin' on no *servant*!'"

With a shrug she concluded, "So I jes' 'bleeged ter show him back out de do'."

There was a pause. Then, mechanically, Dorcas retrieved the soup and plied the spoon until it was all gone. Watching anxiously, Fibby at last ventured, "Wuz you 'spectin' somebody?"

"No." Eyes downcast, Dorcas handed back the empty bowl. "Thank you, Fibby. That was good."

"But it wa'n't no kinda meal. Wan' I sh'd bring—?"

"That was plenty." Dorcas rose, unbuttoning her dress. "I should take your good advice and believe that Mrs. Parbury will have forgotten all she said in the morning. Good night, and thanks again."

Still doubtful, Fibby departed. The door closed on a very different Dorcas: one who no longer gave a damn whether her employer's wife ended her days widowed, crippled, and servantless.

Who after a sleepless night decided it was no more than the bitch deserved.

"Siskin! Where the devil have you been?"

It had taken some while for Abner Graves, editor and publisher of the *Intelligencer,* to realize that his missing reporter had returned, for the pressroom was in darkness relieved only by kerosene lamps. Under its low ceiling resounded the slide-and-thump of the steam press. It was terribly hot, and the air stank of oil and tobacco smoke.

Joel tilted back his hat and removed from his mouth a large cigar, about half burned. "With the man who gave me this," he answered.

"You're drunk!" Graves barked, advancing on him.

"I guess maybe a trifle tipsy," Joel conceded. "But it's all in a good cause. I have news for you, Mr. Graves. Solid news. There's going to be another *Nonpareil.*"

"You call that news? Everybody knows about Captain Parbury and his fantasies! I told you to get an interview with Hamish Gordon. I'm not interested in second-hand river-column boiler-plate!"

"So who do you think is going to pay for the new boat?"

There was a dead pause. At length Graves said, "Stop the press." And when the noise had died down: "Siskin, if this is a prank you'll never work for any paper in the city again."

Joel's cigar had gone out. Leaning to relight it at the chimney of the nearest lamp, he said, "I've been with Gordon since eleven this morning. I was his guest at lunch and dinner. Played cards with him and lost six dollars that I want reimbursed.

"He came here looking for something to invest in. He likes transportation. He used to be a railroad man back in Scotland. He thinks the steamer will be competitive with the railroads for at least another twenty years. And when he saw the *Atchafalaya* he was instantly consumed by the ambition of surpassing her." A note of awe crept into his voice. "Here's something strange. Often and often I've seen that phrase in novels and histories and thought of it as license on the writer's part. But today I witnessed the event. I saw Gordon transformed by a decision reached on the spur of the moment."

By now the pressroom staff were hanging on his every word. "So what happened?" one of them demanded.

"I carried him to the Pilots' Guild as soon as our boat docked—"

"What boat?" Graves rapped.

"We were making an excursion aboard the *Plott.* It's all in my notes." Cigar between teeth, Joel clapped his hands to one pocket after another, failed to locate them, and gave a shrug.

"Never mind! It's in my head, which is what counts. As I was trying to say, I took him to the Guild parlor, thinking Parbury would be there, but we missed him by an hour. He had gone to dine at Martineau's with a bunch of other rivermen.

"There we were told he had not arrived and was not expected, but just as we were leaving we ran across Captain Woodley. A lucky chance made me inquire whether he had seen Parbury. Yes, he had, at Griswold's, only a quarter hour before, and he was certain the captain intended to continue to the restaurant.

"By this time Gordon was like a man in the grip of fever. Nothing would satisfy him but that Woodley accept his invitation to dine while awaiting Parbury. And what Woodley could tell him about the model of the new *Nonpareil* served only to fire his imagination further.

"But—and this was really rather funny!" Joel tried his cigar one more time with conscious theatricality, knowing how engrossed he had made his audience; finding it beyond hope, he threw the butt into the nearest cuspidor.

"Somehow," he resumed, "we had omitted to mention that Parbury is blind. Both Woodley and I had talked in glowing terms of his skill as a pilot, and Gordon had taken it for granted he would be chief pilot and nominally master of the boat he was constructing in his mind's eye.

"So he was considerably shook up when Parbury was led to join us, and from the look on his face as he watched the mess the old man was making with his food, I judged the project must fall through. I can imagine Gordon's enthusiasms dying as quickly as they kindle. But by this time Woodley had had a good deal to drink, and suddenly he thumped the table and said he longed to see a steamer that would run out Drew's, and he would sell his own boat and put the proceeds towards the new *Nonpareil*.

"Parbury almost wept at that, and clasped his hand and explained to Gordon how Woodley provided dolls' furniture for his model, and Gordon insisted on seeing this famous model, and the second he laid eyes on it he was in raptures. I left them to it, with people like Dermot Hogan and Colin Trumbull pleading—I swear, pleading!—for the chance to pilot her on her maiden voyage! I never saw the like before! And if they fit her out as lavishly as they've been promising, then she won't cost a stiver less than a quarter million!"

After long hesitation Graves reached a decision.

"Bring me a chase," he ordered. "No need to waste time by writing all this down—I'll compose it directly in type. Anything to add, Siskin?"

Suddenly weary, Joel reached to the wall for support.

"I did pick up another story," he muttered. "There's going to be a society wedding. But I guess you better hadn't print that. Far's I can make out, not even the bridegroom knows about it yet."

## 1ST MARCH 1870

# NOT SINCE
# THE ECLIPSE

〜〜〜〜〜

"No other steamer, not even the far-
famed Eclipse, could vie with her in
size, capacity, burthen or cost. Everything about her is on the grandest and
most magnificent scale, while nothing
has been omitted that science or
money could furnish, in making her
the most complete steamer for passengers and business combined, that
has ever yet been seen on our Southwestern highway."
—*New Orleans Times*, April 15,
1865; quoted by Leonard V.
Huber in *Advertisements of
Lower Mississippi River
Steamboats 1812–1920*

 Humming "The Water is Wide" and having occasional re-
course to the banister rail, Hamish Gordon made his way up
to his hotel suite. Though accounted the finest in Cincinnati,
"Queen City of the West," this six-storey edifice belonged to the pre-elevator age,
and clients lodged on its upper floors were to be pitied.

Not that he had been relegated to such remote accommodation.

He had been lionized in this city so boastful of its new suspension bridge, so
smug behind its levee crowned with huge posts used to moor steamers when high
water lifted them practically level with the warehouse roofs. Nonetheless he
looked forward to leaving, for he found the atmosphere slow and provincial compared to New Orleans. He would say good-bye forever when the *Nonpareil* made
her maiden voyage, next week at latest, sooner if her trials went well tomorrow—
no, today, he corrected himself, remembering it was already half past midnight.

This evening he had brought his endeavors to a climax with a lavish dinner at
which he had toasted the boat, her owners, her builders, and the crew carefully
recruited for her during the winter. In the course of his speech he had even
obliged Parbury to compound their outstanding differences, by making careful
and always indirect allusion to the disputes which—everybody knew—had punctuated their association so far. There had been a time around the turn of the year
when each was blaming the other for mistakes that threatened to wreck the undertaking. Fortunately from Gordon's point of view, Parbury had intemperately
published his accusations; his partners had been more circumspect. Now the boat
was finally ready, albeit months overdue, Gordon had suggested to the company it
was time for all such insults to be withdrawn, and in the general bonhomie Parbury could not refuse without seeming ungracious.

After his professions of camaraderie, Gordon felt free to disregard Parbury's
views on their last and longest-standing disagreement: a triviality that had been
allowed to balloon into a matter of principle.

From the start journalists had compared the *Nonpareil* to the *Eclipse,* and the
latter had carried a fine quadrille band; surviving advertisements attested the fact.
Parbury, though, was opposed to "wasting" money on musicians, while Gordon's
opinion was that whatever railroads could not offer must be exploited to the
utmost.

Lately, as though conscious that his dogmatism was absurd, Parbury had refrained from mentioning the matter. And after tonight, Gordon told himself, there
was nothing to stop him telegraphing the *Nonpareil*'s agents at New Orleans,
Oliver Knight & Co., instructing them to hire a band and have it standing by on
the wharf to publicize her arrival.

Doubtless Parbury would rebuke him for extravagance, but in a short time the
results would speak for themselves, Gordon was sure. He maintained that adver-

tising and publicity were the Jachin and Boaz of success in business. So a nice loud band would attract attention and pay for itself.

Naturally there were cases where blatancy was inappropriate. Sometimes, woman-like, fame was best courted by being shunned for a while . . . as he had demonstrated on reaching New Orleans. He had refused to talk to the first reporters who showed up, aware that if he did so he would be forgotten in a few days. By biding his time, then yielding unexpectedly to Joel, he had ensured lasting notoriety, because from that moment on everybody felt flattered by acquaintance with this mystery man. The·Marocain brothers had gone so far as to bribe him into patronizing their bank; at least they had sent him a couple of expensive gifts, and the implication was clear.

When he had eventually deigned to visit their establishment, they had practically begged him to let them handle the financing of the *Nonpareil*.

Not for the first time he chuckled at his own ingenuity, and thrust his key into the door of his suite.

"What the de'il—?"

Gordon bit off the words as he entered the middle room of the three-room suite, which he was using as an office. He had taken it for granted that Matthew would be in bed in the room on the right. Instead, here he was in nightshirt and slippers, head slumped among a scatter of documents and obviously fast asleep.

*Now* what was this fool playing at? Gordon took a stride toward the table, intending to shake Matthew awake. His foot brushed a sheet of paper fallen to the carpet, a private letter in a formal copybook hand. Automatically he picked it up. It was so brief, he read it at a glance.

*My dear Nephew,*

*Against your impending Birthday I write to convey my good wishes and trust the speed of modern Railroads will bring my note to hand before the date. I will not write at length, for you do not do so any more. You offer the excuse, Mr. Gordon allows you little leisure. I advance the same reason but citing my Clientele.*

*Your aff'nate Uncle Ray*

"Oh, you're back, sir. Didn't hear you come in. Did it all go off okay?"
Fighting a yawn, Matthew sat up.

Gordon did not look at him at once. Sometimes he thought he had never really had a childhood; certainly he had had none to leave such glowing memories as others claimed to cherish. When things went badly with his parents—which was most of the time—the bairns bore the brunt of their ill temper. He had been beaten regularly until he was old enough to hit back.

Being orphaned was no excuse for this soft boy to cower in the shelter of youth indefinitely! He might still look like a child, but it was high time he started acting like a man.

"Greensickness," he said suddenly.

"I beg your pardon, sir?"

"I said greensickness! That's what's wrong with you!" Gordon doffed his hat and cape. As usual Matthew made to take them. Gordon checked him with a scowl. "If I'd wanted a valet I'd have hired a valet! You're my amanuensis—you're meant to work with your head, not your hands."

Matthew licked his lips. "I do, sir. To the best of my ability."

"Then why didn't you use your head and tell me you had a birthday due?"

"I—uh—I felt it a matter of purely private concern . . . sir."

"You didn't believe I meant what I've always said: I take a personal interest in the well-being of my employees?" Gordon's tone was heavy with sarcasm. "When is this birthday, anyhow?"

Blushing now, Matthew muttered, "March first, sir."

"You mean today!"

"I—I guess I do by now." With a glance at a wall-clock.

"And how old does that make you?"

"N-nineteen."

"Nineteen, hey? I was right, then. Greensickness, that's what ails you! Here!" He fumbled in his vest pocket and produced a small key. "Yonder stands a tantalus. There's Scotch whisky in the right-hand bottle. Pour two glasses and we'll toast your anniversary."

Taking the key reluctantly, Matthew said, "Sir, I've never partaken of strong liquor—"

"It's time you did!" Gordon snapped. "And there's no' a finer introduction tae the glories o' Bacchus than ma whusky! *Dae as ye're tell't!*"

During their travels there had been not a few occasions when Gordon's accent reverted to the dialect of his youth. It was a storm warning. Trembling, Matthew made haste to obey.

This time, at least, he was fated to escape his master's wrath. He filled the glasses to the prescribed height and set them down with correct ceremony. Satisfied, Gordon indicated he should resume his seat, lifted his drink, and said sententiously, "To your twentieth year!"

Hoping he was not obliged to gulp it at a draught, Matthew sipped the whisky and with relief found it pungent but not unbearable. He was even able to feign a nod of approval as he set his glass down again.

Which seemed to impress Gordon, for he said with near-cordiality, "Why did you decide to keep your watch night *this* way? Here I find you sitting up until all hours of a freezing night, poring over"—he reached for a sample of the documents—"last week's expenditures, and the retainer paid to Mr. Hogan to make sure he'll be here in time for the downriver trip, and an indent from Mr. Woodley, and a bill for a piano, and— Ach! Did I order you to do this?"

"No, sir!"

"Then why do it? To impress the night watchman, is that it?"

"Impress—? No, I swear it! It was just that I couldn't sleep. So I thought it best to use the time."

"And did you?"

Miserably Matthew shook his head.

"Greensickness, then," Gordon repeated with satisfaction. Emptying his glass, he held it out for refilling. Matthew was prompt to comply.

And ventured as he relocked the tantalus, "Sir, you've said that more than once, and—"

"And you don't understand what I mean by it," Gordon cut in. "You only ever heard it applied to sickly girls. Is that right?"

Matthew hesitated. "I don't believe," he admitted at last, "I ever heard the term before. But of course I have been largely raised out of contact with young ladies. The Lord chose not to bless my parents with a daughter, as I'm sure I've told you. So . . ."

"You'll have to grow out of it," Gordon declared, exactly as though Matthew had not spoken. Glass cradled between clasped hands, he gave the clear impression of pondering a weighty subject.

Matthew nervously risked a second sip.

"Elvira," Gordon said at length. "Aye. She would be right for you. . . . Nineteen and never tasted liquor! Never had a woman either, I'll be bound! Or am I wrong? Sometimes you thin frail bairns excite their motherly feelings— Ah, I can read by your face my guess was right! That settles it, then. As soon as we return to New Orleans I'll hold a birthday dinner for you. At the Limousin! And you'll be a man by morning, *an' mebbe warth mair'n a wet coo-pat tae masel' wha pays yir wages!*"

He drained his glass. In a different voice, as though his personality had altered with the action, he said, "To bed with you. I've ordered breakfast at six o'clock. Today's the day for the *Nonpareil* as well as you. Good night."

Stowey & Vandersteen's shipyard was a maze of lumber downstream of the main Cincinnati public landing. It was incredibly untidy, having as much rubbish as usable matériel scattered over its two-acre extent. During January and February this had largely been disguised by snow; with the thaw it was becoming sadly obvious again.

Yet it had proved possible to conjure out of this chaos a masterpiece of grace, elegance, luxury and speed. There she lay, moored a short distance from the slipway that had launched her empty hull—too many months ago!

But now at last she was fully fitted-out, except for final trimmings such as linen for the staterooms and liquor for the bar. And she looked magnificent. She measured better than three hundred feet from her rounded stern to her finely modeled bow, designed to create a plume of spray when she was under way. The tops of her chimneys were formed like coronets, as her predecessor's had been, and these ornaments were barely less than a hundred feet above her waterline. She was more than forty-two feet broad, but in proportion to her length that was so negligible, she seemed pencil-slim. Boastfully tall letters spelled out her name on either wheelhouse, while her verge staff awaited the breaking-out of a pennant

Gordon had had embroidered specially, which bore the steamer's name translated into plain English: *None is my equal!*

Even at rest she was creating a sensation. A crowd had gathered despite the cold, and as Gordon advanced to meet the senior partner of the shipbuilding company, Albert Stowey, he was accosted by two men flourishing notebooks, clad almost identically in check ulsters and derby hats.

"Mr. Gordon!" the first one cried. "I'm from the Cincinnati *Commercial*! Are you going to race your boat against the *Atchafalaya*?"

Gordon halted in his tracks.

"What makes you think there will be any call for a race? Why shouldn't the result be a foregone conclusion? Here's the finest steamer that ever graced these waters! Well crewed and well commanded, why should she not outstrip all competition without the need to race?"

The second reporter broke in. "I'm here for the Memphis *Avalanche*, sir! Speaking of command: what made you appoint Mr. Woodley master of the new boat?"

"You probably know his qualifications better than I," retorted Gordon. "Not only does he own a share in her—at last report he's still the youngest riverman entitled to be called Captain. I'm impressed by precocious success. I made my fortune when I was younger than you are now!"

The man from the *Avalanche* bit his lip, giving his companion time to butt in.

"When will the public have a chance to judge your claims, Mr. Gordon?"

"Tomorrow or the next day, if her trials go well, as I'm convinced they will. Before departing for New Orleans, the *Nonpareil* will make an excursion trip, or two if there is enough demand. And I shall personally insist on journalists coming aboard free of charge on the first trip—to create demand for the second!"

Which provoked a ripple of laughter from the bystanders.

Placated for the time being, the pair withdrew, and Stowey led Gordon and Matthew—the latter trying to hide his yawns—along a winding path between heaps of wood and ironware, which ended at the stage linking the steamer with the shore.

Apart from hellos, no words were exchanged. Stowey had been very glib with his assurances when, after visiting a dozen yards without luck and growing impatient, Gordon and Parbury had investigated this one. Summer was nearly over by then, and while it was true that from Cincinnati down the Ohio and Mississippi were generally navigable eleven months of the year, winters hereabout—and upstream on both the Ohio and the other river that debouched here, the Licking—could be cruel. In February 1856 a rise in the Licking had vomited such a mass of ice that it sank eleven steamers and damaged many more; a year later another six were sunk by ice rushing down the Ohio.

This was therefore not an ideal place to let the contract for an expensive boat late in the season.

But Gordon was too enthusiastic to wait until spring; Parbury was desperate to witness the realization of his dream; and Stowey was free with assertions that his and that other vessel would be clear of the yard tomorrow—next week—at latest by month's end!

And there was one sound argument in favor of, if not Cincinnati, then some other northern city. Down south, factories did not yet exist capable of building engines, boilers and piping light enough to be economic, yet strong enough to withstand the high operating pressure necessary if the *Nonpareil* were to run out her competitors. Stowey & Vandersteen had already built one such steamer, and she was at work and showing a fair profit.

For Woodley this was what counted above all. Having kept his promise and sold his old boat for what little she would fetch, not only was he anxious to have his money working for him again, but also—as he admitted to Gordon in a burst of frankness—on his own he would have had to wait a lifetime before commanding so splendid a vessel, and he was eagerly looking forward to her debut.

So Gordon had put his foot down in Stowey's favor, and there had been one hitch following another, and countless excuses . . . and now they would all learn whether their gamble had come off.

The clerks, caterer and steward of the *Nonpareil* were to join her tomorrow, but her mates, engineers, carpenter and pilots had reported yesterday and were assembled in the cabin, awaiting Gordon.

Woodley had greeted them and found an excuse to slip away. Now he was in the pilothouse, staring—still with amazement—at the reality of his new command.

Who would have guessed that his casual exclamation, meant mainly to impress, would lead to this? His confession to Gordon had been all too candid: he had truly never expected to find himself with such an awesome responsibility.

But he was going to discharge it well. He had sworn a private oath to that effect. He was going to run this boat like fine clockwork. She was going to break speed records, yet never fail to meet her published schedules. Above all, she was going to endow him with the status he had dreamed of long and long.

Or perhaps she had done so already. Half a dozen times recently a wealthy acquaintance had made a pointless bet with him and duly lost. Not until it dawned on him that these unexpected winnings were in each case about enough to pay off an existing debt did he realize that he must have passed some sort of test.

Was it solely his appointment to the *Nonpareil* that had settled the matter? He preferred to believe he had made most of the distance under his own steam.

But there was no doubt the beautiful new vessel must have helped.

And yet, all was not, even now, perfect. He was in partnership—albeit on a small scale—with Parbury and Gordon, and that was fair enough. As time went by he would enlarge his share. But in another way he was still far from being his own master.

Laying one hand on the huge wheel—which, sparing no expense, Gordon had caused to be made of the finest South American mahogany—he thought about the haughtiness of pilots. Some steps had been taken to regulate their arrogance; in his view, not nearly enough. And Drew, damn him, had made matters infinitely worse by training a colored cub, who now thought himself one of the lords of creation—that same who had so insulted him last year when he was teasing the quadroon girl outside Griswold's. He had seldom thought about that episode again, for it was too shaming. Miraculously it had not been noised abroad; of the witnesses to his humiliation, Tyburn had not a grain of malice in his makeup, and Whitworth had been persuaded to silence by the assurance of the job he now held. But would the day come when niggers were to order captains about?

Shuddering, he turned his thoughts into a more positive course.

Granted, it was a stroke of luck that two of the best-reputed pilots on the river had volunteered their services as soon as they learned there was to be another *Nonpareil:* stocky, red-cheeked Dermot Hogan and massive Colin Trumbull.

Even so, Woodley was sorry they were joining under long-term contracts. That had been Gordon's doing. In most other respects they saw eye to eye, but the Scot had held forth at length about the stupidity of hiring and firing on a trip-to-trip basis and lauded the vision of a crew who would grow attached to the boat.

And, Woodley glossed sourly, would wind up thinking it belonged to them. Might as well hymn the advantage of slaves who had grown attached to their plantations. That hadn't stopped them turning on their masters during the war.

No, for all their pretensions pilots were and must remain hired hands. If only he had thought in good time of the scheme he now favored! Since any boat accepting way-business was obliged to make a certain number of intermediate stops, and since conditions on the river could change magically overnight, why should pilots not specialize in one particular stretch and arrange to serve on steamers going alternately up and down—under contract not to a single vessel, but to a packet line? There was no shortage of such nowadays; the free-for-all of prewar years had been rudely interrupted, and cooler counsels had led to the creation of groups of half a dozen to a dozen boats running regularly in cooperation rather than competition.

At least that was the theory. All too often these "lines" broke up in their first season. One boat would gain an edge over the others, and then her captain would reneg . . .

Or was it the captains who defaulted? Was it not more the responsibility of the *hired* pilots, who were not in command but were allowed to act as though they were? There were rumors about pilots who took bribes to miscalculate awkward bends and stranded boats on sand reefs just long enough for rivals to overtake. Once or twice he himself had suspected that the man at the controls of the *Hezekiah Woodley*—

A shrill call came from below. Gathering his wits with an effort, he realized that Gordon was being ushered up the stage—and, simultaneously, that his right hand was still resting on the great wheel.

And moreover that, unless invited, this was the last time he would dare lay a finger on it.

Cursing, he hastened down the stairs.

As Stowey and Gordon reached the top of the stage with Matthew trailing in their wake, they were greeted by a thin, ill-shaven man supervising a gang of black workers busy filling the *Nonpareil*'s boilers for the first time, with hand pumps and hoses dangled overside.

"Eb Williams, fourth engineer!" the man said, doffing his cap and extending his hand. "I just want to say, sir, how proud I am to be working aboard your fine steamer, sir!"

Gordon looked him over thoughtfully, not taking the proffered hand. It was extremely dirty. The fact suddenly dawned on Williams. Face crimson, he let it fall.

"Williams, eh?" Gordon said at last. "I shall remember you."

Before the engineer could say anything further, a man affecting garb like a preacher's appeared from the entrance to the main cabin.

"Harry Whitworth, sir," he presented himself to Gordon. "Second mate. Captain Parbury and the rest of the officers attend you. Come this way."

Someone had thought to light a stove, and it was blessedly warm in here. At the head of the largest table Captain Parbury turned his black-barred gaze on the new arrivals. All around, sipping strong coffee which lent its fragrance to the air, stood men whom Matthew regarded with interest. Until now they had been, with a few exceptions, no more than names signed to a letter.

He had met the pilots, Hogan and Trumbull, back in New Orleans. He had seen the chief engineer, Peter Corkran, when he visited the shipyard to check on progress, and recognized him again now by a discolored patch on his right cheek, as though furnace ash were ingrained under the skin.

But Corkran's deputies were strangers to him: Brian Roy and Victor Steeples, the former gaunt and balding, the latter brown-haired and nondescript.

Also present was a man missing two fingers of his left hand. His hair was gray— what was left of it—and he had lost several teeth also. A chance clue informed Matthew of his identity: from the breast pocket of his coat protruded the yellow-and-yellow of a brass-hinged boxwood rule. So that must be Hiram Burge, who had worked on the old *Nonpareil* and literally begged for a post on the new one. Clearly, given his disability, he could no longer serve as an engineer, but at Parbury's insistence he had been engaged as carpenter. The steamer's woodwork was of good quality; it would call for minimal attention during her first couple of years, and in time he could be persuaded to retire. The pioneering days were past when sometimes a steamer had to make repairs fifty miles from the nearest settlement. Burge's chief responsibility would be to make sure the hog chains were always properly tensioned.

He also clearly caught the name of the first mate, Solomon Underwood, when he was presented to Gordon.

Satisfied he knew everybody of importance, and mentally rehearsing the names of those who would report for duty tomorrow and the next day—McNab, Iliff, Katzmann, Bates—Matthew withdrew into an alcove as Gordon took the chair facing Parbury and sat down, gesturing for Woodley and the other officers to do the same.

"And who exactly may you be?" a voice demanded at his elbow.

Starting, he realized the questioner was the man who had greeted them on deck.

"I'm Mr. Gordon's amanuensis," he said after a pause.

"Is that *so*?" Whitworth said incredulously. "Well, if that don't beat all get out. You always say that when people ask you?"

Matthew licked his lips. He was invariably at a loss when people inquired about his work. It seemed like such an empty occupation. Dignifying it with a high-sounding classical name had served to impress his few friends back at Catskill. During his travels, however, he had met so many boys his own age working at such demanding, *adult* tasks . . .

He gathered his forces and contrived a smile. "Well, Mr. Whitworth," he said, "that's what he pays me for!"

Thinking an appeal to commercial interest would work where all else failed.

There was a pause. Whitworth was getting set to respond, when he suddenly realized everyone else was seated and waiting for him. He ducked into a vacant chair beside Underwood. Throughout the subsequent discussion he kept casting puzzled glances at Gordon, and would have done the same to Matthew but that the boy was at his back.

"We're all here, then," Gordon said. "Except Williams!"

"He's still on deck," Corkran said promptly. "Shall I send—?"

Gordon cut him short with a wave.

"There's liquor on his breath, and it's too early in the day!"

A moment of dead silence followed. At length Steeples said, "For him, Mr. Gordon, it ain't early anymore. He came on board at three o'clock."

"And at that hour," supplemented Burge, "a nip of whiskey can revive the heart."

"You believe in drinking on duty?" Gordon barked. "Then you quit now!"

Burge tripped over his tongue. "All I meant was—"

"I'm doing the talking! I put up the money for this boat, remember, even though she's to Captain Parbury's design!"

Parbury smiled slowly; it was like watching lock gates open.

"Corkran, you recommended this man Williams, didn't you?"

"Yes, sir. I've served with Eb on the *Luke A. Horner*, the *Indian Chief* and the *Battleaxe*."

"And at his age he is still fourth engineer?"

The sally told. Corkran shrugged and looked anywhere but at his interrogator.

"He's a good man in his way, sir. And he has children to keep."

"Is he kin of yours?"

Another awkward pause, then a sigh. "Yes, sir. Married one of my cousins."

"Sir!"—sharply from Underwood. "I've served with men a hundred times worse than Eb. You can't expect perfection on a riverboat."

"Can't I? But I do!" Gordon barked. "So does Captain Parbury! And so does Captain Woodley! Don't you?"—the last directly.

"I would never settle for less," came the prompt reply.

"What are we to do about a man like that, then?"

For a second it seemed the boat's new master was baffled; then, however, he leaned both elbows on the table and gazed with a serious expression to right and left.

"Don't they say no man shall be judged guilty until it's proved against him? With all respect, Mr. Gordon, in my time I've had a whiskey breath on a cold morning like today. So long as any man can discharge his duties, I'll support him. But let him once neglect them, for whatever reason, and . . . !" A snap of the

fingers. Nods welcomed his Solomonic statement, and he added, "Yourself, sir—
you've been known to indulge."

"Not when I had charge of someone else's property," Gordon growled. But the
mood of the gathering was against him.

"The morning of a steamer's first trials, sir," Underwood offered, "is scarcely a
rehearsal for her first paying trip."

"And Eb," Corkran said, "did turn out before dawn to make sure the trials
would go well."

The door from the larboard deck opened. Williams himself came in, smiling
broadly.

"Any time you care to raise steam," he announced, "she's right and ready."

Before anyone else could speak, Parbury rose. "I hanker after the smell of
smoke," he said. "A riverboat don't feel natural without it."

"Move it, then!" Woodley jumped to his feet. "Corkran—Roy—Steeples—get
below!"

Standing shyly in his alcove, Matthew wondered whether anybody but himself
had noticed that the three engineers were already out of their seats before Woodley issued his order.

Patient until full pressure had been reached, Hogan and Trumbull made a final
inspection of the pilothouse, with Parbury on the padded bench behind them.
None of the three was a sentimental person.

But when Hogan ventured diffidently, "Y'know, this is kind of like waiting for a
baby to be born . . ."

The others spoke no word to contradict him.

 It was not so much that the *Nonpareil* came alive as that
residues of life within her were aroused and together made a
new and active whole.

A match was struck. The splinter had been part of a tree scant months ago.

The flame was set to a bit of cotton waste. The fields that had yielded bolls to
make it were still bearing. Moreover it had been dipped in oil, owed to living
things of the far past.

So was the coal heaped in the furnaces, which from kindling wood picked up
the yellow flame and turned it redder first, then hotter.

Borne on bars of iron, the fire gave up its heat to eight iron tubes, boilers
running lengthwise with their furnace doors toward the bow so that the wind of
her going would be added to the suction of her chimneys. The boilers were filled
with water that lately had been part of a process which poets often compared with
life: the stream of a great river.

The breath of fire transformed it. Suddenly it was what men called—with excellent reason—live steam.

To feed the mighty engines lying sternward, pipes interlaced across, above, around the boilers. They were of copper, for the most part; where they met iron their union was cemented with hexagonal nuts of bright new brass. First the boilers, then the piping, then the engines themselves, creaked and sighed, repeating in the context of the finished boat what until now they had only undergone separately.

Meantime the hull too was adjusting. Under the weight of all the water that had been pumped aboard, the wooden portions of the *Nonpareil*, from her keelsons to the flimsiest bit of gingerbread work in the ladies' cabin, settled against each other and the nails and pegs that held them snug. For the first time her loading pattern was established; it was like nearing a magnet to the underside of paper strewn with iron filings and watching the lines of force appear.

The piano in the main cabin uttered its first sound since arriving on board when its bass string resonated to the cry of an iron bar: part of a midships hog chain that accepted more than its share of the burden from the boilers.

Studying it and its fellows, striding busily to and fro in the hold, Burge hoped privately that he looked as important as he felt even though, when he spotted excessive slack in the chains, some anonymous black now had to tighten them.

Thoughtful, intent, concentrated, Solomon Underwood walked the length of the main deck and guards while Whitworth made similar rounds on the boiler deck, seeking any sign of bad workmanship or structural weakness. From the bank Stowey watched with field glasses to his eyes. Gordon had said he would prefer not to have the boatbuilder along during the trials, making it plain that he expected faults and wanted to make it easier for those who recognized them to speak freely. Stowey had had the sense to agree.

There was little solid evidence to back the notion, but the impression was widespread that people did not gainsay Hamish Gordon without paying for their temerity.

So far as payment went: it was no particular secret that when all the accounts had been honored for every item supplied by every specialist manufacturer involved in the creation of the *Nonpareil*, including such miscellanea as ice chests, barbershop fittings, and brushes and polish for the bootblacks, the partnership of Gordon, Woodley and Parbury would have laid out more than two hundred thousand dollars.

Nor was it private knowledge that this impressive sum had been administered by the Marocain Bank.

Confidence in which had consequently soared.

With Matthew at his heels, Gordon prowled throughout the *Nonpareil* as the business of waking her continued. At last he returned to the engine room and waited until the steam gauges indicated normal working pressure: 160 psi.

Then, shouting to overcome the noise—for in this empty steamer every rattling shovel-load of coal was amplified by echoes—he demanded of Steeples as he completed a final round of inspection, "Anything amiss?"

Grinning, Steeples shook his head. "She's tighter'n an old maid's—" he began, and suddenly remembered who he was talking to.

But Gordon chuckled, and with relief the three engineers exchanged smiles. "Where's Williams?" the financier went on.

From gloomy sternward recesses Williams emerged looking as pleased as his colleagues.

"Looks like she's set to go!" he declared.

"Then tell Mr. Hogan we're ready to cast off," Gordon said. "Matthew, come on deck with me."

The chill of the morning had relented, and along with it the traces of mist that earlier had shrouded the water. The crowd of spectators was half as large again; many cheered on spotting Gordon.

Down below, steam was fed to the engines, and they sighed like a giant who, from the moment of setting about his lifetime's task, felt bored with it but by divine decree was not permitted to experience anger.

At the opening of the steam cocks, twin pitmans answered the thrust of the pistons. Huge as trunks of trees—which they had been until they were shaped and bound with iron—they leaned on the cranks that drove the axles that turned the wheels . . . which were marginally less than forty-three feet in diameter by substantially over fifteen feet wide, and fitted with two-foot slabs of solid wood that were still called buckets in memory of the watermills of an earlier day. Gray water became brown foam. Trumbull leaned out of the pilothouse and waved. Fore and aft, deckhands singled off the mooring cables. A ragged cheer went up from the onlookers.

At this hour there was little activity along the Cincinnati waterfront. Anything that moved, even a rowboat, was apt to attract attention.

Maybe it was that motion marked an end to the drab immobility of winter, a return of circulation to the numb limbs of the continent. Maybe it was that some aboriginal process of the kind which led humanity to invent gods and goddesses for spring struck chords in the watchers' minds. It made no odds. The sight of the colossal steamer taking to her natural element was enough to justify anybody's admiration. It was less like a baby being born than the bursting into view of the tremendous creature that the prophets knew: Leviathan.

 At this season the Ohio still ran gently, not yet boosted by the northern thaws that shortly would enlarge it into spate. Light on the water as a settled swan, the *Nonpareil* sidled toward midstream and steadied there, wheels dipping leisurely to hold her level with the shipyard.

She was handsome. All the onlookers were agreed about that. But would she—could she or any other steamer—match the expectations of her owner?

The time had come to find out. Smoke belched from her chimneys; Hogan had rung bells for slow ahead and slow astern on opposite wheels, and down below the hands were wrestling with the larboard reversing gear. With briskness due to novelty the job was over in double-quick time, and the boat proceeded to put about in scarcely more than her own length.

Another cheer acknowledged the feat. But it was no mere circus trick. It was a way of testing rudder and wheels both at once.

Hogan repeated the maneuver in the opposite sense. Then he had to signal stand by, for another steamer came plodding up the reach, the elderly *J.W. Carey*.

As she passed she whistled a greeting, and the *Nonpareil* registered another first in her existence when she replied. Her own whistle was of peculiar sweetness, like a songbird's. This newcomer already possessed an unmistakable badge of identity even before her cutwater had cast up its first plume of spray.

The engineers had examined every pipe and every joint. There was no suspicion of a leak. When the bell sounded for half ahead on both, they were prepared for it, and the pistons ceased shadowboxing with their cylinders and began to jab and pound. The wheels' noise grew loud enough to be heard in the engine room: no longer separate splashing sounds, but a cataract-like rush.

At least the racket would be less overpowering when she was fully loaded . . . but then, of course, her pistons would be punching.

Cork-buoyant as she yet was, she bobbed in most undignified fashion when the *Carey*'s wake reached her, causing Gordon to curse and clutch the rail, and Matthew to wonder whether he should have come aboard at all, and the crew to rush about securing loose items. But that was due to her exceptional construction. Stowey himself had stated that he had never before been invited to build a boat so light in relation to her size. She was certain, he maintained, to skim the water at unprecedented speed.

This was what Hogan now set out to prove. Running down stream was for later, when it came time to find out how she handled when her wheels had to be used for braking. In the whole career of a riverboat there might be no more than a week when that was necessary, but that week might see her run aground or sunk.

First, however, it was essential to establish what she could do against the current. At least, if something broke while heading up, she could drift back to the shipyard by herself.

Ears fiercely tuned to every clue the world of sound could offer, Parbury recognized the bell for full ahead. He flung open the door of the pilothouse and hastened down the steps beyond. Fearing he might fall, Trumbull made to help, but Hogan checked him with a gesture.

"Colin! He wouldn't thank you!"

Trumbull looked briefly at a loss.

"He built a model of this boat, didn't he?"

"Well—sure!"

"Don't you believe he's walked every inch of her in his imagination?"

Trumbull stared at the black-garbed figure making for the forward end of the hurricane deck. The wind whipped his coat tails and threatened to carry off his hat.

But his attitude conveyed that he was waiting for something—

And here it came! For the first time the cutwater created its intended fountain, and a graceful arc of sparkling water rose from the bow. None of it fell on deck; yet Parbury responded, turning to right and left as though to relish the difference in noise due to the spray.

Nodding, Trumbull said, "I see what you mean. Must be a hell of a thing, to have your dreams come true."

"Maybe. Maybe not."

Trumbull shot a keen glance at his companion.

"Too light?"

"You noticed it too?" Hogan countered.

"I can't be sure," was Trumbull's pointed answer, and Hogan promptly relinquished the wheel.

"Well?" he said when the other pilot had had a chance to take her measure.

For a further half-minute there was no reply. Trumbull was staring to his left, gaze fixed on two tall buildings which from here appeared to be moving one behind the other. Hogan forebore to press his question; he knew what Trumbull was doing, even though this particular pair of landmarks was unfamiliar to him.

"I make it eighteen knots," Trumbull announced at last.

Hogan nodded. "Reckon she'll make twenty when she's shook down?"

"I reckon she's unquestionably fast."

"But—?"

"But kind of skittish. Like a horse that got spooked in the breaking."

Hogan nodded again. "Better under load," he suggested.

"Sure to be. Anyhow, her list could always be trimmed with a chain wagon." He meant a wheeled cart loaded with heavy weights, which could be drawn from one side to the other to correct a list.

"And the *Atchafalaya* . . ." Hogan spread his hands.

"She's an old boat now. Machinery wears out. Planks and keelsons warp and iron rusts. Are you going to sign for a year?"

"I guess I shall. You?"

"I didn't hear that any better boat was building."

Agreed on that score, they relaxed a fraction. Trumbull pointed at Parbury.

"Say, Dermot! Which of us is going to break the news?"

"He knows. He felt the sheer she took off the *Carey*."

"Yeah. But did Gordon?"

"He was never aboard a light boat before."

They exchanged grins, perfectly understanding one another.

"How much longer should we run up the reach?"

"Oh, far's you like. Give the folks on shore a show. All good for business. And signal every boat we meet. I like her whistle."

"Me too . . . I guess we got ourselves a berth."

"Sure. But there's just one thing."

Trumbull glanced around sharply. "Something you know that I don't?"

"Could be. I reckon we may have problems with Woodley."

"Wouldn't be surprised. But anything particular?"

"He's a great man for specializing. Thinks boats would keep better time if they hired pilots section by section during a trip."

Scornfully Trumbull said, "It's been tried! Hell, there ain't enough pilots on the river to sit on their asses waiting for a—a *specialized* trip!"

"I can't help wondering," Hogan said meditatively, "whether you didn't hear remarks like that the first time they put a boat into the Cairo-Louisville trade, 'stead of running through. Or the New Orleans-Natchez trade, come to that."

"Not the same thing," Trumbull retorted. "Natchez was the end of the Natchez Trace. It was natural to set goods afloat from there on down—"

"And how is a railroad different from the Natchez Trace in what it does?"

Trumbull sighed. "True enough. We're in a fix. But I surely hope I don't have to sweat out my dying days on *one* goddamn' stretch of river. Might as well turn me into a machine."

"They will, sooner or later." Hogan gave a sour grin.

Trumbull nodded. "Still, just 'cause you see what's happening don't mean you choose to go along with it. All them folks out there!" He waved at the crowd on the main Cincinnati landing. "Don't you believe there's one of 'em who wants to make his living on a riverboat? Wouldn't settle for a railroad or a grocery store, or even a cathouse?"

"I believe it! Just like I believe someone I never met wants to annex the moon. I hope he never makes it while I'm around. Think of seeing it turned red and green to advertise a dentifrice!"

"Ah, hell!" Trumbull launched an accurate gob of juice at the cuspidor. "That's nothing to me. But what if they line the riverbanks with billboards?"

"Railroad company billboards!"

"They're the worst kind!"

"Then take comfort in this," Hogan said. "By that time they'll have driven all us pilots crazy and there won't be any steamers to advertise to."

"Just catfish and 'gators?"

"You catch my drift."

There was a pause. At last Hogan said, "How does she feel now?"

Trumbull pondered his words with care.

"If this is the boat Woodley wants to try out his scheme of specialist pilots . . ."

"Right," Hogan said. "She's one that calls for a pilot specialized in her, not in a particular stretch of river."

Trumbull concurred, grinning. "Contrariwise, however—"

"What?"

"She makes me feel kind of like she could grow on me."

"I feel the same," Hogan said. "If you've no objection, I'll take the helm again. I can't imagine Parbury designing a bad boat. And look at him! He's laughing. Laughing right out loud!"

Down below it was far too hot for anyone to shiver; the fireman feeding the Moloch maws of the furnaces were stripped to undershirts.

Yet Matthew shivered. Never before had he seen the fury of flame transmuted into such colossal power! Something that to him had been the escape from the lid of a kettle turned out to be stronger than a man, a horse, an elephant. To think such flimsy vapor could thrust aside those massy pistons . . .

More than a little envious of his employer's knowledge, he struggled to make sense of the tangle of pipes that today must be inspected inch by inch. As soon as he thought he had one run of the steam lines figured out, he realized the pipe he meant to follow ran behind another and his eye had picked up the wrong branch where it reemerged.

Additionally there were gauges reflecting the condition of the engines and boilers. Some were tolerably simple, like the vertical glass tubes that showed the water level, but others that reported unbelievable heat and pressure on dials as impersonal as a public clock—they defied his imagination, and of course this was no moment to be putting questions. Accordingly he stood aside, one ear cocked for Gordon's command to note down this or that comment in the daily journal which, Matthew now privately believed, was meant for comfort in old age rather than as a reference for current business.

Sometimes, on a good day, it was forgotten for hours at a time.

Now, though, was not such a juncture. In Gordon's barking voice: "Matthew! Keep a careful record of this! Mr. Roy, be so good as to hand me the speaking tube for the pilothouse."

With half his mind still trying to fathom the mystery of the engines, Matthew duly noted down the words.

"Mr. Hogan! As soon as we are clear of the city, look for a sandbank where you can run her aground without damage. I gather this is sometimes unavoidable."

Tinny and faint the answer came.

"Sure it is! But it's bad practice to do it deliberately, sir."

Curtly: "And in my view even worse to carry out high-pressure tests within sight of human habitation!"

From the corner of his eye Matthew registered Corkran crossing himself.

Hogan performed the maneuver flawlessly. Having selected a suitable sandbar, he carried on a short distance upstream; then he put the *Nonpareil* about and sidled her into shallow water. Then he ordered both engines to stand by and let the current ground her bow as gently as a falling leaf. Matthew had taken hold of a stanchion, expecting the shock to knock him off balance. Everybody else, including Gordon, did no more than sway and flex their legs, leaving him crestfallen with embarrassment.

"I'm impressed!" Gordon exclaimed. "And I'll make sure to tell Hogan so. Mr. Corkran, do you not have some such colloquial term as 'daisy piloting'?"

Gravely, though with a hint of irony, the chief engineer returned, "I guess if you was to call Mr. Hogan a daisy pilot he would not feel offended."

"Matthew, make a note of that," Gordon instructed, and continued briskly. "Now are there any sign of leaks? Bad brazing? Faulty unions or stuffing boxes?"

All three engineers shook their heads.

"What about the other man—Steeples? Where's he?"

Hearing his name, he emerged from shadow behind the starboard engine, carrying a wrench and wiping his face.

"Trouble?" Corkran called.

"Fixed it," was the succinct response. "A badly packed gland."

"Anything else?"

"Not so far's I've seen. Her piping's lighter than I'm used to for the pressure, and it was put up by a firm I never heard of before, but that's been the way of it since the war."

"So at design pressure she functions as intended," Gordon said, and all the engineers affirmed it.

"Excellent. Now, Mr. Corkran, shut down your doctor pump and overload your safety valves."

For a moment there was dead silence between them. It extended so far, now the rattle of rakes and shovels had ceased because the furnaces were no longer being fed, that Matthew could hear the slap of ripples on the hull.

Then Corkran turned slowly and gazed at the nearer of the twin pressure gauges. It was calibrated to 240 psi.

"She won't bend that needle on its stop," he said at last.

"I don't intend to try," Gordon retorted. "But—"

He broke off, as though abruptly reconsidering what he had had in mind to say.

"What?"—from Williams, taking a half-pace forward.

Matthew was sure this was the moment for public revelation of Gordon's railroad background, a secret that, to his knowledge, the financier had so far shared only with him. It had been edited out of Joel's article in the *Intelligencer*. But instead of making a frank avowal of his origins, he chose another course.

Gruffly he resumed, "I'll never go into a speculation without twenty percent margin to cover me! No more would I trust an engine that won't take twenty pounds over normal pressure!"

"Fair," Corkran conceded, and the others relaxed along with him. "Brian, shut off the doctor like he says. Eb, get one of your hands to bring a fire rake to move the pea with."

Gordon started and swung round.

Each of the *Nonpareil*'s eight boilers was fitted with a fusible plug below regular water level against the risk of overheating. The first had its own safety valve, for use exclusively when it was fired up by itself to drive the doctor engine and the bilge pumps. This was why there were dual steam gauges. Under normal conditions they gave identical readings, because the boilers were cross-connected to keep the water level constant and fed into a steam drum running transversely across their tops, on which was mounted the master safety valve. It was of the type known as a pea valve, which at a certain pressure would force a metal poppet out of its tightly machined seating and allow steam to escape. To control its blowing-off point, a lever with a protrusion on the underside lay across it, hinged at one end, free to move at the other, but there bearing a sliding weight like the load on a steelyard.

The weight for the *Nonpareil* had been carefully calculated; it now rested about halfway along its range of travel.

"Is there no way to adjust that pea without calling for a fire rake?" Gordon demanded.

"Sure," Steeples said. "Send up a nigger on another nigger's back—"

It had been intended for a joke; Gordon quenched the engineer's flippancy with a glare.

"Before we leave for New Orleans, there will be a pole with a steel hook hanging on a bracket *there!*"—pointing at the nearest bulkhead—"so that nobody working in this engineroom need ever risk being scalded by a steam leak! Once I saw a man die that way, and I never want to see the like again!"

"Aboard a steamer, sir?" Corkran inquired.

"No. No, in a factory." Gordon gave a kind of shake, like a dog emerging from water. "I never knew his name, but his skin peeled off like an onion's. Get that rod made up. I'm amazed it isn't standard equipment already."

Ordinarily when a steamer was hove to, the sound of the doctor busily topping up the boilers was as loud a noise as could be heard in her engineroom. The sudden cessation of its thump-and-pump felt uncanny. There was a noticeable tremor in Corkran's voice when he said, "Here's Brian, and I guess Eb will be back in a moment. . . Brian, all shut down?"

"Tight as she'll go," Roy answered, and took station where he could watch the gauges.

Then Williams returned, followed by a coal-dusted man brandishing a fire rake. "Pete, I said to keep the fires up until you shouted, right?"

"Right," Corkran acknowledged, and took the rake. At full stretch he drew the pea along its bar. "Shooting for one-eighty," he muttered.

The needles reached and trembled at 175. "More!" Gordon commanded. Corkran obeyed, and they vibrated past 180.

"Any sign of strain?" Gordon rapped. Williams and Steeples disappeared into dark recesses, tracing the pipes with the aid of kerosene lamps but relying chiefly on the keenness of their ears.

The tension became intolerable. Matthew felt he had held his breath clear through until the glimmering lamps reappeared.

"All tight!" was the unison report.

"Then she'll take two hundred," Gordon said, and turned to Corkran. "Move the pea again."

"It'll do you no good in practice, sir," said the chief engineer. "Since the act of '52 the inspectors seal your valves before every trip. There were too many tales in the early days about levers being weighted down with flatirons."

"The inspectors aren't here yet. Won't be until tomorrow. And in case of need seals can be broken. Give me the rake."

Corkran hefted it. He said, "You want to risk blowing up us-all *and* your investment? I guess you have us thoroughly insured! Who's to inherit?"

Gordon chuckled throatily. "Who's to die?"

And instead of using the rake to slide the pea farther out, he hooked its teeth over the bar and leaned on it.

The gauges moved upward less rapidly than the heartbeats of those about him: 185—190—193—195—197 . . . Matthew bit his lip and clenched his fists, and was relieved to realize the older men were doing the same.

197—199—*200!*

There was a banshee cry of escaping steam and Matthew jumped in terror. But it was no burst. Gordon had let go the rake and the valve had blown off as intended. He had proved his point, and no one was disposed to argue with him now.

When the noise died away, he said to Corkran, "Inform the pilots we can get under way again. If anybody wants me, I shall be on deck."

Only then did those present realize that someone else had joined them. For a voice demanded, "Did she truly stand two hundred to the inch?"

With improbable confidence Parbury advanced into the only clear space among them, relying on his cane and his memory of having come this way before . . . more in imagination than reality. He halted almost square in front of Gordon.

"Well?" he insisted. "Was it two hundred?"

"Aye."

"Then *don't tell the newspapers*. Some day it may be useful to have power in reserve. Will the trials continue now?"

"I just said they could," Gordon grunted.

"But what did Mr. Woodley say?"

"I . . ." Gordon blinked, while the engineers exchanged glances. "I assumed he was in the pilothouse."

"Not when I left it."

"In that case—" Gordon had begun when the subject of their exchange arrived as promptly as a pantomime demon.

"She seems to have taken no harm from being run aground, which is a mercy! Burge and I have checked her fore and aft. But with respect, Mr. Gordon!"—this with a glare—"you might have let me know what you were planning. And why didn't you restart the doctor yet?" he added, rounding on Corkran.

"Mr. Roy was just about to," the chief engineer muttered. "I'll signify when we can back off."

While the *Nonpareil* was making her easy way back to the wharf, Parbury reentered the pilothouse. Trumbull, who had the wheel, exchanged glances with Hogan and, on receiving a nod, stepped back with a flourish.

"Care to judge the feel of her, Captain?" he invited.

"Would I not!" Parbury answered, and marched across the floor, letting fall his cane. He was within an inch by dead reckoning when he had to start groping. Finding the smooth wood under his fingers, he gave a deep sigh.

"She feels just like I always dreamt," he said.

Hereabouts the river was broad enough and traffic light enough for the pilots to leave him safely in charge for more than ten minutes before Hogan was obliged to resume control: the next bend was a tricky one, and a White Collar Line steamer—recognizable from far off by the white bands on her chimneys—was making across it to take advantage of slack water.

With visible regret Parbury relinquished the wheel, about to say something . . . but at the same moment the pilot of the oncoming vessel sounded the two blasts which indicated that he wanted to pass larboard to larboard.

Not waiting for permission, Parbury located the whistle lever and gave it the tugs called for to show agreement.

With a guilty smile, like a boy caught stealing cookies, he murmured, "I like the sound of that there whistle!"

"So do we," Trumbull said heartily. "It announces the approach of a boat as good as any on the river."

"I waited a long time to hear that," Parbury muttered. "And it falls sweeter on my ears than even the fine note of her whistle. I thank you, gentlemen. From the bottom of my heart I thank you for making an old worn-out man feel alive again. You salvaged the engines out of my sunken hull and I'm afloat the way I used to be."

Uneasily glancing at Trumbull, Hogan said, "You should say such things to Mr. Gordon and Mr. Woodley. We two are just hired hands."

"Oh, they paid for her," said Parbury with contempt. "I guess you have to say they made her possible.

"But it takes a pilot—don't it?—to make her *run!*"

The trials of the *Nonpareil* came as a godsend to river correspondents short of copy.

Before she reached the upstream end of her initial run, the most daring—or foolhardy—of them had retreated to the shelter of the telegraph office. The operator grew tolerably bored with the constant reappearance of such phrases as "mystery financier" and "outdoing the *Eclipse*."

Those few who took their task seriously resolved to hold back in the hope of securing an interview with Gordon, or Woodley, or best of all Parbury, whose reputation among river people was secure.

But it was not a time that favored authenticity. The legacy of all the news falsified during the war militated against factual journalism. *Sensational* was the watchword—*get there first* was the slogan.

Therefore the descriptions of the *Nonpareil's* performance that went out by cable were weird and sometimes wonderful, and all but a handful stated she was certain to take the horns of every other boat in service. Stories voicing reservation about her were predictably demoted to an inside page.

However, as soon as news broke of her acceptance by the owners, one incontrovertible fact did emerge. At last there was a steamboat on the river which a man might sanely back to beat the *Atchafalaya*.

## 8TH MARCH 1870

# FIRE TONIGHT, ASH TOMORROW

~~~~~~

"It was in New Orleans that the famous gamblers who flourished before the American Civil War learned the tricks of their trade, and it was New Orleans that started the gambling fever that swept like wildfire throughout the United States after the war. . . . Wholesale bribery and blackmail of politicians and police kept the saloons open, and by the end of 1850 there were over 500 'sawdust joints.' . . . Most of these waterfront shacks (they could hardly be called casinos) were completely corrupt, and honest games of craps could be found only in private homes."

—Alan Wykes,
*Gambling*

 The world had gone insane! Or else the *Nonpareil* had been transformed from a mere steamer into some fantastic vessel from the factory of Monsieur Verne! At any rate, the place she had today brought Matthew to bore scant resemblance to the New Orleans he remembered.

He had been impressed with the sobriety and gravity of the persons he had met here in Gordon's company, who included the bankers Marocain, the steamboat agent Mr. Knight, and even some of the entourage of Governor Warmoth, though a hoped-for appointment with the governor himself had fallen through.

Now, unpremeditatedly, the *Nonpareil*'s maiden voyage—successful enough in terms of cargo, for she had carried a vast consignment of Northern made goods, from axe blades to cream separators, but with not nearly enough passengers—had terminated on the Fat Tuesday preceding forty days of Lenten abstinence.

Which, of course, was why so few passengers had booked. Those who would have been glad to do so a week earlier had already left. Nobody in his right mind, so it was claimed, would miss Mardi Gras in New Orleans. In the old days it had been little more than a riotous orgy. Since the establishment in 1857 of the Mistick Krewe of Comus, and in imitation of it the Twelfth Night Revellers, the Krewe of Rex, and the Knights of Momus, it had been formalized into a city-wide party offering parades, masquerades, balls, singers, dancers, clowns . . .

And in the midst of this gaiety Matthew was feeling sick with terror, while at the same time tormented by a crazy urge to laugh, for Hamish Gordon was showing the world that he had knobbly knees.

A huge steamer trunk had accompanied him from Europe which generally remained, tightly roped, in the strongroom of whatever hotel he and Matthew were patronizing. For this special occasion, however, it had been opened and disgorged a suit of Highland formal dress redolent of camphor: a kilt of blue, red, green and white tartan, densely pleated; a sporran made of badger fur which supplied its lack of pockets but hung at such a level as to make its wearer, when reaching for money, grope about in a manner Matthew regarded as indecent; a green velvet jacket with silver buttons; a white lace jabot; stockings with garters that matched the kilt; shoes with silver buckles; and an ivory-handled knife worn in a sheath inside the right stocking. This last was no toy. Gordon had displayed its razor-keen edge while they were dressing at the St. Charles. Determined to spare no expense in making his amanuensis' birthday memorable, he had ordered him full evening dress and a set of pearl studs, to make up the first part of his gift.

The second was to be dinner at the Limousin. That would be tolerable—just. It was the third part that was filling the boy with dread.

Last night he had lain long awake, tormented by the horns of the worst moral

175

dilemma life had so far inflicted on him. Revelry was going on all about him then, too; the *Nonpareil* was making excellent time and even the normally abstemious Parbury had been persuaded to join the celebration Gordon called for. Seizing his chance to slip away, Matthew retreated to his stateroom and tried to sort out his feelings.

On the one hand, he admired his employer, albeit reluctantly, and Gordon made no secret of his interludes with prostitutes; since he recruited Matthew there had been eight, and one had entailed visits to a doctor.

By the same token, Matthew had known since arriving at his uncle's hotel that men and women had relations outside marriage and that what they did together was pleasurable. Last summer a boy staying there had further enlightened him with the aid of French postcards filched from his father. As a result, part of Matthew's mind was aglow with excitement to think he was at last to be admitted to the world of full-grown men.

On the other hand he had been brought up to believe that the delights of the flesh were sinful, and that rules and customs governing bodily functions were God's hallmark setting the rational creation apart from the beasts. On a less-than-conscious level he could not credit the act his parents must have engaged in to generate himself.

Nor, inevitably, could he do as he desperately wanted: pray for a successful outcome to his first encounter with a woman. To pray for help in sinning seemed like the grandest style of blasphemy.

When at last fitful sleep overtook him, however, he had a vivid dream which made him laugh so much he almost woke himself. He saw Adam and Eve disporting themselves in the Garden of Eden and realized that until Satan called it so sex had not been wicked.

One final surge of that sense of well-being returned when Gordon, resplendent in his Scottish garb, emerged to inspect his protégé.

"Enough to turn any girl's head, aren't you—*just?*" he said with a broad grin, deliberately tagging on the Americanism. "You keep that up, and not only that . . . !"

With a jab of his elbow into Matthew's ribs.

Then, in the disarming fashion typical of him, one moment before the boy could take offense he went on: "Should be his father who does this office for a young man! I trust I'll prove an acceptable surrogate. At least let me say: were your parents still among us, they would surely be proud to see you now."

But even as the carriage Gordon had hired rolled through the delirious streets, Matthew's faint optimism leaked away.

He felt as though he were about to sit an examination in a subject for which, though all his life he had been warned about it, he had never yet managed to find an honest textbook.

Let alone a less than lying teacher.

Just before the carriage halted in front of the Limousin, Matthew saw a white man crawling on hands and knees, drooling and moaning like an animal. His shirt was foul with the red wine he was still intermittently vomiting. Passers-by, spat-

tered to their boot tops with mud—for the street was as usual a quagmire—
hooted with laughter at the spectacle.

"One who can't take it!" was Gordon's blunt comment.

Seconds later the entrance hall closed on them like the jaws of a marble shark
with people for teeth. Signs outside announced that a band had been specially
engaged for tonight, under the direction of M. Gaston d'Aurade of the Grand
Philharmonic Hall, and there it was, playing as though trying to drown the chatter
of the seething crowd. In retaliation all voices were raised near screaming pitch.
Matthew thought of Belshazzar's feast, and trembled.

Waiters relieved them of coats and hats and ushered them to where Woodley
was sitting with some of the others to whom Gordon had extended invitations.
For most, the notice had been too short. The Marocains were committed already
as were the Moyne family, who were members of the Krewe of Comus and attending its Mardi Gras ball along with Arthur Gattry escorting Louisette; Hugo
and Stella Spring were at another similar ball, while Parbury had bluntly retorted
that, even had he not been engaged for dinner with colleagues from Pilots' Guild,
he would not have patronized an associate of that traitor Drew.

But Hogan and Trumbull, and Ian McNab and Sam Iliff, had been glad to
accept. Matthew was less than happy to find the clerks joining in his—"his"—
birthday celebration; both, as he learned during the trip from Cincinnati, were
married men, and the older, McNab, had a son Matthew's age.

And yet . . . and yet . . . ! At the back of his mind hovered the possibility that,
pearl studs and nine-course meals and his first woman notwithstanding, his true
birthday gift was apt to be a set of guidelines, which would enable him to steer
between the shoals of public and private morality. In the world of childhood anything so much as a guilty rub of the genital organ was sinful and punishable. In
the world of adults fornication was admired, even applauded. So was adultery,
provided it was not with a friend's wife. Or . . . No, that could not be exactly
right, because—

Well, anyhow, maybe they were only here to indulge some other weakness,
like gluttony.

His muddled thoughts were cut short. All of a sudden Gordon was introducing
him to—

"Mr. Barber! My amanuensis and protégé Matthew Rust whose anniversary I
plead guilty to having overlooked in the excitement of commissioning the *Nonpareil!*"

"Many happy returns, young fellow!" Barber said, offering a hand. But it was
clear he was primarily interested in Gordon, for a second later he was saying,
"Since this morning Mr. Woodley has been regaling me with tales of your new
steamer's unparalleled velocity!"

"I'll warrant telegraph messages beat him to it," Gordon riposted smugly.

"Yes, of course, and just as well, for you were barely in time to reserve my last
table tonight."

"Still, we made it," Gordon said, affably patting him on the arm. "And you
made one *extra* reservation, didn't you?"

Barber sketched a bow. "I surely did. And Elvira is an admirable choice. "She will be awaiting Mr. Rust at the end of dinner."

 Under his ruffled shirt front, under his gold-embroidered vest, Gaston felt his heart ought to be swelling with pride. It kept declining to oblige.

Why? After so many trials and tribulations he was back at the hotel his cousin had founded, on a one-night contract admittedly, but in the presence of a glittering company. Surely they could not all be deaf to his skill! Surely someone was bound to notice how brilliant a sound he was conjuring from this scratch bunch of musicians, half white, several mulatto, one discreetly shadowed at the rear of the dais who was *excessively* African . . . but all to some extent schooled and capable of reading.

An ironical meeting had taken place earlier in the day. The mustachioed leader of the band parading in support of a strike on the waterfront last fall had heard about work at the Limousin and arrived with a bagful of battered instuments, certain of being hired. But, as Gaston had suspected, he proved unable to read even the simplest arrangement. He had found work here in the end, but not what he was expecting. In a borrowed jacket much too tight for him he passed and repassed the bandstand, carrying loaded trays like any water boy, and each time favored Gaston with a murderous glare. That too should have lifted the conductor's spirits. It was amusing, *n'est-ce pas?*

Yet as the evening wore on he grew ever more despondent.

Then of a sudden he spotted the millionaire he had so nearly met aboard the *Isaiah Plott.* Luck was on his side after all. Now he must call forth miracles of melody and tone. Tonight must mark a breakthrough!

Must.

Today he had learned that the Grand Philharmonic Hall was unlikely to pay its way beyond Easter. There was talk of conversion to a roller-skating rink, to compete with the one at Mechanics' Hall on Dryades. If that happened his contract might be extended: for a year at a reduction of twenty percent . . .

With all his might Gaston willed that his miscellaneous band should touch the heart of the financier. He whipped the air with his baton like a stagecoach driver hurrying his team through a pass in Indian territory.

But these were players used to going their own way. All his exertions made no discernible difference to the music, nor the audience's reaction.

Gaston's heart ceased trying to swell.

To the fuming Manuel, however, even that much success was something to be jealous of. Could that jumped-up French idiot outplay the musicians he hired? Could he play at all? Perhaps the piano, genteel ornament of ladies' drawing rooms, but could be handle a man's instrument? Could he march all day in hot sun with a trombone or a tuba? He'd melt like lard before the band reached the end of the street!

After swallowing his pride because so many of his friends assured him that— short of playing at one of the grand balls—this was the plum of the Mardi Gras jobs; after being kept waiting so long for an audition that there was no chance to find another booking tonight; after being obliged to don this horrible straitjacket and wear out his arms with the weight of all this food and wine and liquor and tread the same damned path to and from the kitchen for hours on end; after all these affronts to his dignity, Manuel José Miguel Campos y Gomez was on the verge of eruption.

He sincerely hoped he was going to get through this night without doing what he most wanted: hurl a laden tray at Gaston's resplendent vest.

But it was going to be hard.

 For only the third time since the invitation was extended, Drew planned to take up Barber's offer of accommodation at the Limousin.

He had hoped not to be at New Orleans for Mardi Gras. He had spent Thanksgiving and Christmas of last year with Susannah and her children; they had proposed he return to St. Louis at this season, and he had intended to do so. The vagaries of the river being what they were, he had nonetheless been obliged to lay over here, and with spring coming on he felt it convenient to resume his regular trade and his regular day of departure: Thursdays, for Louisville.

Which in the ordinary course of events would have been most welcome. Every winter he chafed under the restrictions climate imposed, to the point where once Tyburn had declared he must be a railroader at heart, risking a blow from his knobbed staff.

Ketch got away with it. No one else could have. Not even Drew's ex-cub Fernand.

He thought frequently about Fernand. Although their parting had been almost as acrimonious as their coming together—he never having forgiven the youngster for invoking a law he loathed—he kept tabs on his former pupil's progress and was gruffly pleased whenever he secured a post superior to the previous one. Fernand had spent last summer in the upper-river trades, chiefly between St. Louis and Vicksburg, after a long spell of drudgery in short trades on the lower river. Drew approved. In his view all pilots should always keep abreast of what was going on throughout the river system, old-fashioned though such an attitude might be compared with the specialization some of the younger captains were advocating.

But then, the noisiest among them was not himself a pilot.

"A little learning is a dangerous thing!
Drink deep, or taste not the Pierian spring:

There shallow draughts intoxicate the brain,
And drinking largely sobers us again."

That was a quotation he had become extremely fond of, for it matched his own opinion to a T. He kept resolving to locate someone who could tell him what "Pierian" meant.


During Christmas at Susannah's he had talked in glowing terms about Fernand, to the point where—with the sort of gentle insight he had come to love in her—his sister-in-law inquired why he had not kept on the young man as a permanent co-pilot.

Taken by surprise, Drew produced an unpremeditated answer. "Oh, I taught him what I could! Maybe one of these days he'll realize he needs to know more, and I'm the likeliest to help out. Maybe not. But it's in the nature of young men to break loose and make their own way in the world. Their own mistakes, too."

Susannah nodded wisely. "Those, at least, whose fathers have not so behaved as to render the prospect of adulthood unattractive . . . You should bring him to meet me, Hosea. You make him sound like the sort of son I always imagined you would want."

At first he was inclined to be angry: did she even yet not know that the reason he was single was because he cared more for her than any woman he had met? Then the deeper import of her remark hit home, and he heaved a sigh.

"You're right. I'd hire him back tomorrow if he asked."

That same evening Elphin, proud of the theology he had imbibed at college, tried to advance a defense of slavery based on the curse of Ham, whose descendants were doomed to be hewers of wood and drawers of water.

"My boy drew no more water than most, and less than some!" Drew barked, making another of his rare attempts at a joke. "And there's a fair slice of Ham in him!"

But the company thought he was referring to something else, so his play on words fell flat.

Not, indeed, that the atmosphere was conducive to merriment. Susannah was as well as could be expected; she suffered with aches in her joints, and there were signs of the poor nervous co-ordination that later might become paralysis, but she was able to lead a fairly normal existence. Jerome, on the other hand, was declining and could only rarely join the family. Most of his time was spent either in bed in a darkened room, or attending an expensive steam-bath establishment where vapors based on pine extract, sulphur and mentholatum gave temporary relief from his wheezing and coughing.

Maintaining his late brother's family was proving costly. Now and then he was afraid he might say so out loud. Perhaps it was as well that chance had landed him here.

At all events he would have been happy to pass today as he generally did in port: carrying out inspections, eating his meals alone and retiring early with a volume of poetry to the stateroom which was far more of a home to him than any building on shore—including the one he had bought for Susannah.

But one thing prevented him. On waking this morning he had discovered, moored in plain view, the new *Nonpareil* aswarm with sightseers.

Briefly he had been tempted to go look her over himself. Better sense had prevailed, and he had done no more than examine her meticulously through field glasses. He had been told most of the details of her construction, since river gossip had centered on it for months past. What he saw confirmed his already-formed impression. Probably she was as fast as claimed. Conditions would have to be absolutely favorable, though, if she were to outrun the *Atchafalaya*. She looked top-heavy. In his attempt to reduce her underwater cross section, thus increase her speed, Parbury had overreached himself.

The rival boat's presence, however, loomed on the horizon of his awareness like a storm cloud, and it was not long before he realized it would be unbearable to remain here overnight with the city rejoicing about him and himself brooding over the all-too-distinct possibility that the *Nonpareil* might boast unseen resources. It was after all true that she operated at a pressure fifty pounds higher than the *Atchafalaya*'s . . .

Therefore he sent a message to Barber and, when all was secure about the boat and two armed watchmen had been set to stand overnight guard, quit her to enjoy, if he could, some small share of the festivities.

 From the instant of her putting in hand, the new *Nonpareil* had effected a transformation in Miles Parbury. Publicly he had controlled himself in the old days, well enough for his acquaintances to forgive him when he did lose his temper—as who would not forgive anyone that sacrificed his eyesight for a cause they too believed in? Privately his behavior was a different matter, especially when his insomnia and his wife's acutest fits of rheumatism coincided.

But the sudden restoration of self-confidence, due to others and particularly Gordon and Woodley giving evidence of their faith in him, worked a wonder. Soon he was even heard humming songs popular when he was a boy.

Now the *Nonpareil* had made her first run and been proved fast, he was in seventh heaven.

Not that his rediscovered happiness pleased Adèle. Instead she resented it, because day by day, bar occasional deceptive remissions, her plight grew worse. Then, to compound her misery, she began to lose teeth. Since she was no longer fit to leave the house, a dentist had to be found who would bring his instruments and chloroform to her. Dr. Malone recommended one. Competent he might be; he was also casual, and after suffering his ministrations Adèle went back to an old tune: how Dorcas had betrayed her by not fetching the Electric Doctor. On days when the pain was fierce, she would scream that Dorcas was hurting her deliberately when helping her to her commode, or the devotions she grimly persisted in.

So far Dorcas had resisted the temptation to turn her mistress's charge from fantasy to reality. But it was getting stronger, for at the moment when she learned that Fernand had been turned from the house with an insult, something deep within her, already eroded by her parents' rejection, had seemed to crumble. What to call it? Charity, perhaps, not in the modern sense of scraps of food and cast-off clothing for the deserving poor, but her meed of loving-kindness. When she looked at herself in the glass next morning, she recognized that she had grown older of a sudden. The light of youth had been put out behind her eyes.

Hitherto she had fought the annoyance she felt at Mrs. Parbury's reproaches, the captain's attempts to fondle her breasts under the pretext of blindness. Henceforth she had no qualms about deceiving them for her own advantage.

The following day she had to escort Parbury to the Pilots' Guild again. Instead of returning at once, she continued to Griswold's and brazenly marched in—discovering to her vast relief that the customers included women, quite respectable in appearance, rather than just men as she had feared. Into Mr. Griswold's own hands she delivered an envelope superscribed *M*r *Fernand Lamenthe, late of Str. Atchafalaya. To be called for.* It contained a note begging him to make contact by any means possible. And she had signed it: "With fondest love."

If she had lost charity, she had gained patience, or was obliged to. Ten days elapsed before she heard from Fernand, for he had secured a trip to Memphis— an engagement few pilots cared to undertake, as the city was continually ravaged by yellow fever. She occupied the interim making inquiries about Cherouen. It was not long before she convinced herself that his refusal to attend Mrs. Parbury was not due to having too many patients, for he was accepting others every week . . . all wealthy. All *extremely* wealthy. But her mistress told her she was lying.

And then more patience was demanded of her. Willing though he also was to pledge his love, Fernand made it plain that during his time as a cub he had resolved not to marry until he was not merely a qualified but an established pilot, commanding the Guild's full rate. To support a wife and family on his present earnings, he would have to go on accepting every trip he was offered, no matter how clumsy a tub the boat was or how disgusting her cargo.

Within a year—two at most—he should at last be admitted as a full-fledged member of the river fraternity. Already some of his influential colleagues, like Barfoot and Tyburn, were complaining about the way he was cold-shouldered, risking the Olympian wrath of Parbury and its dutiful echo among the Parbury Pirates.

Let the breakthrough come this summer! Dorcas prayed for that with all the fervor at her command. But not at church. True, on learning that Fernand was Catholic, she had temporarily breached the wall of Mrs. Parbury's detestation by agreeing to accept instruction and making a spectacular conversion. Now she attended mass at least twice a month and likewise made regular confession. But this was all sham. She enjoyed planning what she would say to the confessor, calculating how to make it credible without ever quite telling the truth.

She had an excellent model to imitate. The next time Mrs. Parbury woke in agony following her servant's reception into the church, she decided the conversion was a trick to disguise the fact that her husband was being unfaithful with her. Thus encouraged, Parbury's pawing and poking redoubled. Dorcas wanted to slap his face. But she mastered herself and made out she was content with a reproof no fiercer than a mother's to her child. Meantime she was milder than that mother's milk to her mistress, and when the priest next called he was able to damp down the fires of her fury. Still, the embers smouldered—on Dorcas's side too.

How much longer must she endure? How much longer must she feed the captain with false compliments, or beg forgiveness of his wife for offenses she had not committed?

Stifling all such thoughts, she closed the house door and resignedly allowed Parbury's hand to enfold hers. Ordinarily, because of the unpredictable schedules of its members, the Pilots' Guild could not hold a carnival celebration; the level of the river might prevent too many people from attending. However, last year a steamboaters' convention had been held in New Orleans and much business had been successfully transacted. In the first flush of enthusiasm it had been agreed that any participants who could should meet again on Mardi Gras at Martineau's, the restaurant most patronized by river folk.

Thither Dorcas must now guide her master, despite the fact that every street was awash with riotous crowds.

But she was prepared to brave anything. For she also had a rendezvous tonight.

 "Isn't it wonderful?" Imelda Moyne gushed at her husband, clasping his arm with one hand while vigorously fanning herself with the other. And added, turning to her son for confirmation, "Auberon, isn't it *magnificent?*"

While in Europe, Auberon had attended parties in a Venetian palazzo, the castle of a German duke, a château on the Loire whose owners had contrived to remain its owners despite three revolutions, and sundry embassies. He had repressed his democratic principles long enough to bow before royalty and nobility who could trace their ancestry back past Columbus. In consequence even this, the finest of New Orleans's Mardi Gras balls, was signally failing to impress him.

Admittedly some of the biddies were stunning, particularly those who had abjured the ugly fashion of the crinoline and were wearing gowns with the bustle now popular in Europe. A handful were even swinging their butts, when dancing, with movements that would do credit to a cooche-cooche girl. But it was all for show, like the vast loads of jewelry they—and even more their mothers—were sporting in the harsh radiance of the gasoliers. One could not imagine them fainting handily into a gentleman's arms, as their European sisters did on the least excuse.

Moreover he suspected that the caviar had been spun out with paddlefish eggs and the butter with something resembling that ingenious new French food for the poor, margarine, about which several people had interrogated him this evening because, as they said, now they had to pay servants wages as well as keeping them they were being bled dry by the expense.

Still, the wine was drinkable and there was plenty of it. Feigning to agree with his mother, Auberon helped himself to another glass from a passing tray and went back to his conversation—if such it could be called—with Arthur Gattry's sister Violet and her husband Morton Farmiloe, who had somehow been convinced that the future was to be made secure for sugar planters by a process to transform molasses into a dry hard substance like celluloid.

At least Farmiloe's small talk was marginally more cheerful than his wife's. Last time she had come here it had been to hear Gottschalk play, and she was telling anybody who would listen how cut up she still was about his death.

Louisette was dancing with Arthur, as befitted a girl and her betrothed. Her persistence had worn down her parents' opposition; the engagement had been announced on New Year's Day and the wedding set for early April, although some considered Lenten weddings unlucky.

Auberon too would gladly have taken the floor, if only to escape. But every girl to whom he had contrived an introduction had displayed a full card. Really it was vexatious! And there was a distinct shortage of jolly fellows of his own age with whom he could at least have cracked jokes. If only Joel . . . But that was halfway past repair.

"Excuse me! You have lately been to Paris, I understand—the city of my ancestors, as it happens."

Turning in response to a tap on his shoulder, Auberon answered lightly, "Oh, they say good Americans go to Paris when they die, so I decided to be ahead of schedule."

And found that the man addressing him was taller than himself, black-haired and sporting a black moustache, with red highlights on either cheekbone and at the tip of his nose. Conveniently, the Farmiloes had been distracted by people on their other side, while his mother and father were moving away to congratulate the family of a girl who, like Louisette last year, had been attendant on the "queen."

Grateful as much for that as for this, Auberon accepted a slim hand-rolled panatela from a tortoiseshell case which the stranger proffered. The tobacco was outstanding. He said so.

"Ah, you're a man of taste. I was put on to these by my chief nurse. Apparently some relative of hers is in the business."

Valetudinarianism being common in New Orleans, it was on the tip of Auberon's tongue to express sympathy. But "chief nurse" did not sound like what an invalid would say, and in the nick of time he corrected himself.

"Do I take it you're a medical man?"

"Denis Cherouen," the other said, offering his hand. Introducing himself, Auberon shook it warmly. By all accounts this was one of the few truly progressive people in the city, ever alert to modern ideas. Report had it also that he was a sporting type, a connoisseur of quadroon girls, and was as ready to oblige the ladies as the gentlemen with his professional services when some unlooked-for consequence of obedience to the behests of Cupid needed rectification. On that score Auberon had so far escaped lightly. But there was, of course, another medical matter on his mind . . .

"You're Parisian yourself?" he probed.

Smiling, Cherouen shook his head. "No, but my father's father met his wife there, and they married before removing to the New World."

"You've visited France?"

"Perhaps I shall one day. But currently there's little to interest men of my calling at Paris or indeed elsewhere in Europe."

Auberon looked puzzled. "Forgive a layman's ignorance, but according to the press many significant advances have recently been made by European *savants*—Dr. Pasteur, for example."

"Never believe what you read in the papers! The quacks now being so blatantly puffed adhere to the pernicious germ theory of disease. As though a vital organism could be reduced to its original clay by a process that amounts to nothing more than putrefaction! No, sir: the vital spark is forced out of the human frame by a far subtler and more aethereal enemy, the *inverse*—as it were—of the power which speaks to us from the skies and inheres in all organic matter. From the valiant fire of lightning to the sparks a comb may draw on a dry night, and as I predict astronomers will concede before the century is out from the very stars, including our own Sun!—from all these mute witnesses that the Lord has set before the eyes of the unseeing, the truth declares itself to those who are prepared to receive it! I've proved it over and over in my practice."

As he spoke his voice had risen to a declamatory pitch; on the last sentence it dropped back to a matter-of-fact level.

This was precisely the kind of talk Auberon had dreamed of hearing for a year or more, since the increasing frequency with which he now coughed blood had driven him reluctantly to a series of European doctors, none of whom could offer him anything better than a bed-ridden life in a mountain sanatorium—the last way he wanted to spend his time on Earth. He had never heard Cherouen's name mentioned in conjunction with tuberculosis, but that reference to putrefaction had struck home.

He ventured, "You think the European doctors are dishonest or just misguided?"

"A little of each," Cherouen sighed. "Ah, but it's inevitable, I guess. The stultifying impact of that ancient continent, where the very air must by now be saturated with the residue of outworn superstitions—this alone suffices, I submit, to explain the credulousness and bigotry of such people. They have elevated ordinary cleanliness—for who in his right mind would wish to go about in garments soiled with pus and sputum, let alone have it directly on his skin?—they have hoisted this simple natural principle on to a plinth of gold, and there made oblation to it like a pagan idol! Well was it said by Ambroise Paré, their humble and nonetheless brilliant predecessor, 'I dress the wounds and God heals them.' Would his modern successors had half his nobility of spirit!"

He shook his head lugubriously, then collected himself. A smile broke across his face.

"One of my besetting faults is to lecture strangers! Do forgive me. We are here to enjoy ourselves, not ponder matters of life and death."

"Enjoy," Auberon repeated thoughtfully. "Well, sir, to tell the truth I was better entertained the day I went to view the Paris morgue."

Cherouen raised one eyebrow. "Perhaps I should revise my opinion of the air of Europe! In that remark I detect considerable insight."

That came close to making Auberon bridle; he had had his bellyful of being patronized. But he bit back the reply he intended and looked a question instead.

"You're correct in dismissing occasions like this as worthless," Cherouen stated. "Why? Because they never give free rein to our basic impulses. Is a horse, that can gallop all day and jump great obstacles, a better horse for being broken to carriage harness, docked, put in blinders? Is a man better for being starved of what his wild ancestors took for granted, an active and dangerous existence punctuated by delirious bouts of such joy as no words could recapture?"

Cautiously, for this was a controversial subject, Auberon said, "You seem to accept the doctrine of the survival of the fittest."

"How can any rational person fail to?" Cherouen cried. "And how can anyone fail to see how this sort of shallow pastime is undermining the vitality of our race? Did not the Romans establish mastery over their decadent neighbors by force of will? They had the right idea! They kept their people permanently at the sticking point by the shows and games they held in their arenas, to remind the populace that life and death are a hand's breadth apart, and regaled themselves with orgies afterwards." His voice had been rising again; once more it dropped to the pitch of confidentiality, and he turned to fix Auberon with magnetic eyes.

"How debased is the man of today in comparison with his ancestors! Then, the supreme combination of brawn with brain created its own reward—gratification of the physiological necessity which since time immemorial has corresponded to, and in the course of evolution resulted in, longevity and ascendancy. I allude, you realize, to the frequent discharge of the seminal vesicles, which in our ancestors' case answered to possession of the greatest number of females, hence to the maximum number of progeny. It cannot be otherwise than beneficial, even today, to copy the example which our forebears set, particularly when we are besieged and beset by members of a patently inferior species *following the very course I'm recommending*! Is it a secret that when Dr. John and Marie Laveau seduced ladies of respectable family into joining their beastly ceremonies, what they hoped to do was plant the inferior seed of Africa in competition with the European strain?" Cherouen drained his glass and added savagely, "It's happening! Happening all about us! Out in California the Chinese are at it and have been for a generation. Soon enough the Indians will be given their chance too! Men of our race will have rendered themselves decadent, like the last Romans, thanks to prissy 'morality' and devitalizing 'good manners'! And our women, or rather what should have been our women, will give themselves willingly to the stronger and more virile barbaric races. When I witness a spectacle like this"—he made a large gesture with his empty glass—"I don't look *at* it, I look *past* it. I foresee doom for the white race in America, because the vacuous ceremonial it took Europeans

millennia to develop is being imported ready-made, saving us the trouble of being
the instruments of our own downfall. I don't know why I decided to come tonight.
I wish I hadn't."

A strange and heady excitement was taking possession of Auberon by now.
Even before leaving for Europe he had heard of the teachings of the Comte de
Gobineau; during his travels he had again and again encountered reference to
them. Many Frenchmen and Italians, sympathetic to the Southern cause, had
sorrowfully shaken their heads when thinking of the difference it might have made
had followers of Gobineau been able to put the "peculiar institution" on a proper
scientific basis, therewith to defy the North and the world at large. Combined
with Darwin's, his ideas . . .

Auberon looked covertly about him. There seemed a fair chance of slipping
away unnoticed.

"I wonder," he said sidelong, "whether you would care to—ah—remove to a
more stimulating environment."

Cherouen's lips parted in a broad grin. "A place where—shall we say?—a white
man may plant his seed on the fertile ground of an inferior race?"

"Precisely."

"Then let's go."

 In the city ruled by revelry there were many who did not
join in. Some could not afford to. Some held that carnival was
a device of the devil, and ostentatiously headed for the cathedral or one of the countless other churches. Some had devotions of their own to
attend to; that dark faith which ran like a subterranean Mississippi through the
lives of so many Orleanians shared its holy days with the Christian calendar, and
several of its saints and patrons too.

And some were simply too unhappy.

Caesar had been sacked.

So far this year things had gone tolerably well for him. True, his increasing
prosperity had aroused the jealousy of the others lodged under the same roof,
whom he had begun to think of as friends for want of anybody closer, so he had
been obliged to move out, but the white man whose stand-in he had been for so
long had taken to uttering hints about getting a better post and leaving Caesar
half, instead of a quarter, of his pay. Thus encouraged, he had found himself a
*chambre garnie* in a house owned by a Creole landlady who before the war had
been kept by a rich white man—but he had died of a Union bullet.

At first she had been reluctant to take in Caesar, with his dark skin and "bad"
hair, but the prospect of regular rent persuaded her. He had had no difficulty
keeping up his payments, even though the promised increase had not yet materialized. Apart from a few drinks at a weekend, and a woman when the need be-

came unbearable, he spent little on himself. Most of what he earned, he saved. To what end? He often wondered. Vaguely he imagined renting a small house where he could set up as a machinery repairman. Now and then, too, he thought of remarrying. But the urge to raise children had left him long ago, and while there were whores willing to take his money, that was enough.

But last payday his unofficial boss had failed to show up. His diffident inquiries among the white men who also worked on the wharf provoked scornful laughter; didn't he know that Ed's cousin had fixed him a plum job on a brand-new boat, so he wouldn't be coming back?

Furious, but hiding the fact behind a meek expression, he decided he had nothing to lose by presenting himself to the paymaster and pointing out that he had been running Mr. Williams's crane longer than Mr. Williams himself, so he deserved his wages. The paymaster was not an unreasonable man.

But luck was against him.

In the office he found one of the firm's northern directors, who had come to New Orleans partly on business, partly to spend Mardi Gras here. Caesar, not knowing who this stranger was, explained his case—and the northerner exploded with rage. That one of their expensive modern cranes had been left in the care of a nigger was disgraceful! Get rid of him right now and find a white engineer by Monday!

There was nothing that could be done.

Miserable in his neat lodging house, where the other tenants would not acknowledge his existence even by being rude to him, he had moped away the weekend, knowing it was pointless to look for other skilled work until the holiday was over. Tonight he could stand it no longer. He had drawn on his savings and set out for the place where he had formerly lived. Perhaps those who had driven him away might be in a better mood, pleased to see him again. Or if not him personally, then his money. It should be enough for a barrel of beer and a quart of whiskey and some po'boys. And maybe someone would mention a job he could apply for.

Bribery, Caesar thought bitterly.

But how else could one survive in this sick world? Not by fighting; that had been shown. At least money was a kinder weapon than a gun.

 Single-handed, all afternoon Eulalie Lamenthe had been making the house ready: stripped the beds and turned the mattresses, drawn the curtains, covered mirrors, and shut away anything else that might give back a reflection, as the blade of a knife or the bowl of a spoon, for fear an uninvited witness might behold what was to pass.

She had two servants; they had leave to join the merrymaking. There remained a risk they might have overheard something she let slip. To silence them she laid on a platter an ox's tongue surrounded by grass plucked from a grave and drove a nail through it, muttering the while something between a curse and a prayer.

She was trembling. The import of what she had done was starting to weigh upon her mind. When she first consented to accept the burden of Athalie's knowledge, she had thought of little save her son, whom she could surely protect if she possessed such magic, although she had not forgiven him for defying her and becoming a pilot. The Marocain brothers were going from success to success, and ironically among their latest triumphs was the financing of the *Nonpareil,* which everyone said would break all records and become the most profitable steamer on the Mississippi. If only Fernand had dug his heels in, then with the help of his mother's new powers he could by this time have recovered his proper share of the bank, perhaps broken away and founded a firm on his own. Instead he had opted for a career as chancy and rock-strewn as a rapids.

Moreover, he mocked at her beliefs.

But they were founded in reality. With every new scrap of information she acquired from her cousin, Eulalie became more convinced of it. And one terrifying truth above all obsessed her now.

She had been assured, when she made her pact with Athalie, that she had already paid for her learning. Her man—her two daughters—what more could be required?

But there were those who said that the god known to his followers as Damballah was the same Christians called Satan. And everybody knew what Satan charged for the making of a witch. To have given souls before the event was not enough. One must be surrendered afterward as well.

She had dismissed Cudjo for making too many suggestions about another offering. For all she could tell, he might have gone over to the intruder nobody knew, Mam'zelle Josephine. She half hoped he had, for that would imply he had lost interest in furthering her own power.

Fernand had rebelled against her. He had insulted her. And was still her son!

Some said he was involved with a woman—a servant, pretty, but besmirched with a bastard that luckily had not lived. Very well; most men had *affaires* before marrying. But a marriage was the least she wanted from her boy! He must live long enough to father a family, and never mind who his wife was!

Yet she had sworn to Athalie she would carry on her work. That meant confronting Josephine. To battle her would call for all Athalie's skills and maybe more. Therefore there could be no question of evading the full price.

The dilemma was giddying. Sometimes she thought her head would burst apart.

From the front door came a startling knock. She froze like a deer at bay. Suddenly she felt trapped by her clothes, by her body, as though her spirit wished to shed all impediments and flee. It was too soon for callers to arrive! The tall clocks and the small ones agreed; there were many in the house, that she was about to stop because their ticking might disturb tonight's ceremony.

So who could it be?

Her breathing grew easier. Perhaps some Mardi Gras prankster? Perhaps there was no one on the threshold now, the person having run off—

But the knocker rapped again.

In darkness she braved the journey and let the door gape on its security chain. Alphonse had ordered it fitted; he prized his mistress.

On the threshold was a very thin high-yellow girl, her eye whites enormous in her shadowed face. At the side of the street waited a carriage, its driver statue-still with whip and reins poised.

"Who are you?" Eulalie whispered.

Convulsively the girl thrust toward the narrow opening a magnificent white lily. By reflex Eulalie took it, though she knew she might be making a dire mistake.

"From Mam'zelle Josephine," the girl said. "Your cousin Athalie is dead."

She spun on her heel and fled toward the carriage. Eulalie was left immobile, in her hand the flower and in her mind a vision of unspeakable disaster.

 Of late Parbury had taken to embracing Dorcas before parting from her at his destination, with many protestations of fondness and dependence. She suffered that, and would have to do so for a while yet. Tonight, though, infected with carnival spirit, he not only embraced but kissed her, and but for a prompt turn of the head would have made it on her lips.

She disengaged gently, reminding him that this was a public place, and wished him a pleasant evening with his friends. It looked probable; Martineau's was ablaze with light, and strains of lively music drifted from it.

A doorman appeared and greeted Parbury, and Dorcas was able to hurry away in vast relief. Leading Parbury to believe she felt affection for him had rendered her life infinitely more bearable, for now he took her side automatically in any dispute with his wife. But the risk was growing that one day he might assail her virtue, and she was revolted by the idea of a blind man old enough to be her father taking pleasure from her body.

On the other hand, Fernand . . .

The moment she rounded the corner she transformed herself from the meek person the Parburys knew into the other Dorcas, the version reserved for her lover. A few months ago she had bought from a second-hand dealer a man's opera cape of fine black gabardine with a lining of red silk. With the help of Fibby she had altered it into a wholly reversible cloak. Mrs. Parbury, who had only seen its dark side, had grudgingly approved her servant's economy.

A twitch sufficed to turn it inside out, and it was rich red with black border and collar. Several men whistled at the effect, and she favored them with a smile before setting out for the corner near Griswold's where she and Fernand regularly met.

* * *

His face lit up at the sight of her. Casting her arms around him, she kissed him shamelessly, drawing back at last to say in a near-gasp, "Here's your scarlet woman again, Mr. Lamenthe!"

With a laugh he took her arm.

"Where shall we go? What shall we do? There's so much to see tonight!"

"All I want to see is you," she said, her tone suddenly intense. "Oh, Fernand, I wish we didn't have to wait so long to get married! And even if we do—yes, I know, I know!"—checking him before he could recite all the reasons—"I wish we could go somewhere and make love. Real love. Total love. My darling, I so much want to be all yours!"

She spun around to confront him, taking his hands in hers.

"Is there *nowhere*?" she concluded pleadingly.

He hesitated. Though he no longer lived at his mother's house, where his visits grew increasingly rarer, there was no question of taking her to the place where he lodged while in the city, since it was run "on respectable principles, for gentlemen only."

At length he said, "There's only one place I can think of."

"We'll go there! Right away! Is it far! Must we take a streetcar?" Her eyes sparkled.

"But"—as though she had not spoken—"there's a risk."

"Life is dangerous if you live it properly, and I want to!"

"A risk you might be taken for—for a harlot." Fernand uttered the words with difficulty.

"Which is not something you want said about your future wife?"

"Naturally!"

"But *I* don't care! I love you and I want you!" Abruptly she was almost crying. "Where is this place?"

"I was thinking of . . ." Once more a pause. "I was thinking of the Hotel Limousin."

"Oh, yes! The one with an entrance for ladies who aren't ladies!"

"How did you hear about that?" he demanded, taking her arm again and resuming their walk, for the crowds were constantly on the move and it was impossible to stand in one spot.

"Never you mind!" she retorted with a toss of her head.

He gave her a sidelong stare, then smiled against his will.

"But that's not why I suggested it," he said. "They have—well, their regular girls. An outsider would be thrown back on the street if she tried to go in that door! No, I had in mind something more fundamental. They say the owner, Mr. Barber, is making amends for a shameful episode in his past. At all events people like—"

A scowl accompanied the next words; he always so detested having to utter them.

"—*like us* may freely patronize his premises. This can't be said of all hotels."

"Praise God that there is one, then," Dorcas said positively, "Take me there.

Let us dine in public and spend the night together and not be ashamed of our love any more!"

"But if you don't come home surely the Parburys—"

She cut him short. "Fibby is to say I already am indoors. Neither of them will doubt her."

Fernand gazed at her with such concentration, he almost tripped over a drunken man sprawled on the banquette.

"Are you wondering whether you want me for your wife after all?" Dorcas demanded, real fear in her voice.

"No, a million times no! I was thinking there's nothing in the world I want more. But . . . Well, tonight there may be no vacant rooms."

"How can we be sure unless we go there?"

"You're right." Once more he halted, and this time hugged her close. "Oh, my darling! If we can—if we only can—I shall forever date our marriage from tonight!"

"Me too," she whispered close to his ear. "Now let's hurry!"

Piercing the hubbub of the Limousin's lobby, a voice called, "Say, Captain Drew!"

Delivering his overnight bag to a bellboy, Drew glanced around.

"Siskin, sir—Joel Siskin! New Orleans *Intelligencer!*" Shedding overcoat, hat, gloves and cane into the charge of a waiter, the reporter revealed himself in evening dress of good cut but shabby and fractionally too tight. He added, "I've interviewed you aboard the *Atchafalaya.*"

For the sake of politeness Drew inquired, "Are you here on business?"

"Not in the strict sense, thank heaven." Joel brushed back a stray lock of hair. "No, my work's over for today. Took longer than I expected, though. Result is, I'm late. I'm to join Mr. Gordon's party. Seems that boy of his is making his birthday tonight."

"Hamish Gordon? Is he here?"

"And Captain Woodley. You didn't know?"

"I just arrived," Drew muttered, eyes roving the hall.

"I . . ." Joel hesitated. "Dare I ask what you think of the *Nonpareil?*"

"No!"—reverting to his habitual curtness.

"Have you seen her? I believe she's—"

"Mr. Siskin, you said you were through with work for today. That holds for me as well."

"Fair enough, sir," Joel answered with a sigh. "I'll ask again, though, soon as opportunity presents . . . Or maybe I could ask Mr. Lamenthe."

"What?"

Joel pointed through the dense throng, but at that moment the band, which had been taking a breather, struck up again with a lively quadrille, and what he started to say was drowned out. An instant later, having been apprised of Drew's arrival, Barber appeared, Jones and Cuffy at his heels as always.

"Hosea! Good evening! I've reserved space for you to dine. It's at the common table, I fear, but . . . Why, Mr. Siskin, isn't it? Mr. Gordon has been asking after you."

"I'll go and make my apologies," Joel said, and excused himself.

"If you'd like to eat right away—" Barber resumed, addressing Drew again, and checked on realizing that the other was paying no attention.

"Is something the matter?"

"Hm? Oh!" Recovering with a start, Drew shook his head. "Siskin said he'd spotted my ex-cub—Fernand Lamenthe. I guess you don't know him. At any rate I never saw him here."

"Oh, but I do," Barber corrected. "And you did see him here at least once, while he was still working for Ed Marocain."

Before Drew could say anything further, he turned to Cuffy.

"Find Mr. Lamenthe and inform him that Mr. Drew would like a word!"

Having made inquiries, Fernand returned dispiritedly to Dorcas, who was waiting at the entrance.

"There's no room anywhere," he muttered. "They can't even find us seats for dinner. I was afraid this might happen."

She looked at him with hurt, betrayed eyes: her fairy prince failing to deliver a miracle . . . but she had renounced belief in miracles.

"Then we'll go somewhere else—any place where people don't point the finger! Fernand honey, you're a man, you must have been places like that!"

So much was he at a loss to know what to say to this improbable new Dorcas, he had found no answer before Cuffy materialized at his side.

At the same moment a chance movement of the crowd allowed a clear view across the hall, and there was Drew beckoning with his knobbed staff.

"We better at least say hello," Fernand muttered.

"Glad to see you again!" Drew extended his hand. "I hear you're doing well."

"Thank you, sir. You too, I hope. Ah . . . Dorcas dear, this is Captain Drew that I've talked so much about. Miss Dorcas Archer, Captain, my"—abruptly aware of the absence of a ring, but finishing anyhow—"fiancée."

Drew looked at her as though assessing the lines of a steamer, and at last shrugged, as to say, bachelor-fashion: *women are much of a muchness*. Then he added hastily, "I hope you'll be very happy!"

"As do I," Barber put in; he had been temporarily distracted by some report from a bellboy. "But you must forgive me; I'm called away. Hosea, your seat will have to be at our common table, as I said, but it's being held against your presence."

"Thanks," Drew said from the corner of his mouth, and went on, "You're eating here too, are you?"

Fernand shook his head, and Dorcas said in a firm clear voice, "We asked whether it was possible, and they told us all the places are spoken for, so we shall have to go elsewhere."

"Oh, but that'll never do! Barber can make room for me on short notice, and I guess that goes for my friends too. He owns half my boat, damn him, and I get little enough in return—though thank God he's never meddled with the running of her! It's not ordinary for a lady to sit at the common table, but then I take the impression that Fernand wouldn't get mashed on an ordinary girl." With a nod. "I'll fix it."

Turning, he threw over his shoulder, "Besides, I have a proposition to put to you, Fernand."

For one terrible moment Fernand thought Dorcas was going to stamp her foot and march away. Then she yielded in resignation. A waiter took her cloak, revealing a dress that, by contrast with those worn by other women present, was drab and out of style, for she had never allowed Fernand to buy her clothes. Nonetheless head after head turned as they followed Drew.

The ground floor of the Limousin had been laid out as a vast suite for assemblies and balls. Barber had found it more convenient to divide it up. One section formed the dining room; another, an antechamber to the gaming rooms on the floor above; a third served as a salon for ladies waiting to meet gentlemen to whom they had not been formally introduced—as he sometimes expressed it with a chuckle.

Tonight, most of the partitions had been removed. The salon remained intact, but the dining room was no longer cut off from the main entrance hall, and the antechamber survived only as a group of sofas and armchairs jammed together under dust sheets.

To this area—too near the band for comfort—they had transferred the common table that normally stood in the dining room.

There were half a dozen vacant seats. Drew steered for them. The headwaiter objected, claiming that he had reserved only one place, and the others were booked for clients who doubtless had been delayed, while Drew asserted that it was their bad luck if they couldn't keep a schedule.

He won. Dismayed, for they had been hoping for the opposite outcome, Fernand and Dorcas made a pretense of consulting the menu. Drew scrutinized them keenly under his bushy brows.

Abruptly he said, "I guess your minds aren't too set on food right now."

Fernand's nostrils flared like a startled horse's.

"Boy, you know me by this time—or should. I'm going to be blunt. You're eager to get married, right?"

"Sure we are," Fernand snapped.

"And the lady's with you by herself. Just a minute!"—raising his hand as though it were his staff, which he had ceded into the charge of a waiter. "I don't mean nothing to her derogation. I mean some young ladies don't get to go anyplace without a chaperone. And they're the sort that come equipped with a marriage portion. And before you do like you're given to—blow your safety value for no good reason—let me guess why you two ain't hitched up already."

Dorcas leaned back, crossing her arms, as though on the verge of explosion herself. Drew disregarded her.

"You drawing full pilot's scale yet?"

"Ah . . ." Fernand swallowed. Finally he shook his head.

"I been told not. Just a *minute!*"—to a waiter trying to take their orders. "I know it's not for want of talent. I'd hire you back tomorrow. Said so at Christmastime to my sister-in-law. How about it? I'll pay you what I pay Ketch Tyburn—I got him for this season—less fifty dollars. And next year the rate he gets. Is it a deal? I guess on pay like that you could plan the wedding, right?"

Fernand was on the point of seizing Drew's hand to conclude an agreement on the spot, when Dorcas said, "This Mr. Tyburn—is he the one who was there at our second meeting?"

"Yes—why?"

"I don't think he can be as good a pilot as you are."

Both men blinked at her in amazement. Drew, his mood improved by his defeat of the headwaiter, said, "Why so, my dear?"

"Has Fernand told you how we found each other again? No? Then I shall."

In a few crisp sentences, omitting the identity of Cherouen and her employers, she recounted her ordeal with Woodley and Whitworth. In conclusion she declared, "So you see, Mr. Tyburn couldn't decide whether to do anything or not. So I don't understand how he can be as good a pilot as Fernand, because you taught him, and everybody knows you're the best on the river."

Fernand stifled a sigh of relief. He had an existing contract to work out before he could accept Drew's offer, and news of it might dampen the captain's enthusiasm, so he had feared Dorcas might settle the matter the wrong way by complaining about him being paid less than the senior pilot. Finding the story's end turned with such a neat compliment, he was delighted . . . all the more, because it showed Woodley in such a bad light.

Drew beamed indulgently. "Luckily for me, Ketch isn't indecisive when he's at the wheel. But he's getting on, and plans to quit long-trade work next year. Which is why I want to sign your young man in his place. I trust you have no objection?"

"You'd better not," said Fernand's eyes, as plain as speech.

"It's a deal, then. Waiter, a bottle of the champagne Mr. Barber drinks. We'll toast our new partnership."

And when the wine was brought—which was quickly, for a supply was constantly on ice—he declaimed as he lifted his glass, "'I fill this cup To one made up Of loveliness alone, A woman of her gentle sex The seeming paragon!' Edward Coote Pinckney who died in 1828 at the tragically early age of twenty-six. Who are you, Miss Archer? Who sent you on the errand where you met Fernand?"

She hesitated. Then she told him. He was taking a swig of champagne at the time. He hooted with laughter and the wine ran down the wrong way and he wound up croaking and coughing and somehow in spite of all still laughing.

 "You remember Mr. Siskin, don't you, boy?" Gordon
boomed.

Matthew forced a smile and rose to shake Joel's hand.

"Congratulations, and many happy returns!"

"Thank you!"

Then he was free to sit down again while Joel was being ushered to a place at
the far end of the table. He had been overwhelmed by what Gordon had ordered:
turtle soup, broiled red snapper, stuffed crabs, turkey with glazed yams . . . and
there was more to come. Mechanically he picked at the food and occasionally
sampled, more or less at random, the glasses before him, which contained red
wine, white wine, and water. He had refused whiskey.

His companions were doing their best to be agreeable: Gordon at his right,
Woodley at his left, beyond them the two pilots, conspiratorially chuckling at
jokes that to Matthew seemed pointless, and occasionally erupting in roars of
laughter. Their gaiety was infectious, bringing smiles to faces at adjacent tables.

But the guest of honor felt weaker and giddier by the moment. Lacking appetite because of his apprehensiveness, he had eaten little; wishing to seem neither ungracious nor ungrateful, every time someone toasted his birthday—and
here was Joel doing the same—he had responded by taking a generous gulp of
wine . . . thinking also of Dutch courage.

Now the room was blurring unless he concentrated hard, and there was a sour-
ness in his belly that kept making him remember the man down on all fours and
vomiting.

He began to believe he had made a terrible mistake.

A tap on his shoulder. He glanced up. A dumbwaiter had been wheeled to his
side, bearing a dish with a great silver cover. Beaming, Barber was poised to
remove it, asking permission with a twitch of his eyebrows.

The boy could only nod.

Disclosed, lifted up, placed before him with a silver knife beside it, here came
a cake in the shape of—well, a heart. It was iced with pink sugar. Where the side
incurved, a triangular—a deltar—zone of grated chocolate surrounded a candle of
bright red wax. Striking a lucifer, Barber lit this and provoked applause and cries
of "Speech! Speech!"

Forewarned, Matthew had drafted a pageful of elegant phrases. But there was
nothing elegant about the symbolism of the cake. Staring at it, he felt all his
memorized compliments blow away.

"Come on!" Woodley cried. He was growing very drunk, and his cheeks shone
with perspiration. "Cut the cackle and come to the—cake!"

Matthew seized his chance, and the knife. Rising, smiling as best he could, he
said, "Gentlemen, far be it from me to interrupt this evening's pleasure with a
lengthy address! Let me merely thank everyone who has consented to help mark
my anniversary in such memorable style, and above all of course my employer,
Mr. Hamish Gordon!"

That was precisely to the company's taste, and earned him claps and cheers while the waiter cleared away debris from previous courses and set out fine china plates, confectionery forks, more glasses, and bottles of brandy, rum, and the inevitable whiskey. Moving as in a dream, Matthew leaned forward and puffed out the candle, then awkwardly divided the cake. Its interior was rich; dark yellow, dotted with fruit, separated into layers by heavy cream. The others sampled it with forks and fingers and complimented Barber as they wiped stray cream from their lips. Matthew put a portion in his mouth. Somehow chewed it, somehow swallowed it, found he was being handed a glass of cognac and compelled to swig. . .

The macabre thought crossed his mind that from his private parts something else was now more likely to come pouring out than what a man was supposed to spend when with a woman.

But his time of waiting was over. With peculiar clarity he heard Barber whispering in Gordon's ear that the young lady who had been requested was in the salon and at Mr. Rust's disposal.

 Most of those who had been at the common table when Drew arrived with Dorcas and Fernand had adjourned to the gaming rooms, and those for whom the vacant places had allegedly been reserved had so far failed so show up. The waiters took advantage of this opportunity to lay clean covers.

During the lull, there was a commotion in the main dining room and all heads turned.

Escorting Matthew, here came Gordon and Woodley, grinning and chortling. The boy was trying hard to smile, but kept biting his lower lip. Joel, jumping from his chair, made to intervene, but Gordon grunted something that might be interpreted as "This is none of your business!" He followed anyway.

Forewarned, a waiter darted to open the door of the ladies' salon. Through it could be glimpsed a pretty dark-haired girl in a low-cut evening gown, rising from a sofa.

"Elvira my dear!" Gordon boomed, thrusting Matthew ahead of him. Woodley followed and closed the door again, so sharply that it almost banged Joel on the nose. He stepped back, cursing.

"Mr. Siskin!" Drew rapped. "What's going on?"

Pale, shaking from suppressed rage, Joel answered, "The damn' fools think it's funny! But if I'd known what they had in mind I swear I'd never have come!"

"Why?" Fernand demanded.

"It's the boy's birthday," Joel muttered. "Gordon's giving him his first woman. And they've made him so drunk he can scarcely stand in the regular sense, let alone—"

Abruptly he realized he was not talking to an all-male audience. "Miss, I'm sorry!" he blurted to Dorcas.

Before she could react, there was a crash from the salon. An alert waiter flung the door wide again. Matthew had tripped on a rug, tried to save himself, caught at a fringed tablecloth, and pulled down a tray laden with a complete coffee service.

"Now look what you've done!" Gordon rasped, hauling him to his feet. "This isn't how I expected you to act tonight! Here, Elvira! Take him away and make a man of him!"

With a shrug the girl let them try to drape Matthew's arm around her bare shoulders. But the boy kept closing his eyes and moaning, and Gordon and Woodley grew angrier by the moment. When a third attempt failed, Gordon stepped back with an oath.

"Well, yon's a fine end tae yir birthday party! After a' the trouble I went tae—a' the money I spent! Ye thankless son of Auld Nick!"

He drew back his hand as though to slap Matthew sober, but Woodley caught his arm. He had realized how many people were watching.

Everything beyond the immediate vicinity seemed to recede, as though they were aboard a riverboat when just enough mist lay on the water to make the banks hard to discern, yet it was by no means foggy and the pace of events continued without slacking.

For, harassed and weary because during this evening he had had his bellyful of customers who regarded themselves as more important than the rest of his clientele, Barber strode from the direction of the main entrance, saying, "Gentlemen, this is absolutely the best I can do for you right now, and if you don't care for it, I'm sure there are other places you can go!"

The gentlemen were Denis Cherouen and Auberon Moyne.

"Why, Joel, my dear fellow!" the latter exclaimed. "I was thinking of you only a minute ago. I—"

And broke off, for the scowl Joel bent in his direction was calculated to bring him out in blisters. Wholly misunderstanding, assuming this to be repayment for slights committed earlier, Auberon snapped his mouth shut and turned away.

But his companion was oblivious of that.

Of late Cherouen had taken to pince-nez eyeglasses, for it was the fashion among professional men, and he, like all doctors, hoped to shed the legacy of quacks and leeches and disreputable barber-surgeons and be admitted to the same company as ministers and lawyers. Donning them, he stared at Matthew with the owlishness of the not-quite-drunk.

"He seems unwell," he opined.

"Unwell!" Auberon echoed. "I've heard it called by plainer names. He's tight!"

"Not because he chose to be!"

That escaped Joel and earned a glower from Gordon.

"What do you mean by that?" Woodley demanded.

"I reckon, exactly what he says." Ponderous, like a wreck being raised, Drew stood up and lumbered around the end of the table as Gordon and Woodley returned, abandoning Matthew to Elvira and the waiter. Elvira's gaze shot arrows of disgust after them, for by now the boy was starting to retch.

"Mr. Gordon!" Drew said, raking the financier in his exotic garb with a broadside of a glare. "Do you have children?"

"I'm no' marrit!" Gordon barked. "An' what is it tae dae wi' yirsel'?"

As though he had not spoken, Drew ploughed ahead. "Now I have no children of my own body, but I do have three nephews and a niece as well. I—"

"You better watch your tongue!" Woodley exclaimed, storming forward.

"Why? Because I wouldn't make a boy my nephews' age as drunk as you've made him? Because I wouldn't butcher him to make a Gordon holiday?"

"What the de'il d'ye mean?" Gordon rapped, seething, while Joel tried to make himself look small. By now it was plain there was bound to be a ruckus. From their distant table Hogan and Trumbull were dispatched by their dismayed companions, charged to investigate. Up to now the music had prevented them from hearing clearly, but Gaston, as nervous as any of the customers, had brought the current piece to an end at the next double bar.

More than a hundred pairs of eyes followed them as they crossed the room. They were fellow pilots; accordingly Drew exchanged civil nods with them before continuing to Gordon, "You told off Eb Williams for a whiskey breath."

Disconcerted by the change of tack, Gordon was momentarily at a loss. Woodley broke in. "Do you pay to keep spies on other people's boats? Maybe that's where your money goes! We've all been wondering for years!"

During his time as a cub, Fernand had discovered how in fact Drew's earnings had been spent. He was on the point of attacking Woodley when Dorcas managed to calm him down.

In any case Drew needed no assistance.

"No, I found out because the river is my business and I take pains to learn what's going on. And what I learned in that connection was that a rich stranger who don't mind getting drunk himself *or* making his pet boy drunk and foolish to amuse his pals won't allow a hard-working engineer a nip of whiskey in a misty dawn."

"Why, ye—!" Gordon was poised to rush at Drew, but Woodley hampered him long enough for Hogan and Trumbull to lend their support. Gordon's face was bright red by now, his eyes bulbing, his fists balled, his breath coming in great gasps. In the salon doorway Elvira was on her knees at Matthew's side; the boy was moaning with eyes tight shut and mouth ajar. Cherouen had made no move to assist her, but was standing fascinated, as was Auberon, like spectators at a cockfight waiting for the last moment to place bets.

Sensing trouble, Barber had contrived to send a message to his bodyguards. Taking advantage of the distraction afforded by their arrival, he said in a soothing voice, "Gentlemen, this is a blot on our Mardi Gras celebrations! Go back to your tables, please! Youngsters like him"—a gesture towards Matthew—"haven't had the chance we've enjoyed to case-harden our livers. He'll get over it by morning."

"But they made him drunk deliberately, to mock him!" Drew roared.

"Who said so?" Gordon shouted.

"That damned reporter," Woodley growled, pointing. With a fist. "I knew you shouldn't've invited him!"

\*　　\*　　\*

Covertly to Cherouen, Auberon whispered, "Oh, isn't it a main? Isn't it just a perfect main?"

Bright-eyed, Cherouen nodded, producing a cigar and glancing around for a light. One of four waiters stranded here by the developing quarrel was prompt to supply his need and looked relieved at having something ordinary to do. Swarthy, he wore a luxuriant moustache, and his jacket was far too tight for him.

"Don't blame him!" Drew rapped.

"Why not? If it wasn't his idea, where did you get it from?" Woodley insisted.

"I figured it out by looking!"

"I see! Same as you *figured out by looking* that he"—a stab of the finger toward Fernand—"was the best kind of cub for you to take on! I guess like finds like in God's good time."

Fernand was by this time ready to break Woodley's nose, but Dorcas doggedly restrained him.

"No!" Drew bellowed. "Same way I can figure out by looking your *Nonpareil* wouldn't beat my *Atchafalaya* no matter how you rigged the odds! This boy of mine is solid!" Stepping back half a pace, he clapped Fernand on the arm. "Your pretty new boat is all sham and show! Just ask her pilots! Colin—Dermot—speak the truth now!"

"Are you suggesting"—this from Auberon with the delicacy of a surgeon inserting a scalpel—"that your boat will outrun Mr. Woodley's under any and all circumstances?"

"Yes!" Drew blurted.

"Fascinating! Then you would doubtless be prepared to race."

Nervous, the other diners at the common table were slipping away for fear of being involved in a brawl. They checked and exchanged glances, their thoughts reflected on their faces.

A race between the *Atchafalaya* and the *Nonpareil?* Now there was a notion to be conjured with! Instantly it called up memories of antebellum days: the *Queen of the West* against the *Morning Star;* the *Baltic* versus the *Diana;* the peerless *Eclipse* beating the *A. L. Shotwell* by a scant fifty minutes over one thousand three hundred and fifty miles from New Orleans to Louisville, slashing the record to less than four and a half days and packing into every hour better than twelve and three-quarter miles—this against the current of the mightiest of navigable rivers. Immortalized in prints from Currier and Ives, these and other famous contests had fascinated a whole generation.

But since the war, with much of the river under direct military law and the grip of the steamboat inspectorate tightening, there had been scarcely any similar events. None had excited half the interest of the races that the old-timers now harked back to with sighs of regret, despite the testimony of records showing how often it was while racing that steamers were wrecked by snags, pilot error or—worst of all—boiler explosions.

Moreover, and this gave a special point to the idea, tomorrow Lent began. Forty days of abstinence made a depressing prospect to anybody patronizing the

Limousin, particulary in view of its proprietor's superstitious adherence to the strict observances. He did not enforce them on customers against their will, for that would have been commercially disastrous, but a succession of forty Fridays, however ingeniously the cooks evaded the spirit while obeying the letter, grew inevitably boring. And boredom was what the gamblers, the sporting men, and the *filles de joie* feared most. In other words, four-fifths of the Limousin's clientele.

Abruptly Woodley burst out, "Well, if Hamish won't say it, I will! The *Nonpareil* will take the horns off you—old man!"

It was as well that Drew had surrendered his knobbed staff; otherwise he would have smashed it down on Woodley's head. Instead he chose weapons of another kind, borrowing from a book of Scottish ballads that had been his companion on a slow trip.

"I know something of what happens to gamblers and drunkards on the river, and they do not take the horns from decent sober men! Think on the fate of my late brother—it's no secret! As for your precious friend, he knows damn-all about steamboating, even less than you! But I reckon he may well be fast, having cut his skirt so short it will never hamper his legs! Wager he can't outrun Johnny Cope and I'll take you on!"

Speechless with rage, Woodley made as though to rush at Drew, but Gordon thrust him roughly aside.

"Skirt?" he roared. "Skirt? This is the kilt of my ancestors, the *feile-beg*! And in the tartan of my clan, what's more! Apologize or show the sky yir yellow gut!"

With unexpected swiftness he caught up from his stocking the ivory-handled knife he had earlier shown off to Matthew. A woman screamed, not Dorcas or Elvira, as he advanced menacingly on Drew.

It was not the first time such events had occurred under Barber's roof. Almost wearily, he was preparing to signal Jones to take care of the matter—Cuffy was faster, but let it once be noised abroad that he had authorized a black man to lay hands on a white one, and . . .

Then two things happened suddenly and simultaneously, and the world felt like a different place.

For a long moment Manuel could not believe his luck. Then unholy joy flooded through his being. This he understood! In the fishing village where he had spent his childhood, empty months might drag by with nothing to vary the monotony except a knife fight. Since arriving in the *Estados Unidos* he had scarcely seen, let alone participated in, one worth remembering. These *Norteamericanos* used fists or pistols, the one barbaric, the other brutal. But the knife was subtle . . . ! Whoever would have imagined that this silly fat-paunched man in a skirt as short as a chorus girl's understood the art of the knife? But he held his weapon correctly, and if his guard were a little—

No time for such reflections. Action! He snatched the cloth off the nearest table, spilling wine over the two gentlemen and one dubitable lady who sat there—but no matter—and with a deft gesture wrapped it around his left forearm. It was no substitute for a leather cape; still, it was what he had to hand. These people had ordered roast turkey, and it was being carved on a nearby dumbwaiter. The carving knife, equally, was no replacement for a proper fighting knife, but, alas, his own reposed in a pawnbroker's shop, so . . .

Equipped after a fashion, he set forth headlong to intervene between the Scotsman and the grizzle-bearded American who was boldly standing his ground, though unarmed. Manuel felt a stir of admiration. If only—

The room spun dizzily. He was down on his butt on the hard tiled floor and the carving knife had struck with such a jolt it stung his arm clear to the elbow and his fingers had opened by reflex and *what* was that noise he could hear? Laughter? It couldn't be! *El Señor Dios* would not permit . . .

But He had.

The conductor had tumbled off the bandstand in a dead faint just as Manuel drew level.

Hissing curses, he struggled to stand up. A heavy hand fell on his shoulder: the head waiter, come to drag him away because of what he had done with the tablecloth.

Almost he cast around for the knife again. But his fury was vain, and it evaporated. Shoulders slumped, he turned obediently, while someone brought smelling salts for Gaston.

Barber smiled. The change in the world was illusory after all. It usually was. He completed his signal to Jones, and the latter delivered a perfectly timed blow. The *sgian-dubh* went flying across the floor. Gordon yelled!

"You'll pay for that!" he roared, rounding not on Jones but on Barber. "You have no right—"

"On the contrary. All these people will witness that I acted with the utmost correctness. Gentlemen?"

With a gesture he drew attention to the customers who had left their tables, either to watch what they hoped might become a full-scale fight, or en route to the gaming rooms. They had arrived in time to see Gordon pull his knife. Now they concurred with Barber.

"Thank you!"—with a bow and flourish. "No, Mr. Gordon, it is you who will pay. Settle your party's score and go sober up! I am not one to hold grudges. Come back tomorrow or another day and behave like a gentleman, and you'll be welcome. But not tonight. And leave that knife! Send for it tomorrow. It will be in my office. Cuffy, bring it there right away."

The black retrieved it and disappeared.

"Take your boy with you," Barber concluded curtly, pointing at Matthew, death-pale and horribly ashamed, leaning on the salon door jamb. "And next time he makes a birthday, don't fill him so full of liquor!"

"Hear, hear!" Dorcas said unexpectedly. Giving her first an astonished glance, then a broad grin, Elvira clapped her hands. Her coiffure was in ruins and Matthew's vomit had stained her skirt.

The financier favored both women with a scowl before resignedly turning away. Relieved at such a relatively peaceful outcome, Fernand, Drew, and Dorcas resumed their chairs as Barber urged those who had intended to go up to the gaming rooms to do so now, for there would be no more excitement down here. He signaled to the musicians, and despite lack of a conductor they struck up a lively strain. All seemed as calm as before.

But the dying coals were stirred by a sharp poke from Auberon.

"Say, Joel, which paper do I look in tomorrow for an account of this affair? The *Intelligencer,* ain't that right?"

Gordon checked and swung half around. Drew's brows clashed in a monstrous frown.

Bright-eyed, Auberon advanced on his cousin. "You won't let a chance like this slip away? If you do, you're not the boy I grew up with. 'Famous financier draws knife on steamboater at sink of iniquity!' I can see the headlines now. What's more, Captain Woodley is prepared to back the *Nonpareil* against the *Atchafalaya.* He said so, and you heard him! Two scoops for the price of one!"

"Don't waste your breath," Drew called. "So long as I'm alive, the *Atchafalaya* will never race. My partner could tell you as much. Couldn't you?"

Barber forced a smile, but his eyes were darting hither and yon in search of a way to break this unwelcomely renewed impasse.

"Tell you one thing," Drew continued. "You may know less'n a row of beans about steamboating, but the way you told off Gordon you'd make a right good mate—a better mate anyhow'n *he'd* make a deckhand!"

With a bellow the financier tried to fling himself at the older man, but Hogan and McNab were prompt to restrain him.

Ignoring the abortive attack, Drew said, "Good night, Fernand—Miss Archer. I've changed my mind about putting up here. The company is bad for my digestion. Fernand, you'll wait on me in the morning?"

Fernand nodded vigorously.

"Capital. Say, here's good news—might cheer you up." He clapped Barber on the back as he passed. "Mr. Lamenthe is rejoining the *Atchafalaya* for the coming season. We resume our weekly trips to Louisville on Thursday next. And that"— with a jut of his chin at Joel—"can go in your report along with Gordon's drunken rage!"

Woodley had been fuming. Now he exploded. "Louisville! Naturally! Because we've advertised the *Nonpareil* for the St. Louis trade, and you're afraid to meet us!"

Drew looked him frostily up and down. "You're free to pick the trade you run her in," he said. "Won't make her any better suited to the work."

He pushed past. Woodley made to seize him, but a warning tap on the shoulder from Jones prevented him.

"Let him go," Gordon said sullenly. "The rest of you clear up and come along. Someone find a cab for the boy. He can go right back to the St. Charles. But I'm damned if I'll let him spoil *my* evening!"

Their expressions making it plain that this was not at all the way they had expected things to pan out, the clerks and pilots followed him away, and after a final oath aimed at Drew, Woodley did the same.

This time it really looked as though the situation were going off the boil.

But one thing remained to be attended to.

Swiftly Barber caught up with Joel and Auberon—*damn* these European-edu-
cated sprigs who thought their families' money had turned them into lords!—and
accosted the former.

"Mr. Siskin! I respect the *Intelligencer* very much, for I've known Abner
Graves ten years or more, but . . ."

Joel gave a fixed grin, and he broke off. There was something bare-boned about
the reporter's look.

"You want this kept out of print," he said. "You want to offer a fat price to keep
me quiet. Well, damn it, I'm not for sale. I've been bought already, and I'm not
too proud to admit it. There isn't a journalist in the city who can say he's never
taken money under the table, or if he does he's lying. But not me—now! *I need
this!*"

All in a tone not much louder than a whisper, but of burning intensity. Barber
hastily shifted his ground.

Contriving to look aggrieved, he said, "How could this be kept secret after so
many people saw it happen? The best I can hope for is to beat a few rumors
before they start. Ain't that so?"

Taken aback, Joel nodded.

"Then we understand each other," Barber smiled. "Write what you like, for as
they say the only bad publicity is no publicity, but many of the best-known sporting men of the city are among my customers. I wouldn't wish them to be misled
into making pointless bets just because Captain Woodley has a loud mouth."

The request seemed wholly reasonable. Joel wavered and gave in. Smug in the
conviction of success, Barber turned to Auberon.

"Mr. Moyne, disappointed though you may be to lose your chance of wagering
on the *Nonpareil* . . ."

His voice died as Auberon shook his head.

"Oh, they'll race in God's good time," he said with an air of horribly convincing
authority. "But it will not be against you that I lay odds, sir, having seen what I
have tonight. Now let me seize this overdue opportunity and renew acquaintance
with my cousin. Joel, it was thanks to your advice that I took to coming here. Yet
I've never seen you here before, have I? Won't you be my guest the rest of the
evening, to make up lost time? Are you already acquainted with Dr. Denis
Cherouen?"

Ignored, furious, Barber strode away.


"Fernand!"

He looked at Dorcas fondly. For a while during the clash between Drew and
Gordon he had been afraid that—like women he had seen aboard boats in trouble—she would lose her head.

On the contrary: when he had been on the point of eruption she had shown
more good sense than he.

But what was she trying to tell him? Half-hidden by the drawstring mouth of
her reticule, something glinting . . . Abruptly he recognized the heavy brass tag
attached to a room key.

"Captain Drew forgot it!" she whispered exultantly. "He's gone! We can use it instead!"

"Dorcas darling! But—"

"But what?" She set her jaw at a mutinous angle.

A deep breath. "Well, if anybody were to—"

"*I* think," she interrupted, "you're seeing ha'nts! Who's to suffer? I told you, Fibby will lie for me!"

Terribly torn, he poised irresolute.

Then, miraculously, he was rescued by the headwaiter inquiring whether the cost of their meal was to be put on Captain Drew's account. In a flash he saw the solution.

Affecting casualness, he took the key from Dorcas.

"No, only bill the captain for what he had. But since he changed his mind about staying, he ceded his room to us. Here's the number; charge our dinners to it and I'll settle the whole score in the morning."

Within minutes Barber learned of the unauthorized arrangement. His first inclination was to send Jones to see Fernand and his woman off the premises, for he was in a foul temper by now. He always liked to feel in control. Coming on top of what had so nearly been a stabbing, Auberon's snub—about which he dared do nothing, for the young man spent lavishly every time he came here—had been the last straw. Part of his fury had found outlet in tongue-lashing that crazy temporary waiter, who was now back on the street; later, he looked forward to telling Monsieur d'Aurade what he thought of a bandleader who couldn't be relied on to distract the crowd with nice loud music when trouble loomed. But for the moment he was working with an excess head of steam.

Nonetheless he canceled his initial impulse. Half the rooms in the Limousin would tonight be occupied by unmarried couples; no question of morality entered in. Yet—*control* . . .

The day might come when the fact that a rising young pilot had slept with his girl before marrying her might prove useful. It felt like leverage.

"Let 'em get on with it," he muttered. "But make sure nothing's omitted from their bill!"

 Shoulders hunched and pockets empty, Caesar limped homeward. It had begun to rain. Of all the ways to end up on Mardi Gras—!

But he was lucky to be here. He might have been in jail. He and his friends had been having a little harmless fun—a few drinks and a bite of food, some music, a dance or two with girls who had wandered past and accepted a shouted invitation—and some meddling prune-faced church-loving old bitch had sent for the Metropolitans.

Who had been only too glad to break up the party, seize the unconsumed liquor, and arrest the guests who were too drunk to escape. What made it hardest to bear was the fact that some of the police were as black as he was.

So that was the end of the money he'd spent, money he could have put toward his machinery repair shop.

But everybody knew the bosses from the governor down were corrupt, taking bribes and blandly denying it; likewise, the Emancipation, which had been hailed as the dawn of a new age, was proving to be the same old story told in a different accent.

One day soon, therefore—

A gust laden with raindrops made him huddle against the nearest building. For the first time since turning into the street, he took stock of his surroundings. Opposite where he had halted, flaring gas lamps illuminated the façade of the Hotel Limousin. Reluctant to face the rain, a group of well-dressed men—and one extraordinarily dressed—were pushing the youngest of their number into a cab. The door slammed and it trundled off, its place shortly taken by a carriage whose wet, tired driver scarcely even looked down as his passengers climbed on board.

Then there was an interruption. Caesar watched passively, as though a show had been put on especially for him in the theatre of the world.

Gathering around him what shreds of his dignity remained, Manuel emerged dejectedly from the rear of the Limousin.

If that *maricón* of a Frenchman hadn't—!

But he had.

Plotting futile revenge, he checked as he rounded the corner of the building. There, getting into a carriage, unmistakable in his kilt, was the rich Scotsman. Perhaps he might understand the motive that had driven Manuel to react in the way he had. Maybe Scotland was a little like Mexico, if its people used knives.

Wind-buffeted, holding his hat on, he marched over. "Meestair Gordon?" he called.

Eyes half-closed against the rain, Gordon glanced around.

"You are not to think," Manuel declared in his best English, "it was of anything personal I brought my knife against yours!"

"What did he say?" Gordon growled at Woodley.

"It's the crazy waiter," Woodley muttered. "Ignore him."

"I am not waiter!" Manuel cried. "I am musician—damn good musician! But I understan' also knife, and want say I admiring Scotchman who can use knifes!"

Gordon finally consented to pay Manuel his full attention.

"Oh, you!" he said. "You were set to gralloch me for no good reason! If it hadn't been for that bandleader—"

"He is no musician!" shouted Manuel. "He is fraud—fake—phony, compare' to me! How many instrument he play? One, two maybe? I play all, all!"

"What do you want me to do about it?" Gordon snapped.

Woodley gave a harsh chuckle. "Send him to Knight's," he proposed. "That band they had waiting for us on the wharf was no great shakes. Maybe someone like this is what they need—a bit of hot sauce to spice 'em up!"

Standing close by, both Trumbull and McNab smiled at the idea, and the former called, "He's right, Mr. Gordon! Never did hear such a poor apology for music as today!"

"Oh, do what the hell you like," Gordon grunted, and sank into the cushions of the carriage.

"Okay," Woodley said, turning to Manuel. "Now in the morning you go to Mr. Oliver Knight's office on Magazine. Tell him Captain Woodley wants you to join the band on the *Nonpareil*. Say it was lousy this morning and we're relying on you to put it right. Got all that?"

Manuel was standing with mouth ajar, overwhelmed. This was infinitely more than he had expected. But before he could speak, Woodley had fished a coin from his pocket.

"I guess you didn't get your pay from the hotel because of what happened. Here's carfare, and for tomorrow."

He scrambled into the carriage and slammed the door.

The departure of the carriage broke the spell that had been holding Caesar immobile. With squelching shoes he trudged onward. Another half-mile and he would be home.

Not that he any longer wanted to think of it as such—nor this city. Maybe he should scrap his idea of mending machinery. Maybe he should raise enough to buy a plough and a mule and a plot of land and find someone enough like Tandy not to make him dream forever of a dead past . . .

At all events he did not want to spend another Mardi Gras in New Orleans. As of today he would be primed for any chance to get away.

 In darkness amid tumbled bedclothes, Fernand spoke close enough to Dorcas's skin for her to feel the waft of breath. "With my body I thee worship . . ."

Sighing with contentment, she combed her fingers through his hair.

"There was a time when I was ready to hate Mr. Barber on hearsay," he said at length. "I guess I've learned a lot about the world since then. I guess I've grown up."

"Sometimes . . ." Her voice trailed away. He prompted her.

"Oh, nothing really. I was going to say: sometimes I wish I hadn't grown up. So often I feel sad. Cold inside. As though from now on and for ever I shall see the bad side of everything before I see the good one. As though one day I may stop believing there is a good one."

"Does that go for me too?" he teased.

"No!" She grasped his right hand tightly. "No, and so long as I can cling to that I guess I'll be okay."

"That'll be as long as you want," he said fervently.

"Promise?"

"Yes, I promise."

"Then we're married," she said. Her tone was of delighted surprise. "And the Lord's our witness. Love me again!"

 Sometimes on a broad stretch of the Mississippi, with the river bank-full and the air calm and the surface marred by scarcely a ripple—certainly nothing brash enough to call a wave—there is a change perceptible before it grows visible.

Abruptly it is as though the water slopes: flowing downhill, rather than downstream, toward you. And it may not be in the direction proper to gravity.

There are clouds approaching; however, they have not by a long way reached this spot. Nor, so far, is there a gust of the wind that reason says must be bearing them along.

This lasts a little while, and then, like a pattern of birdshot, a lash of raindrops strikes the water. The change has happened: there *are* clouds overhead, there *is* wind, and the air that *was* warm, *is* cool. Reflections that lay comfortably intact have broken up. A myriad separate splashes launch interlocking ripple rings. The water is shattered until a new integrity emerges: the form and pattern that we call a storm.

 Accepting another drink, vastly relieved to find that under his veneer of European sophistication his cousin Auberon was still his cousin, Joel said, "But why are you determined to bet on a race that Drew and Barber swear can never happen?"

The magic word *race* had rippled out from the moment of its utterance. By this time, and it was not yet midnight, the countless tongues of rumor were transforming Auberon's spur-of-the-moment proposition into news. Raising their voices to compete with the band then abruptly dropping to a whisper for fear someone not yet party to the secret might overhear, people right in this room were treating the idea as solid fact.

"Old man, I've sworn it shall," Auberon murmured, smiling sleepily as though the matter were no longer of much interest to him. But that was one of his recent mannerisms, and Joel had not taken a fancy to any of them. He persisted.

"So how are you going to make sure it does?"

"I'm not," Auberon sighed. "I'm leaving it to them"—with a nod towards the gossipers.

Joel sat bolt upright. "Damn it, man! Do you or do you not want me to feed this load of horse apples to the *Intelligencer*?"

"Indigestible," said Cherouen from his chair next to Auberon. He had spoken scarcely a word for some time, and clearly was very drunk indeed. Joel found the situation infuriating. His first chance to pump the doctor whose fame was more than citywide now, and the man was incapable of doing more than bend his elbow!

Working in journalism had strained his charitable instincts. However, by dint of vast effort he persuaded himself that Cherouen's condition might be a reaction against the strain of his practice. Thrusting all that to one side of his mind, he resumed pestering Auberon.

"Some people," the latter said at last, yielding ungracefully, "cannot resist a challenge. Cato Woodley's one. You saw how he rose to the bait!"

"But for all he's nominally master of the *Nonpareil*," Joel objected, "Gordon put up the money for her. Is he going to risk his investment—?"

"His?" Auberon cut in. "You ought to ask my father about that. Aren't you still on terms to call him Uncle Andrew?"

"Since . . ." Joel began. And hesitated, rephrasing what he was about to say. "Since the war"—there, that was much more neutral and far safer!—"as you know, we've drifted apart. And I've never wanted to exploit family contacts for professional advantage."

"Which, I guess, is why you'll never make your fortune. Well, I'll cut across a bend for you. Father made inquiries and found out that the money for the new boat was raised by the Marocain brothers."

"Oh, everybody knows that!"

"But does 'everybody' know how much?"

Particularly during the winter those employed in menial tasks at places like the Limousin found solace from boredom in gambling on whatever came handy.

By now the image of a race between two great steamers was taking on credible form among the porters and stable-boys. There was much time to kill in their kind of work.

Already people who had never seen either vessel were prepared to take sides: the older and nearer to being worn out, versus the newer—flashier, less well proven. Abstracts grew into concretes as easily as clouds turn into rain.

Very slowly Joel said, "I see. Well, then—how much?"

Auberon formed the words with relish. "Seventy percent."

"Seventy!"

"So I'm told. And do you know who holds the balance?"

"Ah . . . well, I guess Woodley has a piece?"

"His old wreck fetched scrap value," said Auberon with disdain. "He holds about ten per cent, and borrowed most of that. Hell of a note for a master to own a tenth of his boat, ain't it? But I notice you didn't say Gordon first."

"I took it his portion was included in the seventy percent," Joel said, startled. "Isn't it?"

"So far I have no proof," Auberon murmured. "But the story goes, he holds no more than Woodley."

"You mean the Marocains advanced that much against the pledge of someone who could only raise a tenth of the cash himself *and* knew nothing about steamboating?" Joel shook his head in wonderment. "Old Edouard must be spinning in his grave!"

"You miss the point. Even the Marocains couldn't be that foolish."

"But they did advance . . . Oh!"

"That's right. On the word of somebody who does know steamboating. Has done all his life."

"But a blind man, down on his luck? It seems crazy either way."

"There's alleged to be a very particular reason."

"What?"

"Not a *what*. A *who*. Drew's protégé."

Joel sat rock-still for a moment. At last he said, "Can they really hate him that much?"

"You do know who he is, then? For a while I suspected you might not."

"Oh, it made a few paras—steamboat master with Northern sympathies insults the South by taking on the first colored steersman, that kind of thing. So we looked into the guy's background and he turned out to be Ed Marocain's nephew. But he was squeezed out of what should have been his share of the family business, and his mother lives in a run-down house she can't afford to maintain, and the brothers won't help her. Isn't that enough of a revenge?"

"Seemingly not. I suspect because they're afraid he's going to do better than they are. Make more money, acquire more status in spite of his color. They want to spike his guns."

"I know where I've seen that girl before," Cherouen said unexpectedly. His diction, despite his drunkenness, was perfect.

"What girl?" Auberon demanded.

"The girl sitting with Drew and his pal. It was your mention of Parbury that brought it back."

Auberon and Joel exchanged glances. The former said, "Very interesting! Because we never actually mentioned that party's name."

"Didn't you?" But that was irrelevant to Cherouen. He continued, "She was sent to my house once. Works for Mrs. Parbury. Wanted me to treat her rheumatism. I don't mean hers, but her mistresh'sh—*damn*." On that tricky obstacle of a word his control let him down. He took another sip from the glass he was cradling in both hands.

"Is he going to do well out of this new boat of his?" he concluded with total concentration.

"Parbury?" Joel said. "Oh, I guess so, even on a one-tenth share. But naturally not so well as if she could run out the *Atchafalaya*."

Auberon's eyes were alight with excitement. "She works for Parbury, does she? All kinds of hell will be let loose, then, when Parbury gets to hear that his pretty prize is quitting him for a man who works with his most detested rival."

"Does pretty matter to a blind man?" Joel countered. "Besides, it takes two to made a race, same as a quarrel."

"Then I'll be the other one," Auberon said with a shrug. "Or someone will . . . Look here, Jewel!"

It was the first time since returning from Europe that he had employed the childhood nickname. Joel grinned.

"Yes?"

"You keep on saying there won't be a race. I say there will. Back your judgment!"

Joel's grin grew even broader. He felt in his pocket for the ritual two cents. "I say no race," he declared.

"And I say yes race," Auberon retorted, solemnly imitating him. "Within—oh, let's say before the end of this year?"

Joel nodded.

"Well, you just settled your own hash," Auberon said. "Now there will have to be a race. I'll go make it absolutely certain." He got to his feet.

"Then I don't think I'll accept her as a patient," the doctor said unexpectedly. "Not unless— Or maybe I guess I should. Hell!"—with sudden vehemence. "I'd best ask Josephine when she gets through with her mumbo-jumbo."

Realizing that Auberon was on the verge of departure, he reached out an unsteady hand. "Don't go! I wanted to explain what a headache my chief nurse is. Headache, get it? 'Physician, heal thyself!' There's nothing I can put my finger on, but sometimes I feel she doesn't take electricity seriously. Or ozone. Cares more for her superstitious simples, even after the years we've worked together . . . As though some weed torn up from the side of the road could stand comparison with the vital force that informs the human frame, the essence, the *quintessence* of life itself!"

Having achieved his peroration, he slumped back and began to snore. Joel rescued his glass and set it on a handy table.

Turning to Auberon with wry amusement, he checked, then shivered visibly.

"Someone walked over your grave?" Auberon asked.

"I guess . . ." Joel shook himself, like a dog emerging from water. But his smile did not return.

"What's the matter?"

"I don't know." Joel looked up, as though he could see through the ceiling and out into the midnight sky. It was just on twelve, and before he could say more a clock across the room chimed the official start of Lent. Several people crossed themselves.

Eventually, not looking at his cousin, Joel said, "You know the Greek myth about the Fates who weave the destinies of men?"

"Sure: Clotho, Lachesis and Atropos. I always used to think it was from Clotho that we got our word cloth. I was kind of disappointed when someone told me it wasn't."

Joel ignored the wisecrack. "Just now, all of a sudden I felt we were at a point where the threads come together and make a knot. The lives of certain people intersecting at a certain moment . . . Like the electric charge that draws down lightning."

"Oh, I've had my bellyful of electricity from Cherouen! When he got talking to me at the Comus ball, I thought he was going to be worth knowing. Instead he turns out to be a gabby drunk . . . I've changed my mind about promoting my race any more tonight, anyhow. I guess it can take care of itself for a day or two. I'll go play some poker. You coming?" And in a lower tone: "If you're not flush, I can help out."

Very pale, trembling from the intensity of his experience, Joel shook his head.

"Thanks, no. I'd better get on home. Most other times I'd have quit long ago, gone running to Abner at the office and been the first to tell him about Gordon pulling a knife on Drew. But he's not working tonight, so I ought still to be the one. If I'm not, and he finds out I was there, I'll have the devil to pay, of course." He forced a smile, extending his hand.

"Good night, then. And . . . and it's good to meet you again."

Cocking one eyebrow, Auberon murmured, "I'd been kind of missing you, as well. As for Loose—!"

"Oh, last time we met she swore she never wanted to see me again."

"Why do you think no gambler worth his salt will bet with a woman? It may be too late to coax her out of marrying that soak Gattry, but someone ought to try, and it might as well be you. Think about it. Good night!"

 Insight afflicted Drew also as he returned to the lonely comfort of the *Atchafalaya*. Pausing at the foot of her stage, he saw a broad puddle that reflected the light of a torch: briefly disturbed by nothing more than a few ripples, then a heartbeat later pounded by a fusillade of rain drops.

For that instant it stood as the necessary metaphor for the whole huge Mississippi. The configuration of new weather was complete, and a storm without rain, without gales, overlay the water and the land.

## 22ND JUNE 1870

# A DIFFERENCE
# OF DOLLARS

"An extended experience enables us to say, that the qualities which will most effectively fill the cabin of a Western boat are not (generally speaking) the greater stability and experience of the captain, the safer or more substantial construction of the boat, or engine, but rather, a reputation for speed, which promises a progress of a few more miles a day, or the difference of a few dollars less in the price of the passage. It is in vain to hold it out as an inducement to passengers, (we have seen it tried,) that any boat is furnished with the patent safety-valve, or supplied with life-preservers; another lying alongside, which has proved the faster in a trial of speed, leaves port crowded, while the empty cabin in the former causes captains and owners mentally to resolve, that the next boat they build, shall at all events be a fast one."

—*The North American Review,*
quoted by Louis C. Hunter in
*Steamboats on the Western Rivers*

 Emerging on deck, grateful for the whisper of a breeze to relieve the heat, Woodley spotted Gordon and Matthew approaching amid the bustle of the St. Louis wharf.

The financier was assiduously promoting a scheme to revitalize river traffic by organizing steamers into superlines of fifty or a hundred boats. But Woodley could tell he had drummed up no support here. Of course, if the *Nonpareil* had been returning her expected profit, it might have been a different matter. As things stood . . .

He fumed inwardly. Once again his ambition was turning to dust and ashes. He had expected miracles of this steamer; to bring them about, he had worked harder than ever in his life, and obscurely felt he was *owed* for doing so. True, Parbury treated him with respect. But . . .

Nonetheless he gave the expected and politic greeting as Gordon ascended the stage, beard limp with sweat.

"Good morning! I trust all went well?"

"Nothing went at all," Gordon snarled. "Damned fools can't see further than the ends of their noses. And those are going to be burned by the railways any day!"

"Wasn't even Mr. Grammont interested?" Woodley demanded. It was no secret that he had long been looking for ways to invest his surplus capital, nor that he had taken shares in a railroad that, on its first day of operation, had sustained a spectacular derailment involving half a hundred casualties, himself and his wife among them . . . with the result that they were now so prejudiced against this more modern form of transport as to have refused to let Dr. Larzenac travel that way, though precious hours might have been shaved off his journey.

Gordon snorted. "Don't talk to me about Grammont! He's gone into a decline along with his two bairns. Won't talk to anyone except the French doctor. And his woman is worse by far. I swear she thinks the world will end if she loses one of her precious offspring! Isn't that so, Matthew?" he added, rounding on the boy.

"I beg your pardon, sir?" Matthew parried. Despite the summer weather he was very pale. Woodley's second clerk, Sam Iliff, was much given to helping boys in trouble and had lately recruited one as a mud clerk at his own expense; he had repeatedly expressed concern about Matthew's health, and Woodley was against his will becoming worried himself. Scandal of the sort that would follow the boy's illness or even death aboard the steamer was the last thing he could afford.

But in his view half the trouble lay with Gordon, and here was more evidence, for the financier rasped, "What the de'il dae I pay ye for—tae ston' there wi' yir mouth ajar catchin' flees? Tak' ma coat tae the cabin!"

It took Woodley a moment to realize he meant "flies." During that time Matthew turned crimson, muttered an apology, and, seizing the coat Gordon peeled off, vanished.

215

Glaring, Gordon said, "If I'd guessed what a loon he'd prove tae be, I'd ne'er hae ta'en him intae ma employ."

"Mr. Gordon, I thought I heard your voice."

In waistcoat and shirt-sleeves, gilt-rimmed pince-nez on his nose, Ian McNab advanced from the office. Despite his and Gordon's common Scottish ancestry, they had never got on, for they were as far apart in temperament as one country might well produce.

Woodley's attention was abruptly fully engaged.

Holding out a folded letter, McNab continued, "Our agents here, sir, have favored me with a copy of this communication from the Marocain Bank—and I may say I read it with a heavy heart."

"May Auld Nick tak' the Marocains . . . !" Gordon composed himself, however, and when he spoke again the thick accent was gone from his voice.

"What do they have to say that can't be said to me directly?"

"They're asking, sir, whether there is any reasonable chance of the *Nonpareil* paying the interest on the loan you extracted from them to finance her."

"But we're paying off our loans!" Woodley snapped. "We may not be turning the profit we hoped for, but—"

McNab's eyes switched to the captain, though his head did not move; there was something alligatorlike in the shift of attention that sent a shiver down Woodley's spine.

"Not the loan to the boat, sir. The loan to Mr. Gordon personally."

There was a pause. Suddenly giving an ingratiating smile, Gordon took Woodley by the arm.

"Och, but it's hot in the sun! Let's find a cool drink, shall we?"

Woodley brushed his hand aside. A huge and terrible suspicion was gathering at the edge of his mind.

"A loan?" he repeated. "But no mention was made of any additional funds . . ."

"It's news to me as well," McNab grunted, extending the letter. "But you should read it, Captain."

"There's no need!" Gordon exclaimed. "I know what they're on about."

"I don't!" Woodley seized the letter and cast his eye down it, and with every line felt his fury being fueled. If this were correct, then Gordon must have lied a score of times! Here the Marocains were claiming he had raised capital for the boat on note of hand!

"It's all because of the *Alabama* claims!" Gordon barked. "How could I possibly have foreseen that?"

Woodley hesitated, remembering references half-registered in sundry news reports: there was a grand international lawsuit in progress, because the victorious Northern states were suing Great Britain on account of damage done by British-built Confederate-manned warships, one of which had been called the *Alabama*.

"Until the case is settled, they won't allow me to transfer money from Britain to America!" Gordon declared. "But I have a lawyer at work on my behalf in—"

McNab interrupted. "That's as may be, Mr. Gordon. But what are we to do about the *Nonpareil*? So far we've been running with her hold half empty and scarcely more than half the staterooms booked. Regardless of the *Alabama* claims, this costly steamer is operating at a deficit, and that deficit is greater than I'd been led to believe! Can you take your oath on rectifying that?"

He snatched back the letter from Woodley and confronted Gordon, quivering with rage.

"I'll not call you a liar, sir—not yet! But I will complain of being grievously misled!"

During the next few seconds Woodley felt a great calmness take possession of him.

"I want all officers to assemble in the cabin," he said crisply. "Someone call Captain Parbury from his stateroom. I've been discussing with him a possible solution to our problems."

 Instead of the strip of plain black stuff he had formerly used, Parbury now bound his eyes with a silk bandanna: a gift, he had told several people, from Dorcas. Clearly he was very proud of it. Woodley, however, was not the only one to wonder whether he knew it was a riotous tangle of all the colors modern dye chemistry afforded—purple, orange, mauve, green . . . It was taken for granted it had been given as a practical joke.

In Parbury's presence, though, all thought of mentioning it evaporated. As though the realization of his dream steamer had lent him extra substance, one tended now to think of him as larger than life. He seemed taller, more gaunt, in every way more extreme than those around him. Caring little for himself, he was devoted to the *Nonpareil* and expected the same dedication from her crew. In Woodley he fancied he had found it. Accordingly the older and younger captains were getting on well. But Woodley feared that sooner or later Parbury's illusions might be shattered. If the *Nonpareil* failed to pay her way, he would be obliged to sell his share and try another means of earning his living. And he detested the prospect of reverting to a lowlier status. For wholly selfish reasons, therefore, he was as concerned about the poor financial performance of the steamer as Parbury about her inability to corner the *Atchafalaya* and run her out.

Parbury had taken his place at the bottom end of a table in the main cabin. All around, steward Mort Bates's black tenders were dusting, polishing and cleaning. Ordinarily they chatted and sang while about such dull work. Parbury's entrance had hushed them instantly. It had become one of Woodley's ambitions to make that sort of impact on people.

Some day, maybe . . .

The mates, clerks and engineers were assembled, and only the pilots had not yet appeared, when Gordon marched into the cabin, looking daggers, and slumped into his usual chair at Woodley's right. Behind him, as ever, followed

Matthew, whom he had haled out of his stateroom with a curt command to bring his book and come at once.

Only now, with an awful sense of impending doom, did Matthew realize he had snatched up the wrong book. Gordon had meant his journal. Instead his hand had fallen on a volume about Scottish tartans which he had spotted in a St. Louis bookstore and immediately bought, thinking that a knowledge of this subject might ingratiate him with his employer. Gordon was becoming more and more irascible; the least mistake on Matthew's part drove him into a fury.

Yet when things were going well he could be charming and generous. He had even (how long ago it all seemed now!) brought himself to apologize the day after the Mardi Gras débâcle, blaming his behavior on his rough upbringing and that in turn on the pitiable condition of Scotland.

Suffering his first hangover, Matthew had considered resigning, thinking that if he pawned his birthday presents he could raise enough to get him home. But the idea of confronting his uncle was daunting; he allowed himself to be persuaded to carry on . . . only to be met with constant reproaches and insults.

If there were someone he could talk to! But there was no one aboard close to his own age, apart from Iliff's mud clerk Anthony Crossall, and Matthew found him coarse and ignorant.

He was becoming very lonely and rather frightened.

But he had an immediate problem to cope with. Cautiously he assessed his chance of stealing back to collect his journal without calling down another of Gordon's thunderbolts, and decided it would be best to lay down his book and leave the cabin visibly empty-handed. He did so, and inevitably came the rasping question, "Boy, where are you off to?"

In a tolerably steady voice he answered, "I don't know that my pencil will last out the meeting, sir. I'd best bring another."

Gordon grunted but made no further comment. Next to him Woodley glanced at his watch, frowning. "Where the devil are Colin and Dermot?" he muttered. "Matthew! If you see them, say we're all waiting!"

"Yes, sir!"

Miraculously the pilots arrived just as Matthew was returning to the cabin. Under cover of the distraction he was able to gain the alcove, a little distance from the table but well within earshot, where he customarily sat during meetings. And froze. Whitworth, chewing one of his usual panatelas, was leafing through the book he had left there, shaking his head. Realizing Matthew was back, he glanced up.

"This yours? With all the pictures of men wearing skirts like music-hall dancers?"

Not waiting for a reply, he slapped shut the book.

"More I learn about you and your precious Mr. Gordon," he said in a low but savage tone, "the more I wonder why you're not in jail!"

Dimly aware of what he was implying, Matthew ventured, "But those are only pictures of Scottish national dress, Mr. Whitworth."

"You should wear it yourself, then," Whitworth snapped. "Then there couldn't be any mistake about you!"

With a final glare he took his place near the foot of the table, between Underwood and Burge, opposite Bates the steward and Hans Katzmann the caterer. Everybody looked expectantly at Woodley.

"Gentlemen, I've called you together because we're in trouble. Worse trouble than I formerly believed. Mr. McNab knows what I'm talking about, and Mr. Gordon better than either of us."

Gordon scowled and hunched further into his chair.

"What sort of trouble?" Peter Corkran demanded. "Far as her boilers and engines go, she's running fine. Right?" He sought confirmation from Roy and Steeples. Eb Williams was not present; from the beginning he had preferred to avoid these discussions.

"I'm not talking about that," Woodley said. "I'm talking about the fact that we're not getting our proper share of either freight or passengers. Has the *Nonpareil* somehow acquired a bad reputation?" As he spoke, he gazed fixedly at the pilots on his left.

"Why look at me?" Hogan demanded. "If I weren't happy with her, I'd never have signed my contract."

"Same holds for me," Trumbull snapped. "She's handling fine, now she's been fitted with the chain wagon."

As always at the faintest whisper of criticism of his darling, Parbury cocked his head like a hound sniffing the breeze. But he said nothing.

"Right," Hogan concurred. "When she's loaded she acts like a lady and shows just the turn of speed we were hoping for. We've taken the horns in a handful of short trades already. Trouble is, she doesn't get a chance to prove how long she can keep it up. It'd help"—with a glare at McNab—"if we didn't have to make so many way landings!"

"We're having to take any cargo we can get," McNab retorted. "You want her well loaded, we want her to pay her way! So we're obliged to!"

"But why?" Woodley barked. "Why are we not flooded with requests to carry freight and passengers both?"

"Try hiring new agents," Iliff suggested sourly.

"Knight's are a good firm and they're doing their best," McNab insisted. "So are our other agents up and down the river. No, the trouble is, though I'm sorry to have to say it . . ." He hesitated, looking at Parbury and at once away again, and concluded, "People are afraid of these rumors about a race. There's danger in it. Who'd want his goods to float home by the water, scorched and sodden? Or travel that way himself?"

"Danger?"—from Gordon. "In a boat that I personally tested to two hundred per square inch?"

"We haven't been allowed to make that public," Iliff said meaningly, in his turn glancing at Parbury. "But Ian's wrong, anyway. People aren't scared of a race. They're hoping for one. They think they're doing us a favor by not overloading her. Think a lighter boat is more likely to run out Drew's!"

"If that were so," Hogan objected, "putting that card in the papers should have fixed the trouble."

On their last visit to New Orleans they had seen an advertisement from Drew denying that the *Atchafalaya* would race with any other steamer. At McNab's insistence Woodley had published a similar statement.

"Anyway, that argument only affects freight," Trumbull said. "Before the war, when there was the least chance of a race, you couldn't buy passage on either boat for love or money. Where are the sporting fraternity? They ought to be coming aboard in droves!"

"Before the war!" Hogan countered. "Things have changed."

"The amount of money that's been bet simply on whether there will or won't be a race says you're wrong," Woodley declared. "Mr. Parbury and I have discussed this at length and reached complete agreement."

Gordon started, as though suspecting goings-on behind his back. Woodley looked straight at him as he continued.

"There's one way to settle the matter. There must be a race, and we must win it."

Parbury gave an emphatic nod, and his cadaverous face broke into a Halloween grin.

Response was about equally divided into relief and dismay, and for a second Woodley was afraid of a shouting match. Then into the air burst an explosion of music—of a sort. During their last trip Manuel had had to fire one of his cornet players for drunkenness, and now he was auditioning a possible replacement, who was very loud but conspicuously off-key.

"Crazy Dago!" muttered Whitworth. Underwood chuckled; Burge did the same. The tension faded, giving Woodley his chance to go on.

"Whatever you think," he stated flatly, "so long as Drew holds the horns for our regular trade, the *Nonpareil* will never be the automatic choice of shippers and travelers. We'll go on begging for our fair share of business, and for a splendid boat like ours the notion's crazy!"

"Damned right!" exclaimed Gordon, who was now paying full attention. Whether he had expected a public interrogation concerning his debt to the Marocain Bank was impossible to judge, but his alarmed reaction to McNab's challenge was over, and his manner was back to normal. Turning to the pilots, he added, "She can do it, can't she?"

There was a pause; Trumbull and Hogan exchanged glances. At length the latter said, "There's no doubt we can make a very fast run. But how can we force Drew into racing? I believe his card where I wouldn't believe ours, Captain—with respect! He never has raced any of his boats, and he won't start now."

Parbury spoke up sharply. "That's simple! We're due to leave New Orleans next Friday, July first. Give us a quick trip downriver and we'll leave on Thursday instead, Drew's regular day. If we pull away from the wharf together he can't pretend we're not racing as far as Cairo."

"If I know him," Corkran said bitterly, "the moment he sees we're stripped for a fast run, he'll decide to stay over an extra day and leave us to race the clock instead of him."

"If he does," Woodley said, "the whole world will know why. And people who backed him to win will be so disgusted, we can look forward to taking over his Memphis and Vicksburg and Greenville business, can't we?"

His tone of confidence was infectious. Those who had been minded to voice objections, even McNab, seemed to think better of it.

"And do we have to strip her?" the captain pursued. "I'm not sure Drew gained much advantage by taking out windows and removing guards. At all events the *Nonpareil* has a far finer line."

That earned a smile of approval from Parbury, who put in, "At least her decks ought to be painted white, though."

There were general nods; that was a wartime trick, designed to make the most of moonlight and even starlight.

"I'm not so concerned about that," Trumbull said with a frown. "What's more important is that we have sufficient freight to ballast her. Can we get enough cargo for St. Louis, or at least for Cairo? Or would we have to make it up with way-landing cargoes? That would mean more stops and longer ones."

"Why not ballast her with fuel?" Gordon proposed.

Both pilots looked at him stonily. Hogan condescended to reply.

"Fuel has to be kept on the move, Mr. Gordon—towards the boilers. For a high-speed run you need solid freight in exactly the right positions. Besides, there's a question of cost."

Iliff had brought a file of documents with him. Now he handed a list to the pilots.

"Here's what we have engaged for our next upriver trip. Will it be enough?"

As one they shook their heads. Hogan said, "You'll have to make certain we have another hundred tons of St. Louis freight. Never mind what—just get it. Do you have a list of passengers?"

"Here. Of course some will cancel when they learn departure is a day early."

"But a good few more will insist on joining," Trumbull said.

"That doesn't matter," Woodley put in. "Just so long as we accept none who won't go clear to St. Louis with us. The ones we're engaged to convey to way stops can be transferred to other steamers or take their chance riding an empty coal flat. I want delays cut to the bone. On the way down we'll leave messages to have fuel ready at the proper points, and . . ." He hesitated, glancing sidelong at the pilots.

"And," he finished with forced brightness, "we'll cable for pilots to join us under way, to spell you so you're always at your freshest in the pinch."

For a long moment Hogan and Trumbull digested that, plainly wondering whether to take it as an insult or a wise precaution. McNab resolved the problem with a remark that amounted to surrender.

"I can tell you've given a deal of thought to this, Captain," he murmured, and everybody was glad to accept the formula, even the pilots. After sighing with resignation, Hogan put the next obvious question.

"Like who, *Captain?*"

"I thought Zeke Barfoot out of Memphis, and Joe Smith and maybe Tom Tacy out of Cairo, because it's getting kind of tricky towards Cape Girardeau."

Two weeks ago, at just that spot, Hogan had almost gone aground. He was unable to object without being reminded of it; Woodley's tactics were impeccable. He gave a sullen nod of consent. At once the gathering was transformed by excitement. Unwilling to admit it, all of them had been looking forward to a showdown.

Parbury gave a gentle cough.

"But so as not to make a liar out of Mr. Woodley . . ." he said. The point registered at once; he amplified it nonetheless.

"Nobody should state that there is to be a race! It's safe to say we're attempting a fast run—that much will be clear from our refusal of passengers for way stops, and the rates we shall have to offer to secure enough cargo for St. Louis."

"Ruinous!" McNab was heard to mutter behind his hand.

"The hold and staterooms will be full at top rate on the trip after!" Woodley murmured equally softly.

Parbury went on: "But if something goes wrong—not that we expect it to, but *if* it does—a deal of money has been wagered, as Mr. Woodley reminds us. One would not want people disappointed. We know we plan to race if possible. Drew will guess it straight away. Shippers and shipping agents will likely do the same, and some passengers too. But let them draw their own conclusions. Don't give 'em one ready-made."

Outside, the music resumed. Either the offender had been told to sling his hook, or Manuel had forcibly retuned his instrument; this time the sound was at least bearable.

Over it Woodley stated, "Captain Parbury is correct! Remember what he said, and abide by it."

Hogan looked him square in the face. "Captain, you talk an awful lot about what's being bet on this race. Would any of that money by chance be yours?"

Woodley only smiled. He was intending to turn the question with some comment about having entire confidence in the boat—because he had in fact bet a great deal, more than was wise—but before he framed the words Whitworth chimed in, stage-whispering.

"At least it'll give the niggers something to occupy their minds, if you can call them minds . . . !"

There was a gust of laughter. Woodley slapped the table and rose.

"About your duties, then! And make sure she's completely fit to take the horns!"

Humming, Woodley lit a Havana cigar—a smoke he had taken to in imitation of Gordon. He was extremely pleased with himself. He felt that for the first time he had exercised full captain's authority aboard the *Nonpareil*. Necessarily he had still shown deference to Parbury, but by now he was confident of becoming his own man. He would have died rather than admit it publicly, but since taking up his present exalted post a great realization had dawned on him. Command was not something you could buy, as he had at first imagined. It was to be earned, or learned, or maybe the best word would be *gained*.

For weeks, for months, he had been obliged to describe the difficulties he was having to his acquaintances, particularly those he used to gamble with, to excuse his apparent loss of interest in his old haunt, the Limousin. But it was impossible to make people who had never worked for a living—who, even if they had seen service, had been granted officer rank because they were born to appropriate status, not because they were equipped for it—understand that there were subordinates who weren't servants, or slaves, and could not simply be told to obey or quit. The standing of a pilot, in particular, was baffling to young men accustomed to being waited on since they left the womb.

It was also still making Woodley seethe in private. Obtaining Hogan's and Trumbull's consent to the engagement of specialists for individual stretches of the river was a triumph, the first step on a road that would lead to him being truly in control.

Not that the credit was wholly his. Accidentally, by obliging his pilots to sign fixed-term contracts, Gordon had given them a stake in the success of the boat. When they quit, it would do their future prospects no good at all if the *Nonpareil* had run at a loss during their time with her.

The news of Gordon's financial unsoundness had not come as a complete surprise; once or twice in New Orleans he had heard rumors and scoffed in the hope they would go no further. But someone was keeping the story alive, and presumably that someone had an interest in belittling the *Nonpareil*. Perhaps he had bet more than he could afford on this race that kept not happening; perhaps he had a grudge against Parbury, or Gordon, or even Woodley himself; perhaps he had been bribed by Drew to sow tares!

As things had turned out, everybody had wound up on the same side, all wanting—all needing—a record run.

When it was over, and he had claimed the horns off Drew, then if ever in his life he would be able to respect himself. Instead of an old blind man—instead of a fat foreigner—when people thought of the racing steamer *Nonpareil*, they would associate her name for evermore with Cato Woodley!

## 29TH JUNE 1870

# ON THE TURN
# OF A CARD

~~~~~~~~

"Of late, European telegrams have recited in glowing accents all details of yacht races in British channel and Atlantic ocean. We are gravely told by the cable that Mr. Asbury, on board his yacht, the Cambria, is coming to America with prizes of the immense value of £250. How insignificant the contests of these miserable little sailing vessels, contrasted with this pending between magnificent steamers on the greatest river in the world, and how trifling these gold and silver cups with which victors are rewarded in European yacht races, when here, in this remote quarter of the globe, a single steamboat captain is said to have staked money and property to the extent of $200,000—£40,000—on the issue of the struggle . . ."

—Memphis *Appeal* editorial,
1st July 1870, quoted by
Manly Wade Wellman in
*Fastest on the River*

Across the darkened offices of the *Intelligencer*, Abner Graves bellowed, "Siskin! Isn't your piece ready yet?"

Late though it was, the steam presses were working full blast. Speech less than a shout was not worthwhile.

"Just a minute!" Joel called back, and for the dozenth time compared the two concluding paragraphs he had drafted for his article. One stated that there would be a race when the *Atchafalaya* and the *Nonpareil* left port at the same time, and one referred readers to the steamers' respective advertisements as evidence that there would not.

The bulk of his text was a résumé of what Drew had told him this morning (and it was a journalistic coup to have secured so long an interview with that thorny character), followed by some remarks by officers of the *Nonpareil*. He had hoped for Woodley or Parbury; both, however, had declined on the grounds that advancing their departure to Thursday had made them far too busy. Why, then, the advancement? He had at least been able to ask the second clerk, Mr. Iliff. But his reply was thoroughly unsatisfactory: "Commercial reasons!"

Following all this equivocation, what else could he include to make up his word count but reference to the heavy betting that was going on? He was kept *au fait* by Auberon, who took malicious delight in reporting who had laid how much, at what odds, on the success of which steamer.

At first Joel had cared not at all whether he won or lost his two cents. What mattered was to get back on good terms with his cousin. If there had been a secondary motive, it ceased when Louisette became Mrs. Arthur Gattry.

Little by little, however, he had begun to think that not having his own way for once might do Auberon good. His time in Europe had made him so overweening! And a couple of weeks ago Joel had been firmly convinced that this was how it would pan out, for Drew had inserted an advertisement in the paper that was to run until canceled. A galley proof of tomorrow's river advertising column lay beside him; he reached for it and once more read the familiar words:

### A CARD

*Having proved that the steamer* Atchafalaya *can make a fast run, I take this method of informing the public that reports of her intending racing, are not true. Passengers and shippers can rest assured that she will not race with any boat leaving the same day. Business intrusted to my care, freight or passengers, will enjoy the best attention. Verb. sap.*

H. DREW, *Master*

He had been even more encouraged when a response from the *Nonpareil* appeared, also with instructions to let it run. Here that was again too:

227

### A CARD TO THE PUBLIC

*Reports having been circulated that the steamer Nonpareil is going out for a race, such reports are not true, and the traveling community are assured that every attention will be given to the safety and comfort of passengers. The running and management of the Nonpareil will in no way be affected by the departure of other boats.*

CATO WOODLEY, *Master*

True or false, though? Auberon—with, for a change, at least a shadow of proof—had described bets that Woodley had placed months back, when his gambling cronies mocked him for taking up a demanding occupation instead of living by his wits. And in the first flush of enthusiasm for the new boat, other people could easily have been dragged along and later regretted their rashness. So far, so logical.

But money was still being laid on both contenders, and Auberon was giving names and figures. Some were surprising.

Who then, beyond Woodley, was inspiring confidence in the *Nonpareil?* The Marocain brothers? It would be in their interest in one sense, inasmuch as they had huge sums secured by her success in trade; contrariwise, though, let it but be whispered that a banker was gambling with his clients' funds, and . . . !

True, they harbored a double grudge against Drew, not only because he had recruited Fernand, but also because he, however inadvertently, had triggered off the panic that came near to ruining the bank five years ago. But the risk of a second similar panic was too great. No, it couldn't be the Marocains.

Her pilots, then? Many pilots did wager on much inferior steamers. Some had even been known to bet against themselves—but that had been a great scandal long ago, well before the war. Organizations like the Pilots' Guild existed now to prevent such corruption.

Parbury? Oh, anything he said about the *Nonpareil* was automatically suspect!

Some other of her officers? But report held that they were backing her, if at all, with petty sums.

Could Gordon have stirred up such a wave of support? Hardly! River people, while polite in public, were contemptuous of his notions about steamboating.

No, none of these answers fitted the case, Yet, if it were the boat's own qualities that had drawn so many people to back her, why was she earning less than older, slower boats, almost as though shippers and passengers were treating her as above their station? Parbury wasn't that much hated! Nor was Woodley!

Joel turned once more to the galley proof beside him. Running his finger down advertisements for insurance and excursions and missing freight, he eventually came on two items, one above the other:

*FOR LOUISVILLE. The magnificent passenger steamer Atchafalaya (Capt. H. Drew) leaves today at 5 p.m. for Louisville and is receiving for all landings on the Mississippi and Ohio. Messrs. E. Motley, R. Wills, D. Grant, clerks. The Atchafalaya has splendid accommodations for passengers with competent officers.*

*FOR ST. LOUIS. The new and very fast passenger steamer* Nonpareil *is receiving as above and leaves at 5 p.m. I. McNab, S. G. Iliff, clerks. Superior accommodations with polite obliging officers. Competitive rates for all freight. C. Woodley, Master.*

Seeing that the *Nonpareil* was no longer inviting goods for any but her ultimate destination called back vividly the sound of Auberon saying, at the start of Drew's record-breaking run to St. Louis, "That settles it!"

Against such vigorous denials? It could be. It looked as though Woodley—or Parbury—was determined to force a speed trial at least as far as Cairo. For the purposes of the gamblers, that might suffice. How could Drew evade the challenge? By claiming that his "card" was to be taken literally? But that would be on a par with the ancient trick, played by many losing boats, of tying up to some way landing and putting ashore an empty barrel, thereby entailing "unavoidable" delay.

Anyhow, would the customers tolerate that let-out? Not in a million years. Thanks to a whispering campaign, for which Auberon might conceivably be responsible, more and more stress was being laid on the fact that the *Atchafalaya* was the older boat, and her long reign must naturally end.

Sheer repetition had built up a pressure of its own, moreover. Probably for every person who had read the captains' disclaimers, there were a hundred who had been assured by word of mouth that a race was inevitable. Which counted for more—being in control, or the wave of public expectation? Joel's mind remained obstinately poised between the two.

Oh, this trade of journalism, this creating of ephemera that today might conjure up a grand sensation, but tomorrow would be used to light the fire—it was all a far cry from his boyhood ambition of becoming a great poet . . .

"Siskin!" Graves shouted again. "I want your copy and I want it *now!*"

Abruptly he reached a conclusion. For her record run the *Atchafalaya* had been stripped to bare essentials. If and when Drew and Barber resigned themselves to Woodley's challenge, they would no doubt go to even greater trouble than before to ensure their boat would run as fast as possible. But such preparations took time. This morning, when he spoke with Drew, there had been no sign of them. Therefore there would be no race tomorrow.

The logic satisfied him. He was able to deliver his article, make for home, and sleep unworried until morning.

# 30TH JUNE TO 4TH JULY 1870

# AS UNAVOIDABLE AS WAR OR WEATHER

~~~~~~

"From their first appearance upon the Mississippi, riverboats raced often and fiercely. . . . Sweating firemen fed their furnaces to almost incandescent heat with pitch pine and sides of rancid bacon. Then, sometimes the water level in a boiler sagged below the danger point and the intolerable compression of steam drove out a rust-weakened patch of iron shell or a loose rivet with a sudden explosion like that of dynamite. The other racked boilers exploded in turn, sundering the timbers of the hull and shattering into toothpicks the cabin overhead. Again and again, at the very moment of victory, a winner blew up and foundered, scalding and drowning both crew and passengers."

—Manly Wade Wellman,
*Fastest on the River*

 Huge and hollow, a place of brown English tile, pillars that bore no load, and draped derivatives of classical statuary, the Grammont mansion in St. Louis resounded at dawn to the loudest noise it had heard since the sick children were confined to bed.

First the mistress of the house screamed and smashed things. Then, more quietly but with no less violence, she uttered curses, especially against Dr. Larzenac.

And finally, when she was hoarse, she issued orders.

 From daybreak onward New Orleans was baked by the sun and belabored by a hot dusty wind. It was no weather to walk abroad unless one must, especially in fashionable garb: high hats and long coats, embroidered vests and heavy boots for men; long skirts and long gloves, bonnets and bulging bustles for women who could afford to dress in style.

Yet, as though one were to break a pot of honey near an ants' nest, the population of the city seemed to reach a common decision: they would swarm along the wharves and levees. Ten, a hundred times as many denials would not have shaken the conviction of the public that there was bound to be a steamboat race.

Here was evidence of the truth Edouard Marocain had been at pains to din into Fernand: on its way through the world, money exerts as much force as a mighty river. What had begun as a freshet of funds wagered among people who had been at the Limousin on Mardi Gras had grown, here fed by a quarrel, there by an old grudge, somewhere else by vanity and the wish to appear party to secret information. Now there was not an exchange nor coffeehouse where $75 could not get you $100 that the *Atchafalaya* would beat the *Nonpareil*.

And there was no shortage of takers, either way.

Among the poorer people of the city—the "emancipated" blacks, who in sad truth were sometimes worse off than in slavery days, and the French and Italians and Spanish and Portuguese, who headed for the south of the country as automatically as Swedes and Germans headed for the north—betting was just as rife. Black roustabouts who had never learned to read, so that when toting cargo ashore they had to follow colored flags instead of written signs, were nonetheless able to figure odds in their heads and keep book with a knife and wooden tally. Newly arrived foreigners who had as yet not learned the language managed quite as well in their own way. The sides to be taken were furnished ready-made. Apart from older versus newer, and record holder versus challenger, opinion had other lines to polarize along. Some blacks wanted Drew to win because he had trained Fernand, or because he had refused to put his boat at the disposal of the Confederate army. Some, by contrast, wanted to oppose not him but Barber, because the rumor Fernand had heard long ago—about returning ex-slaves to their former master—still haunted his path.

Likewise some immigrants preferred to back the *Nonpareil* on account of her French name, and others because, every time she arrived or left port, the band she carried gave a free performance.

Nor was New Orleans the sole city to be galvanized by the prospect of a race to set alongside the classic contests of ante-bellum days. Almost every paper from St. Louis to the Gulf, save a few whose proprietors were taking a moral stand—more against gambling than on behalf of passengers whose lives might be at risk—had reprinted the ringing slogan disseminated by the Associated Press, its author unknown but suspected of being right here in New Orleans: "Win or burst, sink or swim, survive or perish, Blucher or Sunset, Drew against Woodley, the *Atchafalaya* versus the *Nonpareil*!"

All of a sudden people at Baton Rouge and Natchez, Vicksburg and Greenville, Bolivar and Napoleon and Helena and Memphis, and scores of other places scarcely large enough to figure in *Conclin's Guide*, had realized that, if there was to be a race, it would now be possible to work out roughly when the boats would pass. Like an epidemic of fever, heady excitement spread north along the Mississippi, and calculations of probable arrival times vied with calculations of odds.

Inevitably, though, interest was keenest at New Orleans, for the boats themselves were here. This fact dawning on sensation seekers, they moved in the direction of the river. Some never came in sight of the water; some, determined not to miss the spectacle, bribed watchmen to let them into warehouses with high windows, or persuaded strangers to invite them up to balconies and roofs. A handful of daring youths scrambled onto the dome of the St. Charles Hotel. This was the happening of the day. For the first time ever, there was *no* audience at the Grand Philharmonic Hall for the matinee performance, and the newer, smarter Academy of Music on St. Charles experienced its worst day since its recent much-heralded opening. Dancing, roller-skating, cycling—all the city's favored pastimes lost their fans.

Seizing their opportunity, excursion-boat owners announced special trips to begin at three or four o'clock, so that passengers could view the steamers when well under way. Tickets were a dollar each. They were eagerly snapped up.

Also the city's peddlers made a killing, selling cool drinks, pralines and mirlitons, po'boys and red beans and rice.

Last evening, at the regular hour for quitting port, the *Mary Crayford*, for Natchez, and the *Jedediah Sprague*, for Baton Rouge, had been delayed by mechanical faults. There had been complaints from their passengers.

Today the boats' respective masters were amazed by petitions that they remain here until five in order not to miss the departure of the racing steamers.

Both refused, for there was perishable freight to be considered. But it took much argument to convince the petitioners that they would enjoy a grander spectacle at a later stage.

It was as though a sense of history in the making had descended on the city—on the state—on the river.

 About mid-morning a messenger brought Louisette a note from Auberon. Reading it made her eyes sparkle. Not looking up, she said to her husband, "Arthur dear, don't you find the heat and the dry wind unbearable?"

There was something in her tone that made Arthur nervous. He took a generous swig of sazerac before countering, "So?"

"I'd like to go for a trip on the river."

"Very well, if you wish. Where to?"

"North. A long way north. And on a luxury steamer. I'd prefer the *Nonpareil*." There was a dead pause. Eventually he said, "Is that note from your brother?"

"Well—yes."

"But I'm your husband. And you know perfectly well the *Nonpareil* is going to race. And in your condition—"

He advanced the point in a tone of finality. Having got his bride pregnant immediately—with more enjoyment than he had expected, but less than he looked forward to from a girl at the Limousin—he felt he had for the time being discharged his marital responsibilities, and had more or less resumed his bachelor existence.

At that she flared up. "My *condition*? It's only been three months—not even that! And certainly for the next year and probably for ages afterwards, I'm going to be treated like some rheumaticky old crone and fed on mush and promises, and first I'm going to look like a barrel and then I'm going to be hog-tied to a noisy smelly digestive tract with a loud noise at one end and no sense of responsibility at the other! I want a final fling! And—"

Struck by a sudden thought, she leaned forward.

"You've been betting on this race, haven't you?"

"Well, it's expected that one should," he answered carelessly.

"And were you planning to see the outcome personally?"

"My dear, I—"

"*Were you?*"

"Well, Hugo had mentioned—"

"Hugo? What about Stella?"

"I don't believe—"

"You don't believe he'd mentioned it to her before mentioning it to you. How like a man! Well, I promise you, Arthur Gattry, *you* have *not* married a girl like Stella, who can be stored in a closet when you don't want her around!"

Defeated, but muttering curses against Auberon, Arthur gave another sigh.

"Well, I guess we could perhaps—"

"Perhaps nothing! All my life I've heard about steamboat races and finally I have my chance to take part in one! You send directly to get a stateroom on the *Nonpareil*—and while you're about it, make sure Hugo doesn't come alone! If he leaves Stella at home I shall never speak to him again!"

"Modern marriage," murmured Arthur under his breath.

"What did you say?"

"Ah . . . I was just wondering: what if all accommodation has been booked?"

"Auberon says it hasn't," she countered, triumphantly flourishing the note. "He got space for himself without any trouble, and hopes we can join him on board at four o'clock."

Arthur drained his glass, not looking at her. After a moment he said, "Why didn't you come straight out with it? Why that rigmarole about wanting to get away from the heat and dust?"

"I . . ." She hesitated. "I don't really know. Except"—with a sudden reversion to her normal manner—"whatever I ask for, you always want to refuse, so I thought this time I'd make it impossible!"

"Not so modern after all," Arthur muttered.

"What?"

"Nothing. I'll go reserve that stateroom right away."

 At Cherouen's house the doorbell rang. Alone in her room, Josephine Var gave a start of alarm. Her heart pounded and her mouth was dry. After a moment she had to sit down while a fit of giddiness passed.

Oh, this was so terrifying! Of all the foul tricks fate could play, was this not the worst: to be chief nurse to the most famous doctor in Louisiana and fall prey to a sickness neither she nor he could cure?

It had begun gradually, with numbness in her toes that spread to her ankles. Now her feet were actively painful. Her own remedies having no effect, last week she had revealed her plight to Cherouen.

Seeming excited at having her appeal for help; the doctor at once uttered reassurance; he had always maintained that electrotherapy was especially suitable for disorders of the nerves, whether inflammatory or neurasthenic. And put off his next patient so she could have treatment at once.

Neither that nor subsequent treatments had done any good. And now worse was happening. On the skin she had always been so proud of despite its recognizably mulatto shade, dark patches were appearing—the reverse of what she was trying for!

She barely suppressed a whimper.

On top of everything else, her sickness was now laying her open to attack on the psychic level. Eulalie had issued a challenge to her, to be taken up on St. John's Eve. But she had been too unwell to leave the house that night.

Could her condition be due to ill-wishing? But why should Damballah make her vulnerable to it? Oh, if only Cherouen would get on about his afternoon rounds! She wanted peace to consult the omens.

Then, abruptly from the landing outside, the doctor's voice raised in a shout: "Josephine! Where the devil are you? This is urgent!"

The door was flung open and he strode in, brandishing a cable message.

"At least the woman has sense, even if her husband doesn't!" he exclaimed. "Listen to this! 'Philip died this morning Marie relapsing come immediately by fastest steamer bring all equipment fee and expenses guaranteed Amelia Grammont'!"

Flushed with triumph, he looked for an immediate response.

But she felt detached from herself now the giddiness had passed. She said without intention, "You've been hoping one of the children would die, haven't you? You were so angry when they sent for Dr. Larzenac, so cocksure that you could have done better . . . and here you can't even cure your own nurse!"

"Don't take that tone with me!" he barked, and in the next moment relented. "I'm sorry. In the excitement of receiving this cable I forgot how unwell you are. I was going to ask you to accompany me. But in your present state—"

"I wouldn't be too good an advertisement for your methods, is that it?" Wearily she forced herself to her feet. "But I'll come, I'll come. What do you want me to do?"

Prompt to forget his solicitude, he said, "I must apply to Mr. Barber, because it was through his offices that the *Atchafalaya* was made available for Larzenac. By a miracle she's in port. Even though she's advertised for Louisville, that needn't be much of a problem. It was the same before . . . Are you *sure* you're well enough to come?"

She mastered herself with vast effort. "Of course I am!" she snapped. "Anyhow, it'll do me good to get away from this house for a while. I sometimes think there's a miasma about places where sick people gather."

"You'll be arguing for the germ theory next!"

"I wouldn't care what theory it was if I got back the feeling in my feet!"

At her fierceness Cherouen hesitated. He said finally, "Well, in spite of the tension it will entail, a river trip could do you good. I hope it will."

"So do I . . . What are you planning to take?"

"Charlie and Elmer are seeing to the equipment." He meant the gardener and coachman. "I want you to tell the patients to depend on their magnetic salves for two or three weeks. Say it's to monitor the restoration of their natural recuperative powers."

"Very well," she sighed, and headed for the door.

When the men were getting set to load the cumbersome electrical machines, it was not without malice that she inquired, "Aren't you sending someone to tell the papers?"

And she was not entirely surprised when he answered, "I already did."

Seizing his hat and coat, his gloves and whip, he hastened off in the cut-under buggy he drove himself on the first stage of his route to the nationwide renown he dreamed of.

Whenever the *Atchafalaya* was at New Orleans, Mr. Caudle—who in spite of all had remained Drew's agent here— sent around letters for her crew that had been directed in care of his office. Invariably one was from St. Louis and bore the delicate script of Susannah Drew.

Today the postmark was as usual, and the envelope . . . but not the writing. The letter was from Elphin, and reported a sudden decline in his mother's health.

Sorting out facts among his nephew's protestations of trust in the Lord, Drew felt a terrifying suspicion grow in his mind. Was this what Elphin pretended to believe, a mere summer fever, or was it the final onslaught of the foul condition Jacob had bequeathed her?

His immediate reaction was to seize the speaking tube beside his bedhead and order David Grant to his stateroom on the double, while he composed a telegram instructing Elphin to obtain the best medical advice regardless of cost. He knew very well, he thought, what he wanted to say. Yet he kept the boy waiting a full minute, pencil poised, before making up his mind how to sign the message. *Uncle Hosea? Hosea Drew?* Or simply *Hosea?* And with or without some sort of salutation: *affectionately,* or *anxiously,* even?

In the event, conscious of David's impatience—well concealed, as ever; this boy had learned to disguise his emotions—he settled on a compromise and wrote: *Your anxious uncle Hosea.*

Scarcely had the door closed again before he was regretting that he had not dared to say: *Give her my love.*

Up to the moment he set eyes on the envelope, he had been tolerably pleased with life. The gamble he had taken—he, who feared the gambling instinct as much as he hated it—seemed to have paid off: his record run to St. Louis had by luck started on a day when the *Nonpareil* was hundreds of miles away, and careful planning and careful maintenance had led to a successful outcome. Here lay proof that—as he had always insisted—there was no need for a race to demonstrate the qualities of a fine steamer.

On the other hand, if Fernand had been unwilling to rejoin the boat he had trained on, or if that faulty pipe in number four boiler had blown again, say at Dog Tooth Bend or the Devil's Race Ground . . .

Oh, why was it his doom always to live through disasters that never happened? The fact was, the boat had stood up to the punishment she was given, and the horns were his, and that was reality enough to have kept both his staterooms and his hold full throughout the season. Freed from his inherited debts, he was amazed how rapidly profits could mount up despite railroad competition. At the

Guild parlor, when other pilot-captains grumbled, he shook his head in silent puzzlement. Like Barber, they must be squandering their earnings; that was the only conclusion he could draw. By this time next year, if things continued as they were going, he would have enough saved to finance a brand-new boat from his own resources, perhaps not quite so large as the *Atchafalaya* but incorporating several improvements which ought to make her even faster. She was to be called the *Susannah Drew* . . . naturally. And as soon as she was launched, he would be able to sell the old boat and tell Barber to get lost. Their acquaintance had done little to make him like the other man. At best he could achieve a grudging respect. However, he would always detest the use Barber put his partner's hard-won money to: more gilt and marble, more flash girls, another consignment of French wine . . .

But until this morning he had been in clear sight of an end to all that. The arrival of Elphin's letter made the air chill, the prospect gray. If, in order to keep Susannah alive, he had to buy the time of doctors at the sort of fee it was rumored people like Cherouen were now demanding—

Why, goodbye to the new steamer, and to independence from the smug son of a bitch who had enabled him to commission this one!

Outside, the roar and clatter of the wharf continued as laden drays rolled up and the freight hoister chugged away the hours. Customarily, about this time on a day when they were due to start another trip, he would go the complete rounds of the vessel, checking on the minutest detail, from the order in which barrels were stowed clear to the stock of soap provided for the laundress.

But not every day brought a letter like this.

After a long moment of contemplation, he reached to the shelf where he kept his current reading and withdrew a volume that contained a poem he had been led to accidentally. He knew of nothing else by its author, whose name was Dunbar, and the language was sometimes impenetrable; still, that lent it a numinous quality and made the words more relishable on his tongue. A stern solemnity taking possession of his mind, he began to read silently but with movements of his lips:

> *I that in heill was and gladness*
> *Am trublit now with great sickness*
> *And feblit with infirmitie—*
> *Timor mortis conturbat me!*

The editor had at least been obliging enough to furnish a translation of the refrain.

As the stanzas rolled on, becoming a catalog of forgotten names much like certain passages of the Old Testament, the sense of religiosity which his favorite poetry could entrain became overwhelming. Lowering the book, he stared into nowhere for a while; then, abruptly, he did something that would have delighted Elphin, and awkwardly got down on his knees to beg his Maker that Susannah might be spared at least until they had a chance to meet one more time.

But the phrase "mourners' bench" kept coming between him and what he wanted to say, as though by premonition that she was already past the medicine of prayer.

Or perhaps because in his heart of hearts he knew he still wanted to do what he had desired when they first met: take her in his arms and make her his.

He remained kneeling a long time, fighting the urge that threatened to possess him: cancel the trip to Louisville and make straight for St. Louis instead, with all the resources and tricks he had rehearsed on his record run to get him to Susannah's bedside before she died.

The means existed. Cannily, as Burns would have said, he had guarded against the risk that Parbury—memory returned the image of the young reporter who had called yesterday, and with it came the jocular correction, "Woodley"—might force him into a race against his will. Today that danger was at its most acute. But there were always dodges to evade the clash . . .

His mind was wandering. As far as the ridiculous idea that, if the *Nonpareil* had not been two berths distant, he would already have started issuing orders to throw cargo back on the wharf, transfer passengers to other steamers—

Oh, no! That smacked of insanity! And insanity was the due of those who did not resist their animal instincts, but yielded to them, like Jacob!

Determinedly he heaved himself up. Replacing the volume of poetry, he took down the Bible Elphin had given him as a Christmas present the year he decided to study for the ministry. Not surprisingly his own gift to the boy had also been a Bible; his, however, had been much less ornate. Over that, there had been some malicious laughing and joking in the family—

Why, this mind of his was becoming as fractious as a steamer in shoal water with a fast current! He heaved a deep sigh, as though hauling on a rope attached to some enormous weight, and let the book fall open on the bed, closing his eyes and stabbing down with one finger. Consciously he regarded this practice as superstitious; nonetheless he retained a degree of credulity, which it solaced. He performed the ritual only at crises.

Haste caused him to catch the corner of several pages and double them over. He opened his eyes in fury to a crumple of confusion somewhere in II Chronicles, a list of town names as forgotten as Dunbar's fellow poets.

An oath half-restrained accompanied his mastery of the impulse to fling the Bible on the floor and stamp on it. He restored it to its usual place and stormed out, deciding to carry on with his regular round of inspection so as to distract himself from the hateful thoughts now infesting his brain.

Suddenly on the wharf: the clatter of a carriage approaching at high speed. It was forced to brake. Its horse neighed and whinnied. There were cries—insults and curses. And then a familiar voice was heard, at its loudest and between cupped hand:

"Hosea! Hosea Drew!"

Descending from the pilothouse, heading for the clerks' office where at about this time before departure it was his custom to receive reports from the *Atchafalaya*'s officers, Drew started and glanced around.

"Barber?" he breathed.

Above him on the steps Fernand likewise reacted, and from the window of the pilothouse Tyburn stared out. The three had been agreeing the watch roster for the trip; they all preferred to change the order each time so as to refresh their acquaintance with every part of the river.

Balked in its progress by confused heaps of goods, the carriage halted. Two men climbed down, one Barber, the other familiar to both Drew and Fernand, though neither could put a name to him as yet.

At the foot of the boat's stage stood watchman Eli Gross. Recognizing Barber, he ushered him and his companion aboard. By the time they reached the deck Drew, Fernand, and first mate Tom Chalker were there to greet them, the latter by coincidence, for he had only been intending to deliver Drew a message.

"Hosea!" Barber rapped. "You'll have to cancel the trip to Louisville! There's another emergency at St. Louis! You remember meeting Dr. Cherouen at my place, the night of Mardi Gras?"

The doctor stepped forward, hand outstretched. "Captain, we weren't introduced on that occasion, but when I learned who you were, I regretted missing the opportunity."

Perfunctorily shaking hands, Drew looked at Barber. "What do you mean, 'have to cancel' my trip? You don't exercise any right of command, remember!"

Wheezing and puffing as ever, Tyburn had by now clambered down from the pilothouse. At almost the same moment Wills came from the office to see what was delaying the captain. On spotting Barber, he stepped back long enough to tell his senior partner Motley to come with him.

"Do you always have to snap like that?" Barber countered. "I told you there's an emergency. Doctor, show the captain your telegram from Mrs. Grammont."

Cherouen produced it with a flourish. "Exactly as I predicted!" he exclaimed. "Adhering as he does to the nonsensical germ theory, the doctor from Paris has failed. It may well be too late to call me in now, but I'm resolved to do my utmost."

Engaged in conversation, caterer Ernest Vehm and steward Lewis Amboy, who was due to retire after this season, approached along the main deck. Vehm was the only person on board who owed a direct debt to Barber, except for Drew. When the *Atchafalaya* was first commissioned, Barber had given her two of his best cooks, several waiters, and a selection of the Limousin's finest wines and liquors. Consequently Vehm's eyes lit up as soon as he noticed Barber, and he hastened forward—only to register, a moment later, that he would do better not to interrupt.

Having taken in the telegram with the sweeping glance he used to sum up a report posted at the Pilots' Guild, Drew handed it back.

"Convenient!" he said, and with a thumb over his shoulder indicated what he meant: the *Nonpareil.*

It took a while for Cherouen to grasp the significance of that gesture. In the interim more of the officers joined the group. Ealing had as usual been checking the wheels with Walt Presslie, who was considerably changed from the gangling tow-haired boy Fernand had first seen, for hard work and good steamboat food had turned him into a husky young man capable of wrestling reversing rods single-handed. Josh Diamond had been working with them and also arrived to report. Jack Sexton hovered in the background; he had recruited a dozen black deckhands whom Motley had to enter in the payroll. These too formed an audience.

Such was the attention concentrated on the two steamers that the appearance of Barber and Cherouen had created a great stir along the nearby waterfront. This further departure from routine sufficed to bring most work to a halt, regardless of the threats of overseers. The boat separating the rivals was the much smaller *Lydia King*, which both overtopped by the height of their hurricane decks; within a matter of minutes officers and crew aboard the *Nonpareil* were seen gathering with telescopes and field glasses, and some optimists on shore ran that way, hoping for a few cents' tip for bringing news to her.

Then the circuit closed in Cherouen's mind, and he took half a step towards Drew, lifting his fist. Reflexively the captain raised his heavy stick. The blow aborted.

Not so the blistering words.

"You think I faked this?" the doctor roared.

"Did I say that?" Drew retorted.

Just at that point Fonck and O'Dowd emerged, dirty, red-eyed, blinking at the sun, along with the black gang leader of the firemen, who would look over the new deckhands and pick the strongest to shovel coal.

Without planning, Drew found himself standing before a tribunal of his personnel.

And a phrase from Elphin's letter kept revolving and revolving in his mind: "The Lord willing, Mother will be of sound health when you return to this city. But at the present . . ."

Temptation? Common sense? His brain felt like a whirlpool. A decision lay within his grasp which was so utterly unlike any other he had ever made that it frightened him. Moreover it contradicted a pledge made to himself long, long ago . . .

And was he now the same person? Would he be breaking an oath or acknowledging a simple truth?

Muddled, inchoate, like the spring floodwaters of the Mississippi, his thoughts raged and roared and swirled and he stood mute.

Events from his past flashed into consciousness, along with apt lines of verse such as he had made his mottos for a while before finding something yet more striking and suitable. For years he had been unable to think back to his youth dispassionately. The betrayal he had felt when marvelous brilliant Jacob went insane had cut so deep into his soul, he was afraid to remember the pleasure and excitement he had had as a boy from ideas that Jacob sparked in his mind.

And yet there was no way he could have known Jacob would rot at the core!

Just prior to his record St. Louis run, he had come on a recent poem by Mr.

Emerson, and the image of turning down a Louisville trip in favor of one to the city where, if ever he retired and sank roots on land, he would most likely settle, shone at him from its first verse:

> *Good-bye, proud world! I'm going home:*
> *Thou art not my friend, and I'm not thine.*
> *Long through thy weary crowds I roam;*
> *A river-ark on the ocean brine,*
> *Long I've been tossed like the driven foam;*
> *But now, proud world! I'm going home.*

Had not someone once said of him—he knew not who, but the phrase had currency enough to reach him at several removes—"Hosea Drew seems set on managing without friends"?

But there was one person beloved in his life.

And once a man in a buggy had struck at him with a whip.

And Ed Marocain's unworthy heirs were hoping to see the *Nonpareil* take the horns for the St. Louis run.

And there was a foreign financier whose ideas of initiating a boy not much younger than Fernand into the world of manhood was to get him disgustingly drunk in a public place.

And there was a man who, having lost his sight in a battle between kinsmen, thereafter hated anyone who had dismissed the war for what it was before it started: a pointless bloodbath over quarrels time would mend.

And there was a man right in front of him who owned half of what he himself had made possible, and beside him another who perhaps might possess the power to heal, to cure, to vitalize . . .

And there was one person beloved in his life.

The silence grew. With a shock of horror Drew became aware that not only those immediately about him, but countless hundreds of onlookers, were hanging on his words.

He found none. His throat was far too dry for speech.

Then, blessedly, blunt Dutch Fonck stepped forward and demanded, "What the hell goes on?"

The words unlocked Drew's tongue, and with it the rest of his frame. He was able to set down his staff, lean on it, and gaze frostily at the doctor.

"Mr. Barber, whom you all know," he declaimed in the kind of voice he ordinarily reserved for a night of gales, "wants us to dump the cargo and passengers we've taken on for Louisville and make another fast run to St. Louis."

His eyes shifted briefly to Barber, then fixed on Motley and Wills as though to counter some imagined objection.

"This is the Electric Doctor that you've heard about, I'm sure. The cost of taking him to St. Louis the same way we took the doctor from France is underwritten by the Grammonts—if we're to credit the telegram Dr. Cherouen showed me."

On the verge of eruption, Cherouen thought better of it. Partly he was distracted by the arrival of Jones and Cuffy; they had been occupied in parking Barber's carriage, and there was precious little space to spare within a hundred yards of the waterfront.

"But," Drew went on, "the message doesn't order him to come by the same boat Dr. Larzenac took, only by the fastest boat. Right over there"—flinging up his stick to point—"lies a steamer advertised for St. Louis, and her master claims she can outrun ours. Dr. Cherouen, why didn't you apply at once to Captain Woodley?"

Ever so slightly, he stressed the last word but one. A chuckle rewarded his veiled gibe, echoed by several of his listeners, while on the fringe of the group the uncertain black recruits felt it advisable to join in. Glancing around to see where the laughter had taken its rise, Drew noticed that David Grant had stolen out of the office without permission and was eavesdropping.

Under normal circumstances he would have been annoyed. This soon before leaving port, the boy should have been busy at his bills of lading. For once he had done the right thing. Making sure he was observed, Drew gave a vastly exaggerated wink. A sense of confidence was growing in him. He felt, looming at the edge of awareness, a possible ideal solution to the predicament he was in.

And that was something which, half an hour ago, he would never have believed.

The hilarity around him, though, was making Cherouen fume for the affront to his dignity. He burst out, "Captain, you know damned well the Grammonts are reliable. Hell, you took their pay before!"

"Sure I did," Drew said with equanimity. And waited. He had a reason. Thanks to five years' intermittent observation of Barber, he had learned to read the latter's face much as he read a stretch of river.

And some such unconscious clue as those which had made him a master pilot had prompted him to conclude, the moment Barber and Cherouen appeared, that what was worth hearing would come from the former.

Cherouen blasted on, "So what the devil are you doing just *standing* there instead of—?"

A tap on his arm from Barber interrupted. "Doctor, I think I know Captain Drew better than you do."

The hint was taken, but Cherouen looked more furious than ever as he glanced at the wharf, seeming to search for something not yet in sight.

"What's he expecting?"

The quiet question came from Fernand, who had made his way to Drew's side. But the captain had no time to mention the equipment referred to in the telegram before Barber was launched on a patently prepared speech.

"Hosea, you need look no further than your own chimneys to learn why Dr. Cherouen is appealing to us and not to Woodley!" He flung up his arm, and automatically the eyes of those aboard and ashore followed his movement, fixing their gaze on the gilded antlers that swung between the smokestacks. "Far be it from me to judge the merits of competing schools of medicine, but this I do believe: no matter who the parents of a sick child may be, that child deserves the finest care doctors and nurses can provide! But"—the shift of tone was perfectly timed—"*all* researchers at the forefront of discovery need support, doctors as much as those pioneers who design and develop new steamers, new machines and tools, new reapers and—and lathes and saws!"

His partner's head of steam, Drew privately decided, was not quite adequate for the run he had undertaken. That also lent him confidence.

But Barber's peroration was impassioned enough, and made more than just Cherouen nod vigorous approval. The officers and crew of the *Atchafalaya*, for weeks past, had basked in popular approbation; it had given them a taste for flattery, and for a boat to set out to break her own record, rather than a rival's, was almost unprecedented, so that was warranted to raise their status even higher. Without another word being spoken, Drew knew he had their full support.

Meditatively he said, looking down at the deck, "Dr. Cherouen, is it true your methods can cure any disease?"

"I trust I have too much humility to make such a ridiculous claim," was the stiff reply. "But I can safely state that they have shown remarkable results in cases which other medical men had given up as hopeless."

"You employ some sort of machinery?"

"Electrical machines, sir. Built to my own design. Unique in the world!"

"How much space do they take up—a wagonload, two loads?"

"Ah, you're going to do it!" Barber exclaimed, clasping his hand with an expression of thankfulness.

Drew glanced at him sharply. "Haven't said so yet! But I know why you're so eager to make me!"

Barber smiled uncertainly.

"You've been betting on the *Atchafalaya* all this season, haven't you? Ever since the *Nonpareil* started work! I know! They may hate my guts at the Guild parlor, but that's not the only place on the river where you can hear gossip. You know about the debts my half-brother left, which I had to sweat blood to pay off. And it galls me, sir—galls me!—that half the profit I turn in every season goes to the man poor Jacob died in debt to. Don't argue with me!"—hefting his stick again, with a scowl. "You're a partner in my boat by sufferance, not by right. These men around me are the ones who count: the ones who work to make her run. Mr. Fonck!"

"Sir!" The chief engineer stepped forward.

"Are her boilers and her engines sound?"

"As they ever were, Captain! Ah . . ." He hesitated.

"Except the mud-drum pipe in number four?"

Relieved, Fonck gave a nod.

"And we know about that, and there's nothing to be done short of laying her up while we break out the furnace floor and make a new one." Out of the corner of his eye Drew was watching Cherouen. He saw the doctor flinch in the manner of one having second thoughts. And continued, "But she'll do for normal work?"

"I'm sure of that, sir."

"Well, then, we're safe, for everyone knows that *Atchafalaya*'s fastest runs are part of her normal work, hm?" Without waiting for a reaction, he turned to the carpenter. "Mr. Diamond, how about her hull and upper works? All sound?"

"Yes, sir. But if we're to match last month's time, we should strip her glass as we did before, and—"

Drew interrupted. "If it proves necessary, we can do it under way. I'm not convinced anything but her guards and swinging stages offer great resistance to the air. I've talked about it with Mr. Lamenthe, and we're agreed that sometimes it's better and slicker for the wind to go around."

"That's so," Fernand declared, as with a pointing finger he indicated something Drew had failed to notice. At the foot of the stage where Gross stood guard, several early-arriving passengers were giving instructions for their bags to be unloaded from a carriage. Nearby, a few others were sitting on their belongings for lack of better seats; these were intending to take deck passage and, because they were paying the lowest fare, must put up with being relegated to the last.

Drew took in the situation and shrugged as he continued to the clerks, "Mr. Motley—Mr. Wills—how many passengers have engaged for Ohio ports?"

Motley snapped his fingers at David. "Bring the register, boy!" he ordered. But David started to recite from memory.

"Cabin passengers for Louisville, eight; for Paducah—"

"Captain!" Cherouen cut in. "Are you or are you not going to accept my proposal? If you do, then your passengers will have to find alternative means of travel!"

"I am trying to establish," Drew answered coldly, "whether it is worth my while from a commercial standpoint. Unlike Mr. Barber, I am not a gambling man. I weigh and calculate my prospects in advance. The same holds for my clerks. Young David's feat just now will indicate how seriously I and they apply this principle in all departments."

"Come to the point, man!" Cherouen raged. "Or I shall think your first advice was sound, and I should have gone to Captain Woodley!"

By this time crewmen had gathered from all over the boat, waiters and tenders as well as deckhands, learning in whispers from those first on the scene the reason for this confrontation.

"Doctor," Drew said after a pause, "I can afford to make the run for you, even though it'll mean unloading cargo that's now being brought aboard—on two conditions!"

"What are they?" Cherouen barked.

"First! As soon as you have attended your patient in St. Louis, you will also attend and treat Mrs. Susannah Drew, my sister-in-law. Your usual fee will be met."

"Done!" Cherouen exclaimed. "I'm always ready to help anybody in distress!"

"Except maybe for Mrs. Parbury?"

"How—?"

The betraying word escaped before Cherouen could change the form of the question into "What the devil do you mean?" instead of "How did you know about that?"—his obvious first intention.

Drew felt a warming sense of power infuse him. Silently he thanked Dorcas for telling him about the errand she had been on when Fernand refound her. For an instant he could have believed that his whole reason for taking on a colored cub against the massed hostility of the river community might have been so that in time he could wield that wounding a weapon against the Electric Doctor.

But he was not going to allow anybody on board who could give him orders, except another pilot during his watch. It had been allowing someone who was not a pilot to give him orders that had been the downfall of Parbury.

Larzenac, in fractured English, had made it clear how indebted he was to the *Atchafalaya* and her crew for the safe and speedy journey to St. Louis. It was hard to imagine Cherouen deigning to utter thanks. More likely he regarded it as beneath his dignity.

Drew was saved from the need to reply by another interruption from Barber, who said in a soothing tone, "Hosea, you haven't mentioned your second condition."

Now for it!

He drew a deep breath, feeling years of principle blow away on the dry hot wind.

"For the first and only time in my life, Langston," he said—and it was also a first time as he spoke, for never before had he addressed his partner with the informality the other took for granted; mostly he preferred not to address him at all—"I propose to lay a bet. And it's with you. I bet my half of the *Atchafalaya* against yours that I can win a race with the *Nonpareil*. If Dr. Cherouen's equipment is aboard earlier than five o'clock, then we'll take a true timing of our run and match it against hers. If we leave together, which right now seems very likely"—he consulted his watch—"because it's a quarter of three already, and we have considerable freight to off-load . . . Well, then, we'll simply run her out."

"Done!" Barber said at once, "You're not a gambler, as you say, and what you've just done makes that clear. Either way, I gain! If the *Nonpareil* beats you I'll have your half of the *Atchafalaya*. If you win, I'll clear so much from my own wagers, I shall never miss the pittance I receive from you. Say, what's happening?"

There was a commotion on the wharf again. Every head turned, to see a wagon laden with machinery of brass and glass, of rubber and iron and gutta-percha. In amazement several onlookers crossed themselves or muttered charms.

Cherouen had been about to remonstrate with Drew, perhaps for not taking seriously his mission of mercy. But the sight of his precious apparatus drove all other thoughts from his head. He dashed back down the landing stage, shouting.

Drew instantly started issuing orders.

"Tom, Jack! Get your hands to work off-loading cargo! Euclid, send to Caudle and tell him he'll have to make alternative arrangements for it. Roger, go the rounds of the passengers and find out whether they'll stay with us and take their chance of being put ashore by yawl or coal flat, and if not, refund their fare. Spare me David for a little; I have an errand for him. The rest of you, go make sure she's in tiptop shape when we cut our line and start to run!"

By this time the news had overflowed to the wharf. Here and there a cheer went up; then suddenly there was a roar of exultation from the bowels of the *Atchafalaya* herself, signifying that word had reached the firemen. They too shared in the status the steamer had achieved and were as eager as her officers for further glory. Tension made the air as electric as any of Cherouen's machines.

When the officers and crew had melted away to their duties, except for Fernand, Tyburn, and David Grant, Barber stared at Drew in puzzlement.

"I kind of get the idea," he said at length, "you were expecting this."

"When you can't dodge any more, there ain't nothing you can do but beat the daylights out of the bastard picking on you," said Drew.

"Meaning me?" Barber exclaimed. "Hosea, I assure you—"

"Don't give yourself such airs!" Drew glanced toward the *Nonpareil;* it was clear the news had reached her, for the crew was galvanized into frantic activity. "I don't mean you. Nor Cato Woodley, either—the lousy punk! He may think he's a man, but I won't credit it until he does something men do, like making up his own mind. No, it's Parbury who's after me. Always has been. Can't say I blame him, I guess, but—oh, hell, you know he didn't want the *Nonpareil* just to earn a decent living. He wants her to hold the horns for every trade in the river. And what does she have so far? A few odds and ends it wasn't worth my time to go collect! Now, today, he's going to be satisfied. He and you have forced the race I didn't want."

"But I assure you, ever since Mardi Gras I've been—"

"You've been saying one thing and hoping for the other! Don't waste breath on denying it! You're a gambler like I'm a riverman. It's in the blood and bone!"

"As you say," Barber sighed, and added, "When do you think you'll get away?"

"I told you already: as soon as the cargo we don't want is on the wharf. Won't be much before five."

Barber inclined his head. "Very well. You have staterooms to spare, presumably. I'll take one; Dr. Cherouen another, and his chief nurse a third. I believe I see her over there by the wagon."

"Apply to Mr. Motley," was Drew's chill response. "You'd best be quick. By the look of it, Eli is having trouble standing off an assault by the sporting fraternity. Any friends of yours among them? I guess there may be."

Indeed, at the foot of the stage Gross—who had just been joined by Wills—was being besieged by people of all walks in life: a couple of young men, well dressed; two or three older and shabbier, apparently after work; a woman whose heavily painted face suggested she might not follow the most respectable of occupations, along with a man whose dress and manner were contrastingly quiet, perhaps a professional sharper who had realized, like her, that as soon as a boat was committed to race it must attract a lot of wealthy bored young men . . .

"I suggest you make those reservations right away, Mr. Barber," Tyburn said softly. "Looks like there's going to be pressure on space."

Still the other hesitated, bracing himself to put an all-important question. At last it emerged with the suddenness of a champagne cork.

"Hosea, the *Nonpareil*'s the newer boat. With all respect to Mr. Tyburn and—ah—Mr. Lamenthe, and of course yourself, thanks to Parbury's influence in the

Guild Woodley can call on the best pilots on the Mississippi, and reportedly he's done so. Moreover he's refused freight or passengers for any way-landing. What makes you so damned confident?"

"I've done it before," was Drew's curt reply.

"Yes, but—"

"Okay," the captain cut in. "I'm devious—is that what you want to be told? I believe in precautions. On our downriver trip after taking the horns, I left messages at every place where we refueled coming up. My agents are instructed to make exactly the same preparations for any later run, on receipt of one word by telegraph. David! Get the cable addresses of our agents—unless you know them by heart, too—and run like blazes to the telegraph office. The word you have to send is *expedition*. Got that? Go!"

The boy grinned in wholly uncharacteristic fashion. Then, even more surprisingly, he bounced high in the air and turned a cartwheel along the deck. A gang of hands busy with miscellaneous freight gave him a cheer. There was suddenly a festive atmosphere aboard the *Atchafalaya*. It did not in the least accord with Cherouen's view of the solemnity of his mission.

"You're on a won bet," Drew said sourly to Barber. "And much as I regret it, so am I."

For a long while before he was able to resume his duties Fernand stood like a man in a trance, staring out over the familiar riverside view as though seeing it for the first time.

Never had he expected that this moment would befall him. To be a pilot on a racing steamer!

And if the *Atchafalaya* did win, why, from then on for the rest of his career he would be able to command the highest rates on any of the western rivers. Even if his boat lost, the publicity alone would be enough to transform his circumstances.

What it boiled down to was that his chance of marrying Dorcas had suddenly come a year closer.

He had scarcely seen her since Mardi Gras, though frequent notes assured him it was not because of coldness on her part. On the occasions they had been able to steal a few hours together, she had explained. Her mistress's condition was deteriorating, and in parallel motion with it Parbury's demands grew more fretful and insistent, as though he were becoming senile enough to resent that his wife should enjoy more of their servants' attention than he did. Sleeping together again was out of the question. Not one night went by without Parbury or his wife ringing for some sort of service: a drink, something to eat, a visit to the commode.

And Fibby was not well enough to cope alone. She had developed a growth in her abdomen and was in constant pain except when she took medicine obtained from a friend, which seemed mostly to be alcohol and opium and made her vague and forgetful.

At least, so Dorcas had assured him, Parbury's attentions had become no more unbearable, and for putting up with them he sometimes gave her presents. It dismayed Fernand that his future wife should be augmenting her portion this way; however, when he remonstrated she reminded him that it would bring their wedding day nearer, and no price was too great to be rid of the Parburys once for all.

Already, because this season was going well, Fernand knew he could afford to set her up with at least one servant in a house at least the match of Parbury's. But this she had refused. She wanted to make certain their first home was a splendid one, befitting a top pilot. It looked as though she had once more been proven right. By this time next week . . . !

Old dreams as well as new surfaced in Fernand's mind. He recalled his long-ago intention to invite his mother aboard one of the steamers he had charge of, and for a while he toyed with the notion of sending for her, and indeed Dorcas too.

But Drew's sober, calculating attitude stood as a model for him now, for he had seen its effects. He knew such distraction could be fatal. For this trip he must concentrate his mind absolutely. Better to return in triumph and be greeted like a hero home from the wars.

Besides, suppose Eulalie started planting charms all over the boat . . . !

"Mas' Lamenthe!" a voice shouted. He roused with a start. Here came one of the deckhands, grinning for the honor of being sent in search of someone who was such a credit to "the race" . . . at least according to the black press of Louisiana.

"What is it?"

"Sah, Mas' Vanaday de inspector come here an' de cap'n say he busy, will you talk to um?"

Fernand sighed. Well, it was only to be expected. Back when he first signed up with Drew, the steamboat inspectors had been constant visitors aboard the *Atchafalaya*, though their attentions had shifted elsewhere when it became obvious that she was being operated to the highest standards.

But the rumor of a race was bound to bring them running. Just so long as they were equally strict with the *Nonpareil*, all would be well.

Even so, it would be half an hour wasted.

"Tell him I'm on my way," he said gruffly, and followed the hurrying deckhand at a calm pace imitative of his mentor's.

 "The lowdown sneaking son of a bitch!" Woodley raged, staring through his field glasses. "Drew's unloading cargo that was put aboard this morning! He's not making a regular commercial run!"

Given the news which had been brought a few minutes before, that was unsurprising. The officers standing around him held their peace, except for McNab, who said sourly, "Wasn't that what you were hoping for, Captain—a chance to prove our boat is better? Well, here it is."

"I don't trust him!" Woodley rasped. "He'll leave an hour ahead of schedule and claim it was at the same time as us!"

"We can make certain that doesn't happen," Hogan said, lowering his own glasses. Trumbull was still in the pilothouse, which afforded a better view than this spot on the boiler deck.

"He'll leave when he damn' well chooses!" Woodley insisted, having missed the point. "And if we leave at the same time, and Parbury isn't here—Mr. Iliff! Send your boy to bring Captain Parbury. Give him money for a landau. Go on, do it now."

"What about Gordon?" Iliff countered.

"The hell with him! If he's not aboard for a record run, I for one won't miss him . . . What in *tarnation* are they taking off that wagon?"

"Must be Dr. Cherouen's machines," Hogan suggested.

"Oh, yeah. I guess— What is it?"—rounding on an anxious deckhand who had arrived at a run.

"Captain!"—with a sketch for a salute. "Mr. Underwood says they're trying to come on board!"

"Who are?"

"Uh—all kinds of people. Says he can't stop 'em all forever!"

With a sense of the world falling apart, Woodley strode to the rail and looked down. At least twenty people, including a few women, were laying siege to young Anthony, who had as usual been assigned the routine job of checking that those who tried to board had paid their fare. He glanced up, desperate for assistance, and a moment later Whitworth arrived with a couple of burly deckhands. Having spoken rapidly to Anthony, he shouted to the captain.

"Sir, you got to get a clerk down here! He can't make 'em believe we're taking passengers for St. Louis only!"

Woodley took a deep breath. "Okay! Iliff, you relieve the boy, send him to Parbury like I said. McNab, get Bates to assign you a couple of tenders who know how to handle cash. Paying passengers are paying passengers, even if they are idiots who only want to say they've taken part in a race. Corkran, you and Roy raise steam at once! Is Steeples here? Williams?"

"Vic's below," the chief engineer answered. "But I don't know about Eb. He should be here by now."

A chill tremor went down Woodley's spine. He concealed his reaction.

"Find him, damn it! And I mean at once!"

 Having spent the morning on an entirely different story, which had worked out well, Joel had taken time for lunch before returning to the *Intelligencer* office. Confident the copy he was about to deliver would be publishable, he was feeling tolerably pleased with himself when he pushed open the door.

A blast met him, hotter than the wind outside, hot as a steamer's furnace.

"Siskin! Where the hell have you been? And what the devil did you mean by giving me *this* last night?"

Choleric, fuming, shaking a copy of today's paper like a club, here was Abner
Graves breaking all his own rules and storming into the pressroom instead of
insisting that Joel come to him.

Feebly Joel said, "What?"

"This arrant nonsense!" Graves jabbed his finger on the relevant column.
"Where you took your oath there wouldn't be a race between the *Atchafalaya* and
the *Nonpareil!*"

A terrible leaden sensation gathered around Joel's heart. "You mean something's happened to alter the logical conclusion I—"

"Logical!" Graves bellowed. "If that's what they teach as logic in the fancy
school you went to, we can manage without it! The *Atchafalaya* is dumping cargo
for Ohio ports, and the *Nonpareil*—as you damn' well know—has been refusing
goods for anywhere except St. Louis. If that doesn't spell a race, I'm a
Dutchman!"

Joel clenched his fists. He could see his job vanishing up the chimneys of the
rival steamers like the fumes from a pine knot.

"Get over there at once!" Graves roared. "Get aboard the *Nonpareil* even if you
have to take deck passage! I'm arranging by telegraph to have your dispatches
picked up along the way, and if the *Atchafalaya* ever gets into the lead I want you
to overtake her by train and report from her as well. And before you ask: no, you
may not go home for your baggage! You shift your ass down to the wharf just as
soon as you grab hold of this documentation I've prepared!"

Dismayed, Joel began, "But, Mr. Graves—"

And stopped dead. An idea had erupted in his mind that previously he would
never have dared to voice. Timorously he put it into words.

"Mr. Graves!"

"*Yes?*"

"If you're so angry about my getting it wrong last night, then why—?"

"Why the hell am I sending you in spite of it? Because you may have no more
sense than a bedbug, but you write so well you had me believing the garbage you
turned in. Me!"—in an aggrieved tone. Then, with a sudden resumption of his
normal manner: "Come on, this way! Move!"

Joel tossed his draft for today's piece on the handiest table and obeyed, his
heart singing.

"I say! Arthur! Hugo! Hello!"

The high voice cut through the racket of the riverside. Arthur
glanced around. He was ill-temperedly overseeing the dis-
charge of Louisette's baggage from the carriage that had brought them. She had
insisted on four hatboxes and a trunk fit for an Atlantic voyage, not to mention two
changes of costume for her maid Bertha. Arthur saw no reason for the latter to be
along; he had left his own valet behind, since the *Nonpareil* boasted a comprehensive staff of cabin attendants.

And Stella had inflicted a scarcely less burdensome load on Hugo and their respective servants. If the steamer did not actually founder under the weight, Arthur reflected sourly, she might well be handicapped by it.

His eye fell on the man who had shouted: Auberon, of course. But he was late in reacting. Louisette had recognized him instantly and jumped down from the carriage. Nobody could have guessed she was pregnant; Bertha had had—so she declared—no trouble lacing her into her slenderest corset. It had been in Arthur's mind to consult some doctor or midwife concerning the stage at which tight lacing might affect the child, but other things had interfered. As soon as this trip was over, however . . .

"And how are you, old fellow?" Auberon inquired, using his worst mock-British tones. At least he had refrained from asking in French, which was a mercy; most of the time he delighted in phrases borrowed from European languages, because they were tremendously impressive to girls whose families were never going to let them venture far afield for fear they might be "spoiled" before a desirable match was found.

Arthur looked him over. His cravat was loose; his boots were scratched and dusty; his cheeks were flushed; his speech was slurred . . . When, Arthur asked silently, was he going to learn to hold his liquor like a gentleman—like himself? The more he learned about the family he had married into, the more he felt their son and heir would have been better educated had he been sent to sweat out five years on a hog farm.

But if his bets on the *Nonpareil* were lost, Arthur would have no one else to turn to for help in recouping his fortunes. Exactly why he had wagered so much, he could not recall, but he did remember where and with whom. It had been at the Limousin, and Barber had been boasting so about the steamer he held a share in . . .

At all events the figure was twenty thousand.

Accordingly he swallowed his pride and warmly shook Auberon's hand, thanking him profusely for having notified Louisette about the race.

Auberon was in too boisterous a mood to respond. He took his sister by the arm and hurried her toward the boat, yelling orders over his shoulder at her maid. Stella followed, and with a sigh Arthur joined Hugo Spring in completing the transfer of their belongings.

 Nervous, Anthony was received by Captain Parbury in a dark salon crowded with overstuffed furniture. Conscious of his instructions to return at once, he blurted out his news, afraid the old man might explode with rage.

On the contrary: he uttered a gusting sigh like one who has struggled long and hard and come to the end of his task.

He asked a single question: "Does Mr. Woodley still plan to leave at five?"

"I guess so, sir," the boy answered. "Leastways he didn't tell me no different."

"Good!"

Parbury was seated in a high-backed leather chair. At his right, various necessaries reposed on a lacquered papier-mâché table, including a brass bell. By touch he found and rang it.

Scarcely a moment passed before a slim girl with huge dark eyes, dressed in a drab stuff gown, came to inquire what he wanted. Her voice was tremulous, and Anthony was relieved to find he was not the only person the old captain overawed.

"You've packed everything for my trip?" Parbury said.

"Yes, sir. It's all ready."

"Pack for yourself as well. This time I want you to come with me."

There was an instant of total stillness. The hot oppressive air seemed to congeal.

Eventually the girl raised her head.

"I don't want to be blown up," she said flatly.

"Dorcas, my dear!" With perfect accuracy he caught her hand and drew her to him. He appeared to have forgotten there was someone else in the room. "Didn't I tell you this morning? There's no question of being blown up! But there's going to be a race, one to set alongside the famous races of before the war, and the winning boat is going to be *mine!*"

On the last word his fingers clamped convulsively around hers.

"Dorcas—Dorcas my *dear!* You have conceived some affection for me, surely? For me who took you in when Dr. Malone says you could have died on the street? Tell me you have!"

His blind face, ludicrously crossed by the gaudy bandanna she had given him, turned beseechingly upward.

"Of course!" she cried, trying to tug her fingers free as his other hand groped around her skirt to press her to him. "Of course I owe you more than I can ever repay! But—"

"Then why won't you come with me? I'd regret it to the end of my days if you weren't with me at the supreme climax of my life! Have you not guessed that I love you?"

Anthony wished with all his heart he could be a thousand miles from this grotesque confrontation.

"But your wife!" Dorcas burst out. Parbury interrupted.

"Wife? You know what kind of a wife she's been to me since I came back from the war—*and* she let my only son die while I was away!" The accusation came out raw and bleeding. "If there were any justice in the world . . . But there's none. Take what you can and make the most of it: that's the rule experience has taught me. But, Dorcas!"—his voice growing gentle—"there's one thing that's comforted me in my darkest moments. You gave me courage to continue until I found someone to make the steamer of my dreams a reality. Now she's set to run out her keenest rival. Come with me! Lend me your eyes!"

Once more there was a pause. Then, unexpectedly, Dorcas said, "How much time do I have?"

Parbury tensed. "You're coming? You *are* coming?"

She ignored the question, and continued, "But when you say *pack*, you forget I own nothing to pack anything in! I have little enough in all conscience—a few gowns, shoes, stockings, bodices . . . That and I guess soap, towel, a hairbrush and comb, the sort of things I pack for you, would fill a bag like your old carpet-bag with the broken lock."

"Take it!" Again he pressed her hand fervently. "I'm a blockhead not to have thought of that before!"

Released at last, she kissed him lightly on the forehead. Turning away, she gave Anthony an immense, exaggerated wink: a streetwalker's wink, accompanied by a lascivious passage of her tongue across her lips.

He was so startled, he almost failed to react when she beckoned him to accompany her from the room. Outside, he tried to break away, mindful of his orders to go back to the boat, but she sternly checked him.

"Tell your driver to wait a little longer! How is the captain to get to the wharf as quickly as that landau can take us? And Mr. Woodley will not dare leave without him. I'll be with you in a quarter of an hour."

The door of her room creaked as she was tossing all her belongings into the shabby but still usable bag. From the passage Fibby whispered, "Dorcas honey, what yo' doin'?"

"The captain wants me to go with him on this trip."

Fibby gasped, crossing herself. "Honey chil', how'm I gon' tell Miz' Parbury?"

"*I'm* going to tell her," said Dorcas savagely. "I've been looking forward to this for a long time. Just exactly at the moment when I get set to walk out the door on her husband's arm, I'm going to tell her what he ordered me to do and how he bribed me to do it."

She snapped the bag shut. Its faulty lock flew open again at once; she shrugged and made do by buckling the strap.

"Poor Fibby!" she said, claiming her cloak from a hook behind the door. "But I'm doing just what the captain told me. He said, 'Take what you can and make the most of it.' So I'm going to."

Having twirled the cloak around her, black side out, she turned her back and retrieved from under the bed the purse in which she had stored her coin-by-coin savings . . . and one thing far more precious: the engagement ring Fernand had bought her after their night at the Limousin, which she wore only when she was away from the house, which Mrs. Parbury and even Fibby had never seen.

The fat black woman was making a valiant attempt to follow, but so far she was badly astray. She ventured, "Yo' gwine be de new missus? Miz' Adèle gwine to de hospital?"

"Oh, wouldn't he like that—just?" Dorcas exclaimed, chuckling gleefully. "But I don't want to live in a poky house like this any more."

"You got a better job!" Fibby burst out, as the thought habits of slavery days finally broke down and she remembered that nowadays a servant could find a new employer without waiting to be sold.

"No, I—" Dorcas began, and was interrupted by a shout from the front of the house.

"Dorcas! Aren't you ready yet?"

"Coming, sir!" And aside to Fibby: "Damn him, he'll spoil my surprise for Miz' Adèle if he yells like that! I don't have a better job, Fibby dear. I got the gentleman Miz' Adèle turned away, and he *is* a gentleman for all he came calling on a servant, and he's going to be rich, and he's going to win the race against Captain Damn-your-eyes Parbury! And when I'm living in a beautiful new house in the Garden District, I won't forget you, I promise. I'll send for you to come and work for me. And Captain and Mrs. Parbury may *rot*!"

 "And another thing!" roared the bankrupt proprietor of the Grand Philharmonic Hall, who had called together everyone on his payroll so he could vent his rage on them in the empty auditorium.

Gaston could not stop himself trembling. He knew the rest were looking to him for guidance. He had been here longer than anyone except a few of the stage-hands, and the conductor was after all a person of some consequence . . .

But all he could think of was that he was now sure to be out of a job along with the humblest emptier of cuspidors.

He had been struggling for weeks to find an alternative post, and failed. Gallingly, there was one new permanent orchestra in the city now: at the Limousin. It should be he, Gaston, who was directing it! But after the débâcle of Mardi Gras he had not dared go back . . .

What was he to be reduced to? Conducting the quadrille band aboard a steamboat, like that madman who had tried to get into a knife fight with Mr. Gordon? A man who could not read a note of music, yet leading his own band! It was cruel! What had he done to deserve this torment? Why had he ever come to this dreadful country?

"Mister Dow-raid!"

The call came from the foyer of the theatre. It was a light voice, a boy's.

"Mister *Dow*-raid!"

Gaston had been in America long enough to hear his name mispronounced in every conceivable fashion. This was one of the commoner. He shouted, "In here—this way!" And walked briskly toward the exit. The theatre owner stood blinking, having lost the thread of his tirade.

The door swung wide just before Gaston reached it and a telegram boy marched in. He was well known here; sometimes he called two or three times in a week, bringing confirmation or cancelation of future engagements to the current batch of touring artistes. It was the first occasion, however, that he had brought anything for Gaston.

Hastily handing over a tip—which he could ill afford at this crisis in his life— Gaston seized the message. As he read it, a strange calm overcame him.

Some ten days ago, sleepless at midnight, he had suddenly decided to write a letter. Experience had taught him that setting his woes on paper made them easier to bear.

But to whom? It had to be someone who spoke French, naturally. He regularly wrote to his family, but to salve his pride he always put the best complexion on what he had to report, even though he had been unable to stop himself complaining about not getting the job at the Limousin. However, of course, the present owner owed nothing to its founder's cousin . . .

Inspiration struck. Despite his Breton name, Dr. Émile Larzenac was a fellow countryman, and might be sympathetic to a stranger's plight.

With only the faintest intention of mailing what he wrote, Gaston plunged his nib into the inkwell. Dawn found him still pouring out his heart on the page. At last he slumped exhausted on his bed, and almost missed the matinee as a result.

But to his surprise and delight, when he came to reread what he had set down, he realized he had struck precisely the right note. He had neither boasted about his talent nor moaned about his ill treatment; he had merely described his qualifications, indicated a couple of his ambitions, explained what made it hard to fulfill them in New Orleans, and requested the advice of a compatriot—in what leisure he might find from attendance on his patients—as to whether conditions at St. Louis might be better. He had expected to appear embittered; instead he had confined himself to an excusable degree of disappointment.

Casting his bread upon the waters, he addressed an envelope to Monsieur Émile Larzenac, Doctor of Medicine, in care of Monsieur Grammont, whose residence he found mentioned in one of the daily papers.

And committed it to the mails.

Here, now, miraculously, was the answer, not from Larzenac but from Mrs. Grammont. He read it again, marveling:

"Come St. Louis direct music funeral my beloved son accompany Cherouen medical doctor instructed take fastest steamer today expenses paid your fee $1000."

"Hope it's good news," the delivery boy said as he turned to leave. "Been chasing you half the day! Better be worth it!"

"Oh, yes, it is very worth!" Gaston declared. And then, as a sudden thought struck him, his face fell. He snatched out his watch. Would there be time to go home and pack, get to the wharf, find out what steamer Dr. Cherouen had hired?

"D'Aurade, damn you!" the owner barked. "Come here! I haven't finished."

Gaston looked at him; at the telegram; back again. How could he face working any longer for such a disgusting barbarian? Never mind if he missed the boat and arrived in St. Louis after the funeral was over—the lightning had struck, and he must not disregard his cue.

He snapped his fingers loudly under the boss's nose. "You may not be finish! But me, yes! I hope I see you now the very last time, *salaud!*"

Conscious of making a grand exit, he spun on his heel and quit the building. Only when he was safely clear did he break into a run.

"Hey, nigger!"

The shout was loud enough to disturb Caesar from his gloomy musings. He turned his head.

"Yes, you!" said the white man advancing on him, who wore a broad-brimmed hat and long-skirted coat and chewed an unlit panatela. "Want some work? Or are you too damned bone-idle, like most of your kind?"

Since losing his steam-crane job, Caesar had had to endure worse. He was overdue with rent; he had had to pawn his best boots; he was resigned to putting up with any kind of insult so long as he got paid. His slavery smile had come back as a regular habit. He put it on now and rose to his feet. Most of his "bone-idle kind" were half-starved. It made sense not to stand when you could sit.

Glancing around, he found that a commotion had developed while he was dozing. Around the *Nonpareil*, the *Lydia King* and the *Atchafalaya* there was a crowd shouting as though a fight were on the brew. Well-dressed men were waving canes and ladies were fanning themselves against the dry heat and both were pushing and elbowing their way toward the stages where harassed officers were trying to control them.

"Get on over to the *Nonpareil!*" the man who had roused him ordered. "Tell Mr. Underwood that Mr. Whitworth sent you—got that?"

"Yassuh!"

"Let me hear you say it!"

Caesar dutifully repeated the names.

"All right! You're to help load baggage! If we don't muster enough hands we'll never leave on time!"

And with a glance at his watch and a ferocious scowl he was gone in search of more recruits. It had not occurred to him, Caesar reflected bitterly, to offer a rate of pay.

But he did as he was told, anyhow.

These past few days a terrible sense of betrayal had dominated the existence of Eulalie Lamenthe. Since the episode of the lily she had gathered all her own forces. And, inevitably, spent more than she could afford . . .

Though she must survive on cornmeal mush and blackeyed peas, this was not too great a price. For recently she had dreamed that a stranger without a face was trying to bind about her waist a girdle that could never be unknotted. The sign was unmistakable. It was not Damballah who wanted the death of her only son, but a jealous rival, perhaps someone who had never born a child of her own.

Insight struck like a knife. Was this upstart Mam'zelle Josephine a mother?

Because if she was not—!

Virginity was permissible in the Christian context, but in the light of the old religion from Africa what it reflected was failure: deformity, or repulsiveness, or derangement, or the effect of a curse. Once, long ago, she had hinted at this aspect of her beliefs to Alphonse, but he had never taken her—or any woman—seriously. He turned her remark with a French epigram. In those days she had understood the language well enough to follow what he was saying: "Of all sexual perversions, chastity is the least comprehensible."

He had been content to treat the idea as a joke. For her it was absolutely real. And now she came to think of it, while more and more rumors were clustering around the mysterious Josephine—there was even a song about her—none referred to a child or any other relations. (To be called "Mam'zelle" did not, naturally, signify virginity. Conjuh women were seldom referred to as "Madame"; the married ones, the vast majority, were generally called "Tante" or "Maman." Already Eulalie was "aunt" to half a thousand people she had never met.)

Gathering her courage, she read the omens and found them favorable. Accordingly she sent out those who had been Athalie's followers and were now hers to noise abroad the fact that she was prepared to encounter her arch-rival on the night of nights, 24th June, the feast of St. John Baptist for the orthodox, but a date with very different meaning for those who hewed to the competing creed.

Nothing happened.

But the following day, when she was fully expecting that those who had defected to Josephine would shyly steal back, that didn't happen either.

Meantime a terrible conviction gripped the city: there was to be a race between the *Atchafalaya* and the *Nonpareil*. Knowing Eulalie's son was pilot of the former, people kept inquiring whether they should bet on her. Most of them would do so anyhow, for the honor of the race—the other kind of race.

Her dreams became a hell of disasters and explosions. It was vain to try and comfort herself with the advertisements the respective captains published; for each, there were a dozen contradictions in the news and editorial columns.

She had become more than ever estranged from Fernand over the past months, and often lay awake into the small hours, mourning the fact. The sole cause was that she was doing her best for him—sacrificing herself to protect him with armor stronger than steel. She was convinced of that, and consequently regarded him as ungrateful.

Yet he was still her son, and he *must* be married and *must* father an heir before he died . . .

All this morning people from the neighborhood had been setting off for the river. From occasional cries Eulalie had been able to piece together that they were planning to witness the start of the race. At last she could bear the temptation no longer. She too set out for the wharf, her heart hammering insanely, her mouth dry, her vision overlaid with the image of her son as he had been when he was young enough to be dutiful.

And in her purse she carried as a gift for him the most precious of her magical possessions.

 Luncheon at the Moynes' when a guest was present was a lengthy and formal event; dish succeeded dish to the accompaniment of proper wines and intolerable vapid smalltalk. Gordon fretted. He had no special wish to be here. But after the failure of his visit to St. Louis, he needed to use every minute of the *Nonpareil*'s stopover to drum up support for his schemes. He would have preferred to invite Andrew Moyne, and other people whom he knew to be looking for fresh investments, to meet him tête-à-tête at the St. Charles. His account there, however, was embarrassingly large by now, so for the immediate future it looked as though his domicile was going to be aboard the steamer. A fine pickle to be in!

At long last Mrs. Moyne withdrew, and he was able to accept with relief her husband's suggestion that they adjourn to his smoking room along with Matthew—who had sat through the meal like a specter at the feast, mechanically picking at what was set before him and speaking scarcely twenty words.

But as they were crossing the entrance hall, there came a hullabaloo from the servants' quarters. Voices could be heard raised in a quarrel; someone banged a door.

A gong used to call people to dine stood on a table at the foot of the stairs. Moyne struck it with his fist and shouted for his butler, while Gordon glanced anxiously at a nearby clock. Time was slipping away, and he fully intended to be aboard the *Nonpareil* for her record run. So instead of explaining his project in detail he would have to present a curtailed version—

What had the butler just said? Moyne was turning round.

"I do apologize, Mr. Gordon! But it appears the *Atchafalaya* is dumping Ohio River cargo. Some of my staff who have been making bets on the chance of her racing have got overexcited by the news. . . Is something wrong?"

Between set teeth Gordon forced out, "Can we believe this?"

Moyne, puzzled, consulted the butler, who insisted that the person who had brought the news was trustworthy.

"Woodley knew where I was!" Gordon muttered into his beard. "He could have—Mr. Moyne, you must excuse me. I have to cut short this most enjoyable meeting. Matthew, call the carriage and— Boy, don't you hear me? Why are you standing there like a plaster dummy?"

Pale as paper, biting hard on his lower lip, Matthew spun blindly on his heel.

"That boy of yours doesn't look well," Moyne observed.

"Doesn't act well, either," Gordon grunted, shrugging into his topcoat. "Lily-livered little bastard! I'll wager it's the idea of the *Nonpareil* racing that's made him so upset!"

"You mean there is going to be a race?"

"Maybe, maybe not!" Gordon snarled. "If half what I've heard about Drew is true, he'll stop at nothing to leave early and then claim it was a level start! I must get back at once! But. of course"—suddenly regaining control—"if there is a fair race, the *Nonpareil* is sure to win, and she'll be a splendid nucleus for the line of steamers I propose. So if you're inclined to place a bet yourself, Mr. Moyne, I counsel you to back the *Nonpareil!*"

 During their last downriver trip, Parbury had spelled out over and over what must be done if, against all odds, Drew accepted that a race was inevitable and took the obvious step of trying to get away first, so his wake would hinder the pursuing vessel.

Woodley had been resentful of this gratuitous tuition. Now, by contrast, he was glad of it. He was able to issue far more precise instructions to his men than he could have done without it.

However, as the time of showdown approached, he began to lose his borrowed confidence, and checked his watch more frequently, and wondered what in hell was keeping the old devil. He even started to feel that he should have made more of an attempt to trace Gordon. Though exactly what a foreign financier could usefully do on a high-speed run was a question without an answer. It was just that over the past months he had grown used to working in impromptu committee. Even this trip had been jointly planned, and on his own Woodley felt irresolute.

Sometimes he wondered what it was like to be Drew, governed by no man, capable of outfacing even Barber, although sacrificing as the price of his independence the colossal fortunes one well-starred gamble might reap on the river. Sometimes he dreamed: if only I had been master of the *Atchafalaya . . .* !

Still, everything seemed to be going fine. Lots of last-minute passengers were appearing, enough to ensure the voyage would turn a handsome profit. Even McNab had been seen to crack a smile.

When, as was inevitable, Vanaday the steamboat inspector came aboard, Woodley greeted him with only the faintest hesitation. Somewhere at the back of Gordon's mind indubitably lurked the notion that if all else failed they could break the lead seals on their safety valves. At first Woodley had accepted the notion; it would take a few bribes to sort matters out afterward, but he had assumed the financier could easily afford them. Evidence that Gordon's money was locked up in Britain had come as a blow—but if need be, he reasoned, he could pay the bribes himself out of his probable winnings.

Even so, he wished it had been Sweet assigned to today's duty, or someone else tractable, for Vanaday had a reputation for strictness. Had he not been the one to condemn the old *Atchafalaya?*

Disguising his apprehension, he escorted the inspector on his survey of the boilers, piping, and engines, and thought all was going flawlessly.

Then disaster struck.

Rounding a corner among the stacks of wood being readied for the furnaces, they came upon a man sprawled like a dead starfish with a whiskey bottle clutched in his hand.

Woodley's heart sank like a steamer holed by a snag.

"I know him," Vanaday said after a pause. "By the list your agent supplied, he's your fourth engineer."

Woodley took a deep breath. "Not any more," he said grimly.

"That's correct, Captain," Vanaday murmured, tucking his documents under his arm and bending to feel in the slumbering man's jacket pocket, from which he retrieved a greasy engineer's license.

"Withdrawn," he said succinctly. "He can appeal, but I shall oppose him. Have you had trouble like this before?"

"Oh, my God," said a soft voice behind them. They glanced round to find Brian Roy, carrying a pipe wrench which he let fall in horror to his side.

"Well?" Vanaday continued, as though the newcomer had not spoken.

"Nothing like this," Woodley declared. Roy echoed him.

"No, he's always trimmed his drinking bouts until he was safe ashore. Must have been the prospect of a race that unsettled him."

"A race, is it?" Vanaday repeated thoughtfully. "Well, I'm sure I don't have to tell you that if word of your racing gets to the Cincinnati Underwriters, you may kiss good-bye to your insurance."

Bluffly Woodley replied, "When they see how well she runs, they'll cut our premium!"

"That's as may be," Vanaday said. "But I expect to see this man put ashore."

"Yes, of course!" Woodley snapped. "We'll just have to make the trip with three engineers!"

"That's your decision. But don't overwork them in search of any records, or I'll have an addendum to make to my report. I can find my own way back to the stage."

When Vanaday had gone, Corkran arrived and learned the news in a couple of brief, bitter sentences.

"Manage with three engineers?" he said in dismay. "Captain, we can't!"

A nod from Roy confirmed the statement. Williams simply lay there, his faint smile commenting ironically on the argument.

Woodley drew a deep breath, conscious that on the outcome of this depended his authority.

"Dump Eb ashore!" he bellowed. "The wharf is littered with soberer and better engineers!"

"Like who?" Corkran demanded.

"You should know better than I do! But I'm sure there must be an engineer out there who'd give his eyeteeth for a berth on a racing steamer! Go look for one!"

"What can I say you'll pay him?" Roy countered.

"More than he's getting now!"

"And if that's more than you're paying us—?"

"Damn it, man! If he helps us win we'll all be rich!"

That worked. Roy hastened back to the guards. Following more slowly, Wood-

ley was infinitely relieved to see a carriage arriving, from which stepped the unmistakable figure of Parbury.

 Steady toil, even for a scant half hour, had revived Caesar. As
though the blood flow enlivening his stiff limbs brought with
it memories of the time when he had striven against an
enemy while handicapped by worse than misery, he found himself responding to
the orders he was given, to the weight of the bags and bundles he was shifting,
to the mere acknowledgment of his existence which he had so sorely missed waiting for work that wasn't offered.

Therefore when a drunken white man was carried off the *Nonpareil* he paid
attention.

In his nostrils rose the scent of hot oil and burning logs. His fingers felt the
roughness of cast iron.

He recognized that man. For months on end he'd done his work on quarter-
pay.

 It was a squeeze: as when in a bend where the channel,
though deep, was exceptionally narrow, steamers bound up-
river that dared not lose way because the current was too
strong were meeting others heading down whose rudders did not give enough
control to divert them across the stream.

If there were not collisions, at the irreducible least there would be anger. Captains and officers and crew of boats involved in such a muddle tended to bear long
grudges afterward.

To the brash bright accompaniment of Manuel's band, which he had led out as
usual at the one-hour mark to advertise the *Nonpareil*'s departure, this kind of
clash was now occurring between people.

For the crowds converging toward the river had become so dense, they were
obstructing streetcars. Joel abandoned his and ran the final stretch, aware that one
or other steamer might leave ahead of time, and by no means certain of boarding
the *Nonpareil*. Graves had given him a retainer adequate for cabin passage, but
he did not relish the prospect of making the trip without a razor or a change of
socks, so he had stopped off at one of the many shops where sailors and riverboat
crew pawned their belongings and forgot to reclaim them, acquiring some basic
necessities and a worn carpetbag to put them in. This had cost him at worst ten
minutes. He hoped it was not too much. It wasn't.

He arrived at the wharf just as Parbury, stick in hand, was being helped from a landau by his servant Dorcas. A youth who looked vaguely familiar was attending to his baggage.

Among Joel's most valuable stock-in-trade was a memory for faces. A moment's reflection reminded him: that was the *Nonpareil*'s mud clerk. Logically, then, Parbury had been especially sent for. Time was running out!

He pushed his way toward the old captain, disregarding insults and once or twice dodging a blow. But his attempt to attract Parbury's attention was fore-stalled. Someone else came charging down the *Nonpareil*'s stage. Him too Joel recognized: the boat's chief engineer, Peter Corkran.

The flow of eager passengers had been doubly interrupted. A deckhand was coming down with a couple of shabby carpetbags. Two more followed, carrying a man who was plainly drunk. Some of the onlookers reacted with excitement, but Joel failed to get a clear sight of the toper's face.

At all events he must be someone quite important.

Corkran and Parbury were engaged in anxious, low-voiced conversation. The mud clerk was summoning help with the bags; his signal was answered by a black man with a limp who also looked improbably familiar. But Joel had no attention to spare for him. He was wondering whether Dorcas might recall him from the Limousin. She was standing aside, glancing this way and that like a trapped animal.

A touch of reassurance, Joel reasoned, might be welcome. And she really was too pretty to be wasted on a blind man!

He was rehearsing a suitable opening line when something altogether unex-pected happened.

Reaching for one of Parbury's bags, the limping black man checked and turned.

"You say you need an engineer, suh?"

Instantly he clicked into place in Joel's mind. Of course! This was the steam crane driver: Caesar something! He thrust forward, determined not to miss the answer.

Parbury glanced around, head cocked in the characteristic attitude of the blind.

"Who said that?"

"I did, suh!" Caesar stepped forward.

"You're an engineer?"

"I sho'ly am!"

Corkran tried to break in. Parbury continued oblivious.

"You worked on a steamer before?"

"Nossuh! But I dare swear that's about the *only* kind of steam engine I never worked on, saving the railroad kind. I got my learning in a sugarmill. Then I drove a steam crane right here on this wharf."

"So why aren't you doing that right now?" Corkran barked. And added to Par-bury: "Don't let him fool you, sir. He's just a loudmouth nigger."

"Shee-*it!* That man you done hauled ashore a minute back—!"

"Save your breath," Corkran advised curtly. "If niggers was fit to do more than shovel coal, we'd have 'em in the engineroom already."

Flaring up, Caesar snapped, "Ain't there *one* boat got 'em in the pilothouse?"

"Now you mind your tongue!" Corkran blasted. "Quit wasting our time! No black man ever got a steamboat engineer's license, and I'd lose mine if I hired someone unqualified! Get back to work, damn you!"

And he took Parbury's arm to lead him away.

Joel hesitated a long moment. He had been raised by slaves, like most of his class and generation. Also he had retained a clear memory of how sad this man's face had been when he said advertising for his lost wife and children had produced no result. He was constantly under the impression that a great debt remained to be discharged toward those who had served so many so faithfully, and that war had not been the right way to go about it.

His hesitation ended. "Mr. Corkran!"

The engineer glanced at him in surprise.

"Mr. Corkran, I reckon any man who could serve a twelve-pounder gun single-handed could be trusted with your valuable engines!"

Uncomprehending, Corkran blinked. Caesar reacted with amazement and a gap-toothed grin. But Parbury's response was altogether different.

"You know this man, do you—whoever you are?"

"Joel Siskin, Captain. From the *Intelligencer*."

"Oh, yes. I place you now." But Parbury's head was weaving back and forth, snake-fashion, as though scanning for some clue to Caesar's identity. He went on, "A nigger? Served a field piece by himself? Is that the truth?" And clenched his hand on Corkran's arm so tight the knuckles paled.

"Yes, Captain."

"There wasn't but one man in all the war did that," said Parbury, half to himself. "Not that I got to hear of, anyway." He spoke as though the racket of the waterfront had suddenly been removed to a great distance. "And if he's the man he claims to be, he'll answer questions only I can put. You!"—with abrupt force.

Caesar snapped to attention as though it had been Sergeant Tennice addressing him.

"What were you shooting at?"

"A steamer, suh!"

Parbury tensed. "How many times?"

"I didn't help fire the first salvo, suh. One of the guns got stuck an' I was set to chop it free. I guess that's why I 'scaped when everyone else got killed or wounded real bad."

"How?"

"Shot from the steamer hit a hoss. She rear up an' spill a limber in our campfire."

"So that was it," Parbury murmured. "And then you fired some shots by yourself?"

"Yessuh." Caesar licked his lips. "Three. But I got hit in the leg. Left me with a limp like you see—uh—like the gentlemen with you can see. Couldn't get off no more."

"It was enough," Parbury said softly, and tore away the silk from his ruined eyes. Few had seen the desolation of his face. The left orbit was a pit, covered in sunken shriveled skin; the right a mass of brown keloid, slightly shiny, as though the heat of the hell he had lived through had firmed it the way an iron stiffens starch.

He had never found out—had never dared ask—how it was he did not drown. But there had been coma on a muddy bank, and waking to knowledge of his loss . . .

Here was the man responsible. He had thought about such a meeting, long ago; he had thought of torments and punishments and sweet revenge.

But now he had stood at the bow of his masterpiece; he had heard the thump of her engines, been spattered with spray from her cutwater, held her wheel and steered her on an imaginary Mississippi, half memory and half dream.

And as he had felt even while it was raging: war is like the weather, unstoppable.

Moreover he was elated because a sweet-natured, affectionate young lady had consented to accompany him on his most memorable voyage. And she also, he had been informed, was "colored."

Miles Parbury drew a deep breath.

"Mr. Corkran!"

"Yes, Captain?"—somewhat surprised.

"Set this man's hand in mine! Black, white . . ." Parbury indicated his scars. "What difference does it make to anyone like me? The war's been over long enough. Nigger or not, I salute him as a brave and clever soldier!"

Awkward, unwilling, but overwhelmed by the force of Parbury's order, Corkran brought the hands together.

For a moment they squeezed; then they parted and Parbury was saying, "Take him aboard, Mr. Corkran! Check him out! If he knows what he claims, call him a striker to get around the license problem, but pay him an engineer's wage. The laborer is worthy of his hire!"

"But if Mr. Woodley—" Corkran countered, adopting the last available objection. Parbury cut him short.

"If Mr. Woodley could have designed the *Nonpareil,* he would have. He didn't and I did. Stop wasting time!"

Corkran made to speak again but thought better of it. With a harsh nod to Caesar he led the way.

Joel, looking on, reflected that there was going to be a miniature war in the engineroom. All kinds of possible articles stemmed from this clash of personalities. Perhaps, after the race was over, he might make a short story of it, or even a poem . . .

But imagination was running away with him. He forced his attention back to the present. Someone else had been found to shift Parbury's baggage, and young Anthony had returned to guide him. Joel seized his chance.

"Captain!"

"Yes, Mr.—uh—Siskin?"

"My editor has instructed me to cover the race from the *Nonpareil.* May I come with you?"

"Hm?" The blind man seemed distracted for some reason. "Why not? I know

there are masters who won't have journalists aboard, but the more they print in
the papers about our victory, the better it will be for trade . . . Is Dorcas there?
Miss Archer, I mean?"

Joel glanced about him. There was no sign of her. Anthony spoke up.

"I guess she went ahead, sir."

"Then we'll find her on board," Parbury said with conviction—and, a second
later, remembered he had doffed his bandanna.

"Mr. Siskin," he muttered, "would you be so kind . . . ?"

"Of course." And Joel busied himself tying a neat bow.

"I have been told . . ." Parbury said, but the words trailed away.

"What, sir?" Joel prompted.

"I have been told I present a repulsive aspect without some form of bandage.
Well?"

It was the most difficult question Joel had ever answered. But after only brief
hesitation he was proud of what he was able to reply.

"That may be true, sir, to those who are ignorant of what you suffered in a great
cause. But those who love their country may gaze unflinching on a hero's
wounds."

"Well said," Parbury murmured. "I'll remember that. And because of it I'll tell
my officers to give you all possible assistance."

 "How are you feeling?" Tyburn asked Fernand over his
shoulder. Of the entire crew of the *Atchafalaya*, which num-
bered more than a hundred, the pilots had least to do during
the period prior to departure, and they were simply keeping out of the way in the
pilothouse. Tyburn was scanning the crowd with field glasses; Fernand was reclin-
ing on the padded bench, beating time to the *Nonpareil's* band.

He affected a debonair tone as he replied, "Pretty well, considering."

"Never raced before, did you?"

"You know damn' well," was the nettled answer. "You?"

"Yeah, a couple times before the war. Once on the *Reuben Corner* when we
beat the *Tillotson* to Natchez, and once on the *Tomahawk* when the *Red Flower*
beat us to Vicksburg. It don't feel so different while it's going on. You're just plain
too busy to notice . . . Say, don't I see your girl down there?"

Fernand started up. "Where?" he demanded. Tyburn yielded the glasses.

A pause; then: "The devil! You're right! What in thunder brings her here now
of all times . . . ? Oh." He had shifted his gaze toward the *Nonpareil*. "There's
Parbury going aboard. Guess she must have had to guide him as usual."

"But she's heading this way," Tyburn murmured. "Tacking like a yawl in a
thunderstorm. I figure you could do worse than mosey down and see what's itch-
ing at her."

\*       \*       \*

There was an altercation in progress on the boiler deck. Cherouen was holding forth while Barber and Drew kept trying to interrupt. Motley stood by with a file of papers, visibly impatient, and several deckhands whose next job depended on the outcome were also listening. Seemingly overcome by the heat, Josephine was leaning on the guard rail.

As he descended, Fernand was pounced on by the captain and informed about the dispute. Cherouen was insisting that the steamer must leave now, although it was barely half past four. Quite apart from the fact that half an hour was likely to make little difference to the fate of the Grammont girl, Drew and Barber had forgivable reasons for disagreeing with him. To the latter what counted was that an early start would serve as grounds for people to cancel their wagers because one of the ill-defined rules had been broken. And the former was equally determined to do everything in strict form, because half his steamer was at stake.

Having summed up the situation, Fernand spoke with assurance that made Cherouen still angrier.

"Captain, you're correct. I myself won't run the risk of taking her out ahead of time. Up through Gretna Bend, Greenville Bend, clear past Carrollton, the water's littered with small boats whose owners know five o'clock is when the big steamers come through. Right about now they'll be moving out of our way. By the time we get up there we'll have a clear run. If we started now we'd have to pick between them like a horse in a herd of hogs. We could lose as much time as we hoped to gain. And I'm sure Mr. Tyburn would agree."

Without waiting for Cherouen's attempted rebuttal, he pushed past. He had been spotted. Dorcas was waving to him.

That something was wrong became plain before he reached the foot of the stage. Slipping between yet more late-arriving passengers, he expected her to embrace him as usual, heedless of who might be looking on.

Instead she gazed at him with a hurt expression, clutching a carpetbag which, as soon as he had his wits about him, he took from her. He was overjoyed to see she was wearing the ring he had bought her. But the moment her hands were empty, she started twisting it nervously around and around.

"What's the matter?" he demanded in a near-whisper. "Are you frightened about the race?" They had spoken about the dangers of racing more than once; she had undertaken to try to dissuade Parbury from the idea, and there had almost been a row . . .

She gave an empty shrug. "No. Not any more. You've got to take me with you."

"What?"

"That's what he wanted to do." With a nod toward the *Nonpareil*. "Ordered me to come with him. I know why!"

A sudden cold horror bloomed in Fernand's mind. He thought of all the times she had laughed about the old man's ineffectual fumbling, which she tolerated because it made life simpler and brought her presents, and the objections he had only half made because he was forever afraid of offending this lovely girl whom he had met by a miracle.

"Has he—?" he began, and checked, not knowing how to phrase what he needed to ask. "Has he attacked you?"

"He would if I went on his boat! I only just managed to slip away. Fernand, you must take me with you!"

"But . . . !" In his head a clock was ticking: ten minutes remained until first bell, the single loud stroke that warned all who were not passengers to go ashore. By then at latest he must be back in the pilothouse, though Tyburn was scheduled to take her out.

"Where else am I to go?" Dorcas cried, and tears suddenly magnified her lustrous dark eyes. "I can't go back *there*, and I don't have much money and I don't have any friends! All I have in the world is you, Fernand!"

She collapsed with her face buried against his shoulder, weeping bitterly, while amid the bustle a few people found time to glance at them incuriously. Such scenes were not uncommon on the waterfront.

For the space of three long breaths Dorcas wondered whether her gamble was after all going to come off. She could almost read Fernand's mind, how he was weighing the pros and cons.

He had never heard of any pilot taking his girl aboard, married or unmarried, unless he owned the boat. Most steamers maintained an atmosphere of rigid propriety. Some forbade gambling, some were strictly temperance, though the majority tolerated both cards and liquor. But one point all agreed on: single women and single men were segregated, to the point that one pair of illicit lovers had been forced to marry before the captain, the enraged balance of the passengers declining to let the boat proceed if they did not.

And, being colored, Dorcas would be relegated to the "freedmen's bureau," and that was immediately adjacent to the officers' staterooms. Their being so close would inevitably—

*And the hell with it!* thought Fernand exultantly. This was one of the few occasions in his life when he had held the whip hand. Drew had been favorably impressed when he met Dorcas; he might have reservations, but he was unlikely to refuse her passage point-blank—especially since if he did he would lose one of his pilots. And after the race he would be among the best-known pilots on the Mississippi, and the lingering disadvantage due to his color would fade away.

Taking her arm, he said, "Come on, then! It's sort of irregular, but I can fix things with the captain."

She resisted for a moment, gazing sadly at him.

"Fernand, if I've done wrong—"

"Parbury's the one who's done wrong," he snapped. "And I want to rub his nose in the fact! After what he did to you—"

"Tried to do," she corrected timorously.

"Bad enough! Come on, we have to hurry!"

 "What does that damn' nigger woman think she's doing?" Gordon raged as the driver of the landau in which he and Matthew were arriving at the wharf had to rein his horses sharply because she ran across in front of them.

Matthew said nothing. The woman reminded him a little of his own mother; she had been dark and slender. They were perilously late in getting here, but that was Gordon's fault. He had insisted on going via the St. Charles and collecting a mountain of baggage, muttering the while statements to the effect, "When the *Nonpareil*'s set some records, they'll listen to me then!"

Matthew had not troubled to note the remarks in his journal. The regard he had had for his employer was fast vanishing. Gordon had been extravagant all the time he was failing to convince other people that his ideas for reforming river traffic were sound. Now the financial pressure was on, he was growing worse-tempered by the day. Even Matthew's most ingenious devices were met with scorn, like buying his book about Highland costume.

That, though, was more than going to pay for itself. And at least the designs were colorful. There had been little color in Matthew's existence recently.

"Driver, stop here!" Gordon shouted, seeing how dense the crowd was. "And bring our bags to the boat!"

Feigning alacrity, Matthew opened the door and jumped down, turning to help the other. He was rudely brushed aside with a grunt that might have meant, "Think I'm a woman, damn you?"

Matthew sighed. The more that kind of thing was done to him, the more firmly his mind was made up. As soon as this trip was over, he was going to quit, come what may. He wished he could do it right now; however, it was quicker and cheaper to go by train to New York from St. Louis than from New Orleans, and some trace of his former ambition did endure, so he was prepared to stick it out a little while yet for the sake of having taken part in the steamboat race. It was one thing for a girl to see a Currier and Ives print on the parlor wall. It could be another for her to meet a young man who had been there, seen and felt and smelled it all.

Whenever he reached that point in his musings, though, he was reminded about Mardi Gras again and felt ashamed.

Perhaps it wasn't worth fretting so much about women. A man didn't *have* to be a husband, after all. But if bachelorhood turned you into a person like Gordon, it was obviously better to get married.

 Since boarding the *Atchafalaya*, Josephine had been feeling giddier and weaker. Voices and other sounds seemed to reach her from far away, as though her reserves had been used up in supervising stowage of the electrical machines . . . which had been unable to remedy the creeping numbness in her limbs.

Perhaps if Cherouen had not abandoned all concern for his patients in favor of this chase after fame and fortune—perhaps the machines might have helped in the long run . . .

Like a blade of chilling steel an image transfixed her.

With ever-lessening vigor she had continued to fan herself with the purse she always carried. The movement stopped in midair. She was staring across the wharf to distract herself from Cherouen's continual complaints. Everything looked very small, very distant and incredibly sharp, as though she were gazing down the wrong end of a telescope.

And she had just seen . . .

"Oh, how could I have been so *blind?*" she whispered to the air.

"But I keep telling you!" Cherouen thundered—at Motley and Tyburn, Drew having sensibly found some other duty to attend to. "When you took Larzenac to St. Louis, you weren't so nice about the proper departure time, were you?"

"We'd been getting ready for two days!" Tyburn retorted, with something as near bad temper as his nature permitted. "They cabled us before the liner left Europe! And you turn up on no notice at all, demanding that Captain Drew make over his boat to you as though you were an officer commandeering a stray horse! *Were* you an officer in the war?" he concluded with sweet venom.

Unmistakable despite the distance, there on the wharf was Eulalie Lamenthe. Once Athalie was dead—so Josephine had dared to hope—she would reign un-challenged over that portion of the city which her employer would not notice if he trod in one of its leavings, for he was fixated on "modern" and "progressive" treatment. The purpose of being a doctor was not to heal, but to exercise power. Had the stupid man finally realized? Was that why he was dashing off to St. Louis like a boy chasing a jack-o'-lantern?

But it didn't matter. His electricity could never help when what was—what must be—at the root of her problem was supernatural.

Of course! The tingling numbness invading her body was the sign of a curse that must have been pronounced by Eulalie in revenge for her cousin's death. *I never thought she'd be so powerful so soon!*

Now she must have come to gloat. For if she could put so successful a spell on Mam'zelle Josephine, there was no telling what she could do to a steamboat! Why, at the first bend she might make its boilers explode!

At exactly that moment the band on the wharf broke into a tune she recog-nized—who better? For it belonged to a song about herself, "Mam'zelle Jo-sephine."

She had been so proud when she first learned of it. She still had no idea who had written it, but its catchy lilt had at once made it a favorite with all the musi-cians in New Orleans, from ragged street boys with jew's-harps and cigarbox fid-dles to the pianists in the smartest hotels.

But right now it convinced her that her worst fears were well founded. Her religion had taught her that chance did not exist. Every event was the decision of a god, and the gods were the decision of Damballah.

So it could not be by coincidence that precisely *now* precisely *that* tune was being played . . .

Frantic, Josephine straightened and ran toward the stage, her steps inaccurate as a drunkard's. Cherouen called after her in amazement. By then she had almost reached her goal, but the effort cost all her resources, so she could be unbalanced by a trivial thing like catching the strap of her purse on a projecting hook and spilling its contents and as she bent down to reclaim them, thinking even as she did so that she should not, for she must quit this ill-starred, this doomed, this accursed vessel *right away*—

The world swam upward into a funnel of mist, and she fainted.

The fit of unconsciousness was brief. It seemed that a bare moment had passed when she opened her eyes again to find Cherouen's familiar features looming over her. But they were set in a most undoctorly expression, and he was waving something furiously at her, something she remembered having been in her purse.

There were other people nearby, but they didn't matter.

Cherouen was almost hissing, such was his rage. The words seemed at first not to apply to her; then abruptly they broke through and became real.

"You crazy bitch! Begging me for help when you were doing this to yourself! Fool! Idiot! Blockhead!"

The thing he was holding: a bottle of the skin-lightening preparation she had ordered from New York, where it was so fashionable nowadays among society ladies . . .

"Arsenic!" Cherouen ranted. "How the hell do you expect me to cure you if you're poisoning yourself with *arsenic*?"

He spun around and pitched the bottle overside. Then he made to punch, not slap, her face. She cried out, scrambling to her feet; he would have come after her and made sure the blow landed, but someone seized his arm. Another person, she thought, tried to catch hold of her, but she eeled aside and somehow—she never knew how—descended the stage. Those in her way, including Wills and Grant who were trying to stem the flow of would-be passengers, took it that she was insane or drunk, and for fear of being attacked or vomited on gave her room to pass.

She was half-convinced that when she reached the wharf she would be confronted by Eulalie. But there was no sign of her.

Faintly she could still hear Cherouen's storm of insults. Her sluggish thinking fastened on what he had last said. He didn't want her to lighten her complexion. He was saying it was done by poison because he didn't know how to do it for her. Wait, though: her skin hadn't grown much lighter, and some patches were actually darker . . . Her own anger burgeoned. What was the use of living in a doctor's house if he couldn't help you when you did something—well—ill-judged? It was human to make mistakes, wasn't it?

And calling her those foul names was the last straw!

She clenched her fists. She was going to revenge herself on Cherouen somehow! But that would mean following him to St. Louis!

Simultaneously, on other levels of her disordered brain, fear grew in measure

with her anger. If she left New Orleans she might return to find her work un-
done, her followers convinced she had deserted them. Yet if she stayed, she
would be vulnerable to Eulalie, who was now so strong she could convert a harmless medicine into poison!

And, on the level of anger again, she felt a molten eruption of hatred against
the boat that was to carry Cherouen—

And a fireburst of relief at not being aboard her because she was cursed by
Eulalie, who right now must be enjoying the special favor of Damballah . . .

Her thoughts churning like the water behind a steamer's wheels, Josephine cast
about for a course to set, and suddenly decided that all she needed to do was wait
until someone relieved her of the need to decide again. Perhaps forever. She
therefore stood passive, waiting.

What she did not realize was that she was talking to herself nonstop, so that
anybody within earshot might know the chaos ruling in her mind.

 *As though I didn't have enough on my hands, the old fool has
to lose his head over some dime-a-dozen yellow girl!*
What made it worse, of course, was that it should be the
same girl who, along with Lamenthe, had made him look ridiculous in front of
Tyburn and Whitworth . . .

Woodley kept a stern face, but there was no way of hiding what had happened.
The moment he discovered Dorcas had not preceded him on board, Parbury's
wrath had burst out like high-pressure steam. In vain Woodley himself, the clerks
and other officers, had attempted to calm him. The more they pleaded, the more
he brandished his stick and the louder grew his cries of treachery and deceit.
Emerging from the cabin with glasses and cigars in their hands, the majority of
the first-class passengers were looking on. Woodley sweated; he didn't give a hoot
what the deck passengers thought, but among those who had taken staterooms
were the people he was relying on to tell the world that the *Nonpareil* was efficiently managed as well as speedy. Above all, there was that damned reporter
whom Parbury himself had escorted up the stage!

He cast around for some line of argument that might hit home. Perhaps the girl
had misunderstood her instructions. Perhaps she had been overcome by the heat.
Perhaps she was afraid to travel aboard a racing steamer. There were a thousand
possible explanations. Though, of course, if what he was hearing was a sample of
the way Parbury spoke to her at home, it could well be she had simply reached
her breaking point and seized her chance to run away.

Was that—? No, not young enough. For a moment he could have believed he'd
spotted Dorcas, but it was illusion.

Now, of all times, for this to happen—less than five minutes from first bell, less
than twenty from the actual start of the race! He cordially wished he could clap
Parbury in irons.

*     *     *

"I know what's become of her," Auberon muttered to Arthur and Louisette. "Don't you, Joel?" he added with a chuckle.

"I could make a guess," the latter answered slowly.

"Out with it, then!" Louisette ordered.

"Parbury doesn't know it, but—" Auberon's chuckle turned to a giggle. "But this girl he's mashed on is mashed on that darkie pilot of Drew's. I think if she has to be on one of the boats she'd rather it was the *Atchafalaya*. Right, Jewel?"

"It's very likely," Joel admitted, frowning. Luckily his telescope had been at the *Intelligencer* office; he raised it to scan the other steamer. But of course it was absurd to think the girl would show herself at the moment.

"Darkie pilot?" Arthur said sharply. "The one Drew trained himself and hired back for his record run?"

"The very same. Drew's kept him on for the season."

"Hmm! I thought the only other pilot on his payroll was Tyburn. That makes a difference. Everybody says Lamenthe is so determined to make his mark, he drives himself as hard as he drives his boats. Maybe we should have chosen the *Atchafalaya* after all."

"Then you'd have missed my dee-light-ful company," said Auberon, and added, nudging his sister, "Anyway, would you trust your wife to somebody like that when she's in an—ah—interesting condition?"

"Shut up, Obe!" Louisette hissed.

But his mind was already on a different tack. He said in an altered voice, "Joel, lend me your 'scope . . . Thanks. Now that is very strange indeed!"

"What can you see?" Arthur demanded.

Disregarding him, Auberon went on, "Joel, you met Cherouen on Mardi Gras. I guess you must have tried to interview him, right?"

"Sure. I went to his place a couple of days later. But all I got was such a puff, my editor said he wouldn't run it without being paid."

"Sounds typical," Auberon remarked drily. "I dropped in on him too, about— well, another matter. And I met his chief nurse, same as you must have. Take a look and tell me if that isn't her standing alone like a stump in a burnt field." He handed back the telescope. "And if it's true that Cherouen is on the *Atchafalaya* and determined to be at St. Louis quicker than Larzenac, her reason for not going with him should be very interesting! I'm going to ask her about it."

"Obe, it's almost time to leave!" cried Louisette.

"Don't worry," he soothed. "I'm what the English call a bad penny—always turn up. Coming, Joel?"

The reporter hesitated a second. But the rumpus around Parbury was dying down; under the combined onslaught of the officers, who had now been joined by Gordon, he was at last showing resignation, although the fury on his face had been replaced by a cold anger. Possibly someone in the know had told him where Dorcas had most likely gone—

Oh, that was for later. Right now his duty was to exploit to the utmost his privileged position. There were going to be a great many reporters covering this race, but from shore, because their editors were unwilling to risk the chancy schedules of steamers being driven to their utmost. At just the time when an edition was closing for press, they might be stranded on a sandbar, or tied up for repairs miles from the nearest telegraph office. Graves was taking a considerable gamble on sending Joel. It behooved him to add every scrap of inside information to his reports.

"I'll tip the guy on duty to let us back up the stage!" Auberon proposed, divining the grounds for his cousin's reluctance, and hurried him away.

At just the same moment Woodley was finally able to make for the *Nonpareil's* huge, gleaming brass bell and give it the single tap that warned all those not traveling to return to shore.

Scant seconds later, the sound was answered by a chime from the *Atchafalaya*. Then, and only then, like a collective sigh of relief, the bells of other boats were rung.

That symbolized something crucial. No other steamer moored at this wharf was going to pull out until the rivals had their chance to get clear.

 Grinning satanically, Manuel signaled the bass drummer to give the extra thump that instructed the band to stop playing at the next double bar. He was feeling very pleased with himself. To think the boat he was on was going to win a race and be famous all the way to New York, maybe to Europe!

The calamity of Mardi Gras still haunted his dreams; never had he made such an idiot of himself! Had he not, though, been mortified by working as a waiter . . .

Well, it was over. The good Lord willing, and His Mother, he would never do the like again. For the time being, he was content. He was making a handsome salary, and he enjoyed the acquaintance of Mr. Katzmann the caterer, and Mr. Bates the steward, and many others. What chiefly occupied his mind as he led the band back on board was the choice of music to accompany tonight's supper.

Safe aboard the *Atchafalaya*, having secured a stateroom on the strength of Mrs. Grammont's cable, Gaston heard the music stop with relief. To have his head filled with such trivial noise while struggling to compose his funeral anthem—why, the notion was intolerable!

Someone had said, in his hearing, that this steamer and the one with the raucous band were going to race all the way to St. Louis. If so, he sincerely hoped the other boat would remain permanently out of earshot, either in front or behind.

But this one, doubtless, would be in front, for had it not already carried Dr. Larzenac, and was it not now carrying another doctor with a French name? When he came aboard, Cherouen had been involved in some kind of *hurluberlu;* accordingly Gaston had made no attempt as yet to become acquainted. Since, however, each in his own way they were both bound on the same errand, it could only be a matter of hours before they were as bosom friends.

So much did the prospect cheer Gaston, he was annoyed to find himself whistling the tune "Mam'zelle Josephine," which the band had been playing when it quit, instead of a solemn stately theme, as he had intended.

And then, suddenly, a gang of black workers on the *Atchafalaya's* foredeck started to chant in unison, apparently to give the time for some menial task like coiling ropes. Gaston shivered. These barbarians! These savages!

Perhaps, though, some of what he heard would ultimately contribute to his tone poem about the Mississippi. Recently he had been thinking he might get back to that project.

He wished he could afford to stand a round of drinks at the bar. That way, as he had seen on excursion boats, one might readily buy conversation, if not friendship.

But if Mrs. Grammont changed her mind before he reached St. Louis . . .

Of such stuff are nightmares made. He concentrated on the spectacle before him, striving to translate the rough utterances of the Negroes into what he regarded as real music.

 All of a sudden Eulalie realized what a sight she must look, having dashed out of the house in a dress barely better than a wrapper, then come across town in overcrowded streetcars which had left her sweating and panting and with her hat awry.

She was not usually careless of her appearance. It was concern for her son that made her so today.

A few minutes still remained to complete the errand she had set out on. She glanced around for something that would offer a reflection, spotted a tolerably clean window, and hurried toward it, groping in her purse for a comb.

Something infinitely more important met her fingers.

Reassured by its solidity, she smiled. Then the overwhelming pressure of her surroundings dismayed her again: so many people, so many horses and mules, wagons, carts, bales and containers and crates and sacks and chains and ropes, and above all so *many* steamboats! Like a frightened bird, her mind darted this way and that; she found herself wondering why she had never before visited her son at the boat he was working on, for what she saw struck her as more real than the abstracts of money or even jewelery which had made fortunes for the family of her Alphonse.

She had dealt too much in symbols lately: herbs, bones, feathers, blood . . . None meant what it appeared to mean, but was a mere echo of a greater reality.

To outdo this array of engineering masterpieces ornamented with decoration more spectacular than many a millionaire's mansion—that defied her imagination. She felt as though she had come to a holy place, a temple to gods she had never dreamed of.

Suddenly she was no longer puzzled about Fernand abandoning the bank.

While she stood transfixed by her fit of insight, there came a clang-clang-clang of bells, dwindling into distance, as though the signal were being given for a ritual to begin. She came to herself with a start.

Thrusting her comb back in her purse, she withdrew instead the other, heavier object she had seized as she ran out of the house. It had been a gift from Alphonse the day he took her virginity, and she had particularly asked for it: a crucifix of solid silver. She might be vowed to the darker Lord. Her son was not and never need be. Assailed as he was by Mam'zelle Josephine, this might yet serve to guard him on his perilous journey.

The tangle of beliefs that hedged her mind like a thornbrake would have been the despair of any theologian. It bore far more resemblance to the mundane world than to an idealized cosmos. Nevertheless it served its purpose.

Determinedly she made for the *Atchafalaya*.

 And *still* they came!

Struggling at the foot of the *Atchafalaya*'s stage to control the flood of would-be passengers, Wills sweated and shouted to ensure that no one would be left ashore who had a right to come along, nor anyone aboard who should have quit.

His task was being made no easier by the row behind him. Exactly what was going on, he could not be sure, but he had registered that first this damnable doctor had insisted on leaving at once, then he had quarreled with his nurse and driven her back to the wharf, and *now* he was ordering Drew not to leave until she had been brought back to him. Crazy! Perfectly crazy!

Suddenly he brightened. He had caught scarcely a glimpse of this nurse when she arrived, but he did recall she was colored, slender, and obviously harassed. A woman approaching him matched that description. Moreover she was brandishing a silver cross as though it were the most important thing in the world. That could explain where she had vanished to. Wills was a lapsed Baptist, but he retained a degree of faith in Christian symbols. Maybe this had some part to play in Cherouen's healing.

At that moment Cherouen himself was bellowing, "Damn you! Why did you let her go? Didn't *any* of you see what happened to Miss Josephine?"

*She* had been on board this boat Fernand was piloting?

It had been Eulalie's intention to deliver the cross to some trustworthy officer and then hurry home and conduct protective rites until the race was over. Acting at a distance, she knew her powers. It was always safer, as in any magic, to be at a place the enemy did not recognize.

But hearing that of all names made her rush out of the crowd.

The clerk's eyes lit up. "Say!" he exclaimed. "Is it you we been waiting for?"

"This is for Mr. Lamenthe! I must give it to him!"

For all Wills knew, there was some link between Cherouen and Lamenthe; at any rate both were French-type names. And the quicker this was sorted out, the sooner the race would start, the better the chance of winning.

Haste overtook him just as Cherouen was persuaded that because of what he had said there was negligible chance of Josephine returning.

"Go on!" Wills ordered, and in Eulalie's wake signaled for the stage to be lifted, baffling frantic latecomers who still were waving money at him. The freight hoister was already stowed. On the day of any ordinary departure, things would now settle to an orderly routine. But today was very different.

Abruptly it dawned on him that hearing the shout of "Josephine!" must have persuaded him that the quadroon woman was the person sought, and he had let her on board without a ticket or other authority and it was too late to do anything about it. The deckhands were singling off to one line, and the stage was already at a balance, and Motley was ordering him to stop hanging about, and all of a sudden he registered the forces unleashed by the prospect of the race: the masses of humanity on the wharf, on the boats nearby, and on the excursion steamers which were riding so low in the water one could picture steamboat inspectors commandeering a launch and rushing out to serve committal orders for endangering the lives of passengers.

Alarmed at the avalanche of events let loose by a conflict between what after all were mere machines, Wills gathered his papers and rushed up the stage.

Cherouen checked him.

"*Did* you see Miss Josephine?"

"Didn't she come up just ahead of me?"

"What? Oh, you infernal idiot! *She* wasn't Josephine—didn't look like her, even!"

Wills stared in disbelief, because he had no faintest notion why the doctor should pick on him, and then the hush that was gathering along the waterfront reached them, like the mood of service at a shrine. There was a not-exactly-silence, for the hiss of steam and the drone of machines disturbed the air, but there was no wind to speak of except a dry harsh dusty breeze the same as this morning's, and as always at this time of the afternoon the sound of drays and freight hoisters came to an end, the work having been done which would see the scores of steamers on their way.

For a distance of ten, perhaps fifteen steamer-breadths up- and downstream of where the *Atchafalaya* and the *Nonpareil* were moored—the latter lacking the upstream advantage of the former by two berths—there was stillness. By thousands there were more people nearby than ever before; noise might have been expected, but the watchers fell quiet, even the eager active ones who had climbed roofs.

*Hush.*

 While he was escorting Dorcas aboard, Fernand's heart was pounding and his mouth was dry, as though he were a cub again and faced with a tricky night crossing that he knew Drew—on principle—was not about to help with.

For this was the real-life enactment of a dream he had consciously discarded, which had caught up with him nonetheless.

The chief clerk was approaching the head of the stage, giving final instructions to the second mate. Not releasing his arm from Dorcas's, Fernand hailed them. All around, passengers who had signed up for the thrill of a race were already searching for distractions to alleviate the boredom of waiting until five o'clock. He was proudly conscious of how many eyes were on him and his companion when he said in a loud clear voice, "Dorcas my dear, this is Mr. Motley, and Mr. Sexton. Gentlemen, my fiancée Miss Archer, who for urgent personal reasons desires to accompany me to St. Louis."

They were too startled to do other than bow politely.

Fernand continued smoothly, addressing Motley, "You'll see she is suitably accommodated, won't you?"

The clerk hesitated. All his puritan instincts could be seen rising in his face, stiff as his collar.

"We had planned to keep the freedmen's bureau closed this trip," he said finally. "And in any case such proximity of an unmarried woman—excuse me: young lady—to the accommodation of her intended would certainly excite comment."

Before Fernand could explode at the implied insult, there came a bellow. Spotting Motley from the hurricane deck, Drew shouted, "There you are! I've been hunting— Stay put! I'm coming down!"

Motley strode to meet him. Fernand did the same, urging Dorcas along.

"Motley, I told you everything must be set to go by ten of at latest!" Drew barked. "Woodley's lying downriver, and that makes it twice as likely he'll try to cut away early! Fernand, what the devil are you—? Oh." With awkward politeness he clawed his blue cap off his gray and balding head. "Miss Archer, ain't it? I guess you came to wish good luck to your young man. Things being as they are, though—"

Fernand cut in and explained. Drew blinked.

"Sure, we have empty staterooms! Let her have the best of 'em! Fernand can afford it, as you damn' well know!"

Motley countered, "But what if the other passengers—?"

"They can swim ashore if they'd rather! Stop wasting my time! I have a race to win and a problem with this crazy doctor who can't make up his mind if he wants his nurse back or not! Fernand, get up to the pilothouse, damn you! Now!" And aside to Dorcas: "Sorry about the language, Miss Archer, but with a pilot for a husband you'll hear it all eventually. 'Some early learn to swear and curse'—and some late, with better reason!"

With a grin Fernand thanked him, and led Dorcas to the boiler deck, where he spotted one of the black women who doubled as maids and laundresses. He issued crisp instructions, handed over Dorcas's bag, and gave one final injunction.

"Darling, I'm afraid I have work to do, but as soon as I can I'll come and seek you in the cabin, near the water cooler, okay? And if anybody questions your right to be there, tell 'em they must answer to me." He kissed her cheek. And wondered even as he turned toward the pilothouse stairs why her face felt so cold on such a cruelly hot day.

Sharp as ever, Tyburn said, "Are you going to take her out instead of me? I guess you'll want to, now your girl's aboard."

Fernand hesitated fractionally. Then he broke into a broad smile.

"What brings her here, anyhow?" Tyburn pursued. Fernand cast around for words—Motley's comment of a few minutes ago had reminded him acutely how he had already enjoyed her body in a way approved, it seemed, by everyone except the Church—and managed an adequate summary.

Tyburn gave a wise nod. "Yep. A man not gettin' any younger, with a sick wife—a girl that good-looking under his roof . . . I guess she done the right thing to cut and run."

He heaved his bulk around on the leather bench.

"And something else too. She done you a favor, I'd say. She just gave you a reason for honest hate. I read it in your face. Now you really want to beat the *Nonpareil!*"

Before Fernand could tell him how right he was, the speaking-tube whistle from the clerk's office sounded. Expecting captain's orders, Tyburn unhooked it and listened. A moment, and his face changed. He looked oddly at Fernand.

"Say, are you dead set on sharing your moment of glory with all your womenfolk?"

Fernand gave him a blank stare. Tyburn offered him the tube. He took it and heard Anthony's voice.

"Mr. Lamenthe, there's this lady here says she's your mother and wants to give you something before we leave!"

The world seemed to spin around Fernand. His first thought was: *She's probably bringing me trickenbags!*

And then abruptly he grew calm. He felt very old—no, very mature—and cynical as he replaced the tube.

"Guess there's time for me to see what she wants," he said with affected casualness. "But it's lucky she's still pretty nimble. She's sure going to have to dash down that stage when the old man sounds three bells!"

 Head still ringing with visions of Eulalie and Cherouen's frenzied reproaches, Josephine abruptly realized she was standing among a group of curious onlookers, mostly white but some black, all dirty, all ill-clad, and all men. They were wondering aloud whether she was drugged or in liquor.

Memory swooped back to her. She recognized what had happened. For a while she had not been herself.

And her faith allowed only one explanation. She had been possessed.

She knew the feeling well, of course. On a dozen nights in every year, when Cherouen believed her to be visiting relatives in Algiers whom she was ashamed to introduce because they were black and backward—but she was loyal to them nonetheless—she let herself be taken over by a god in the presence of a handful of trusted friends, sworn to a secrecy whose breach would lead to worse than mere damnation. But not since childhood had she been possessed in daylight and without desiring to be. (Then it had been said she suffered from fits; she learned better later on.)

The gods did nothing without a reason. There must be a purpose behind this invasion of her mind.

As a flower grows from a seed, conviction blossomed. She gazed around, disregarding the bystanders' comments. None of the gods she called on would do anything to harm her except to avenge an insult, she knew that. But she must have insulted one of them, because otherwise Eulalie could not have inflicted such agony on her feet and legs. This therefore was most likely a final chance to redeem herself and the god's honor. By being separated from Cherouen she was at a disadvantage. If she lost the money he paid her, she would be in the plight of any back-street wise woman, and the privacy she prized would be at an end. What might compensate?

Logically, saving her life.

For an instant she thought she had the answer. Eulalie planned to destroy the boat Cherouen was on; by leaving it, she had escaped. But that did not fit! Her own son was aboard too!

Oh. Wait. It did fit. It fitted perfectly. What a way to make the final sacrifice before entering into all the powers formerly possessed by Athalie! What a grand offering to Damballah!

Josephine shivered in awe. There was not enough ruthlessness in all her being to match so tremendous a deed.

And then her roving gaze caught sight of Eulalie herself on board the *Atchafalaya,* being escorted along the main deck by a gentleman who must be one of the officers, for he was dressed in the highest style, from his tall silk hat to his brilliantly-polished boots. So little time remained until five o'clock, it was impossible to believe she was merely on a sight-seeing tour. She must be intending to take passage.

And commit suicide!

Hopelessly confused, Josephine tried the alternative possibility: that the attack—for by now she was convinced there was to be an attack on one of the boats—was aimed at the *Nonpareil*. If that was true, how would it be carried out? Something like a stake, probably, a piece of wood in a crucial and strategic spot, turgid with doom . . .

"You think there's something aboard the *Nonpareil* which is supposed to spoil her chance of winning?"

The question came from outside the narrow compass of her awareness. She answered as best she could.

"I don't think it. I know it."

"What, then?"

She was able now to register whom she was talking to: a couple of newly arrived white men in their twenties. She had seen them before, though not together. It dawned on her that she must have been musing aloud.

"Well, what?" the younger man said again impatiently.

"I guess it could be . . ." She passed her hand wearily across her forehead. "Oh, I said already. Like a stake!"

"How do you know?"

"It's something I can do. It's a power."

"Power—*dynamis*!" A snap of the fingers. "They don't say a stake of it, they say a stick of it. Could it be a stick?"

"What *are* you talking about?" interposed the older one.

"This stuff, Mr. Nobel invented. Dynamite! They talk about a stick of it—and can you think of anything better to wreck a steamer with?"

"Obe, I think you're—"

"Drunk? I don't believe it. But in any case I have too much money riding on the *Nonpareil* to take the slightest risk! And if you're going to be aboard too . . . Here, ma'am: my arm."

She took it after a brief hesitation.

"Come with me. We're going to tell the captain of the *Nonpareil* all about this."

"No!"

"Why not?"

"I have to go to St. Louis with Dr. Cherouen! I work for Dr. Cherouen!"

"But the *Nonpareil* is going to St. Louis too, and what's more she'll get there sooner. . . What's wrong?"

She had started and bitten her lip.

"N-nothing," she forced out.

"Well, then! If there's such a thing on the *Nonpareil,* you can describe it, seek it out?"

"I could try, sure."

"Let's go, then!"


The omen was too plain to resist. She had thought the man who offered his arm looked familiar. It had taken a long time to see past the new moustache and the effect of several years' growth, but suddenly she realized what she had overlooked when he came to consult Dr. Cherouen. Auberon was her half-brother.

And, wits dulled by arsenic and laudanum, never thought to inquire whether he, or his companion, recognized her as well.

She merely did as the god who had possession of her ordered.

Enough of what had passed between Auberon, Joel and Josephine had been overheard for another rumor to take its rise: there's a plot to blow up the *Nonpareil*!

Miraculously, like wildfire encountering a shower of rain, it was damped down at once by the general hush of expectation.

Otherwise there would have been fights by the dozen as those who had backed the *Nonpareil* accused those who hadn't of being responsible for her destruction.

"That's to replace Eb?"—incredulous, from Steeples.

"At least he's sober!"—in a nettled tone from Corkran.

"Only because he didn't make enough today to get drunk yet!"—from Roy, and the sally earned a round of harsh laughter.

"But *why*?" Steeples demanded.

"Parbury says. Seems this is the guy who sank the last *Nonpareil*."

That created as near to a dead pause as was conceivable in the engineroom just before departure.

"I'll be damned," Steeples said at last. "I heard some tale like that, but . . ." He looked Caesar over curiously. "You fired the gun that sank Parbury's last boat? And made him blind?"

"I didn't know until today," Caesar said. "I shot at a steamer, and I never knew it was his." He spoke in his most educated tones.

"Here's a change from your reg'lar loudmouth nigger," said Roy. "Nine out of ten on 'em, they'd make out they captured New Orleans single-handed!"

But this second attempt to provoke a laugh failed. The others were too concerned about getting the job done.

"What's that gauge read?" Steeples said suddenly, shooting out his arm. Caesar answered promptly.

"One-fifty-six. You're a little below nominal working pressure."

"Who told you what pressure we—?"

"Save it, Vic," Corkran cut in. "Everybody on the river knows we're running at one-sixty. But this—this *man* never had charge of anything bigger than a steam crane. I guess that don't signify too much, because the last job Eb had before joining us was the same."

Caesar bit back the comment he was tempted to make.

"But it comes down to this," Corkran went on. "We accept him or we handle the whole trip ourselves. That means one-man watches. Do we want that?"

"Hell, no!" Steeples snapped.

"Okay! So we put up with it." Corkran's expression made it clear that he was no happier than his colleagues, but he pursued the matter no further.

"You—uh—Caesar! You know the bells? The signals from the pilot?"

"No, sir. But if you explain them twice, I surely promise to know them the third time."

"Know how to pack a leaky union?"

"Had to do it a hundred times, sir. Also I can sweat a sleeve on a leaky pipe while it's still under pressure. Also I been shown how to use hemp to stop a leak without shutting down a boiler—I never did it myself, but I guess you gentlemen did, and anyhow the machinery on board this fine boat ain't too likely to create such an untoward happenstance!"

He was overdoing it, trespassing on the border of the in-group technique whereby blacks parodied the high-flown talk of white people. Miraculously none of them realized. Only Roy still looked hostile.

"What's eating on you, Brian?" Corkran demanded. "We don't have too long before—"

"He is," Roy cut in, and indicated Caesar's greasy old clothes, his boots worn through, his galluses supplemented by string. Being out of a job this year of grace was not a kindly experience.

"How a man looks don't affect—"

"I don't want his fleas! I don't want his bugs!"

"Mm-hm." Corkran turned to Caesar again. "I guess I didn't mention that, nor Captain Parbury. Do the work or not—and you'd better, else we'll flay the hide off you—you bunk where you can along with the other niggers. Understood?"

For a long moment Caesar wrestled with rage. He put his hand to his chest, groping for the charm that had so often lent him strength.

"Hah! Makes you itch, don't it—talking of fleas!" Roy crowed.

Caesar managed a sickly grin and dropped his hand back to his side.

The lump under his shirt, which he had grown so accustomed to . . . was no longer there. He had obeyed the injunction to wear it until the string perished. Today must be the day. Perhaps he had burst the thin strip of leather straining to lift a heavy load. It didn't matter. The power of the trickenbag was spent, and henceforth it was up to him to make the best of what offered.

He resolved to do so. After all, there was one colored man working as a pilot now! Why not a colored engineer? Maybe that was the end product of the charm's potency. Maybe it didn't signify failure when the thong broke, but achievement.

To gain this much ground against the constant ill will of white folks was already a sort of victory.

Adopting his most deferential tone, he said anxiously to Corkran, "Suh, I guess we don't have too long before dishyear boat moves off. Never mind where I gwine bunk down tonight—I figures you do better teach me dem bell signals!"

Hearing, even as he spoke, how his voice was moving back into the protective thicket of nigger ignorance. And sensing what an impression this "good nigger" had made on the engineers.

Roy spoke for them all when he said, "I guess just so long as after sinking the last *Nonpareil* you don't do nothin' to sink this one too . . . !"

A flicker of superstitious alarm showed briefly on the others' faces; clearly they had not thought of that. But now it was too late for worrying. The signal came from the pilothouse: *stand by!*

It still lacked several minutes of five, but they knew that clocks and watches differed vastly, and meridian time was far from public time.

"This way!" Corkran barked, and fatalistically Caesar followed where he was bidden.

Half-hopeful, half-fearful that Dorcas might reappear and oblige him to present her to his mother, Fernand descended to the main deck again, very conscious of how close it was to the moment of departure.

With a *grande dame* manner such as Alphonse had schooled her in, Eulalie offered her cheek to be kissed.

"I will not delay you, Fernand," she said with chill formality, and for a moment one might have believed she wore a regal velvet robe rather than a housedress that had seen better days. "But . . . Take my arm. Lead me around the deck. I have no wish to let people eavesdrop."

Matching the stiffness of her manner, Fernand complied, not without an anxious glance toward the *Nonpareil*.

"I know," she said when they had taken half a dozen steps together, "you mock me for my faith."

"I find it hard to reconcile with the one you and Father raised me to," Fernand said after a moment.

"Oh, at bottom I think it's all one. For some people, mine is a better way of looking at the world. But the point is—!"

She gave him an earnest look.

"You're in terrible danger, Fernand. I know. And it's likely to be because of this foolish race."

Fernand almost groaned, though he preserved his outward dignity.

"Mother, I've lost count of the number of dire warnings you've uttered. And here I am, in my skin."

In a colder tone than ever, she said, "This is the first time I've visited one of your boats. I expected at least a polite reception. Particularly since I went to some trouble to bring you this, which will protect you if anything can."

She produced the silver crucifix.

"Take it!" she instructed. "Keep it close so long as danger lasts!"

He hesitated. "Take it!" she repeated, and thrust it into his hand. Then she resumed her casual manner and urged him once more to stroll along the deck. If for an instant they were stared at by neither passengers nor crewmen, then the weight of all the eyes on shore was overwhelming.

"I know you feel contempt for me because I didn't trust you to make a go of your new career, but—Oh, Fernand, you must believe I love you!"

She swung around, and abruptly he realized that the eyes she turned on him . . . were haunted.

Before he got over the shock of that insight, she was practically babbling.

"They say I want to sacrifice you and it's a lie! They're all lying, all of them—behind every bush and every tree they're lying about me, saying I'm going to murder you for the sake of the power Athalie had! Never believe that, no matter who says it to you!"

It took Fernand a long moment to make himself accept that his *maman* was actually speaking the words. He felt as though some stray current of unreality had carried his mind into a backwater where nonsense reigned.

But that settled it. He had been right not to bring Dorcas to meet his mother.

At least this crucifix was an advance on what she had given him in the past: ugly smelly bags of greasy felt containing Lord knew what foul bits and bobs. When he got home, though, he must find help for her: less a doctor's, probably, than a priest's . . .

But it was time to escort her back on shore. He was framing an acknowledgment something less than insulting when—

*Ding! Ding! Ding!*

Three taps on a steamer's bell, the signal for departure! And by the roar that went up from the wharf, it could only have come from the *Nonpareil!*

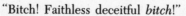

"Bitch! Faithless deceitful *bitch!*"

After uncountable variations, Parbury's venom against Dorcas had settled down to that rhythmic phrase, repeated over and over. He was seething like a pool at the foot of rapids, waiting for a surge to make it overflow.

As best he could, Woodley was occupying himself with the business of departure, already wondering whether the race would have to be postponed. He hoped desperately it would not; he needed his anticipated winnings. On the other hand the old man exerted such influence . . . The exudation of his bad moods had been known to induce sickness among boiler-room hands.

And already, despite the efforts of Gordon and of Parbury's oldest colleague Burge, the atmosphere on board was souring like milk left in a warm place. The excitement that had obtained since the decision to provoke the race was suddenly threatened by apprehension. The black workers had been singing nonstop—revival hymns, songs remembered from plantation days, new inventions with words that were sometimes harshly satirical—but that had died away within the past few minutes. Ordinarily, too, the crew cheered when at the one-bell mark the banner was hoisted which Gordon had had hand-embroidered: "None is my equal!"

This time more applause rang out on shore than on board.

Having made a hasty visit to the office and from there, by speaking tube, checked that all was well in the pilothouse, Woodley returned to where Parbury was standing on the boiler deck, sightless eyes staring into the past, bony hands tight on the stick he so much hated having to carry, lips moving in endless repetition of a string of insults.

Woodley was about to address a final plea to him when into a fleeting silence broke words just loud enough to reach someone who depended chiefly on hearing.

"Blind old fool! Someone should have told him long ago—his girl is mashed on the darkie pilot!"

Parbury jerked and swung around, blank gaze turning upward—for the words had come from the hurricane deck—and lifted his stick as though to kill someone. Anyone.

"You heard that?" he rasped at Woodley.

"Heard what?"

"Don't mock me! Out with it, damn you! Is it true?"

Woodley sighed and gave ground. "I guess you're just the last to know, Cap'n. Word is, Lamenthe plans to marry the girl at the end of this season."

There was a long terrible pause, during which Parbury's face crumbled like a statue's exposed to much weathering.

"Captain Woodley!" A tap on his arm; he glanced round to find Auberon beside him, pointing toward the head of the stage, where Joel stood comforting a colored woman, handsome but apparently unwell.

Impatient of the distraction, he growled, "What is it?"

"A plot to wreck your boat is what I make of it!"—and added details in a low and rapid voice.

Woodley's heart sank. He hoped against hope that Auberon had kept this wild assertion to himself until now. For it was not incredible, given that such vast sums were being wagered. But if some sort of false alarm were to delay their departure, it would be disastrous, and in any case the man was plainly drunk. Anxious to prevent him announcing his claim at the top of his voice, he tried to urge Auberon away.

But Parbury caught his arm.

"You've got to run him out now! You've got to, now!"

"I'm going to beat Drew anyway!" Woodley retorted. "Didn't I promise?"

"The hell with Drew! I'm talking about Lamenthe, God damn his soul and rot his carcass! What's the time?"

Attracted by the commotion attending Auberon, Gordon had drawn close enough to overhear. Now, looking anxious, he produced his watch and announced, "It's five to five."

"They mustn't get away ahead of us!" shouted Parbury, his fury erupting like flame taking hold of oil. Brandishing his stick, he thrust toward the bow.

"Think there's any substance to Moyne's story?" Gordon muttered.

"If I thought so, I'd call off the trip this minute!" Woodley retorted, putting his bravest face on the matter. But, thus distracted, he failed until it was too late to realize what Parbury intended. Only as he saw the stick raised high in the air did he remember how perfectly the blind man had always been able to find his way around the *Nonpareil*.

Her great brass bell, a survival of the days before steam whistles became the accepted mode of signaling from boat to boat, was mounted at the forward end of the deck above, the hurricane deck. But part of it overhung the boiler deck. At his full stretch and with the full length of his stick Parbury was able to reach up to it.

And on it he struck three times: the order to depart.

Instantly the well-organized drill he had devised and Woodley had conveyed to his crew went into effect. Only one stage was out, and that at a balance; the other one had been withdrawn as soon as the last baggage had been stowed. An especially nimble deckhand with a hatchet remained on the wharf. So did one line through a ringbolt; the others had been stealthily hauled in. The hatchet slashed the line; the deckhand rushed up the stage and his very weight lifted its heel clear; the pilothouse bells rang for full astern and the *Nonpareil* stood out into the river with a churn and rush of water.

A roar exploded from the crowd. People waved hats and flags, and if they were too poor they improvised with rags and empty sacks. Some let off firecrackers. A few shot pistols into the air. Assembling his band at the stern, Manuel was taken by surprise, thinking a minute yet remained before they must strike up, but he hastily organized his men and with frantic waves of his baton evoked a stirring rendition of "Pauv' P'tite Lolotte."

Hundreds of people within earshot knew the song, and some loud-voiced improviser launched a new verse that fitted the tune:

> *Hey!* Atchafalaya *dyin'!*
> *Hey!* Atchafalaya *dyin'!*
> *Hey!* Atchafalaya *dyin'!*
> *Gon' be lef' behin'!*

More and more, as the verse caught on, people could be heard clapping wildly: those who had bet on the *Nonpareil*.

While those who had bet on the older boat contained themselves in silence, as must the crew of the *Atchafalaya*, and her passengers, from captain to fireman, from stateroom to corner of the hold. Parbury's scheme had been apt, and simple, and flawless. "If we have to lie up at a berth downriver of the *Atchafalaya*," he had said, "we must at all costs cut across her stern and leave her to flounder in our wake. That way we can gain a lead she will never make up."

So it turned out. There was no way Tyburn could back into midstream without a collision. Fuming, he was forced to signal stop engines.

Woodley felt awe at the forces he had unleashed as the *Nonpareil* went full ahead and the *Atchafalaya* was at last free to pull out and wallow in her wake.

While hordes of yawls and pirogues and skiffs scattered before the charging steamers, Parbury forgot Dorcas who had been a chance intruder in his life, and even his son who had been scarcely more than that, and remembered only his dream come true. Abreast of St. Mary's Market, he was told that the *Nonpareil* was one full minute ahead of her challenger and uttered a yell such as had not been heard since the desperate moments of the war.

Woodley made haste to confirm that yell with a gunshot. And counted seconds as the *Atchafalaya* struggled after, in the roiling surges of the *Nonpareil's* wake. Only in still water could paddles take a full grip; were it already stirred by other vessels, they beat air.

By his watch, and those that others were consulting, more than fifty seconds passed before an answering gun was fired aboard the *Atchafalaya*.

The sky resounded with shouts from the rival boats, from others now pulling out, from the New Orleans and the Algiers sides of the river: to the north, mostly sightseers and the curious at leisure; to the south, mostly those who were stealing half an hour from the labor that was all that stood between them and starvation.

That, and perhaps a won bet on one of these great steamers.

Cato Woodley snapped shut the cover of his watch. At the same moment Hosea Drew did likewise.

It was like the closing of a door through which there could be no return—like the breaking of ice in a narrows—like the consignment of a corpse to its grave . . . which also called for bells to be rung.

From this dead-reckoned instant there was no turning back. The race *began*.

 Making a shadow for herself with the vast cloud of smoke pouring from her chimneys, the *Nonpareil* sliced through the water, her upperworks gleaming white, her silk banner proudly flying, her high-pressure engines thrusting with the even rhythm of a fine-mettled horse—and suddenly to the joy of the crowd, she wore a rainbow. The careful fluting on her bow created the fountain of spray for which she was now famous, and the afternoon sun patterned it with brilliant fleeting color, gorgeous as a peacock's tail. Responding exuberantly to the spectators, her pilot sounded and again sounded her sweet-toned whistle. Ferryboats, excursion boats, launches, all other vessels cleared out of her way, and everyone on board them waved and shouted their appreciation of so splendid a spectacle.

Crowned on her chimneys with red and gold coronets, she looked every inch heiress apparent to the queenship of the river. Her wheels smote the water with such violence, she caused a surge from bank to bank within yards of quitting the wharf. Backing out almost faster than was safe, the *Atchafalaya* found herself trapped.

There was room for two such boats to pass in either Gouldsborough Bend or Gretna Bend, and Tyburn did his utmost, as did her engines. Not so modern nor running at such a pressure, they were nonetheless larger, and while her wheels were smaller in diameter, their buckets were broader and thrust aside more water with each revolution.

But this gallant attempt to seize the lead immediately was doomed. With a sort of contempt the *Nonpareil* sidled into the path the other boat was trying to take and set her pitching and rolling. It was as though the *Atchafalaya* were contending with a double current. She was forced to fall back.

When St. Mary's Market appeared on the starboard, the firing of the customary gun momentarily broke the rhythm of Manuel's band, which would as usual continue to play until the *Nonpareil* reached open country, then adjourn to the cabin for its series of regular recitals. Those who laid claim to the most reliable watches were in agreement: already the *Nonpareil* was proving faster, for even on her horns-taking run the *Atchafalaya* had not done so well up this stretch.

And already she looked, if not beaten, then beatable, for she lacked the crisp first-season newness of the challenger. She had been repainted when the fitments removed for her record run were restored, but that had lost her most of her gold leaf, which was not worth replacing on a boat with at most two years' life ahead, more likely one if this was a profitable season. Drew had never thought in terms of frippery like silk banners or special cutwaters or unique whistles. He was concerned with performance, not appearance.

But there was one factor working on his side.

The captain, crew and owners of the *Nonpareil* could look forward to the profits that thus far had eluded them if their steamer won. But if the *Atchafalaya* beat her, what Drew would gain, for the first time in his life, was freedom.

 "Glasses, boy!" Gordon snapped at Matthew, who with due leisure unslung the binoculars on their leather strap and passed them over. They were at the after rail of the *Nonpareil's* hurricane deck, the best place to view the pursuer, where in consequence almost all the cabin passengers had congregated. Below, the deck passengers were doing likewise, and in their permitted areas so were the hands currently off duty.

But they had come here less for the sightseeing than to avoid Parbury. He was so afraid for the safety of his precious steamer, he was half-convinced by Auberon's yarn about a plot to wreck her, which the other officers had summed up as a drunken fantasy, and as a result of his persistence a garbled version was reaching the passengers—a potential disaster . . .

Having heard the "evidence" and satisfied himself it was worthless, Gordon had stalked away from the argument.

"What a pack of nonsense!" he growled for the latest of many times.

"Sir, why are you so sure?" Matthew ventured. "Surely there's some real risk that people who have bet too much—"

"It's a trick! Someone wants us to tie up and search the boat!"

"But how can you *know*?" Matthew persisted.

"Now is it reasonable to believe that Cherouen would tell his chief nurse to get lost, on his way to the biggest coup any American doctor could wish for?" Gordon breathed heavily, loosening his collar with one finger; it remained very warm and out on the water it was also humid. "Besides, who brought her on board? A journalist—and Auberon Moyne!" The last name was delivered in a tone of finality. For him it was the clincher, though it meant nothing to Matthew. After a pause he added, "I see Barber over there—and don't he half look sick! Here, take a keek."

Adjusting the focus, Matthew persisted, "But what does Mr. Moyne have to do with it?"

Gordon glanced at him sidelong. "Hmph! If you don't know how much young Moyne has staked on Drew, it's small use my telling you!"

He meant it as another of his regular half-insults. It seemed that that was the only technique he knew for maintaining his ascendancy over others, and occasionally it deteriorated into sneering. It occured to Matthew to wonder why, if Auberon had backed Drew, he should have chosen to ride the *Nonpareil*, even if he planned to delay her; what gambler would wish to be aboard the losing boat? But with Gordon in his present mood, it was pointless to go on talking to him.

He concentrated on what the glasses showed. And felt a tremor run down his spine, part awe, part gladness—at the majesty of the spectacle, and at the good sense he had displayed in deciding not to quit his job until after this trip. His vague fear that Parbury might be more right than Gordon concerning Auberon's story faded like mist at sunrise.

Here at last was just the kind of event he had been dreaming of. Every throb of the engines seemed to strike an answering chord in his body. The wake spread out astern like a trailed coat, defying challengers to trample on it, and there was the challenger, not so fine as the *Nonpareil* and nonetheless a splendid sight.

Moreover his ears rang with a marvellous medley of noise, and the smell—the unique, unparalleled smell of a riverboat at maximum power—assailed his nostrils and aroused some primeval instinctual response. He thought of running from a forest fire, and then of learning to tame that terror at the cost of burned fingers. Some people were saying nowadays that human beings were descended from monkeys. If so, they had surely come a long way.

And, even as he mused, the buildings on the right bank grew fewer; the towers and churches and domes of New Orleans proper dwindled and gave way to the lower structures, mostly private homes, of Jefferson and the recently incorporated Carrollton. Plantations of tobacco and humble truck gardens supplying the city's needs met his eyes, and even now patches of near-wilderness, the latter perhaps marking where some struggling landowner had lost the battle against sickness, or falling prices, and abandoned his holdings. Many such, he knew, would be black—freed slaves who had secured the reversion of property formerly belonging to supporters of the rebel cause and who found such hostility against their produce that sometimes they were literally unable to give it away.

Down here he had met many friendly, courteous, educated people. But there was still a stench of hatred that might take generations to die out. He looked forward to going home.

"See Barber, do you?" Gordon demanded at last. "Hah! I wonder what he's thinking! It won't be pretty, that's for certain!"

"I'm afraid," Matthew said, relinquishing the glasses, "he is a little too far away for me to make out details of his expression."

Lately it had dawned on him that his employer was far from a subtle man. It was possible to make quite barbed remarks directly to him without his realizing their true import.

Matthew proposed to go on doing so at every opportunity, secure in the knowledge that he had stumbled on a secret Gordon wanted kept at any cost.

"Not satisfied with delaying me, you're making me look a complete fool!" Cherouen raged. "You took Larzenac to St. Louis fast enough! And here you are trailing the *Nonpareil!* One could almost believe you'd bet on her!"

That was too much for Drew and Barber both. Barber barked, "You'll withdraw that, sir! I don't take lightly to the impugning of my honor!"

"And you damn' well know there's a good reason for me not to dawdle!" Drew rasped.

"Then why didn't you leave when I wanted you to?" Cherouen countered. "If you had, I wouldn't have found myself without the person I depend on most!"

"You drove your nurse to quit the boat," Drew said frostily. "You said she was going crazy because she'd been taking poison. You want a crazy woman beside you at St. Louis? Heaven help the child you're called to attend!"

Cherouen became ever redder in the face, and after a fuming pause exclaimed, "Well, you'd better get me there in good time, that's all. Otherwise I'll make sure the Grammonts never pay you a cent."

"You're amazingly certain of your own fee," Barber said curtly, and turned to go.

At the same moment, a faint cry was heard from below, just audible against the clamor of the engines. While Barber was still wondering whether it had been illusion, David Grant called from the clerks' office.

"Captain! Mr. Tyburn—speaking tube!"

Drew hurried toward him.

"Yes?"

"Cap'n, the doctor engine blew a packing gland. Walt's been hurt. They signaled me to cut engines, but I figured I should check with you first."

"They shut the doctor down?" Drew demanded, his graying brows drawn instantly to a frown. He knew better than anybody how short a time the *Atchafalaya* could run at this punishing speed without her boiler level being topped up.

"Had to, right away—!"

"Cap'n!"

Drew glanced round. Dutch Fonck was in the door of the office, his expression grim. Drew's heart sank further.

"Yes?"

"We got this guy Cherouen on board, we better make use of him. Ketch told you what happened?"

"Yes! How's Walt?"

"Got scalded pretty bad. Right shoulder. Missed his face, thanks be. Needs dressing, though."

"Show me!" Drew snapped, and thrust the other man ahead of him.

In the cavern of the engine-room Walt lay pale and gasping. Ealing and O'Dowd were already stripping the faulty gland, using wrenches as long as their forearms.

"Not so bad as it looked!" O'Dowd announced as Drew appeared.

Walt groaned. Drew glanced at him.

"Did he say something?"

"Before he so much as swore," Ealing said, "he called out to cut engines. And we would have, but that Mr. Tyburn said no! Now he wants to know whether it was safe, and so do I!"

"We can run twenty minutes at full power without the doctor," Drew said flatly. "I never had to do it, but I made the calculations when she was being built. Get that pump fixed and don't cut engines until I give the order!"

The engineers broke into identical broad grins.

"That's the way to win a race!" approved Fonck, and they all set about their work with redoubled efforts.

Drew bent to Walt's side. In the gloom it was difficult to make out what his injuries amounted to, but his shirt-sleeve had been torn away and it was plain that a huge blister was forming.

"I'll try and get Dr. Cherouen to tend you," Drew muttered. "But I guess it won't be to his taste to come in here."

"You best—not take—me on deck," Walt forced out in successive gasps. "Could start—a panic!"

It was delivered as a joke. It was also bitterly accurate. To have it known that this serious a setback had occurred in the first half hour would cast doubt on the boat's capacity to complete her run. That would lead to people insisting on being put ashore at way stops Drew did not intend to make and above all to Cherouen slandering him again and threatening to do the same on arrival—if they did arrive . . .

Even as he was hesitating, Walt furnished the answer.

"Leave me right here until they start her up again! I don't reckon I'll die beforehand!"

"Good man," Drew said softly, straightening.

The faulty gland was apart now; the pipe ends dribbled a little steaming water that ran down shreds of greased hempen rope. Irregularly packed at its last overhaul, the union of threaded brass sleeve and nut had deformed the pipe. The crack through which steam had burst was no more than a thumb-joint long, but it had bulged outward much like the blister now gathering on Walt's shoulder. Strictly it should be cut clean out and a new section welded on, or at the very least a piece of larger pipe should be sweated over it and brazed in place. But that would involve changing the union for an oversize one, and cutting a matching piece of pipe for the engine side of the joint, and . . .

O'Dowd's suggestion of binding it with wire and wrapping more packing around the repair was an old steamboater's dodge.

But it was scarcely what you would expect aboard a record-breaking giant.

Drew strode to the bell board, where the speaking tubes were also located. Seizing the tube for the pilothouse, he roared against the racket of the engines.

"Ketch!"

"How's it going?"

"The rate the water's dropping, we can maintain pressure for about fifteen minutes. That may be long enough to fix the doctor. But if you want full ahead again more than ten minutes from now, I doubt we'll get it back without risking another burst. What's it like up there?"

Tyburn uttered a colorful curse. "We just came in sight of a goddamn' coal tow taking up half the river and steering like a drunken cow! I swear she's on hire to a railroad!"

"Trying to get between us and the *Nonpareil?*" Drew was instantly suspicious.

"No, she's ahead of us both and I guess we'll both slide past her somehow. But you don't generally reckon on a chute in this wide a reach, and she's going to make us one. Most other traffic is behaving sort of polite to us."

His voice suddenly became more serious. "Hosea, how is it down there?"

"More exciting than I care for," Drew answered dryly, and hooked the tube back in place with one hand while fishing out his watch with the other.

All but two of the precious minutes remaining had leaked away when Fonck wiped his eyes and stood back, letting his wrench fall to his side.

"Let her see some steam," he said harshly, and O'Dowd cautiously opened the feed valve. The pump began to move, gently at first, then rapidly. A parody of hush had descended; now it broke apart in shouts as it grew plain the mend would hold.

"Well done," Drew said curtly, and made for the speaking tubes again. The first crisis was past. How many more there could be in a journey as long as this, he knew from long and sometimes cruel experience. But he had confidence in his boat, and his men.

"You may keep running at full speed," he formally instructed the pilot.

"Not right now!"—and in the same second came the half-speed bell. "We caught up with that coal tow, and she surely is more like a floating towhead than— *Thank* you!"

He had sounded two whistles before Drew called him; at long last two answering whistles could be heard, indicating the towboat's consent to being passed. The full-speed bell followed prompt, even before the engineers had had a chance to react to the earlier order.

It was going to be *that* kind of trip. But they had, of course, known that all along.

Drew waited just a little longer, watching the water in the gauges rise to a safe height and listening to the chant of the firemen forty feet forward, keeping time to the pounding of the engines:

> *"This ol' shovel* [crash!]
> *—kill' mah daddy!* [crash!]
> *Gwine kill me, boy* [crash!]
> *—gwine kill me!* [crash!]"

But they sounded amazingly cheerful at the prospect.

Then it was time to persuade Cherouen to soil his hands for an injured engineer.

Having the two women who meant most in his life aboard a steamer he was piloting was turning into a nightmare for Fernand. It brought back the agonized sensation he had experienced as a cub, keeping the midnight-to-four watch in a tricky reach with only the moon to guide him.

Dorcas's arrival had elated him, like any lover. He was still capable of being transfixed by her beauty, and the memory of their stolen night together shone like a beacon on his life's course.

Moreover, to have his mother aboard for a race would in principle have been the ideal way of convincing her he had been right to quit the family firm.

But to have both at once . . . ! It was the unkindest cut fate had dealt him in years. The two had never met; when they did, his mother was bound to dislike Dorcas, being without a marriage portion and moreover having lived in servitude; and heaven alone could guess what Dorcas would say and do, for she had always been utterly unpredictable. Sometimes she was brazen, as when she turned her cloak to scarlet and kissed him open-mouthed on the street, yet moments later she might recall that she had a post to keep and start casting glances to every side for fear some acquaintance of Parbury's might recognize her.

Yet all these shifts of mood had served to make her seem deep and mysterious, and in her he sensed an analog of the river to which he had committed his life, scarcely knowing what he was about.

His mother, by contrast, he believed he understood. And whatever had driven her to practices which, if they were not absurd, must be unspeakably dangerous, had been done when he himself was still too young to intervene.

Therefore it was with a tolerably clear conscience that he approached the state-room assigned to Dorcas before seeking out Eulalie, traversing a cabin empty save for one black tender at the bar. The sky as yet being light, almost everybody was on deck, gazing at the trail of smoke the *Nonpareil* was leaving up ahead.

But he had been around the deck first, and there was no sign of either of them. Therefore . . .

"Dorcas, honey, it's Fernand!"

"Oh!" She unbolted the stateroom door at once. It had to open outward, for lack of space within. Eight feet square, this was generous accommodation, containing a bed, a closet, a mirror, a laver, a stool, and a shelf that did duty as a vanity, with a piece of rough toweling spread on it to prevent scent bottles and suchlike from sliding about in rough weather.

And, after glancing over his shoulder to make sure they were effectively alone, she allowed her mouth to melt on his.

For moments only. Then she thrust him away and began to cry.

"My darling, my darling!" Fernand burst out. She shook her head, standing back, and smiled although tears were still coursing down.

"I'm sorry. It's just so horribly different from the way I wanted it to be!"

Clasping her hands, Fernand said excitedly, "But that's what I was coming to say to you! Let's not mind! Let's just be glad we have each other, and after this race we can forget all about Parbury and his miserable old stick of a wife, and of course if we win . . . But that's the most important thing. You know we got away to a bad start, so I'm going to have to work very closely with Mr. Tyburn, and I shan't always be able to pay you the attention you deserve, you lovely lovely lady!"

He tried to kiss her again, but this time she pushed him aside with all her strength, and her huge eyes grew very wide and her mouth trembled as though to renew her weeping, and . . .

And with a leaden sensation Fernand turned to discover who, through the door he had only pulled to and not latched and which had swung wide in answer to the steamer's rolling, was gazing at them from the doorway of a stateroom opposite.

A flash of out-of-body awareness overtook Eulalie as she emerged into the splendid cabin—vastly more impressive at the moment for being empty—as though she were in some supernal shrine of Damballah and gazing down on herself at a crux of her existence.

For there stood her son kissing a girl.

She had not seen a man doing that for . . .

That was her conviction for the space of three heartbeats. Then memory flooded in and took possession of her.

She might not have seen that. But she had been watched when doing something far more shameless.

The world she lived in was a strange, strange place, even to those who knew it well. Yet it was neither crazy nor even illogical. Given the basic assumptions—for instance, that power might be exerted over others without their knowledge and at any distance, but for this talent a price must be paid far exceeding the cost of ordinary political or financial power—everything else followed tidily.

Finding herself committed to a trip that would last four days without touching shore (she had learned this from the laundress, who was concerned about finding her a change of clothes among the stock kept for newly recruited crew, assembled in accordance with Drew's miserly instructions from items left behind by forgetful passengers), she felt at the mercy of the divine force that, people said, was demanding the sacrifice of her son. But she was fated to resist. She must salvage something from the wreck of her life.

Elsewhere she might have fought against the conclusion. Here, where every atom of the air resonated with instability, she was helpless. Never in her life had she been in a building as huge as this cabin that was not securely rooted on dry land. Like a cathedral it evoked religious feelings. Like a ballroom it evoked the pleasures of the flesh. The very thrumming of the engine sent quivers down her spine. She thought of the night when (it was never provable, but she felt certain) this intractable son of hers had been conceived. Calendars and doctors might argue it was earlier or later, but she recalled the way her frame had been half torn apart by the lips and tongue and hands and spear-armed haunches of her lost Alphonse . . .

That was a ceremony fit to make a man.

At the very beginning she had thought of sexual congress as being pierced. Which was why she had asked for the silver crucifix on that of all days.

Now what was most important was to create a posterity for Alphonse . . . and Fernand, if he was doomed in spite of all. She had heard about his involvement with a girl, presumably this one. Seeing her for the first time, she approved two things: she was not dressed like a whore, though with such looks she could have been among the most successful; and even in her alarm at finding they were being watched she had not let go Fernand's hand.

Summoning all her self-control, smiling as though there had never been a moment's disagreement between her son and herself, Eulalie advanced across the worn but still colorful carpet.

"My dear, why have you never brought your young lady to meet me? I'm certain we shall like each other very much. Even though I don't yet know your name . . ." The smile grew dazzling; she had forgotten none of the charm that had enraptured Alphonse.

Five minutes later they were chatting like old friends while Fernand stood by in amazement. What could have made him imagine his mother was less unpredictable than Dorcas? A scant hour ago he had been convinced she was off her head, whereas now . . .

Taking his leave on the grounds that he must confer with Drew and Tyburn, he left them to it, baffled.

Was he ever going to understand women? They were more inscrutable than the Mississippi!

 At the hour-and-a-half mark they were abreast of Red Church, symbolic of Europe's greatest impact on the New World. As yet it was too soon for the competing boats to feel the true force of the river. Moreover there were plantations and gardens on either bank, and the water was still aswarm with smaller craft, including some belated steamers working down, hours or days overdue because of grounding or mechanical trouble.

Later, in the huge broad reaches out of sight of habitation, where the water seemed sluggish until one tried to fight its flow and learned the hard way about its sheer mass, and where the only sign of life might be a beetle come to blunder against the pilothouse window, or a grasshopper welcoming the chance to see the world, then things would be very different from this interlude of merrymaking.

For the time being, the passengers on both boats were on deck, waving at spectators on shore, mocking the steamer behind or cursing the one ahead, applauding and gossiping and taking the occasional drink—alcoholic if their morality permitted. The stewards sold little solid food; no one seemed to have time to think about appetite.

But the bars did land-office business.

 Eventually the contempt of the *Nonpareil's* officers—or perhaps the fact that he was sobering up—bore it in upon Auberon that his vision of a wrecker's plot was absurd. He did not admit the fact in so many words, but abruptly turned away with some

muttered remark about arranging a stateroom for Josephine at his expense. Joel, embarrassed by his transient credulity, made no move to accompany him.

When in a little while he rejoined the company, he acted as though the whole affair had never happened.

Parbury appeared equally satisfied, but was still desperate to be distracted from the recollection of Dorcas. Aware that Gordon and Matthew had field glasses, he had forced his way to where they stood staring at the *Atchafalaya*'s smoke plume, surrounded by the rest of the cabin passengers.

"Where is she now?" he demanded for the uncountableth time.

Growing weary, Matthew did his best to make an estimate.

"Ah . . . I guess about a half-mile behind."

"Not a yard more than one quarter!" Gordon barked, and retrieved the glasses. "Boy, your notion of distance is—" He muttered the rest into his beard, suddenly remembering there were ladies in earshot, including Louisette and Stella.

"You mean she's gaining on us!" Parbury roared, and at once Gordon realized his error. But he made no apology.

"I mean we are holding our lead," he said coldly, "as we have expected all along, have we not?"

"It's not good enough!" Parbury rasped. "We ought to be gaining all the time! We—"

"It will be enough to win," Gordon cut in.

Parbury seemed on the verge of explosion, when by good fortune the band struck up in the cabin and black waiters began to parade around the deck, tapping gongs to announce that from now on full meal service would be available.

"About time," Gordon grunted. "I did scant duty to my luncheon, being over-concerned with courting Moyne!" And instantly tried to bite back the words, having momentarily forgotten it was Louisette and Auberon's father he was referring to. Luckily neither they nor Arthur had noticed.

In the case of the Gattrys, perhaps they were still too wrapped up in each other after such a short period of marriage. But Auberon had been distracted by something else, to which he had drawn Joel's attention seconds earlier.

Josephine was approaching, walking like one in a trance.

A little while after starting the medication intended to heighten her color, Josephine's discomfort had driven her to dependence on the tincture of cannabis Cherouen had used to relieve her after being raped.

The numbness in her feet and fingertips remained; the darkening patches on her skin grew larger; anxiety evolved into agony. Therefore she tried laudanum. There was always some at hand, because Cherouen regarded a few standard remedies as stopgaps tolerable until electrical techniques were fully understood.

Now opium, arsenic, and shock due to being rejected by her employer, had created a state where she enjoyed almost angelic detachment from the world; she could observe it, heedless of the fact that she had lost her purse with all her various "medicines"; that belonged to a universe she still inhabited but need not be touched by unless she chose.

This was no special surprise. She had been taking such events for granted since her initiation into the rites of Damballah. Semistarvation, sleeplessness—for the proceedings began at dusk and lasted until dawn—and firm conviction concerning the nature of what was about to happen sufficed to make a reality of what skeptical people would term delusion. She had never emerged from one of the night-long ceremonies without deep reaffirmation of her original beliefs, even when she was obliged to be at greatest pains to conceal her identity from her followers. She was always masked when she participated in such services; she dared not be recognized if her adorers crossed her in the street.

But she had for some time been aware that a crisis was approaching, and a race between two steamboats, one of which was piloted by the son of her arch-rival, was clearly just the sort of event she must prepare for. She had expected and planned to be on the *Nonpareil*, of course . . .

Some portion of her mind attempted to disagree. It was outvoted. It was not protective to the ego of the master witch, Mam'zelle Josephine, to recall how she had been taken wholly by surprise when Cherouen announced his invitation to St. Louis.

Therefore it was with indelible conviction that she had known all along about this divine decree that she emerged from the stateroom where she had been given the chance to refresh herself. She was not thinking about anything practical, like leaving the boat and heading back to New Orleans, or even the possibility that the *Nonpareil* would reach St. Louis first, so she might greet Cherouen on his arrival. Her powers of reason had been usurped by the god. What other explanation was there? It fitted together, it was logical!

Which gods were not.

But it was possible to extract from this situation a plan of action. She must be on the wrong boat for a purpose. Her half-brother had urged her to come aboard; perhaps he sensed that purpose. At all events he must have had grounds for what he had done. Therefore it behooved her to be polite to him and go along with what he proposed. She must seek him out again at once.

Beyond that she could not see. Her thoughts danced like the mosquitoes celebrating sundown.

"Ma'am!" Auberon said, and his face was flushed and his clothes were crumpled but his manners were still impeccable despite the amount of liquor he had taken. "I owe you an apology for having rushed you on board, and of course I know now that the interpretation I put on what you said was foolish."

Interpretation? She thought about what she had just heard and recalled, faintly, something about wrecking, or . . . No, it was too long ago.

"I checked with Mr. McNab, the chief clerk," Auberon pursued. "And he told me . . . Joel, I forget the details. Refresh my memory."

Looking acutely embarrassed, Joel said, "According to Mr. McNab, while the *Nonpareil* will never actually tie up until she makes St. Louis, arrangements could be made to transfer you to one of the small boats that are bound to turn out to greet us at Baton Rouge; and if you're short of funds, we could give you enough for a ticket back to New Orleans . . ."

The words trailed away. Josephine was beaming sunnily.

"There must be a reason for my being here," she said. "I trust in my Lord. Not the least of the signs I have received is your kindness"—to Auberon, with a sketch for a curtsey.

"But I jumped to a stupid conclusion!"

She looked at him inquiringly.

Confused, he said, "When you started talking about sticks, I imagined . . ." He hesitated, pulling out a silk kerchief to wipe his face. "At any rate I don't understand why you aren't with Dr. Cherouen on the *Atchafalaya!*"

"It was fated," Josephine said solemnly, and with grand pantomimic exaggeration aped his face-wiping. "Oh, but this heat grows unbearable! Will you not escort me within?"

Joel and Auberon exchanged glances, equally astonished. Then the latter gave a sudden grin and offered his arm.

"There's little more to be seen up here," he said. "At least until full dark. Then the sparks from her chimneys may make a show. And I'm told they're going to light beacons on the banks for us, since the moon is less than a week past new. So we might as well investigate the cuisine. I'm told it's better than average. Joel, will you join us?"

But, not waiting for an answer, he continued in the same breath, "What happened to Louisette and Arthur?"

"They sloped," Joel replied. "I have the impression the excitement was too much for Loose."

"Could be. Arthur once mentioned that taking a girl on a river trip . . . But I'm certain you have work to do, don't you?"

Every time they met now, Auberon seemed to be acting more and more strangely, Joel reflected as he watched his cousin leading Josephine to the cabin, heedless of the heads that turned on every side; some wore disapproving scowls. Yet a short time ago he had been talking with admiration of the racial theories of the Comte de Gobineau.

Oh, no doubt he was doing it deliberately, *pour épater les bourgeois*, to quote one of his favorite European catch phrases—

Joel's thoughts ran abruptly aground on a name: Var. It was common enough in New Orleans for him not to have made the connection before, but suddenly it dawned on him.

This Josephine must be Auberon's half-sister!

And if he'd realized, he wouldn't be calling her "ma'am!"

He thought of rushing after them; then began to chuckle inwardly. For a moment he had been conned into believing that ridiculous story about dynamite, and revenge would be sweet. Maybe this was a shock which Auberon deserved.

Then all concern for his cousin was dispelled as he heard a shout from the bow, where off-duty deckhands were keeping informal lookout.

"Hey, man, fire come down from heaven, *yeah!*"

And, within seconds, it was no longer a mere shout, but the making of a song, using a tune Joel was familiar with whose words were about stars falling from the sky: *number one, number two, my Lord . . .*

Along the west bank around Bonnet Carré, bonfires were springing up, one beyond another, marking out the river's course toward the darkling north.

 The *Nonpareil* felt divided into two unequal parts: on one side, the gaiety of those to whom the race was just another exciting event in a life kept well stocked with distraction against the risk of growing bored; on the other, the seriousness of those to whom the contest was in deadly earnest.

No doubt, Hogan thought as he cast an eye astern to determine whether the *Atchafalaya* was still in view, anybody involved in this clash of titans could trade on it when applying for other jobs, down to the lowliest fireman or deckhand. It had been such a long time since any similar race occurred, and very possibly this would be the last of all.

But if it were, he wanted to be aboard the winner. And he knew the same held for Trumbull. The latter had not gone below once during the three hours that had so far elapsed of the four-hour watch, and had eaten a sketchy supper off a tray.

They could faintly hear the band playing for the cabin passengers, most of whom had been driven inside by now, the night being too dark to see much except the bonfires, which were growing fewer as the boat cleared the denser areas of habitation, and moreover full of flying insects, which, if they did not bite or sting, all too often found their way up sleeves or skirts.

Revelry, however, was far distant from the minds of the pilots. They were high above any lights that might diminish the acuity of their eyesight; they had their ears more keenly attuned to the thump-and-pound of the engines, the plashing of the wheels, the faint creaks and subtler rubbing sounds of the hull structure and the guards, than to the quadrilles Manuel was leading on violin, and Hogan had ordered the boat's silken banner replaced by the bulbous white-painted night-hawk as an aid to setting course. Even so . . .

Inevitably it was impossible now to run at full speed, for the night drained the world of clues to location, making a waste of darkness and not-quite-darkness. If only the moon had been full . . . Perhaps they should have waited until it was.

He had not realized he was speaking aloud until there came a grunt from Trumbull, which sufficed to indicate agreement with the opinion he had already arrived at: it was as good to win a race under unfavorable conditions as favorable, and likely better. It merely reduced the chance of new records.

So long as they didn't meet something really disastrous, like a coal tow aground on a mid-river sand reef . . .

While he was thinking along these lines, long practice and a trained sub-conscious were enabling him to lay the *Nonpareil* into the marks that would take her past the sawmill on the west bank until she came almost level with the point on which stood Jefferson College. Then it would be necessary to line up on the courthouse, and then on Contrelle Church, exactly as though they could head straight for Donaldsonville . . . except they couldn't, since a spit of land lay between, and they would have to swing another hundred degrees to starboard, and go to larboard again to round Hampton's Point, and creep through a string of tricky snag-strewn shallows in order to reach that town . . . but by then his four hours would be blessedly up and he would have heard from Trumbull the welcome words, "I got her!"

The intensity of his concentration was tiring him much more rapidly than usual at this stage of a trip. He was angry with himself because of that. He was still tolerably young, only in his forties; he should not grow weary so soon! A few brief years ago he had been able to stand two watches in succession and still return a good fast time and never so much as brush a sandbar . . .

Was that one, looming black-on-black to larboard? He had his hand reflexively on the backing bell rope before he was able to reassure himself: an illusion.

But there was a distraction happening, which perhaps was to blame for his lapse. They heard the quiet complaint of the stairs leading to the pilothouse as weight was placed on each tread in succession. A little dim light crept in also as the door opened and its polished wood caught the fugitive reflection of a poorly shielded lamp.

He was about to snap at the intruder when he realized it was Woodley.

"How are things below?" he inquired.

"We finally quieted Parbury down."

"Gagged him?"—from Trumbull.

Woodley gave a harsh laugh. "Made him tongue-tied, anyway! Gordon got him to toasting our success. One thing I'll say for Gordon: he can drink his share. Anyway, the old man's dozed off, and with luck when he wakes up he'll have forgotten he ever believed that idiot Moyne."

"And about the servant girl too?" Hogan murmured.

"Oh, heaven knows." But recollection of his embarrassing first meeting with Dorcas made Woodley want to evade that sort of question. He turned to gaze sternward. Yonder loomed a patch of red faint as the tip of a cooling poker; even as he looked, there was a flurry of sparks to emphasize it.

"She's keeping up well," he said. "Too well for my liking."

"She's lost her length since sundown," Hogan contradicted. "She'll lose more overnight . . . Quiet, please. There's a bar just ahead."

Here were treacherous shallows created as the meandering current spilled silt on the outside of the bend, which were never the same from one year to the next. He waited a heartbeat to make sure she was in her marks; then he tugged in rapid succession on the larboard full-ahead rope, the starboard half-ahead rope, and the wheel itself, giving the rudder purchase to swivel the steamer through a quarter circle in barely more than her own length.

Massive, magnificent, looking from shore at night more like a fairy palace obeying Aladdin's genie than any mode of human transport, the *Nonpareil* groped for the deep safe channel. Trumbull and Woodley held their breath. There were no snags here, for "Uncle Sam's tooth-pullers" had been back on the job long enough to keep them under control, but there was the ever-present risk of a floating log, or—worse yet—a sawyer, a tree with its root end carrying enough dirt to prevent it showing on the surface. As the dirt dissolved, sawyers might bob up from deep water without warning.

But there was no more than a whisper of ripples to add to the noises the boat was making as she swung tidily on to her new course. Trumbull gave a quiet murmur of approval, and even Woodley was sufficiently moved to clap Hogan gently on the shoulder.

"Think we'll make it?" he demanded after a pause.

It was less than a tactful question. Hogan answered anyway.

"You make sure Pete keeps the engineroom as trim as we keep things up here, and we'll romp home. And by the way," he added, "what about this nigger you hired in place of Eb?"

"Parbury insisted—" Woodley began, then broke off and once more uttered a laugh, but it was unconvincing. "Hell, sounds like I take orders on my own boat, doesn't it? Didn't mean that. But it seemed like a fair way of calming him."

Both pilots were aware that Parbury had not yet learned of Dorcas's defection when the black engineer was hired. They exchanged glances which said, to their keen dark-adapted eyes but not to Woodley, that they would rather be winning a race under anyone else's command.

"Howsomever," Woodley went on in haste, "I spoke to Roy, and seemingly he's been working hard and understands the job. I had a word with the reporter, too—Mr. Siskin—and he says he really did have charge of a steam crane by himself."

"Dermot's right," Trumbull muttered. "They're taking over everything."

"Beat the *Atchafalaya*," said Woodley drily, "and you'll help keep 'em out of one place for a while yet."

They gave nods of sage agreement. If one thing united them with their captain, it was disgust at what Drew had done: admitted a colored person to the sanctum sanctorum. There should not be a pilot with nigger blood! Any more than there should be a woman pilot, or Chinese, or Redskin!

The band's music had died away. There was no sign of it resuming. Hogan said, "Are people turning in?"

Woodley shrugged. "I guess some of the single men will carry on awhile yet, but most of the passengers have gone to their staterooms."

There were some who had no staterooms to go to, but they were never regarded as worth mentioning in such a context.

There was a brief silence between them. On the larboard shore a few lights glimmered, and then there was a ragged group of explosions: four or five people letting off guns. Hogan grinned and reached for the whistle lever.

Meditatively Trumbull said, "I guess the reality of a race is never quite what you expect. First watch should be up when we draw level with the White Hall. I'll take her then, but right now I got to go downstairs."

When he had left, Hogan said, "Think it's going to be smooth from now on?"

Woodley took his time over answering. "Depends," he said at length.

"On—?"

"Tomorrow's hangovers, damn it!" He hesitated again, then burst out with unprecedented frankness.

"Oh, *hell*! Parbury thinks he owns this boat! Gordon knows he owns it—except he doesn't! You heard about his money being locked up in England?"

"Sure."

"Okay, then!"—with renewed firmness. "And I sold my old boat to buy a fair and honest share in the *Nonpareil*! What did Parbury bring to her? A reputation, hollow as a blown egg! What did Gordon bring? Another goddamn' reputation, for conjuring money out of thin air! Ain't that what a financier does?" He gave the word a mocking pronunciation: fine-an-*sheer*.

"You didn't mention someone who brought more than just a reputation," Hogan said.

"What do you mean?"

"Doesn't matter who owns a steamer. Doesn't matter who ships freight on her, who clerks for her, who books passage. She goes where the pilot tells her." Hogan sounded as though he were smiling; the dark was too intense for Woodley to discern his features.

"So?"

"I guess you have considerable stakes riding on this race" was the oblique response. Woodley snorted.

"Sure! And I'm not alone!"

"But right now *we are*," Hogan said softly. "Nobody to hear me say this except you. You better listen good because I'll never say it again. You're going to have to forget about bringing other pilots aboard."

Woodley's voice became abruptly shrill. "Are you out of your head?"

"No, I'm coming to my senses." There was another rattle of gunfire on shore and he tugged the whistle lever again. "I want to win this race. So does Colin. We're the only two who know her vices. She's unique. And in any case we don't want *hired help*." He stressed the term and thereby converted it into an obscenity.

"Shut up, damn you!" Woodley barked. "We'll do as I—"

"Captain," Hogan said silkily, "you insisted on signing me and Dermot to one-year contracts, which nowhere make mention of other pilots taking over. We'd like to win the race, but we shall be no worse off if we don't. I guess you didn't reflect too much on the fact that it isn't done for pilots to make more than a token bet on a race they're taking part in. The Guild don't lay down strict regulations, but they're informally observed. And everybody in the Guild, and everybody the Guild approves of, will know why and how come the *Nonpareil* didn't quite win."

He chuckled. Trumbull was coming back; his weight made the stairs cry again, and the same flash of wan light as before matched the swinging of the door.

"I'll be back on watch in four hours," Hogan concluded. "We'll be some place around Baton Rouge. From there you can send telegrams to Zeke and Tom and Joe Smith, tell them not to worry after all. Think about it . . . Colin, you got our drift?"

"I guess so," Trumbull answered. "And it makes good sense." Ceremonially he laid his hand on the wheel and uttered the customary phrase, "I got her!"

Mopping his face, Hogan said as he turned to leave, "Got to do something about the lamp reflecting on that door!"

Solitary, Harry Whitworth prowled the decks of the *Nonpareil*. They were abnormally empty except near the bows, where a group of deckhands were whiling away time by improvising verses to well-known tunes like "De Las' Sack."

Normally, of course, there would have been—on the main deck at least—bodies stretched out all anyhow, and the same down in the hold if the weather was bad: people who could not afford cabin passage, sometimes whole families. They littered the smart boat like garbage on a slum street. Whitworth hated them. He far preferred what he found tonight. Everything was neater and tidier than usual, and neatness and tidiness were cardinal virtues in his universe.

He allowed himself only one slight irregularity. In a while he would be entitled to a rest period. He would ignore it. Watches on most Mississippi steamers were four hours on, four off, although there was an increasing tendency on the towboats to switch to six and six. Both were too short to suit Whitworth, who had slept badly since childhood and tended to look down on those who were not insomniac as either lazy or unfortunate. The most frequent exception to the standard schedule was a watchman's routine of twelve hours on and twelve off, from dusk to dawn as near as made small difference. But that was a disappearing post. Old-fashioned, Drew still kept up the custom; wanting to seem progressive, Woodley had made no mention of it when drawing up a list of officers to be hired. Had the pay for a second mate on a brand-new boat not been far better, he would have gone hunting for another watchman's job.

"Hunt for another job"—that phrase came close to summing up his career. He was forever grasping at opportunity; no one could say he let it slip by, though now and then his wife tried to. They saw one another infrequently nowadays. She lived in Paducah, near her folks; he was more like a boarder than her husband when he went there, so he kept his visits to a minimum.

Nobody could accuse him of inefficiency, he was sure of that. He was thorough, he was punctilious, he understood his duties and carried them out to the letter, and his few mistakes had each entailed a burning lesson; never to be so neglectful again.

Yet here he was in the second mate's post when many men with less experience had been promoted to first, and not a few had bought part shares in the boats they worked on . . .

If the war had gone the other way, it would have been different.

That was his firm conviction. There was no other logical explanation for his plight. The Northern victors had broken down the fences surrounding the inferior type of humanity, which in its collective wisdom the South had erected. With the end of slavery those whom God had branded on their very hides had been released to carry their dirty habits, their disregard for the rights of property (and what greater infringement of such rights than depriving their former owners of their most valuable possessions?) and their foul so-called religion which bordered on black magic, into the heart of cities, into the homes of formerly respectable people, into professions that once were jealously protected by those who had created them. What had niggers invented? Some said the banjar, that instrument which all too often made the night hideous aboard a riverboat. But did they ever invent a steamer? Or a gun?

And his resentment did not stop there. He looked down on Dagoes, too, and on the slow-spoken Irish who chose to emigrate to the South because there were more Catholics here, and indeed on anybody who did not speak the English he had been raised to, the language in which the King James Bible had been couched.

He was still smarting at the fact that Drew had fired him because he objected to a coon being trained as a pilot. During Fernand's apprenticeship he and the captain had argued constantly; Whitworth thought it shaming for a white man to be talked to that way, and had finally said so. Not only had Drew dismissed him, which was bad enough—now he had rehired Fernand. Incredible! Disgraceful! And it would be worse yet if by some mischance the *Atchafalaya* won this race . . . but that wouldn't be allowed to happen. Couldn't. Mustn't!

Nonetheless, on the surface things had worked out well. Possibly the fact that he had witnessed Woodley's humiliation by Fernand, yet never spoken about it to anybody else, had something to do with securing his present post.

However that might be, he had thought more and more about quitting the river, and during his latest refreshment in New Orleans had gone so far as to invest some of his hard-won capital in a stock-in-trade, which reposed in his state-room against the risk that the *Nonpareil* might lose.

He saw no obvious reason why she should. But some people were so fallible! Parbury, for instance, around whom the whole enterprise revolved: what imp of Satan possessed him today? Not content to associate himself with a man who kept a self-confessed bum boy, not content to get mashed on a colored girl young enough to be his daughter, now he had set a nigger engineer to work alongside white men! It was disgusting! Even Corkran, for all he bore an Irish name, conducted himself with tolerable dignity on duty, though on shore his manners had been known to lapse.

Firemen with four hours' nonstop shoveling behind them were emerging on deck, sweating and gasping and shouldering one another aside for a drink of water. Vic Steeples had come with them, just recognizable in the lurid light from the furnaces. Whitworth headed that way and accosted him.

"Say, what about that darkie engineer?"

Stretching enormously, Steeples uttered a reluctant answer. "I guess he warn't lying when he said he knew his trade."

"Uppity niggers shoul'n't be taught a trade like that!"

"Guess someone shoulda told Eb that. But I'm surely glad we don't have to work this trip with only three of us."

"He standing the next watch?"

"Yeah, with Brian. Pete'll be out directly."

"He trusts him that much?"

"It's like I said," Steeples grunted, and with a cavernous yawn he moved away.

Fretful, disappointed because if any of the white engineers could find fault with Caesar it would likely be Steeples, Whitworth made a mental note to be around in four hours' time and catch him going off watch, tell him to bunk down right *there* near the other blacks, not to imagine that because he was playing at white man's work he was entitled to a white man's privileges.

Too many niggers and immigrants taking bread out of decent folks' mouths—that was the trouble with America today!

 The distance between the boats had altered little since they left New Orleans; the gap, give or take a few hundred yards, represented the advantage stolen by the *Nonpareil* when she cut loose early. Not here, not immediately, but within a day's run, there were places where her rival's wake would no longer discommode the *Atchafalaya*, and superior skill in piloting would make all the difference.

That was why Drew felt renewed confidence as he strode the hurricane deck. For the river was nothing like a formal racetrack. Right now, for example, the *Nonpareil* was visible on an easterly heading across what the untutored eye might mistake for clear water. It was barely a foot deep; the headland here reached out treacherously beneath the surface and the channel bent around it like a hairpin. Therefore the *Atchafalaya* was making almost due west.

Glancing around in sudden alarm, Drew was relieved to find nobody watching him. It was not unknown for a passenger to ask why the boat was going the "wrong" way, and a conversation of that sort was the last thing he wanted right now, especially with someone who had bet on the race.

But the deck passengers were lying down where they could, while many of the cabin passengers had also retired. Barber, like some oriental idol, still presided at a long table scattered with cards, glasses and ashtrays, mulcting the survivors—including some who had the air of professional sharpers—with the skill that had carried him from his sleazy shack to the Limousin.

Paradoxically, though Drew never expected to admire his partner, he was more and more tempted to like him.

Cherouen, on the other hand, whom he wished he could admire, was proving a miserable customer. First there had been all that fuss about his machines; then the row with his nurse, who had sensibly fled; then the row with anybody who might have stopped her but didn't . . . It had taken all Barber's charm to persuade him that he ought to stand by his original decision and put up with the consequences. A good few drinks had served to firm the conviction, and at long last the Electric Doctor was safely stowed for the night.

Perhaps it would not be a good idea after all to have him treat Susannah . . . ?

But any man could act oddly under stress. He himself was aware of a change in

his attitude: he could not stop running over points of detail he knew he had
attended to, as though rehearsing them in memory could arm his steamer against
the risk of failure. Why should he expect better of Cherouen?

For a little while Drew's mind became solely occupied by perception. He saw,
without reacting to, the dim *Nonpareil* crowned with red sparks, easing now behind the next headland, her image barred into segments by isolated willows at
first, then partly obscured by a denser clump, then wholly hidden by cottonwoods, save for her chimney tops and their glowing stain on the sky. Around, he
was aware of the lie of the land, the pattern of the current, the whole vast complex process which formed the Mississippi.

What in the world were puny humans doing, tackling this leviathan greater
than any affronted by whalers, demeaning it to a mere convenience for gaining
gold?

Suddenly he shuddered. He had believed he was remembering a poem he had
read. Now it dawned on him that was untrue. His thought had welled up from
within himself, as though he too had it in him to make a poem.

But the way it went over into words was not poetical as he understood the
term. One could see that a modern poet like Mr. Whitman was following the
example of, say, the Psalms, if with no great success. How, though, could the
experience and vocabulary of a steamer captain be fitted for poetry? He dismissed
the whole notion with a fierce effort.

Yet some regret lingered.

He knew the sensible thing to do was snatch a rest in case he was called on for a
turn at the wheel. When Dorcas came aboard he had expected Fernand to take
the boat out instead of Tyburn, in order to show off. Then when his mother
showed up too . . . !

Oh, it was all most irregular! He wished he could afford the luxury of losing his
temper over it.

But having made his bet with Barber he was constrained. He dared not risk
upsetting Fernand, who one day was apt to be a better pilot than his teacher, if
more highly-strung. . .

Enough of this brooding. It was leading nowhere. He turned toward the pilothouse stairs, offering himself the excuse that he was too overwrought to sleep.

The darkness of the pilothouse was eerie. Faint by way of the bell tube under
the breastboard came a ghostly echo of the racket in the engineroom.

Fernand was at the wheel. At one end of the bench behind him, carefully sited
so that no glow would reflect off the window, Tyburn was smoking a meditative
last cigar before snatching some rest.

Both of them glanced around on Drew's entrance, but neither spoke until he
had walked to the window, gazed for a moment at the *Nonpareil,* and joined
Tyburn on the bench. Then the latter said, "She's a flash boat. But she won't
make it."

Drew glanced sharply sidelong. "What makes you say so? Long as she has this
much of a lead—"

"She won't keep it," Fernand cut in, making a minuscule adjustment to the

*Atchafalaya's* heading. A tall cottonwood had come up on the skyline, which this year for the first time slanted enough to serve as a mark.

"Why not?"

"She's swinging overwide in the bends."

"That's so," Tyburn confirmed. "In principle she ought to have the legs of us. But even without Walt, since nightfall every bend is giving us . . . not much, but a yard or two."

Drew gave a satisfied nod. "So where would you expect to try and pass?"

Fernand and Tyburn exchanged glances. "We were talking about that," said the latter. "Figured we might try the reach north of Ellis Cliffs, up towards Como Landing. If not there, then any other place where she's too light to be manageable. Directly before a coaling stop would be ideal."

Drew thought that over and said at length, "I guess you have a fair point. We'll try it, anyhow . . . But here's a question, Fernand. How long have you been up here, that you've talked it out? I'd have expected you to stay below with your—womenfolk."

One could almost sense the heat in Fernand's cheeks as he worried over his best answer.

"Captain, you should think yourself lucky! With both of them on board, I'd never dare make a mistake—now would I?"

Tyburn burst into a full-scale laugh, and after a moment Drew so far relented as to accord the joke a chuckle.

Much relief showed in Fernand's voice as he concluded, "No scandal, sir, I promise you, will mar this trip."

"Scandal?" Drew snorted. "Long's you marry the girl before it starts to show, I don't give a damn! I'm more concerned about disputes and disagreements which might affect my junior pilot's concentration. How's your mother getting on with your intended?"

"I was telling Ketch," Fernand said after a brief hesitation. "Swimmingly. It's hard to believe, but . . . We ate supper together. They were like old friends."

"*Like* is not the same as *being*," Drew said heavily. "But I hope you're right. . . Say, don't I see a boat coming down? Who can she be at this time?"

It was a gentle probe of Fernand's competence, such as he had often used when the latter was still his cub. Sighing, Fernand answered, "She'll be the *Treasure Chest*, most likely. Unless of course she's the *Dinah Shine* ahead of schedule."

"Or another goddamn' coal tow!" Tyburn grunted.

"I surely hope not! When towboats start to run by night . . . !" Fernand spat at the cuspidor, accurately despite the darkness.

"How are things below?" he added, making a pointed effort to change the subject.

"Oh!" Drew sighed. "The passengers we don't care about are finding out that a steamboat race is dull and lengthy. I mean the ones who came aboard at the last minute to watch over the money they've bet. Some are beginning to imagine we're doing less than our best; I have my eye on a couple who are drinking a lot and arguing even more. A few are complaining that they chose the wrong boat, naturally."

"Cherouen?" inquired Tyburn.

"Gave over when Barber got him drunk enough. I—" .

Fernand seized the binoculars that reposed on a ledge close at hand and peered at the oncoming steamer.

"I'll be damned! She is the *Dinah Shine*! Never tell me the *Treasure Chest* is grounded!"

Tyburn made to say something but thought better of it. It was not the first time he and Drew had sat like this and waited to see what Fernand would do. Long ago, he recalled, he had disliked Drew. Then, watching what a transformation he was working in his cub, he had realized there was much of the man beneath the surface.

Like the Mississippi.

Here the river was curving around in a huge shallow arc, traced anew by last winter's floods. Somewhere in the waste of water, which pilots learned by day and had to remember by night when riffles on the surface were invisible and only silhouetted trees and rocks and nearby rises in the ground could serve as clues, there was a deep safe channel.

Even by day the route of the *Nonpareil* would have confused anybody following her, the wake interacting with the natural flow of the current. It was consequently of some importance that the correct side be chosen to pass the *Dinah Shine*.

Half a minute slipped away; a minute, while neither of the older men commented and Fernand simply steadied the wheel with one hand and the glasses with the other.

Then finally, with an air of decision, he set by the glasses and reached for the whistle lever.

*One!*

Drew and Tyburn relaxed. That was exactly what either of them would have done in the same situation. Working down with the current, the *Dinah Shine* was less controllable. Passing starboard to starboard meant that in this bend, where Donaldsonville was fading astern and there would be no further clear marks until past Dominguez Landing, up around the Louisiana Institute, the upstream boat would benefit from deeper water.

But almost instantly there came a challenge: two short blasts on the other whistle.

They tensed. Drew said, "What in heaven's name—?"

Tyburn broke in. "Ain't he standing off to east'ard like he means to tie up?"

The clues that led him to this, vague and subtle as the undeveloped image on a photographic plate, would have been impossible to explain in words to anyone who had not been long in the profession.

"No," Drew said softly. "He's just giving us room. I wonder if he did the same for Woodley."

"I guess," Fernand said cynically, "it's more for the benefit of his passengers than either him or us."

He released half a dozen brief notes as though scrabbling over a message inscribed in sand, then made plain his agreement with the other pilot's proposal: two whistles loud and stately.

At once the *Shine* repeated her signal and laid off into the shallower water. She was a fine sight in the clear night air. Many of her lights were still burning; people could be discerned waving from her, and strains of irregular music drifted across the water as though a scratch band and a group of drunken passengers had decided on separate melodies.

Hereabouts, also, there were people on the bank who had stayed up to watch. A couple of dying fires gleamed dimly red, each surrounded by a group of sleepy young men. This would almost certainly continue clear up the river by day and night. Steamers were commonplace enough, but racing steamers were worth weariness to see.

Such onlookers, though, would grow more scattered as the voyage progressed. Already the trees were dense; the *Nonpareil* was hidden behind a stand of cottonwoods, her location marked only by the glow on the underside of her smoke plume. Farther up, landings would be isolated, miles apart, the loneliness being almost hurtful to travelers accustomed to cities. There was a saying that summed it all up: "Wait till you get beyond Baton Rouge. There's an awful lot of nothing up there . . ."

Yet to those who understood it, as Drew sometimes explained to his sister-in-law and nephews, the Mississippi itself was company of a sort: better company, he would say, than a horse to someone riding range. (The younger boys were indulgently permitted to buy dime novels, most of them featuring real-life heroes in impossible adventures, fighting outlaws or Indians and miraculously escaping certain death in every other chapter.)

By every wave and ripple the river spoke to those who knew how to listen.

The *Dinah Shine* dwindled astern as Fernand laid the boat into her marks for the next bend, and as the last few passengers retired and even the most sleepless of the deckhands ceased their quiet singing, Tyburn doused his cigar and stretched, rising.

"See you at change of watch," he said, clapping Fernand on the shoulder. "'Night, Captain."

Elsewhere they had long been "Ketch" and "Hosea"; never, though, in the pilothouse.

Drew grunted by way of answer. Then, for a little while when they were alone, he spoke to Fernand somewhat in the manner of a father. What he said made the younger man's ears burn. Then he left him alone, having delivered a final compliment to salve his wounds.

At some point around midnight Fernand said to the air, "Damn, but it's a shame the old man don't have kids. I guess that accounts for a lot of what he's doing these days. Well, he had the chance, and . . ."

After which he thought a lot about marriage, and how much easier it had been made in prospect by his mother's amazing reaction to Dorcas.

Thus reminded of Eulalie, he fished out the silver crucifix she had given him and set it on the ledge beside the fieldglasses. After which, as though rid of a burden, he stopped dreaming about the future and concentrated on eroding the *Nonpareil*'s lead.

 And now this did begin to look like a race between steamers instead of human beings. Both boats were almost wholly in darkness, save for smears of red when furnace doors were opened for more fuel—less often than by day, for even with the best and keenest pilots it was hazardous to run at night. Indeed, within a generation's memory it had been unthinkable except when the moon was within a day or two of full. Then the habit was for the pilot to instruct the captain, "We shall tie up here till sunrise, sir." And the command was resignedly obeyed.

Progress had changed that, as it had changed many things. But the steamers remained: vast, purposeful, announcing their presence with roars and hisses. From the distance of the banks it was impossible to detect the people on board; the great machines seemed to be acting of their own volition.

Now and then they passed other vessels adhering to the older tradition: here a smaller steamer engaged in the way-landing trade, delivering coffee and nails and gunpowder to such private jetties as Parbury had known in childhood, never aspiring to ascend beyond Baton Rouge or at farthest Natchez; there a towboat that had sidled its monstrous clutch of barges into the shallows, grounding them securely until dawn; then again something rarely seen so far south, one of the last of the timber rafts that long ago had composed much of the traffic on the Mississippi, with a sort of hut at the stern to shelter her crew and a great sweep for steering— this too laid up overnight, and indeed having no business on the bustling modern river. Such rafts were now generally broken up at Natchez, but likely the lumber it was made of had been contracted for by a New Orleans builder cutting the meat on his client's contract to the bone.

Once or twice their wake disturbed alligators. By day this would have been a signal for half a dozen gentlemen to fetch rifles and start shooting; now it was a mere distraction for a handful of insomniacs and the men on watch.

Also they startled birds: wild turkeys on a sandbar made a machinelike rushing sound with their wings as they rose blindly into the night, and occasionally owls complained at this intrusion into their domain of darkness.

But any boat running at night might have the same impact. It was to people that the passage of this pair was exceptional.

Here the Mississippi twisted and writhed. Leaving behind Claybourne Island and the Louisiana Institute, five and a half hours after departure the steamers were heading due west. Six hours after, they were heading north, passing the mouth of Bayou Goula to larboard; almost immediately after that they were heading east, using St. Gabriel's as a marker but not relying on it wholly, for the channel shifted deceitfully hereabouts. Once or twice the *Nonpareil* slowed almost to walking pace, and Trumbull feared he might have to send out leadsmen, but the risk passed and he was able to lay her into the reach above the hundred-mile mark, bow slanting toward Plaquemine in the narrow but clear channel between the bank and the pair of islands that every year grew larger and would eventually create a cutoff, shortening the river and leaving an oxbow lake and perhaps isolating Plaquemine from the outside world. It had happened to many other ambitious towns.

The hundred-mile mark was reached at about six and a quarter hours from New Orleans: better by several minutes than the time set by the *Atchafalaya* last month. About then Parbury came up to the pilothouse, enough recovered from the drink he had taken to inquire about their speed and exclaim with satisfaction at what he heard. Miraculously he seemed to have forgotten about Dorcas for the time being.

Shortly, though, he dozed off again and snored away the reach dictated by the long and treacherous sandbars opposite the mouth of Bayou Jacob, where steamers were obliged to turn through almost 180 degrees and head east again, lining up now on Manchac, with due care for the silt washing out of Bayou Iberville. The pilots knew these bayous better by their appearance than by their names. Often the local people had names that appeared on no map or chart; often the names on maps were unknown to the settlers.

Astern, sometimes masked for a while by trees, the *Atchafalaya* made her solemn way upstream. Perhaps it was the lack of the special cutwater that so elegantly provided the *Nonpareil* with her moving fountain; perhaps it was the deeper note of her engines, or her broader beam and marginally shorter waterline . . . but she looked the more purposeful of the two, as though a heavy-shouldered hound were on the trail of a deer.

Yet, if the order had been reversed, the pursuer might have brought to mind a mountain lion unhurriedly wearing down a stockier prey: an aging plough horse?

Bruly Landing loomed ahead on the west bank. It was time to change watches; another four hours had passed, and both boats were beating the record. Scarcely three minutes separated them; the distance had opened and closed and opened again, and now there was going to be some chance of a level run in competition, despite the darkness, for upstream of Bruly Landing a northeasterly reach was as straight and as safe as any on the southern Mississippi, to and beyond Baton Rouge.

 About midnight the company in the cabin of the *Nonpareil* dispersed with rash promises to rise in time to watch the dawn. Joel was enormously relieved. He himself had no bed to go to; Graves's advance had been meant to cover the cost of a stateroom, but he preferred to husband the money, knowing that he would have to be up at all hours if he was to ensure that his reports were sent ashore at the proper times. Right now, specifically, he must prepare an account of the first day of the race to be telegraphed from Baton Rouge, where a launch was supposed to collect it. Under a flaring lamp, with the liquid in his inkwell rippling back and forth as the boat breasted sluggish surges, he drafted and blotted and scratched out and rewrote. Plain facts were easy enough to set down: the *Nonpareil* was in the lead,

the *Atchafalaya* had failed to overtake her, the captain was delighted and his co-owners were overjoyed and all along the banks people were turning out to cheer. So much was simple.

But even as he struggled to fix that on the page, he knew there was something else, deeper, more significant, that he could never define in words—or at least not until he had the chance to recapture emotion in tranquility. That was the sensation of *being here*, compounded not only of sights and sounds but of vibrations, smells, hoarse orders and maladjusted machinery and food left too long on a galley stove, and the live excitement of passengers and crew.

He achieved a draft that satisfied him tolerably well, and yet it was not right, it was not the whole truth. While he was rereading it for the fourth or fifth time, shortly after one o'clock, he drowsed.

And was awakened scant minutes later by his name being called.

"Joel—I say, Joel!"

Coming to himself with a start and narrowly avoiding knocking over the inkwell, he glanced around. In the dim light of the few lamps which were kept on overnight, he made out his cousin-in-law emerging in a handsome silk robe from the stateroom he shared with Louisette.

"What is it?" Joel said around a yawn.

"Something's wrong with Loose."

Instantly he was fully awake.

"I came out to find her maid. I guess she's been put away somewhere with the other servants. Did you see—?"

But Joel had pushed past him into the stateroom. It was palatial as such accommodation went, better than all except the finest on a transatlantic liner, but it was still like being shut up in a chest.

On the bed, broad enough to serve as a double if the occupants were reasonably slender, Louisette was tossing and turning in her nightgown, the coverlet thrown aside. Her eyes were closed, her mouth open; she breathed in gasps and now and then moaned. A lamp, lit by Arthur before he came out, showed her pale skin shiny with perspiration, and when Joel caught her wrist, he found her touch clammy, her pulse strong but slow.

He whispered her name. Her eyelids rolled back, and on recognizing him she forced a smile.

"Oh, Jewel! I don't want to be a nuisance! Why don't you tell Arthur to stop worrying? I guess I ate something that disagreed with me, that's all."

"Are you in pain?" he demanded. "Where?"

She gestured vaguely at her belly, and even as she did so her hands folded over and she gasped in renewed agony.

"Abueron has been hinting," Joel murmured sidelong to Arthur, "that you've . . . well, begun your family."

Dry-lipped, Arthur nodded.

"And I couldn't help noticing how excited she was by the race. Sometimes tension— But hell! I'm no expert!"

"We don't have a doctor aboard, do we?" Arthur muttered.

"I guess not. But—!" Joel snapped his fingers. "By a miracle we wound up with Cherouen's nurse! Do you know where she's been put?"

"Is something wrong?" inquired an unfamiliar voice, and they glanced toward the door. Framed in it, serious-faced under a black hat, was a man neither of them knew, who hastily averted his gaze on realizing Louisette was *en déshabillé*. "I'm Harry Whitworth, second mate," he added. "Couldn't sleep, thought I'd take a turn around, make sure all's well."

Arthur and Joel started to speak at once, and within moments other staterooms were opening to reveal cross expressions on sleepy faces. A fat, sour-voiced woman—who had, she declared, objected to being lodged next to a darkie—was finally able to identify the room allotted to Josephine, over on the far side.

As Whitworth departed with a promise to seek out Woodley, Joel rapped on the indicated door and whispered urgently, "Miss Var! Miss Var! We need your help!"

Josephine appeared shoeless but otherwise fully clad. She seemed little rested, but summoned enough energy to order everyone else out of the stateroom and shut the door so she could examine Louisette. At first the latter objected, but then lay resignedly still.

After three of four minutes she reemerged and addressed a point halfway between Arthur and Joel as though uncertain which was the husband.

"She must be put ashore as soon as possible. She's in danger of losing the child."

During the examination Whitworth had vanished. Now he returned, announcing that the captain would be here in a moment. But by then the cabin was awash with people. Auberon had appeared, belting a robe about him, prepared to be furious at the noise that had awakened him until he realized its cause; Gordon also, shouting for Matthew as though still half asleep and unable to react to what was actually happening; Matthew in his turn, barefoot and in a nightshirt, suddenly alarmed as he realized how many people were gathering and retreating in order to dress more decorously; Hugo and Stella Spring, who seemed to have concluded that the boat had struck a snag and was sinking . . . Moreover a number of men who were respectable enough to enjoy cabin facilities but either could not afford or had chosen not to book staterooms, who had been dozing on deck in canvas chairs, came sleepily to investigate.

At the focus of all this, Louisette lay striving not to moan aloud.

Belatedly her maid arrived, bringing some sort of sleeping draught. Josephine seized the bottle, inspected the label, withdrew the cork and smelled the contents, then gave a grudging nod of permission: all mannerisms copied from Cherouen. To her this was a weird experience, much as though she were caught up in a vivid dream.

For it required no gift of prophecy to predict what Woodley's and Gordon's reaction would be to the news that there was a woman aboard who risked miscarrying and must be landed at the earliest opportunity.

But it was neither of them who put that reaction into words. Instead it was

Parbury, to whom light and dark were one, descending from the pilothouse by the guidance of his cane and still more than a trifle drunk.

"This woman is Cherouen's nurse, isn't she?" he rasped when the situation was explained. "And he's aboard the losing boat, isn't he? It's another trick to delay us! She tried before, remember—wanted us to stop and search the boat for an imaginary stick of dynamite! When that didn't work . . . I'll lay Mrs. Gattry is in on the conspiracy, too, playacting for all she's worth!"

There was a faint gasp from Matthew. Then Auberon took a long stride to confront Parbury.

"By God, if you weren't blind I'd call you out!" he exploded.

Just in time Joel caught him by the arm. At the same moment Whitworth returned with Woodley, who barked in an attempt to assert his authority:

"I will not tolerate a brawl aboard my boat! Sir!"—using the tone he only adopted toward Parbury when his patience was exhausted—"both Mr. Gattry and Mr. Moyne have backed the *Nonpareil*, and what you just said was unworthy! We shall have to do as the nurse says."

Gordon thrust his way to the front of the little crowd. "But Moyne backed the *Atchafalaya!*" he declared. "I'm sure of it!"

"No, he's been backing us—" Woodley countered, and was cut short by Auberon.

"Only enough to keep up the odds! Upon my honor as a gentleman I want the *Nonpareil* to win!"

The wind out of his sails, Gordon pursued doggedly, "Well, then—at any rate, can't Mrs. Gattry be put ashore in one of these things you call a yawl?"

Matthew giggled at the unintended and ridiculous rhyme; Gordon glared at him.

"My sister will be treated as she deserves," Auberon whispered, very pale. "Not like a package—like a human being and a member of the gentler sex!"

"And anybody who says different will have me to answer to," chimed in Joel. He pointed to the windows on the starboard side. Ahead, lights were gleaming on the bank. Producing—and remembering to wind—his watch, he continued, "I guess there's a good hospital in Baton Rouge, and plenty of doctors! She must go ashore!"

From within the stateroom came a faint cry. "No, no! I just ate something I shouldn't have, that's all!"

"Now hesh yo' mout'," said Josephine firmly, reverting to the kind of phrase she ordinarily would have died rather than utter. "Ain't no bad food gon' make yo' belly chu'n so! I done felt yo' womb a-creepin'!"

And, with sudden dismay, she recollected there were strangers including men within earshot, and subsided. But she had won her point. Woodley slapped his hands together.

"Mr. Whitworth, since you're here and handy! Up to the pilothouse, tell Mr. Hogan we have to put in at Baton Rouge long enough to land a sick lady and her husband. The wharf will be clear at this hour. We shall lose only a few minutes at worst, and the *Atchafalaya* is still too far astern to catch up."

He put all the conviction he could into the statement, because he wanted—

needed—to believe it was so. And letting a pregnant woman die on board would be far more of a smirch on his captaincy than losing even this longed-for race.

All who had laid bets relaxed visibly. To shave the lead was not as bad as losing it.

"You are certain, are you, Miss—uh—Var?" Woodley ventured as a last hope. She nodded firmly.

"No doubt of it, sir. I guess it's the excitement. A lady in her condition shouldn't have come aboard."

"It was her idea," Arthur said defensively. "She insisted!"

Ignoring him, Auberon demanded, "But she will recover?"

"Oh, sure. She's young and in good health—a few days' rest and a doctor's care will see her fine. But not if she continues with the trip."

"Okay," Woodley sighed. "Do as I said, Whitworth. Ask the pilot to let me know how much time we lose so we can deduct it from the total in case of arguments."

The gathering broke up. Immediately Joel rushed back to the table where he had left his draft report and sat down, dipping his pen to scribble a hasty addendum.

"I don't want this in your rag!" Arthur rapped.

"You can't stop me saying that the *Nonpareil* is making an unexpected stopover!" Joel flashed. "Don't worry, though—I'll keep it down to generalities."

Arthur hesitated; then turned away, grumbling, to comfort his wife.

But within a very short while comfort had turned to recrimination. "Thanks to *you*," Joel clearly heard, "I could lose every cent I've bet on this race!"

Poor Louisette. . . but there was no time for Joel to think about the fate of others. Unless this story was ready to be sent ashore in less than ten minutes, he would have to wait until their coaling stop at Natchez before he could telegraph anything to the paper, and that would waste all the advantage due to having a reporter on board.

Heedless of blots and erasures, he made his pen fly over the pages.

 Fernand's first watch of the trip had started tolerably well but ended badly. Shortly after Drew left him, the *Atchafalaya* had come upon a lot of floating lumber, which the *Nonpareil* had encountered in a broader reach where it caused far less trouble, and he had had to play safe at bends where the leading boat's wake disguised the familiar wrinkle of sand reefs. To his shame, he had lost as much as he had gained by the time Tyburn came yawning to relieve him.

Four-hour watches really were too brief, even though the sheer concentration involved meant that it took exceptional endurance to maintain speed over a longer period. Perhaps when the Guild and the government and the Army all got together and the river was properly marked with buoys by day and lamps by night, every boat might safely adopt the six-and-six system of the towboats. But that might well not be in Drew's time. He was old-fashioned despite being progressive: a paradox often found in elderly pioneers. The first captain to work with a colored pilot might also be the last to give up the short watch.

On a normal trip Fernand found it easy enough to snatch catnaps. Right now his brain was infinitely too busy; it pumped and thumped like a doctor engine, full of images of his mother, and Dorcas, and what little he recalled of his father, and Drew, who had in some sense taken his father's place—but too late, so that they met as men, not as man and boy—and Cherouen, with his haughty manner and overready temper, so different from the reassuring bluntness of Malone, who had very likely saved Dorcas's life, and . . .

Well, there was at least one matter he could set his mind at rest about. He went to inquire after Walt Presslie. He was, it turned out, safely asleep; according to Ealing, he had declared his injuries were not as bad as they looked and sworn he would be fit for light work in the morning.

That was a relief, for there were bends and narrows up ahead where the lack of a single engineer could make a vast difference to the boat's speed. Fernand ordered himself to turn in and made his slow way up to the texas. Just before going inside, however, he cast a final glance around. The *Atchafalaya* was pushing now into the straight reach above Bruly Landing; he was able to discern the church astern to larboard and the characteristic clumps of trees left by land clearance on the east bank, which he was used to navigating by.

Tyburn was keeping up a very fair speed. But there were still too many pieces of lumber in the water for Fernand's liking.

Then he turned his gaze directly ahead and was scarcely able to repress a cry of amazement. It looked as though the *Nonpareil*— No! The *Nonpareil* was indisputably putting about, in a manner that could imply only one thing.

She intended to make a stop at Baton Rouge.

Impossible! Woodley's clerks had gone to the greatest pains to ensure she had neither freight nor passengers for Louisiana ports!

He darted up the stairs to the pilothouse, shouting.

Drew beat him to it by a fraction. Coatless, collar open, hair untidy, he was staring at the *Nonpareil* with equal disbelief. In the almost total blackness of the pilothouse she could be seen much more clearly.

"A breakdown?" Fernand burst out.

"The good Lord knows," Drew said with a shrug. "But it gives us an opening. Ketch, you thinking what I'm thinking?"

Tyburn hesitated. "We're still meeting an awful lot of floating logs," he said at length.

"*And* we're farther behind than I figured we'd be at this time," the captain murmured, not looking toward Fernand. But the words bore barbs; his cheeks grew hatefully hot, as they much too often did. When would he outgrow this juvenile reflex?

"It is our best chance before Red River Cutoff," Fernand said in the firmest tone he could summon.

"I concur," Drew said with utmost formality. "If you care to ring for full speed ahead, Mr. Tyburn, I shall raise no objection."

"Yes, *sir!*" said Tyburn, and reached for the rope. Fernand felt a pang of envy. Serpent's-tooth sharp, the realization came that, had he been here to take the wheel at starting time, it would have been to him that Drew issued his unprecedented instruction. Dorcas—his mother . . . The thoughts tangled up together and were firmly thrust aside. He must take the wheel again at five o'clock, and up around Angola, Red River, Mansura, there were a bunch of the trickiest bends on the whole Mississippi. Watch and learn must be his motto; between them these men beside him mustered sixty years' more river time than he did.

But at all events Baton Rouge was about to enjoy one of the grandest spectacles of the century: a steamer passing at top speed in the dead of dark.

Another bell?

For a moment Fernand failed to register the signal. Calling out the polemen? That was reserved for picking your way through shallows, beating off mosquitoes by day and waving moth-infested torches by night, and in either case at less than walking pace.

Then a cheer rang out from the forward end of the main deck, and there was a tremendous hurrying and scurrying. Belatedly it dawned on Fernand what was happening. Old and canny in the ways of the river, Tyburn was resuscitating a technique that probably had not been used since "befohdewoh." Already one could hear the excitement as Chalker and Sexton organized their men into gangs. The boat's hull seemed to speak in answer to the shifting weight, for more than thirty deck crew had signed on for this trip, and that amounted to a fair load.

Within a minute the first fire basket was lit and lofted, and the most venturesome of the men could be seen advancing on the forward guards with the long poles normally used for shallow soundings. Not tonight. By groups of three and four they were to fend off any driftwood that showed in the harsh yellow glare of the fire baskets—a second now, a third, and the final fourth hung on chains to keep their pitch-fed flame from infecting the wooden upperworks.

Fernand shivered. It would never have occurred to him to give such a signal. Did they know the pilot was gambling with their lives? One log too large to be diverted, and pole and men alike could be whipped overboard and lost in the dark and seething current.

Perhaps they knew; perhaps they didn't care. He could not tell which possibility was the more frightening.

But the bells, and now the flaring light, had roused the deck passengers. They were shortly joined by people from the staterooms, including Barber, who usurped the speaking tube from the office to demand what was going on.

"We have a chance to pass her!" Drew shouted, and the wind the boat was making explained the rest.

Writing the record of her passage in a script of sparks, the *Atchafalaya* raced toward Thomas Point, while her passengers and crew joined in the cheering from the banks. Later the papers said all Baton Rouge awoke to greet her passing; most respectable citizens, however, cursed the racket and went back to sleep. Some on board her also swore: polemen who had thrust at nothing much, making too valiant a lunge at what proved to be an empty barrel or a bundle of drifting weed, and almost spilled overside. The densest of the lumber had been carried past and the water was clear again.

But that was nothing to the curses from the *Nonpareil*.

 After delivering his report to the astonished owner of the launch Graves had hired by cable, by merely handing it overside, Joel returned to the boiler deck. Leaning on its rail, Auberon accosted him; being in nightwear, he had taken his leave of Louisette before she was wrapped in white sheets and carried to the wharf on an improvised stretcher, where she now awaited the summoning of a doctor.

"And how, pray, do you intend to describe this setback in your next dispatch? I can just guess how you depicted our early triumph! Superior skill in the management of the vessel will always tell—is that not close to what you said? And doubtless this will become an errand of mercy!"

He coughed as he concluded, and from the pocket of his silk robe produced a handkerchief with which he covered his mouth in a manner that was somehow guilty. Joel was seized with a wild surmise. But he was too pleased at having got his report away to make any comment . . . and also more than a mite too tired.

Besides, any attempt to make this stopover appear to be what Auberon had ironically termed it was doomed, for Arthur was in a filthy temper, still shouting about how his wife had cost him a fortune because she had insisted on coming.

"Are you delighted by my sister's choice of a partner?" Auberon murmured.

He coughed again, and this time was not quite quick enough to hide a dark stain on his handkerchief.

Oh, no . . . !

Full realization crossed Joel's weary mind. Yet Auberon was speaking again before he could, catching his arm and pointing.

"Look at Parbury! Look at him waving that stick like a conductor with a disorderly orchestra!"

And indeed the image was exact: the blind man was standing near the bow, visibly boiling with rage.

Auberon gave a sour chuckle. "Ah, the stability of the Old World has much to command it, but for stimulation of the glands and guts, give me the New World!"

Joel faced him squarely. "Obe! I don't like that cough of yours!"

"Oh, it's only a nuisance! But listen, will you?"

He pointed over the rail. From the main deck words reached them with sculptural clarity. The voice was unmistakably Gordon's.

"He paid ye! He bocht ye! It's thanks tae what ye did that we're o'erta'en!"

Confronting him, hands on hips, was Josephine. Her riposte was just as fierce.

"If I were a man you'd never dare insult me so! When I was an army nurse I

watched better men than you cry like babies, and if you give me cause I'll make
*you* weep!"

"Now that," murmured Auberon, "sounds like a woman one might respect. I'll
take her side on principle."

He strode away, giving Joel no chance to raise again the question of his cough—
or his awareness of Josephine's identity.

The *Atchafalaya* drew level at that moment and roared past. Roared like a
maddened beast! Like a twin-headed dragon rearing back to strike at an enemy,
as though a serpent and an angry swan were to be combined at the whim of a
sorcerer, then fed with coals and lava, she charged up the reach uttering such
fiery breath as might have made a Saint George quail.

Joel stood a long while transfixed by the spectacle, his head ringing with such
phrases, hoping he might remember them long enough to note them down for his
next report. Eventually he looked down again, expecting to see Auberon and
Josephine still arguing with Gordon. They had moved out of sight. But what he
did see drove all thought of them from his mind.

The stage was about to be withdrawn. Leaving Louisette and her maid on the
wharf, Arthur was coming back on board.

Abruptly beside himself with fury, he rushed down the stairs.

"What the hell are you doing?" he shouted above the roar of the engines as the
pilot called for full astern.

Scowling, Arthur spat overside. "She'll be all right. She has her maid with her,
and plenty of money."

"That's my cousin you're—"

"Cousin or no cousin, she's a damned fool! I told her she wasn't fit to come on
this trip, but she pleaded, she wheedled, and finally I gave in. Now look what's
happened thanks to her pigheadedness! The *Atchafalaya's* in the lead!"

"And that's a reason for abandoning her when she may be in danger of her life?"

"Too late to do anything about it now," Arthur said with a shrug, and turned to
go.

Joel caught him by the shoulder.

"I won't let you get away with this," he promised between clenched teeth.
"From now on I shall pillory you in every story I file, as the man who cares more
about his money than his bride!"

He looked around for Auberon, in search of moral support, but he was not to be
seen. His heated tone, though, had drawn the attention of a dozen other bystanders; they knew what he was talking about, and there were nods of approval.

Arthur's mouth worked. He too sought someone to take his side, but by chance
none of his cronies happened to be nearby. After a moment he beat a retreat,
while the *Nonpareil* rounded bows-on to the current and went ahead full pelt.

To small avail. By the time she was square in mid-channel, the older boat was
breasting Thomas Point with ten clear feet of water under her and the chance to
run a dead straight course to Lobdell's Stores before having to slacken speed
again. And it was her turn to generate frustrating wash.

Having—like many others—found it impossible to sleep, Manuel crept cautiously along the main deck toward the bow. He had learned never to mingle with

"respectable" passengers; however, from those taking deck passage he hoped to find out what was going on.

Luck was with him. He came unobserved upon Parbury, Woodley, Auberon and Josephine—the latter standing a little apart—and heard Auberon say, "I observe this delay has cost us six minutes. Had the *Nonpareil* made as good time in the present reach as did the *Atchafalaya,* she would still be astern of us, would she not?"

"Of course that's so," Woodley answered bluffly. "Anyone who says different is a liar."

"I'm glad to hear you say that. Mr. Gordon has gone storming off in a rage because he believes I bet heavily on the *Atchafalaya*. It's not true, any more than the slanders against Miss Var voiced by"—a meaning pause—"*certain people* are true! And I hope to hear no more of any such nonsense! I admit I did lay some money on Drew, back in April, which is doubtless what Gordon got wind of, but that was solely to ensure that interest in the prospect of a race was kept up. I was betting against myself. In the upshot I plumped for your boat as the likely winner. If you want my support when it comes to calculating actual times, you have it."

Parbury's face was etched with lines as deep as desert shadows. He said, "No use making claims like that. We got to pass her in our turn. I'll get back to the pilothouse, I guess."

Auberon turned to Josephine, offering his arm. "Ma'am, I'm much appreciative of the aid you rendered to my sister. Allow me to escort you back to your stateroom."

For a moment she looked at him with a trace of bewilderment; then she acceded and they moved away.

Manuel judged it politic to do the same; one could never tell when these unpredictable gringos might lose their tempers because they were being overheard. He backed rapidly out of sight around the nearest corner.

And Joel, coming in search of Auberon to tell him about Arthur's presence, bumped square into him.

There was a flurry of apologies, and by the time they were over, Auberon and Josephine were ascending the stairs to the cabin again.

Oh, let it rest for the moment. Auberon would find out about Arthur soon enough . . .

Looking more closely at the man he had collided with, Joel said, "Oh, you're the musician, aren't you? I guess I ought to interview you some time."

Manuel, amazed, stood to attention. "You wish to interview *me,* señor?"

"Why not? You must know as much as anyone about—well, the way passengers behave on a riverboat, to start with!" Joel was very tired and also much distracted by his confrontation with Arthur; he scarcely knew what he was saying.

"Oh, I want to do!" Manuel exclaimed. "It is an engagement for when I am not busied with the music! You are a *gentleman,* sir! I shake our hands!"

Having with some difficulty parted from Manuel, Joel reentered the cabin—now once again deserted—amd stretched out on a chaise longue. They were thundering toward Fausse Rivière, having covered 150 miles in less than nine hours.

Even though most of the way so far had been in darkness, both boats were ahead of the record for the distance.

Spectators, passengers, owners, crews and bettors alike were getting splendid value for their investment of money and/or interest.

And what matter, Joel asked himself as he shut his eyes in the hope he would not oversleep the dawn—what matter if the *Nonpareil* had been overtaken? A few changes of lead would make for a more dramatic race.

And if the *Atchafalaya* did win, it would be a poke in the eye for that son of a bitch who'd married Louisette.

 The rest of the night was a story of weaving back and forth in bends that became unexpectedly and sometimes frighteningly shallow, a summary of all the reasons why the Mississippi steamer had developed in the way she did, with a liner's hull sitting on the draught of a scow. Names hung in the predawn air, full of memories and expectations, disappointed or yet to be put to the test. Fausse Rivière, testimony to a wrong guess, slid astern to larboard, opposing Prophet's Island; what prophet— the explorer who said, "This will prove to be a river joining the greater river," and when it turned out a mere bayou had to suffer the mockery of his companions? Waterloo recalled a terrible battle and Francisville a saint who would not even tolerate the killing of animals. Pleasant Harbor passed, and Morganzie, and Fisher's Store, and Tunica—and then suddenly there was the fast clear reach, 204 miles from New Orleans, which in the memory of men still working on the river had not been there; formerly it had been necessary to swing southwest, due north, and almost due east in order to gain a few miles northward from Tunica. Therefore it was known by the same name in two languages: Racourcie Cutoff.

And a little higher there was another cutoff named for the Red River, which in turn was so called because of the red soil it washed out of its hinterland in time of flood. In turn, again, there was an island named for it: 215 miles from the start of the trip.

Behind this island was the other river, which bore a name now being made more famous even than it had been yesterday.

"Captain!" Fernand said when sunrise was painting the eastern sky.

Drew had not returned to his stateroom, but lain down on the leather bench, where he had slept clear through the last change of pilots. One eye opening, he muttered, "What?"

"Know where dawn will see us?"

"Where?"—in the tone of one who has seen too many dawns to care.

"Close as this boat has ever been to the river she's named for." Fernand shivered, although the morning air was already warm. "Kind of like an omen!"

Drew's eyes were comfortably shut again. "I guess your mother knows more about omens than I do," he grunted. "What I care about is hard facts. Where's the *Nonpareil?*"

"I see her smoke," Fernand murmured. "I guess about three or four miles back."

Drew sat up. "We gained on her?" he demanded incredulously.

Forbearing to mention how little of the credit belonged to himself, Fernand handed him the glasses that rested beside his mother's crucifix.

"Thunderation, but it's true!" the captain crowed a moment later. And in a fit of enthusiasm sounded a blast on the whistle before shamefacedly returning to the bench.

Where in a little while he dozed off again.

 Friday . . . and the rising sun shone on a portion of the Mississippi where there were long-established settlements, comparatively close together. Yet already they were like mere notches cut into the aboriginal woodland, temporary roosting places for migratory man, perched clear of last year's flood but perhaps not of this year's.

But the eastward sky was exceptionally beautiful: a color symphony easing the velvet dark away.

Here, around Point Breeze and Black Hawk Point and Fairview Landing, there were some of the awkwardest bends on the river.

Under normal trading conditions a boat might well go slowly through here, pausing occasionally to consult her leadsman. During a race . . .

Sheer exuberance, rather than confidence, made Fernand signal full ahead as he gazed about him at the bright new day. Drew snored behind him; Tyburn would remain in his stateroom until a few minutes before nine, for it was his custom to take breakfast at the wheel—coffee and rolls brought by the texas tender. He was on his own.

Taking over at five in the morning, he had been amazed to discover what a lead Tyburn had conjured up from the *Nonpareil's* check at Baton Rouge. Now they had a clear run until the coaling stop at Natchez, which would fall, most likely, around the middle of Tyburn's next watch . . . though Drew himself would insist on tackling the delicate operation of sliding her between the flats, so they could refuel without needing to stop. He had done this on their earlier record-breaking run, with the same aplomb as when he had accepted Dr. Larzenac off the *Franche-Comté.*

Proud though he was of his achievement as a pilot, Fernand knew he was no more ready to imitate that kind of maneuver than to copy Tyburn's flat-out rush past Baton Rouge, relying on his polemen.

Yet he was learning all the time. Something strange had happened to him since he first laid hands on a riverboat's enormous steering wheel. He had learned to think without words, to divide his mind between the reflex pattern of controlling the steamer and the totally rational one that governed the rest of his life. Now and then he thought about one day owning a boat, and his mind rebelled at the idea of having to calculate freight charges and figure out duty rosters for his crew, because it was too much like keeping track of debits and credits for the Marocain Bank.

Yet he must not forget the precept Uncle Edouard had made the pivot of his existence! The more he traveled this astonishing river, the more he thought of the old man's dictum that money and the Mississippi were alike, sometimes destroying, sometimes creating, according to principles which humans as yet had failed to comprehend.

Caught as he frequently was between two courses of action, as for example when he had to weigh the chance of grounding because there was an exceptional amount of cargo in the hold, against the fact that if he brought it to port quicker than expected he would surely secure more cargoes in future, he often found himself appealing to imaginary authorities. One was his father, who in his childhood had seemed tremendous and infinitely capable; another, Drew.

But the person on whom he strove to model himself was, increasingly, Uncle Edouard.

Why? Out of gratitude? That scarcely entered into it; whatever the old man had done had been guided by a degree of self-interest, at best. Out of jealousy of Richard and Eugene? Never! Fernand's lot was now so superior to his cousins', he wondered how he had ever been able to endure the whims and caprices of rich bored stupid idiots.

It had come to his ears that some of that group had been seen boarding the *Nonpareil*, including the former Louisette Moyne, around whose new husband a scandal was evolving. Gossip being such a popular pastime in New Orleans, from a servant's chance remark a whole fantasy world could be elaborated in a day. But Fernand suspected that what he had heard was more factual than fantastic. Mrs. Imelda Moyne employed enough black staff for her to be a common subject of conversation, while her husband had behaved in most irregular fashion before and even after his wedding, not infrequently with colored mistresses. Why—?

The association of ideas abruptly swung his mind over like a spate finding a new cutoff. On the roster of people to whom he made mental appeal, why did his mother not appear? After all, she had turned up in what she must have regarded as his hour of trial . . .

He glanced at the crucifix on the windowsill. But he found himself unable to pursue that line of thought either. The moment he pictured his mother, that image was displaced by Dorcas.

Pangs of guilt flashed through his mind. He fought them valiantly, just as he had fought Drew's most ill-tempered accusations of incompetence when he was a cub, not on the grounds that he had been right, but that no one could charge him with knowing he was wrong. Perhaps that was the proper duty of a mother: to interfere in her children's lives for the best motives, regardless of whether the act led to the best outcome.

Proper or not, it certainly seemed to be the commonest. There had been long nights spent right here, when Drew watched and criticized and sometimes talked of himself, his half-brother—vastly encouraged on discovering how much Fernand had been told about him—and his sister-in-law and her family. He must be very attached to them; had he not made it a condition of taking Cherouen that Susannah be treated by him?

Yet he, even he, had often grouched about the way she treated her sons, like a broody hen protecting eggs, especially the one who couldn't breathe without his aromatic medicine.

And what was life going to be like for Drew in old age?

The question struck like lightning from the subconscious level of Fernand's mind. Thinking of his mother, he could not escape the concept "older"; thinking of Dorcas and right now marveling all over again because from the moment they met the two had behaved like friends, he could equally not escape the idea "I/father" . . .

And naturally enough he had to recall the precious night he and Dorcas had stolen, courtesy of Drew and Barber . . .

And last night Drew had lectured him, and—and . . . !

It came together suddenly. He knew what and why and how. This trip he had thought of as a prolongation of the adventure that had lured him out of the Marocain shop was not a continuation of anything. It was a first step on a new road. What now came to mind was a vision that made him shudder: of countless unknown employers, all white, all prepared to apply stricter than normal standards to a colored man, and then to double that because he was also famous.

And much of that would hold true for his marriage. The children he had by Dorcas would be little, if at all, darker than himself. They might of course have hair as crinkly as sheep's wool. They might be slim with huge deep eyes, or round-faced and thick-lipped—

Never mind! What they were sure to be was *in trouble*. At the best schools— and a successful pilot could afford them—there would always be white children prepared to sneak behind the teacher's back, to throw away a colored boy's exercise or tear his clothes or call him such foul names that he broke down crying and dared not tell the master why.

But here was Fernand: at the wheel of the finest steamer on the whole damned river system! And his kids were going to do even better—spit in the eyes of the other kids, white or not, tell the teachers to teach the truth, go out into the world and tame it like a circus lion! Hell! For thirty years or more people had been laughing at minstrels dolled up in blackface. Wasn't that long enough?

Wasn't it time to laugh *with* and not *at*?

And why was he thinking about this anyhow when, according to all the novels he had read and all the plays he had seen, he ought to have been concentrating on nothing but Dorcas?

Because without falling in love with her he could never have learned to think this way, any more than he could have learned the wordless skills now ingrained in his hands and eyes without falling in love with this bitch of a river.

In the real world, all this time, he was smashing the golden path of the new day's sunshine into magnificent fragments, rousing whole crazed roosts of shouting

birds, frightening alligators into sluggish motion, enraging the engineers and firemen with his demands, annoying the stewards trying to lay tables for breakfast,
amazing and delighting the passengers, and impressing the drowsy Drew as he
yawned and stretched and got up off the bench. Sternward rose two gray plumes
of smoke: one might be the rival boat's, one the sign of a steamer Tyburn had
passed around 4:30 A.M.

Having consulted his watch, still yawning, Drew peered under bushy brows
through the forward windows. After a pause during which Fernand's heart
pounded worse than Dorcas could provoke, he said, "You're laying into Black
Hawk Point."

"Yes." There was no sense in saying more.

"Palmetto and Jackson's?"

"Have to." With a scowl. "I'd rather go by Island 118 and straight to Hoovers. I
dasn't."

He waited for the Olympian verdict that was sure to follow. It never arrived.
Drew merely grunted, stretched anew, and made for the stairs with some comment about "'freshing up and getting coffee."

Fernand relaxed with a gusting sigh. Then it occurred to him to check his own
watch.

With a considerable shock he realized what Drew had omitted to say.

At this stage of the trip the *Atchafalaya* was twenty minutes ahead of her previous record.

And there was certainly no other steamer, *Nonpareil* or otherwise, within three
miles of her downriver. Maybe five.

In the same instant he was easing the boat into an improbable but necessary
curve, because here the old channel was silting up and the new one hardly established. A sense of strength rightly applied flowed up his arms and seemed to
permeate his brain. Drew could have challenged his judgment; a teacher with his
former pupil had the privilege. And the boat was worth—well, its formal price
didn't matter, but half was Barber's, and Drew wanted to win it off him, so . . .

Memories of Edouard flowed back, the old faint voice discussing the impact of
money.

Regardless of all that, he had been allowed to continue on his breakneck course!
He had come out of night at full split; he was running no faster now than he had
been in the half-light of false dawn; he had added to the *Atchafalaya*'s lead while
sheer good luck ensured that he neither heard nor felt so much as a twig brush
the hull.

Drew, however, was prepared to accept it as the reward for skill.

This, he thought with a tremor of awe, is why I admired Edouard and do
admire Drew; why I may love but can't respect my mother; why I despise my
cousins and their butterfly wives; why I hope to love and cherish Dorcas and have
children to whom I can pass on this lesson.

*I have been trusted; let it show me how to trust.*

In a little while he would greet Dorcas and his mother, escort them to breakfast, taste the first hint of what life would be like as a married man, console the
former for what Parbury (damn his guts!) had done to her, comfort the latter as

best he might for the fact that he did not believe in her magic: walk the tightrope path between sympathy and insult which was so like steering the monstrous bulk of the *Atchafalaya*—

A shriek on the edge of hearing! His hand was flying to the backing bell rope before he was able to dismiss what he had reacted to. Like being touched on a naked nerve, the scrape of an underwater obstacle, most likely a rotting branch, had triggered all his pilot's reflexes. But none of the consequent signs had followed, not even a crunch as it shattered on the implacable buckets of the nearer wheel. It had washed away, was gone.

Image after relevent image pestered him: girls he would never see again, yet never forget; temporary crewmen on the many boats he had now piloted . . .

Which led him back to the men he had met serving under Drew, and Drew's stake in this race, and a delicate question of judgment: whether he should rush onward and trust his luck would hold, or yield to caution and chance letting the *Nonpareil* close the gap.

He stared at the huge flat expanse of water ahead, and glanced back, and shut his eyes for a second and tried to sense the pattern of vibrations reaching him from the giant pistons. It seemed normal to the point of being monotonous, which doubtless must be why he had paid it less and less attention during the course of his watch.

Therefore there was no reason to slow down, except lack of confidence in his own skill. From below he could hear voices, even someone singing. The news was abroad that the *Nonpareil* was far astern, and there was laughter.

Why disappoint the thrill seekers? Why not enjoy a challenge to himself? Earlier it had been reflexive; this time it could be conscious.

Taking a fresh grip on the wheel, he resolved to lay the steamer into her next marks at unprecedented speed.

*What am I doing here?*

From a night full of despairing dreams Gaston woke to indescribable strangeness: a low ceiling, confining walls—as in Mr. Poe's celebrated *nouvelle* concerning a refined torture of the Inquisition—and an all-pervading throb, as though he had slept in the guts of some colossal beast, close enough to its heart to feel its pounding.

He rolled off the bed and was within arm's reach of the one tiny window, decorously curtained. Peering out, he found he was looking directly toward one of the most gorgeous sunrises he had ever been privileged to see.

The reds and golds, colors of vitality and action, wiped his mind of pointless fears. Here he was, having cast his bread upon the waters, doing exactly what he had promised himself so long ago: undertaking a voyage up the Mississippi. And there was music of a kind, barbaric though it might be, for idle deckhands were passing time with a mournful chant. He fancied he could make out words he had heard before, concerning judgment day and the fall of stars from heaven. Well, if he were ever to compose the tone poem he had originally imagined, he must accept the crudity of North America and incorporate what raw materials it

provided. After all, so trivial a theme as a common chord had served as inspiration
for great composers of the past . . .

His spirits revived. Suddenly he was hungry too.

Within ten minutes of waking, fully clad and donning his best silk hat, Gaston
d'Aurade emerged to face breakfast and a whole new life.

Eulalie had scarcely slept; when she did doze off, the engines' throbbing became like the beating of drums and carried her away to a ceremony in a vast and
distant place, where she knew none of her fellow celebrants and where she had to
offer her body in turn to countless violent strangers. There was a fire in the center
of a ring of dancers. She strove to shape its glow into the form of the crucifix she
had brought to aid her son. Again and again, just as she thought she could detect
the outline of the cross, came another hot uprush from the embers and a hideous
sketch for a human face leered at her with black pits for eyes and a great maw full
of tonguelike flames.

Yet, paradoxically, when she awoke she was somewhat comforted, as though
she had paid an asked-for price. As yet she dared not guess what it was. There
was one terrifying possibility—that she had set in train the very events which
would lead to the loss of her only son—but she was incapable of facing the idea.
She clung rather to the recollection of having acted in a proper, indeed, a dignified, manner when this young man, born of her loins but grown into an alien,
presented his intended wife.

Memory confirmed her first opinion. Here was not what she had been afraid of,
some flirty little fortune hunter with a roving eye and a stock of jewels, gifts from
her previous admirers. On the contrary, although she was undoubtedly beautiful,
this Dorcas seemed meek and polite and affected a respectable style of dress.

A meek daughter-in-law would be an admirable acquisition.

Today, therefore, she resolved to cement the acquaintanceship and establish
dominance . . . not that she verbalized the latter impulse. She had feared a mistake; now she knew she had done perfectly right to arrive aboard her son's boat on
this trip. There were bound to be, had already been, slights to suffer that were
due to her—and Fernand's—color. Never mind! They might smart awhile, but
they could never touch the heart of one who was heiress to a greater fortune than
any white slave-owning family had ever enjoyed, the mystical and magical bequest
of Athalie whom thousands worshiped.

When she discovered that the *Atchafalaya* had overtaken the *Nonpareil*, she
made up her mind to perform a necessary rite today, perhaps with materials
begged from the cooks. There were bound to be chickens on board.

And let the mysterious Josephine remain a mystery to her grave!

It had taken Barber a long time to get back to sleep after the episode at Baton
Rouge. Along with everyone else who had been roused from bed by the overtaking, he had relished the spectacle of the *Nonpareil* frustrated at the wharf. But
even his best field glasses could not inform him of the reason for her stop. Gross,
however, had assured him it could not be due to mechanical breakdown. He had

been an engineer and lost his certificate on grounds he preferred not to go into, though sometimes he hinted they had to do with besting his captain in a barroom fight.

But the moment the notion of breakdown entered Barber's head, it began to plague him. Not since her maiden voyage had he traveled aboard this vessel he half owned. Since then, had not an alarming coughlike sound developed in the starboard cylinder, or a new shrill wheeze in the other one? Did not the wheels creak over loudly in their bearings? Were not more frightening groans uttered by the hull and upperworks every time the *Atchafalaya* crossed a contrary current or the wake of another steamer?

Above all, had not the junior engineer been severely scalded within a few miles of the start? Today he was informed that the man should be fit for work, but one needed an authoritative opinion.

He pondered all this as he sat in a barber's chair, being shaved by Jones.

At last, while the surplus lather was being wiped away, he said, "Cuffy! Go invite Dr. Cherouen to take breakfast with me. And don't let him say no!"

Cuffy departed obediently. Rising, retying his cravat before the mirror, Barber asked his reflection whether he had made a sound decision, betting so much on the older boat. If she lost, would he be left in sole ownership of a vessel of use for little except scrap? Even if she was capable of earning her living for a few more years, he would have to find a new captain, new pilots, new crew . . .

No, she must win the race, if only because were she to lose it would cost him at least forty-eight thousand dollars.

Of course, there were supporters of the *Nonpareil* who had bet as much again . . .

His heart fluttered and trembled in a sensation all gamblers knew. Privately, he sometimes compared it to falling in love.

But that was not something he had much experience of.

Dorcas could scarcely tell whether she had been awake or asleep between midnight and dawn. Even now she wished she might not be awake. The shift and shudder of the room where she found herself, the trembling of the bed she lay in, the rattle of tooth glass against water carafe, the flicker of dust in shafting sunlight—for it was already proving a clear bright day—all, all conspired to mock her plight.

And who was to blame for it? Herself alone.

She strove to think of Fernand and was briefly comforted. A man, that one, not a boy! Tough and trusty, and with a skill to support her, to make him and her both rich after they were wed. And with certain other talents . . .

She tried to think only of him clothed, his smiling face as he doffed his tall hat and made a bow, and was unable to escape recollection of his bare body. She did not picture it; she had indeed not seen it save as a series of sliding shiny planes by a glimmering lamp. But her hands knew it, and her skin, and her inmost being. He had convulsed her into what was almost terror, as though volcanoes had erupted. Perhaps that was what made sure of his achievement. One night had not cost other girls such a grave penalty; Fibby had lain with her man for more than a year, and his seed fell on barren ground.

For herself, here was only the second time of her life, and it was the second disaster. (What had been the name of the boy with eyes like chips of sky? She had realized with dismay on waking that she no longer knew it. Yesterday she had!)

Turned out of her home, forced to move to a city anonymous and incomprehensible, she had found sanctuary, a lover, a husband, and a future. Had she lost them again?

Her thoughts spun giddily. She began to weep, tears coursing her flawless cheeks like crystal insects. She was indescribably afraid of what she had done and only half understood why. An older and wiser woman could have explained, but the new life growing in her had no skill to communicate.

Expulsion from home for making love, loss of her child, equated in her head with expulsion—by choice—from the Parburys' house, where she had been secure after a fashion. She had been reborn at New Orleans; now she had to endure a third birth, into responsibility and marriage and motherhood . . . question mark. This life also might end before it properly began. But at all events she knew one thing. She could never again be what she had been: a dutiful daughter, a dutiful servant. She had failed in both roles.

Now she was condemned to be forever Mr. Lamenthe's "scarlet woman." And it had taken such tremendous effort to break the links that bound her to the past, to transform herself for a few brief hours to please him! How could she be that other amazing version of Dorcas for days, weeks, years, a lifetime?

The prospect was unbearable. She lay alone, quietly sobbing. Eventually someone knocked at the door. If only it could be Fernand, or Dr. Malone, who had saved her before . . . !

But it was doubtless a servant, who went away.

Last night nervous tension—it was always nervous tension, exacerbated this time by having to tend Walt, whose injuries reminded him of the war—had driven Cherouen to drink too much. Consequently he had retired comparatively early. Yet, he had been unable to sleep for a long while. The fact that he had overlooked something as blatant as Josephine's use of arsenic had struck at the foundations of his self-confidence. He had come to rely implicitly on that woman. How could she have been so *stupid*?

Above all: without her, was he going to be able to cope?

And what a fool he was going to look if the *Nonpareil* reached St. Louis first!

That was his last thought before he was claimed by slumber so deep he knew nothing of what happened at Baton Rouge, until . . .

"Doctor!" And a firm, repeated knock.

"Who is it?" he growled, eyes still closed. "What d'you want?"

"Mas' Barber's Cuffy, sah! He sent me to tell you we's in de lead dis mawnin'—"

Instantly, though bleary-eyed, Cherouen was awake and marveling.

"—an' to ask ef you'll take breakfas' wid'm, sah."

"Sure I will, just as soon as I'm dressed," Cherouen declared, and climbed

cautiously out of bed. His head throbbed almost as badly as the engines, but he
hummed a lively tune as he drew on his clothes.

"Seen your girl today?"

Fernand started, having thought himself alone in the pilothouse. Tyburn was
not due to take over for some while yet, and he had assumed that Drew's rounds
would occupy him longer than this. Here he was, though, standing at his shoulder; all of a sudden it was like being a cub again.

But the feeling passed in an instant. He had had a good watch up to now.
Jackson's Point had been safely rounded; he had made a flawless passage of Dead
Man's Bar, named for a corpse seen, long ago, snagged on a flood-uprooted tree in
mid-river. Boys among steamer crews liked to frighten passengers and first-timers
with the eerie name, evoking ghosts.

Now the toll of islands was reaching 117, 116; yonder to larboard lay Lake
Cocodrie, baptized by French explorers who marveled at the hordes of alligators
they found there. Beyond Ellis Cliffs, those soft-faced slabs of land raw from the
touch of the Creator, there remained only Como Landing before their first coaling
stop at Natchez: 279 miles upstream from New Orleans as the river ran at present—and who could guess how far next year?

Except, of course, there would not be a stop. There would be a mere pause,
just as during their last St. Louis trip. It was a fine clear morning, and by noon it
was going to be swelteringly hot. Everything was working out just fine. Apart
from . . .

When he answered Drew, Fernand's tone was scarcely that of a lover eager to
see his betrothed.

"Not yet, Captain! I guess when I go off watch."

"I got her," Drew said, laying his hand on the wheel. "I didn't see her in the
cabin when I passed through just now, and Ernest said she hadn't been in earlier.
Start acting like a man with responsibilities—go rout her out and feed her a decent breakfast."

Having made a hasty detour to change his shirt and run a razor over his face,
Fernand almost collided, as he entered the cabin, with a man taller than himself,
impeccable in gray, with a small moustache and imperial beard like his own. Each
knew he had seen the other before; neither could coerce memory into recognition. They therefore exchanged apologies and went their ways, and later on kept
sneaking puzzled glances at one another.

But for the next few moments this encounter was driven out of Fernand's mind.

He looked down the colossal vista of the cabin, thinking what a contrast it
presented with the last St. Louis trip. Astonishingly they were running better
with all the window glass in place, and even with the deadweight of guards and
swinging stages. Maybe this was a paradox like the fact that for a given power and
breadth of hull a longer boat would always prove faster than a shorter one. Maybe
it cost less in terms of effort to have all the air pass by the upperworks than to let
it come whistling through.

Or maybe their superior speed this time was due to the fact that the river was at a more favorable level, near bank-full, so they were wasting less time on hesitation and second thoughts. At any rate the cabin this morning was most impressive. The linen was as white, the glassware as brilliant, the cutlery as heavy and numerous, as usual.

Of course, most of the places laid were for people not on board.

Of those who were . . .

Fernand's eyes roved across the few passengers present. Red-faced and yawning, Cherouen sat next to Barber, engulfing a deal of hot coffee and seemingly nothing else. Apart from those two, and Barber's attendants, there were only a bunch of nonentities along for the thrill, going to and presumably returning from St. Louis for the mere relief of boredom. To one who must work for his living, for his future wife, for his eventual family, their presence was a sort of insult.

Fernand was disturbed to find himself thinking in this manner. He recalled Uncle Edouard and his reference to "your respectable revolutionary heritage," and a shiver ran down his spine. He forced himself to make a move. Nodding to Barber and Cherouen, he headed for the water cooler, his gaze searching the zone beyond, wondering what these people would have felt had they been aboard for the Larzenac trip. None so comfortable then!

His attention was abruptly diverted. A head of lustrous black hair, a cheek and hand of rich creamy gold, eyes dark as pits at midnight: seated by herself at one of the tables for four, the most beautiful woman in sight, the only beautiful woman in sight, cynosure of all the men who clustered at the midships end of the common table. In particular the man in gray was ogling her . . . but who could blame him?

Then time ran aground for Fernand on the reef of awareness that very shortly he was going to need spectacles, an intolerable nuisance for a river pilot.

It wasn't Dorcas he was looking at . . .

His recovery was prompt. He marched up to her, bestowed a kiss on her cheek, emphasized the final word in his greeting: "Good morning, *maman!*"

Noticed that all the starers bar one reverted their attention to their food, the exception being the man in gray. But perhaps his interest could be explained by his semirecognition of Fernand, for he smiled and bowed as best he might when seated.

Vehm himself took Fernand's order for coffee, a dish of fruit, dry toast and honey. Trial and error had made it clear that if he ate more in the morning he was apt to doze during his next watch.

Most of those present were taking a more substantial meal: Eulalie was demolishing with dainty ferocity an omelette that overspread her plate, while Barber was at work on fried eggs and grits. Cherouen, by contrast, had now called for an eye-opener, by the look of it a sazerac. Fernand reflected on what a couple of those might do to a doctor before he had to treat his first patient, and resolved not to fall ill during this trip.

And also to inquire again about Walt as soon as he got the chance.

After a too-long delay he was able to ask, "*Maman*, have you not seen Dorcas yet?"

Mouth full, contriving to remain gracious and lovely, she shook her head.

Fernand caught the eye of a hurrying waiter and formulated a rapid message. Shortly Vehm returned.

"Miss Archer has not yet appeared," he announced. "Do you wish me to have a maid waken her?"

"No need," said Eulalie, having disposed of her omelette. She lifted her coffee cup and drained it, wiped her lips with a huge stiff white napkin, and pushed back her chair. "I'll go. If she is to be my son's wife, it's my duty to do what I can for her."

There was a double-edged quality to the remark which made Fernand suddenly apprehensive.

"Of course!"

The exclamation came from the man in gray, leaning back after ingesting a brioche powdered with sugar.

"*Monsieur!*" he continued, addressing Fernand, who would rather have been left alone. Rising, he approached and offered his hand. "Are you not a customer of that disgraceful *boîte* my efforts could not rescue, where I am happy to say good-bye for ever—the Grand Philharmonic Hall?"

It was true that Fernand had visited the place. Unenthusiastically he took the proffered hand, and without waiting for further invitation the other sat down on one of the unoccupied chairs.

"I present myself! Gaston d'Aurade, musician and composer! Bound for St. Louis on a mission which combines grief and joy! I must be directing music at the funeral for the boy of Madame Grammont who is died."

Fernand was anxiously staring after Eulalie, wondering when she would return and whether Dorcas would be with her. Gaston continued unheeding, his English improving as his confidence grew.

"But it is not, as you say, completely a bad wind, for my mission affords opportunity for a project I imagine since many years: a suite for orchestra to capture the essence of the Mississippi—a tone poem, I think it is said in English. The subject is a ripe one, do you agree? One might even transform the barbaric noise of the Negroes into an element, because they haunt the night as naturally as birds and—and alligators, and so forth." A wave of his carefully manicured hand. "From a waiter I learn you are a pilot, yes? Please allow me to inquire you concerning typical phenomena that presents the river at the different seasons."

A waiter arrived to top up Fernand's coffee cup; seeing Gaston seated before an empty one, he automatically filled that, too, and the act was taken as authority to remain. Reaching for cream and sugar, making himself comfortable, Gaston added, "For example, I think to utilize noises of waterfalls, big winds, and breaking of ice. You have seen all these, no?"

Fernand ignored him. Where was Dorcas? Was something wrong? Had she been taken ill?

If so . . . if so, how did she view the fact? Had she been raised to a creed like his mother's, which claimed that disease was due to magic influence, or did she accept modern theories of infection by bacteria? It was a shock to Fernand to realize how little he knew about his fiancée's beliefs and fears. Even when she told him she was making a conversion, it had been in an offhand manner, as though disposing of this potential barrier to their marrying were trivial. On the sole occasion when the subject of Catholic doctrine had arisen between them, she had sidestepped the issue by mentioning how much more she liked the priests who called on Adèle Parbury than the ministers she had met at home. If her conversion had been heartfelt, should she not have ensured he was present when she was received into the Church?

There were some who believed in the Church's power but were not obedient to it . . .

He slid his hand into the side pocket of his coat, groping for the crucifix, which he had not wanted to leave in the pilothouse, and wondered whether instead of Dorcas taking instruction he should himself have converted to the starker practices of some Protestant sect. The lonely nighttime reaches of the river did not make him feel closer to God, only further away from humanity.

But it was impossible to think deep and pivotal thoughts with the race under way and the intersecting crisis of his mother and his beloved about to focus on him, and this strange garrulous man who was so contemptuous of Negro song and so proud of being hired for a funeral, like a professional mourner, putting questions that sounded as though at any other time they might be fascinating.

Effortfully he contrived a few answers and made them more or less polite.

At the very moment when Eulalie reappeared, her expression grave, inspiration struck Fernand and he saw how to rid himself of Gaston. Interrupting the next of that seemingly interminable sequence of questions, he said, "Ah! Suddenly I recall where we saw each other. Not at the Philharmonic Hall—at the Limousin, last Mardi Gras. And now, if you'll forgive me, my mother and I have personal matters to discuss."

Memory of his disastrous public collapse overwhelmed Gaston. Worse yet, as he looked at Eulalie, he obviously reheard his patronizing comment about the "barbaric noise of the Negroes." Scrambling awkwardly to his feet, he hurried away. Later he was seen at a table on the leeward side of the deck, much occupied with manuscript paper, pen and ink, and remained there until the sun declined and the mosquitoes became too troublesome to be borne.

"What of Dorcas?" Fernand demanded of his mother as she resumed her chair.

She took a roundabout route to her answer, avoiding his gaze.

"You know her very well?" she parried. And after a pause to ponder on her choice of words: "You know her *intimately*?"

Fernand automatically glanced around for fear of being overheard, but nobody was paying them the least attention; the party at the common table was breaking up at word of an oncoming steamer—Fernand's pilot instincts informed him she would most likely be the *Cariboo*, on her regular run down from Vicksburg— while Cherouen and Barber were desultorily chatting.

Of course! He ought to have thought about that long ago! In a sense, last night at least, he had . . .

His mother regarded him with a wan smile. "Your father," she murmured, "was a—a *manly* person. In that, as in many other things, you plainly take after him. However, since marriage is possible, I counsel you to arrange it as soon as may be." She gave a light silvery chuckle. "I never imagined I'd look forward to be-coming a grandmother! Nonetheless I confess it would be a comfort to my old age to see my only son securely established in a fine home with a lovely bride to take care of him. She is lovely, you know. I say so in all honesty. I hope her spirit matches her appearance."

"I too!" said Fernand fervently, his mind racing. But he was at a loss for words.

Eulalie had laid aside her reticule. Retrieving it, she rose, as regal in her much-worn dress as any queen.

"She has promised to join you in a minute," she said. "I feel you will have lots to talk about. When you want me, I shall be taking a turn around the boat. I have one or two things to attend to."

Rising, he stammered, "What sort of things?"

"Oh!"—in the lowest possible voice above a whisper—"I know you don't be-lieve in my powers, but they are real, and you are in very present danger."

"Mother! For years you've been warning how lightning may strike from a sum-mer sky, an oncoming boat might run against us, a boiler pipe might burst! And here I am!"

At the back of his mind was what he had half forgotten because she had been so courteous to Dorcas: her outburst concerning her enemies' charge that she would sacrifice him . . . What crazy nonsense!

Yet, as he looked at her calm face, he could almost sympathize with her in the hell she had created unintentionally for herself.

"Never mind," she said composedly. "Just keep the crucifix by you at all times. But remember, I'm not speaking of natural, accidental dangers, but of deliberate ones. Due perhaps to so much money having been wagered on the *Nonpareil*."

Upon which she walked away, forward along the cabin, through the area tradi-tionally reserved for single men. Amboy made to check her, but then realized that since almost everybody had gone on deck to watch the other steamer, it was not worth making a fuss. Indeed, as she passed, Barber half rose and sketched a bow, which she acknowledged with a broad smile. Another moment and she had left by the forward door, tilting her hat against the bright sun and the breeze.

"Fernand!"

He swung around. Here at last was Dorcas, looking ravishing despite a trace of redness about the eyes. He wanted to crush her to him, for what his mother had said had transformed his world on the instant. Now he must think of himself as Fernand Lamenthe, founder of a legitimate line of descendants! He wanted to embrace not only her but all the new lives that would spring from her womb.

He dared not, however; he must be content to kiss her passionlessly on the cheek, supervise delivery of hot chocolate and rolls and butter. He burned to put the central question, but had no chance until she had eaten and drunk and the waiters were too busy clearing away used crockery to pay any heed.

Then he asked her.

Her face turned to stone, her mouth sucked in, lipless, as to suppress an un-bearable admission. From that he knew the answer anyhow. He caught her hand and said, choosing his words with utmost care, "I want to hear you say yes! Be-cause I want you for the mother of my children! Because I love you!"

Her eyes brimmed with tears.

"Oh, Fernand! I'm so frightened! I have nobody but you in all the world. And I don't know whether even you are to be trusted— No, let me finish! You've no idea how hard I prayed, all through the night, to be allowed to trust somebody at long last."

That was so close an echo of his own feelings, Fernand could only insist, "But I do love you! And we'll get married as soon as we return to New Orleans!"

Her fingers tightened on his. "I so much want it to be true!"

"It is!" he declared. And, to his horror, felt himself overcome by a gigantic yawn. He frantically tried to apologize, but still with tears wet on her cheeks she broke into laughter, and all their unspoken thoughts—of the past, of Parbury, of Eulalie—blew away as with infinite relief he found he was able to join in.

Coffee and cocktail combined at last to quiet the pounding in Cherouen's head, despite setbacks due to Barber's unaffected appetite. It being Friday, his breakfast was meatless, but it was nonetheless substantial. A bowl of cornmeal mush swimming in molasses and cream gave way to a mound of grits topped with two fried eggs. Butter dripped from accompanying piles of toast. Cherouen did his best not to look, but even awareness of it made him queasy.

Finally he was enough recovered to start talking, and by and by he turned to the subject of Josephine, in which his companion and host displayed a polite interest.

"Eating arsenic!" he exclaimed. "I'd heard that crazy so-called 'fashionable' women were doing that in New York last year, but I never imagined she'd be such a fool. She ought to know, after working with me so long, that all that stuff is poison—pure poison! Calomel and antimony, sulphur and blue vitriol: all nonsense! At best they may have a palliative effect, but to restore true health you must vitalize the system as a whole . . . which in her case is impossible, of course."

Barber looked a polite question.

"Her system's tainted," Cherouen amplified. "It's the African blood. Must be. Nothing else could make her act so foolish except her wish to hide the outward signs."

Barber, with the greatest delicacy in the world, murmured, "And this applies also to the fashionable ladies of New York?"

Without waiting for an answer, he inclined to Eulalie as she passed, then changed the subject.

"Shall we go and view the other boat?"

"I didn't know she was in sight!"

"Ah, you mean the *Nonpareil*. I was referring to the southbound steamer we're about to cross. But it would be interesting to know how far we are ahead of our rival. Cuffy, send to inquire of Captain Drew."

To Cherouen he added dryly, "I imagine we are not alone in wishing to be told."

He snapped open his watch, and concluded, "What's more, before noon we shall witness the amazing arrangements our captain makes for coaling on the run. We shall be at Natchez in unprecedented time."

"And at St. Louis too," Cherouen muttered.

"So we all hope. Come along."

 Since the *Atchafalaya* steamed triumphantly past, a miasma of ill temper had permeated the *Nonpareil* like river fog. Inevitably it was densest where the work was hardest, in the boiler room and engineroom.

And so far as Caesar was concerned, it ultimately concentrated on himself. Already he had made two grave mistakes.

On being turned out, by Whitworth but on Steeples's order, before his four hours' rest were over, he had muttered, "Is this the freedom I was fighting for?"

That was bad enough, since it earned him a clout on the head, which he dared not repay. But worse was to follow. While he was still rubbing his eyes, he sensed something amiss in the web of piping that fed the engines, and stood stock-still to analyze it, perhaps as his ancestors might have done in dense forest, judging the path of some unseen predator. And then, without waiting for instructions, he had gone and put it right: a union on a high-pressure steam line that vibration was gradually shaking loose. All it called for was a heave on a wrench, and the like must certainly be done a score of times during the voyage. But his not asking permission angered Steeples and earned him many curses before his stint was over.

Caesar had realized something must be wrong with the *Nonpareil* the moment he recognized Eb Williams being carried off her, drunk. But now it came vividly into focus. Throughout his childhood he had been aware there were good and bad slaveowners. During the war he had seen how there were good and bad officers in the field. Now he was discovering there were good and bad commanders on the river.

He was a little surprised. He had been briefly able to gaze out over the Mississippi before weariness felled him, and had felt a shiver run down his spine at its majesty, its impersonal power, against which even the greatest engines might not prevail. How could bad men endure the pressure of such an implacable opponent?

Perhaps the answer was that in the long run they did not. But the long run, as ever, had not arrived.

What galled him above all was that he knew he had more feeling for the machinery than Steeples: maybe not as much as the chief engineers, Corkran and Roy—whom he had seen reacting as he felt they should, freezing and cocking their heads as a suspect noise broke the even rhythm of the pistons, then dismissing it wordlessly as negligible—but the skill to isolate and rectify a fault before it caused any harm. Had he not proved it? Yet the cascade of resentment at loss of the lead was washing over him, and beyond him the powerless laborers who fed the furnaces.

This human failing was a fault as bad as any a machine could show.

Still farther behind? How? Why? Waves of black suspicion welled out, above all from Parbury—who, thanks to his blindness, was forever distrustful and now felt he had suffered the betrayal to end betrayals—while Woodley prowled from stem to stern, seeking any cause for complaint, as though a dirty towel or a badly coiled rope could affect the steamer's speed. Gordon, who cared nothing for the *Nonpareil* but much for what he had bet on her, merely snapped and growled, usually at Matthew, who was least likely to snap back.

Sober counsels were attempted, to little avail. McNab truthfully observed that the *Atchafalaya*'s claim to so great a lead was based on cries from people along the bank, without a watch among them. If any had a clock at home, it was not to be believed: since when were cheap country clocks accurate? Also Hogan and Trumbull, red-eyed already, were at pains to point out that when dawn broke the *Atchafalaya* was in easier water, but there were shoals and reefs ahead. And over four days, was half an hour all that significant?

All of which arguments had a certain force. Yet they did not prevent ill feeling from building up. Parbury barked at Woodley as though he could somehow have refused to stop at Baton Rouge. Gordon treated Joel as though, by his family connection with Arthur and Louisette, he could have done something to delay the crisis. And, naturally, all minds reverted to Josephine and her confused warning about disaster. The fact that both she and Auberon had retracted their claim did little to dispel anxiety.

So far there was no sign of Auberon. He must be still asleep.

Joel worried about him. Now his first dispatch was safely on its way, and a while remained before he need prepare one to send ashore at Natchez, so he had time to think about that stain on his cousin's handkerchief. If it portended what one might assume . . .

But in that case, why had Auberon never mentioned it? Since Mardi Gras they had become friends again, albeit not as close as in childhood; so one might have expected—

"Meestair Shishkin!"

Joel started and swung around. Advancing on him was Manuel, moustachios bristling and hand outstretched. With a sinking heart Joel remembered how he had pledged himself to interview him.

Yet it was not, surely, too great a chore? Anybody could talk to the officers and crew; the bandmaster enjoyed a unique position and might furnish scandalous copy of the kind that sold newspapers best.

Affecting a jovial manner, he said, "Señor! Join me for breakfast!"

During their repast, while he dutifully noted down whatever Manuel could tell him in intervals between preening—he had never before been the guest of a passenger here in the cabin—Joel had something else on his mind, constantly distracting. Arthur had put in an appearance, his expression defiant, as though challenging the world to comment on his decision to remain aboard. Spotting Joel,

he had taken a place as far away as possible at the common table. But his eyes
kept shifting every time there was the noise of a door opening. Small wonder.

In the meantime Joel made frantic notes, wondering how much of what Manuel
was recounting Graves would regard as fit to print and thinking it would probably
be too little to justify spending all this time on it.

At the back of his mind he was calculating at what point, if the *Nonpareil* fell
even farther behind, it would be worth leaving the boat and overtaking her rival
by railroad. Conceivably one might even cut across a narrow neck of land on
horseback . . . No, that was too chancy.

Not that railroads were totally reliable either; had they been, possibly the
Grammonts would have overcome their notorious prejudice and sent for the Electric Doctor by that route. But if the train were delayed, it would be by a spectacular amount, involving the slow and costly conveyance of new rails from the nearest
depot. Even if a steamer ran aground, she could quickly refloat herself without
outside aid. On a commercial average, therefore, it made sense to trust the tried
and true steamboat.

How long this would last was anyone's guess. Long enough, Joel decided, to
warrant doing his duty by his paper and getting the best material back to it from
every stopping place, or even slowing-down place. He composed himself to go on
listening to Manuel, keeping one ear alert for the appearance of Auberon. All his
instincts indicated that when the latter set eyes on his brother-in-law there would
be hell to pay.

But there was still no sign of him when Manuel, with visible regret, finished
eating and announced that he had to go and round up his musicians.


"Excuse me, sir!"

A question at the top of the speaker's voice. Leaning on the forward rail of the
hurricane deck, lowering his telescope, Joel turned in answer.

"I see you have a map, sir!"

Indeed he did: a copy of Schönberg's *The Mississippi, Alton to the Gulf of
Mexico, As Seen from the Hurricane Deck*, glued to canvas and folded accordion-
fashion.

"Does it give the name of those bluffs?"

Although it was already out of date, thanks to changes in the river's course, Joel
was able to answer that one.

"Those must be Ellis Cliffs. In which case we're about two hundred sixty miles
from New Orleans."

He had to shout because ahead lay one of the straight stretches where the
*Atchafalaya* had built up her lead and the pilot was hoping to close it, so the
pounding of the engines was making the entire hull vibrate.

"Thank you!"

After that, for a minute or two, there was no further conversation. It was a
stifling day; thermometers were registering in the eighties, with the promise of
topping ninety before noon. The river lay gray-green across the landscape like a
nightmarish mold, fringed with trees almost as gray, the usual willows and cottonwoods and in the distance hickory and white oak which, to achieve full growth,

required longer than the river was prepared to grant. In the shrub-low vegetation that bordered the water, creatures moved as the approaching boat alarmed them: terrapins, more frequently an alligator, most often a flock of birds. Always and everywhere insects swarmed, but their main assault would be at sundown, as usual.

Hereabouts there were few signs of human habitation. Some slight smoke drifted up from a spot astern, but might be due to a short-trade boat overtaken earlier, laboring up from Baton Rouge to Vicksburg like a cart horse being out-stripped by a thoroughbred. Soon they would sight Como Landing and beyond that would be the near-twin cities of Natchez and Vidalia, facing one another across the immense bosom of the waters, linked by memory—the saying went—as much as by the struggling ferries that plied between them.

But the land was poor in this area, and too liable to flooding. Disillusioned, a generation of would-be farmers had quit and trudged north, and now their shacks and hovels and barns of bits and pieces lined the banks at other spots just as vulnerable to the Mississippi's whim. To testify to their former presence, they had left a few wind-battered structures, roofless, warping, rotten, and a scattering of rusty implements too heavy to take away.

If the land had been worth the having, plantation owners would have seized it, as they had done a bend or two higher: Quitman, Fairchild, Zachary Taylor who had gone on to become a general. The lesson had been learned the hard way: it was imperative to be greedy, so as to have enough left over to insure against the depredations of the river. Freed slaves and poor whites stood no chance. The rich could spend their servants, and if an acre or two of truck garden were washed away, it was not they who hungered.

Suddenly Joel realized that the questioner had remained hovering nearby. He said with a start, "Oh, you're Mr. Gordon's amanuensis, aren't you?"

Half-flattered and half-abashed at being recognized, Matthew held up before him—like a shield—a book in an embossed leather slipcover.

"We last met at the Limousin the night of Mardi Gras," Joel continued. "And I'm glad to have this chance of saying I was made ashamed by what they did to you."

Matthew's small-featured face froze for a second, his mouth turned down at the corners. Conscious of a *faux pas*, Joel offered his telescope, which was accepted with alacrity.

"How far ahead do you reckon she can be?" Matthew said after a careful survey of the horizon.

Very much aware that several people had noticed the telescope and were hovering nearby, hoping for the loan of it, Joel answered with premeditated loudness.

"Too far to be caught up in a hurry!"

At the words the onlookers reacted with animation. Joel hoped that discussion of the possibility of being beaten might supplant last night's gossip about the threat of wrecking that he had helped to trigger off. He was embarrassed when-ever he remembered how he had fallen in with Auberon's absurd gloss on Josephine's few wild words.

Where was she, anyhow? So far today there was no more sign of her than of Auberon.

Matthew was persisting with his questions. "Think she's already made a coaling stop at Natchez?"

"It won't be a stop as such," Joel said. "Not unless she still has passengers Drew didn't manage to get rid of before departure. Even if he does, he may perfectly well just pitch them overside into his empty coal flats! Now he has the lead, he's not about to yield it in a hurry. Would you?"

Matthew gave a nervous grin and headshake, returning the telescope.

Joel accepted it, glancing uneasily around. Suppose at this very moment Arthur and Auberon were meeting elsewhere on the boat . . .

Well, if they were, there was nothing he could do about it.

Rapidly, for distraction's sake, he went on talking to Matthew as he closed the telescope's leather case.

"What's more," he amplified, "it isn't at Natchez that the real strain will be felt. It's beyond, in the reach south of Bruinsburg."

"Why?"

"Why?" Joel echoed, as much for the bystanders' sake as Matthew's; his earlier ploy had failed to distract them completely, but given that they presumably knew he was a journalist, they must be forgiven for expecting him to have inside information. "Because south of Bruinsburg, between Rodney and Waterproof Landing, was where Captain Parbury lost the former *Nonpareil*."

"Is that so?" Matthew breathed. "Does he know?"

"How could he not?" Joel countered, astonished.

"I mean being blind and all . . ."

"Oh, I get you. No, blind or not, I swear he knows every reach and bend on the river. And there's a very special reason why on this of all trips it's going to rankle if we don't regain the lead."

For a moment Joel was tempted to explain how Parbury had hired the man who fired the fatal shot. But he thought better of it. He might be the only reporter aboard; there could, though, all too easily be people who hadn't yet heard about Caesar and would earn a few dollars by selling the information to a local paper. In any case it was time for him to finish his next report; Natchez was drawing near. He wondered whether, before then, he might corner and grill Parbury concerning his feelings, but decided to reserve that for tomorrow. His conversation with Manuel had given him plenty of material for the time being. He must, though, have a word with Woodley.

Sensing he was no longer welcome, Matthew murmured thanks for the loan of the telescope and moved away. One of the other passengers tried to press Joel for the "special reason," and Joel parried neatly. The bystanders dispersed. He was about to go in search of Woodley when he noticed that Matthew had left his book behind. Picking it up, assuming it to be a continuation of the journal Gordon required the boy to keep, he idly opened it at a page marked with a slip of paper.

And found it was an illustrated account of Scottish tartans. The marked page dealt with Clan Macrae.

Doubtless Matthew was trying to ingratiate himself with his employer. Not that it seemed to be doing the poor devil any good . . .

Tucking the book under his arm, intending to return it at the first opportunity, Joel returned to cabin level. And found his worst fears confirmed, for the first thing he spotted was Auberon, immaculately clad, freshly shaved, unnaturally bright-eyed, approaching Arthur, who stood at the bar talking to Hugo Spring.

He rushed inside, arriving just in time to see Auberon touch his brother-in-law on the arm, quite lightly but very firmly.

"Good morning, Arthur," he said.

Arthur muttered some sort of reply. Glancing around to see who else, apart from Hugo and the tenders, would witness the confrontation, Joel saw a dark, thin figure sitting in the neutral ground near the water cooler, leaning back with eyes closed: Josephine. But she seemed to be paying no attention.

Meantime Auberon had more to say. Much more.

"Forgive me for touching you without invitation. But I had to convince myself you were real. I thought it was a bad dream I was having when I walked in and saw you. I thought it impossible that you should have sent my sister ashore in her condition and returned aboard yourself. *Quite* impossible!"

"I told her not to come," Arthur growled. "She insisted, no matter how I warned her."

"Some would say," Auberon gibed, "that a man whose wife can make him give in against his better judgment *has* no better judgment."

"If I had gone with her it wouldn't have done any good!" Arthur snapped. "She started arguing that it was because I tried to stop her coming she got these pains. Nonsense, of course! If you ask me, it had more to do with the vanity which makes her insist on tight lacing even now. I've told off that damned maid of hers more times than I can count, but—"

"So you dismissed her in the care of this untrustworthy servant," Auberon cut in, scalpel-neat. Arthur straightened, flushing; his eyes were red from drink and lack of sleep, and he was unshaven and his cravat was loose. He looked worse today than Auberon yesterday.

"Furthermore," the latter continued, "you are now taking refuge in insulting Louisette. I admit I expected no better of you, of course. However, it gives me grounds for telling you what I plan to do. If you were any sort of a gentleman, but for the fact that it is unmannerly to make a widow of one's own sister, I would call you out. I'm certain Joel would be glad to act as my second, wouldn't you?"—with a sidelong smile. "Since your lack of decency makes it out of the question, I shall simply ensure that the other passengers treat you in the manner the English call 'sending to Coventry'—in other words, decline to speak to you for the rest of the trip. If your behavior results in the death of my sister or the loss of her child, I shall take the skin off your back with a horsewhip. Is that clear?"

He was smaller and slighter than Arthur, but there was such menace in the last few words, it seemed for a moment that he towered over the other like a wild beast, fangs and claws bared. The illusion passed, and he was affably addressing Hugo.

"I trust, sir, you will set a fashion for the rest by removing yourself from the company of this loathsome cad. I now plan to seek out the officers and enlist their support against him. Joel, you are presumably better acquainted with them than I am, having interviewed them. Be so kind as to perform the necessary introductions, will you?"

He turned away. Arthur tossed down the last of his drink, caught him by the shoulder and swung him around, and punched him as hard as he could at the base of the breastbone. Auberon doubled over, gasping—and with the gasp came a sudden bright flow of blood from his mouth and nose.

"Stop, you damned fool!" Joel shouted, seizing Arthur's wrist. At once they were surrounded by stewards and tenders, black and white, and Arthur, panting, yielded after a brief struggle. Meantime Auberon gasped again, making a horrible bubbling noise.

"Mam'zelle Josephine!" Joel shouted. "Here, quickly!"

Taking his cousin by the arm, he led him to a chair and used his own handkerchief to mop up the blood. Arthur stood staring dazedly, muttering at last, "I didn't mean to do that. Just wanted to shut the bastard up!"

Josephine, opening her eyes, assessing the situation, hastened over. With professional expertise she looked at the blood, noting what a brilliant color it was, then felt his forehead and took a few counts of his pulse.

Straightening, she said, "Get him to bed at once."

"I'm all right!" Auberon protested.

"That was a vicious blow!" Josephine declared. "It must have done severe harm! Whoever hit you should be thoroughly ashamed! You and you"—indicating the nearest waiters—"help me take him to his room."

Arthur made to follow, but Joel checked him with a glare.

"Carry on, and it won't just be poor sick Auberon you have to deal with, but me! Didn't I warn you last night? For Loose's sake I'd rather not, but if Auberon isn't well enough to horsewhip you, I'll strip your reputation away instead of your skin, I'll write two reports to be sent from Natchez. You can choose which one goes ashore. Why not pack your bags?"

And he stalked off in Josephine's wake.

When Auberon had been made comfortable and they had closed his stateroom door, Joel said in a low tone to Josephine, "It wasn't just being hit that did the damage, was it?"

She shook her head wearily.

"Of course not. Why didn't they send him to one of those fancy sanatoriums they got in places like Switzerland?"

"I don't think they know. If you mean his parents."

"That figures. Runs in the family. Don't notice things right under their noses!"

"You mean he hasn't realized who you are?"

She shook her head again, this time with a faint smile. "Tell him about it one day, I guess. . . You knew, didn't you? Right away?"

"Well—I worked it out."

"And you're a reporter?"

"Mm-hm."

"Bet you write the best stories in the paper."

Joel forced a smile.

"Think he ought to be put ashore at—?"

She cut him short. "Better he goes all the way to St. Louis. They say northern climate is better for cases like his. In fact I guess he ought to go clear to the North Pole. I'm surprised he didn't sign up with Dr. Cherouen, you know. You heard he went to see him?"

"Yes."

"His ozone treatment does seem to have been helpful to some TB cases . . . Anyway, don't you worry. I'll take care of him."

"Uh—there's the question of your fee." Joel fumbled coins from his pocket and made to offer them, but she closed her hand firmly over his, thrusting it away.

"No call for that! I don't have too much else to do this trip, do I? Now you go explain to the captain."

He glanced round. There indeed was Woodley striding along the cabin. Josephine gave Joel a firm push and reentered the stateroom.

Well, at least from here he could segue into the interview he had been intending. He pulled pencil and notebook from his pocket, looking around for Arthur.

But of neither him nor Hugo was there any sign.

 Elation grew and grew aboard the *Atchafalaya* as she drew closer to Natchez. She was running as though she were brand new and the engines' rhythm was clock steady. For the passengers on the upper deck, the back-breaking gut-wrenching work which made that possible was remote, invisible, except when by turns the begrimed and sweating firemen were allowed a minute's breather on the guards and appeared like very fiends, gasping and spitting gobs of sooty phlegm.

It was known that Drew had made a speciality of fast coaling. His technique was admired yet rarely copied, calling as it did for a skill that few possessed. People on board who ordinarily thought of coal as the concern of servants suddenly developed a vast interest in the technicalities of transferring it from shore to flat—as the barges were called—and flat to steamer. Those who had condescended to take in such data in the past were unexpectedly at the center of attention. How rapid, how alchemical, must be the transformation that converted black random lumps into vapor, heat, and the power to keep those huge wheels lashing the brown water!

But even those who had bet most heavily on the *Atchafalaya* were not worried about the time she was likely to spend refueling. However long she took, the *Nonpareil* was certain to take longer.

From the moment Drew relieved Fernand to let him take breakfast with his mother and Dorcas, it had been obvious that the regular watch roster was going by the board. The tension was so tremendous, no four-on, four-off system could be adhered to.

Tyburn knew the approach to Natchez particularly well, and was by mutual agreement bringing her into the reach below the city. Drew would take the wheel personally when the coal flats came out. Tyburn was signaling for them now with repeated blasts on the whistle.

And beyond that . . . Well, with luck the lead they had would be increased here; using Drew's methods, they reckoned to waste only four or five minutes on refueling, while the other boat might easily lose ten. So the helm could be left to the junior member of the team. Fernand fretted and frowned as he mentally reviewed every shift in the channel, every new-fallen tree this summer had shown him.

As to the lead, however:

"How far behind is she now?" Tyburn demanded as he sidled by the great sandbar southeast of Como Landing, which was bound to grow up in a few years and reroute the river.

Field glasses to his eyes, Drew said, "Better than twenty minutes. Could be close on thirty."

Fernand was feeling light-headed. The prospect of becoming a married man kept intruding on his concentration. He said musingly, "Like we predicted! Lighter she gets, the more she takes a sheer at every bend! But I reckon Parbury can *feel* as much as you or I can calculate. When she leaves Natchez she'll be just nicely balanced, with as much coal as she needs and no more, for fear it make her wallow."

Tyburn and Drew exchanged approving looks.

"What follows from that, then?" Drew pursued.

"She's going to do her damnedest to overtake before nightfall . . . Mary mother of God, why didn't I see that sooner? Of course! She's bound to try and pass us in the reach above Waterproof—somewhere in Petit Gulf and probably south of Island 111!"

"Why?"

"You know damned well— Excuse me." Fernand wiped his face. "But I should have spotted it sooner. Shouldn't I?"

There was a pause. In the meantime Tyburn altered course skillfully to avoid some floating logs and sounded the whistle again, this time to warn off an over-eager excursion boat.

"Ah, I guess no man is to blame when he finds a woman to steal his heart," the captain said at last.

Fernand grinned.

"That's a fine sentiment, sir. May I know where the quotation comes from? I'd like to note it down."

"Quotation?" Drew returned blankly. "I don't believe I ever saw it written."

"Then you have the making of a poet yourself!" Fernand exclaimed.

But the compliment was wasted. There was a sudden flurry as the excursion steamer threatened to lose way in the path of some idiot's sailboat that he had crammed with girls in fashionable dresses too cumbersome for them to be any help in a crisis of rerigging, and when it was over Tyburn stepped back from the wheel with a huge yawn, surrendering command to Drew.

"You got her, Captain," he said with formality. "I'm off to catch a ration of sleep."

Looking after him as he ponderously descended the stairs, aware of the way in which the population of Natchez—lately claimed to have topped the ten-thousand mark—had bloomed at windows and along the shore like a millennial crop of mushrooms, Fernand wryly realized that in truth he had far to go before he became a seasoned pilot.

Still, his sharp observation concerning Parbury had struck home.

If only there were some way to free his mind from the distractions caused by having Dorcas and his mother on board! It was the essence of a fairy-tale curse, visited on the fortunate one because he did not think things through.

"For someone who reportedly did not see military service," Cherouen pronounced sententiously, "it must be admitted that Captain Drew possesses a remarkable grasp of organization and discipline. On a good day, that is."

Sycophantic chuckles greeted the remark. His reputation had been enough to ensure him a group of hangers-on for the duration of the trip. But no one replied. All were too involved in watching Drew's famous refueling-on-the-run. Ashore, many people had witnessed it before; that did not diminish their excitement.

With their brawny crews paying out long thick hawsers, two flat barges of the largest size were being floated out from shore by the action of the current; the ropes served to position them, aided by men with poles and sweeps. Each was stacked as high as was safe with coal—in boxes rather than bags, for the wood too could be burned.

As Drew slowed the steamer and aligned her on the gap between them her deckhands assembled on the guards under the direction of her mates: Chalker to starboard, on the Natchez side, and Sexton to larboard, the Vidalia side. The river here being so broad, however, those at Vidalia were enjoying a poor view or none at all, unless they had put out in some of the boats that, numerous as mosquitoes, threatened to clog the racing steamer's passage. Drew sounded his whistle savagely, and a few took the hint, but others pressed still closer—dangerously so.

Suddenly Gross appeared on the foredeck. Though no longer young, he still boasted a fine and resonant voice.

"Fair warning!" he bellowed. "Our pilot will not slow or put about for any vessel in our path! I say again: we shall not slow or put about if you get in our way!"

That did it. Hastily looking around them and discovering they were apt to be crushed between the *Atchafalaya* and the coal flats, several young men leaned frantically on their oars and were able to make use of the steamer's bow wave to get clear—but only just.

Even as they were dispersing, though, yet another small boat closed in: this time a battered steam launch uttering thick smoke and horrible noises from machinery long overdue for repair. Standing at her prow was a man cupping his hands to his mouth and shouting. Fragments of his words reached the ears of those aboard the *Atchafalaya*.

"Reporter—Memphis *Avalanche*—hundred dollars . . . !"

Fernand was at Drew's side in the pilothouse. To him, between clenched teeth, the captain said, "That idiot looks like he's going to try and cut across our bows! Go tell him to get lost! Take a pistol to him if you must, but see him off!"

With alacrity Fernand darted down the stairs.

The barge crews flung lines to the steamer, and they were made fast: Chalker's in less than ten seconds, Sexton's in well under twenty. At once Drew signaled full ahead, and the barges closed on the steamer's sides while a human chain seized box after box of coal, to the accompaniment of rhythmic chanting, and hurled them on board. By the time both flats were empty the steamer was clear of the city and her deck crew was exhausted, but there was fuel and to spare for even the most extravagant run to Vicksburg.

Whereafter all should have gone with the smoothness of a well-made watch. With their cheering crews the barges were to be cast loose to drift back on the current, so that the *Atchafalaya* would be free to charge ahead again, swinging around Rifle Point and its fledging of immature willows. It had all happened before.

But Drew's guess about the steam launch was only too correct. Instead of giving up, the reporter had passed money to the boat's owner, more pantomiming than speaking his order to get ahead of the *Atchafalaya* at all costs. Tucking the fee away, the owner—a melancholy-faced man in clothes much stained with soot and oil—pushed his steam valves to their widest, and the row from the engine achieved such a peak, it momentarily outdid the thunder of the larger boat.

Seeing this, Drew shouted down the speaking tubes for yet more power, intending to leave this nuisance behind.

But even as the engineers hastened to comply, Fernand spotted something that was eloquent of calamity.

Not quite all the tree trunks loosened by the river's gnawing had gone by. Here came another—and it was colossal! No mere soft cottonwood or flexible willow, but a white oak of thirty good years' growth . . . and if Drew put about to miss it, he would surely sink the launch beneath the *Atchafalaya*'s starboard wheel.

While if he did not, it would strike the larboard wheel and break Lord alone knew how many of its buckets!

"Keep cursing him!" Fernand yelled at Gross. "Blister his goddamned hide until it bleeds!"

And raced back to the pilothouse, three steps at a time.

Even as he flung open the door, however, he knew Drew had come to the only possible conclusion. He heard the bells for full astern on both, and his heart sank as he thought of all the headway this would cost.

He glanced astern and stiffened. There! The *Nonpareil*, with a clear reach ahead of her, being greeted like her rival with cheers and pistol shots and fireworks.

And the *Atchafalaya* shuddered, stem to stern.

"We hit the log!" he exclaimed.

"It was that," Drew answered grayly, "or sink the launch and drown the fools aboard."

At once he seized the speaking tubes again, issuing rapid orders to Diamond, Fonck and O'Dowd. "One cracked bucket!" was the burden of his message, and by the time Fernand gained a view from the larboard window deckhands with hatchets were already swarming out to smash away the paddlebox and manhandle another bucket into position.

"Just so long as we didn't spring the pitman . . ." Drew said, more to himself than Fernand, and waited for a report from Fonck. It was favorable: the impact had been gentle enough to do no worse harm.

"Thanks be," Drew said at last, wiping his face. "I'm on an errand of mercy, so they tell me, and sending even such blind idiots as those to a water grave would haunt my conscience all my life. But I wish with all my soul it hadn't happened in plain sight of *them!*"

One thing at least had turned out well. The launch's engine, overstrained, had sprung a steam leak, and now she was being carried helplessly downstream by the current, the reporter still shouting hysterical promises of enormous bribes to anybody who could put him aboard the *Atchafalaya*.

"Serve him right," said Drew contemptuously. "Half the time when you waste an hour talking to 'em, they get it wrong when they write it down." And added, leaning out of the wide-open larboard window, "Don't just stand there like you're growing roots, you sons of perdition! *Hump* yourselves! Going to be a year getting that bucket fixed? Lively now! Ain't no funeral you're bound for 'less it's your own! *Get* the lead out of your breeches!"

A cheer answered this tribute from "Old Poetical," and wood chips flew wildly. But an even more rousing one came from astern as the *Nonpareil* stormed into full view.

"Jump to it!" Drew roared. "Jump, or I'll strangle you in your own guts, you lazy spawn of unrighteousness! I don't want to see you move—I want you to move so fast I *can't* see you!"

Over his shoulder, in a hasty aside to Fernand: "Is all well down on deck?"

"You can't guess which way Cherouen will blow," Fernand answered sourly.

"Yeah, I guess not. . . But I surely wish it hadn't been young Walt who got scalded! Nimble as a monkey, him! That's who we need out there on the wheel!"

Fernand gave a sober nod. The untrained deckhands were doing their best, but even so . . . He checked his watch anxiously. Far too much time was leaking away.

Moreover, lacking power, the *Atchafalaya* was being carried downstream like the launch.

Suddenly there were heavy footsteps on the stairs, and Barber stood glaring in the doorway.

"What happened?" he demanded. "And how much longer is this going on?"

Not turning, Drew said, "Didn't you see that fool reporter doing his damnedest to get drowned?"

"Of course I saw him! And why the hell wouldn't you take him aboard? It could do us all kinds of good to have our lead published in the papers!"

"It's happening already," Drew snapped. "We can manage fine without some inky-fingered son of a bitch pestering the passengers." Without waiting for a reply, he leaned out of the window once more and shouted, "*That's* more like it, you clubfooted offspring of Belial! Get that bucket bolted fast and maybe your mothers will recognize you when you get home!"

A speaking tube shrilled; he seized it. The voice was Fonck's.

"Cap'n, we found something else!"

"What?" Drew barked.

"Had a backup of pressure when we hit that log. Got to fix a sprung union."

"Bad?"

"Needs slacking and repacking. Five minutes?"

"Make it two!" Drew twisted his head around. "I see the *Nonpareil* too close for comfort!"

"Yeah, but she still has to refuel."

"Sure, but even so . . . Hey!"

"What was that?" Fonck demanded.

"I guess we got the time you need," Drew said slowly. "But hurry it up anyhow. I didn't ask for this and they could claim the race because of it."

"What?"

"Tell you later!"

Drew slammed the speaking tube back on its hook and, together with Barber and Fernand, stared at what was happening astern.

One of the coal flats they had cast off was floating across the river instead of being homed to its wharf. Perhaps the crew were too partial to the *Atchafalaya* . . . but if that flat blocked the course of the *Nonpareil,* or worse yet collided with her, then many people would call off their bets.

"I didn't ask for that," Drew repeated under his breath. "I swear I didn't. But I could name a hundred who'd not believe me."

For a long and painful minute they stood as though petrified. Then came a cry from the men working on the wheel: the new bucket was in place.

But by then, having avoided the coal-flat as the current bore it to one side, the *Nonpareil* was heading for her own fuel-barges, and still Fonck had not reported a cure for the leaky union.

"Got it!" he shouted an unbearable eternity later, and added, "Full ahead whenever you like, Cap'n!"

"Now!"

But the *Nonpareil* was coaling up, and the precious lead won by her rival had been cut in half. Now it was nip and tuck.

 Exactly what had caused the delay to the *Atchafalaya* was not apparent from the *Nonpareil* as she stormed toward Natchez to the accompaniment of even louder shouts than had greeted her rival, plus her own band of music.

Never mind! Here was a God-sent opportunity to make up distance!

"Just so long as we lose no more time in coaling than she did, we'll close the gap!" Woodley predicted to Hogan, who had the wheel, and Parbury gave a long-drawn sigh of relief.

The air crackled with tension as they drew close to the wharf, with the *Atchafalaya* being born backward toward them—and one of her coal-flats also, while men with sweeps madly flailed the water.

"If that's one of Drew's tricks . . . !" Woodley whispered.

But it wasn't. The crew of the flat were as eager to avoid collision as Hogan was, and the encounter cost them at most a few seconds. Call it accident . . .

But now they were to make their own coaling stop, and because Drew had been here first, the best-positioned flats, nearer the center of the river, had been claimed. They had to slow more than the *Atchafalaya*, and they took longer to lash the flats and start unloading them.

Well before the job was finished, the *Atchafalaya* was once more under way at full power.

Gordon marched importantly off to oversee the refueling, leaving Matthew in possession of the field glasses through which, during the morning, he had stared in frustration at the leading boat.

That suited the boy splendidly. He was scanning the shore, spotting scores of beautiful girls, some demurely tagging at their parents' heels, some hanging shamelessly on young men's arms.

Determination mounted in him. Sooner or later he would have a girl. Not one bought for him by his boss! One of his own choice! It *must* be possible!

The recollection of Gordon, so pompous and absurd in his "national dress," was about the only thing related to his disastrous evening at the Limousin that made Matthew want to laugh. But he preferred staring at the girls and thinking how much better they would look than Gordon in skirts as short as the latter's kilt.

Particularly since he could not possibly be wearing it by right—

*Oh, no!*

What had he done with his precious book about tartans?

Even as he set forth to search for it, however, a hand fell on his arm and a much-hated voice rasped in his ear.

"Boy, they say you have field glasses! Tell me what's going on!"

Parbury had a fierce grip, and his visage was grim enough to arouse childlike terrors. Matthew cast about desperately for rescue.

"Lost your tongue?"

"I don't know what you want me to say, sir!"

"Tell me what you see, that's all! Boxes of coal are being brought aboard, right?"

"Why, of course!"

"Are they flowing smoothly, like midstream water?"

"Uh . . ." Abruptly Matthew caught an inkling of what Parbury was driving at. "No, sir! I saw one dropped a moment ago."

"Dropped! You must be lying!" His clawlike grip closed tighter.

"I swear it, sir! Clear over the side of the barge!"

"Dropped!" Parbury repeated the word as though savoring its bitter taste, and released Matthew. "Oh, it's always the same! Want to learn a lesson, young man? No matter how hard you work to make something perfect, someone else can always ruin it. Tell me the names of the foremen down there"—with a jab of his forefinger toward the coal flats.

"I don't know them, sir. Never saw them before."

"But you were aboard last time we coaled at this wharf!"

"That was coming downriver at night!" Matthew cried. And before he could stop himself: "Have you forgotten there's a difference?"

Parbury became a statue for the space of half a dozen heartbeats. Then he relaxed like the miracle of Pygmalion, and actually laughed. Short and dry the sound was, but it was laughter.

"I was about to teach you a lesson, and you taught me one. Good luck to you, boy. You should go far!"

Whereupon he swung around and, by memory and the use of his stick, stalked away while others hastily stepped aside. Even the first-time passengers had learned by now that Mr. Parbury was the person not to cross.

He left Matthew wholly unaware of what he was supposed to have done.

Then coaling was complete, the band rose to a joyous pitch of loudness and a new degree of dissonance that made Manuel wince even as he whipped the players to greater and greater volume, and at last the *Nonpareil* was able to swing back into midstream. Other steamers made the welkin resound with their whistles.

Up ahead, still in plain sight, was the *Atchafalaya*. The delay caused by the reporter had slashed the gap between the boats.

And Arthur Gattry had made no attempt to go ashore.

"How does she feel?" demanded Woodley anxiously, up in the pilothouse.

"Better" was Hogan's succinct reply as the lines from the coal flats were shed. "Just as well. Here he comes. You know what he's going to beg for, don't you?"

Woodley looked blank.

"Hell's name!" Hogan exclaimed. "What point do we pass this evening?" He would have said "afternoon" in other company; it was a regionalism.

Comprehension dawned.

"Think she can make it?" the captain said eventually, just before the door was flung open.

"If not now, then never," Hogan muttered, and made a fly-swat gesture as yet another sailboat with a retarded blockhead at the helm threatened to cross the *Nonpareil*'s course.

On his way up to the pilothouse Parbury was as ever aware of the people who made way for him, unseen, unseeable, but *there*. He sensed them much as he had sensed obstacles hidden in the river in the old days, one being much like another, to be avoided if possible. Occasionally, however, somebody ventured to address him and was thereby singled out. This time he knew from the voice it was Whitworth, who had formerly served with Drew and might have a comment worth paying attention to.

"Slow job, that coaling, Captain! Just like to let you know I'm sorry. None of my fault! I worked the hands just as fast as I was allowed!"

"Someone ordered you to slow down?" Parbury countered, his blank gaze not turning.

Alarm colored the answer. "Of course not, sir! It's just that I wish we'd had the advantage of Captain Drew's system. We should have sent ahead precise orders for the coaling, and—"

"Well, if you think you can run the boat better than me and Captain Woodley," Parbury snapped, "you'd better go buy your own, hadn't you?"

He made to push by, raising his stick. But Whitworth said, "Sir, there's one more thing."

"What, damn it?"

"The handkerchief you bind your eyes with."

"What about it?"

"Sir, I think it's about time someone explained that it's dyed like a harlot's ribbons and quite unbefitting to yourself."

For a second Parbury stood silent. Then he said in the chillest tone he could muster, "When I want your opinion about my dress, Whitworth, I will ask for it. Get about your duties, and I mean *now*!"

But as he made his way to the pilothouse again, that remark burned.

If it were true, then a foul trick had been played on him.

Had he maybe also played one on himself?

Immediately before departure, he had made a magniloquent speech. That was all part of an attempt to hide from himself as well as others the fact that he was suddenly frightened. He had always tried to disbelieve in omens and portents, but the dream he had had yesterday morning still haunted him, all the more because Dorcas—whose color he had never cared about because he had never seen it—had deserted him for Drew's fancy nigger pilot, and because he had learned, for the first time, that his former *Nonpareil* had truly been sunk by a single man, and him also black.

Was he to be doubly doomed, despite his grand gesture in forgiving Caesar?

Yet so far this dream child of his was running admirably. Straight ahead and level pegging, he still believed she could outstrip the older boat. Since she grew more skittish as she lightened, though, it made good sense to strive for the lead while she was still heavy in coal.

It was with that thought in mind that he entered the pilothouse to a welcome that was hearty yet somehow insincere.

"How much time did we waste on that sloppy job of coaling?" he demanded, pulling out his repeater to make sure he had something to listen to instead of Woodley's reply. The latter hawked and spat, but left speaking to the pilot, who adopted an optimistic tone.

"Not enough to signify. There's the *Atchafalaya* still in plain sight."

"I want her astern!" Parbury blasted. "When shall we overtake?"

With a trace of a sigh Hogan said, "Could be as soon as Fairchild—Island 114. More likely at Petit Gulf."

Parbury relaxed a trifle, though his expression remained grim. "That's where you're surely going to try?"

Surprised more than annoyed, Woodley glanced at him. "Hell, with all the money I have riding on our win, we got to do it soon or risk being left permanently in the lurch! If only to keep Gordon out of my hair, I'd do it soon! Why ask such a pointless question? Don't we all want to win the race?"

"I keep wondering about the witch woman," Hogan said.

"What?"—from Parbury and Woodley simultaneously.

Looking as though he was sorry to have raised the subject, Hogan said reluctantly, "When I was last off-watch I heard that word's gone round among the darkies that this nurse of Cherouen's is some kind of—I don't know—high priestess!"

"Ridiculous!" Woodley scoffed. "Chief nurse to one of the most modern and scientific doctors in the world? Doesn't bear thinking of!"

Parbury said, "But our coaling did go awful slow. Didn't it? And one box got dropped overside!"

"And she came aboard with that story about dynamite!" Hogan amplified.

"That wasn't her—it was this crazy Auberon Moyne!" Woodley objected. "And they both withdrew what they'd said!"

"Fact stands," Hogan said obstinately. "*And* it was on her say-so that we had to put Mrs. Gattry ashore!"

There was a moment of dead pause. The cheering of the Natchez crowds was far away; even the thrum of the planking receded, though the engines were at full pressure and full revolutions.

At long last Parbury exhaled sharply and sat down on the bench.

"Just don't let her stop us overtaking," he grunted. "By Island 111 at latest! Understood?"

And he retreated into the darkness of himself.

Slowness in coaling was a technical matter. What counted for most people aboard the *Nonpareil* was that the other boat was now not only within what appeared to be striking distance, but visibly not gaining. Although the weather was very hot, although this new load of coal proved of less than perfect quality and the chimneys were soon uttering clouds of smuts warranted to ruin clothing, although there was a plague of insects hereabout, people crowded on the foredeck and laid spur-of-the-moment bets. Delighted, Manuel kept his band blasting away louder than the engines.

Almost the only person who was less than pleased with the music was Gordon, but it was plain that until the *Nonpareil* was in the lead again he would not be pleased with anything. He had even been curt to Joel, who could give him publicity.

Not that the latter would have welcomed another interview with the financier. He had enough problems to keep him fully occupied, as well as far more copy than he could cope with.

Auberon's attempt to have Arthur ostracized had collapsed when he was confined, shivering and sweating, to his bed.

Recruiting support among the other male passengers, who apart from Hugo were sporting men and gamblers, despiteful of women, let alone wives, Arthur was now swaggering around, growing ever drunker and even boasting about not leaving the boat at Natchez.

Therefore Joel had kept his promise. The dispatch he sent ashore, by prearrangement, via the foreman of the starboard coal flat, contained the most virulent denunciation of Arthur's behavior he could contrive without naming him.

By tomorrow dawn it would have been copied by newspapers across the nation; Joel was sure of it. He had been long enough in the trade to know a "good story."

So the instant word reached Arthur—as it was bound to, since newspapers had come aboard with the coal at Natchez and no doubt the same would happen at the next stop—Joel was going to be in trouble. He had no hope of rallying support to his cause, except perhaps among the officers, who would rather there were neither quarrels nor fights on board.

But then, he didn't want to. Louisette had chosen her husband; Joel's dreams had blown away on the wind, and now, in his role as reporter, he was hoping to do no more than state the facts, and if one fact turned out to be disgraceful to his cousin-in-law, so be it.

He had, after all, no wish to hear that Louisette had died in childbed.

Even so, it would be politic for him to avoid Arthur, or make sure whenever they met it was in company . . .

Above, the band had given up for a while. But music had not come to an end. Making his way along the cabin, intending to pay one more call on Auberon before starting work on his Vicksburg report, Joel checked in mid-stride.

From the area of the main deck where off-duty hands could lounge about, a slow and sleepy chant that long ago must have been a hymn had suddenly been transformed into a driving chorus that kept time with the boat's engines. There were footsteps passing at a run above and below; shrill cries and orders rang out, and ragged cheers.

Joel stared ahead. Yes, there was the *Atchafalaya* looming so close one might have picked off her passengers with a squirrel rifle!

Everything else vanished from his head as he feverishly checked his map.

Ahead lay a broad straight reach from Quitman's past Island 114 to Coles Creek Point. And beyond the next bend . . .

The thump-thump of the engines quickened; the chanting of the deckhands kept in time. Frantically folding his map and uncapping his telescope, Joel rushed toward the forward end of the main deck, shouting, "We're going to overtake! We're going to overtake!"

To his dismay he found he was far from the first to reach the same conclusion.

On a pile of old sacks Caesar lay dreaming. He had thought himself too weary, but maybe sleeping at this unaccustomed hour had something to do with it. His dream meant that his slumber was not restful. There was a person in it who should have been Tandy but was not. With the passage of the years her face had grown dim in memory; he had long been resigned to the fact that if they met on the street they would pass without a glance.

But it disturbed him greatly when he realized, half rousing, that the face this ought-to-be-Tandy wore belonged to the nurse, Miss Var.

"Wake up there! Wake up!"

He was being prodded. Rolling over, cursing, he found one of the black firemen gazing at him apologetically.

"Leave me be!" he mumbled, renewing acquaintance with all his aches and pains: his war injury, another tooth going bad, plus the effects of his last watch in the engineroom.

"But we gon' overtake de *'Chuffalaya!'*"

Something deeper than words communicated to Caesar now. The boat's hull was vibrating at an unprecedented pitch. He thought of the maze of pipes he had seen below.

And also of the part of the river they must now be approaching.

Yawning, he got to his feet. "On my way," he said resignedly. "Right here is where Mas' Parbury would have her bust her boilers rather than lose the race."

"Bust her boilers?" the fireman echoed, looking surprised. "No way dat gon' happen! Not wi' Mam'zelle Josephine aboard."

"Who?"

The word crept out between lips that felt as stiff as leather. His hand flew to his chest, but the trickenbag of course was gone . . .

"It sho'ly mus' be her!" the fireman declared. "Even de w'ite folks b'lieve in her!"

"What yo' talkin' 'bout, hankachief-head?" Caesar grunted as he drew on his boots. "Think yo' pullin' mah coat?"

"Hey, it come straight from dishyear tender saw de cabin folks treatin' wid her!"

Was it possible?

Caesar hesitated for a long moment, wondering whether in truth the woman he had dreamed of might be the mysterious genius to whom he owed his present good fortune.

And then—as a roar came from Steeples, wanting to know why he was taking so long—started suspecting it might not be so good after all.

With her lead shaved to the fineness of a whisker, the *Atchafalaya* strode past Rifle Point and swung sharp to starboard. Drew had kept the watch instead of ceding it to Fernand, in view of the risk of being overtaken. Now he laid into the outer edge of the channel, as was customary, where the current was least swift.

That, thought Fernand, might be all very well on an ordinary run, but it made for a longer course, and . . .

He glanced anxiously astern. The *Nonpareil* loomed so close, through field glasses he could identify Woodley and Gordon on the forward end of her hurricane deck, and the outline of Parbury silhouetted at the pilothouse window. Passengers and crew alike were shouting and clapping in expectation of passing into the lead.

On either bank the patches of cleared and settled ground grew fewer and farther apart as they left Natchez and Vidalia behind. Even so, there were always people watching, in small, often ragged groups, with a horse or mule nearby, or possibly a wagon. How they had heard about the race, how far they had had to come to witness it, there was no way of guessing. But there were onlookers where Fernand had never before seen a sign of life apart from birds and muskrats.

Now up toward Quitman's, and the larboard turn that would take the boat around Island 114, Fairchild Island . . . and still Drew was laying her into the easy water. Meantime whoever held the helm of the *Nonpareil*—and by his style Fernand was prepared to bet it must be Hogan rather than Trumbull—was steering a shorter path, defying the current, calling on all the resources of higher pressure. Vast clouds of smoke rolled up like the banners of an advancing army.

Worried, Fernand glanced at Drew and was astonished to see that he looked almost happy. In the tangle of his beard his lips were moving, shaping near-inaudible words. At first Fernand imagined he might be muttering curses; then he leaned closer and realized that in fact he was reciting a poem under his breath. He caught a snatch of it.

"*And they signalled to the place,*
'*Help the winners of a race!*
*Get us guidance, give us harbour, take us quick—or quicker still,*
*Here's the English can and will!*'"

"What's that, Cap'n?" Fernand demanded. "I don't believe I know it."

"It's by Mr. Browning," Drew answered as he laid the *Atchafalaya* into her marks for the short straight reach to Coles Creek. He sounded completely unperturbed by the nearness of the *Nonpareil*. "Tells how a Breton pilot led the French fleet through a narrow channel and saved it from the British. I felt it was kind of apt."

Encouraged, he now began to declaim aloud.

"*Then the pilots of the place put out brisk and leapt on board;*
'*Why, what hope or chance have ships like these to pass?' laughed they;*
'*Rocks to starboard, rocks to port, all the passage scarred and scored . . .'*"

He continued, word-perfect, recounting how Hervé Riel the humble fisherman took precedence of the admiral himself and, at the wheel of the ninety-two-gun *Formidable*, pride of the French navy, followed a passage too shallow for a ship of twenty tons to the haven of Solidor, leaving the enemy baffled.

Listening, Fernand began to understand the source of this improbable solitary man's inner strength.

But the *Nonpareil* was closer than ever when they rounded Coles Creek Point and swung first southwest and then northeast opposite Waterproof Landing.

And here came Hogan's challenge now!

Even as Drew felt for the slacker water at the outside of the bend, with the lead cut to less than a hundred yards—less, indeed, then the overall length of either of the giant steamers—even as the band on the *Nonpareil* struck up a rousing tune and was answered by a defiant song from the *Atchafalaya*'s deckhands—even as it appeared inevitable that by cutting across the bend instead of taking the slackwater course the trailing boat was bound to seize the lead . . .

Drew paid back in kind and with interest the trick that had been played on him when leaving New Orleans.

Quite calmly he reached for the engineroom speaking tube and said, "Dutch! I want half astern on starboard and then half astern on larboard, and then full ahead on both again, fast as you can."

And put the wheel over to starboard so hard the hull cried out, and passengers and crew staggered as they lost their balance, and the giant paddles came close to lifting clear of the water, and the whole colossal mass of the *Atchafalaya* swung halfway to broadside on and back again.

"Mary mother of God!" Fernand shouted as he saw what Drew had done, and could not prevent himself from clapping his hands.

Instead of just the wake from the leader's wheels, the *Nonpareil* was now about to be struck by a miniature tidal wave. One could clearly see it advancing across the calm surface of the river; one could discern the alarm it was provoking aboard the other boat. For Drew's timing was impeccable. Hogan had taken his vessel as close as was safe to the inside of the bend, where the channel shelved rapidly. She was less than half her own width from shoal water.

And the impact of the wave sufficed to close that gap.

Her starboard wheel met mud, and flung it up, and dragged her around until her bow was pointing almost at the bank, while the music from her band dissolved into a ragged mess of discords and her passengers screamed in terror. Hogan was quick to order stop engines, then slow astern, but his attempt to overtake had failed.

Just to make certain, Drew now steered the course the *Nonpareil* would have taken, so that even as he struggled to fight her free of the mud, Hogan saw the *Atchafalaya*'s wake come slapping and chuckling against the hull. There was never any way to overtake another boat from dead astern. Drew had served notice that so long as he held the lead, he would use any means, fair or foul, to retain it.

During the tensest part of his maneuver Drew had interrupted his recitation. Now he brought it to a premature conclusion at an appropriate stanza.

*"The peril, see, is past,*
*All are harboured to the last,*
*And just as Hervé Riel hollas, 'Anchor!'—sure as fate,*
*Up the English come, too late!"*

He gestured for Fernand to take the wheel, and as soon as he had sat down on the bench and wiped the sweat from his face and under his collar, he leaned back with a sigh and with amazing rapidity fell fast asleep.

 In the *Nonpareil's* pilothouse Parbury and Woodley stormed and raged. Hogan, his face stiff as wood, held his tongue until the boat was once more in deep water, though by now a good mile behind. At which moment it turned one o'clock, so that Trumbull ascended the stairs to take his watch.

Handing over, Hogan swung to confront the two captains.

"There's not a pilot on the river could have done better with this boat!" he roared. "She's so light, even fully coaled, she takes a sheer from a dead mosquito dropping in the water!"

"If that's what you think about her, I'm going to have my replacement pilots after all!" Woodley shouted back.

Parbury turned his head sharply. "But we're going to have specialist pilots, aren't we?" he demanded. "We agreed on Tom Tacy and Zeke Barfoot and Joe Smith!"

"And these idiots think they're too good at their job to need assistance!" Woodley raged. "Trying to blackmail me—that's it, blackmail me!—into forgetting the idea!"

"But we're used to the way the *Nonpareil* handles!" Hogan retorted. "Nobody else is!"

"Yes," Woodley sneered. "So well used, you just ran her into mud. Didn't you?"

There was an electric pause. Suddenly Trumbull said, "If you don't keep quiet, you're short one pilot as of now. How the hell can a man think with this racket going on?"

"He's right," Parbury said heavily. "I guess if I'd been in Drew's position, I'd have tried something of the same kind. If luck's on his side now, it may not be tomorrow. And the race is far from over."

The despondency felt by the officers of the *Nonpareil* naturally infected the passengers as well, especially those who stood to lose heavily if their boat was beaten. Among the first to yield to it was Gordon, whom lack of sleep and too much liquor had made morose. Having taken his usual heavy luncheon, he sat down in a wicker armchair on the main deck and shortly fell asleep, his face still set in a scowl. That suited Matthew perfectly. It gave him the chance to corner Joel and inquire whether, by any chance, the reporter had seen his book about Scottish tartans.

"Oh, my God!" Joel exclaimed. "I'm terribly sorry! Yes, I did pick it up. But then this trouble broke out with my cousins, and . . ."

He swallowed hard, spreading his hands apologetically. "Perhaps I left it at the bar," he suggested after a moment. "Perhaps the tender picked it up."

But he hadn't.

Why, though—Matthew asked himself as he continued on his fruitless quest—should anybody want to steal such a specialized work? He made inquiries, but no one remembered having seen it. After an hour or so, he was resigned to its loss, and that of the expensive leather case he had bought to protect it.

Which quite wiped out his satisfaction at having a respite from Gordon's irascibility.


Auberon had slept throughout the abortive challenge. When he woke in mid-afternoon, to find Joel in the stateroom as well as Josephine, he grew furious on hearing the news and insisted on rising. Very pale, very bright-eyed, he parried every comment Joel made about his illness, although he winced when he put any strain on his belly muscles.

In vain they tried to restrain him; he was not to be persuaded. He kept vowing vengeance on Arthur, no matter how often Joel emphasized that his reputation had been ruined by the dispatch sent to the *Intelligencer*.

Eventually, realizing of a sudden that he was too weak to make an issue of the matter, Auberon gave a sad smile.

"Don't worry, Jewel," he said. "I'm not going to have a duel with him on the foredeck. I must admit that was in my mind—and wouldn't it have been a story for you? But I am going to make sure he doesn't enjoy the trip!"

Turning to Josephine, he gave a half-bow.

"Ma'am, I appreciate the trouble you've been put to. Many thanks."

She gave him a stern stare.

"Why aren't you under a doctor's care? I saw the blood you coughed up. I know what it means!"

Auberon shrugged. "Oh, your boss would ascribe it to the air in the Old World being permeated with decay, wouldn't he? So now I'm back home, I should be getting better, right?" He made the most of the bitter joke.

Joel caught his hand. "But you will promise me—won't you?—to consult Cher-ouen when we reach St. Louis."

"I had that in mind when I met him at Mardi Gras," Auberon said. "Having got to know him, I'm not sure I'd trust him to tend a horse, let alone a human being."

Seizing gloves and hat, he concluded, "Now I prescribe for myself a little light refreshment. At the bar. That is, unless Arthur is there ahead of me, and his buddy Hugo, in which case I will be a good boy and content myself with being served at a table on deck." And he marched out.

"No arguing with him, is there?" Joel muttered to Josephine. She gave a wan smile.

"No, he's too much like—our—father."

"Would you perhaps care for some refreshment? This trip should have been a chance for you to rest and relax, instead of which it's turning out to be a tour of duty, and it's partly my fault, so . . ."

She shook her head.

"You're most kind. But I prefer to take care of myself, and I'm sure you must have professional obligations to attend to. Will you not have to send another report ashore at Vicksburg?"

"As a matter of fact, yes," Joel said with gratitude. "But if there's anything I can do, call on me, won't you? Particularly if—"

"If he breaks his word to stop short of a fight with Mr. Gattry?"

"Exactly."

A glance passed between them that conveyed perfect mutual understanding.

Then, returning along the vast length of the cabin, Joel was free to consider once more the possibility that he might leave the *Nonpareil* if she was still trailing, say, at Memphis, and overtake the *Atchafalaya* by rail.

On the other hand, a reporter had tried to get aboard the other boat at Natchez and been refused; Joel had heard him go by in the broken-down launch, sharing his troubles with the world at the top of his voice.

A decision had better be postponed.

But a little later on he noticed something odd. Josephine was sitting alone at a table in the after section of the cabin. Without noticeable appetite, she was picking at a dish of cold food left over from luncheon, forcing herself to eat as though taking some necessary medicine and sipping occasionally at a glass of champagne. She must, Joel deduced, have come aboard with plenty of money; no wonder she had refused his derisory offer.

But money could not account for the way three black waiters danced constant attendance on her, like courtiers in the presence of more-than-ordinarily intolerant royalty.

Little wheels began to turn in the back of Joel's mind. That name Josephine . . .

However, the implications refused to come clear, and anyhow he had far more important matters on his plate.


"You there—Caesar!"

The voice was Roy's. With a sinking heart Caesar turned as he made to go out on the guards for a few blessed breaths of clean air.

"Yes, sir?" he said, expecting to be called back to deal with some petty emergency.

"Well done," Roy said, approaching to within arm's reach. He wiped sweat from his face with his grimy shirt-sleeve.

"I beg yo' pardon, suh?"

"I said well done! I saw you when we grounded in that bend. You got to the reversing gear before anybody give the order, didn't you?"

Caesar swallowed hard. "I just kind of figured that was apt to be the next signal come down from the pilot, suh."

"And you were right. Like I say, well done. Keep it up."

"Thank you, suh. Thank you very much!"

As Roy told Steeples and Corkran a few minutes later, when recounting what he'd done, "Niggers is like horses and dogs. One reward is worth a dozen whippings!"

Having slept a few hours despite the racket of the racing boat, but as ever unable to go back to sleep once he had wakened, Whitworth roused uneasily well ahead of the time he was supposed to return to duty.

But all watch schedules were being fouled up anyhow.

Having washed and shaved and dressed, he took up anew the book he had found lying in the cabin this morning. Thinking it must be the journal Matthew kept for Gordon, he had quietly purloined it to peruse in private. Now there seemed to be a fair chance of the *Atchafalaya* winning after all, he stood to lose more than he could afford, having rashly placed bets on his own boat, more to spite Drew than because he was by temperament a gambler.

Perhaps, he thought, he might gain some usable information about this shameless foreign pervert and his fancy boy—information he could translate into cash. Not that he had plans to remain much longer on the river; chance had put him in the way of a brand-new commercial discovery, with immense financial potential, of which he was carrying actual samples to show to the businessmen of St. Louis. This could well be his last-ever river trip, except as a first-class passenger.

He had been most annoyed to discover that the book was the one he had seen before in disguise, full of pictures of men in skirts, as though Gordon's habits were somewhere in the world regarded as acceptable.

While he was asleep his annoyance had grown into anger. For a while he was inclined to open the window and hurl the book into the water.

Then a better idea struck him.

Loathsome or not, Gordon had bet even more heavily on the race than he had; moreover, if the *Nonpareil* lost, she would take even longer to return a dividend on the financier's investment.

Having found and returned this book might be the key to a conversation with him, which could have all sorts of implications.

He decided to hang on to it until tomorrow morning.

 In the cabin of the *Atchafalaya* there was a permanent party going on, chiefly at Barber's expense. Toast after toast was drunk to the skill of Hosea Drew.

Among those who remained apart were Dorcas and Eulalie.

Within a very short while the latter's charm had eroded Dorcas's mask of gloom, and by the time the *Nonpareil* attempted to overtake, she was so impressed by the older woman's worldly wisdom, she took her by the arm to watch the beating-off of the challenge from the deck.

"Fernand always told me this was the finest boat on the river!" Dorcas enthused. "I guess we just saw proof of it!"

"But the race is far from over," Eulalie countered soberly. "And there are all kinds of other dangers to be faced."

"Why, I know about *them*!" Dorcas exclaimed. "In fact, yesterday morning I was trying to . . ."

Her voice tailed away as she remembered to whom she had been talking about the subject.

"My dear?" Eulalie prompted. But she shook her head and fell silent.

"At any rate," Eulalie resumed when she was sure the girl was going to say nothing further, "I wasn't referring to the obvious risks, like running aground. I meant . . . My dear, you do love Fernand, don't you?"

Eyes very bright, Dorcas nodded.

"I'm sure you do," Eulalie affirmed, laying a comforting hand on hers. "As of course do I. But I'm not sure you understand the real world we live in, a world of forces as invisible and implacable as lightning, so that a careless thought, even, can tip the balance between good and bad luck, success and failure."

Dorcas looked at her blankly.

"When I came aboard—not intending actually to make the trip, to be honest—I brought a gift for Fernand. Has he shown it to you?"

"I—I guess not."

"Shame on him . . . though perhaps he was preoccupied. It's a crucifix. Of solid silver, one of the noble metals."

"In my family," Dorcas said nervously, "we were forbidden the use of idols. Even photographs were disapproved by my aunts. They were very pious people."

"Well," Eulalie said judiciously, "it is true that the power of symbols is better left alone if you don't understand how to harness it. You see . . ."

And for the next hour she led Dorcas into a bizarre and fascinating universe, where the shadow might become the reality, where the gesture might become the act, where the token might become the wished-for truth. Overwhelmed, the girl drank it all in, because this matched so much more closely the actuality of her experience than what either ministers or priests had tried to make her believe. When eventually Eulalie confided that for the greater protection of Fernand and his steamboat she proposed to conduct a small ceremony, in which Dorcas could be of help, she gulped and nodded and passively followed her to the kitchens.

The black cooks were not at all surprised on being asked for the blood, guts, comb and wattles, feet and feathers, from a rooster.

Later the maids and stewards, about their endless work of cleaning up, saw red-brown smears at inconspicuous points around the vessel. With relief—especially on the part of those who had heard the rumor that Mam'zelle Josephine was aboard the rival boat—they left the charm marks where they were.

 A little farther upstream the settlements were crowded close, some large enough to be dignified with the name of town: Rodney, Bruinsburg, St. Joseph, Grand Gulf, Palmyra, New Carthage . . .

But even where the banks looked desolate, they were still dotted with people who must have trudged long miles and waited long hours in the baking sun. Perhaps they had heard rumors from boats obliged to deliver some petty necessity at Hard Times Landing, or to refuel at Turner's Woodyard.

However that might be, their patience was to be well rewarded.

 The *Atchafalaya* had just rounded Coffee Point. The *Nonpareil* was, as usual, making better time up the previous reach, but there was no way she could catch up before she must again slow to make the point in her turn. The whole race was going to be like this, unless there were groundings or mechanical breakdowns: the gap between them would continue to open and close concertina-fashion. At the wheel Fernand allowed his mind to wander for a moment, to delicious thoughts of Dorcas.

Abruptly his mood of optimism ended. In the doorway appeared Josh Diamond saying, "I got bad news."

Fernand's heart sank.

"What's wrong?" he demanded.

"That trick the captain played to ground the *Nonpareil:* it strained the rudder post. I thought I'd better tell you personal. Don't want too many rumors flying around."

Drew was still slumbering on the bench; they kept their voices low to avoid disturbing him.

"So how bad is it?" countered Fernand, his mind full of images of the boat's stern, where the broad vane of the rudder hinged on the main vertical member . . . which also took much of the load from the fore and aft hog chains. A sidewheeler could be steered on wheels alone, but it was not something he had ever tried, nor did he want to learn the knack of it in the middle of a race.

"It ain't fatal!" Diamond answered sharply. "Take us a while to put a couple of cramps around the post, that's all. But make the most you can of this reach."

"*Reach?* It's no more'n a pause between bends!"

"Make the most of it anyhow. Too sharp a turn, and—" He rolled his hand over as though spilling a little pile of sand from the palm. A shout came from below. He turned to leave.

"Sounds like they got my forge set up," he said. Fernand checked him.

"How long?"

"No longer'n I can help!"

As the door closed, Fernand reviewed his predicament and a shiver crept down his back. There was scarcely a worse point for this to happen. Not only was there a string of bends ahead; for a minute or two he had been noting the smoke of an oncoming steamer. In a short while he should be able to identify her. It was a little early to meet the *Judson Clegg*, but they hadn't yet raised the *Annie Hampton* or the *Red Swan*, and she might equally well turn out to be a stranger doing a casual run in the lower-river trade.

Cautiously he chose a course which would not put too much strain on the rudder post, realizing as he did so that all by itself this would inform the pilot of the *Nonpareil* that his rival was in trouble.

How long before the clue was picked up and acted on?

For a little longer it seemed his fears were going to be unfounded. After all, here the river twisted like an intestine, so that a boat going up from Island 110 to 109 was running parallel to but on almost exactly the opposite heading from another making upstream from 106 to 105, the other side of the narrow point where Palmyra was precariously located. Where the channel kept doubling back on itself, and moreover where a number of steamers were scheduled to be coming down about now, was the last place a pilot would normally choose to try and overtake.

Of course, a race wasn't normal. . .

He glanced sternward, and his mouth went suddenly dry. As though reading his rival's thoughts, the other pilot—it must by now be Trumbull, Fernand calculated—was piling on the pressure. Once more great gouts of black smoke were gusting from the *Nonpareil*, while her band assembled and her off-duty hands cheered and stamped at her bow. The defiant silken banner slapped back and forth.

What to do? Should he wake the captain?

Of course not! A second later Fernand was ashamed of himself for even considering the idea. He was no longer a cub; he was a qualified pilot with as much experience as any of his own age.

Besides, there was a term he had heard during discussions about steamer racing: a *fighting* pilot. He wanted to be one of those.

So why should a little problem like a strained rudder post handicap him? Coolly and reflectively he started to reassess his situation from basic principles.

The *Nonpareil* was bound to try overtaking in the same way as before: cutting across the inside of a bend against the faster current but covering a shorter distance. What she had been unable to do when Drew sent her aground, she could very probably do now the *Atchafalaya* was compelled to tread gently.

And she was fast. With increasing nervousness he watched her closing the gap for the second time today: lean, elegant, almost composed-looking in her gaudy gold-and-white livery. Beside her the *Atchafalaya* appeared dowdy, wearing the signs of age from stem to stern.

All that apart, the two of them were amazingly well matched, as though some supernal balance had been struck in advance: so much gain for higher pressure, but so much for wider buckets; so much for a more slender hull, but so much for energy not wasted on making pretty fountains at the bow . . .

And to think the *Nonpareil* had been designed by a blind man!

But she labored under one great disadvantage: having a master who was not himself a pilot. Fernand drew a deep breath, having just realized there was a possible way out of his predicament.

It all depended, though, on whether the oncoming boat was the *Annie Hampton* or the *Red Swan*. For the latter was a line boat, owned by an anonymous group of businessmen, while the former was the personal property of a man who, like Drew, had worked his way up from the bottom.

Tensely he searched the gaps in the trees for hints to her identity, and as for the first time he caught a clear view he crossed himself and muttered a prayer of thanks. The collars on her chimneys were blue, not red. It was the *Annie*.

But she was already laying off into slack water, on his side of the bend, prepared to waste time in order to give the passengers a treat by letting them watch the racing steamers thunder by. That was exactly what Fernand was most afraid of. With her weakened rudder post the *Atchafalaya* could not cut across the *Nonpareil*'s bows, and here the river was too wide for her wake to affect her pursuer.

Urgently he reached for the whistle lever and sounded one long blast: the signal that he wanted to pass starboard to starboard.

For an agonizing moment there was no reply from the *Annie;* then, somehow inquiringly, she returned a double blast—why not larboard?

Deliberately Fernand sounded another long blast, and after a pause another, and then another still. Any pilot on the river could read that language: "I am coming ahead in the slack water at all costs!"

Since this was normal practice when two steamers met, the pilot of the *Annie* had no choice but to comply, unless he was willing to risk a collision or ground his boat.

She was, though, older and slower than the racing steamers, and it took a heartbreakingly long time before, with a resigned single whistle, she put about and made for her proper course.

Now all depended on the reaction of the *Nonpareil*.

Sweat was running into Fernand's eyes; he wiped it angrily with his sleeve as, taking care not to put too much load on the rudder, he brought the *Atchafalaya*'s head gently around and into the next short reach, leading between New Carthage and Palmyra—where, as ever, the crowds had turned out to watch, and many of them had taken to boats that constituted a hazard to navigation. Needing no orders, though, Chalker and Sexton had mustered their polemen, and Gross was back shouting the standard warning that their pilot would not slow for other traffic.

But any moment now there was the terrible sharp bend before Killacranka Landing, where the boat must be put about in not much more than her own length to head toward Island 105, where there was another bend—this time to larboard—of more than a right angle.

Fernand reached for the speaking tube.

"Dutch! I got to put her through the Killacranka bend on wheels and let the rudder drag. Stand by to give me a dead stop on the starboard wheel!"

"You going to take her through full ahead on the larboard?" Dutch shouted back.

"The *Nonpareil's* breathing our smoke, and I can't swear the *Annie H.* will cross her nose in time!"

"The *Annie*—? Say, I got it! I heard you whistle, but I guessed it must be for the crazy fools putting out in boats from Palmyra! I'll send Walt out on the guards and watch for trouble, but so long as he says you're not apt to tear the wheel loose, you got what you want!"

Hearing that, a great calm came over Fernand. He had set the boat up as best he knew how. What happened now was up to fate.

Then from astern began a series of angry blasts on the *Nonpareil's* whistle, and he relaxed a fraction and allowed himself to grin.

Madly waving and cheering, the passengers on the *Atchafalaya* and the *Annie Hampton* saluted each other as the two boats crossed and passed. A few people were afraid they were coming too close; one might have tossed a biscuit from deck to deck.

It was safe enough, however. The moment the smaller and lighter boat caught the bow sheer from the larger, she was automatically carried farther over into the deep channel, and therefore into the very path the *Nonpareil* had hoped to follow. Hence the frantic whistling.

In a straight reach free of islands and towheads there need have been no problem. Hereabouts, though, the *Annie* was within her rights, and no hearing of the Pilots' Guild would have ruled otherwise. She went on blasting the signal to pass starboard to starboard, and the *Nonpareil* was forced to yield and swing over to the New Carthage side, to precisely that area of water where the *Atchafalaya's* wake could once again delay her.

Fernand delightedly pictured the frustration in her pilothouse.

"Just exactly what I'd have done," said Drew quietly.

Fernand started; he hadn't realized the captain was awake.

"Carry on," Drew added before the younger man could answer. "You got the makings of a fighting pilot. Always thought you did."

There was no time to preen over the compliment. Here came the Killacranka bend. Dead stop on starboard—*now!*

The wheel complained, but took the strain.

And there was no way of gaining advantage in the next short reach, to Island 105, and before the *Atchafalaya* had to make her next turn, Diamond came sweating and weary to report completion of repairs.

Triumphant, Fernand showed the *Nonpareil* a clean pair of wheels past Island 104, then Warrenton, where he finally met the *Red Swan* and *Judson Clegg*, then into Diamond Bend. He felt that virtue had gone out of him and left him weak, but he also felt immensely proud of himself.

Now ahead loomed Vicksburg, where they were both to refuel. Drew took the wheel, and this time the coaling went without flaw, gaining a few more precious minutes. Then Tyburn took over, and Fernand had the chance to rest.

They were one day and about half an hour into the four-day race. At Vicksburg they were three hundred and ninety-five miles from New Orleans. They were making better than sixteen miles an hour.

Every record for the distance had been smashed.

 "God damn him for a stupid fool!" Woodley raged in the pilothouse of the *Nonpareil* as the *Annie Hampton* slid by in the deep channel with her cheering passengers sublimely unaware of the setback their boat had caused. "Has Drew bought him? Why didn't he just go aground on the outside of the bend until we were safely past?"

"I know the captain of the *Annie*," Parbury said stonily. "He's a member of our Guild." He paused long enough to let the reproach rankle in the ears of Woodley, who was not. "You wouldn't have to buy him. And what happened was not of his choosing."

"What do you mean?" Woodley snapped.

"Ask Mr. Trumbull," Parbury said. Only a faint tremor in his voice had thus far betrayed the enormous effort it was costing him to accept this new disappointment, so close to the watery grave of his old boat. He made his way out; shortly he was to be seen in his favorite position on the foredeck, where the spray from the cutwater could just touch his face.

Sighing as the door swung to, Trumbull said, "He's right, Captain. That Lamenthe is smarter than most people give him credit for. I don't know if Drew taught him that trick or he figured it out for himself, but he was within his rights. You can't oblige another boat to go aground to suit your convenience."

"I wish our toy cannon could sink her, then!" Woodley barked. "When's our next chance to overtake?"

Trumbull shrugged. "Dark's coming on," he muttered. "It won't be until tomorrow."

"Thank you very much!" Woodley exclaimed, and stormed out.

Trumbull scowled after him; then concentrated—and not without success—on making up time lost by their slower coaling.

 A breeze had sprung up and it was cooler now, but most of the passengers were still in the cabin, where Barber was continuing to spend lavishly on refreshments for his guests, some of whom he had never met before. Cherouen was taking full advantage.

But there was no sign of Dorcas or Eulalie.

Eventually Fernand spotted them sitting by themselves on the afterdeck. Wide-eyed, Dorcas was leaning forward across a white-painted table, hanging on the older woman's words.

He had no chance to hear what they were talking about, though. As soon as she saw her son approaching, Eulalie jumped to her feet.

"Why, you poor boy!" she exclaimed. "You look worn out! You can't have had any proper sleep since we left New Orleans!"

That was perfectly true, and Fernand was relieved that he wasn't going to have to apologize for leaving them again in a few minutes. He kissed his mother perfunctorily on the cheek and embraced Dorcas—though she turned her mouth away—before slumping into a chair. To a waiter he said, "Bring me a sazerac and make it fierce! And for you?"—turning to his companions.

"Tea," Eulalie said firmly. She had never grown used to her son drinking anything stronger than wine, and rarely did so herself. Dorcas gave a timid nod of agreement. The waiter hastened away.

"How is the race going?" Eulalie inquired after a pause.

Now was his opportunity to boast a little. Fernand gave a shrug.

"Very well, thanks to the good fortune that brought that other steamer along just at the proper moment. I was able to insist on her taking the usual downriver course, so she baffled the *Nonpareil* when she tried to overtake. Captain Drew was very pleased."

"So we're still well in the lead?" Eulalie pressed. And exchanged a secret glance with Dorcas, who smiled broadly.

It dawned on Fernand that something was amiss. Had these two actually not realized that the *Nonpareil* was trying to pass?

He put the question in so many words. For a few seconds they hesitated; then Eulalie said, "Well, we have been keeping to ourselves."

"Nobody else told you?" Fernand demanded.

"As I said, we've been keeping to ourselves."

Fernand glanced along the deck, anger burgeoning in his mind. How dare these people ostracize his mother and his wife-to-be when the outcome of the race, and the winning of their bets, depended on him?

But Eulalie laid a hand on his. "We're getting properly acquainted—we don't mind in the least. Do we, Dorcas, my dear?"

"Not at all!" Dorcas declared. "I only wish you'd introduced me to your mother sooner, Fernand. She's perfectly charming!"

*Some of the time*, he glossed grayly. But he was too weary to argue. When the waiter returned, he gulped his cocktail and rose.

"Do please forgive me! I have to be back on duty in"—he checked his watch—"three and a half hours, and I need some rest."

"Are you getting enough to eat?" Eulalie inquired solicitously.

"Oh, the texas tender brings anything we ask for from the kitchens. Don't worry! Perhaps tomorrow, if all goes well, I can enjoy lunching with you."

Bowing, he kissed each in turn, and tried and failed to master a gigantic yawn.

"What a profession!" Eulalie said, shaking her head. "To have to work four hours on, four off . . . It isn't natural to the human frame!"

"Steamboats aren't natural," Fernand said more curtly than he had intended.

"No more are ocean liners, or railroad trains—ploughs and harrows, come to that! Don't fret about me, please. I love my job. I wouldn't settle for any other."

When he had gone, Eulalie said softly to Dorcas, "You see what I mean? He really believes it was just chance that brought the other steamer to the right place at the right time."

Dorcas nodded. For her the afternoon had been a revelation. Eulalie had shared with her secrets such as she had never dreamed of.

"Please tell me more!" she begged. "How I wish I'd met you sooner! You could have taught me how to handle that monster Captain Parbury!"

 Sunset and the light wind of evening saw the two boats threading their way through the bends upstream of Vicksburg, past Duckport and Millikinsville, past Pulhan's Academy—lone outpost of learning in a wilderness—Campbellville and Terrapin Neck. Famous names alighted hereabout by sheer chance, like Brunswick and Transylvania, were intermingled with accidental, personal commemorations: Wilton's Landing, Walker's Island.

Later a great writer was to say of Fort Smith, Arkansas, that there was no fort there and the people had forgotten what Smith it was named after.

But here it was not the passage of time that undertook erasure. A single season's shift in the course of the river might wipe out a settlement so completely, no one was left to speak its name save those puzzled pilots following the next spring rise who would mutter to the wheel, "This is where such-and-such a town used to stand."

Its fragments might by then be drifting across the Gulf of Mexico.

Indeed, around mid-morning near the mouth of the Arkansas River they were scheduled to reach a place facing just that doom: the proudly named Napoleon which was being worn away by the river like wood under a carpenter's plane.

The distance between the rivals remained more or less constant now. Where one had to slow, the other made up time; where one was checked by drifting mist, the other had clear skies.

Tallulah and Providence slid by, to the usual cheering, bonfires, and occasional fireworks. A little ahead of midnight the *Atchafalaya* passed Ashton above Island 92, but before she had reached Princeton, on the other bank, people were applauding the *Nonpareil*.

A little higher up, there were patches of deceptive shallowness where they had to send out leadsmen; then traditional cries resounded in the night—"Mark three! And a half twain! Ma-ark *twain!*"

At which they had to seek a deeper, safer course without even the assistance of the moon.

Meantime the passengers settled down to the wearing away of the night. A few still preferred to remain awake, though they could look forward to small distraction before the coaling stop at Greenville, around four o'clock. Some who had retired lay sleepless; Gaston was among them, his head ringing with the echo of the day's noises.

Joel sat by himself in the cabin, struggling to compose his next report. But his mind was fractious. He was concerned about Auberon, who seemed feverish and kept muttering curses against Arthur. Moreover he was now more than half-convinced the *Nonpareil* would never overtake, so that if he were to cover the race properly he must take a train from Memphis to Cairo. But would Drew let him aboard the *Atchafalaya*?

Josephine lay sleeping for the first time in a long while without nightmares, as though separation from Cherouen was beneficial. But she dreamed, even though the dreams were not horrible enough to wake her. She had been danced attendance on all day by the black staff of the *Nonpareil* who let it be understood that, despite her efforts at secrecy, they knew who she was. She dreamed that tomorrow they would come to her and beg for the advantage of her powers to overtake the *Atchafalaya*, and that she would graciously deign to oblige.

Yet a shadowy figure loomed in her dream who wore a kerchief across his ruined eyes, and he was too like the image of a certain deity brought to life for her dreaming to be entirely pleasant.

Eulalie slept dreamlessly; she had concluded before she retired that her fears of defeat were illusory. Now she had met her son's intended, she knew she was in arm's reach of a far more important success: she was to have grandchildren, and her rule over Fernand would be continued by his wife. She was naïve; she was ignorant; she came from the Protestant background that laid far less emphasis on faith than did the Catholic; but even so . . . !

And if, as rumor said, Mam'zelle Josephine was to be identified with this nurse about whom Cherouen complained so constantly, then the charms she and Dorcas had put about the *Atchafalaya* should ensure victory. A new, young, enthusiastic disciple was notoriously valuable in such a case.

Dorcas, by contrast, was unable to sleep at all. She kept feeling the curve of her belly where a new life was growing. It had happened before, but then it had led to a disaster. This time—she had been so assured by her man's mother, which amazed her—it was to lead to fortune, and delight, and achievement.

She grew frustrated after a while, touching her skin through cloth, and stripped herself as naked as when Fernand took her in the Limousin. After that her fingers strayed away from the swelling mound below her ribs and became very busy to the accompaniment of what were not exactly visions, but compounded more of recollected contact.

She wished with all her heart that Fernand could be here beside her. After the race was won . . .

She moaned a little as she attained perfect visualization—except it wasn't visual—of his hard sleek body over hers.

Langston Barber regretted only one thing about the day he had just passed: the fact that he was obliged to be polite to Cherouen, whose claims—both medical and personal—he had summed up, as he would those of anybody intending to bet against him.

He had concluded that the man did not even believe in his own cures. He had seen how resentful Cherouen was when called on to dress Walt Presslie's scald. Surely any doctor should willingly help any sufferer, were it only to bandage a cut finger!

He was considering laying bets against the survival of the second Grammont child in consequence.

Walt himself was poised halfway between fatigue and guilt. Though his blistered shoulder hurt far more than he admitted, he was able to contribute again to the common effort. But he was having to work one-handed, and when it came to heavy jobs like going astern he was left at a loss. Dutch was taking things as they came, and there were a couple of white firemen who could be trusted to go as they were told, whom he had roped in as temporary strikers.

It galled Walt, though, to think that accident had prevented him from pulling his full weight in such a momentous run.

Staff in hand, Drew spent those waking moments when he was not in the pilot-house wandering from deck to deck, mustering a smile and a polite word for the passengers who complimented him on the efficient running of the *Atchafalaya*, snapping a curse at any member of the crew who was neglecting normal duties because there were so few passengers and so little cargo this time, or because it was a race and somehow different from a regular run. But luckily there were few calls for reprimands. Most of those who worked for him had joined the boat reluctantly; his reputation had preceded him and he was held to be a hard taskmaster. Yet they had come back to sign on for another and still another voyage, sometimes after trying other steamers and finding conditions worse. Little by little he had come to think of himself in terms he had run across in an English novel about schoolboys, which meant nothing to him but which for lack of anything else he had passed an evening reading. There was this head teacher defined by his pupils as "a beast, but a *just* beast!"

To have kept one's word; to have kept faith . . . Surely that would be enough to defend oneself before the eventual throne of the Most High.

Therefore he had made a conscious effort to mingle praise with punishment. Therefore, even more on this trip than on the previous record-breaking one, he was able to say, "Well done!"

To even the lowliest of the dirty, flea-ridden, greasy-garbed, black-nailed, stinking niggers camped out on the foredeck, snatching an hour or two's repose between shifts: people who with the best will in the world it was hard to recognize as belonging to the same race as Fernand, with his flawless manners and his impeccable attire.

But then there had been years—so many years!—when he himself begrudged the cost of soap, let alone a new coat or shirt, because he was hag-ridden by Jacob's debts . . .

Then, he must have looked not altogether unlike this rabble: holes in his boots, his beard untrimmed, everything about him signaling poverty to the world. Why, that morning when he first met Fernand, the boy's appearance must have put his own to shame, and he was a clerk in a store!

It was a different world he was looking back into from the standpoint of now. One thing only had remained constant.

But he was afraid to think about Susannah and the children. He was coming to wonder whether even the Electric Doctor would be able to help her. The more he thought about that sad letter informing him of her ill-health—the more he talked to, or rather put up with, Cherouen—the more he grew depressed. Consciously he was aware that the boat was running beautifully and that his crew were tuned to their finest-ever pitch. Against his will, however, he felt a terrible sense of foreboding. He knew he ought to spend more time asleep in his stateroom, confiding the race to Tyburn and Fernand. It was impossible. Every time he turned his feet that way, he thought of some other thing that might go wrong, and felt bound to investigate. His eyelids were stinging, as though they were rimmed with hot sand; his stomach churned because he hadn't eaten a square meal, or at a regular time, since leaving New Orleans.

It hadn't been like this on the last fast run. Then, he only had a plain ordinary job to do, and he was doing it to the best of his ability. Now he was being pursued, he understood why he had never wanted to race. It was like being a runaway slave hearing the hounds and the patterollers on his track. It was like being doomed to pay off his inherited debts all over again from scratch, because this time half his heart was at stake—his precious steamer!

He had thought, when proposing his bet, that having enough money to finance a new boat, more fitted to compete in this age of railroads, would be sufficient to cushion him against the fear of losing.

It wasn't.

In a way his decision to hide from the war had never managed—for then he had had his personal justifications to shield him—this experience was bringing it home to him that at heart the reason he was not a gambler was because he could not, could never, face the fact of being defeated.

To have married, and got it wrong: that would have been a defeat. Imagine being Parbury, with his only child dead, his wife a crippled whining misery, his eyesight lost in the moment his proudest possession went to the bottom!

And yet somehow Parbury had come back, and there he was on his rival's heels, as it were tap-tapping with the stick he carried not because it was useful to discipline lazy deckhands but because without it he could not find his way . . .

Sleepless, agitated, Drew became more convinced by the hour that fortune had smiled on him too long.

 On first discovering that Whitworth found it impossible
to shake off his watchman's habits, so that he prowled the
night away, eyes sharp for any irregularity, Underwood had
thought he might be trying to usurp the privileges of his senior.

However, it had not been long before the *Nonpareil's* first mate realized how
lucky he was in having a deputy who could manage with four hours' sleep, even if
he did take them at improbable times. Being himself of a constitution that called
for a more normal ration of repose, he was glad to make an unofficial rearrange-
ment of the watch system. Tonight he had agreed to turn out for the coaling stop
at Greenville. Until then, he was snoring to his heart's content.

Woodley had not been informed. It might be safest to let him learn by degrees.
Surely, though, it was better for him to have his first mate properly rested before
such a crucial event?

Nonetheless Whitworth walked circumspectly, alert for trouble of whatever
kind. He was expecting a crisis between Auberon and his brother-in-law. The
latter was drinking more than he ought, in company with Major Spring and—who
else?—Gordon, whose purse despite his financial problems appeared to be bot-
tomless. Luckily Auberon appeared to defer to the darkie nurse and the reporter,
though much of the time the latter was running around bothering people for their
opinions of the race. So far he had not cornered Whitworth; doubtless he eventually would.

And if so, what would he say? That regardless of the outcome he planned to
leave the river for good?

Whitworth was of two minds . . . no, three at least. The chance that had come
his way not long before leaving New Orleans was perhaps a once-in-a-lifetime
opportunity. To become a commercial representative for a product already in
enormous demand back east: that was pregnant with possibilities! Of course, he
would have to settle in St. Louis, and his wife had never wanted to leave
Paducah, but their marriage was effectively at an end anyhow.

And there was something beyond that mere promise of financial success. There
was something which rang around his skull whenever he looked at Josephine and
saw how the waiters and stewards danced at her every whim. He had seen one of
them actually hand her money!

Wrapped in a scrap of paper. Bearing a message—or a prayer? Who could say?

But there was no doubt about it: this woman had some kind of a hold over the
colored crew. And here the *Nonpareil* was lagging behind despite being faster.
Coincidence?

Also the nurse had ordered the stop at Baton Rouge. Coincidence?

Also a black engineer had been hired for the trip. Coincidence?

And if in fact some supernatural influence was at work—which in his view any
rational person must admit to be possible, for he had often witnessed the effect of
luck charms on the fate of others, though he himself had never profited by any he
had bought—if so, then was it not time that some very natural influence indeed

were brought to bear on behalf of this boat which, by all reasonable standards, should be outrunning her opponent?

Except that the *Atchafalaya* had a colored pilot, and today he had frustrated the *Nonpareil*'s best attempts to overtake.

By sheer skill? Or because all these goddamned niggers were in cahoots with one another?

The last passengers found their way to bed, and the weary waiters and tenders, yawning as they cleared away dirty glasses and emptied ashtrays and cuspidors, shut down the lights in the cabin. There had been no fight after all.

Whitworth turned his steps towards the pilothouse. He was never entirely welcome there, and he knew it, but at this stage of the race Hogan was holding the wheel, and he found Hogan the more tolerant of the pilots. Trumbull was brusque; Hogan was at least polite.

Parbury was in the pilothouse also, but dozing. There had been no sign of Woodley for an hour or more; presumably he was napping in his stateroom.

"All secure below, sir," Whitworth said formally as he entered. Here, even to his dark-adjusted vision, there was only a faint glimmer of light, but the white-painted decks cast back what starlight was to be had, and in a little he was able to make out something of the banks.

"No trouble with the passengers?" Hogan inquired as he made a minuscule adjustment to the wheel. "Not even with the witch woman?"

Whitworth started. He said after a pause, "You mean the nurse?"

"Nurse?" Hogan gave a harsh laugh. "Well, I guess she may cure some of her followers if they believe enough."

Astonished, Whitworth said, "Then you noticed—"

"Noticed what?" Hogan cut in. "How every time we try to overtake the *Atchafalaya* something happens to prevent it? We got away first! We should have held the lead clear to St. Louis. But Cherouen's on the other boat, and his nurse somehow found her way aboard ours. And here we are, trailing 'em!"

"I've been thinking exactly the same," Whitworth said.

"Have you, now? Well, congratulations!" Another minute adjustment of course; they were running on a dead slow bell, but in the distance could be discerned sparks from the *Atchafalaya*. As so often happened hereabouts, their courses were a hundred and fifty degrees apart, thanks to a sharp headland.

"I'd be a sight happier," Hogan said savagely, "if I didn't think there was a connection."

"You really—?" Whitworth began.

"Yes, I really!" Hogan snapped. "I was brought up by my parents, who remembered life in the old country. For all the Church said or did, there was a grain of truth in the tales they used to tell. And darkies are closer to nature than you or me. They understand things we've forgotten as we grew richer and more secure. Falsely secure!"

"Once I was on a boat," Whitworth said slowly, "where we had a gray mare aboard. Took us more than a day to clear the Grand Chain."

"Ever had a preacher aboard?" Hogan said. "I did once. Might as well have been going astern, all the headway we could make from Natchez to Vicksburg." He chuckled, once more turning the wheel by an imperceptible trifle. "Broke all the records for overtaking towheads, I believe! Least, though, he was an understanding person. Didn't mind when we put him ashore to finish his trip by muleback."

"Women big with child," Whitworth said, and waited for a response.

"I had a few of them," Hogan said ruminatively. "Didn't make the connection until now. You mean this Mrs. Gattry we had to put ashore."

"Well, it was while she held us up that the *Atchafalaya* snuck by."

"Bad news," Hogan said, and reached for engineroom bell ropes. Here was a bend they would have to take at walking pace; he was giving an early warning.

"So what about men who dress in skirts?" Whitworth ventured. "And what's more, act like . . . I don't know a word bad enough for that kind of thing."

"Hmm?" Hogan had been preoccupied for a moment; now he glanced around . . . not that any details were to be made out in the gloom.

Abruptly he realized what Whitworth was driving at, and exclaimed, "You mean Gordon? Hell, everybody dolls up like that in Scotland! Y'ain't seen pictures of what Julius Caesar and that bunch wore? Like nightshirts! Glad I don't have engineers dressed that way, myself. Imagine 'em clambering over a broken wheel on a bad night!"

Obdurately Whitworth persisted, "But that boy of his! He came right out and said it was true!"

"What?"

The gravelly voice was Parbury's. Waking, he creaked to a seated posture.

"I chose Gordon to be my partner in creating this here boat," he stated flatly. "I won't hear a word against him 'less it's proven solid. What did his boy say?"

Whitworth stumbletongued. "Why—why—he said plain as I hear you now that he was Gordon's . . . Well, he was . . ."

Parbury rose to his feet, reaching for the familiar landmarks around him. Once upright, he towered over them both.

"*What?*"

"It's not the sort of thing I generally talk about, but I took it for granted everybody knew!" Whitworth licked his lips, recalling their last conversation.

Parbury bent his blind gaze Whitworth's way; it was impossible to tell whether he had discarded Dorcas's bandanna or whether its colors had merely blended into the murk.

"If you're implying what I think, you're insulting me as well as him! Gordon's manly enough to suit me, and that's that! Mr. Hogan, how do we stand concerning the *Atchafalaya*? Did we not pass Island 88 a while ago? Are we not bound up towards Point Worthington?"

Hogan said with respect, "Even when you're asleep, Cap'n, you don't let much escape you!"

Shut out by this exchange, Whitworth made his way stealthily to the door.

He was shocked, as a riverboat might be on going aground at full speed. What had he misunderstood?

\*    \*    \*

Tired, but too overwrought to sleep, Joel made his way to the forward end of the boiler deck. At present the *Nonpareil* was running easily in a broad expanse of what looked to the layman's eye to be clear water, but he was aware that following the channel was a different matter from simply avoiding the banks. He shivered as he thought of the risks the pilots were facing, and was glad he did not have their job.

Not that his day had been an easy one. It had come as a grievous shock to realize that the cousin he had so admired had fallen prey to the Pale Death which had stalked other of his idols: John Keats, above all. And had not the same dreadful sickness stolen away the child-bride Mrs. Poe?

Yet he was resigned to the sad truth that disease struck at random, and carried off each time more of the old silly notion that God was always just and merciful. To Joel, the deity seemed now more like a gambler, prepared to shrug off losses and start over on another set of human predicaments. And if the world's best doctors were like Cherouen— Poor Auberon!

That much said, harder visions now assailed him, associated with the Duelling Oaks in New Orleans. Try as he might, he could not hide from the fact that he was growing scared on his own behalf. When those bitter lines he had penned, attacking his cousin-in-law, appeared in papers that might be received as soon as Greenville, he could himself be in danger.

Unless, of course, Graves had edited them out . . . but why should he? The way Arthur had treated his pregnant bride was disgraceful, and the world should know of it!

Sighing, he struggled to compose himself, so that he might polish off the rest of his next report. Equally sleepless, a black deckhand below was crooning an old plantation song with subversive intent: "Run nigger run, patteroller ketch you!" Maybe that could supply the image he needed to conclude his piece—the relentless pursuit of the *Atchafalaya* by her rival.

However, perhaps the moral was inappropriate. Because the man being chased got away.

"Hello!"

A soft challenging voice from behind. Joel spun around. He relaxed as he recognized Whitworth.

"Sorry, sir," the latter said. "Didn't mean to startle you . . . Say!"

"Yes?"

"I guess you're a literary kind of gent, ain't you?"

"I allow you might call me so. Why?"

Whitworth hesitated. He said eventually, "This boy of Mr. Gordon's."

"What about him?"

"Well . . . ." It was clear Whitworth was having trouble finding the right words. "Well, when I first met him he called himself by some sort of fancy name. He said Gordon pays him to be his—something. And I'm darned if I can recollect what."

Suppressing his annoyance, for he had not wanted to be interrupted, Joel searched his memory. "What kind of name?" he said finally.

"*I* don't know!" Whitworth gave a shrug. "Some long word with *s*'s in it."

"Amanuensis?" Joel offered.

"That's it!"

"What about it?"

"Well—uh—what does it mean?"

Joel cudgeled his brains. "I guess you could render it pretty well by 'confidential secretary'," he suggested at length.

"Nothing else?"

"Not that I ever heard of. And now, if you'll excuse me, I have to write up my next column."

At just that moment there was a cry from the sleepless hand at the bow.

"'Ware drift!"

Whitworth darted for the nearest stairs, shouting, "Polemen! Polemen on the double! Move, you sluggards—move!"

Shaking his head in puzzlement, Joel reentered the cabin and resumed the laborious task of organizing his thoughts into readable prose.

At the end of his piece he added a note directed at Abner Graves, stating that if the *Nonpareil* did not regain the lead by tomorrow sundown, he would definitely take the railroad from Memphis and try to join the *Atchafalaya* at Cairo.

Reports from the losing boat were that much less effective.

But in his heart of hearts he mainly wanted to leave the one that carried Arthur.

The miles rolled by, more slowly than by day, but at a respectable rate nonetheless. Here the river had shortened its course and names commemorated the fact: New Cutoff, Old River, Old River Lake—one of the countless sloughs, known in river dialect as "slooze," where stagnant water now offered breeding grounds for mosquitoes. They were coming into yellow-fever country. Few diseases since the Black Death had had the privilege of undoing the creation of a city, but that fate befell Memphis when an epidemic hit.

Memphis was for tomorrow night, though; midnight or the small hours, according to what the Mississippi allowed.

Of course, there was a chance that all records would be broken again during the daylight run. Memphis by eleven was at least a possibility. As she lightened, the *Nonpareil* grew harder to handle, requiring maximum use of her chain wagon and losing perceptible ground. But even she, when Phisick Island loomed—memorial to the discovery of a healing herb—was comfortably ahead of her own previous best and "ticking along," as Brian Roy declared exultantly, "like a railroad watch!"

This was not a popular image among steamboaters; he made the remark precisely once.

Why, though—*why*—Caesar kept puzzling, had Woodley not made the same arrangements for refueling as the *Atchafalaya*'s? He himself was of course busy manhandling the reversing gear or running from gauge to valve to stopcock with wrench in hand, all the time the *Nonpareil* was rounding to her wharf, collecting her coal flats, swinging out into the current again. But reports came to him. The black deckhands were shyly proud of the fact that there was one of their own working as a full engineer, even though he was compelled to sleep like them on piles of sacking, while the black waiters and tenders found means to slip him food and drink and talk about Mam'zelle Josephine.

If indeed this was the actual person. Caesar wondered why, if so, she had chosen to be aboard the trailing boat . . .

But the charm he had bought from her was gradually receding, like the memory of Tandy and his children. Now he was baffled to the point of frustration by the contrast between the speed with which the *Atchafalaya* coaled up on the run and the slow, painful process the *Nonpareil* was constrained to.

There were black-owned steamer lines around Louisiana. Would they be interested in someone who came to them and said he had seen the high-speed method in operation and could copy it?

Caesar guessed not. His cousins (for he could not call them brothers, being much lighter in color than himself and referred to as Creoles, not Negroes) were in his view far too concerned to imitate the proven successes of the whites rather than the risky innovations that ensured white supremacy.

But his mind was too weary, and his body too fatigued, to pursue thoughts as deep as those. In the engineroom, quite apart from the grudging compliment he had been paid earlier by Roy, he was now earning an occasional pat on the back from Corkran and even Steeples when the noise was too great for speech.

That must suffice.

He tumbled on to his improvised couch and was asleep before the *Nonpareil*, half an hour in arrears against the leading boat, swung into Spanish Moss Bend.

Greenville was noisy! Here, instead of staying up late, people had gone to bed and risen early in full possession of their faculties, which included pistols and fireworks. Much of them had been expended on the *Atchafalaya*, but enough remained to make the racket that greeted the *Nonpareil* impossible to sleep through.

Groggy, resplendent in his silk robe, Matthew made his way down the cabin in search of coffee for his employer. One or two deck passengers had sneaked into the cabin during the night, and as they were causing no trouble, Whitworth had let them be. However, since people would be appearing for breakfast shortly, he had decided to return and rout them out. This was how he came upon Matthew in the wan light ahead of dawn.

Clearing his throat, he said, "Say, Mr. Rust!"

Unaccustomed to being addressed so formally, especially by this of all people, Matthew blinked at him.

"Can I help you?"

"Well . . . Well, Mr. Gordon is asking for coffee!"

A snap of the fingers; a drowsy black man roused to duty; a salver, jug, and cups and bowls.

"I guess we could use a little of that," Whitworth said heartily, and poured two cupfuls at the bar before letting the tender deliver the rest to Gordon's stateroom.

"How is your boss, anyhow?" he demanded.

Matthew gave a thin smile. "Got a head like a bear's, as usual."

"Still having trouble getting money from home, is he?"

"Oh, yes! He thought he'd figured out a way around the problem—he planned to have the money sent to Paris first, then transferred here. But now there's talk of war between France and Prussia, so that's fallen through too." Sipping his coffee, Matthew looked and sounded puzzled: why was Whitworth suddenly being polite? The older man hastened to offer a plausible explanation.

"Say, I guess I been rough on you once or twice, ain't I?"

Another uncertain smile.

"Well"—with a shrug—"it comes of the way I've always earned my living. I've had it pretty tough. Not had much time for fancy things like books and writing. I guess you can get to look down on people because of that, think because they couldn't hold their end up in a fight they can't amount to much. But I was talking with Mr. Siskin, and he's kind of a regular fellow. I guess if you go on in your line, you could wind up like him one day, hm? I mean, like writing in the news-papers and all?"

"It's one of the things I'd certainly like to try," Matthew admitted cautiously. "I've been hoping to talk to Mr. Siskin about it, but he's always so busy, of course."

"Grab him this morning, then," Whitworth advised. "Our next regular coaling stop is Helena, and we'll be there around four or five o'clock. 'Less he wants to pitch something overside at Napoleon, I guess he'll have time to spare before his next report."

He drained his coffee. "By the way," he added, "I think I got something of yours. Didn't you leave your book lying about, the one with pictures of the way they dress in Scotland?"

"Why, yes!" Matthew exclaimed. "I've been hunting high and low!"

"I put it in a safe place; no need to worry. Right now I'm kind of busy, but I'll give it to you later, okay?"

"I wish I might have it right now," Matthew ventured.

"Sorry, boy. I'm on duty. But I'll get it back to you, never fear."

He strode away, leaving Matthew biting his lip. He was more puzzled than ever and now considerably worried. Why had he been fool enough to leave a slip of paper in the book, marking the page that revealed a secret worth, if his guess was right, hundreds of dollars? There was no call to remind himself of the place. The discovery was burned into his memory in letters of fire.

But there was nothing he could do about it. At least, he consoled himself, the mate was unlikely to take more than a passing interest in the book.

As for Whitworth, an idea had come to him that was buzzing and buzzing around in his head and at every pass seemed more attractive.

It had not been given to him many times in his life to be tempted of the devil.

But there were those who would have said that this was when it happened to him beyond a peradventure.

Beside her laver when she woke, Josephine discovered a bunch of flowers filched from a display intended for the cabin, and a little heap of sweet cakes, candy, and fresh fruit.

It was an offering.

For the first time in longer than she could remember it seemed less than unbearable to face the morning without the aid of hemp or laudanum.

She made obeisance to her dark lord in consequence.

Then she went in search of her half-brother and found him sick enough to be condemned to bed.

A little after dawn Gordon emerged for breakfast. But he made it clear with scowls and grunts that he was in no mood to renew the acquaintanceships of yesterday.

Nobody was surprised. The news this morning was bad enough to cast a general gloom. The *Atchafalaya* had improved her lead, adding to it the minutes gained by her quicker coaling. Was today to be a story of staring wistfully after her receding smoke?

It felt very much like it.

In an attempt to lighten the mood, Manuel entered the cabin and sat down at its piano, tinkling out popular tunes. Since he was self-taught, his harmonies would have caused Gaston to cringe, and indeed some of the more musically inclined passengers moved ostentatiously away as soon as they had finished breakfast.

But so did those who were not musical at all. Gordon was one. Having snapped several times at Matthew, he finally walked out and took station on the afterdeck to light his first cigar of the day. Whitworth, who cared no more for music than did the financier, seized his chance.

"Mr. Gordon!"—in a low voice.

"What the hell is it now?"

"I know how to stop the *Atchafalaya*."

"What kind of nonsense are you talking, man?"

"I mean exactly what I say." Whitworth moved confidentially close, producing and lighting one of his own panatelas. Now that he had actually broached his idea, his course seemed plain. And if he had gauged Gordon correctly, this was the one person on board who would make a cold-blooded judgment of the possibilities. Financiers were notoriously ruthless. Everybody said so. Whitworth had never met one before, but so far the Scotsman had matched their reputation.

"Matthew says you didn't get your funds from home yet," he continued.

"Damned little rapscallion! What business does he have talking about my affairs?"

"I asked with the best intentions, sir," Whitworth said placatingly. "I mean, it's no secret—is it?—that if we don't win, a lot of money will be lost. Not only yours, but Captain Woodley's, Captain Parbury's . . . even mine."

Gordon found the end of his cigar coming apart and spat flakes of tobacco to leeward; there was a brisk breeze this morning, and the new sunlight lay brilliant on the water. But this part of the Mississippi, around Catfish Bend and Cypress Bend and Bolivar, though broad, was so serpentine that boats doubling back and forth along it had no chance to display their full speed. Merely to look at such a sequence of bends conveyed to the lay watcher all the frustration felt by the pilot of a trailing boat as its rival piled on the coal. That was why Whitworth had chosen to approach Gordon now. Later, in the straight reaches above Island 74—past Victoria, Scrub Grass Bayou, Concordia and Laconia—they would be making good headway and able to believe that, if fortune smiled, they might catch the *Atchafalaya* while she was struggling through Horse Shoe Bend.

But by then the *Nonpareil* would be light again, and less manageable. Gordon was primed and ready to listen.

Whitworth sighed with private relief as, from within the cabin, a ragged chorus announced that some people at least were cheerful enough to join in a song at this hour of the morning. That reduced the risk of their being interrupted.

Which would be disastrous.

"Come to the point!" Gordon invited.

Covertly, after making sure they were unobserved, Whitworth drew from his coat a light-brown cylinder and displayed it between his hands.

"Do you know what this is, sir?"

"For a moment I thought you were going to offer me a better cigar than this damned thing!" Gordon retorted, as he found the end of his coming apart altogether. "No—what?"

"Did you ever hear of a firm called Mowbray's, in North Adams, Massachusetts?"

One could almost hear Gordon searching his memory, as a gambler might riffle through a deck of cards to spot the marked ones.

"I believe I did," he said after a pause. "Powdermakers, aren't they?"

"They went beyond that," Whitworth said. "This here"—he made the cylinder vanish again into his pocket—"is their very latest. Mica powder. Stabilizes nitroglycerine like nothing else—better than rendrock, better than dynamite."

"What in the world are you doing with it, then?"

"I had a stroke of luck. During my last refreshment in New Orleans I fell in with someone from back east who'd come out here to let monopoly contracts on behalf of Mowbray's. Had with him a caseful of demonstration samples. But he took sick and couldn't pay his doctor bills. Decided he was too ill to go ahead with the deal. So I paid the doctor and took the stuff in exchange. I'm thinking of quitting the river, you see. I figure up around St. Louis, and further west, there's going to be a lot of call for this kind of thing—blasting out railroad tunnels, for example."

"So?" Gordon said. But his expression indicated he had already leaped to the same conclusion as Whitworth.

"So if someone left the boat at Memphis and rode the L & N to Milan and then the Mobile & Ohio to Cairo, he could be there ahead of the *Atchafalaya*. If we haven't overtaken her by then, of course."

There was a period of silence, except for the singing from the cabin and the inevitable noise of the engines and paddlewheels. Now and then a bird took fright.

Then, before Gordon could speak again, there was a commotion. They had come in sight of a sternwheeler towboat sluggishly butting a dozen barges upstream, so now there was going to be further delay.

"I know the woodyard where the *Atchafalaya* will refuel," Whitworth pressed. "Same one we always use!"

"You mean at Cairo?"

"Sure!"

"How's Woodley going to manage without his second mate?" Gordon asked acutely.

Whitworth hesitated. He said at length, "I guess I hadn't figured out that kind of detail."

"You might simply be lost overboard . . ." Gordon sucked a corner of his moustache into his mouth for a second. "No, that's too complicated. But I guess some way could be worked out . . . What do you want?"

Whitworth relaxed. He said, "A stake to get me to Cairo and a piece of what you win."

"They may declare all bets void if the *Atchafalaya* doesn't make it to St. Louis."

"Think they'd dare? Who's to say it wasn't a boiler explosion? Drew's last boat was condemned by the inspectors!"

"What kind of a piece?"

After careful calculation: "A quarter!"

"Twenty per cent!"

"A quarter! Without me you don't win anything."

"A quarter if you come up with a foolproof scheme to explain your disappearance. A fifth if I work one out."

"Done!"

"Good, that's settled. When do we reach Memphis?"

"Late tonight. Eleven, maybe midnight. All depends."

"Gives us plenty of time, then."

"Yeah . . . I guess we can't exactly appoint a stakeholder, hm?"

"We can't tell anybody," Gordon said, taking out another cigar—and then, on second thought, another still, which he offered to Whitworth. "Throw away that horrible object," he added. "Have something fit to smoke."

"You weren't too pleased with the last one," Whitworth observed pointedly, making no move to take the gift.

Gordon shrugged and put it away again. He said, "What made you approach me and not—well—Parbury?"

"I figure he wants his boat to win on merit and won't do anything to help her along. Besides . . ." Whitworth hesitated a moment, then gave a wry grin. "Besides, I told him about that kerchief he's been wearing."

"I see," Gordon muttered. "Well, about time somebody did. Why not Captain Woodley, though?"

"The way I work it out, only the person who stands to lose the most if we don't get to St. Louis ahead of Drew would listen to me."

"And you think that's me?"

"It sure as hell ain't me, sir. Like I said, I'm even going to have to ask you to stake me to the train ride. And a little lagniappe with it. For expenses."

The singers in the cabin had exhausted their repertoire of well-known chorus songs, and someone was trying to arouse enthusiasm for "The Old Rugged Cross," as though in preparation for the prayer meeting that would inevitably be held tomorrow. It was not a great success, for the vigorously rhythmic bass Manuel beat out had more to do with the spirituals performed by the Negro crew than anything to be heard in a respectable church. More people were being driven away than attracted by the music. Time for this secretive conversation was running out.

Gordon shrugged and produced his billfold.

"If you don't make it," he said softly, "I shall swear on any number of Bibles that this discussion never took place. If you do, come back to me, and instead of hustling blasting powder, you can look forward to a steady job at two thousand a year, and your first year's salary will be on account. Is that okay?"

"No," Whitworth said boldly. "I already make two thousand, and I'm only a second mate after far too long. Double it."

"I'll double the down payment and put you in the way of what will make far more for you in the long run."

"Promises don't cut ice," Whitworth said scornfully.

"Five thousand out of my winnings!"

"We agreed a quarter!"

"A fifth!"

The hymn died away. People began to emerge from the cabin.

"So the deal's off, is it?" Whitworth said, and turned away with a shrug. If it had all ended there, he would not have been uncontent. To have had an international financier at his mercy for a few minutes was in itself an achievement.

But Gordon caught his arm.

"Damn you! If we don't best 'em I'll lose a hundred thousand. I can't let that much go! That stuff of yours—is it very powerful?"

"Not as much as dynamite. Far safer to handle, though."

"It would make a convincing boiler explosion?"

"One would blow up the boiler directly above the furnace."

"Would a lot of people be—uh—killed?" The last word emerged in a whisper. Contemptuously Whitworth said, "I guess a few of the firemen might catch it."

"Would the boat sink?"

"Oh, sure! What the hell else would you expect?" Aware of his temporary ascendancy, Whitworth was determined to enjoy it. "Take Drew with her—and his nigger pilot, with luck!"

The *Nonpareil* was being obliged to creep around the towboat like Parbury fumbling across a strange room. This was no way for the challenger in the greatest steamer race of the century to be acting!

Almost choking, Gordon forced out, "Then do it, damn you! And I'll be glad to my dying day that it was you, not me, who thought of it."

"You'll feel differently when you collect your winnings," Whitworth said serenely. Drunk on power, he turned away and began to work out how he could convincingly strand himself on a Memphis coal flat.

 "Ah, Captain!" Cherouen exclaimed as he came on Drew, staff tucked under his arm, at the stern rail of the *Atchafalaya*'s hurricane deck. "How are we doing today?"

Unhurriedly Drew completed his current business, which was to bite off a fresh chaw.

"Thus far," he said at length, "we are comfortably ahead of the best time for the distance, which is our own. Will that suffice?"

"And she continues to run well?"

"Dr. Cherouen," Drew said meditatively, "I don't know too much about the practice of medicine, but I did hear tell that by listening to the noises a body makes, you can figure out whether the lungs and belly are working right."

"That's what a stethoscope is used for," Cherouen said stiffly.

"That's the term. Matter of fact . . ." Drew turned with one elbow on the rail and looked directly at his interlocutor. "Matter of fact, it was this here Dr. Larzenac who told me the way of it. Showed me, too, to pass the time when we were just about in this stretch here. The second full day of the run is always kind of monotonous. Time hangs heavy."

The first gob of juice was ready; he aimed carefully to leeward and let go, then resumed.

"Said it was one of his countrymen that invented the gadget. A Dr.—Lannic, would it be?"

"Laënnec," Cherouen said reluctantly. "René Laënnec."

"That's right. And I thought then what I'm thinking right now."

"Which is—?"

"Which is how odd it is for a doctor to have to ask me whether my boat continues to run well!" Drew straightened, eyes flashing. "You ought to realize, sir, that I not only hear but feel the very vibration of the engines, which is the heartbeat of the vessel. The least cry from the wheels, the faintest irregularity, will alarm me, awake or asleep, as a mother can sleep through the racket of a thunderstorm yet waken to the whimper of her child!"

"I wouldn't doubt that for an instant," Cherouen said, as though amazed to be challenged so brusquely after what he had intended to be a friendly opening. "A stethoscope, after all, is a means to magnify just that faint *irregularity*"—he stressed the word to emphasize that he was echoing it—"which a trained observer would already have identified within his own organism."

"You mean to imply that someone who pays as much attention as I do to the operation of a steamer might equally learn to attend to malfunctions in his breathing or digestion?"

"I do indeed and would argue beyond it. Have you ever been subjected to a sphygmomanometer? Did your precious Dr. Larzenac possess one? Did he keep his hand in by measuring the blood pressure of your crew?"

Drew was for once taken aback and let it show. Cherouen smiled.

"I suspected as much. This is a simple enough device, as easy to comprehend as the—well, the steam-pressure gauges which I saw when you called me to help your engineer. I propose to inspect his burn again this morning, by the way, and change his dressings, though I admit that until I have all my equipment set up I can't do half what I would wish to."

"A pressure gauge for people?" Drew hazarded.

"Why, yes. An example of the way in which medicine is making true progress. One binds a cuff around a limb—the upper arm is convenient—and, after inflating it with a simple air pump, reads off the pressure of the blood in inches of mercury, and this is informative, since there is a limit to the elasticity of veins and arteries, just as there is to the rigidity of the pipes and tubing in your steam engine."

"Ah, Captain!"

The call came from Fernand. Freshly shaved, spotlessly clad, he was approaching along the deck, ignoring passengers who would have liked to question him.

"What are you doing here?" Drew growled. "You need another hour's rest before you take the wheel again! Else you'll be a candidate for this new medical device I was just hearing about! Did I understand it correctly?"—glancing at Cherouen. "You run yourself too hard, high pressure builds up, and you get the counterpart of a boiler explosion?"

"Very good!" Cherouen said with the slightest possible hint of patronization. "Except the burst is most likely to occur in that most precious and most fragile of our organs—to wit, the brain. Where it may lead to paralysis and death!"

Fernand, not understanding, blinked at each of them in turn.

"To sum it up, young man," Drew said heavily, "don't overdo things or you'll wear yourself out before your time! But to be honest, Doctor, right now I have no special worries concerning my protégé. Nor need you have, despite your views about African blood! I never had a better pilot under me than Fernand here, and I only wish he would rest more and spend less time fretting. I'll make a guess about what's roused you, and it's not your fiancée!"

Fernand gave a grin. "Captain, you must have read my mind! No, I'm at ease about Dorcas. I shall join her directly, but she's talking with my mother, and they get on fine, so that's one of the married man's worst problems taken care of. I only wanted to know what we shall do at Cairo when we have to put off passengers."

Cherouen started. "I understand we set out without any commitment to ports other than St. Louis!"

"I just talked with Mr. Motley," Fernand said. "For the chance of being aboard a racing boat, several people said they would come along anyway. Grant is making out a list of those who changed their minds and want to be transferred for Louisville."

Drew chuckled.

"Tell him to cable his list from Memphis to Cairo, attention of the master of the *Luke S. Thrale*. Won't cost him more'n an hour or two to cross us south of Island Number 1. And he's expecting some such message."

Fernand gave an exaggerated shrug and turned to Cherouen.

"I did hear you had doubts about coming with us, particularly when the *Nonpareil* got away first. I suspect you don't anymore! Excuse me!"

And he spun on his heel and strode away.

"You had doubts about me too," Cherouen said after a pause.

"I didn't say that," Drew growled. "If I had, would I have invited you to attend my sister-in-law?"

"Oh, I'm used to it," Cherouen said, unable to resist the impulse to preen a little; he was conscious of gaining a kind of victory over Drew. Especially since he had committed the error of admitting how much he depended on his nurse, who was aboard the rival boat, he had been looking for a chance to mend his fences in this fashion. "During the war, particularly, my ideas were often overruled by bigoted officers still stuck in the mud of fifty years ago . . . By the way, has there been news of the lady?"

"Not yet," Drew admitted gruffly. "But I hope to find a cable at Memphis or even Helena."

"I trust the news will be excellent. If not, you know you may rely on me to bring to bear the best of modern scientific aids. Now, if you'll excuse me, I think it's time for an eye-opener."

He sketched a bow and made for the cabin.

On his own, Drew pondered dismally whether he was ever likely to learn to make accurate judgments about people. He had decided to dislike Cherouen; yet here he was talking calmly and reasonably, displaying a level of knowledge comparable to, say, a skilled engineer's. And all his working life Drew had been used to the fact that in any steamer's engineroom one might find a foul-mouthed unqualified unpopular shabby dirty man capable of improvising in an emergency and saving the day. Draw out someone like that on any subject but his own, and one could easily get a false impression . . .

Yet a suspicion lingered. For all this smart talk about a human body being like a steam engine, a vein was not a copper pipe. A belly was not a furnace. A heart was no mere pump, and the brain not a pilothouse!

To fix a fault aboard a steamer, you took mallets and crowbars and wrenches and bar-stock iron and fired up a forge and chopped away spoiled parts and hammered and nailed and brazed new ones into position. Even if the body did emit signals that could be converted into a height of mercury, like reading the approach of a storm off a barometer, the analogy did not automatically follow. A chart of the Mississippi was not the river itself, nor could any number of years of study substitute for direct experience. How could Fernand have learned in his clerkly role what he now comprehended about steamer operation?

Even Motley, on Fernand's testimony, had overlooked what Drew had assumed the rest of his officers would take for granted: that he must be a step ahead and thinking about precautions that might aid them in the race . . .

Yet why should they? Why would any of them do so when none of the *Atchafalayas* had raced before? When he himself had never stood to win or lose a bet on any boat he was commanding?

When, moreover, he himself had been haunted night-long by the suspicion that things were going altogether too well?

This inability to guess what people around him would think or feel was Drew's longest-standing fault, and he knew it by now—or should. Had he not experienced a powerful lesson when he was driven into partnership with Barber, at first hating him, then growing to be grateful against his will and ultimately realizing that within his own narrow world the man had a code of honor—not everybody's, but at least consistent upon its own terms?

Even so . . .

Suddenly Drew chuckled, struck by a recollected passage from William Cowper. He recited it to himself, well pleased:

> "I would not enter on my list of friends
> (Though graced with polished manners and fine sense,
> Yet wanting sensibility) the man
> Who needlessly sets foot upon a worm."

Yes, that would categorize Barber very nicely.

And—speak of the devil! Here came not the man himself, but his bodyguard Jones, stiffly smart in his livery despite the intense heat. Drew sighed.

"Morning, Captain! Mr. Barber's compliments, and could you have a word with him?"

For a second Drew was tempted to say that if Barber wanted to talk to him, he could come in person. He thought better of it. He was no longer the person he had been when the last *Atchafalaya* was condemned. He was learning how to unbend.

And compromised.

Taking out his watch, he consulted it before answering. "Very well, provided it's only for a moment. I want to make my rounds and get up to the pilothouse."

Barber, plumply cheerful at the morning's news, beamed at Drew on his appearance in the cabin. He had breakfasted well, as ever, and now had returned to a position near the bar. He proposed buying the captain a drink, knowing it would be refused; that formality disposed of, he said, "Several of us would like to know whether—so long as we keep the lead—we shall make any special attempt to break further records on this trip."

"So you can make more bets?" Drew said after a pause.

Barber inclined his head.

"No, sir!" was Drew's retort. "It's enough to be well ahead of our previous time over the whole distance. The longer we run, the greater the risk of mishap. Simply to cut the time from Greenville to Helena, or Memphis to Cairo, set by fresh boats which were in the short local trades, would be pointless. Of course, I'm not saying we shan't do it! Right now the *Atchafalaya* is running as sweetly as she ever did. I was telling Dr. Cherouen so a while back."

All the time he was talking, he was acutely aware that everybody in the cabin was straining to catch his words.

"But I'd be a fool, and a bad commander, if I overstrained her now!" he concluded.

"I told my friends that would be your view, and I'm glad to have it confirmed," Barber said. "There's no use in tempting fate. The way I understand it, today's run is mostly along the portion of the river where bends succeed bends, and sheer superiority in speed is as nothing compared with skillful piloting. Am I correct?"

"You are perfectly correct!"

"Then you've set my mind at ease, and I thank you. Are you sure you won't . . . ?"—with a wave at the bar.

"I have too much at stake, remember," Drew said dryly, and with a touch of his cap to the passengers marched away.

But he had told Barber less than the whole truth.

He did indeed hope to shave every record for the rest of the trip. It merely galled him to think that gamblers would make unearned money from his efforts, and those of his pilots and engineers . . . come to that, his firemen.

Nothing as trivial as money was involved. What concerned him was the fate of Susannah. He had expected news at Greenville, perhaps even at Vicksburg. There had been none, and he trusted his agents in both those cities.

If nothing was to hand at Helena, he must send a cable of his own, requiring a reply at Memphis, copied to Cairo.

He wanted to hurry, if only to give himself insufficient time to disbelieve again in Cherouen's ability.

 "It's no damn good!" Hogan muttered under his breath at the next change of watch aboard the *Nonpareil*. "Chain wagon or not, it's no damn good!"

Both Trumbull and—more violently—Parbury, who was now almost shaking with fatigue, reacted as though they had been given an electric shock.

"What the hell do you mean?" demanded the latter.

"I mean we're running fine so long as we're running heavy! But every ounce of coal we burn, we lighten her, and . . . Oh, hell! You've felt it! You can feel it through the soles of your boots!"

After a pause Trumbull said, "I guess I have to agree. I wish I needn't. But—"

Parbury was on his feet abruptly, towering over them. "But we coaled-up at Greenville!" he exclaimed.

The pilots exchanged glances. Hogan said at length, "I know, sir. But we already burned away so much of our edge. We *got* to be heavy in a good long reach. Then we can surely overtake."

One could almost hear Parbury's brain at work as he mentally surveyed the river, not in any fashion that a mapmaker could have understood. He said, "Past Napoleon—"

"Oh, sure!" Hogan cut in. "There's a plenty of 'em! All with bends between where we lose ground!"

"Are you giving up?" Parbury demanded.

"No! 'Course not! Only—"

Trumbull cut in. "If we ran heavier beyond Napoleon, we could take advantage of such reaches as there are."

The idea was clear in an instant. There was no doubt in any of their minds that along a dead-straight course the *Nonpareil* was faster than the *Atchafalaya*.

Probably Drew would not dispute it, either. But it was a question of entering a long reach close enough behind the other boat to prove the point.

"It makes sense to me!" Parbury rasped. "Next town we pass that has a telegraph office, send the necessary message!"

"Surely Mr. Woodley—" Trumbull said, as a matter of form.

"The hell with him, and Gordon too! You're *right*, damn it! If we're no further behind by the time we reach Napoleon, the extra weight will see us quicker in the bends!"

He concluded in a chilly, bitter tone: "That is, if we don't lose as much time in the coaling as we hope to gain."

The pilots exchanged glances, Hogan's as much as to say, "Sounds like he's clutching at a straw!"

And Trumbull's: "Aren't we all? And can you think of any better idea?"

It was settled.

"Fernand!" Dorcas jumped to her feet in high excitement. "At last!"

"Sit down!" Fernand exclaimed, and eased her back into her chair with maximal solicitude. Overnight, news reports had made their way upriver faster than the racing boats, and one paper had been sent aboard at Greenville; from it he had learned that the *Nonpareil*'s first setback was due to the need to send ashore "a lady in an interesting condition," and he had absolutely no wish to find the same happening to the *Atchafalaya*.

Given the circumstances under which he had first met Dorcas, it was a very reasonable kind of apprehension . . .

"Forgive her," Eulalie smiled. "But, as I've learned, she is very devoted to you, Fernand."

"Even so, she must take great care of herself!" he declared, and glanced around for fear of being overheard. As before, however, the two women were well away from everybody else.

"Don't worry," Eulalie said. "You may rely on me for that."

"Thank you. Thank you very much." Fernand wiped his forehead with his kerchief; the weather was dreadfully hot. "In fact," he added, remembering his purpose, "I do have to make haste up to the pilothouse. But I came to assure you that if you don't mind eating somewhat later than usual, I can keep my promise to join you."

"Oh, wonderful!" Dorcas exclaimed. "Is yours a very difficult task today? Hereabouts the river winds, but it is very wide, isn't it?"

Delighted by such a perceptive question—and not a little by the chance to impress by talking shop—Fernand said, "Oh, that may be how it looks to the untrained eye, but I assure you it's not so simple! Where the river's wide, it's also

shallow. Where it's shallow it flows sluggishly—which helps a boat making upstream, naturally, but also allows the deposit of silt."

Dorcas looked at him uncertainly.

"The fine grains of earth and dust which the river picks up in its higher
reaches," Fernand amplified. "Tiny in themselves, but when you multiply them
by countless millions, they create bars and reefs and eventually towheads, that's
to say bars with trees starting to grow on them. If sufficient time passes without a
major flood, the tree roots bind the new soil and make it resistant to the water;
then the next flood has to find a fresh channel. Which is why from season to
season we always have to feel our course carefully. Last year's channel may be
silted up; last year's headland may be this year's cutoff."

"Fascinating!" Dorcas breathed. "You've spoken of such matters before, but
seeing it in reality is very different!"

Fernand preened, quite forgetting that these were the two who had completely
overlooked his brilliant coup of yesterday. Eulalie smiled a private smile. She had
been instructing Dorcas in the art of humoring a man, and the girl was proving an
apt pupil.

Beaming, Fernand caught Dorcas's hand and pressed it to his lips for a second,
then let go but continued gazing into her eyes.

"So you don't feel your prospective husband has chosen a métier beneath him?"
he suggested.

"Why should you think for a moment—?"

He cut her short. "*Maman*, have there not been times when you said I'd made
a grave mistake?"

His voice was full of unspoken apologies for their past quarrels about signs and
charms and symbols and the performance of rituals he did not believe in . . .
though it was clear that if the same subject arose again, the same things would be
said.

"As Dorcas says," murmured Eulalie, "seeing the reality makes a vast difference."

She was rather proud of the ambiguity she introduced into that polite reply,
like a conjurer distracting his audience.

"Tell us about this part of the river," Dorcas urged. "That is, if you can spare
the time."

"Well, perhaps another minute or two . . ."

Whereupon, for much longer than a minute, he expounded on today's run: the
flat and boring country they must pass through, where the Mississippi wandered
in such a random manner that sometimes a steamer would be heading literally
straight for her point of departure; the impending fate of Napoleon, a proud city
with a courthouse and a theatre and a Marine hospital and its own newspapers
and a thriving river trade, destined to disappear unless a miracle overtook it,
thanks to the ceaseless shifting of the river in its bed, for the very land it stood on
shrank, winter by winter, and it must ultimately be laid low as efficiently as by an
earthquake; the promise of their first sight of high ground since Ellis Cliffs at
Helena, and the change in the river's character up there; the indescribable con-

trast between the broad plains of the lower river country and the rough and rocky upper reaches; the menace of the Devil's Race Ground and the Grand Chain, and all the graveyards of wrecked steamboats that littered their course to St. Louis . . .

"And you," said Eulalie, "keep claiming your profession isn't dangerous!"

He was late arriving in the pilothouse for the first time in his career. Tyburn gave him a long keen look, which made him feel grateful that Drew was still making a tour of inspection.

"I figure you're pleased at how well your fiancée is getting on with your mother, hm?"

"How in the—? No, don't tell me. You can read me like the face of the water, ain't that so?" Fernand grinned. "I got her. Anything special you need to tell me?"

"Only that women can be trickier than the Mississippi. But I guess right now you don't want to hear about that."

"I sure as hell believe they're unpredictable." Fernand shook his head, making a tiny adjustment of the helm as he began to feel the current. "Any more trouble with that rudder post, by the way?"

"Josh did a perfect job on it. Rock-solid now."

But Tyburn still did not make to leave the pilothouse. He said after a pause, "Something else is eating on you."

"I guess so," Fernand sighed. "Way I hear it, the groomsman at a wedding has to be a bachelor, right?"

"It's customary," Tyburn agreed.

"Think I dare ask the captain?"

Tyburn stared for a long moment. Then he gave a snort like a safety valve blowing off.

"Why the hell not? Why should he go to his grave without being asked at least once? But I warn you of one thing."

"What?"

"You know this sister-in-law of his. They're very close. And she's sick. Don't try and fix the day until she's better. If she ever is better."

"You think it might be that bad?"

"I know it is. I've tripped with Drew since before you met him, remember, and this is the first time I've seen him trying to cut time for the sake of cutting time. And it's not just because he's bet his half of the boat against Barber."

"I thought—"

"I'm sure you did. Just take my word for it. His sister-in-law's health is preying on his mind, a fact which, if you weren't so starry-eyed about your girl, you'd have spotted of your own accord."

Tyburn stumped ponderously away. And on the stairs met Drew and exchanged greetings, while Fernand bit his lip and struggled manfully to bear in mind that however much he was involved with Dorcas—and the idea of showing off his piloting skills by running narrow chutes had crossed his mind—his first obligation must be to the boat and all the hopes and fears that rode with her.

*    *    *

To Gaston's mingled amazement and delight, there was a sort of structure about this trip that closely paralleled the form he had had in mind for his tone poem about the Mississippi. The frenzy of departure—the silence of night—rapid initial progress punctuated by coaling or meeting another vessel—now a long, adagio section that would represent a full third of the entire elapsed time, when such sounds as bird cries and the chanting of the deckhands might conveniently be allowed scope . . .

Oh, it was all falling patly into place in his head. He was covering sheet after sheet of paper with scribbled melodic lines, to the extent that he feared he must go beg more pages from the clerks. Who had, as it happened, been much more courteous to him than the other officers or even passengers. He fretted a little about the lack of attention paid him as a composer at work on a major concert piece, but he had spent enough of his life among strangers to accept that there would be periods of neglect.

If only he could force himself to pay attention to the duty laid upon him by the Grammonts! He ought to be converting the notes pouring through his head into solemn settings of the mass, or at least into slow marches and requiems.

No matter how he strove to inspire himself with melancholy, though, from the fate of the vanished or vanishing towns they passed—he had high hopes of Napoleon, in view of its name—he was unable.

Never in his entire existence, not even crossing the Atlantic, had he experienced such vivacity, such liveliness, such a sense of drive and purpose. Even though, since dawn, the smoke of the *Nonpareil* had been well astern, while other steamers and towboats and excursion boats had punctuated the progress of the *Atchafalaya*—even though he was assured that the fortunes of the race might at any moment be reversed, he still felt a thrill pass through his frame as he watched the officers, especially the captain and pilots, going about their business with the dedication of a conductor directing a great orchestra. And it would be a great one, were all the participants musicians! Gaston had made inquiries of those officers who were in a position to spend time gossiping with passengers, and had learned that altogether there were more than a hundred crew aboard, down to laundresses and barbers . . . for the sound but ironical reason that it was cheaper to hold them on the strength than let them go and risk not finding a replacement. And the same held good for the *Nonpareil*.

How like the predicament of an impresario whose programs might call for a harpist, or a second tympanist—or a performer on any of a dozen unusual instruments—when finalizing a series of concerts in order that the advertisements be sent to the printers in good time!

Not that Gaston had ever operated on that heady level . . . but he had heard about similar problems at his conservatoire in France.

And that entailed another, alarming consequence. Suppose what he composed for the funeral at St. Louis were to require musicians who did not exist!

Straining his ears, he could make out at the limit of audibility the *Nonpareil*'s orchestra, announcing her presence with all the force of her bandsmen's collective lungs. Hereabouts the river doubled back on itself yet again, so that only a headland intervened between the antagonists; besides, the country was so empty there was little noise to compete.

All of a sudden, illogically, Gaston found himself wishing he were aboard the same boat as that unschooled Mexican. He at least had nourishment to sustain him: a band, physical people to play instruments, the chance of actualizing what went through his head.

What had Gaston to make do with? There was a piano in the cabin, certainly, and last night he had ventured to sit at it for a while, but people kept pestering him to play popular tunes when all he wanted was to try over a few of his more striking inspirations in the hope of rendering them gloomier and more funereal. The same would doubtless happen today, and he had been advised, or rather warned, against attempting anything of the kind tomorrow; it would be Sunday, when pastimes such as piano playing were regarded as improper by many of the people on board, unless it was to accompany divine service . . . and even that was considered daring, inasmuch as the instrument lacked the dignity of the harmonium.

Oh, well: he must simply trust to luck. On his arrival he must at once interview all available musicians, find out what they were capable of, sit up all night if necessary preparing scores adapted to their skills, choosing the most solemn themes and incorporating, perhaps, a few well-known hymns. A woman like Mrs. Grammont was bound to have her own favorites.

He could do it all right. But the prospect reminded him of the chores he had been called on to perform at the Grand Philharmonic Hall, which he had expected to leave behind for good.

 The *Nonpareil*'s gamble on making an extra coaling stop at Napoleon was paying off in far better handling. One could almost hear a mechanical sigh of relief from the steamer as she swung into the broad reaches of the afternoon. Here she could again exploit the extra power of her high-pressure cylinders, and her cutwater threw up its fountain for the first time in far too many miles.

Still, though, there seemed little prospect of overtaking.

Parbury had left the pilothouse and resumed his favorite station near the bow. By now the passengers knew better than to pester him; his acid tongue had delivered many a rebuff since the start of the trip. But Joel decided this was too good an opportunity to miss. The old man's personal comments would perfectly round off the dispatch he planned to send ashore at Helena.

If only he had known in time about the unscheduled stop! But Matthew had been bombarding him with questions about becoming a reporter, a job for which he was plainly unqualified, and . . .

Well, it was too late to worry about that now. At all events, here was the person he needed most to talk to.

As he drew close, he realized something had changed about Parbury's appearance. The heat was stifling and the sun's glare off the water dazzled him for a moment, so that he could only make out the gaunt profile. It called to mind an Indian chief, defeated by the wiles of the white man, yet defiant to the last. Strip away the coat and pants and boots, garb him in war paint and buckskin . . . Joel nodded, deciding to use that image in his report.

But the thought of war paint explained what the change was. Instead of the gaudy silk bandanna Dorcas had given him, he had reverted to a plain black bandage.

Small wonder.

He coughed discreetly, as he came within arm's reach. In a gruff voice Parbury said, "Yes, Mr. Siskin? What is it?"

Briefly Joel was surprised, then realized a blind man must doubtless learn to recognize people's footfalls.

"I'd value your opinion about the progress of the race," he said after a pause.

"Say that in my view the *Nonpareil* has had more than her share of misfortune," Parbury snapped, and clamped his jaw tight.

But while Joel was casting about for a way to provoke further comment, he suddenly heaved a sigh and shook his head.

"Perhaps," he murmured half-inaudibly, "I'm not talking about the boat, but about myself."

Joel was prompt to pick up his cue.

"Sir, no one could deny that you've deserved better of the fates!"

"Couldn't they?" Parbury said. "Ah, but they do. Even my nearest and should-be dearest . . ."

He firmed both hands on the rail, setting his shoulders back. Now that the *Nonpareil* was rushing ahead under maximum power, the spray—which normally did no more than sprinkle this part of the deck—was thickening. Joel took care to shield his notebook.

But Parbury took pleasure in the flying droplets.

At length he said, "I don't know why I'm going to talk to you . . . Oh! Yes, I do. It's because you brought me face to face with my own past. Reminded me, in a moment of terrible adversity, that I have done things I need not be totally ashamed of . . . Speaking of being ashamed, though: I just realized I've been guilty of a sin of omission. I've taken no steps to find out how that brave black soldier is making out as an engineer."

"Well!" Joel said crisply. "I spoke earlier to Mr. Roy, and he pronounced himself completely satisfied."

"Ah, that's good news. So it can't be because of him that we're lagging. I did wonder for a little. I guess that fool Hogan's talk about the witch woman put it into my head."

Sensing a lead, Joel said, "I haven't heard Mr. Hogan mention that subject."

"I'd hope not!" Parbury snapped. "I have no time for such superstitions! No more should he!"

"But talking about a witch," Joel persisted, "was he referring to Miss Var?"

"I guess so"—reluctantly.

"In what connection?"

"If you don't know, I'm not about to tell you!"

"I have noticed that the colored crew do seem very obsequious to her."

"I reckon he saw the same and built some crazy private notion out of it. I wish she weren't on board, anyhow. It was bad when she arrived with all that talk about wrecking the boat—"

"Sir, to give her her due, she did not actually say anything of the kind. My cousin misunderstood her; he and I have done our best to clear up the point."

"Oh, a denial stands as much chance of overtaking a rumor as—as we do of running out the *Atchafalaya!*" Parbury retorted bitterly. "How far ahead is she now? Do you have field-glasses?"

"Just a telescope, sir. But I don't need it. Her smoke can be plainly seen. According to what Mr. Trumbull told me when I last spoke with him, we've halved the distance."

"Yes, I'd been told that!"—with a trace of impatience. "We'll always do better in the straight reaches, but in the bends, with insufficient cargo for stability . . . Frankly, Mr. Siskin, when I devised this boat, I never expected her to be short of cargo! I imagined we'd be turning freight away on every trip. Is it not ironical that we should have taken on fuel merely to serve as ballast?"

"May I quote that, sir?"

"You may not, and if you print it I'll deny it! I take you to be an honest reporter, unlike some, for otherwise I'd not have let you come aboard."

"I'm immensely grateful that you did!" Joel assured him, making no reference to his intended departure by rail from Memphis.

"And so you should be. But so should I be to you."

"How's that, sir?"

Parbury pondered a long while before answering. Of all the people in the world he might talk to, was not a reporter the last he ought to choose?

And yet it was a very special debt he owed this man. As he was coming aboard on Thursday evening, he had been on the verge of making a complete fool of himself. But for the intervention of this Siskin, by now he might be mocked all over the boat—hell, all over the river!—as the idiot who lost his head over a servant girl.

It was unbefitting for one who might properly be called a hero to behave in such a childish fashion.

Almost without realizing he had put thoughts into words, he said, "I guess it should be enough for any man to see his greatest dream come true. It's too much to ask for another as well."

He fell silent anew. Joel, sensing he had more to say, ventured, "Do you refer, sir, to the tragic loss of your son?"

"You're too damned smart for your own good," Parbury said, but his tone was resigned. "But—oh, the hell with you and your tricky tongue! Yes, you figured it out. Even being aboard this magnificent boat which I dreamed of for so long . . . She is magnificent, isn't she?"

"One of the finest spectacles the river has ever presented—elegant in all her lines, imposing, and as I can personally testify, a pleasure to travel on!"

"I'll tell Mr. McNab to quote you next time he drafts a card for the press," Parbury said with dry humor. "Even so, can you not imagine how much more complete my satisfaction would be were I in the company of . . . ?"

His voice tailed off. Joel suggested, "Someone near and dear to you?"

"What else? Had my son lived, by now he would have been my apprentice. Sickness stole him, and then my wife also, in any sense that a woman *is* a wife . . . I oughtn't to be talking this way."

"I shut my notebook," Joel said, suiting action to word. "I put away my pencil. But I promise you my deepest sympathy."

Parbury sighed more heavily than before. "Yes, it's a sad fate for a man to be cut off from his fellow human beings. Stranger though you are, you gave me back much courage when you spoke of my having suffered a hero's wounds."

"I gather," Joel said delicately, "that you have been disappointed by someone else dear to you . . . ?"

"Hah! Perhaps it was a blessing in disguise. But—well, was it altogether foolish of me to imagine that, lacking a wife in all but name, I might take a mistress? How many famous people in New Orleans were born of mothers in—in . . . what's that damned French word they use?"

"*En plaçage*," Joel said. And added, "In my own family there have been such connections, and many of them most respectable."

"I had such dreams," Parbury mused. "After the *Nonpareil*'s victory, I was going to set her up in a house and comfort my old age with the sound of children's laughter. I kept thinking of the story of King David and the Shulamite."

Joel was beginning to feel immensely flattered. He was prepared to bet that never in his life had Parbury spoken so openly about such personal matters. It sounded, curiously, as though he was surprised at the words emerging from his lips.

He remembered how Drew had also been unexpectedly forthcoming, and for the first time considered the possibility that he might grow reconciled to working as a newspaperman, seeing that he had the key to opening men's hearts. But one day in the far future there must also be poems, and stories, and novels. He could not print what Parbury was telling him. Yet it must not be forgotten. It must some day, somehow, be shared.

"All of which," said Parbury as though no time had passed, "explains why I was so . . . disappointed." Briskening: "Do I delay you? Do you not wish to send a dispatch ashore at Helena? I feel the boat slowing; I reckon we're about up to Island 61 and meeting the current through the Old Town cutoff."

Joel stared in frank disbelief. With all the power of two keen young eyes, he could not have been so positive about the speed and position of the steamer.

Parbury had meant to conclude their conversation, though. He would have felt churlish to try and continue; there did, however, remain one more thing to be said.

"Sir," he stated, fumbling, "I'm privileged. Today I have looked on a hero's wounds again, if of another kind. They are nothing to be ashamed of. I wish the *Nonpareil* all possible success, and you with her."

He spun on his heel and hurried away. He was afraid that if he stayed any longer he might burst into tears.

Meanwhile . . .

With enormous effort Woodley maintained a polite façade in the presence of the passengers. Inwardly, though, he was seething. As though one unscheduled stop (and damn the Gattry woman and her baby!) had not been bad enough: now his pilots (and damn Parbury for being in cahoots with them!) had visited another on him!

And yet he could not raise professional objections, for since Napoleon she had indeed been faster through the bends . . .

But even that was not sufficient! He wanted to blame somebody—find a scapegoat for the obvious fact that again and already she was light enough to escape her pilot's control now and then. "Running off" was the polite term. Of a horse one would have said "bolting."

Time after time his spirits rose, as racing straight ahead the challenger gained. Time after time they sank as, halfway through a curve, he heard the engineroom bells announce the pilot's order for half-speed.

Those pilots! Damn them too! Both already near exhaustion, both too proud to consider the engagement of specialized reliefs for the tricky upper river.

What would happen if the cables he had sent canceling their engagement had failed to get through, and Barfoot, or Smith, or Tacy, or all three, turned up as originally arranged? Would Hogan carry out his threat to ground the *Nonpareil*? How could he, without being drummed out of the Pilots' Guild?

But by the same token, how could he, Woodley, prove that he had actually sent the cables? At the very least he would wind up in a shouting match.

It was not a prospect he looked forward to. He would far rather that they overtook, and made it soon. This afternoon's run was an ideal location for a challenge. The river was very broad, and often the channel was ill-defined, so it was impossible to repeat either Drew's trick, or Fernand's. Besides, tomorrow being Sunday, a good few boats in the shorter trades were now laying up until Monday morning, their owners regarding Sabbath work as sinful.

Ahead could be discerned the high ground rising to the west of Helena, indicative of the change that would follow in the river's upper reaches. Woodley tensed. North from Island 64 the river was straighter, over a longer distance, than at any point in the previous six hundred and sixty miles.

Were his pilots going to take advantage?

Suddenly the wind against his face grew noticeably stronger, and he gave a sigh of relief. The note of the engines had quickened and the wheels were hurling great waves on either side. He resolved to visit the engineroom and urge the men to even greater efforts.

This decision was not entirely unconnected with the sight of Matthew approaching with the expression that presaged a message from his master. If Gordon wanted to see him, he could damn' well come himself!

It was no special pleasure for the captain when he discovered that Gordon was in the engineroom ahead of him, arguing with Corkran about ways to increase pressure without breaking the inspectors' seals on the safety valves, and wanted Woodley's authority to back him up.

Right now, though, nothing risky seemed warranted. In this blessedly long straight stretch, the *Nonpareil* was gaining so fast, it was like watching a clock's hands closing on noon. When the *Atchafalaya* was at Island 64, her rival was at 66. But when she reached 61, the pursuer was at 62. When she entered Horse Shoe Cutoff and struck up toward Friar's Point and the Yazoo Pass, the *Nonpareil* was making a final tremendous burst before Helena, and by the seven-hundred-mile mark one might have fired a gunshot from her bow and had it land on the *Atchafalaya*'s deck. Her band played exultantly; her passengers' cheers outdid those from the shore, where as usual it seemed the entire population of the vicinity was assembled, down to babes-in-arms.

"Five minutes!" Woodley breathed. "I swear we've cut it to five minutes, not a second more! And if you make allowance for what we lost at Baton Rouge—"

He was back in the pilothouse. Against the imminent refueling both pilots were with him. So was Gordon, on sufferance. But Parbury had chosen to remain on the foredeck and called Matthew to him; he was receiving a move-by-move description of what happened, suspicious of error ever since learning that fuel had been dropped overboard.

Glancing around with a sour expression, Trumbull said, "If we don't lose time in the actual coaling, we're okay."

"Why should we?" Gordon demanded. "Underwood and Whitworth have their men ready, don't they?"

"Drew's snatched the outer pair of flats," Hogan cut in. "So we have to make do with the pair nearer the bank, which takes us into shallower water."

"Even so—" Gordon began, but Trumbull hissed him quiet, reaching for bell ropes.

The *Atchafalaya* picked up her flats without stopping and men swarmed over her sides like bees. They stripped the coal, though, more like locusts, and a bare four minutes elapsed before they cast off the flats. The *Nonpareil*'s hands tried to match them but failed. They took six minutes.

And then exactly what had so nearly occurred before did happen. Poorly controlled by the men with sweeps who were supposed to guide them back to the wharf, the *Atchafalaya*'s flats were borne by the current directly across the *Nonpareil*'s best course . . .

"I'll cancel all bets!" Woodley raged as Trumbull had to back on both and force the flats clear with the wash from his wheels. "There are rules to be observed before a race can be called fair and square, and Drew's making a God's plenty of 'em! All bets are off!"

"Don't say that!" Gordon exclaimed. "Don't we need our winnings? I swear I do! And all's not lost. I have—" He hesitated. "I have another resource."

"Like the ones you were suggesting in the engineroom?" Woodley countered.

"More likely he wants to bribe the witch and get the evil charm taken off us!"

Trumbull snapped, with a sidelong glance at Hogan, who bridled.

"Aren't there too many strokes of bad luck—just *too many?*"

"Nothing like that!" Gordon insisted. "But you're right, Mr. Hogan. Aren't we all agreed that beginning with Mrs. Gattry's trouble we've had setbacks that made the race unequal?"

"Anybody who saw us this afternoon would have to admit it!" Woodley declared.

"Very well!" And Gordon broached an excuse for Whitworth's departure which had come to him while reading a newspaper sent aboard at Napoleon. "Can you manage without your second mate between Memphis and Cairo? That is, if we haven't already overtaken?"

Woodley and the others exchanged puzzled looks. "What for?" the captain said at length.

Smoothly Gordon explained. "According to the newspapers, some of Drew's passengers who booked for Ohio ports want to be transshipped at Cairo. Drew has cabled for a steamer called the *Luke S. Thrale* to be standing by."

"So what?" Hogan grumbled. "I know the *Thrale*. So does Colin. She's a regular in the Cairo–Louisville trade. What of it?"

"We've had delays. Why shouldn't Drew put up with one for a change? Suppose this boat that's scheduled to take off his Ohio passengers doesn't show because she's met with a convenient breakdown? It could be worth the time we need!"

Woodley was smiling already. The pilots were not so sure. It could be read in their faces that they would have preferred to win entirely on their merits and those of the *Nonpareil*.

But the chance of that was receding, and it was better to win than lose.

At length Trumbull said heavily, "Silas Crowne is master of the *Thrale*, and he likes the feel of money. Won't bother him to be late at Louisville, whether it's us who pay him, or Drew."

"I guessed you'd feel that way," Gordon said. "And I figured out—don't tell him I said so, of course!—we could manage most easily without Whitworth upstream from Memphis. I'll go find him right away and settle matters."

Flinging open the door, hastening down the stairs, he was amazed how easy it had been.

 "I'm going to stand a full watch out of here," Drew announced suddenly as the *Atchafalaya* headed away from Helena. Luckily this was too small a community for there to be as many light craft as at previous ports of call, so they had made excellent time again. The one steamer in this stretch at the moment, a hundred-and-fifty-footer in the Paducah–Vicksburg trade, was tied up at the wharf and had duly exchanged whistled salutes. Her apart, there was scarcely anything on the water, bar an old black man jug-fishing from a rowboat.

"Suits me," Tyburn said after a pause. "I'd rather stand off the *Nonpareil* when she's running light. Want me to take the next one?"

"Fernand can follow me," Drew said without looking round. "Call on you about Memphis, okay?"

"You think there might be fog tonight?"

Fog?

Fernand kept his thoughts to himself, but his mind was busy. The idea of being forced to tie up for fear of going aground, which not the most experienced pilot on the river could totally avoid when visibility was reduced to less than the distance between the pilothouse and the verge staff . . . Surely not on this of all trips! Heaven forfend!

But he had seen no threat of it. Yesterday there had been mist in treetops alongside the river; today had been clear and much too hot. Also there was a good breeze.

"Do I think there might be fog tonight?" Drew said, in a tone suggestive of asking the air rather than his human listeners. "I surely hope not! I didn't see any sign so far, and I guess we regularly meet it, if we do, a sight further north."

So much a mere passenger might have said, having made enough trips up and down the Mississippi.

"But," he continued, reaching into his pocket for a plug of tobacco, "I do recall that north of Memphis we have to negotiate Paddy's Hen and Chickens and the Devil's Race Ground."

There was a brief but electric pause. Eventually Fernand said with a gusty exhalation, "Ketch, he's right. You'll handle her better up there than I can."

Not until he finished did he realize he had for the first time called Tyburn by his privileged nickname.

The fat man stood dead still for a second. Then he gave a shrug.

"Well, if that's all that's eating on you . . . Fine by me!"

The door closed behind him.

It had been in Fernand's mind to mention, here where the next stage of the run was rigidly prescribed by the deep channel—there were no chutes past Prairie Island, or 59, or Battle Island, or at least none that any sane pilot would risk except at extreme flood levels—the possibility of Drew being best man at his wedding. He had discovered the capacity to ache with longing. Dorcas was still the most beautiful woman he had ever set eyes on. Her voice still sent quivers down his spine. Now that he knew she was carrying his child, he wanted to enfold her in his arms in a dark and private place and somehow imbue her with the confidence needed to bring it to birth. He was unable to escape recollection of that red stain on her petticoat . . .

But he couldn't until the race was over. And in the meantime he knew his mother was cultivating her acquaintance, and the constant reminder of her views, which consisted in the crucifix weighing down his pocket, troubled him.

In the last analysis he was afraid that one day his wife too might yield herself to a one-eyed conjurer.

How could he speak of such fears to anybody? Since cutting himself off from those he had known in childhood—and most of them were no loss—his whole circle of friends had been among river people. Tell them about magic, or the worship of Damballah, and they would not merely scoff; they would review their acquaintanceship with him and decide they could manage without!

He must therefore get married to Dorcas as soon as possible, and never mind what rites the ceremony was performed under. Then he would have a husband's right to separate his wife from his mother and—

All that, though, was for later. What could he do until the race was over?

Except contribute his utmost to winning it!

Therefore he cleared his throat and said, "Captain, I don't mind your saying that to Ketch. You're right. It is a hell of a difficult stretch, especially at night."

"You could run it as well as I could, damn' near," Drew answered gruffly.

"Then why—?"

"Because it *isn't* the only thing that's eating on me!"

With impeccable precision Drew laid the *Atchafalaya* into her marks past Island 59, making toward Dunn's Landing, where he would have to swing hard to starboard for Peyton and then back again, almost on a reverse course, into Walnut Bend.

He cast a glance sternward. There in clear sight, having lost a little, but only a little, during coaling, came the *Nonpareil* with both chimneys sparking.

"Next time they try and take us will likely be . . . Oh, hell! You tell me!"

"Grand Cutoff, above 54," Fernand responded promptly.

"Where else?" There was a trace of bitterness in Drew's voice. "Know something, boy—? I guess I must cure myself of calling you 'boy' now you're to be married. I apologize."

This was so unlike the usual Drew, Fernand was at a loss. He compromised. "Know what, Cap'n?"

"What. . . ? Oh, I remember what I was going to say. This takes all the pleasure out of piloting."

The only thing Fernand could think of to say was, "All?"

"Ah, you're young yet. You're not old and cynical like me. But you were with me on our last run to St. Louis. Was I the same then?"

"Well . . ." Fernand licked his lips. "You didn't stand to lose half the boat if—"

"That's nothing to do with it! Except . . . Oh, hell. I guess it is. I never liked the idea of racing in principle, and now it's happening to me I like it even less. And on top of that . . ."

"What?" Fernand advanced to where he could lean on the sill of the larboard window, keeping his back to the declining sun.

"It's gone too damned well so far!" Drew barked.

"How?" Fernand was confused. "Merely because we've trimmed a few minutes off our last run? Didn't we expect to?"

"Oh, it's not that." Drew sounded suddenly very weary. "I don't even know whether I can make clear what's on my mind. But Ketch spotted it."

"He's known you much longer than I have—"

"But not so closely. Strictly a business arrangement. Whereas you . . ." Drew's words trailed away. When he resumed he spoke more briskly.

"You mentioned my bet with Barber. It does have a lot to do with my troubles. I have this sensation as though—as though by betting on my own abilities I were tempting fate. As though," he finished in a lower tone, "something of my half-brother had entered into me."

"Oh, surely not! You're nothing like him!"

"How the devil do you know? You never met him! I spent half my life modeling myself on him!"

"My uncle Edouard told me—" Fernand began in a placatory tone.

"Oh, yes! Your uncle! But it was no substitute for meeting him! Did Edouard tell you how charming he was—how he could flatter the hide off a buffalo and save ammunition?"

"My uncle was no slouch at that himself. Was he?"

Fernand had struck the note. Drew gave a sour grin.

"Right on the nose," he said after a pause. "And you take more after him than your other kinfolk, don't you? But this feeling that I'm tempting fate—can you wonder that it's so strong, when I know I may not see my dear Susannah again in this life?"

"Is it truly so bad, her sickness?"

"It could well be. I've been expecting a cable at every stop, telling me that I've traded her life against winning the race."

"No!" Fernand straightened with a jerk. "That's ridiculous!"

"Is it? Aren't there some things which modern thinking can't explain, for all its marvels of steam engines and telegraphs and transatlantic cables? Where in there do you find room for such a reality as love?"

This time the pause was longer than ever and full of embarrassment. Drew ended it with a curt gesture.

"You don't believe there is such a thing? I thought you were in love with this girl of yours!"

"I am, sir!"

"Then why in tarnation won't you accept that this dry old stick of a steamboat master can feel something of the same kind? If I lose Susannah, half my reason for living will go with her!"

"Sir, I understand that! All the times you've talked of her, and her children, right here in this pilothouse—"

"And if I've opened my heart so much, why can't you recognize that I'm afraid for her, since everything is going far too well?"

"Because there's no rational link between—"

"Rational! What's rational about the thrill that great poetry sends down your spine? What's rational about loving somebody? If I were to be rational about what you're letting yourself in for, I'd say all kinds of cruel things, like what sort of a wife will Dorcas make for a pilot, with her background in domestic service? Don't lose your temper. I'm making the points a devil's advocate must make, and in my heart I don't believe them. I frankly envy what comes into your face when you talk of your intended. It's something that has passed me by. In spite of which!"— with sudden fierceness. "In spite of which I do know there is much of Jacob in me! Equally irrational and equally real!"

"Is there something you want me to do, sir?" Fernand ventured after reflection.

"I think there is. Call me a fool, if you like. But Jacob left his print on me, and he believed in such things. You too have talked in this pilothouse about private matters."

Fernand sensed what was coming, and his heart sank.

"How vastly making a bet on something that is dear to him may change a man," Drew muttered, more to himself. "But I do all the time feel so afraid that my best may not, unaided, be enough—just as with Susannah. My care, my support, my affection . . . Yet she is dying, and I may not bring this doctor to her in time, and even if I do he may fail in his treatment, which most other doctors scorn . . . Your mother!"

"Yes, Captain. My mother."

"She believes, and many others also believe, that she has power to affect the kind of luck that gamblers trust in."

The words emerged with terrible difficulty. Fernand could only stare at Drew, incredulous that he should have uttered them.

"You want my mother to make charms to protect the success of the boat?"

"I guess it comes down to that."

Fernand shook his head. For the moment he had no idea what to say. True, he was afraid of what Eulalie might be saying to Dorcas tête-à-tête. It would be a great advantage to have her embroiled with Drew instead. But even so . . .

"What do you expect me to do? I mean right now."

"Ask whether she will talk to me, that's all. Then go and get some rest yourself. I want you sharp as a needle when you next take the wheel!"

"The captain never needs to ask permission to speak with a passenger!"

"She is a little more than a passenger."

"Very well."

As he descended the steps from the pilothouse, Fernand's mind was in turmoil. Who would ever have thought that Drew was prey to such superstitions?

Truly he must be falling under the influence of his dead half-brother!

He wished he might consult with Tyburn, but it was out of the question. Who else might wield influence over Drew? Motley or Wills? But they would mock and probably not understand why at all costs the captain must be humored. Dutch—? No, for Drew would order him straight back to rest or work.

Maybe the doctor, Cherouen, for all his faults might prove helpful. Fernand stared around. He was on the boiler deck ahead of the cabin. Evening had brought its usual plague of mosquitoes, and everybody had moved inside, including Dorcas, Cherouen, and his mother. Cherouen was talking to them very affably at a table much closer to midships than they had previously ventured, and was standing them wine and mineral water; the bottles were on the table, and several glasses.

And Dorcas was sparkling like the water.

Just as he was about to fling open the cabin door and march in, something caught his eye. He glanced up. On the right of the lintel was a brownish trace.

He looked at it for a few heartbeats. Then he set off in search of more. He found them with no difficulty.

Ten minutes later, not having spoken to either his mother or his fiancée, he returned to the pilothouse.

At that precise juncture Drew was swinging the boat's bows past Battle Island, with the little town of Peyton dead ahead. Fernand waited until they were on course. Then he said, "About that date with my mother . . ."

Drew looked embarrassed beyond description. He said, "It was in the heat of the moment. I wish I hadn't opened my mouth."

This last in a barely heard mutter. Fernand disregarded it.

"You don't need to worry," he said, and walked forward to where he could hold out something for Drew to look at without sparing more than a fraction of his attention. It was a cockerel's foot stained with dry blood.

In the same moment he slammed the crucifix down on the forward windowsill.

"You don't need to worry," he said again. "From stem to stern this boat is littered with luck charms and magic symbols! And that son of a bitch Cherouen, who makes no secret of his contempt for anybody with a trace of black blood, is plying Dorcas and my mother with all the wine the bar can supply!"

The moment the words were out he was ashamed of them, knowing they could scarcely be true; the mineral water would be on the table at his mother's insistence, and the mix in her and Dorcas's glasses would be no stronger than what he had been given as a Sunday treat during his teens.

How, though—*how*—could they possibly be talking with Cherouen on such friendly terms? When Dorcas held him to blame for half her troubles with the Parburys, all her problems with Adèle?

"If that's worrying you," Drew said, "go sort him out! I don't want anything preying on your mind when you stand your next watch. Meantime, let me work out my problems—and that's an order!"

In the other's voice Fernand could hear the rest of the reasons why he was taking the wheel. It was serving for a penance.

As he left, he dropped the cock's foot in the cuspidor.

Fernand took several deep breaths on his way back to the cabin, wondering whether he should try and force Cherouen away, and if so, how. But by the time he entered the cabin the doctor was at Barber's table near the bar, and someone was breaking out a deck of cards. Dorcas and Eulalie were once more by themselves.

Calming but still on edge, he joined them.

"Didn't I see you talking to Dr. Cherouen when I passed by earlier on business for the captain?" He added the last few words to justify not having come before.

"He apologized to me!" Dorcas exclaimed excitedly.

"What?"

"He was very charming," Eulalie supplied. "He sent over a bottle of wine with his compliments, and before I had time to return it—which I suppose I should have done—he came himself to explain the reason. He said he had recognized Dorcas, and remembered her, and would always be sorry that pressure of work prevented him from taking on Mrs. Parbury as a patient."

Fernand stared blankly. "But," he said at length to Dorcas, "you always told me it wasn't pressure of work at all, but the fact that Parbury couldn't afford his fees. He went right ahead taking on richer people. You told me so several times!"

She looked uncomfortable. "Yes, but while he was talking I remembered that I heard about that mostly from Dr. Malone, and Dr. Cherouen says orthodox doctors are afraid of his new methods because they're so successful."

"He also inquired whether, having left Mr. Parbury, Dorcas was looking for another post, because if so, he would give her training as a nurse, with a view to taking over from this Miss Var who has deserted him in time of need." Eulalie sipped delicately from her glass; it did indeed contain, as Fernand had suspected, far more water than wine. "Of course I explained there was an understanding between you two, and he said he would send a wedding present and promised that if need be he would offer medical advice whenever you like."

"Upon his return from St. Louis, naturally," Dorcas concluded.

For a long moment Fernand sat rock-still. Then he shook his head.

"I met a few hypocrites in my life," he said bitterly, "but I guess Cherouen could give the others cards and spades. *Maman,* I always thought you had your ear to the ground among—among our people. Don't you know how Cherouen sends out Mam'zelle Josephine to pick up pretty underripe yellow girls on the pretext of training them as nurses, uses 'em, and turns 'em back on the street if they do something as inconvenient as getting pregnant?" His voice grew heated, though he kept it too low for anybody else to hear.

But partway through his diatribe Eulalie's expression had altered completely. Now she leaned forward, dismayed.

"Did you say 'Mam'zelle Josephine'?"

"That's what everybody calls the Var woman. Why?"

"How long have you known about this?"—fiercely.

"Why, since last fall, I guess," Fernand said, taken aback. "But it's common knowledge!"

"You've known who Mam'zelle Josephine is for that long and you never told me?" Eulalie's tone progressed from fierce to venomous.

"What's so special about someone being called Josephine? There must be hundreds of them in New Orleans—thousands!" By now Fernand was alarmed; he had rarely seen such intensity in his mother's face. Perhaps the last time had been coming away from Uncle Edouard's funeral. He went on hastily, "Besides, it isn't a pretty story, is it? Not the kind of thing I would ordinarily talk about in front of ladies! But what you said about Cherouen just made me mad!"

Eulalie didn't answer. She snatched the wine bottle, slopped as much as she could into her near-empty glass, picked it up, and hurried away in the direction of her stateroom. Half a dozen people glanced after her in astonishment.

Fernand was rising to follow, when Dorcas caught his hand. "No, darling—don't!" she implored. "I understand why she's so upset!"

"Do you?" His voice was grating. "What kind of nonsense has she been filling your head with?"

"It isn't nonsense!"

"I'll be the judge of that! Come on, tell me!"

Her eyes brimmed instantly with tears, but he disregarded them; they came too pat to be genuine. "Tell me!" he repeated. "For one thing you've known Cherouen longer than I have! You were on your way to his house the second time we ever met, remember? And you met his nurse, didn't you?"

"Yes, but I always thought of her as Miss Var!" Dorcas produced a handkerchief and dabbed her eyes. "I never connected her with Mam'zelle Josephine! Or I'd have said so!"

Fernand drew a deep breath. "I want the whole story," he said. "Who is this mysterious Mam'zelle, and why is my mother so upset?"

Then it came tumbling out: all the talk about charms and magic and Damballah that Eulalie had been plying Dorcas with; the story about the rival who was determined to drive down the inheritor of Athalie's secret knowledge; the evil enchantment laid on Fernand's boats to turn him into an unknowing sacrifice; the mystery Josephine wove around herself; her refusal to appear at the place appointed on St. John's Eve . . .

And Dorcas had heard of her before. Fibby had once appealed to her for medicine to relieve some condition she would not describe to Fernand; he deduced it to be a hemorrhage or vaginal discharge. It had worked.

But even Fibby did not know who Mam'zelle Josephine might be; she had dealt, as was the invariable custom, through an intermediary.

"So you see, you mustn't call it nonsense!" Dorcas wound up pleadingly. "Dr. Cherouen told us only a few minutes ago that Miss Var is aboard the *Nonpareil*, and we're still in the lead, so the danger must be fearful . . . Fernand?"

But Fernand had swiveled around in his chair. Spotting a waiter, he called the man over.

"Send Mr. Amboy to me!" he said harshly.

"Fernand, what are you going to do?"

"I'm going to show you what my mother's *nonsense* counts for! You and—and everybody!" He had been on the brink of speaking Drew's name, but he owed too much to his mentor for that. "I never paid Cherouen any mind until you told me what he'd done to you. Then I made inquiries. It didn't occur to me to mention his filthy habits because I thought you were disgusted by him. Turns out you weren't so disgusted after all, hm? But Dr. Malone will attend you and deliver our baby, not a phony like Cherouen! And my mother is just as much of a phony! If she thinks her revolting messes are as important in the running of a steamer as the skill of her pilots and officers, she has another think coming! Ah, here's Lewis!"

He rose to his feet and confronted the elderly steward.

"A little while ago I noticed some dirty marks on the lintel of that door!" He pointed toward the forward end of the cabin. "I also saw others like it on the guards, at the foot of the stairs to the boiler deck, and at the bow and stern, and in several other places. I want them cleaned off right away! And if your men don't get rid of them inside the hour, tell 'em they'll have the captain to argue with!"

His voice was loud enough to attract attention from most of the people in the cabin. He noticed one of the waiters crossing himself as the import of what he was saying sank in.

"I'm very sorry," Amboy was muttering. "I guess I've just been too busy to notice—"

Fernand cut him short.

"Skip the nonsense! Just get it done!"

And he strode away, leaving Dorcas staring after him in horror. A moment, and she too fled for the privacy of her stateroom.

This time there was nothing feigned about her tears.

 By sundown on the Saturday, much more than half the distance lay behind the racing steamers. At the two-day mark, the *Atchafalaya* had been opposite the St. Francis River, some 710 miles from the start—not quite so far in advance of her previous record as some had hoped, yet still averaging almost fifteen to the hour despite reckoning in the slow progress of two nights. Now she was making the most of what daylight remained, dismissing Battle Island and Ship Island and Walnut Bend into the past.

Her crew were jubilant; her officers a little less so. For just ahead lay the Grand Cutoff, north of Island 54, and it would not yet be dark when they entered it, and the *Nonpareil* had consistently shown she was quicker in a straight reach.

Now here she came, freshly laden with coal, into a portion of the river ideally suited for yet one more attempt to overtake.

And what tricks could Drew play this time to prevent her? Repaired though it had been, the *Atchafalaya*'s rudder post could never stand the strain of such a broadside wave as he had unleashed before. Nor was there much hope of meeting another compliant down-bound boat like the *Annie Hampton;* the imminence of Sunday had halved the traffic.

Above all, in the Grand Cutoff the channel was deep, and straight, and wide enough for two boats abreast in equal current.

Fernand had intended to obey Drew's order to get some rest. It proved impossible. He took a cup of strong coffee at the bar and went wandering around the decks and guards, his brain seething. He had known it was possible to quarrel with someone you loved—indeed his uneasy coexistence with his mother was proof of it—but he had never imagined he would reduce Dorcas to tears. Before or after marrying her!

Still in this miserable frame of mind, he came upon Walt Presslie on the larboard guard.

"Wait!" he exclaimed. "How are you?"

The other gave a sour grin, indicating how the sleeve of his shirt had been cut away to make place for bandages. There was a spot the size of his palm where serum was soaking through.

"Reckon I'll last out the race," he said after a moment.

"Is Dr. Cherouen looking after you?"

Walt spat over the side. "Well, he got a laundress to make up a fresh dressing twice a day. Don't hurt too much any more, praise be."

"I wish I'd known about that," Fernand muttered.

"Didn't hear you?" Walt countered. There was so much noise from the paddlewheel, one must speak loudly to be understood.

"Never mind!" Fernand said with a forced smile. "But what about the boat?" he went on. "Figure she'll last out as well as you?"

"Why, she's younger nor me!" Walt said. "Yes, she'll make it. Didn't see anything worse yet than the leak that wished this trouble on me. If she keeps going like she's going, we'll win handsomely. That is, unless . . ." He hesitated; Fernand prompted him.

"Unless the *Nonpareil* can draw level when she's riding low?"

Walt nodded, his expression worried. "That's what Dutch has been saying—excuse me: Mr. Fonck. Says if she comes even with us into a good long straight reach, she's bound to overtake."

"Don't you believe it!" Fernand said, clapping him on his uninjured shoulder. "Not so long as I or Mr. Tyburn or the captain hold the wheel! It's true she's very fast along the straight, but there are always means to stop another steamer overtaking. Were you ever in a race before?"

"No, never."

Feigning a confidence he did not feel, Fernand declared, "Then trust to those who were! We'll beat her yet!"

"I surely hope so." Walt drew a final breath of fresh air and moved away. "I got to get back to work—sir."

"Get along, then—and be sure to tell 'em what I just told you!"

When the junior engineer had gone, Fernand realized he was feeling quite absurdly proud of himself. One well-told, well-intentioned lie . . .

But how to turn it into solid fact?

He hesitated a second, then made for the pilothouse again. He believed what he had said earlier—that Tyburn, better than almost anybody, could see the boat through the perils above Memphis.

Yet no chain of rocks posed half the threat to their hopes that the *Nonpareil* was going to offer inside half an hour.

Fernand stole back into the pilothouse with all the uncertainty of his days as a cub. What Drew had admitted about the difference between racing and merely making a high-speed run had vividly recalled to memory something he had heard Parbury say, on one of the rare occasions he had been able to remain long enough in the parlor of the Pilots' Guild to eavesdrop on its doyen.

Parbury had declared that neither the Mississippi nor storm nor earthquake could be your enemy, but only another human being.

It had much to do, Fernand had gathered, with his experiences in the war.

Hereabouts they were coming into the most mobile portion of the river they had so far encountered. Lower down, it might be a decade, or a generation, before a new cutoff established itself, or an island rejoined the mainland, or a town was abolished. Here, and for hundreds of miles to come, a single season might suffice. Here ill-fortune was to be taken for granted. Even the proud new city of Commerce, at the upper end of Grand Cutoff, was under threat.

A century later, instead of a vital and flourishing community, there would be labels on revetments and guiding lights. Island 56 would be locked irrevocably to the mainland, and it would not be the only one . . .

Fernand was thinking about the future, and even from the narrow standpoint of his experience he was resonating to the fluctuations of the Mississippi. Much of this was already present to his subconscious—such-and-such a cutoff was deepening, such-and-such an island was silting up in the chute to its east or west side, such-and-such a towhead was going to become an island and there would be no number to spare for it, so it must acquire a name!

The prospect of becoming a father was working like a ferment in his brain. Once Dorcas had talked about the way she watched bread dough rising, spoken of something from the very air that could change and alter and make food where none was before . . .

This river could make and break land, and cities, and the hearts of men.

He crept into the pilothouse, therefore, trying to make less sound than a breeze, very much afraid of his momentary impulse to have all the magic charms scrubbed away, which his mother—and Dorcas!—believed essential to success.

And waited, wondering what on earth Drew could conjure up to frustrate the *Nonpareil*, which came thundering into the clear straight run of Grand Cutoff a scant few hundred yards behind, as ever with her band blasting on the foredeck and her whistle uttering its heart-piercing note and generally announcing her presence to the world whether or not the world gave a damn.

"Mr. Motley, you must make it clear to your captain that if he does not deliver me to St. Louis ahead of the *Nonpareil*, my guarantee of the fee for the trip may be void!"

"Mr. Motley, if we arrive at St. Louis later than the *Nonpareil*, my commission to write funeral music may be canceled!"

"Mr. Motley, if we don't beat the *Nonpareil*, I stand to lose fifty thousand!" Mr. Motley . . . Mr. Motley!

It was a sad predicament, Motley found—being the senior officer without obvious duties.

Yet it did have certain compensations. It was a pleasure to say to the people who stood to lose by their bets, "Sir, if you distrust the management of the *Atchafalaya*, why did you make such wagers on her?"

Moreover it was a way of making other people laugh—a rare achievement for someone as solemn and devoted to duty as a steamer's chief clerk—to say, to this fop who spoke with such a funny accent, "*Mossoo*, you weren't driven aboard at pistol point, were you?"

Above all, it was gratifying to say to Cherouen, "Doctor, you had your pick of every boat on the river when you left New Orleans! You selected ours, *when you might have gone by railroad!*"

And that was where the pinch was felt. Canny as his opposite number McNab, without a Scottish name, Motley was first and foremost a commercial calculator. In his view anyone wanting to reach St. Louis in a hurry from New Orleans would for years past have done better to take the cars, disregarding the risk of derailments and washouts. Year by year he had watched the passenger receipts aboard one boat after another decline, while the profits from bulk freight—clean and sweet like cotton or tobacco, or foul and reeking like smoked fish or tung oil . . . Lord preserve him from tung oil!—increased apace.

This racing was a foolishness! In his view Drew should have told Cherouen to ride the railroad and take his chances. He should have told Larzenac to do the same.

But the principle once established . . . Well, here he was at the end of his career, and it was better to be retired from a record-breaking steamer than an anonymous, forgotten one.

Maybe after this trip he would be able to afford a share in a boat of his own, free of such interference by the gambling fraternity. That one would be devoted to safe and silent cargo, free of these lunatic passengers half of whom wanted to enjoy the race and half of whom wanted to follow the *Atchafalaya*'s original course to Louisville. It might even be—heresy!—a towboat.

"Mr. Motley! What about transfers to Ohio ports?"

"We have arranged with the fast and reliable steamer *Luke S. Thrale* to transfer passengers and baggage at no extra cost to yourselves!"

But it shouldn't have been necessary. Other people, warned about the change of destination, had accepted refunds and gone to find another boat. These had said they were happy to go to St. Louis for the excitement of the race, then changed their minds.

It was no way to run a proper commercial service. It offended him, Euclid Motley, who so much admired the rigid logic of his namesake.

Therefore he took especial pleasure in telling the rudest of those who complained that they would have done better not to board a riverboat in the first place.

Some of his listeners began to talk about going ashore at Memphis and taking the rail from there. But not enough to wholly relieve his mind.

 And here it was at last: Grand Cutoff, where the river had slashed a new course from Island 53 to Island 54. It was not very long, but it was broad and knife straight.

Field glasses to his eyes, Fernand looked alternately ahead and astern. Ahead, he was hoping against hope he might spot another boat coming down, which could block the *Nonpareil* as the *Annie Hampton* had. But there was nothing to be seen before the next bend, bar some boys in a flat-bottomed skiff, waving a tattered Union flag.

And, of course, on the banks, the inevitable watchers.

Astern there was the *Nonpareil* coming on at full power. She had narrowed the gap to a quarter of a mile, and the passengers and crew of both boats were beside themselves with excitement. Now, in a plain straight reach like this, she must have the advantage. What in heaven's name could Drew pull out of the hat to baffle her now?

But he seemed remarkably calm, chewing on his quid of tobacco and now and then turning to let fly at the cuspidor. Moreover, as Fernand suddenly realized, it was not merely chewing that made his jaw move; he was once again reciting to himself.

Greatly daring, Fernand said, "Cap'n, I can't quite hear you!"

"Hmm? Oh, I guess not. Thinking aloud more than anything." Drew gave the wheel a precisely measured tug and laid the *Atchafalaya* parallel to the southwestern bank; here that was the slacker water, but it meant he was leaving the shorter course open to the faster boat, and Fernand quailed.

Before he had a chance to say anything more, however, Drew had continued: "'I returned, and saw under the sun, that the race is not to the swift!'"

Although the translation was unfamiliar, Fernand instantly recognized the quotation.

"And I'd be obliged," Drew finished, "if you would deploy those glasses and tell me whether there's anything coming down the chute from the larboard side of Council Island!"

"But—" Fernand began, and could have bitten his tongue off. For the second time this trip he had been guilty of overlooking . . . well, not the obvious; one had to be very wily and experienced to spot what Drew had worked out by reflex.

Of course!

At the head of Grand Cutoff, Island 53, Council Island, was on its way to rejoining the mainland. It had long been safer to take the Austin—eastward—side.

But on every fall of the river, particularly in winter, when so much of its flow was locked into ice and snow, debris up to and including whole tree trunks could get trapped in the narrow chute. Little by little the summer flow loosened it, but it never disappeared entirely—one of the reasons why the island would eventually cease to be an island.

Nonetheless drift was constantly breaking away, and that was what Drew was gambling on. Fernand saw the scheme now, clear as a landscape illuminated by lightning. It was perfectly legitimate to put about to avoid floating logs; when he did so, he would have to cut across into the path the *Nonpareil* was intending to take, thereby swamping her once again with the *Atchafalaya*'s wake. Already the *Nonpareil* was heading determinedly for the starboard side of the channel, and the gap was reduced to no more than twice the length of either vessel.

But everything depended on whether there truly was drift coming down from the chute. Hands shaking, Fernand refocused his glasses and was hard put to it not to shout for joy.

His voice, though, was steady as he said, "I see a pretty fair mess of trees and boughs heading our way."

"Suits me," Drew grunted. Casting a glance over his shoulder, he carried on along the same course.

"How did you know this would happen?"

"Didn't," Drew answered curtly. "Maybe your mother's charms worked the trick."

From the foredeck a sudden shout went up: "'Ware drift!"

Leaning forward, holding the wheel one-handed, Drew flung open the pilot-house window and shouted, "Thank you, Mr. Sexton! I have it in my sights!"

And still made no move to alter course.

Fernand stared in disbelief. Had he misjudged Drew's plan completely? Here came the *Nonpareil*, gaining visibly as every ounce of power was applied to her wheels. Alarmed, despondent, the *Atchafalaya's* crew and passengers alike were sharing his puzzlement. What in thunderation was the old man up to? They were almost halfway along the cutoff, the rival boat was poised to cut through on the inside of the next bend, and—

And the drift was upon them!

At which point, with all the aplomb in the world, Drew put his wheel over to larboard, not starboard after all. The *Atchafalaya's* bow sheer caught the mass of vegetation—mostly willows, with a few larger cottonwoods and what looked like a live oak mixed in with them—and it slithered away to the steamer's right side.

Where, despite the best efforts of her polemen, the suction of the *Nonpareil's* larboard wheel was ready to draw it fatefully in.

"I guess we have no more than half a fathom clearance hereabouts," Drew mused as though talking to himself. "I better not cut the bank too fine, right?"

And at long last turned on to the starboard heading Fernand had originally expected.

So doing, he created a sidewise wash—nothing as fierce as the one which had strained the rudder post, but perfectly adequate to carry the mass of drift up against the *Nonpareil* for all her attempts to evade it. Thanks to the combined racket of all four giant cylinders blasting away, it was impossible to hear the crunch and crack as a willow trunk jammed between the buckets and the paddlebox, but Fernand saw it happen and felt it as though it had been one of his own bones going snap.

A grand huzza went up from those among the *Atchafalaya's* passengers who appreciated what a feat of steersmanship they had just witnessed. Fernand was tempted to join in. He had piloted boats through this stretch of the river a score of times; he had known that the chute past 53 now and then shed such clumps of vegetation, so it was advisable to keep to the east of the channel—and he had taken such matters so much for granted, he would not have been able to guess how nearly one might shave the western side, let alone put two and two together as Drew had done and take advantage of what was normally a nuisance.

Yet the question remained: how could he have been so sure?

At the wheel the captain stretched and yawned and said, "Oh, Fernand, Fernand. . . ! I never knew till now what capacity I have to be a villain! Has she taken much harm, the *Nonpareil*?"

Fernand scanned her with his glasses. She was swinging broadside to the current, thanks to her larboard wheel having been forcibly stopped before the engineers could cut the power to the other one, so it was impossible to judge.

He contented himself by declaring, "Enough to be going on with!"

Drew was laying into the marks for the next bend, heading for Bladsoe's Landing, where they must for the uncountableth time swing back to a southerly heading. Always this infernal frustration, having to backtrack and sidle: two steps back for every three forward . . . but at least now the *Nonpareil* was guaranteed not to overtake!

Fernand could contain himself no longer. He repeated his earlier demand: "How *could* you have predicted that drift?"

"I guess Mr. Barber and his kind would say I was backing an even chance. At least half the times I've passed here in summer since the Grand Cutoff formed, that chute has shed something after being disturbed by the wake of a steamer."

"After being . . ." Fernand's jaw dropped. He snatched his glasses back to his eyes and searched the sky above the next reach, from Bladsoe's Landing to Commerce, where he had not previously looked.

And there was what he hadn't spotted, but Drew had: smoke wisps betraying another boat.

"She'll be the *Cordelia*," Drew said, and turned to spit the residue of his chaw into the cuspidor. "Clumsy tub! Too much beam for her engines! *You've* seen her!"

And indeed Fernand had, tied up at the Vicksburg wharf, but she was in the Vicksburg–St. Louis trade, and consequently he had never met her on the water; only on the *Atchafalaya*'s run with Dr. Larzenac had he worked the long Mississippi since her appearance, rather than turning off to Louisville.

Yet Drew, likewise . . .

Indescribably impressed, he said, "Sir, you were talking earlier about my mother's charms."

Shrugging, looking uncomfortable, Drew said with a trace of defiance, "Sometimes I think I'd call on the devil himself if I could win this race and be sure it was the only one I ever ran!"

"You don't have to."

"What?"

Fernand, moved by a strange impulse, put his arm around the older man's shoulders.

"Sir, there aren't any charms aboard this boat. Not any more. I set Mr. Amboy's stewards to getting rid of them. You did that on your unaided skill and judgment. And you still have more to teach me than you've told me yet. So I want you to be the best man at my wedding, and—and will you stand godfather to my firstborn?"

There was a pause while Drew made yet another of the minuscule adjustments to their course that were dictated by such tiny factors as the wake of the much-abused *Cordelia*. Shortly she must be overtaken—but that would be a trivial problem.

At last the captain said, "It's on the way?"

Fernand nodded.

"I guessed it was possible, but I wasn't sure. Yes! Yes, but on condition!"

"Anything!"

"That you get your head down, damnit! Don't go canoodling with Dorcas now, but get some rest! Because if you run us aground in the dark . . . !"

"I'm on my way! But—"

"What now?"

"But one more question, Cap'n! What would you have done if the *Cordelia* hadn't shaken loose that drift?"

"Same as before: tried washing the *Nonpareil* into the shallows."

"And risked breaking the rudder post completely? The last time was on a bend! How could you do it in a straight reach?"

"That's why I had Josh standing by with his forge alight to make more cramps. You didn't notice?"

Fernand felt himself once more victimized by blushing; he was glad he was behind Drew.

"But on reflection I doubt it would have worked," the captain finished. "So call us lucky . . . *Are* you going?"

"Right away," Fernand declared, opening the door. But he had to add one final comment as he looked toward the *Nonpareil*.

"You know, I bet they're hating us back there!"

 "That son of a bitch has the luck of the devil!" Woodley raged. "Unless he hired someone to cut loose that drift just as we were closing on him!"

Hogan said stonily, as he juggled the *Nonpareil* in mid-river using the surviving wheel and the rudder, "I said we'd been ill-wished, didn't I? There was no way he could have known a clump like that was going to float free just as he came on it. Soon's he saw it, of course, he knew what to do, and there isn't a pilot on the river could have dodged. Oh, he's the wiliest of us all! Now he's using every trick he ever learned or heard of—never mind how dirty, so long as he keeps the lead!"

The pilothouse door opened to admit Parbury, who had been down on the foredeck as usual. His face was gray with fatigue, and his expression a mask of suppressed rage. But his tongue was as acid as ever when he said, "Dermot, how in hell did you let him catch you out?"

Hogan bridled. "I did my utmost—!"

"And you didn't realize that drift was going to be bust loose by the *Cordelia's* wake?"

There was a sudden dead pause. Woodley said at length, "The *Cordelia*?"

"Oh, in heaven's name!" Parbury thumped the floor with his cane. "I have no eyes of my own! I've been watching through the eyes of that boy Matthew! And he told me about the wake ripples! He's bright, that one—could even make a pilot if he weren't so dainty and fine-mannered! Dermot, how often have you been past here and seen a steamer's wake shake off a bunch of logs from the Council Island chute?"

Hogan scowled, but forbore to reply.

"So how do you know about this *Cordelia*?" Woodley rasped.

"Don't you know your steamer schedules? What other boat could be clearing Grand Cutoff about now, except maybe a towboat failing to keep her times? Ah, to perdition with it! How much damage did we take? I heard a crack, but it sounded more like green wood than one of the buckets."

"I'll get down and find out," Woodley said hastily. But he could not forbear to check on the threshold and glance back with a snarling final gibe.

"If it takes too long to fix the trouble, don't blame me! *I* never wanted to hire a cripple as our carpenter, give him a free ride into old age!"

Parbury's face turned perfectly white and he raised his cane and would have struck out by sound alone, only the slam of the door and the clatter of Woodley's boots on the steps came even quicker than the intended blow.

Hogan said after a while, "We've been ill-wished. Short of being drunk or mad, I don't know how I could have overlooked the risk of drift along this reach. Even when I saw him put his helm over to larboard, I didn't realize he was kicking the damned stuff our way so our wheels would suck it in!"

The admission had the grudging tone of a sinner making confession, not because he planned to, but because he had bumped into a priest and been persuaded.

"You're a Catholic, aren't you?" Parbury said.

"Sure I am!"

"So's my wife!" And without further ado he followed Woodley down the stairs.

It was no secret that Hiram Burge, ever since he had been blown up with Parbury on the old *Nonpareil*, was less than prompt about responding to emergencies. Not he, therefore, but Underwood and Whitworth went bellowing to summon every available hand.

One black man, whose name Whitworth did not know, was nimbler than all the rest and was already peering through a breach in the paddlebox when the second mate arrived. He looked carefully at the tangle of broken branches and dying greenery that had jammed the wheel, then, with a ceremonial air, took from around his neck something hung to a leather thong and pitched it into the water, and after it sent an insulting gob of spittle. Then, and only then, did he yell his report.

"Bucket's okay! We just strip her and she'll roll again!"

Whereupon men swarmed down with hatchets and knives and their bare hands and ripped and slashed until the drift was cleared.

But by then the current had carried the *Nonpareil* a long way back down the Grand Cutoff, while the *Atchafalaya* was rounding Blues Point and making for Buck Island, her lead once again increased to a safe half hour.

Gordon had been looking all over the boat for Whitworth since before the cutoff; he had failed to locate him, because he was dozing in a corner of the hold. When he did need to sleep, he needed it without interruption, and anyone might find him in his stateroom.

Coming upon him now, as the wheel was finally freed from broken branches, Gordon seized his arm and drew him aside.

"You take the train at Memphis tonight!" he whispered. "Your business is to delay the *Luke S. Thrale!*"

"What?"

"The *Thrale* is to take on Drew's passengers for Louisville. You're to contact her skipper and ensure she doesn't make the rendezvous!"

And Gordon accompanied that with a monstrous wink.

Whitworth gazed up the reach, seeing how far away the smoke from the *Atchafalaya* was now. Slowly nodding, he said, "So the deal is on."

"Yes! But remember: twenty per cent if I figured out how to explain your disappearance! And I did!"

Whitworth shrugged. "If I need more, I only have to remind you I can talk about our arrangement. But the way you lay out your money, I reckon twenty per cent could keep me in comfort for a good long time. I'll go find a pine log the right size to hide you know what. I just hope they didn't burn them all."

Emerging from the heat and stench of the engineroom, Caesar rubbed his sore eyes and looked about him. In order to free the jammed willow, they had had to unship part of the paddlebox. A group of passengers watched the work, leaning over the boiler-deck rail a few feet above where he stood. Among them—

Totally without intention he called out, "Mam'zelle Josephine!"

She started, putting her hand to her mouth. An expression of terror crossed her face.

"You are mistaken!" she said after a pause. Which made Caesar absolutely certain he was not. Wanting very much indeed to view from close up this mysterious person who had created his trickenbag, he glanced around and spotted a way he might clamber onto the intact upper portion of the paddlebox. Up he went and was on a level with her, while two or three of the firemen, who had also come out on the guards for air, moved close, staring.

"It's true my name is Josephine! It's true I'm unmarried! What is it to you? You speak as though you know me, but I swear you don't!"

The other passengers leaning over the rail looked puzzled and muttered among themselves.

"No, I don't know you," Caesar said. "But I know who you are, and so do plenty of other people!"

She might simply have spun around and marched away; he would not have dared follow her to the upper deck. But she seemed transfixed, like a trapped doe confronted by a hound.

"I had a trickenbag from you! The moment I came aboard, it fell off my neck!"

A gust of excitement rose from the firemen. One of them demanded, "What yoh doin' for de *Nonpareil?*"

"I bet mah las' red cent on um!" came another accusing shout.

"So did I!" The chorus swelled as more of the firemen and deckhands appeared. Josephine began to sway, clutching the rail for support.

"Now what's all this?" inquired a high voice, and Auberon arrived, his cheeks more flushed than ever, his eyes brighter, his hands more eloquent in the air. He laid one comfortingly on Josephine's shoulder. "Don't you men have work to do? You!" He shot out his other arm. "Aren't you Caesar, whom my cousin brought aboard to replace the drunken engineer?"

Caesar gave a sour nod.

"Then get about your business! You're not the only people who've laid bets on the *Nonpareil*—just the only ones who think a race can be won with charms and incantations instead of planning and hard work!"

"If you were in the engineroom," Caesar countered, "you'd never dare say we weren't working hard!"

"What was that?" Auberon dropped his hand from Josephine's shoulder.

"You heard me!" Caesar snapped, and a cry of approval sprang from a dozen mouths. "And I didn't bet anything on the *Nonpareil* 'cause I don't have anything to bet! I just want to go home saying I was on the winning boat and not the loser!"

Auberon licked his lips, dismayed. He was unused to having blacks talk back to him. He tried another tack.

"If you want to help her along, what are you doing out here?"

"Did we run the boat foul of all that drift? And shan't we breathe sweet air while what's the pilot's fault is set to rights?"

"You're apt to start a mutiny if you go on."

The words came flat and penetrating from Josephine. Auberon glanced at her in dismay.

"Best leave such talk to the officers," she continued. "If I were one of these men, I wouldn't stand to hear a passenger talk to me that way! You're not appointed to rule the world, you know! I swear by heaven you make me ashamed of our connection! Thank God our cousin is a decent man!"

Auberon, face dark with fury, had been about to slap her the way he would have slapped any uppity female slave in the days "befohdewoh." Her concluding words checked him in mid-movement, giving her time to round on Caesar and his companions.

"I surely do not know why you think you know who I am!" she shouted. "When this here is my own half-brother and he doesn't know me! So leave me alone, will you? I'm not the Josephine you think I am!"

"But if that's so, Mam'zelle," Caesar countered, "how do you know what Josephine we're thinking of? *It ain't no white folks' business!*"

At which precise instant the roar went up: "She's coming clear!"

"Back to work!" Caesar rapped, turning to slither down the paddlebox. "If she won't help us win the race, we got to do it by ourselves!"

Auberon had been about to stride away, enraged. But Josephine's face crumpled like wet paper and she began to sob. Pity overcame anger; he took her by the arm and led her away, uttering vague words of comfort, as the *Nonpareil* began her second traverse of Grand Cutoff.

A moment later they were accosted by Joel.

"Ah, there you are! I thought for one awful minute Arthur had cornered you and staged a confrontation . . . Hey, what's wrong?"

"You didn't tell me," Auberon said, gazing venomously over Josephine's shoulder.

"Tell you what?"

"You know damned well what! You let me make a fool of myself in front of a bunch of coons!"

"I did *what*?"

"Oh, the devil with you!" Auberon put his arm around Josephine's shoulders and urged her away. "Come, my dear! It seems we have both been cast out; we should console one another."

And as they passed Joel, who was still staring blankly, he concluded, "Knowing how much I care for Louisette, were you afraid I might care equally for my other sister, whom neither she nor I had been told about?"

Joel stood there for a long while, mind in turmoil. Finally he remembered that he had another dispatch to draft, to take ashore at Memphis, that unwholesome city.

Auberon would no doubt calm down. But it would be useless reasoning with him in his present mood. He regretted having uttered that meant-to-be joke about Arthur. His cousin-in-law was drunk and snoring in a corner of the cabin. Privately he gave thanks for the fact.

For the first time he began to appreciate in his guts what it must have been like during the war for families that were divided along lines of conscience to the point where one branch—or even one brother—might take up arms against another.


As Whitworth was heading in search of a pine log he might hollow out enough to conceal explosive, he chanced upon the black man who had been first at the wheelhouse to inspect the damage.

Checking him, he said, "I saw you throw something in the river!"

For a second the other seemed inclined not to make sense of the remark; Whitworth amplified, "Took it off your neck and spat after it!"

The man's face twisted as though he had sunk his teeth in an apple and found it both sour and maggoty. He said, "Till I come on dishyear trip I b'lieved Mam'zelle Josephine was on de culluhd folks' side!"

And he was gone about his work.


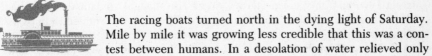 The racing boats turned north in the dying light of Saturday. Mile by mile it was growing less credible that this was a contest between humans. In a desolation of water relieved only by sparse and random settlements, transient as any on the river because hereabouts the Mississippi gnawed at dry land like a wolf gobbling the carcass of a deer, the *Atchafalaya* and the *Nonpareil* resumed their thrust-and-parry as

though they were a pair of fantastic duelists condemned by a supernatural power to strive until at least the magic number of three nights and days had worn away.

And after that would come the resolution of the fray.

 Delayed by the excitement, supper was eventually served in the *Nonpareil's* cabin. There were more staff than customers; it was curious to see this immensely long room emptier than at any time since the maiden voyage. In spite of being under far less pressure than usual, Katzmann's cooks made a dismal showing, as though a universal despondency had overtaken the food as well.

Nonetheless some people maintained the fiction of dining in a floating hotel, calling on Bates's finest wines and liquors. Urged on by Hugo and Stella, Arthur roused himself and came to table to pick at what was set before him, his face a glum mask. He spoke little, and what he did say indicated that by now he was thoroughly ashamed of himself. Alcoholic depression had him in its grip. Sometimes he talked of cabling home from Memphis; sometimes of leaving the boat there and returning to New Orleans by train.

But mostly he confined his replies to grunts and monosyllables, eating scarcely anything and drinking much wine.

A trace of animation did appear in his face when he noticed Auberon escorting Josephine up the cabin from the far end, to seat her solicitously at a nearby table for four thus far unoccupied. When his cousin looked directly at him, though, and drew back his lips in a wolfish grin, Arthur only muttered something incomprehensible and returned to his meal.

Late, the band began to play. Despite Manuel's best efforts, however, the musicians kept falling back into slow tempi and sad keys. Like so many others of the crew, they had bet heavily on the *Nonpareil's* victory, and with every setback it seemed more and more probable that the race was effectively lost.

If the faster boat could not overtake the slower in a dead-straight cutoff, what hope was left?

Entering when most of the other passengers had reached their dessert course, Joel glanced about him and responded—reluctantly—to a beckoning invitation from Auberon.

Dropping into a chair placed for him by an attentive waiter, he said, "I thought you and I weren't on speaking terms! And I also thought you should be in bed!"

"I have tried to tell him," Josephine sighed. "But he's determined to burn both ends of his candle."

"And why not?" Auberon spread his hands. "I didn't want everybody to know, old fellow! That's what I chiefly hold against Arthur—apart from his foul treatment of Loose: the fact that he made my affliction public!" He gulped a mouthful from the glass before him; it held champagne.

Leaning forward, he went on confidentially, "Also I'm sorry I snapped at you.

You're as good a friend as I have in the world, and—and . . . well, introducing me at long last to Josephine was a welcome act, even if you did leave me to find out who she was. And even if she thinks that I ought instantly to turn into a whining invalid, assailed with stinks and smokes from carbolic balls and God knows what else, fed on a diet only fit for babies, in spite of all that, I'm obliged! You won't do the same, will you? You won't say that this damned illness has to make me old before my time? I want to use what time I have left—use it to the full!"

That final outburst might have been overheard by half the people present, except that—in a vain effort to rouse their spirits—Manuel whipped his band into a fortissimo. Joel suddenly felt his eyes fill with tears.

What would he choose to do if he knew tuberculosis had doomed him to an early death? It made all kinds of sense, Auberon's attitude. Had not tens of thousands of men and boys died in the war without being given a chance to say yea or nay? It seemed nobler to make one's own decision instead of leaving it either to some anonymous general or to the insidious progress of a disease.

He was ill-accustomed to speaking of such deep matters; while he was still hesitating over a reply, Auberon had to stifle a cough in his napkin. Though he folded it rapidly after wiping his mouth, Joel caught sight of a trace of red on the cloth. He turned to Josephine.

"When Arthur hit him, it caused real harm, didn't it?"

She gave a sober nod. "If he would behave like a normal patient, I'd have him in bed right now. Only rest can help him."

A speculative look came and went on Auberon's face. But he commented lightly, "Why, you'd not deprive me of my chance to go out in a blaze of glory, would you? When we reach St. Louis, if Arthur is still aboard, I'll take pleasure in making my sister a widow . . . or letting Arthur turn me off, if he can. Wouldn't it make the greatest climax to your series of dispatches if you could report that duel on the foredeck which we were talking about?"

"It might," Joel said curtly as the waiter delivered to him a charred steak and some dismal-looking vegetables. "But I wouldn't be here to report it."

"What?" Auberon tensed.

"I'm leaving this tub at Memphis. Going on by rail to Cairo. After what happened this evening, I don't believe we have a snowball's chance in Hades."

And thrust a wedge of meat into his mouth and chewed busily.

After a long pause Auberon said, "Then I might as well fix that duel and hope to come off worse."

Joel checked in mid-movement. Having swallowed, he said, "You can't be serious!"

"Why not? Every cent I have is backing the *Nonpareil*. I looked forward to spending my enormous profits during my last few years on earth."

"You just cling to that idea of *years!*" Josephine said in a tone of sharp reproach.

"That's right!" Joel agreed. "Besides, a lot of bets are going to be declared void because of what Drew's been getting up to. The tricks he's pulled can't be called fair, can they?"

"The world is under no obligation to be fair to anyone," Auberon said, and with a sudden shift of mood gave precisely the kind of boyish grin he had exploited during childhood to escape a scolding. "Yes, I guess I can take the cheap way out if I must, though I hate the notion . . . Change the subject! I propose a toast!"

Reaching for his glass again, he raised it high.

"May my newly discovered sister become a more beloved member of our family than my loathsome brother-in-law!"

Whereupon he completely ruined the effect by adding, "Well, when I go, someone will have to take my place in your hearts, because I'm bound to be sorely missed, *n'est-ce pas?*"

Out on deck with the rest of the black crew, Caesar was finally tucking into his much belated supper. He had no idea what kind of meal the white engineers were being given, but if there was one advantage this job had over any other he had ever taken on, it was in the quality of the food, so he doubted whether what they were getting could be half as good as this: black-eyed peas stewed with plenty of onions and great chunks of ham floating in the pot liquor, fresh cornbread, and as much hot sauce as you wanted to spice it with.

Even if he had to put up with a dozen of Steeples's kind, he decided as he wiped round his pan with the last of the bread, it could be worth it to feel his belly so well and warmly lined twice every day.

Maybe this was what he had been assured by Mam'zelle Josephine's expensive trickenbag. Maybe this kind of thing represented the limit of her power, while machinery, including steamboats, was beyond her reach, because it was white folks' business. Maybe she should be forgiven for her failure.

Then one of his bad teeth started to give off twinges, and he went in search of water to rinse his mouth, and before he had the chance to think more deeply about Mam'zelle Josephine, fatigue overcame him and he tumbled on a handy pile of sacks and fell asleep, aware up to the very last moment of wakefulness how soon he would be routed out to help manhandle the reversing gear at Memphis.

There were some, though, who had no stomach for any kind of food or drink tonight, and among them was Cato Woodley. What profit or pleasure was there in being captain of the finest new boat on the Mississippi if an older boat held the horns for every trade you could mention?

Damn Parbury! How could he have been so stupid as to imagine that a blind man could design a functional steamboat? Damn Gordon too! What had possessed him to put his trust in a foreigner with a sweet tongue and a ready line of credit? When the Marocain bank foreclosed on its loans at the end of this voyage, good-bye *Nonpareil*!

And good-bye to his proud title of captain! There wasn't the faintest hope the new owners would retain him in that office!

Not that the *Nonpareil* was running badly. Through dusk and into dark she was once more racing fleet-foot up the water, her engines regular as a healthy heart-beat. It was just that so far she had never been in a position to let her pilots show off what she could really do. Drew, Tyburn and Lamenthe had made sure of that!

Or was it entirely due to them? Was it not just as much that through their stupid pride the pilots of the *Nonpareil* had let themselves become overtired, so that they failed to see what traps were being set for them? Hadn't Hogan admitted that he'd forgotten about the risk of drift breaking away from the chute at the head of Grand Cutoff and tried to blame his shortcomings on the woman Var?

Why the hell shouldn't a racing boat call on the finest pilots, the greatest specialists? It would be fairer than most of what Drew had done, to start with!

Short of putting Hogan and Trumbull under arrest, though, how could he stop them carrying out their threat to run deliberately aground if their authority was challenged?

So all that was left was Gordon's notion of sending Whitworth ahead by rail to Cairo (and why Whitworth?) to catch Captain Crowne and ensure that when the *Atchafalaya* reached there, she would be delayed in transshipping her passengers for Ohio ports.

How could it possibly work? Unless the gap were once again to be reduced to a few hundred yards, Drew would simply call on any and all other means to rid himself of this unwanted burden, and if none came to hand, he would carry right on up the Mississippi and let the passengers complain till they were hoarse. Short of a court of law, there would be no redress.

So musing, Woodley glanced along the deck, and there by heaven were exactly the people he was thinking about: Gordon and Whitworth, speaking in whispers. He made for them.

"Someone's coming!"

The deck throbbed; birds complained at being disturbed on their way to nest; the light level was at the indeterminate point where neither day vision nor night vision could claim mastery. From the cabin came the strains of Manuel's attempt at cheerful music, which nobody applauded. A whole menagerie of intractable animals beset the *Nonpareil*'s course toward Norfolk and Grayson and ultimately Memphis: Buck Island, Cat Island, Cow Island . . .

"It's the captain," Whitworth said after a long enough pause to make out details. With the onset of night he was once more in his element. The prospect of what he had pledged himself to do had terrified him; later, exalted him. Now it felt like a sheer necessity.

A deckhand passed, checking to make sure no lamp was in a position to reflect light into the pilothouse; at the same time shades were being drawn across the cabin clerestory. They waited until the man had gone by. Then Gordon said bluffly, "Not so promising, eh?"

"You know damned well," Woodley answered with a scowl. "You, Whitworth! Do you honestly think this harebrained scheme to bribe the master of the *Thrale* will work?"

There was a dead pause.

"If it doesn't," Gordon rumbled at last, "we do have another resource."

Whitworth caught his arm, but Gordon shook him off.

"Hell, if nobody else agrees with us, *he* must! Cato, how do you like the idea of the *Atchafalaya* bursting one of her boilers?"

Woodley stared at the other's face, seeking for hidden meaning, but darkness and the mass of beard combined to hide it. He said, "What's going to bring that about—a charm from Miss Var?"

"Not exactly," Gordon said, and continued, smoothly lying. "There's an old railwayman's trick, which I learned when I was a boy. I taught Harry here the way of it. That's the real reason I want him to go to Cairo ahead of us. I don't think the *Thrale* being delayed will force Drew to slow down or wait over, any more than you do. But now we have a second string to our bow."

"What is it?" Woodley demanded. "If it involves him getting on board, how's he going to manage that?"

"I'll go out with the coal flats," Whitworth said.

"And get into the engineroom without being challenged? And what happens to you when the boiler blows? I think you're spinning a yarn!"

Gordon and the mate exchanged glances.

"We're going to have to tell him," the former said heavily. "Cato, how much do you stand to lose if we don't beat the *Atchafalaya*? It's no secret that the Marocains will foreclose on my loan and take my share of the boat; I imagine they'll dismiss you and appoint another captain, right?"

"It's about the best I can look forward to," Woodley muttered, and produced a cigar from which he savagely bit off the end.

"That leaves us no alternative, then. If the *Atchafalaya* is still leading when we hit Cairo, there will be something in the fuel she takes aboard guaranteed to blow one of her boilers."

Gordon concluded sweetly, "Like I told you—an old railwayman's trick!"

Woodley's lips were suddenly dry. He licked them nervously. "Sink her?" he suggested.

"Not unless she's built like a raft of eggshells. Crack the iron, blow the fire door open if it's shut, flood the boiler room with scalding water, generally create chaos. Enough to delay her but not sink her."

Whitworth started to say something, then thought better of it and gave a shrug. He had one of his own panatelas between his teeth; he struck a light, offering it first to the captain.

Drawing the first smoke, the latter said, "Traceable?"

"Nope!" Whitworth declared. "Besides, did you never hear of something being left in the coal by mistake—a blasting charge that didn't go off?"

"That's what it's going to look like?"

"Pretty well."

"How the hell do you hide it inside a lump of coal?"

Once more Gordon and Whitworth glanced at one another; some of Woodley's questions were too acute for comfort.

"Not coal. A pine log," Whitworth explained.

"Hollowed out and filled with powder, hm? No, don't tell me. I prefer not to know." Woodley drew hard on his cigar at the risk of making himself cough. He was staring into the dark, where sky and land now merged so closely, only an expert eye could tell them apart.

"So we send you ashore at Memphis," he resumed. "Just one trouble with that idea. The reporter told me he wants to be landed there too."

Gordon said at once, "Then we ought to persuade Mr. Siskin that it will be to his advantage to stay with us. I'll get to work on him as soon as he finishes at table. He's with his cousin and the colored woman—I saw them just now."

"What's the connection between them? I mean Moyne and Miss Var?" Woodley demanded.

"She's one of his father's by-blows," Gordon replied. "I'm surprised to hear you ask."

"Why the hell didn't you tell me when he brought her aboard with all that folderol about our being in danger?"

"Keep your temper! I found out so easily, I thought it must be public knowledge!"

"Maybe she wasn't entirely wrong," Whitworth said, and sucked his cigar into a brilliant red eye against the night. "She just got her boats mixed up."

Gordon gave a harsh laugh, but Woodley was in no mood to be amused. He said, "Look, if Siskin does wind up on the same train—"

"I got sick relatives at Cairo," Whitworth interrupted. "Besides, Mr. Gordon just said we don't have to worry."

"I did hope so much," Woodley said slowly, "that we'd win this race fair and square and aboveboard."

"After what Drew's been doing," Whitworth snapped, "playing fair means losing, don't it?"

Woodley straightened and snapped his fingers.

"Got it! *This* is why you're going ashore at Memphis! I wasn't able to cancel my engagement of Zeke Barfoot, who was supposed to join us there!"

"But if you sent a cable—" Gordon began.

"I don't know it got through, do I? Your orders are to find him on the wharf and tell him the deal's off, but he'll get something for his trouble anyhow to keep that damned Guild of theirs sweet! Except you *won't* find him—will you?"

A slow grin spread over Whitworth's face. "*I* get it! Because I'm delayed, I miss rejoining the boat and have to overtake her at Cairo!"

"It's thin," Gordon worried.

"But the wharf will be crowded, and it'll be easy to think I spotted Barfoot only it wasn't him after all!" Whitworth crowed. "Cap'n, you have your wits about you, that's for sure!"

"And we won't send a yawl out for Siskin," Woodley amplified. "Tell him if he wants to go ashore, he has to run across the coal flats, same as you! And we won't give him a nigger to carry his baggage, either!"

"What will that do to our reputation as a fast and courteous boat?" Gordon objected.

"Talking like a riverman now, aren't you?" Woodley said with barely veiled contempt. "Sounds like you've been reading the cards we put in the papers! So one reporter gets smudged with coal dust! What's that against the certainty that the *Atchafalaya* will burst a boiler trying to beat us, and we'll be in St. Louis not just hours ahead of Drew, but days?"

"If he makes it at all," Whitworth said, and added hastily, "On this trip, I mean. She's by far the older boat, remember; they may think it worth scrapping her for the sake of the insurance and the engines."

"I hope that's all you mean," Woodley said, and turned to Gordon.

"Go find Siskin and get him good and drunk and change his mind!"

\*    \*    \*

Norfolk and Grayson, President's Island and Fort Pickering—they receded one by one behind the *Nonpareil*. But at every mile's mark, the *Atchafalaya* had been there first.

Drew's eyes were sore and his belly was grumbling and his mouth was full of the foul taste due to chewing too much tobacco. He knew he must eat at least a snack, though he had no appetite, and then seek his bed, though he expected to get little rest, because he would be needed at Memphis.

Wearily, therefore, he ordered a sandwich to be brought to the clerks' office beside the cabin, where Gaston had been persuaded to sit down at the piano and tinkle out a succession of dance tunes. Indefatigable, Barber had led out Dorcas and was guiding her steps through an unfamiliar measure, while Cherouen looked on glowering from the bar, and Eulalie sat smiling—almost smirking—as though at private memories. Below, in the engineroom, everything was proceeding as it should. Walt Presslie, whose scalded shoulder was giving cause for concern despite his insistence that it scarcely hurt any more, was on duty with Ealing during this easy stretch; Fonck and O'Dowd would take over when Memphis neared. Diamond had inspected the hog chains and the strained rudder post and pronounced them sound enough to last till dawn without attention, while Gross had reported all in order among the off-duty hands.

Altogether this was far too like a Saturday night on any regular run for Drew's contentment. He was still haunted by the same feeling that had driven him to make that embarrassing appeal to Fernand—which, by a mercy, the latter had disposed of tactfully. Nonetheless, Hubris, as he had learned from reading poetry, was always followed by Nemesis. Or, putting it in plain English, "Pride goes before a fall"—*vide* the Book of Proverbs.

But where the hell was the flaw that would cause the fall?

There ahead were—at last—the lights of Memphis. Fernand could not remember when he had suffered through so miserable a watch. The contrast with the exhilaration he had felt at dawn was indescribable. It seemed to him that about the only mistake he hadn't made was the archetypal one of the legendary cub left alone at the wheel by night for the first time, who sounded the backing bell with six fathoms under the hull. But he was convinced he had swung absurdly wide, because it was dark, through bends that by day he could have shaved closer than a barber's razor. And this was not simply because, earlier in the trip, he had felt a snag rap at the hull, demanding to be let in; no harm had come of that minute error.

No, it was because every now and again he had found his attention wandering, and always to the same subject.

Dorcas.

From below drifted the strains of the piano and intermittent laughter. Was one of the people laughing his fiancée? Occasionally his ears, keen to single out noise in the darkness, identified the hoarse bullfrog boom of Cherouen or the baritone-turning-into-titter of Barber. But, as he realized with dismay, he had not heard Dorcas's laugh often enough to recognize it.

When a hush fell, though, what his perception instantly flew to was the over-riding sound of the *Nonpareil,* and every time she appeared louder.

Who was at her helm now—was it Hogan, was it Trumbull? He had lost count. On a regular run one could tell, for the pilot of another boat would match his opposite number, watch for watch. This trip was different. Now he was reduced to listening for clues in the wind, hunting for tricks of style that might not be conclusive, for after so long working in double harness, one might have copied from the other.

Fernand strove to guess and always failed.

The sole conviction which obsessed him was that during these early hours of night the other pilot was gaining on him because he was not worrying about marriage and fatherhood.

Therefore it was with astonishment that Fernand heard his captain say, as he opened the pilothouse door and in the same instant snapped shut the case of his watch with a crisp little click, "You held the lead very tidily, boy! Now go see to your womenfolk, because I got her!"

Fernand swallowed hard, feeling the blood rush to his cheeks as usual, glad of the dark.

"Are you all right, sir?" he contrived to say in a fair approximation of his normal tone.

"I'm fine," Drew answered. "Caught myself a nap, and I'll be back in bed when we clear Memphis and Ketch takes over. Go find Dorcas—she's in the cabin, where they're holding a whale of a shindig! None of 'em want to turn in before we finish coaling!"

As Fernand turned to go, he added quickly, "One more thing!"—producing a sheet of paper from his jacket.

"Yes, sir?"

"There ought to be a cable waiting for me. If not, have this one sent. Here's the money."

Taking the message, Fernand said, "It would be about your sister-in-law."

"Yes. What else?"

"I'll give it to Tom Chalker," Fernand promised. "It'll be his gang that mans the shoreward side."

Chalker was mustering his men on the main deck. Fernand gave him the message, the money, and his instructions; if a cable did come for Drew, it would be brought by someone leaping nimbly over the coal flats; and if it didn't, then . . .

So at last he was free to seek out Dorcas before going to bed. He needed his rest; he was so tense, his very bones were aching.

He must fight fatigue a little longer, though. Must!

\*    \*    \*

Entering the cabin was like walking into another world. The air was heavy with tobacco smoke; the tables were laden with bottles and glasses; earlier, card and dice games had been in progress, but they were abandoned now, and everybody was concentrating on the dancing . . . such as it was.

At the piano Gaston was pounding out tunes that, with weariness, came progressively closer and closer to the simple heavy beat and four-square harmonies of the black streetbands he so despised.

Fernand, on the edge of collapse, was overwhelmed by the paradox of what he saw and heard.

He had taken, say, a hundred paces since leaving the pilothouse. What was that on dry land? The boat's own length! Yet here he was in a passable imitation of the grand ballroom at the Limousin. The same musician who had directed the band on that fateful Mardi Gras night was providing the musical accompaniment. The same man who had permitted his all-night rendezvous with Dorcas—thereby standing, in a way Drew could not, godfather to the eventual child—was turning to him, bowing, ceding his partner, demanding that her betrothed take over.

How could Fernand resist? Here she was, eyes wide and sparkling, panting a little from her exertions—and they had never danced before!

Nor had he even imagined that she knew how.

But her tutors tonight must have been apt, for she was even able to punctuate their circuit of the floor with a kiss: at least a brushing of his cheek with her lips as she rose on tiptoe.

There was applause. Cherouen did not join in, leaning on the bar, one hand busy with a cigar and the other with his glass. But the *hell* with him!

Then, just as Fernand was about to relax into what was happening—just as he was about to start enjoying the accident, which seemed in a fair way to curing his earlier dispute with Dorcas, avoiding words—there came an all-too-familiar noise.

The *Nonpareil* had sounded her unique and famous whistle, and it might have been right here in the cabin.

Against orders, one of the waiters flipped up the shade over a glass door at the rear of the cabin.

And there she was! Her chimneys reaching skyward, she loomed against the deceptive darkness of the night, magnified by contrast.

For a heartbeat Fernand was overcome with horror. Then, with indescribable relief, he found himself able to translate the gap between the racing vessels into terms of time, and realized that a good fifteen minutes must separate them, due to be extended—if all went well—by the *Atchafalaya*'s faster coaling. He had been looking at the *Nonpareil*, framed by the window, as though at a picture cast on a screen by a magic lantern. An optical illusion had made her seem infinitely closer than she really was: that, plus the extraordinary penetrating power of her whistle.

Yet . . . And here his pilot's instincts overcame him. Still, the argument in his head ran, she must have made up half the time she had lost during her tangle with the drift in Grand Cutoff. Which implied . . .

"You poor dear," his mother said close to his ear. "You're worn out!"

Which was so transparently true, he made no objection when they urged him to his stateroom.

He wished with all his heart he might keep Dorcas with him, but even as he removed the second of his boots, sleep claimed him.

His last thought was that Dorcas must have forgiven him for making her cry.

 The *Nonpareil* was closing on the *Atchafalaya*—no doubt of it! Because the final run toward Memphis was clear and straight, Trumbull had been able to make up an amazing amount of distance during the last half hour. He had come full ahead from President's Island when Fernand was obliged to slow for the bend at Fort Pickering, and risked the shortest course across that bend. By the time Drew took over, the *Nonpareil* was already getting up speed, as her rival slowed to poise herself for coaling she was pelting onward with all the power at her command and visibly gaining!

Risking everything on his now long-standing acquaintance with this mettlesome yet awkward vessel, Trumbull had done by night what few pilots would have dared by day: run that final bend on memory alone, trusting the bowsheer to sweep aside and, if worse came to worst, overturn the small boats putting out from shore. Anything, so long as they didn't foul the wheels!

He'd made it, anyway. And small thanks he would get for it, what with a captain who was not a pilot, a pilot called captain who could never be one, and an owner who cared mostly about money. What a trio! In his heart he was inclined to refer to them as an unholy trinity . . .

At least Hogan would realize what he had done when he next came on watch. But there was one final chore to be undertaken: linking up with the coal flats. And there was a hell of a racket on the decks below. He reached for the rope that summoned the texas tender, an order to be relayed boiling in his mind like low water in an overstressed boiler. He could not spare attention for any distraction, even music, even song.

Manuel knew no more about the actual operation of a steamboat than your average passenger; however, in common with everybody else aboard, he had sensed the excitement as the *Nonpareil* doubled her nighttime speed in this final rush toward Memphis. It became pointless to continue playing in the cabin; everybody was going out on deck, even those who were so tired or drink-sodden they could scarcely take two breaths without a yawn.

Besides, the pounding of the engines was imposing its own rhythm, fiercer than any the band could muster.

And suddenly a rhyme popped into his head.

"The *Nonpareil*," he muttered half aloud, "is on her way!"

Picking up their instruments to adjourn to the deck, where they expected as usual to play while making this brief stopover, a couple of the musicians overheard: two of the blackest, who took second place whether it was in regard to seating on the bandstand or the right to choose new positions on deck.

They grinned at him, and one of them patted juba on his bass fiddle's back with one hand as he lifted it with the other: thump, thump! His colleague imitated him with a triplet cross-rhythm on his banjo's vellum.

"The *Nonpareil* [slap-slap] is on her way [slap-slap]!"

A passing waiter copied the beat with a pair of spoons, and it acquired a complex percussive obbligato. A tender clearing up the mess along the bar thought for a moment, then dropped sugar lumps into a tall glass and began to rattle it back and forth, improvising a *shac-shac*.

Manuel beamed. This was the kind of music he loved most—invented on the spur of the moment, identified with the event it commemorated, capable of being recalled for a generation afterward and bringing memories with it.

"The *Nonpareil* is on her way!" he shouted, brandishing his baton as he followed the rest of the musicians to the foredeck.

Within less than a minute the slogan had seized the imagination of everybody in earshot. The passengers stamped or clapped to its insistent beat; the musicians, one by one, picked up the tune—less than a melody, more than a phrase—and started to embroider it with trills and variations; the deckhands shouted it with defiant approval.

For a brief span it seemed that the entire steamer was pervaded by the conviction of ultimate victory. Manuel danced with excitement, trying to keep the beat going as the engines slowed abreast of the crowded waterfront.

But already the *Atchafalaya* was beyond the northern city limits, her welldrilled men transferring fuel at an unmatchable rate. And suddenly the message came down from the Olympian height of the pilothouse:

"Mas' Trumbull he say quiet here! Quiet!"

Little by little the singers and shouters and stampers grew silent. Manuel drooped his head and let his baton fall to his side.

To the devil with them all, these cold-blooded *gringos*!

"But, Mr. Siskin, haven't I explained why it could be disastrous were you to publish the fact that you went to Cairo by train?"

Over and over, Gordon had been harping on the same refrain, plying Joel the while with far more beer, wine, and other liquor than he wanted; the table between them was crowded with half-empty bottles. If ever they were to invent the promised device that could repeat human speech, Joel reflected sourly, then it would sound pretty much like Gordon.

He had escaped long enough to finish the report he must cable to New Orleans tonight, but then it had started anew. Abruptly he could put up with it no longer.

With infinite gratitude he saw Auberon approaching, with Josephine hovering beside him like a guardian angel. He was in full fig, but obviously weak, for he was walking with a slim black cane.

Joel leaped to his feet.

"I must take leave of my cousin before I quit the boat!" he exclaimed. "And I have one final thing to say to you, Mr. Gordon!"

By Gordon's side, as ever, Matthew sat; he flinched as in expectation of a blow.

"I'm a reporter! It's my duty to record the facts! And the fact is that thus far the *Nonpareil* has not overtaken the *Atchafalaya!*"

He thrust back his chair and stalked away.

"Obe, old fellow—"

Auberon interrupted him, eyes feverishly searching the cabin. "Has that bastard Arthur decided to go ashore?" he demanded.

"I haven't seen him lately! Nor Hugo or Stella. Are they on deck?"

"*I* don't know! Night air is said to be unhealthy, so my *beloved* half-sister won't let me go and see!"

Pleadingly Josephine put in, "But this is a yellow-fever area!"

Privately Joel felt that any such miasma must already be present in the cabin; what difference could it make whether you breathed the air this or that side of drawn curtains? Mosquitoes penetrated them, after all. Waiters and tenders with a spare moment went around swatting the little devils; nonetheless by morning everybody on board was likely to have been bitten.

He compromised.

"Whether he's going ashore or not, I certainly am! I wish I could stay, but it's going to be better for me to report from the leading boat, isn't it?"

"You're so certain we'll be beaten?"

"If you're in the lead when you get to Cairo, I'll rejoin you!"

"I guess you may do so anyhow," Auberon murmured. "Persuading Drew to let you come aboard may not be as easy as you think . . . But all that aside!" He made a sweeping gesture. "At least let me see you ashore, and we'll get in touch next week in New Orleans, okay?"

He frowned down Josephine's objections, and she yielded.

But as soon as they emerged on deck, Joel was confronted by Anthony Crossall.

"Mr. Siskin! Compliments of Mr. Woodley, and we ain't putting out no stage here!"

The steamer was slowing now as she approached the shore; there was cheering and shouting and people were waving torches.

"What?"

"I said no stage!" Anthony was sweating gallons, obviously unhappy at being deputed for this task.

"But—" Joel checked in mid-word and reached a decision. "Then I'll go ashore with one of the coal flats! And, come to think of it, what are you doing about that extra pilot you were scheduled to collect at Memphis?"

"Mr. Woodley canceled his engagement, sir!"

"I'll do it that way anyhow!" Joel snapped, and spun on his heel. "But tell McNab from me this is no advertisement for the service provided on his boat!"

"Good man!" exclaimed Auberon, and tucked his stick under his arm so he could applaud.

Now the monstrous length of the *Nonpareil* was lining up parallel to the wharf; now the coal flats were being readied by black and white roustabouts; and on shore, isolable because of their serious demeanor—the majority of watchers were jumping up and down with excitement—surely there were some people waiting, or hoping, to come on board?

Anxious, Josephine said, "My dear, you shouldn't stay out here—"

Auberon cut her short.

"I told you, damn it! If I have so little time left, I'm going to cram it to the full!"

"That you, Matthew?"

It was indeed, and he was coming to dread Parbury's harsh tones as much as Gordon's.

But it was too late to dodge. Matthew sighed.

What he heard next, however, was not what he had anticipated.

"Bear a message for me, boy!" Parbury ordered. "Go to the pilothouse and tell Mr. Trumbull that nobody in my time has better run the bend at Island 47—neither by night nor day!" he added with a nudge in Matthew's ribs.

"But passengers aren't allowed in the pilothouse!" Matthew objected; it was one of the first things he had learned about riverboats. Even when Gordon went up there in his guise of part owner, he insisted on his amanuensis remaining outside . . . more, Matthew suspected, to show he was *au fait* with river etiquette than because the pilot would truly have complained.

"Anybody bound on my business may go anywhere aboard this boat!" Parbury rasped. "Go tell him what I said! You recollect it?"

"Y–yes, sir!"

"Then hurry up! And come back at once—you'll find me on the foredeck. I want you to tell me how the coaling goes."

Matthew felt intolerably conspicuous as he mounted the stairs to the pilothouse. The light from the city made a tremendous contrast with the utter darkness of an hour ago. He set his hand to the door, wondering whether he should knock; decided against it, remembering that pilots disliked sudden distraction; and stepped inside as noiselessly as he could.

There was Trumbull, sour-faced, turning the enormous wheel with one casual hand while peering through the forward windows and gauging his approach with impeccable precision. Scant seconds before the *Nonpareil* made contact with her flats, he had signaled stop engines with a quick tug on the proper bell rope, and the whole vast mass of the steamer touched as lightly as a kiss. Instantly chaos boiled over as men rushed to load the coal.

He ordered half ahead and took out a handkerchief to wipe his face. In the same moment he grew aware of Matthew.

"What the hell are you doing here?" he barked.

As best he could, Matthew stammered out his message, his eyes darting hither and yon. How in half a lifetime could anybody make sense of this tangle of controls? Yet, by the same token, how could anything as basic as a mess of ropes and speaking tubes direct so complex and so huge a vessel?

"I'll be damned," Trumbull said softly. "The old devil did notice after all. I thought he hadn't, for he's stayed below these past two hours, despite saying he would spend all his waking time up here . . . Tell him thanks from me! And tell him something else too."

He hesitated, framing the proper words.

"Tell him it's a tragedy he can't stand his watches, for if he could, we'd have the horns!"

Unnerved by the emotion in Trumbull's voice, Matthew hastened away, regretting that he now had no excuse to evade Parbury's command to return.

Given that the *Nonpareil* was coming to a stop to pick up her coal flats instead of nosing into a cable strung between them like the *Atchafalaya*, lack of a landing stage was a small handicap to anyone as determined as Joel, even if it meant running the gauntlet of men intent on shifting coal the other way. The shoreward flat would be almost on a level with the steamer's main deck; he need not even jump.

Clutching his carpetbag, he advanced along the deck.

Just at the point where he was heading for, however, he spotted a kind of ambush. There were Woodley and Gordon talking to Whitworth . . . who was carrying what looked remarkably like the brother of Joel's bag. *Not* what one would imagine a mate on duty required at this juncture.

And as soon as the lines were secured, there went Whitworth at a dead run, while Woodley and Gordon closed on Joel, blocking his way.

All of this was blurred: a montage of black shadows cast by scores of yellow lamps, their flames stirred to flickering by a sluggish breeze.

Joel was about to push the captain and the financier bodily aside, when Hogan (where had he sprung from? But his faint Irish brogue was unmistakable) shouted, "Mary and all the saints! I swear that's Zeke Barfoot! Captain, we warned you not to—"

"Shut your trap!" Woodley blasted, even as Joel registered the presence of a tall, well-dressed man who had stepped onto the coal flat the instant Whitworth passed him, a fraction before the steamer got under way anew. "You! Siskin! Where do you think you're going?"

"Leaving your boat because she's beaten!" Joel retorted, and lifted his bag like a shield in front of his chest.

"You stay with us and tell your readers the truth—that we've been unfairly beaten by tricks no decent pilot would descend to!"

"So what's wrong with your pilots, that they can't give as good as they get?"

That struck home. Both Hogan and Woodley bunched their fists just as the smartly dressed newcomer leaped nimbly on the deck, avoiding the flow of fuel with the ease of much practice. And—

"Don't do that to my cousin, Mr. Woodley!"

The words were delivered in a level, almost sleepy tone, but they were accompanied by the slash of a thin black shadow across Woodley's face. It was cast by Auberon's cane—except it was no longer just a cane. Now from its lower tip jutted a seven-inch blade of wicked steel, released by a twist of its silver cap.

"How do you like my Parisian sword stick, Jewel?" Auberon inquired. "I'd been hoping to test it on Arthur, but he's in a stupor, and it's unsporting to attack a drunken fool. Never mind, I'll find a reason to square accounts before we reach St. Louis! In the meantime, you get aboard that barge before they cast it off!"

The coal was more than half shifted by now; the rumble was continuous, and the men had converted Manuel's slogan into a chant:

> "The *Non-* [hanh] *-pareil* [hanh!]
> Is *on* [hanh] her *way* [hanh!]"

It was amazing how the singing added to the speed of the work.

And here was the man whom Hogan had recognized as Barfoot, and Woodley's attention was enough distracted for him to be saying loudly, "But I sent you a cable canceling—"

"I got it," Barfoot interrupted. "I wish I may never offend any of my colleagues, like Dermot here! But what's to stop me looking at the river?"

His invocation of the immemorial custom whereby any out-of-work pilot might travel free of charge on any steamboat was so disarming that Hogan broke out laughing. This gave Joel his chance to board the empty coal flat moments before it was cast loose.

To the accompaniment of thunderous cheering, the *Nonpareil* swung back into midstream.

But what lingered in Joel's mind was the sight of Whitworth bound—obviously—on some important errand.

What could it be?

As the lights of Memphis dwindled astern, the passengers on both boats began to turn in, not purely through fatigue, but also because only someone who had the feeling of the Mississippi in his, or maybe her, very bloodstream could be interested in what happened when land, sky and water mingled into one impenetrable backdrop.

Nonetheless, this was one of the most amazing portions of the river. A keen and experienced eye, even at night, might read the clues that hinted at another revision of its course, due next year—the year after—perhaps not for another decade. But it would come, given a great enough flood. And then all this series of twists and bends, as the deep channel switched back and forth around Beef Island and Greenock and Brandywine Point, Paddy's Hen and Chickens—those treacherous islands which could smash a hull as thoroughly as a hammer smashes an egg—and ultimately the Devil's Race Ground: all, all would have to be forgotten by the pilots with as much diligence as they had spent on learning it. For it was as grave an error for a steersman to follow an out-of-date map in his mind as not to have memorized it in the first place.

Beyond that they would come to the Chickasaw Bluffs, and Pecan Point, and Fulton at the mouth of the Hatchee, and the tragic site of Fort Pillow, scene of the massacre that stained the name of Nathan Bedford Forrest more deeply even than his founding of the Ku Klux Klan. Sunrise, with luck, would find them rounding the notorious Plum Point en route to Osceola and Ashport.

It was a clear night: no sign of fog or even mist.

But it was a run to tax a pilot by day, let alone in the dark, and every now and again they passed other steamers that had made the safe decision to tie up.

Tossing restlessly, breaking the surface of sleep every time the boat's engines changed their note in spite of his weariness, Fernand was wakeful long enough to feel infinitely glad that Tyburn had the wheel, even though it meant he himself might have to run Plum Point, the grandest challenge, before dawn.

Was this the way for an aspiring bridegroom to behave to his intended?

Dorcas was grieving to Eulalie about the fact that during the voyage Fernand had granted her so little of his time, and devoted part of that to angering both herself and his mother.

Who rewarded her with smooth reassurance.

"You must bear with him, my dear. Men are all like that, each in his own way. Women take second place in their lives, not to themselves—though there are some of that stamp—but to what they conceive of as their duty. And I would not wish any girl to marry a man who had no notion of what was proper, and behooving, and honorable."

Dorcas cried, "It's not honorable for a man to care most about the—?"

She had been going to say "mother of his child." Eulalie read her mind.

"He will be a fine husband and a devoted father!"

"You can say that, when he ordered the waiters to wash away the charms you took such trouble over?"

"They served their purpose, did they not?" said Eulalie with composure. "Are we not still in the lead, despite the rush the *Nonpareil* made? Come, dear; it's bad for you to be up late in your condition. Fernand will still be the same in the morning."

"But not, let us hope and pray, in a year from now."

The point sank in. Slowly Dorcas began to smile. When Eulalie rose from her chair, she docilely imitated her and followed her down the cabin as the *Atchafalaya* plowed her course into the darkness.

At midnight she was exactly eight hundred miles from New Orleans and, in spite of all, had averaged comfortably over fourteen and a half miles for every hour of the race.

 By way of celebrating his triumph—for that challenge with the swordstick had excited him—Auberon insisted on remaining in the cabin until the *Nonpareil* was well clear of Memphis. He made barbed remarks about Arthur, knowing that although Stella was safe abed, Hugo Spring was being adequately taunted, and more than once the

atmosphere grew electric as he hit on a specially venomous turn of phrase. At the piano Manuel did his best to lighten the mood until he was exhausted. Eventually he quit, and Katzmann and Bates instructed their waiters and tenders to clear up and start laying tables for breakfast.

"You'll burn yourself out!" Josephine mourned softly.

"And what's it to you if I do?" Auberon countered, tossing back a final drink, aware it was probably the one too many but not caring. "You didn't even know I existed until this trip began, any more than I knew about . . . Or did you?"

She was very tired, and confused from the effect of the ill-judged medication she had taken recently. She said without thinking, "Do you mean did I know my father had another family, by marriage?"

"Yes!" He leaned toward her.

"Of course I knew. So did your cousin. And your sister. They must have found out, I guess, when you were still in Europe. How long were you away—four years, wasn't it? Was it after you left that you realized you were sick?"

"I think it's monstrous!" Auberon exclaimed, and rapped the floor with his stick. Waiters glanced around, hoping this was not the signal to bring more liquor; reassured, they kept on clearing the other tables.

"What's monstrous?"

"Keeping you a secret from us! I'd have wanted to know about you long ago! Has life been fair to you?"

She hesitated, then made the frank admission: "No! It's been cruel!"

"Even though you wound up working for one of the most famous doctors in the whole of the South—drunken ass that he turns out to be?"

"He was kind to me once. At the beginning. Later . . ." She shook her head. "No, it's gone badly for me."

"Are you telling me the truth?" He gazed at her keenly. "Caesar made a claim about you, and it's confirmed by the way all the coons act aboard this boat." He sat bolt upright. "That's it! I've seen it in Europe, but never in America before. They treat you like *royalty*!"

She made a dismissive gesture, but he caught her hand.

"It must be true, then!"

"I don't know what you mean!"

"Don't be elusive! From my gambling friends I've heard about Mam'zelle Josephine who makes charms and trickenbags! You magicked Caesar aboard Parbury's boat, even though he was the man who sank the last *Nonpareil*! If you can do that, can't you magic away my damnable sickness?"

"Oh, what nonsense!" she burst out, as though just this moment realizing how many people were still in the cabin, even though they were servants. "You shouldn't be here, talking like this! You're unwell!"

"Very well, then," he said with gravity, gathering his stick and hat. "Nurse, be so good as to escort me to my stateroom and prescribe your next treatment! I shall need your guidance, since I see they're putting out the lights!"

And coughed.

She was not quite quick enough to snatch up a napkin; a trace of blood spewed onto his hand as he clasped it over his mouth. The sound was brief, but nonetheless horrible. All eyes turned their way.

"I must put you to bed," Josephine sighed. "Your brother-in-law did terrible harm when he hit you!"

"Ours," Auberon murmured with the first breath available when the spasm was over.

"What?"

"*Our* brother-in-law! And I never thought Louisette could hate our parents so much . . . 'Give me that!"

A waiter was passing with a laden tray; on it was a half-empty bottle of brandy, which he seized.

"Never mind about the cost—I'll pay!" he declared, and rose. Unwaveringly he headed toward his stateroom, with Josephine trailing resignedly in his wake.

The moment the door closed, he poured drinks for them both, apparently again in total control.

"You never really knew our family, did you?" he said. "Even if you knew about us! Sit down, sit down! Your being here is justified: my nurse, my sister! Do you have anyone to go to bed to? And don't pretend to be coy! I recall from my childhood what the devotees of your god were getting up to in the days of Marie Laveau and Doctor John, and often when I was in Europe I wished I could be with them! Often, I mean, after I started coughing blood."

His tone, though emphatic, was soft, almost conversational.

"There's a power in there somewhere, isn't there? I don't know what, but I can see the effects. Your Dr. Cherouen, for instance—isn't he ruled as much by lust as by his medical principles?"

She had, with distaste, obeyed his instruction to sit, and perched on the edge of the bed.

"I don't know what you mean!" she claimed, as before.

"You're not afraid of me, for if you were, you'd already be the far side of that door!"

"What?"

She was utterly bewildered. She sipped from the glass he thrust into her hand as though believing it might offer consolation, while he kicked off his boots and removed his jacket and cravat and loosened his shirt before drinking.

"Oh, God, I wish I'd known of you before all this came about!" he muttered as he dropped on the bed beside her. "I wish even more *you'd* known!"

"What? *What?*"

"About my father, so insulted by the way he was cheated when that damned Scotsman got away with millions on a timber fraud—what am I saying? My father? Yours too!"

He threw his arm around her as she took another swig of the brandy, hoping for release, or surcease, or something . . .

"And to think I had kinfolk who danced in Congo Square all the time I was fretting over what I'd done with Loose and Jewel!"

"What? What?"

"Oh!" He gave a shrug, not removing his arm. "Playing the games any children play. The ones their parents would be angry over . . . But Loose was so sweet, sister or no! We called her that because we'd heard the term 'loose women'!"

He capped the admission with a frantic gulp of brandy and resumed: "But for you it has a purpose, doesn't it? Not just a game, but—something else."

There followed a long pause during which Josephine's mind was in turmoil.

At last she said, sensing disaster yet convinced it could not stem from any words she spoke, "Yes, when we dance in the ancient way, we come together to make a climax. Have you not seen it? Many—many *white* people watch from shadow."

"I thought *you* had never been at Congo Square!"

"How did you know?" Her question was almost a cry; she transformed it into a whisper, remembering how flimsy the partitions were.

"I inquired there for a certain Mam'zelle Josephine," he said. "I was told she made good charms for gamblers. I was losing more than I could reasonably expect to have covered by my—our father."

*Our father!*

That phrase clicked in Josephine's head like the cam of a steamboat's piston meshing into place.

"And here I am doing it again! Joel's right! The *Nonpareil* is bound to lose even if she is the newer boat! And I stand to lose a fortune! I don't mind dying young, but I hate like hell the notion that I may die young and poor! Josephine, Josephine, even if you can't charm me healthy, can't you charm me rich?"

That, though, barely registered on her awareness. The brandy combined with the aftereffects of the arsenic and the drugs she had been taking, and together they conspired to breach all her defenses, like the conflux of three tributary rivers overwhelming the levees puny human beings erected against the might of the Mississippi. Of a sudden she found herself telling him about the rituals she had been obliged to undergo to acquire her powers—powers of which Cherouen understood nothing, obsessed as he was by mechanical devices . . . as though a machine could match the complexity of a person!

In turn he described to her the misery of being his parents' son, the designated heir to the Moyne millions—depleted, surely, but at worst by half, so that ninety-nine out of any hundred would still feel jealous of the luxury he was alleged to be enjoying.

And envied her, who, regardless of what humiliations were forced on her, had at least a profit to look forward to: a thing earned by her efforts, or at least her submission. What could he *earn*? Moreover, what could he look forward to, save a premature and loathsome death?

The *Nonpareil*, still trailing despite the finest efforts of her crew, rumbled onward through the dark. It came to Josephine as in a vision that some great magic was required. She had forgotten her loyalty to Cherouen; let him find someone else to do his pandering! Here was flesh of her flesh, bone of her bone!

If a little disguised behind the pale skin she herself had hoped to wear one day . . .

Therefore when Auberon progressed from leaning his cheek against hers to supping at her lips with his, and when he started to unhook her bodice so he could lick and fondle her full breasts, and when he put aside his glass and blew out the lamp, too impatient to turn its wick down, too eager to bear her backward on the bed beneath him, she thought of this consummation as a ritual that would defend the *Nonpareil* and herself, and him, against all the perils of the Mississippi.

She had never before taken pleasure in the body of a man. But now she moaned and sighed and laughed and sometimes wept, as though all her life she had been waiting for this moment, and now it was upon her she had no faintest notion how to profit by it.

Lightening as her coal burned away, the *Nonpareil* "took another spell of running off" around three A.M., and embarrassed Hogan terribly by grounding on a bar of soft mud. By the time he had backed and freed her, he had once again lost precious miles of distance.

Parbury was snoring on the bench, oblivious.

But almost as gaunt, and almost as tall, and equally spectral in the darkness, Zeke Barfoot stood beside the starboard window.

His unspoken reproachfulness was colored by what he might have said, had he a mind to:

"I've served with Lamenthe and seen how well Drew taught him!"

Hogan wished with all his heart the other hadn't been there. But it was contrary to all the customs of the river to drive him out.

For the first time he began to wonder whether Woodley, when he spoke of hiring relief pilots, might not have had a valid point after all.

 The Memphis depot of the Louisville and Nashville Railroad was one of the godforsakenest places Joel had ever been in. It was not so much that at this dead hour after midnight most of the people moving back and forth under the great echoing barnlike roof had no destinations to go to, but were pretending to be on business in the hope of eluding the agents long enough to find a quiet corner and lie down for a rest—waifs of the war, many of them, even after the lapse of five years. Nor was it that the air stank even worse than a riverboat's engineroom, with the fumes of burning wood and coal and hot oil cross-mated with the stink of penned livestock: pigs, cattle, sheep, waiting restlessly for the next stage of their journey to slaughter.

No, it was chiefly because here the machines were seen to lord it over the humans. Like tamed elephants whose training might yet break at a careless gesture, beyond an iron grille—which at a richer city would have been ornamental, with curves and flourishes, but here was strictly functional—there loomed the new monsters of the machine age: the common 4-4-0 locomotives with their enormous cowcatchers and their boilers sloping up just ahead of the cab as though they were the muscular hindquarters of the mechanical beast, and in addition a couple of the new ten-wheelers, the 4-6-0's which could haul even more cars faster, farther, and cheaper.

No wonder they needed to be caged.

Feeling insecure on hard dry land, even after less than two and a half days on water, and realizing for the first time what was meant by the phrase "sea legs," Joel gazed at them for a long minute. He had grown up with riverboats; he admired their luxury, their comfort, their ornamentation—in a word, their style.

They had the grace of swans.

Whereas these trains were more like boa constrictors snaking across the landscape on a rigid path, immune from the vagaries of that sleek brown god the Mississippi. No doubt of it: they had the last of the riverboats in their toils, and in a generation probably only the towboats would be left, which could move immense bulk very slowly but on a highway which cost nothing to build—though, given what the Corps of Engineers were planning, much to maintain.

A wistful echo of what Gordon had said aboard the *Plott* crossed his mind, and he decided he too did not much look forward to the time when the continent would be constricted in a corset of iron rails.

But there was no time for such musings. He had a schedule to check, a ticket to buy, and a cable to send, and he must hurry.

At least the clocks here showed, to within a minute or so, the same time as his watch, which he had set in New Orleans. As soon as the river began to slant northwest again, above Cairo, there would be problems far worse than those experienced in the lower river, where the westing on one day's run would be roughly canceled out, as evidenced here, by the easting on the next.

It was not until, ticket safely in his pocket, he was waiting in the line at the cable office—busy, even at this hour, with people sending messages public and private—that Joel spotted a familiar figure on the concourse.

Whitworth.

Then it was his turn, and he passed over his dispatch, prepared to explain any unfamiliar symbols or abbreviations. But he was used to writing full copy, rather than an outline for the subeditor, and it went clear past the final DNQ—the do-not-quote where he explained his intention of trying to board the *Atchafalaya*—with no hesitations. The clerk scribbled a note of the charge and nodded him toward the cashier, reaching for the next text to be transmitted.

Considerably the poorer, he left the cable office and set about tracking down Whitworth, for he did want to know the reason for his presence.

It smelt of news.

Growing light-headed with fatigue, Anthony entered his so-called "stateroom"; in fact it was half of one, partitioned off by a wall little thicker than paper. He welcomed what privacy the division allowed, though, for next door was Whitworth's room, and he

was forever turning in or getting up at unlikely hours, a task he seemed incapable of doing quietly.

Tonight at least, Anthony reasoned, he could sleep without interruptions.

But the moment the light from the lamp he held fell on his bed, he realized it was half covered with clean washing: not his.

Oh, that damned fool of a laundress! This was far from the first time she had left Whitworth's belongings in here! He had informed Mr. Bates the steward, to no avail.

He gathered up the clothes with determination. Not that Whitworth could have immediate need of them, having got himself stranded at Memphis. But if, on his return, he found the stuff dumped all anyhow he might complain, and make more impression on the silly woman than a mere mud clerk.

He marched out, arms loaded, and kicked open the next door. Having thrown the clothes on their owner's bed, he hesitated.

Perhaps it wasn't politic to offend Mr. Whitworth. He could easily find out that it wasn't the laundress but his neighbor who had made such a mess of his belongings . . .

Sighing, Anthony looked around for a place to put them tidily away.

His eye fell on a valise under the bed, and he started. He had never seen that before. Setting by the oil lamp he had brought in, he knelt down with a sense of great daring and tried the lock. It yielded.

And inside . . .

Rows of brown cylinders. With one missing from the top layer. And some documents.

He picked one up and held it to the lamp, and a thrill of dismay ran through him. It was a printed prospectus headed with the name of a firm called Geo. M. Mowbray, in North Adams, Massachusetts.

And it boasted about the finest available explosives for earth moving and mining.

A moment later he was rushing out the door again, the document clutched tight in his hand. He checked in mid-stride as he remembered the lamp—and what a fool, to leave a burning lamp unattended right next to the stuff!

Then he hurried off in search of the captain.

 The train from Memphis to Milan was due to leave shortly before one A.M.: a string of mixed freight and passenger cars timed to connect with a long-distance train on the Mobile and Ohio, which had left New Orleans long after the *Atchafalaya* and *Nonpareil*, yet would overtake them in the course of tomorrow and, if schedules were met, allow Joel to be on the Cairo wharfboat when the *Atchafalaya* picked up her coal flats next evening. Truly the epoch of the steamboat was at its end!

Joel had failed to locate Whitworth when it came time to board the train, but he lingered in the certainty that he must turn up sooner or later.

And there he was! Wasn't he?

No, this man, in much the same clothing and carrying much the same kind of bag, lacked that characteristic moustache—

Yet, he smiled reflexively on showing his ticket, displaying the same gap in his lower teeth. That was Whitworth.

"Hello!" Joel said, with a cordiality he didn't feel. "What are you doing here?"

Whitworth's features froze for a second; then he gave a shrug and scrambled up the steps into the rearmost passenger car.

"Got to overtake the *Nonpareil*," he said over his shoulder as he preceded Joel in search of usable seats. The depredations of the war had been mostly rectified on trains like this one; however, bored passengers could not be prevented from carving initials on the woodwork or slashing cushions in the first class. Moreover some cars stank in testimony to people who could not wait until the next stop before relieving themselves.

Whitworth seemed hopeful of losing Joel; the latter was equally determined to keep up with him. When they came upon four vacant seats together, they stopped, and Whitworth sighed as he dropped his bag.

"Goddamned fool, that Woodley! Know what he did? Cabled extra pilots to come and join us on the way, then changed his mind and didn't make sure it was in good enough time, so when we hit Memphis he told me to run ashore and find the first of 'em—man called Barfoot—and tell him the deal was off. Wasn't looking forward to it, I can testify! Heard he's a mean devil if he's crossed! But he warn't there!"

Shrug.

"So here I am stranded and got to catch up the best I can. I guess you're doing pretty much the same, hm? Hoping to be at Cairo before the *Nonpareil*? Even before the *Atchafalaya*?"

Stony-faced, Joel disregarded that last red herring and made himself as comfortable as might be. There was a pause full of shouting baggage loaders and the occasional hiss of steam, while he pondered whether to tell Whitworth he had passed within arm's length of Barfoot.

But it seemed probable he already knew.

At any rate he was muttering, "I'm going to catch hell from Woodley when he sees me again, and it ain't fair!"

"Oh, forget it," Joel suggested. "At least it means we'll be company for each other on this leg of the trip. Though I guess I ought to say I tend to sleep more than you do."

"Who told you I don't sleep much?" Whitworth demanded, settling down in his seat but keeping one hand protectively on the bag beside him. A black porter came by, carrying the heavy bags of another, portly, puffing passenger, and hoped to set down his load here; meeting scowls, he proceeded reluctantly into the next car.

"I'm a reporter, remember? Keep my eyes and ears open!" Joel gave a disarming smile. "Say, I took the precaution of picking up a bottle of whiskey before I quit the boat."

"I don't care much for hard liquor," Whitworth muttered.

"Ah, come on! It's going to be a long dull trip! I guess you could bend your rule a little? Or sit and watch me put the lot away, if you like!" Joel opened his bag to reveal the bottle and, as the porter came by in the other direction, caught his sleeve.

"Say, I guess you could find us a pitcher of water and a couple of glasses, couldn't you?" In the same moment making a tip vanish into the ready brown hand—he hoped Abner Graves would keep his word to underwrite his expenses.

The porter, instantly beaming, nodded and disappeared.

"Now tell me, Whitworth," Joel continued affably, "what's your honest opinion about the race so far? Don't you think I did the wise thing, quitting the *Nonpareil*? I mean, she seems to be fairly beaten by the *Atchafalaya* all the way so far—"

"Fairly?" Whitworth interrupted with a grimace. "What you call fair ain't what *I* call fair!"

He touched his pockets in search of one of his usual panatelas and discovered he had none there. Snapping open his bag, he extracted a fresh box and offered it to Joel. The latter shook his head but produced matches.

"How do you mean?" he inquired.

And was treated to a positive rodomontade about proper practice during a race on the river, such that a listener might have taken Whitworth for a steamboat master instead of a lowly second mate at an advancing age.

Joel paid little attention. The diatribe had all the hallmarks of a rehearsed defense, like the excuse offered earlier about coming ashore to locate Barfoot.

Moreover he was preoccupied by another question.

Why in the world, he was wondering when the train departed amid a chug-chug-chuggachugga-chugging as the locomotive's drive wheels slipped and gripped—why in the *world* should Whitworth have chosen to pack a bag if he believed he was only going as far as the wharf?

And why, if he *did* pack one, should he have wasted space on a log of pinewood?

Which had clearly been visible when the bag was opened.

 When she fell asleep, Josephine felt that a spell had been worked: as though a channel in her mind had been opened which even the power of the god had not previously created. To her amazement the tingling in her fingers and toes had receded, not yet replaced by normal sensation, but at least reduced to bearable levels, while the hateful dark patches that had appeared on her skin were not so loathsome as to dismay her incredible, unexpected lover.

It was beyond doubt a very great magic, of a kind she had heard about and never conceived of as entering her own existence.

Conceived . . . ?

The word had more than one meaning. But if that followed, such a child would be equipped to work miracles.

Later, however, she began to dream of being beaten with short brown sticks. A hideous sense of danger overcame her and she awoke moaning and at once began to draw on her clothes.

Rising sleepily on one elbow, Auberon whispered, "What are you doing? There's nothing to be afraid of! You've been tending me as a nurse! You've given the kindest possible therapy to a dying man!"

"Danger!" she hissed between clenched teeth.

"What?" He sat upright now.

"I know you and Joel were mocking me when you brought me on board," she asserted in a low but intense voice. "But I do have power, and something was coming through to me—something about a brown stick! And terrible danger!"

Around a yawn Auberon tried to chuckle. He said, "According to the modern theorists in Europe, if you dream of a brown stick . . . Well, you should have been dreaming of a pink one!"

She scowled at him, fastening her bodice with awkward rapidity.

Suddenly from above came a stamping of feet and a shout: "Captain! Captain, wake up!"

She gave a triumphant toss of her head and rushed out of the stateroom. Cursing, still more than half drunk, Auberon struggled into pants and slippers and a silk robe, and hastened after.

The noise was coming from the texas, where the officers' quarters were located. He followed her up the narrow stairs as much by feel as by sight, and found they were not the only ones to have been aroused by Anthony, who stood at the captain's door, thumping on it with one hand, brandishing a paper in the other. McNab and Iliff had both appeared in underwear, obviously furious, and a bewildered black man, presumably the texas tender, was hovering in the background.

Woodley's door opened and he thrust his head out, barking, "What the hell do you want?"

"Captain, I found this in Mr. Whitworth's room! Read it! And a caseful of explosives—rows of little brown tubes! Only not *full*! One is missing!"

By now Auberon had caught up to Josephine. She reached behind her and closed her fingers over his so tightly it was painful. He paid no attention. This was unbelievable! Had she truly seen it in a vision?

Or had she private knowledge more conventionally come by?

"Oh, I know all about that!" Woodley declared unexpectedly.

"What?" Not only Anthony, but Iliff and McNab and Auberon, took half a step closer.

"Yeah!" Woodley rubbed his eyes and yawned. "Seems he's planning to quit the river after this trip, go into business on his own account with an agency for some company back east." With sudden fierceness he added, "Think I'd have let explosives aboard my boat without being sure they were safe? This is none of your regular nitro that goes off at a touch—this is so stable you can hit it with a hammer!"

"But why is one of the tubes missing?" Anthony persisted.

"Hell, how should I know? Maybe he gave it to a prospective customer as a sample! We could ask him if the damned fool hadn't walked straight past Barfoot without recognizing him and got stranded at Memphis! Now get the hell to sleep and leave me be!"

But as he was turning to shut his door, his eye fell on Auberon, standing behind Josephine on a lower step but tall enough to look over her shoulder.

More wakeful now, in better control of himself, he said resignedly, "Mr. Moyne, what can I do for you?"

Auberon's mind raced. His drunkenness was fading; he was coming to be astonished at what he had done, and a little fearful. Making the boldest face he could, he improvised.

"Miss Var was kindly watching by me! You know about my—my illness!"

All eyes were on him, suspiciously: perhaps only because he and Josephine were passengers and this was officer country.

"Hearing the boy shout"—a nod at Anthony—"she thought of an emergency and came to see if she could help. I followed. I felt it unwise for a woman to go about the boat by herself at this hour."

"When she came aboard, she was talking about danger and a stick!"

The unexpected interruption came from Hogan, out of shadow. There was a minimum of light here: one lamp glimmered at the end of the corridor; a trace more came from McNab's room, reflected on its door.

"Hogan!" Woodley bristled. "You're supposed to be on watch!"

"Oh, you beat me, Cap'n," Hogan said wearily. "Zeke has the wheel."

"You entrusted my boat to him without orders?" Woodley burst out.

"I thought they were your orders!" Hogan retorted. "Colin and I believed we could win the race without help. The sin of pride, I guess. Shame though it be to confess it, I was damned glad we had a relief pilot to hand over to! So I hollered 'nuff. But I couldn't stop thinking about what this here woman said—"

"Miss Var!" Auberon supplied quickly.

"Yeah. Her. Cap'n, what makes you so sure that missing stick of explosive isn't still on board? After all, it's Whitworth's, and he's jumped ship!"

Though the noise of the boat was still as loud as ever, this disturbance was enough to awaken more and more people, much as the emergency of Louisette had done. Matthew came up the stairs with a message from Gordon; the texas tender heard the bell that summoned him, and vanished, and returned in less than a minute with a message from Parbury, who was in the pilothouse with Barfoot, wanting to know what the hell was going on.

At the eye of the instant hurricane Anthony stood and trembled, feeling that, had he known what he was about, he would rather have risked being blown up.

Then finally Gordon appeared and shouted his opinion of the news Matthew had relayed.

"I did talk to Whitworth, damn it! I know what's become of yon bluidy tube of powder! As well as meeting Barfoot on the wharf, he hoped to hand over a sample to some client he'd corresponded with! An' if he'd planned tae quit, wad he no' hae ta'en his stock-in-trade?"

That cooled the atmosphere instantly. The officers, still angry but much relieved, returned to their rooms; on his way McNab took the chance to tell Hogan what he thought of his superstitions. The pilot looked daggers but held his tongue.

"Come away," Auberon whispered to Josephine, and she obeyed, moving like a puppet.

But as they were departing, Auberon caught an extraordinary exchange of glances between Gordon and Woodley: from the latter, as it were, *quick thinking*, and from the former, *you may always rely on me*.

How could a mere glance turn into words with such facility?

Despondent, Anthony made for his bed, knowing that in the morning he might look forward to the telling-off of his young life.

On the way back to their respective staterooms Gordon said to Matthew, "Boy, I've been giving thought to what may happen if the *Nonpareil* doesn't win the race."

Matthew looked at him vaguely; had they not all done so, at least for the past twenty-four hours?

"I want you to make some arrangements for us. Book railroad tickets from St. Louis, cable for hotel rooms back east."

"But, sir, even if the *Nonpareil* does lose, surely she will continue to earn her keep? By the end of the trip everybody will at least have heard of her, won't they?"

"If I'd tried to teach you about gambling," Gordon sighed, "I'd maybe have had as little success as when I tried to teach you about women. *Jis' tak' ma wurrd!*"— with a flare-up of his customary temper. "In the morning I shall give you detailed instructions."

"Are you thinking of reneging on your bets?"

The words were out before Matthew could stop them, and for a heartbeat he thought Gordon was going to hit him.

Then the financier contrived a smile. He said in a low, controlled voice, "Never insult me like that again! But if all my funds are still blockaded by the damned English, I must find ways and means to make good my debts of honor—must I not? And it appears that the steamer trade on the Mississippi does not return dividends big enough or soon enough. As the saying goes, I am overextended!"

He gave Matthew what he doubtless intended for a pat on the shoulder; it was more like a slap. Reeling a little, Matthew escaped into his room.

That settled it! He took up his precious book, which Whitworth had duly returned, and once more lovingly inspected the pages that detailed the bearing of Clan Macrae.

Clutching it, he was shortly fast asleep again. His dreams were full of money.

A drowsy black maid came to meet Auberon and Josephine when they returned to the cabin; with a private curse, for what he had stumbled into was growing more attractive by the minute—the decadent, romantic poets he had encountered in Europe had infected his mind with a taste for extreme experience that perfectly matched his view of himself as a tragic figure doomed before his time—he ceded care of Josephine, who by now was crying silently and staring into nowhere.

He would have argued but that he felt a coughing fit coming on, and he had no handkerchief.

For the most trivial of reasons, therefore, because he did not want to spoil his handsome silk robe, he left his half-sister in the maid's charge and rushed back to his stateroom, where he saw blood pour into the laver, not red in this faint yellow glow but utterly black, as in a Poe story.

When he recovered, he found himself wondering whether in some arcane, absurd fashion he had not beaten the wiles of Death, who was riding so close behind him.

Conceivably (and the word struck the same overtones in his mind as, unknown to him, it had earlier done in Josephine's) he had seized a unique chance to perpetuate the Moynes.

Better this way than crossed with the foul strain of a swine like Arthur Gattry!

But he felt abominably weak, and had to fall on his bed and wrap the coverlets around him because he was also bitterly, incredibly cold on this hot night.

The race was taking its toll of the *Nonpareil*'s machinery. In order to match and, with luck, outdo the performance of the *Atchafalaya*'s forty-inch cylinders, when hers measured only thirty-four, she was having to rely entirely on higher pressure.

Which would have posed no problem had the piping, and the supports the piping rested on, and the unions and the valve packing and the rest, been of sufficiently heavy gauge. But Parbury's quest for lightness had proved halfway to self-defeating because, instead of being built up to the standard the pressure called for, his boat had been built down to the minimum the Steamboat Inspectorate would allow. The boat was entirely legal—no contesting that—but her pipes, and presumably her boilers, which would have been admirably suited to the *Atchafalaya*'s 110 to the square inch, or even to 130, were showing signs of dangerous strain at 160.

Such at least was Caesar's opinion after long and weary hours of nonstop hunting back and forth through the maze of steam connections.

He kept finding sources of potential trouble, and so did the other engineers. No longer did Steeples reproach him for taking a wrench to a union without orders; even he was grateful that he didn't have to find out all the problems by himself.

Thus far they had not had to stop while a leaky joint was taken apart, but twice they had needed to snatch the chance offered by a tight bend, when the vessel was going ahead on one wheel with the other stopped to provide drag. It might take only a matter of minutes to "slack and pack" while no steam was being fed to one of the cylinders—a fast tug of the wrench on a hot brass nut, then an equally rapid winding of waxed hempen cord around the pipe, then a steam-tight joint made by putting a four-foot length of pipe over the wrench handle and leaning your full weight on it: tricky, and risking strippage of the screw threads, only possible with a well-drilled crew—but it terrified Caesar how easily minutes might become hours, were an unnoticed weakness somewhere else in the system to be turned into a wide-open crack by the haste and violence of the work.

At the root of their difficulties lay one insuperable fact. When the pipes were under pressure, they were rigid; they might as well have been cast-iron bars, whereas the boat was limber, flexing to every wave and current.

But they were not rigid all the time. Whenever steam was being admitted to the cylinders, the pressure fell somewhat; whenever one engine was stopped, the pressure was cut off entirely, then surged back at full force. In the interim the metal had had the chance to cool down—not by very much, granted, but Caesar had seen long ago, before he took over from the white engineer at the Predulac plantation, how accidentally running cold water through hot pipes could make them crack open. He was dimly guessing at the nature of thermal shock. If it worked with cold water and hot metal, why not with cold metal and far hotter steam? Besides, you could see the pipes strain on their supports; they had a pulse, like a man's. And could not a weak blood vessel in the heart or brain bring about his death?

Every time he was able to quit the engineroom, he was grateful to have survived his watch, and he slept only fitfully, thinking that at any time he might be roused by screams.

He wished he could stop himself from feeling after the trickenbag he had grown so used to.

And also that Mam'zelle Josephine had not seen fit to deny her powers.

 How strange the sensation was of being rattled over rails after the smoother progress of a steamboat! The contrast was infinitely useful to Joel. He was sleepy, and would otherwise have dropped off despite having company.

As for Whitworth, he remained inscrutable. It was impossible to tell whether he was embarrassed at having been caught out in a lie, or even whether he realized he had been lying. Though he did add a word of warning: "I guess it's because I sleep so little that when I do I sleep so deep! I'm glad you're along, otherwise I'd have to rely on the conductor to turn me out at Milan, and even if you tip 'em all you can afford, you can't trust darkies. Like they say, there's God's time, and railroad time, and nigger time!" He gave a harsh laugh.

"You're in favor of this idea of regularizing time into zones?" Joel suggested.

"Sure I am!" Whitworth said bluffly. "Changing your watch every time you move a degree or two east or west—it's all foolishness! Much better to change one hour at a time after traveling a good long distance, don't you think?"

As a matter of fact, Joel did, but for the sake of keeping his mind busy he took the devil's advocate role, and afterward led the conversation down another dozen paths, until shortly before they reached Milan when, with relief, he saw Whitworth beginning to yawn.

"I guess since there's a good long wait before the Cairo train, I could snatch some rest," he admitted. "You?"

Joel shook his head. "I was lucky last night," he lied. "I still feel pretty wide awake."

"That's great. Watch by me during the layover, and I'll do the same for you when you need it, right?"

"It's a deal."

Though how Joel was going to keep his end of the bargain he didn't know. Maybe if there was strong coffee to be got at Milan . . .

Not that he wanted to sleep. His mind was preoccupied with a score of other matters, apart from the mystery of Whitworth's log. How, for example, was Louisette getting on? Cabling her at home was probably useless; she might all too easily have been obliged to remain at Baton Rouge.

What sort of a person could Arthur be, that he let the mother of his child undergo such torment? And what was he going to say and do when his fellow passengers recognized him in Joel's reports? At least one of the papers likely to copy them was bound to have gone on board at Memphis; it was amazing none had been received earlier. When Arthur saw them, would he again attack Auberon, since the author was not available? In that case, would Auberon have the sense to avoid a fight?

Poor devil!

Joel shivered. Perhaps it had been cowardly of him to leave the *Nonpareil* when he was aware that that might happen . . .

As though divining his thoughts, Whitworth started inquiring about Arthur and Auberon's disagreement. Doing his best not to speak overfreely, Joel answered.

Whitworth shook his head. "I guess it can't be good for a man to have too much of this world's goods," he opined sententiously. "A camel through a needle's eye—ain't that the way of it?"

A little put out, Joel raised a question that had been at the back of his mind. "How do you reckon the *Nonpareil* will get on, deprived of one of her key officers?"

"I guess I got my deck crew perfectly trained," Whitworth retorted with a huffy look. "Whether I'm there or not, they'll do their damnedest." A grin twisted his newly-bare upper lip.

"Used to be with Drew, you know! He always told his men, 'Act like you don't know whether I'm there or not! Because I could be!'"

Joel faked a smile at the witticism and went back to yet another of the mysteries about this man: why he should have taken time out to shave off his moustache.

The layover at Milan was indeed going to be a long one. The train they planned to connect with was behind time, though not late enough to prejudice their chance of overtaking the *Atchafalaya*. And the atmosphere was even worse than at Memphis. Since this was not a terminus, there was not a single locomotive in the depot at this hour, and frustrated passengers and night-duty railroadmen wandered about or sat in corners smoking and chewing tobacco and exchanging desultory gossip, under what was little more than a sketch for a roof. At least it was a clear warm night.

By now Whitworth was yawning continually. He pointed at a vacant bench.

"Guess I could do with a little shut-eye," he said. "Say, if we sit with our feet on our bags, it would be kind of hard for anyone to . . . ?"

"Suits me," Joel answered, matching words and action.

Whitworth leaned his head on his arm and soon began to snore. In a matter of minutes he turned around and his feet slipped off his bag. But Joel let a safe quarter hour elapse before he gradually eased himself away and, moving with utmost care, exchanged his bag for Whitworth's. In the dim light of flaring kerosene and naphtha lamps, they looked more identical than ever.

Whitworth stirred but did not awaken; what he had said about needing little sleep, but that very deep, was plainly true.

Hoping against hope he could carry off his pretense of having made a genuine mistake, Joel hastened toward an all-night washroom whose sign he had spotted as they came off their train. There was an attendant, but he was sleepy and uncaring.

As soon as he was sure he was unobserved, he opened Whitworth's bag and removed the pine log. A moment's inspection revealed it had been split down the middle, hollowed out, and reassembled with a peg and a bit of string. A thought sprang unbidden to his mind. When carrying fuel aboard a steamer, or tossing it into the furnaces, who would look twice at this or any chunk of wood?

All the time rehearsing in his head the excuses he would make if Whitworth caught him, he produced the pocketknife he always carried, eased the string out of the way, and pried the log apart. And in its hollow center . . .

A tube about ten inches long, brown, made of thick cardboard, with a wooden plug tamped into each end.

Heart pounding, he turned the thing over, noting that one plug was furnished with a pair of copper wires. He remembered what Josephine had said about a brown stick, and the hairs prickled on his nape.

After what seemed like half eternity, he gathered his wits. Did he have any kind of container with him . . . ? Sure he did: his pocket match-safe.

Hastily he emptied it. Then, using utmost care, he levered out the plug at the bottom of the tube. Inside there was a molasses-dense liquid with sparkles in it.

He snapped his fingers. He recognized this stuff! What a miraculous series of coincidences had led up to *that*! Although almost ruined by his unwise speculation in slaves during the war, his father had never given up hope of recouping the family's fortunes, and among the many notions he had toyed with was the offer of an agency for an explosive developed by a firm back east, using mica to stabilize nitroglycerine, which he had rejected because, having had his fingers burnt so often, he insisted on guarantees the manufacturers were unwilling to provide. So far as Joel knew, the offer of the agency was still being peddled around New Orleans.

But this was the explosive: no doubt of it. Mica powder, it was called.

He poured enough of it out of the tube and into his match-safe to serve as proof if he had to stand up in court. Then he scraped the rest down the drain, re-plugged the tube, assembled and retied the log, and returned it to the bag.

*What a story!*

This was going to make fortunes!

But he must be quick. Any second, Whitworth might waken. Accordingly he marched back to the attendant with a scowl.

"Goddamn it! This isn't my bag! I guess I picked up my friend's by mistake! I'll be back directly!"

Whitworth was still snoring. Much relieved, Joel gently withdrew his own bag, which was resting against the other's ankle.

He started and came awake, reaching under his long-skirted coat. Until this moment Joel had not realized he was armed. It was only a pocket pistol, but at this range . . .

"Easy, man!" he exclaimed. "I spotted a washroom and I want my bag!"

Whitworth blinked, then gave a slow smile.

"Are you ever lucky! When I worked as a watchman, I always used to carry a .44 with a hair trigger, 'stead of this toy here. Coulda blown you clear across the depot! One time a thieving nigger came by, thinking I was dead to the world, and I drilled him square 'tween the eyes. Took a half hour to clean up the blood!"

He returned the gun to its hiding place.

"Say, if you spot any place we can get coffee, I could do with a cup or two."

"I'll see what I can find," Joel promised, and with his own bag in hand marched away.

Back in the washroom, he retched and retched until he had cleansed himself of the terror he had felt when the miniature gun flashed into view.

Never had he been so glad that his family's riches had lasted until the conquest of New Orleans—long enough to ensure he escaped military service, when many boys far younger than himself had been drafted.

But he was not without courage. He couldn't be. What had he just done, steal-ing away that terrible secret from a man who awoke at a touch with a gun in his hand? He had—he had . . .

He had, he thought, saved the lives of everybody aboard the *Atchafalaya*.

Confronting death . . . His guts twitched again, but there was nothing left to vomit.

How could someone face the prospect of a duel, for instance, with frank excite-ment, unless he was drunk, or crazy, or—like Auberon—doomed?

To lend a colorable excuse to his absence, he made shift to wash in the sour cold water and run his razor over his cheeks, heedless of the fact that it needed stropping. Until he was set back by a dismaying yet persuasive thought.

*Had* he saved all those lives?

There could have been another reason why Whitworth was carrying that per-ilous burden. What sort of reason, it defied Joel's weary imagination to work out. Yet the fact stood.

When he came away with his own bag, he had vaguely considered calling for

the sheriff, cabling the *Intelligencer*, and drafting tomorrow's headline: OUR
REPORTER SAVES RACING STEAMER FROM DESTRUCTION!

But he didn't *know*.

Regardless of whether the story was securely founded, a score—a hundred—
editors up and down the country would be delighted to print it.

But if it *was* an error . . .

In that moment Joel knew he was doomed never to be a top reporter, with the
doors of New York and Boston open to him . . . unless he stuck it out for yet one
more day before committing himself.

He was going to have to ride the cars to Cairo with Whitworth, acting as though
he were not party to any deadly secret. He was going to have to watch the other
man until the very moment when the log was tossed into a coal flat destined for
the *Atchafalaya*.

And then delay her, by claiming that that log must be removed and inspected . . . ?

Oh, no!

The more he thought of it, the worse the complications seemed, and he stood
no chance of recruiting—even by cable—witnesses to arrest Whitworth.

What sort of a man must he be, to undertake such a hideous mission? And on
whose behalf? Surely it could only be Gordon's! (A conflux of recollections, especially concerned with the financier's treatment of Matthew.)

Thus something more fundamental than a mere news story began to gather in
his mind. Given an intelligent man, frustrated in his ambitions, still working as a
second mate when his length of service and qualifications—plus such useful talents as making do with a minimum of sleep—would have suggested he ought to
be at least a first mate, maybe even master on his own vessel: what would one
make of such a character in a novel?

A great deal.

The discovery lightened Joel's spirits. He went in search of the promised coffee,
and found it in chipped and clumsy mugs, and by the time their long-awaited
train was signaled he and Whitworth were chatting in the friendliest possible
fashion.

How else should a writer deal with his characters?

No matter how despicable they were . . .

The *Atchafalaya* made astonishing time throughout the night,
because Tyburn worked wonders during his watch. Fernand
ran Plum Point in the clear light of sunrise, and was enormously grateful to both him and Drew for enabling him to get so much unbroken
rest, so that he came fresh to one of the trickiest portions of the river.

Yet all those efforts had not been enough. The *Nonpareil* was still snuffing at
her rival's heels.

And Tyburn had said with a grunt, as he ceded the wheel, "New pilot!"—jerking his head sternward. "That ain't Colin's style, nor Dermot's either!"

"There was talk of Woodley hiring specialists," Fernand began. Tyburn cut him short, around a huge yawn.

"There was also talk of Dermot grounding her if Woodley tried it! Not that he ever came into the open about it, but listening to him in the Guild parlor you could read between the lines. Yet I swear that wasn't either of 'em chasing me!"

"Any idea who?"

"I'd put money on Zeke Barfoot. I know Woodley wanted him because he once tripped with you, didn't he?"

Fernand nodded. "Did me a good turn, what's more," he said, recalling how the gaunt rangy man had reprimanded Whitworth.

"Figures. Also he lives at Memphis. You'd think with the fees he pulls down he could move to a healthier city. But he was born there, so . . ." A concluding shrug.

"You won't have to bother with him, at least. I reckon his watch is about over. Most likely you'll have Colin on your tail."

That was no special comfort to Fernand. He recalled how miserable his last watch had seemed, and how Trumbull had closed the gap on the approach to Memphis, despite Drew having taken over.

And yet he almost caressed the wheel as he laid the *Atchafalaya* into her marks for the next bend. For at the edge of memory echoed that precious compliment Drew had paid him: "You have the makings of a fighting pilot!"

Very well: he was going to fight like hell!

And the chance to prove it came upon him very shortly. Above Ashport, once they had cleared a tangle of tiny islands, there was a straight five-mile run before the channel swerved again into Needham's Cutoff—behind what had once been Needham's Point, before the river's relentless gnawing severed it, and incidentally transferred the land which survived from the Arkansas to the Tennessee side.

With a hand that shook not in the least, he reached for the engineroom speaking tube. Fonck answered.

"Dutch, I guess you better rout out Josh and get his forge to burning. We could strain the rudder post again shortly."

"Is she that close?" rumbled the big engineer.

"She's so close, I reckon I could spit on her."

"You just do your damnedest and we'll do ours!" Fonck promised.

"How are things down there? Any more trouble? And how's Walt?"

"I'm kind of worried about him. His bandages soak through in next to no time. But he claims his burn don't hurt too bad, so . . ." There followed the audible counterpart of a shrug. "He's going to be a real engineer one of these days. But for chrissake don't tell Jim. He's much too proud of having picked him for a striker!"

Fernand chuckled and hung the tube back on its hook. It struck him with a pang that he shouldn't have needed to ask. On any ordinary run, he would have visited the engineroom twice a day, a habit he had consciously copied from Drew. Of course, on this trip he was bound to spend what time he could spare with Dorcas and his mother.

Maybe he was getting his priorities wrong—?

But there was no time to think more on the subject. Here they were entering the five-mile reach, and there was the *Nonpareil!*

Followed the longest twenty minutes of his life.

Here the river was far too broad to make maximum use of the wake, yet it was the only weapon to hand. There were no oncoming steamers or sluggish towboats to be overtaken, which might balk the *Nonpareil;* she was running too far from shore and in water too deep to repeat Drew's trick with a broadside wave that drove her aground. She came late out of the last bend, by a dozen times her own length, but the instant she was clear and straight she used the full tremendous power of her high-pressure steam, and the fountain from her cutwater splayed higher than ever before.

It looked as though what Fernand most feared was bound to happen: she was going to overtake while he was at the wheel, with Dorcas and Eulalie on board to witness his failure.

The pilothouse door opened stealthily, and in came Drew.

For a second hope flared in Fernand's breast: had the captain arrived with a brilliant solution and the intention of taking over the helm?

Not at all. For a while he said nothing, merely chewed meditatively. At length he spat into the sawdust box and said, "Got the legs of us, has she?"

The *Nonpareil* was closing like a greyhound on a hare, her bow aligned on the best and broadest entrance to Needham's Cutoff like a rifle sight on a bull's-eye. A surge of anger washed through Fernand.

"Not if I have anything to do with it!" he declared, and in the same instant inspiration struck.

What would happen if a steamer's mass were to wallow in a chance wind-driven surge? There was more breeze this morning than they had had since setting out, and it was patterning the water.

He pondered a few seconds, and then it came naturally, on a level below logic.

He reached for the speaking tube again and said calmly, "I guess you better warn Josh we're in for some rough weather. Turn the deckhands to and make all secure. Warn the stewards and tenders we could break some crockery. In about two minutes I'm going to ask for a dead stop."

"What?"

"And then the fastest shift you ever made to half astern starboard and half ahead larboard! We could strain not just the rudder post but the whole damned hull, but it's our only chance! She'll pass us before the head of the reach if we don't do *something!*"

"I hope to God you know what you're about," said Fonck seriously. But seconds later it was clear the order had been passed on. Luckily there were not, as yet, more than a handful of passengers up and about, and all those congregated at the stern where their weight would be most useful. The deckhands turned to as instructed, and did their best to make a cheerful noise, but they too had seen how close the *Nonpareil* was looming, and by now the latter's deck crew could be heard chanting: "The *Nonpareil* [clap, clap] is on her way [clap, clap]!"

*Not if I can help it,* Fernand swore under his breath.

Now where was the biggest of these accidental waves? He reached for his field glasses and knocked the crucifix to the floor . . . but there was no time to grope after it.

He had to tug the bell rope for a stop.

The wheels were at rest before they had completed another revolution. Their bearings and supports cried out but stood the strain. Could they take the rest of what he had in mind? He must trust to the design skills of Wenceslas Cleech and the loving care that Drew had lavished on this boat.

In the grip of an emotion halfway between terror and exaltation, Fernand tugged the bell rope again, and—with her rival closing swiftly—the *Atchafalaya,* still rushing upstream with all the momentum of her former speed, swung end for end in what from rest would have been little more than her own length, just as the largest of the natural waves broke on her hull. She rocked—her whole gigantic bulk *rocked*—as though a storm had struck her. But she turned as impersonally as the paddle of a butter churn until she had made a complete revolution, then resumed full ahead.

The effect, Fernand recounted later, was like dropping a boulder in a bathtub.

Although her pilot tried valiantly to steer clear, the *Nonpareil* was caught in what might as well have been a tidal bore—a wave higher than her freeboard, which sluiced her main deck, soaked her waiting fuel, slopped into her hold . . . Meantime one of her wheels lifted clear of the water; then her bow dipped; that lifted her rudder clear; and within seconds, faster than her pilot could recover, she was halfway to broadside on, thereby taking the remaining force of the *Atchafalaya's* backwash where she least wanted it, where it could make her swerve—slowly, but she too weighed over a thousand tons—off her intended course.

Which Fernand, sweating, promptly poached by lining up on Needham's Cutoff in such a manner that the *Nonpareil* would again be running square in her rival's wake.

There were a few ragged cheers from below, but more curses and complaints, for he had tested the steamer to her utmost, and he waited a long moment for fear of hearing he had sprung a leak somewhere in her hull.

No such report came. He relaxed slowly, aware he had accomplished something he could relate proudly for the rest of his life.

But the finest accolade came from Drew, who got down on hands and knees and stood upright again and said, offering what he had retrieved, "Here's the thing your mother gave you . . . Oh, damn it! I thought we were beat at last! And it warn't true!"

Fernand made no move to take the crucifix—just grinned. It didn't seem to matter anymore.

 Tyburn had been wrong in his guess about who would take over from Barfoot. Cursing with all the fury of his Irish forebears, Hogan struggled to force the *Nonpareil* back on her intended heading despite the fact that the hold was awash and the chain wagon had jammed at exactly the wrong point of its traverse.

With sudden sick realization he discovered the trouble was far worse than that. He could turn the wheel one way—to starboard—without the least resistance.

In the same moment shouts came from below, and one horrifying scream.

He did not need to wait for Burge's message via speaking tube to guess what had happened. The shock of being swung halfway to broadside had snapped one of the rudder cables; near its break a crewman had been struck by the rope's end.

Shortly he was informed that the man was not seriously hurt, which could have been a miracle. Once he had seen a big burly fellow killed in just such an accident, his windpipe crushed as efficiently as by a garrote.

But, Burge warned, splicing the rope wasn't the only problem to contend with. Its colossal tension had made it crack like a whip and coiled it around a stanchion which had split and must be reinforced. Moreover there was so much water in the hold it would have to be pumped out, and the fact that the fuel had been soaked would reduce the temperature of the furnaces . . .

The job took what felt like half eternity. Meantime Hogan seethed, and the *Nonpareil* barely held her own against the current, because lacking a rudder he dared not take her into the next bend, and yet once more the *Atchafalaya* raced ahead.

 When the excitement died away, realization of the fact that today was Sunday began to spread aboard the *Atchafalaya*. Even before daybreak the deckhands had raised a drowsy song about Judgment Day:

> *In dat great gittin'-up mornin', fare thee well, fare thee well,*
> *God gonna up an' speak to Gabriel, fare thee well, fare thee well!*

But the reference to having to rise without enough sleep behind you was too clear for anybody to show much enthusiasm.

In the cabin it was agreed over breakfast that a prayer meeting, at least, must be held. Despite his Catholic stance, Barber let himself be persuaded to approach Gaston to provide music for a few hymns. Yesterday the Frenchman had made the mistake of demonstrating the keenness of his ear; a snatch of melody sung or hummed by one of the company had been enough to supply him with all he needed to round out a fully developed arrangement. His performance had so impressed Barber, he had gone to him privately afterward and told him that if his engagement in St. Louis fell through, he might apply for a permanent post at the Limousin.

Which was, of course, precisely what Gaston had dreamed of when he first arrived in the New World.

But now the idea of working to please the fads and fancies of a sporting, gambling crowd was repugnant to him. He was not foolish enough to turn down Barber's offer outright; however, he made it clear that his ambitions lay in the direction of the concert hall.

Subsequently, however, he had passed a bad night. While striving to concentrate on his projected funeral music, he had kept finding his mind drifting off course, toward his tone poem about the Mississippi, and what strains floated through his head were too exultant for funerary use. Traveling to St. Louis aboard a race-winning steamer was perhaps not such a good idea after all . . .

When he appeared—red-eyed, because his mind had gone driving on much of the night like the *Atchafalaya*'s engines—the last thing he wanted was to sit down again at the piano for any other reason than to fix some fleeting fragments of inspiration against his arrival.

But he yielded to Barber's blandishments when the latter neatly pointed out that a succession of sober hymn tunes might be exactly what he needed to make his imagination flow down the proper channel.

It was therefore with some dismay that Gaston discovered, partway through the impromptu service, that he was, not for the first time, picking up the insistent, barbaric rhythms of the spirituals being sung forward. Worse yet, when he strained his ears during a prayer that Motley was offering—as the most devout of the officers, he had been called on to preside—he realized he was also being influenced by the band aboard the *Nonpareil*.

Though in real terms she must be four or five miles behind, the river was doubling back on itself yet again. Across a point fledged with saplings the music from Manuel's little orchestra was borne on the light wind.

It made her seem as close as she had been before Fernand executed his coup. Illogically, irrationally, people felt she must be within an ace of overtaking after all.

 That was the opinion buoying up everyone aboard the *Nonpareil*, now the rudder cable had been fixed.

Or almost everyone . . .

Josephine had slept well after the triumphant proof of her power, which had impressed Auberon and Hogan, at least, if not Woodley or the clerks.

Now she woke to an alarming suspicion that seemed to have carried over from a dream.

Had it been somehow *necessary* for her to engage in that ritual (she could not think of it otherwise) with her half-brother before her abilities could again be manifest?

Or was the explanation simpler? Had she not made her faith apparent enough so that she seemed to be ashamed of her Lord?

She had, after all, hidden from even her most devoted followers . . .

But perhaps the time for pretense was at an end. It could not be kept up much longer, anyhow; the engineer had claimed he was only one of hundreds who knew her identity. She had better make a virtue out of misfortune.

Making herself as presentable as she could, given that she had no change of attire with her and Auberon's haste had torn some of the hooks from her bodice, she set out in search of Caesar.

She found him asleep on a pile of sacks near the verge staff. Close at hand, some of the firemen and deckhands were marking Sunday by singing spirituals. She found a place to sit down beside Caesar, the startled men making room for her, and waited patiently for him to wake. The singing continued until the band appeared for its first performance of the day, a medley of hymn tunes.

Josephine knew very few of the words, but she recognized several melodies and joined in wordlessly with her resonant contralto, not at all dismayed by seeming to give lip service to the rival deity. Damballah, she was satisfied, knew what was in her heart.

Above, on the boiler deck, Auberon made inquiries for her, having discovered that her stateroom was open and a maid was making up the bed. No one appeared to have seen her yet today. It was long before it occurred to him to look for her on the main deck; when he did, she went on singing, paying him no more attention than if he were a total stranger.

 The sound of music and singing also woke Cherouen, but his response was to groan and cover his head with his pillow. He had drunk long and deep last night, mostly at Barber's expense, and he hated the idea of facing the new day. Especially a Sunday.

Though at least this was not a boat that closed the bars and banned cards and other games of chance on the Sabbath. He cheered up a little, thinking about an eye-opener, and then was dragged right back down to the depths of depression by the sad reflection that so far medicine had never come up with a quick, infallible cure for hangovers.

There were, of course, palliatives . . .

After a while he was able to reach his medical bag and stagger to the laver for water to mix a potion with.

All the while he was cursing Josephine for deserting him in his hour of greatest need.

Eulalie woke with a sense of pleasurable anticipation. Like Josephine, she believed implicitly in the content of her dreams, and what remained most vivid from them was the image of her silver crucifix, but immensely enlarged, gleaming above the twin chimneys of the *Atchafalaya* while her son was at her wheel.

Above—or between?

There was a curious and disturbing ambiguity in the picture she could recall: as though the crucified Christ might in fact be hanging between the chimneys, arms outstretched and lashed to them, like the swinging gilded horns that announced this steamer's prowess to the world.

In any case she had wanted to dream of Damballah, not Jesus.

Why, then, was she convinced on waking that she had foreseen something right and to be looked forward to?

Faintly she detected another image trying to.escape from memory and pinned it down. It was of a baby.

Ah!

She rose, washed and dressed hastily, and went to rouse Dorcas. That must be the link. If it was, it wouldn't be the first time a love child had been born with magic powers.

Dorcas too had dreamed: that Fernand had come to her. She woke thinking that the knock on her stateroom door was his, and was bitterly disappointed when she found it was only his mother's.

But she and Eulalie were overjoyed when they found him joining them in the cabin upon the conclusion of his watch.

When they asked how it had gone, he modestly made light of his achievement, which somehow—he could only guess at the cause, though Drew hazarded it might be rudder damage—had delayed the *Nonpareil*. However, he laid stress on the new pilot aboard the trailing boat. He was overheard, and the news spread like wildfire. To his infinite dismay he suddenly found more people talking about that than about his feat of piloting. Those who had imagined the *Nonpareil* to be hopelessly far behind looked for ways to hedge or default on their bets.

Barber was a notable exception. By now he was so confident of the *Atchafalaya*'s victory, he had dispatched cables from Memphis increasing his stakes on her by ten thousand dollars.

He sent Fernand a bottle of champagne by way of thanks.

 Arthur Gattry awoke to as bad a headache as Cherouen's, and even louder music, for Manuel was by then drilling his players through a lugubrious version of "The Old Rugged Cross."

He wished he could lose himself again in the mazes of sleep, but it was useless.

Lying on his back, with cramp in one leg which he continually flexed and reflexed in an attempt to make it go away, he thought about this day and his past and above all about the way he had acted since leaving New Orleans.

For a while he tried to defend himself against himself, as in a court of law. He had made clear from the start that he wanted a *modern* marriage. So why had

Louisette landed him with a child immediately? He expected her to be a charming, pretty companion he could rely on escorting to parties and public functions,
then take home and bed without objections. Babies had no role in his vision of the
future, except insofar as he was marrying because of family pressure, to provide
an eventual heir.

He had been stupid to give in. He would have done better to take a mistress *en
plaçage* like so many of his friends, instead of a wife who claimed an equal share of
his life!

But Hugo and Stella had seemed so pleased with one another, and there was no
boring nuisance of children to worry about yet, and he had taken the necessary
steps . . .

No. He hadn't. In his first flush of excitement at the discovery that Louisette
had what they called a "passionate nature," he had at least once disregarded better judgment and . . .

The band was blasting out another hymn tune now, inviting sinners to repentance.

He bent his head. He *was* responsible. Black depression, infinite misery told
him so. He had grounds to be ashamed of himself, to seek out Auberon and
apologize, to admit he ought to have accepted his cousin-in-law's advice and left
the boat. Especially since she seemed in a fair way to losing and he couldn't afford
to meet his bets if she did.

When was the next stop? Cairo this evening?

As he dressed, he was balancing priorities: his wife and child, his stakes on the
race, and the urgent need for something to take care of his aching head and sour
belly.

Optimistically he checked his pocket flask. It was empty; he made a mental
note to have it refilled.

He was starting to feel himself again.

Woodley had been crowing with pride when the *Nonpareil* arrived in the five-
mile straight so close astern of the *Atchafalaya*. He ascribed all this to Zeke Barfoot's intervention.

"Warn't I right all along?" he kept crying. "Hiring extra pilots to tackle the
worst bits of the river—it paid off!"

Now he was singing a very different tune.

"What are we going to pay Barfoot with?" Gordon grumbled. "Promises and
scraps of paper?"

"You know more about that than I do!" Woodley flared.

"Is it my fault that the English are still locking up my money?"

There was a cough. Because it came from Parbury, all eyes turned to him.

"As I understand it," the blind man remarked, "hiring fresh pilots didn't pay off
yet. We're still trailing 'em!"

"By far less!" Woodley objected.

The prayer meeting was over; they were in the clerks' office, the most convenient place for a conference.

"*Less* is not good enough!" Parbury barked. "And don't complain about not specifying strong enough rudder cables! Some dirty tricks can't be foreseen! What do you say, Hamish?"

"I won't be satisfied until I see the *Atchafalaya* far behind!" Gordon declared, and exchanged secret glances with Woodley. "But above Cairo—yes, I guess we may just do that!"

"Banking everything on Smith and Tacey, is that it?" Parbury countered. "Well, Drew can hire their match at any port along the river! Not that I see why he should. He's proving himself the champion, and Ketch and Lamenthe are in there with him. Don't argue!"—raising one black-gloved hand as he sensed opposition from Woodley. "Barfoot did take over, and I still want to know how much you're paying him and what with!"

Woodley said sullenly, "It was none of my doing. Hogan came off watch when he wasn't authorized and left the boat in Barfoot's charge. I never talked terms with him!"

"You planned to! And if he's a responsible member of the Guild, as I believe him to be, he won't have touched that wheel for less than a hundred bucks! Ain't I right?"

"But we agreed beforehand—"

"Back when we were expecting to be in the lead! And we aren't, and there's Tom and Joe waiting to come aboard, and once they hear what's happened with Zeke, there won't be any nonsense about 'looking at the river'—they'll expect to serve their turn and be paid commensurate!"

"Come now," Gordon offered bluffly. "In principle we did agree to hiring pilots along the way, and we took the question of paying them for granted."

Parbury inclined his blind gaze in the financier's direction. "That's so. But whereas you may conjure money out of nowhere, most of us have to earn it. Or win it!"

He rose stiffly to his feet.

"I sorely hoped we'd pass the *Atchafalaya* above Ashport. But that's not the only straight reach we have today! Between now and sundown we *must* overtake! I leave it to you exactly when, but I expect it!"

He seized his cane and marched out.

When they were alone, Woodley said to Gordon in a low, fierce tone, "God, but I was a fool to listen to you! If the *Atchafalaya* does blow up, someone's bound to connect it with the explosive missing from Whitworth's bag! There's no way of preventing that getting around, thanks to Crossall!"

"Tae the de'il wi' him an' Whitworth!" Gordon retorted. "Forswear yirsel', mon—it'll nae be the furrst time! Ah ne'er spak' a bluidy wurrd anent sich goings-on, an' nae mair did ye!"

"What?"

Gordon mastered himself with immense effort. "Lie, man—lie in your teeth! It was all Whitworth's idea, and nor you nor I was consulted!"

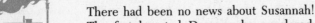 There had been no news about Susannah!

The fact haunted Drew as he wandered about the *Atcha-falaya*, verifying that what Fernand had done in the five-mile straight had not caused detectable damage. It was sheer good fortune (and echoes of his temporary belief in charms resonated in his head) but it was true.

And to think that a pupil of his had come up with a notion his teacher could never have conceived!

Risky? Well—yes, hideously so! But if the next generation was to build on the experience of the past, what else should one ask for?

Better that than some pious fool mumbling over his prayerbook . . . as Jacob had mumbled over his records of wins and losses at the gaming tables.

Drew started. How long was it since he had thought about that? When obliged to visit the asylum, he had barely paid attention to the charts and tables, so carefully compiled, which in the grip of syphilis Jacob believed held the secret of forever winning. Then, Jacob's children had been too young to accompany him or their mother and see the straits their father was reduced to.

It was as well . . .

Oh, how could Susannah have married such a hollow person, bedded with him, borne him children?

*But in those days,* a sniggering demonic voice reminded him, *you too thought he was a great man!*

True, alas! True!

In that instant he could have wished his life as simple as Cherouen's, for the doctor was so convinced of his power to heal, he cared not a whit for the damage he was doing to himself by drinking all day and half the night. Relying, perhaps, on the effect of his electrical machines when the strain grew too great?

Or, indeed, as Barber's—and that was a first! Until this moment he had never thought of Barber as leading an enviable existence. At best he had thought of it as easier than his own, but one might have said the same about, for example, Edouard Marocain, who so completely comprehended the virtues and vices of his customers, who reigned over a private empire whose subjects he knew personally and individually—

Wait! Was that why Fernand had adapted so superbly to the enclosed world of a steamboat?

It could well be.

And if that were so, then . . .

*I have a son.*

The idea had long hovered at the edge of Drew's mind. Only now, when he was reflecting on the brilliant coup Fernand had brought off, did it come sharply into focus. The invitation Fernand had extended, that he be not only best man at his wedding but also godfather to their first-born, had awoken just those dormant emotions that he felt when with Susannah and her children.

Susannah, who was sick and nigh to death!

Confusion threatened. He resolved once more to cable from the next available port; it must be Hickman, this afternoon. There was a telegraph office there, and even—now—a railroad depot.

He was roused from his brown study by the sound of the *Atchafalaya*'s whistle saluting an oncoming steamer. She was, he knew the moment he set eyes on her, the *Bella Brawle:* 190 feet, stern-wheeler, in short trades between Cairo and Vicksburg.

And cursed his knowledge. What would he not have given to be on the path of discovery again, like Fernand now? When all was stale—

So what must Parbury be feeling, whose son had been stolen by disease and who had never had the chance to make good his loss save by creating what he believed to be the finest steamer on the river?

Except she was being denied the chance to prove it.

Then he was being assailed by passengers who wanted to compliment him on eluding this morning's challenge. As best he could, Drew made conversation, all the time thinking how readily, had he been Parbury, he would have swapped this victory for possession of a son as smart as Fernand.

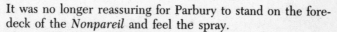 It was no longer reassuring for Parbury to stand on the foredeck of the *Nonpareil* and feel the spray.

The sun's heat burned his face. The water drops solaced that. They could do nothing to salve the hatred in his soul for the pilot who had cheated him today. A man smutched by the taint of slavery, whose ancestors would have been—had the war not happened—kin to those the Parburys might have bought and set to work on their farm!

Except the Mississippi had washed the land away . . .

He drew a rasping breath and admitted to himself that owning slaves and a plantation had never been chief among his ambitions. What was making him so bitter was Dorcas.

Who, so they told him, was both colored and deceitful.

A chance combination of words fell into place, and he touched the bandage across his eyes.

Had she thought about the colors of the bandanna Whitworth had described—a man he had never taken a liking to? Or had she been so simple and unaffected that she thought only about how grateful silk might be on raw skin?

There was little sensation left where his flesh had been beset by flame; his fingertips said so when he dared explore that portion of his face, and he took the fact as a parable of his condition.

Never mind that, then! How could Dorcas have known? She had never touched him there.

What right did he have to read into her actions more than she intended? At his age he was already separated from all females save one—and not his wife.

The "she" in his life was the *Nonpareil*.

Conceivably—here he hesitated—conceivably he had betrayed her, then. By not devoting his whole attention to her, he had been guilty of unfaithfulness.

Dorcas? She was none of his creation; she was a servant, and slaves had been abolished, so he had no control over what she did with her life or her emotions. She might feel a certain kindness for him, but if she chose to marry one of her own kind, especially one who was proving his skill with every mile of this race . . .

Here the confusion in Parbury's mind became total.

Hungry he was for the touch of smooth young skin, warm against his own.

Yet his *self* was committed elsewhere, irrevocably. Into the *Nonpareil* he had poured his heart, his soul, his power to love. He could never have loved Dorcas, and in this moment of near-defeat he recognized the fact.

His son he could have loved. And in a complex, wordless way this boat had become his son, his wife, his mistress.

Nothing mattered more to him in all the world than that she triumph.

 All that fine hot Sunday the *Atchafalaya* led and the *Nonpareil* strove vainly to catch up. Noon saw the champion at risk again, for above Point Pleasant there was a seven-mile reach marred only by a few sandbars, while after the horseshoe bend at New Madrid another such would carry them southerly to the famous Island 10, whose Confederate batteries the Union ironclad *Carondelet* had defied in one of the war's outstanding feats. So little was left of it now, one might imagine that the terrible pounding it had later taken from mortar-boats had smashed it down to water-level. But no effort of puny humanity could match the power and patience of the river.

In both these reaches the *Nonpareil* gained ground, and each time it was not enough. As soon as she entered a bend, she was obliged to slow far more than the *Atchafalaya,* having burned enough coal to make her overlight again. During his next watch Barfoot's lack of experience in handling her betrayed him, and he ran her ignominiously aground, which cost still more precious time.

But lightness could not be the sole reason for her failure to come ahead strong. In the first reach she gained ten minutes, and lost five in the New Madrid horseshoe; in the second she gained only five, though it was the longer, and lost them again rounding Island 10.

She was being held back. A steam leak? It seemed likely! Jubilant, those aboard the *Atchafalaya* waved madly at the watchers who, here as everywhere, had mustered to witness what might be the last of the great river races.

Those who launched boats did so at their peril; Drew was not inclined to slow for lesser craft again. Blast after blast on the steam whistle sent up huge white plumes into the clear air, and, given due warning, they made way.

At Hickman, Kentucky, the entire population seemed to have turned out, but when the *Atchafalaya* thundered past in midafternoon, they were rewarded with little more than a glimpse of her. She was racing at her maximum, packing eighteen and even nineteen miles into each hour. Whereas the *Nonpareil* . . .

It was possible to calculate the pursuing boat's velocity by noting, with field glasses, when her smoke altered direction for bends or known hazards. In the pilothouse with Tyburn, Drew did exactly that.

And was astonished. The *Nonpareil,* theoretically capable of twenty miles per hour, was making more like sixteen!

"If you ask me," the captain said softly as he announced this fact, "Fernand did more damage with that trick of his than we could have guessed."

"More than just a broken rudder rope," Tyburn agreed with a nod. "We're gaining on her now, that's for sure. But if it's so, won't they argue to cancel all bets?"

"Let 'em try," Drew returned grimly. He had the satisfaction of knowing he had done what he could to get a message to Susannah: cast a note overboard wrapped in oilcloth and tied to a chunk of wood, along with enough money to cover the telegraph fee, and seen it picked up by a man in a rowboat who shouted his promise to take care of the matter. He went on: "I'll lay they weren't talking in such terms when they tried to cheat by starting ahead of us, then trapped us in their wake when we might have overtaken. Far as I'm concerned, the first one away had a chance to make the rules, and if they chose not to play it fair, that's their lookout!"

He added after a pause, "But I'd dearly love to know what's holding her back!"

What Fernand had done hadn't helped. But that was not the root cause of the *Nonpareil's* trouble.

Earlier, Caesar had striven to sleep on regardless of the singing around him, until the far noisier band drowned it out. Opening his eyes in annoyance, he discovered Josephine nearby. When the song was over she said to him, "Come to me in New Orleans and I'll make you another bag, better than the one before."

And that was when the problems began. A messenger came to summon him back to work. Despite stinging eyes, foul mouth, and grumbling belly, Caesar judged it best to obey.

She called after him, "It's time for me to make myself known!"

He had no chance to wonder about that. As soon as he arrived in the engine-room, it was plain what had gone wrong. Two joints at once were starting to leak, one on either side, and neither was more urgent than the other. Cursing, because his old wound was paining him and his bad teeth kept issuing little twinges of warning, Caesar grabbed a wrench and set about tackling the nearer, with Roy's help, while Corkran and the other man who had been sent for dealt with the other.

"What's she look like, Caesar?" Roy grunted.

"Looks like we ought to open her right up and braze a collar on the pipe."

"Right, or she may split lengthwise." Roy wiped his sweating forehead; he was so grimy now, as were the other white engineers, a casual glance would not have told them from their colored helpers. "But we aren't going to be allowed to. We just got to slack and pack again."

"Even binding it with wire would help," Caesar offered after a moment's reflection.

"Yeah, that's sound. Then we can run some solder over it, at least. Tighten it as much as you can. I'll speak to Peter."

Aching with fatigue, deafened by the noise, dehydrated by the heat, Caesar was nonetheless comparatively happy as he leaned his weight on the wrench. To have been asked for his opinion, rather than just given an order: it was a breakthrough.

Not that he had ever used the trick he had just proposed. At the sugar mill, or driving his crane, he had always had the time to stop and make repairs.

Shortly Roy was back, grimacing.

"Peter says we don't get a chance to cut steam to either wheel before the New Madrid bend, and that's a starboard one. Then we got the best part of ten miles before we can slow in the Island Ten bend, on the larboard."

"I guess we better pray," Caesar said, and to his surprise Roy gave a laugh—short and dry, but a laugh.

"Yeah, or otherwise Parbury will visit us with wrath from on high! But we got to warn the pilot anyhow, to take it easy less'n he wants us boiled alive!"

Two days and twenty-one hours into the race, the *Atchafalaya* had covered a thousand miles.

The *Nonpareil* was falling behind: the gap widened to thirty minutes again, thirty-five, forty . . . Despondency reigned, though Woodley and Gordon preserved an air of optimism.

And considered whether they should share their secret with Parbury, and concluded not. Were he to discover what they had empowered Whitworth to do, he would take them to small pieces with his bare hands, blind or no.

Besides, if anybody made the matter public . . .

They thought of Joel; they thought of Anthony, and Auberon and Josephine; they shivered in the hot air as they wondered how well Whitworth could hold his tongue.

 During the bone-shaking ride which occupied most of this baking-hot Sunday Joel's thoughts harked back constantly to his first meeting with Gordon. How right he had been to vaunt the comfort of steamboats!

But also how right those people had been who spoke of the American obsession with speed. This railroad journey was going to bring him and Whitworth to Cairo a good three hours ahead of even the *Atchafalaya*, and he was prepared to believe that had it been only three minutes there would still have been a plethora of customers.

Whitworth, in expansive mood, talked a lot about the great drought of 1860, which was when the railroads first began to bite at the cherry of southwestern trade, because the steamers were often unable to complete a scheduled run thanks to the low water level. It had been obvious from the start that he had no special attachment to the river which had given him most of his livelihood; indeed, he dropped hints about a far more profitable job selling some new invention from back east.

Explosives?

But there was never any chance of probing the subject. The moment they overheard talk about the steamer race, their seat neighbors had joined in: drummers, men on the move in search of work, a couple of preachers, someone who claimed merely to be looking over the lay of the land but whose shabby-genteel manner suggested he might be one of those all-too-common phenomena in the younger states of the nation, a black sheep expelled by a wealthy but excessively respectable eastern family.

Slower or faster, there was no doubt which type of transportation held the imagination of the public. Two of the drummers had even placed bets: luckily for them, in favor of the *Atchafalaya*.

Or were they so lucky? They began to doubt it when Whitworth spoke slightingly of her as too old and certain to be overstressed before reaching St. Louis. Why, it wouldn't in the least surprise him, he declared, were she to burst a boiler trying to outrun the newer vessel!

"I know Drew for a penny pincher!" he concluded. "And remember, his last boat was condemned!"

What manner of man could be guilty of such infamy as to blow up a steamer? Joel listened in bafflement. Who had the soulless greed to abet the plan? Or was it entirely his?

Reflection indicated that it might be. The more he observed his unexpected traveling companion, the more he realized he was a very strange person: nervy, high-strung, constantly on the border of outright agitation. When he wasn't actually smoking, he generally was chewing on an unlit panatela. Thinking to lower the man's defenses, Joel again produced the whiskey he had brought. But Whitworth declined, preferring coffee, of which he drank all he could obtain, or, failing that, one of the syrup-and-soda drinks vended during the train's brief stops by salesmen prosperous enough to own ice-making machines.

The preachers did the same. But the others were glad to help dispose of the liquor.

Race fever was apparent at Cairo, too. Half the countryside seemed to have decided to make an excursion, to the delight of those local traders who had settled here on the assumption that—regardless of what people might say about the land being muddy and swampy and given to breeding fevers—the junction of the Mississippi and the Ohio was a strategic point. They were, paradoxically, in favor of the railroads, for river people had their own long-standing trade centers: Mound City, in particular, a few miles up the Ohio, where so many great steamers had been built or fitted out. The railroads, in contrast, were converging here as though drawn by a giant magnet.

The atmosphere of the city was like Carnival in miniature. Ever alert for detail that might lend color to his reports, Joel learned by eavesdropping that the incoming flood of sightseers had begun a whole day ago. Already by yesterday evening the levee had begun to spawn clusters of tents, sprouting like mushrooms at convenient distances one from another, linked by newspaper sellers and gossip mongers who kept a flash flood of mingled fact and rumor at its swell.

Thanks to telegraph messages, it was known that the *Atchafalaya* was still in the lead; that Drew had ordered his coal flats to be made ready on the Missouri shore, where he could save time by not cutting across incoming currents from the mouth of the Ohio; that his few remaining passengers for Ohio ports were to be transferred on the run to the *Luke S. Thrale*. And she was standing by with steam up, heedless of the cost in fuel, for the sake of a part share in this epoch-making run.

Some therefore claimed that the result was a foregone conclusion. Others argued that if the *Nonpareil* had, as was reported, hired extra pilots for the stretch north of Cairo, she still stood an excellent chance, while others yet maintained that the idea had been abandoned. The debate raged furiously.

For here, if anywhere in the entire run, skill must be at a premium over speed. It was not for nothing that the vicious curve of Dog Tooth Bend was nicknamed "the graveyard." Steamer after handsome steamer had gone down in its treacherous maze, adding countless obstacles to the passage of later vessels, especially because during the war and immediately after neither funds nor means were available to raise the metal from sunken boats.

And night was drawing on.

Worse yet, perhaps worst of all, one of the few boats to continue running this portion of the river on a Sunday, the *Phalanx*, arriving from St. Louis, reported stretches in the upper river where there was barely eight feet of water.

Eight feet! When everybody knew the racing boats drew at least nine when fully loaded.

But, of course, neither of them was. Learned disputes broke out concerning the superior advantages of lightness for one or the other boat, while Whitworth kept his secret counsel and sometimes smiled without it reaching his eyes.

Meantime Joel did his best not to, thinking of what was in his pocket safe. He had had deliberately to prevent himself from reaching for it on several occasions when Whitworth wanted a match.

In an odd sense he was starting to feel guilty. Direct acquaintance with his victim was evoking what had frequently brought him to quarrel with his father during the latter's ill-judged speculation in slaves. He would rather have seen him copy Andrew Moyne's venture in matchwood, even though that had brought in its train an even vaster financial disaster. Trees? Lord, they were sprouting the length of the Mississippi as fast as one could keep track! A sedge of willows could anchor a sandbar almost overnight! Granted, pine woods were a little less hasty, but even so, how could one compare the worth of trees with the worth of people?

It dawned on Joel by degrees that he was called on to act as both judge and jury over Whitworth.

He had condemned Arthur's treatment of Louisette willingly enough, for he knew Arthur and—though he had never wished to cast the first stone—the man's drunkenness would by itself have been enough to warrant condemnation.

Also (but this was very remote now, like the echo of a dream) he had loved Louisette.

Yet now, when he held Whitworth's fate in the palm of his hand, and knew there was only one right course for him to follow, he felt guilty about exercising such responsibility. It *was* like owning a slave, and he had hated that since he first realized what it meant.

At the cost of not filing his report from Cairo, which he had worked out bar some figures and times he intended to pick up on arrival; at the cost of maybe not joining the *Atchafalaya*, and sacrificing his career in consequence; at any cost and all cost, he wanted to escape from the duty of pronouncing doom.

Therefore he hung at Whitworth's heels when they left the train and headed for the wharf, instead of making at once for the telegraph office.

Therefore he put up with the older man's snarling comments until they could be borne no longer and Whitworth rounded on him and said, "Say, Mister Reporter!"

Riding the cars they had become "Joel" and "Harry." It was a warning sign, like the thin bright line of light across the sky presaging a storm's arrival on the Mississippi.

"You have a story to send to your paper, don't you? So quit hounding me or you'll miss out on your plan to switch to the *Atchafalaya*! Me, I got plenty of time, if the *Nonpareil* ain't taken her yet! And plenty of business!"

"Such as what?" Joel barked, emboldened by this opening.

Whitworth looked at him for a long while, panatela in one hand, carpetbag in the other.

At length he sighed.

"Hell and all its devils! Look, if you print one word of this I'll swear you're lying, and so will everybody else! But just to get you off my back . . . Drew's hired the *Thrale* to take off his Ohio passengers, right? Well, we reckon he owes us a handicap time, which would be made up if he had to make a proper stop here. How can you compare the speed of two steamers when one had to make a stop and the other didn't? *We* didn't bargain for putting in at Baton Rouge! So they sent me to outbid Drew's offer and force him to make a stop! And if I don't fix it, I'll be less than the dust Woodley shakes off his shoes!"

With that improbably biblical phrase, Whitworth stormed away, losing himself as quickly as possible in the crowd. There were crowds everywhere in Cairo today.

Joel wished for a heartbreaking moment he could believe what the other had told him. But he had felt that pine log: its weight in his hands, its rough surface under his fingers. And inside it he had seen and recognized . . .

He reached his decision without further ado. Whitworth was quite right: he had a story to file, one which must include reference to the *Nonpareil*'s second mate being aboard the train.

Nothing more than that. Not right now.

But after the dispatch was safely on its way, he would be ready to bet anything he could afford on their next rendezvous.

He planned to ride out on one of the *Atchafalaya*'s coal flats, and originally he had simply meant to take his chance of being allowed on board, using the threat of press power to persuade any of the junior officers who got in his way.

But now he had a weapon, and it sat on him uncomfortably, as though he had donned a gun belt and holster.

For he was sure to meet Whitworth at the coal flat, and Whitworth would be trying to toss that pine log into the fuel pile unobserved, relying on the assumption that nobody taking a box of coal aboard would question a fine chunk of burnable wood.

He pictured himself marching aboard the *Atchafalaya* and demanding to see Drew, offering the explosive in his pocket as evidence for the terrible story he had to relate.

And was dismayed to find that merely thinking about it made him indescribably sad.

Should not this truly have been a contest of giants—albeit the giants were machines? Instead, here he was finding it tarnished by the petty concerns of humanity: gambling wins and losses, self-aggrandizement, personal renown!

At the back of his mind had been hovering the notion that he might write a book-length memoir about this race, whether in fictional or reportorial form. Since his time in company with Whitworth, he had been inclining more toward the novel version, which could be a gage for him to throw down in the literary arena. He made a resolution. Unless the *Atchafalaya* actually exploded, he would omit all reference to this loathsome episode.

In the meantime, though, he had that rendezvous to make. For if by some miracle he could produce Whitworth's log to Drew, he would crown himself with glory. He tried not to think about the possibility that Whitworth might realize it had been emptied and fill it again with regular gunpowder, to be had anywhere.

Once embarked on his perilous course, being the taut, nervous person he was, he would never accept a setback. Out west, according to the newspapers, according to the dime thrillers now appearing on bookstalls—especially along the railroads—they spoke of "desperate men."

What Joel could not understand was how such a man as Whitworth could have been deprived of hope.

His best guess seemed trivial, yet it was all he could come up with.

Solitary, wishing to imagine himself as better than he was, Whitworth needed a scapegoat. He had indicated something of the sort during their train ride. It so happened that he had been offended—how, Joel had no idea—by Fernand Lamenthe when he was working aboard the same boat. The notion that a colored man might aspire to pilot's status, while he remained a hireling at far lower pay, was more than he could bear. From that point on he had frozen into the belief that those who, in his childhood, had been regarded as fit mainly to be bought and sold, were conspiring to take over the world.

Sinking a steamer with a Creole pilot at her helm by extension was no worse than shooting a dog, and the hell with anybody fool enough to ship with the black devil in the first place!

It had never come out so nakedly, but it was—was the *taste* Whitworth had left in Joel's mind.

Consequently he went about his business with expedition, eager to reach the wharf where coal flats for the racing boats must even now be being readied.

And armed with something wholly unexpected.

Reading over the text he had to send, the clerk in the cable office glanced up. "You going aboard the *Atchafalaya* now?"

Since the fact was plainly stated in his message, Joel nodded.

"Say, you can do us a favor!"—turning and signaling over his shoulder. "We had a telegram for Mr. Drew, and we ain't got a *one* of our durn delivery boys to bring it to him! Mr. Meldrum!" he added as his chief approached. "Would it be okay if I gave that St. Louis cable for Captain Drew to this gentleman, who plans to join the *Atchafalaya* here?"

"Well, I wouldn't know about that," Meldrum began. Joel cut him short.

"It would be a pleasure! I've often interviewed Captain Drew for my newspaper. I know him well!"

"I guess it might be okay," Meldrum sighed at length. "We figured on sending it care of his local agents, as usual. But every last one of our boys is missing! I guess they're all down the levee, waiting for the boats. And if that's so, I swear they'll get their hides tanned in the morning!"

Triumphantly Joel pocketed the sealed envelope, which would be a passport for him to board the *Atchafalaya*, and signed a receipt for it with a cheerful flourish.

 The reception awaiting the *Atchafalaya* and *Nonpareil* at Cairo outdid anything seen on the lower river. It being Sunday, scarcely any steamers were scheduled for departure, and most of them delayed it anyhow. Those downbound from either Mississippi or Ohio ports, or about to be overtaken on their way up by the racing boats, were

likewise lying over to see them go by, and to hell with passengers impatient to reach their destination, or forfeiture charges on perishable goods! There were so many, there was room neither at the wharfs nor the wharf boats to cope with them all, and some stood into midstream, narrowing the channel dangerously.

Moreover dozens of excursion boats had turned out, and special trains had been run on both the Illinois Central and Cairo & Fulton railroads. The concourse of locomotives and other steam engines loaded the air with smuts that marked the smart white dresses of the ladies and the gentlemen's snowy shirtbosoms.

Rumors abounded—that one or other of the boats had struck a snag, or gone aground, or burst a steam pipe, or collided with a barge adrift from its towboat. Gossip that afternoon was a growth industry.

Little by little, however, as the sun declined, the mood grew calmer, and all eyes turned on the *Thrale*. Brilliant in white and red and gold, though a bare two-thirds the length of either racing boat, she was an outstanding vessel in the local trades, with one year of reliable service behind her almost to the day. Therefore the spectators took her as a barometer. When smoke puffed from her chimneys, they cheered; then they waited anxiously for the first sign of movement from her wheels; then they cheered again when she cast off from the wharf and grew despondent when she merely sauntered downstream instead of hurrying.

But then she rounded to in a patch of dead water at the conflux of the rivers, and even those who had witnessed many previous fast runs—including the *Atchafalaya*'s with Larzenac, including the maiden voyage of the *Nonpareil*—started to urge silence on others, to create a hush requisite for an event so memorable, none present would wish to miss the slightest detail.

And Whitworth, Joel was prepared to bet, had not been within a hundred yards of her.

 Aboard the *Nonpareil* it felt as though they were already doomed to endure the torments of eternity. It was so humiliating to review all her setbacks—not merely the stop at Baton Rouge, but the encounter with floating drift, and the broken rudder cable, and Barfoot grounding her, and, just to top it all, the need to slow for steam leaks!

None had been reported for an hour. They were breathing more easily in the pilothouse. But slowing in bends where they should at least have matched their rival's speed had cost them dear. There was talk not only among the passengers but among the deck crew of treating the race as lost and won, and with less than two hundred miles to go it was a tempting notion.

Yet they were still in sight of the *Atchafalaya*'s smoke, and newspapers brought aboard at Memphis had included the assertion that she too had suffered a steam leak and it had been bad enough to scald one of her engineers.

If once, why not again? At least they were driving her to her limits!

This fortunate scrap of information was a source of great relief to Woodley and Gordon. Now they could hint at what they—

Knew? Well, not exactly. But *expected*.

For those not party to that deadly secret, misery was overcoming hope, and much of it had no connection with the racing steamers.

This morning, when Josephine took her place among the black deckhands, she had experienced a familiar sensation. It had seemed as though some outside force was in control of her actions.

Yet somehow the singing had dragged her back to her normal mode of existence. It was too calm, too weary, to complete the process which, in that past she sometimes had trouble remembering, had cut her loose entirely and delivered her into the grasp of the god. She had expected the feeling to go on when she told Caesar she would make him another trickenbag; that had not been her usual, considered, concealed personality speaking. It was as though this short time away from Cherouen had been enough to persuade her she had been wrong to live in disguise among strangers. But how foreign were the whites to her? She wanted to compare herself to Ruth, who followed love into an alien land; yet alien blood ran in her veins, and—for all she could tell—might soon be pulsing in her womb.

With the failure of the god to take command, she had found herself trapped once more in conventionality. What last night had seemed powerful magic was now disgusting. If only Auberon had come rushing after her to declare his attachment, seized her arm and swung her round to kiss her, that would have sufficed to reconnect her with his people. As it was, he had accepted her rebuff as meekly as though she were no more than a disappointed partner at a Mardi Gras ball, whose toe he had trodden on.

If that was all the impact she had made on his mind, what use had last night's ceremony served?

And there was no future for her among the other of her peoples! How could there be, when they were so cringing and overawed? And *filthy!* Even Caesar, who spoke up like a man, proved on inspection to be clad in rags, to have rotten teeth, to limp on one leg! She who—thanks to Cherouen—had visions of making humanity whole, ridding it of fleas and lice and grime: how could she treat such folk as equals? And how could she any longer be tempted by the notion of lording it over them like Marie Laveau?

And how, above all, could she ever have been so stupid as to think she might cut herself absolutely free from that half of her existence by taking a white man's poison to lighten her skin?

She would never forget, so long as she lived, how Auberon last night had worshiped her dark body. No matter how she now hated the very thought of him!

These contradictions closed on her like ice floes grinding on a winter river. All of a sudden they became unbearable. She had to flee to her stateroom.

There she slumped on the bed and gave herself over to helpless weeping, during which she was chiefly conscious of one desire: that she might make real the visions she had had about a dangerous brown stick, so that this boat might be blown up with her and all aboard.

At some stage Auberon sent one of the stewards to ask if she would join him at table. She offered no reply, but buried her face in a pillow to prevent herself uttering curses.

Much later in the afternoon Auberon was sitting glumly on deck and watching this landscape which had indeed changed, but dreadfully slowly, since the start of the trip. He had never paid to go into a panorama, but he was coming to understand why people might. If the scenery from New Orleans to Alton could be displayed in an hour, with all the famous sights like Fort Pillow and Island 10 and the rest, why waste time on seeing it in real life?

Or was his impatience due to awareness of impending death?

Last night . . .

He had still not come to grips with himself after that extraordinary, terrifying experience. Josephine had kept on moaning and gasping in a deep throaty voice; what few recognizable words emerged were not English but a kind of French, which thanks to his time in Europe he sometimes understood despite the thick, slurred accent. She had spoken, after a fashion, of medicine, and good luck, and charms, and powers unknown to Christian people, and he had had the sense of being caught up in a process far beyond his conscious control.

Today he was wondering whether it had all been illusion. If so, he hoped he might never enjoy such another.

"Auberon!"

A commanding voice at his side. He turned and found Hugo brandishing one of the papers that had been brought aboard; Stella a pace behind; Arthur in the background, scowling.

"Auberon, you've got to use your good offices to prevent Joel libeling Arthur! Here's a paper reprinting a slanderous story, and it's obviously his work even though it isn't credited! Arthur was all set to call him out, but we've persuaded him it would be better to seek an apology. Of course, we know how much you care for Louisette, and so do we all, and I'm sure you're aware that if it had lain in our power we would never have permitted Arthur to act as he did at Baton Rouge, but you must understand that—"

And so on. Doubtless including reasons why he didn't go ashore at the next port and try to make good his ill-treatment of his bride . . .

*My sister.*

The words continued. Auberon paid no attention. He was suddenly launched on a voyage of self-discovery.

During his time in Europe he had thought of Louisette as his one solid link with the idyllic past he had left behind when he quit childhood. To her he had addressed his sentimental letters, enshrining the affection he wished he could have lavished on his parents. Those he had written to Joel had been couched in what he had learned to regard as "grown-up" terms: a trifle cynical, a touch boastful, and above all detached from anything that might be construed as honest feeling.

Because he was trying to run away from all such emotions as of the day he first coughed blood?

No; it went deeper and hurt more cruelly, because those who had bought and sold slaves were accustomed to regard their children too as investments more than as human beings. Joel had said as much in some of his letters, but Auberon had dismissed it as due to bitterness after his father's stupid speculations in black livestock. And, since his return, Louisette had said more or less the same kind of thing. Now he was coming to accept that they were right. If he had not been packed off to Europe . . .

Well, at least when he died he would leave behind a younger brother, in good health as far as he knew, fit to be heir to the Moyne fortune because he was dutiful and obedient and industrious. Let his parents be content with one out of three!

But, in spite of all, he would rather it had been two out of three. He would rather Louisette had married someone—though lacking riches—who was capable, and sensible, and levelheaded, and ambitious: someone, in short, who could have made life fun for her.

Someone not like Arthur Gattry, who was ambitious—yes!—but also selfish, and slothful, and a drunkard. Someone, as it were, more like Joel.

Cousin or not, poverty-stricken or not (by the standards of the Moynes and those like them), Joel was a better man.

Auberon grew aware that there was a silence about him. He had been challenged. He was to mend his fences with Arthur, for the sake of future peace.

But his thinking had one more stage to go. He had to work beyond "someone like Joel" and reach—

It hit him with blinding force, and when he had the chance to take stock of the inspiration, it proved incredibly simple:

*Someone like me.*

Which explained last night to perfection. It ought to have been . . .

*Not my half-sister. My full sister.*

As though the prospect of premature death had held up a mirror to him, one in which he might view his life entire without distortion or the hope of self-deception, Auberon saw everything about him in a cold and pitiless light. Those who stood near, the cabin of the *Nonpareil*, the landscape visible beyond the windows, receded to an illimitable distance. He wondered with what hint of detachment remained to him whether he was running a fever, and if so whether he should call on the nurse who had so kindly tended him before, and remembered she was Josephine, so that was impossible.

Therefore he must go to his grave without care, and he might as well begin now.

He had it in mind to say, "This drunken fool named Arthur Gattry who seduced my sister into marrying him and has betrayed her daily since the wedding, whom I ordered ashore to look after her and who has failed in his marital duty at every port on the river, as witness his continuing presence: him I want to kill. Him I want to see pierced with my pistol's ball through not his chest but his belly, where a child is carried by a woman. Where, for all I know, he sowed the seed of my beloved sister's death, for we have had no news of her."

And that was particularly galling, since cables and telegrams could always be brought aboard even a racing steamer.

They were not, however, still waiting for him to speak. Instead Hugo was say-

ing, "Look, Auberon! Stella and I both agree that since their marriage Louisette
has treated Arthur abominably! He had no faintest intention of bringing her on
this trip, only she insisted until she was blue in the face, and his only choice was
to give in. How was he to know the strain would prove so dangerous?"

At that point Auberon was set to explode.

But realized with a terrifying premonition that he could not do so into words,
only into a violent cough. He felt it gathering at the base of his breastbone: that
familiar hideous tightness which would become liquid in a moment, as though he
were about to drown.

He had to get away.

Rising from his seat, he brushed Hugo aside with one hand while seizing his
handkerchief with the other, and blindly fled from the cabin.

Hugo came after him, calling. He quickened his pace, wanting not to be near
anyone he knew when the paroxysm overtook him. He had hoped to keep his
illness secret for far, far longer. He still dared hope that Hugo and Stella might
believe it was only Arthur's blow which made his blood spurt before. If they saw
him in this predicament . . .

But abreast of the midships stairs leading to the main deck he was convulsed,
and reached for support, and found none. Of a sudden he was half scrambling,
half tumbling, while an unbiddable racking cough flooded the handkerchief—
which he managed to keep over his nose and mouth—with red.

A strong hand caught and steadied him, saved him from falling, urged him to
the side of the guards, let him be until the spasm was over and he was able to ball
up the saturated cloth and fling it into the water.

"Thanks," he muttered, not knowing whom he was obliged to.

"That's okay, sir," said a familiar voice. "My captain when I first signed up with
the Union Army—he had the same trouble."

Blinking away tears, Auberon glanced sidelong. Of course: Caesar, stripped to a
filthy undershirt and greasy canvas pants and giving a gap-toothed grin.

"I just come out for a breath of air," he said, half in explanation, half in apology,
as perhaps for laying uninvited hands on a white man's arm.

"How—how are things in the engineroom?" was all Auberon could think of to
reply.

"Mighty near as bad as they 'pear to be for you, sir. You take to your bed and
call on Mam'zelle Josephine again!"

No surprise in that, Auberon thought. News of how she had tended him before
must be all over the boat.

"I guess I might just do that," he muttered, and with a further word of thanks
turned back the way he had come.

"Auberon!" Hugo exclaimed, hastening down the stairs to confront him, with a
frantic Stella behind and Arthur lagging but following. "Auberon, I say! Are you
okay, old fellow?"

A final ooze of blood invaded Auberon's throat. He hawked and with considerable theatrical deliberation spat at Hugo's feet. The red embedded in the clear
sputum was like the twisting thread of color in an opal.

He thrust by before they had a chance to recover from the shock and betook
himself to his stateroom to finish last night's brandy.

Caesar, uncomprehending, watched him go, watched the others trail in his wake, arguing in low but vehement tones, and then was recalled to duty by a shout.

At least it wasn't yet another steam leak he was wanted for.


"Know what this boat of yours reminds me of?" Zeke Barfoot said.

Those nearby looked at him: Woodley, Gordon, Hogan, Matthew, grouped on the forward end of the boiler deck. The air was full of reproaches. Had this man not actually run the *Nonpareil* into a mudbank? What excuse did he have to offer?

Also Parbury, who stood among them like Banquo's ghost, half turned his black-barred face.

"What the hell are you talking about?" rasped Gordon.

"She's the newer of the boats," Barfoot said, "She may in principle be the faster. But she ain't the tougher. I had that proved to me last time I held her wheel."

Woodley seemed about to say something, but a rap on his shin from Parbury's cane prevented it.

"I want to hear this," the blind man said in a soft but dangerous voice. "Please continue, Mr. Barfoot."

Matthew suppressed a murmur of astonishment and went on feigning attention, more out of habit than because he expected to be called to account after to-morrow.

"Brings to my mind," Barfoot said after a pause, "a cathedral I once read about in Europe. It was to be lighter and more graceful than any seen before. And would have been, 'cept they were too ambitious. There was this little sinking of the ground because the foundations weren't as solid as they wanted, and *down* came the mighty tower and its spire!" He paralleled the crash with a folding downward gesture of his arm.

"What the hell are you talking about—cathedrals?" Woodley barked.

"What he means, sir"—this unexpectedly from Matthew—"is that the *Nonpareil* resembles that cathedral, when the masons overestimated their skill. This boat is fragile, made so in the quest for lightness. But, like the ground sinking, the river is testing her and finding her wanting."

Barfoot bent an approving gaze on him. "You take my drift, young man!" he rumbled. "She's too light! She takes to running off too easily! Her speed has been bought at far too great a cost!"

"You're saying that because you found you couldn't handle her!" Gordon accused.

"Oh, don't worry—it won't happen twice. Not now I know her *vices!*"

All eyes flicked instantly to Parbury, expecting him to erupt in fury at this condemnation of his masterpiece.

To their amazement he said nothing, but lifted his cane and tap-tapped away, bound to rejoin Trumbull in the pilothouse.

Impenitent of the offense he had caused, Barfoot said, "When have you ordered your coal at Cairo?"

Woodley pulled himself together, as from a great distance and many directions.

He said, scowling, "Between five and six. And beyond there, you'll see what she can really do to win the race!"

"Oh, sure! With me, and Tom Tacy, and Joe Smith as well—I contacted them both, made sure they'd join me, for no man cares to look a fool and sign aboard a losing boat without doing all he can to prevent it!—with all of us, and all respect to you, Dermot, naturally, we stand as good a chance of beating Drew as ever we did. Otherwise I'd not have come."

"But I canceled—" Woodley began. Barfoot cut him short.

"Ain't you glad I'm here after all? Dermot is, and Colin. Not because I hold any special love for you, *Captain*"—with a curl of his lip—"but because Joe and Tom and I and lots of others think it time Drew was cut down to size, that's all. For once your first idea was right, and I guess Dermot would be ready to admit it now."

He added, "I did kinda think, though, that this would be the boat to do the job. Now I've held her wheel, I'm not so sure."

Conscious that in some subtle fashion his claim to authority had once again been undermined, Woodley made to say something else, but Gordon caught his arm and gave a meaning headshake. The captain shrugged and turned away.

Over his shoulder he said, "Fight it out between you who has the helm when we coal at Cairo. Just make sure it goes quicker than ever before! Every minute gained improves our chances!"

And he too stormed off.

Placatingly Barfoot offered to those remaining, "At least this race has shown up her weaknesses, hm? They can be put right if she's overhauled this winter. And she's a handsome vessel, I'll admit."

"Looks don't count worth a damn!" Hogan snapped. "But I wouldn't have signed my contract without being sure she was a worthy contender!"

"Worthy contender!" echoed Barfoot, and there was more than a trace of mockery in his voice. "Coming second in a race of two—what do they call that at Metairie?"

It occurred to Matthew that if Gordon lost as much on this defeat as he suspected was probable, he might not be able to extort the severance pay he was looking forward to. The notion was depressing. He barely noticed when Barfoot, as he passed, tapped him on the shoulder and said, "You're smart! I guess Mr. Gordon don't know how lucky he is."

Right.

Mr. Gordon, to the best of Matthew's knowledge and belief, did not realize how narrow his successive escapes had been so far.

If only Joel hadn't left the boat and gone ahead . . .

But on his own he was going to work it out and bring off the coup he had so long planned.

The one remaining question was the one that had just struck him: how to put in his claim before everyone else descended on Gordon like buzzards following a dying cow.

At precisely which point Gordon himself came over and gave a broad grin and spoke in a whisper.

"These pilots aren't half as smart as they think they are, you know! Wait till we get above Cairo! If we don't beat the *Atchafalaya*, you may hang my kilt for curtains and call me Sassenach!"

That being one of the foulest terms in his vocabulary—meaning, as it did, English—he left Matthew totally and indescribably confused.

Seconds later, as though to underline the contrast between reality and what one hoped for, Manuel's band struck up on the foredeck, and the air rang with cheerful tunes.

It did nothing to strengthen the *Nonpareil*'s elegant, refined, beautiful—and fragile—hull.

For the first time it was truly dark inside the head of Miles Parbury.

Since his blindness there had always at least been flashes of remembered light. They had faded—as Dr. Malone had warned they would—but they had come back at irregular intervals, and especially since the start of the race they had been frequent and vivid, whether provoked by his rage at Dorcas's desertion or by excitement at the way the *Nonpareil* responded when he struck her bell three times . . . which had cleansed his mind of hatred and resentment and made him grateful for the mercies still granted him.

Hearing Zeke Barfoot's verdict on his darling, though, he had been seized with violent self-pity.

Bitterness came with the darkness. So did fatigue. He fumbled about him for a place to sit down, realizing with horror that for the first time ever he did not know exactly where he was aboard his own boat.

Then someone was at his side and guiding him and asking whether he might bring refreshment. A tender. By the voice a black tender. The accent made him think of Dorcas, and he didn't want to think of Dorcas. He grunted no and leaned back, and the darkness that had begun with despair grew into the darkness of sleep.

Bringing with it dreams compounded not of images but of mere sensations: disappointment, regret, anger, futility. Now and again his limbs twitched, as he also experienced pain, violence, and resistance.

Eventually the shadow awareness of slumber developed into other and better forms, and when he moved he was feeling remembered skills; his legs responded to the shift of the deck as a rival boat shed her wash into his course; his arms hinted at the movements of a wheel controlling an even grander and finer vessel; until at last he was dramatizing within his skull the expected triumph of his beloved *Nonpareil*.

During all of which time they were preparing, at Cairo, a splendid reception for the *Atchafalaya*, of which it was rightly said by one observer, "There has not been such excitement at the meeting of the rivers since we shook and trembled at the echo of the batteries on Island Ten."

 Of a sudden the *Luke S. Thrale* came to life and put about for the lower river at high speed. The tension was now so tremendous, the sighs and gasps of the onlookers were like the soughing of a breeze in a forest. There still remained the best part of an hour before, on the most optimistic estimate, either of the racing boats could appear at Cairo, yet this event presaged their passage so vividly that many let off fireworks or gunshots.

The *Thrale* sped downstream and out of sight, heading for Island 1, beyond Birds Point and Fort Jefferson and the little town of Norfolk, ready to greet the *Atchafalaya*.

Smoke loomed in the distance as she came up past Columbus and Iron Banks and through Lucas Bend.

By which time there was more smoke on the skyline, and the day being Sunday, there were few vessels that might be emitting it. Surely the *Nonpareil* must still be in the race!

Even now they were placing bets as the cables hummed. Even now—and this was the marvel of it—the outcome seemed undecided, as garbled versions of what had happened to Walt Presslie reached the proponents of the *Nonpareil*, filtered through reprinted newspaper accounts that had been condensed and altered so that an editor might not be accused of stealing his contemporaries' stories.

Even now the contention that the *Nonpareil* still stood a chance was making elderly folk who recalled great races of the past, remembered how over so long a stretch as that from New Orleans to St. Louis there had been at best one, with luck two, changes of the lead, anticlimaxing in a once-for-all contest somewhere in the straight reaches of the lower river—was making them come forth and pronounce oracular judgment: that never since the *Eclipse* beat the *Shotwell* to Louisville had a race been so close-run at the Cairo mark.

The shouting of odds beset Joel's ears as he arrived on the wharf fronting the Mississippi, having traversed the one fronting the Ohio on his way from the railroad depot and found it effectively deserted, apart from a few grumbling watchmen who complained about being paid to stay put when the action was elsewhere. Whenever he heard someone backing the *Nonpareil*, he found himself wondering against his will whether that person was party to the secret of the attempted wrecking.

*Had* Whitworth brought a second stick of explosive with him? Surely not! Yet why else would people be laying out good money to back the losing boat?

He comforted himself with the assurance that he had treated the cardboard tube with utmost care, emptied it as though he were handling a baby, left no trace of his intervention.

But it had come as no surprise at all when he was told that the *Thrale* had put out from shore long before Whitworth could have caught up with her.

So where was Whitworth now?

Logically his target must be the coal yard, and—as it turned out—everyone knew where that was, and whom it belonged to: a certain Mr. Frobisher . . . who had been in receipt of so many cabled messages today, from both Drew and Woodley, that it was right on his river frontage that the missing telegraph boys were playing hookey.

Joel smiled a private smile, and kept on searching.

Among Mr. Frobisher's prized possessions was a steam tug, generally used to break up barge clusters of which some must continue downriver and some be transferred to the opposite one of the upper rivers. Today she was assigned to deliver coal flats by pairs, and there they were lashed together, waiting.

It would be tough luck on the trailing boat if the tug was still occupied with the leader when she arrived.

Joel got the yardmaster to point out Frobisher: a heavyset man, grimy from head to toe. So were all those who worked here among high piles of shiny coal.

"Oh, Christ! Not another of you!" was his reaction to the journalist's approach.

"I'm sorry, but what do you mean?"

"Well, everybody and his uncle wants to ride my flats today! Even a couple of goddamn' *pilots!*" He pointed; on the wharf stood two men sporting silk hats and diamond studs as though bound for some high-class party or society dinner.

Putting together scraps of information garnered during his time aboard the *Nonpareil,* Joel said acutely, "Ah! I guess that will be Mr. Smith and Mr. Tacy."

"You know them?" Frobisher growled. "I wish you'd tell 'em I don't approve of having my barges used for transportation of anything but the coal I'm paid for! But you're not bound for the same boat as they are, right?"

"No! I have this telegram to deliver to Mr. Drew, of the *Atchafalaya!*"

Frobisher gave a short laugh. "Hiring real men, are they, at the telegraph office? Well, I guess they need to. Seeing how many delivery boys didn't go back for more, but stayed right here on the levee, I've been wondering whether there may not be cables awaiting me which ain't got through yet. Ah, to the devil with it! You just stand by. At least you're the only guy lined up for the *Atchafalaya.* For the *Nonpareil* we got three already."

"Would the other be her second mate, a Mr. Whitworth?" Joel ventured.

"Could be," Frobisher allowed. "A cable said to expect someone with a name like that, though I guess it got muddled in transmission."

"I know Mr. Whitworth also," Joel declared, scanning the wharf. He stiffened. "Yes, there he comes now!"

With a touch of his hat to the two pilots, whom he engaged in conversation.

"I'll call him over and present him to you," Joel said on the spur of the moment. "I guess—in fact I'll bet—he will ask which of these flats are reserved for the *Atchafalaya.*"

Frobisher shrugged. "Whichever boat gets here first will have the ones lying furthest from shore."

"Figures," Joel said dryly, and strode toward Whitworth.

Who was not entirely overjoyed to be accosted, but presented Joel to Smith and Tacy with tolerable politeness.

"And what do you make of the *Nonpareil's* chances?" Joel inquired, whisking out notebook and pencil and becoming all reporter again.

They exchanged glances, Tacy said at length, "Slim. But far from nonexistent."

"Oh, very far from that!" Whitworth said with enthusiasm. He seemed to be even more tense and edgy than he had been on the train. Small wonder . . .

Instead of continuing to a full-scale interview, Joel contented himself with half a dozen notes, then turned to Whitworth.

"I promised to introduce you to Mr. Frobisher, who had a cable warning of your arrival. He's over there by the flats. It won't take a minute."

"Oh, if that's him," Whitworth said promptly, "no need for you to take the trouble. You carry on talking and I'll announce myself. Gentlemen!"—with another tap on his hat brim.

Accordingly Joel reopened his notebook and put some more questions to the pilots, concerning the amount of water in the upper river, the possibility of fog, and suchlike matters, which they were willing enough to answer. He only scrawled their replies, though. Most of his attention was on Whitworth.

Who stood chatting to Frobisher until a heaven-sent opportunity arose. A shabby black man with an urgent message hurried from the direction of the shed that served as the coal yard's office. Scowling, Frobisher excused himself.

Thinking he was unobserved, Whitworth promptly set down his carpetbag and opened it as though needing to take something from it: another box of panatelas, as it transpired. To get at it, he lifted the pine log out very quickly and set it down on the riverward side of the bag, effectively concealed from view save to the hands aboard the waiting barges. Rising, closing the bag again, he contrived to kick against the chunk of wood as though it had been there all the time. Pretending to be surprised, he made to knock it into the water, then pantomimed second thoughts, picked it up, and thrust it among the piled-up coal on the nearer of the leading pair of flats. Then he was heading this way again.

Joel felt no pity for him after that.

Nor, curiously, any hatred either. Rather, he was experiencing the calm triumph of a chess player who has watched his opponent blunder into a well-planned trap.

Hastily he said to Smith and Tacy, "Gentlemen, you've been most obliging, and I'm sure my editor would wish me to mark the fact! Since I'm afraid it may well be quite some while before the *Nonpareil* arrives, why don't you take Mr. Whitworth and get yourselves all some refreshment?" He produced some coins and made them jingle in his hand.

Tacy, who was small and wiry and stern-faced, bridled at the offer, but Smith—plump, bluff, ruddy-cheeked—grinned and said, "So neither of us cares for Whitworth much! *I'm* not proud, though, and one day I hope to be rich!"

Heart pounding, Joel waited until the three of them were making their way up to the nearest of the temporary coffee stalls that had appeared to cater for the crowds of sightseers. Then he hurried toward the coal flats.

And was too late to recover the log. The tug sounded her whistle; the men aboard the barges jumped to answer it; and, catching sight of him, Frobisher shouted, "You'll be left behind if you aren't quick!"

Bag in hand, Joel leaped from the whaft and almost lost his footing when the tug leaned into her load like a horse taking a cart's weight on the traces. A high-piled box of coal spilled half its contents, covering the spot where the log was hidden. He stared in dismay, wondering whether he must burrow in search of it. Maybe one of the hands would help. Did he have enough cash to tip somebody? Frantically he fished in his pockets and discovered he had given all his change to Smith and Tacy.

Fatalistically Joel realized that unless he did actually grub for that log, the only proof of his charge against Whitworth consisted of the sludge in his pocket safe, and who was to say he hadn't put the stuff there himself?

But here came the *Atchafalaya* in plain sight, whistle howling! Roars of applause and thunderous explosions welcomed her, and at once his last chance of retrieving the log was snatched from him. Perhaps if he talked to the chief fireman on the steamer and told him to watch out for one large chunk of wood. . . ? But it would be covered in coal dust, indistinguishable from the rest of the fuel.

No, he must trust to luck and common sense.

Nonetheless it was with a frisson of terror that he made his way forward on the coal flat, shouting at the overseer that he had cleared this ride with Mr. Frobisher and brandishing the telegram in its envelope addressed in a florid copperplate hand to Captain Drew, c/o Str. *Atchafalaya*.

The overseer was plainly less than delighted to have him along; however, he swallowed his annoyance and merely ordered Joel to "git on board fastern'n a nigger after watermillions, else you'll find a coal box in the seat of your britches!"

Joel took the advice to heart and sprang on deck the instant the barges were secured. Cursing, the *Atchafalaya*'s deckhands let him pass at risk of being tipped overside.

Tom Chalker, the first mate, stood there shouting: "Yare now! *Move* yourselves! I want to see that coal warmed for the furnace because you rushed it on board so fast! (Who in thunderation are *you*?) Get a move on, you left-footed son of a slugabed and a balky mule! (Don't interrupt, goddamn you!) Where did you leave your *muscles*, you limp apology for a week-old corpse? (Cap'n Drew's in the pilot-house, where else? And won't thank you for disturbing him, so you best not try!) I said *hurry*, you thrice-condemned sons of Belial! I didn't say plant your shoes and wait for springtime! (Telegram? Show it to Mr. Motley and quit pestering me!) *That's* more like it, you wet-draggled coonskin-bin-through-a-'gator bunch of punkin ghosts!"

Meantime, miraculously, the coal was flowing on board at a rate it would have taken machines to better. Already the *Atchafalaya* was heading upriver at full speed again, and Cairo was receding into distance, and then both barges were empty and being cast off—the whole job of coaling having taken at most six minutes—and there was no sign of the *Nonpareil*.

Joel felt a shiver run down his spine, even as he realized that there were people gazing from the upper decks, among whom were a few he recognized and who recognized him: Cherouen, Barber, Dorcas, that strange Frenchman who had been directing the band at the Limousin last Mardi Gras . . .

But he had no attention to spare for them right now. He was simply aware that not even when he collected Larzenac from the *Franche-Comté* had Drew more splendidly exhibited the full-blown skills of a Mississippi pilot than during this refueling. He wished he had been able to witness the transfer of passengers to the *Thrale*, which doubtless would have been carried off with equal panache.

If this was typical of the standard Drew had now achieved, no wonder supporters of the rival boat were having to resort to trickery and maybe murder!

For the very last time he thought about being blown up. Then he wiped the notion firmly from his mind. That chunk of pine contained a cardboard tube stuck with two wooden plugs. At worst it would fizzle in the fire.

Now: where was Motley?

Glancing at the envelope that Joel proffered, Motley said in a gruff tone, "Sure, I'll give it to the captain when he comes from the pilothouse."

"I figured it might be urgent," Joel suggested. "It had been waiting Lord knows how long for lack of anyone to bring it."

"Yeah, I guess that's a point," Motley admitted. He glanced around and caught sight of David Grant.

"Call Mr. Drew by tube from the office," he instructed. "Say this here gentleman fetched a telegram from St. Louis."

David obeyed with alacrity, and the effect exceeded Joel's best hopes. Half a minute later the pilothouse door flung open and here came Drew three steps at a time, staff and cap forgotten. With a bare nod to acknowledge Joel, he seized the envelope and ripped it open.

Joel started to explain how he had come into possession of the message and was ready to continue about Whitworth's explosive, when he saw that Drew's face had set in a rock-hard mask. Even his eyelids ceased to move as he stared into nowhere. Only his fingers seemed alive; they folded and refolded the telegram form.

The *Atchafalaya* had cleared Elk Island and was swinging into the terrifyingly shallow channel that wove past the Dog Tooth Islands before Drew spoke again, and then it was with his attention fixed on another place and time.

Under his breath he recited: *"I that in heill was and gladness . . ."*

From that Joel was able to judge the content of the message, and his heart sank. By his face, so did Motley's.

Then Drew seemed to return from far away, and bent his gaze on Joel. Just a spark, no more, of animation remained in his eyes; he appeared very old of a sudden, and his voice creaked like the hull of a worn-out steamer on her way to the scrap yard.

"I can't thank you for bringing me this news, Mr. Siskin. I would have given an arm and a leg not to receive it. But I guess I have to say I'm obliged by your courtesy, for otherwise I might have been in limbo overnight. I expect you'll be making interviews for your newspaper now you've joined us? And one of them will be with Dr. Cherouen? Then do me one more favor. Wait on him at once and inform him that his attendance on my sister-in-law will not after all be required."

Upon which he turned away and, with heavy senile steps, ascended the stairs to the hurricane deck and then to his stateroom. Before he reached his destination, he crumpled and flung away the fateful paper.

A freak of the wind prevented it from blowing overside as he had intended. An alert deckhand caught it, and a roar from Motley ordered him to fetch it here at once! It was brought on the double, and—suddenly become companions in adversity—Joel and the chief clerk read it together.

MOTHER PASSED AWAY PEACEFULLY BLESSED YOU IN HER LAST MOMENTS
YOUR NEPHEW ELPHIN.

While they were still pondering the impact of this terrible news, they were interrupted by a shout.

Leaning over the texas rail, hands cupped around his mouth, Drew was bellowing at them.

"And tell Cherouen not to worry! In spite of all, we shall deliver him to St. Louis in time no other boat could beat!"

On the last word his voice broke, and he vanished in search of privacy for his grief, leaving Joel to wonder whom, if not the captain, he should tell about having saved the *Atchafalaya* from destruction.

Word of Susannah's death spread throughout the boat as fast as fire taking hold, and brought misery for all.

Especially since Tyburn, who had the wheel after Drew relinquished it, was suddenly obliged to cut their speed. Those warnings about shallow water in the upper river had been only too accurate. The first proof consisted in a grinding of pebbly mud against the hull as he rounded to larboard past the Dog Tooth Islands. It was like the touch of terror on their naked souls. It caused no delay, but there remained Dog Tooth Bend, already in plain sight, and beyond it the stretch known for good reason as the Graveyard, and the Grand Chain—of rocks!—and Steersman's Bend, near Thebes, so named because it called for expert navigation; and moreover night was falling. It was far from dark as yet, but the sun was close to the western horizon.

And though she had doubtless made worse time at her coaling than the *Atchafalaya*, as usual, the smoke from the *Nonpareil* could once more be plainly seen as she pulled away from Cairo, for despite the lay of the land—they were now clear of the great flood plain that made the lower river wander so—there was no intervening hill to blot out the sight of those vast plumes, like a war bonnet on an Indian chief.

And there was something about the view ahead that made Tyburn curse and rub his eyes and reach for his field glasses and curse again.

Mist among the treetops. Thickening. Even before sundown it might visit darkness on them by turning into out-and-out fog.

"Mr. Barber!"

"Why, Mr. Siskin! Came aboard at Cairo, did you? Satisfied the race is lost and won, I take it! Let's drink to that, shall we? Sit down, sit down! Cuffy, bring more champagne!"

Oddly nervous, Joel complied. There was something in the air, here in the *Atchafalaya*'s cabin—tension, hard to pin down. Perhaps it had something to do with the company Barber was keeping. There were scarcely any passengers left now, except a handful who wanted to see the race out for the excitement of it, and most of them were playing cards at the forward end of the room. Among that group he recognized Cherouen, who by the expression on his face was having poor luck. But the others at Barber's table were Dorcas and Eulalie: prim, a little on edge because their host had invited them to sit so far along the cabin, now that the women's section at the stern was otherwise empty. Nobody felt inclined to argue. Here, with his bodyguards at his back, he was as much in command of the situation as though he were at the Limousin. He did, after all, own half the boat.

Which was precisely why Joel had sought him out, needing to . . . give a warning? But the call for that was past.

To share his secret? That came closer. More precisely yet: to let his deed be known and—here he had to be brutally frank with himself—admired. It would be described fully in his next dispatch, to be sent ashore perhaps at Thebes, perhaps at Chester or St. Genevieve, depending on what sort of time the *Atchafalaya* made in this treacherously shallow upper river. But, of course, for the sake of modesty, he must ask Graves to have it rewritten in third person before lauding it in banner headlines. And it would all be very remote at the far end of a telegraph line. He wanted to see the impact of his story on someone else, face to face.

The champagne arrived and was poured only for Barber and himself. He realized belatedly that what he had taken for the same in glasses before the women was actually a mix of white wine and sparkling water.

Clearly Barber had been indulging in nothing so mild. He went on talking and smoking a succession of cigars, for the lighting of each of which he asked permission of Eulalie, but took it for granted so far as to have signaled Cuffy for a match before glancing his question. It was going to be a long time before Joel managed to steer the conversation his way.

He began with a valiant attempt, saying, "Mr. Barber, you are still part owner of the *Atchafalaya*, aren't you?"

"I don't expect to be so for long," Barber replied. He brushed back a strand of hair from his face; he was very flushed, and shiny with perspiration in the warm wet evening air. "Finally I broke Hosea loose from his prudish refusal to lay bets."

"I don't quite follow," Joel admitted, sipping his wine and finding it good.

"You haven't heard, and you a newspaperman? I thought the news would have fled up and down the river like fire on oil! Why, Hosea will win my share of this boat if he beats the *Nonpareil,* and we're in a fair way to managing that, are we not? And I shall never have lost a bet with better grace! *My* natural environment, Mr. Siskin, is not this unstable luxury afloat on the water, contrived of planking painted to look like marble and mirrors cunningly hung to make a cabin seem like a ballroom! No, all that I'll leave to Hosea, and it may console him for his greater loss."

On the last phrase his look and tone became so sad, Joel was startled. He said, "You've heard about his sister-in-law, then?"

"Jones brought the news a minute before you put in your appearance. I sent him to express all our sympathy, but it appears Hosea wants none of it right now. Condolences in their due time, then. But at all events, so long as we beat the *Nonpareil,* I shall regard the bet as lost, and I shall not complain. How do you think of me, Mr. Siskin?"

At a loss, Joel stumbletongued. Barber continued as though he had not been expecting an answer anyhow.

"I have not lived without my share of opprobrium, you know. At our first meeting Hosea himself was prepared to loathe me, and never entirely recovered from it, though I may say with some slight satisfaction that his dislike has evolved from the personal to the general; he will never love me so long as I continue to be a professional gambler. Nor will many others, particularly those whose money I have taken when they believed they were in luck. Never talk about luck to a gambler, Mr. Siskin! Many of them will speak of it to you, but if you view the matter dispassionately, you'll notice that one good reason why Hosea and I have ultimately reached an accord is that I don't believe in it and nor does he. For this run, as for his run with Larzenac, he made exquisite preparation. He left as little as humanly possible to chance. Are not his arrangements for coaling, for example, far superior to those which Woodley made? Has not his policy of engaging and then paying to keep a first-rate group of officers, backed by an outstanding crew, better repaid the time and trouble he went to than all the efforts Woodley made to sign pilots on long-term contracts, then offend them by hiring so-called specialists for the upper river?"

The grammar of his question might be dubious; the logic of his argument was not, and Joel said so with a trace of respect, adding, "I had not believed you so well informed about steamboating, sir!"

"I believe in careful analysis of whatever I invest in," Barber said, preening a little. "It was not luck which carried me from my first gaming rooms at the Fair Ground to my present position of—well, if not of eminence, then of notoriety at least! It was forethought and calculation."

All the signs indicated he was about to launch into a string of reminiscences. Hastily Joel said, "But, sir, there are some things which can't be foreseen. Might I have a word in private?"

Barber checked on the brink of another sentence. He blinked a couple of times, reading Joel's face as he might that of someone who had just raised him in a poker game. Then he tilted his head ever so slightly toward the vacant rear of the cabin. Joel nodded, and he heaved himself ponderously to his feet.

"Ladies, you'll excuse us," he muttered.

Catching sight of movement from the corner of his eye, Cherouen called from the card table.

"Any more bad news for us, Langston?"

"I shall share it if it's fit to be shared," was Barber's reply. And he continued as he accompanied Joel sternward, lowering his voice, "You heard the phrase 'bedside manner'?"

"Yes, of course."

"Cherouen doesn't have it. It could well be a merciful release that Mrs. Susannah Drew has escaped his ministrations, and I hold out no special hopes for the surviving Grammont child. He is so obsessed with his own special methods, he can't descend to the level of us ordinary mortals. You heard that one of our engineers was badly scalded not long after departure?"

"The story was in newspapers brought aboard the *Nonpareil* at Memphis."

"He deigned to attend the poor devil—once or twice. Thereafter he left him alone, though Hosea and the chief engineer and I myself have attempted to persuade him to pay more attention. I'm told Walt's shoulder is suppurating and he's feverish, though he insists on working regardless. Meantime Cherouen blames the loss of his nurse for his indifference. *Did* she wind up aboard the *Nonpareil?* Cuffy tells me a rumor is rife to that effect."

Joel realized with a start that Jones and Cuffy were following them, with tread totally silenced by the carpet.

"Yes, she did," he admitted, not wanting to mention his and Auberon's part in bringing her there. Quickly he added, "And the most amazing thing happened, too! It turned out she is—well, a conjuh woman rather than a nurse!"

"So she *is* Mam'zelle Josephine, is she?" Barber murmured as they reached the end of the cabin. It had plainly been his intention to step out on deck by the rearmost door; however, he had just caught sight of someone leaning on the after rail in a posture eloquent of total gloom. "Stop," he added to Joel. "We'd best remain in here. One wouldn't wish to interrupt our French genius, hm?"

Joel was confused by the change of subject. He had paid no attention to the man outside, though now he recognized him.

"That's the celebrated composer Monsieur d'Aurade," Barber said with a faint chuckle. "At least he will be celebrated, so he claims, if he's given the chance to concentrate on music for the funeral of the Grammont boy. He has been complaining nonstop about the way he's interrupted. He was positively cheering when we transferred the bulk of our remaining passengers to the *Thrale.*"

Which should have given Joel his opening to mention Whitworth and the explosive, but something else took precedence. He blurted, "How in hell did you know about Mam'zelle Josephine? Because so many of your customers patronize her?"

There were chairs and tables here, and comfortable sofas, but neither ashtrays nor cuspidors, smoking and chewing being regarded as exclusively masculine habits. Barber's cigar was spent; he thrust it at Cuffy and the black departed at a run to dispose of it and fetch their glasses and the newly opened bottle of champagne, while Jones handed him a fresh cigar and struck a light.

Dropping onto the nearest sofa and indicating a chair for Joel, Barber said meditatively, "Don't like my men—the waiters, I mean. Nor Vehm and Amboy, who take a share of the tips. Sometimes I wonder how they'd feel if they had to deal with one of these here noblemen you hear tell of in Europe, who won't move without a whole damned squad of flunkies . . . But you were saying"—puffing the new cigar into life—"how did I know about Mam'zelle Josephine?"

Joel nodded, and by reflex whipped out his notebook and pencil.

For a second Barber seemed inclined to tell him to put them away again. Then he changed his mind and sighed.

"Ah, I guess I can tell the truth at last. I can take off the mask, the disguise, the Mardi Gras rig . . . and why not to you, because I think you're an honest reporter?"

Joel stared at him with a distinct sensation of having missed at least one important phrase. But Barber's attention was no longer on him, nor indeed on anything in present time—though by reflex he picked up his glass when Cuffy filled it.

Eventually he said, "No, Mr. Siskin. The suggestion you just offered is of course correct: like Marie Laveau and Athalie Lamenthe, Josephine has served the needs of gamblers, and many have been customers of mine. Far more to the point, I like to keep my ear to the ground where my own people are concerned."

There was a pause, during which Jones and Cuffy exchanged looks of amazement.

"Why the hell do you think I was rubbing Cherouen's nose in my pleasure at the company of Madame Lamenthe and her soon-to-be-daughter-in-law?" Barber snapped at last. "He has often slighted the colored people in my hearing, and I— Damnation, I am making confession because I need a priest and you'll be one for the nonce! All this Sunday I have reflected on my plight, and you come handy when I'm drunk enough to speak out. *In vino veritas!*"

His voice changed abruptly.

"I am a doomed man, Mr. Siskin. Without wife or children and no family that I know about. I have it on the word of a doctor whom I vastly admire, who used to be Edouard Marocain's physician too. Excessive liquor, excess in diet, excess in staying up nights at the tables, excess in everything took its toll of my body, and chiefly, he tells me, of my liver. I shall not collapse tomorrow, or next week, but it is too late to think of marrying and founding a dynasty! Next year, the year after . . . who can tell?"

He gulped more champagne.

"Presumably," he went on, "it's the news you brought to Hosea which has turned my mind into such a melancholy channel, but the sensation is not the less real for being accidental. Though you may not speak of luck to a gambler, chance is what he perfectly comprehends! And the miraculous chance that this winning boat is piloted for much of her run by a colored man has been of extraordinary help in winding me up to this pitch. Mr. Siskin, I acknowledge my status as a Creole, which I have for years denied, invoking Spanish blood to explain my complexion."

Absently he touched his left cheek, brushing it as to disturb a fly.

"Did you ever hear a rumor to the effect that I had hired armed men to restore freed slaves to their former owner?"

Joel gave a cautious nod.

"That was done, but not by me. What I *did* do, and had no credit for, was rescue starving black folk from the city streets and return them, at their own wish, to the country, where they might scrape a subsistence. Then the dispossessed landlord fought a lawsuit and won back title to the land they had settled on, and sent discharged soldiers with guns to reclaim it, and shot those of the new settlers who tried to flee, and . . ." A shrug. "It was a gamble, and one I lost, for I was not rich enough to outdo him in the courts. And in the upshot what *I* did grew confused in the public mind with what someone else did, and that was among the reasons I preferred to go on being regarded as wholly white."

He drained his glass and held it out for Cuffy to refill, the while shaking his head despondently.

"Did no one know the truth?" Joel demanded, finding himself touched more deeply than he would have liked in his role as a hard-boiled reporter.

"Oh, old Edouard knew. Edouard Marocain, I mean. He was all sympathy in his distant, formal way. His name, he pointed out to me, meant Moroccan. In other words 'of African blood'! But he was a man who only discovered late in life how to grant freedom to his feelings. Much like myself, come to think of it. I must pluck up the courage to tell Fernand about this, too. After all, I'm in a better position to stand godfather to his first-born than Hosea is, and he's asked Hosea."

"I don't quite . . ." Joel began, and his words trailed away. Memory supplied the image of Fernand and Dorcas at the Limousin the night of Mardi Gras, and a pattern formed that he had not previously suspected.

"It's a strange other world one lives in under such circumstances," Barber sighed. "Knowing how Athalie Lamenthe willed her powers to Eulalie, who sits yonder like some *grande dame* fallen on hard times and doesn't realize I know this boat was sown from bow to stern with magic charms at her behest—which, at her son's, were wiped away again."

Joel sat still as rock, his head ringing with uncontrollable insights, wondering how he could have been so foolish as to opt for the *Nonpareil* when the *Atchafalaya* was electric with these secret and unguessable events.

He ventured finally, "You must therefore have been aware of Miss Var's connection with my cousin Auberon and ultimately myself?"

Barber sighed and nodded. "Among the reasons I learned to distrust the notion of luck was because, when you look closer, you often find that what appears to have been accidental was nothing of the kind. Oh, I don't mean that the universe is like a great machine, only that it's too complex for any single person to comprehend, and the Deity has preserved a degree of inscrutability which my faith obliges me to respect as a 'divine mystery'! So we lack keys to such confluxes of events as—oh, Fernand meeting Dorcas and giving her into the charge of the doctor who found her a place in Parbury's home, thereby leading to this race, in a way . . . But I suspect you may disagree. You said some things cannot be foreseen, as though you're a mystic rather than a fatalist. What were you referring to?"

Joel remained silent for a while, listening to the boat and thinking how much he would prefer to be a novelist instead of a reporter. He would have liked to omit Whitworth's deed from the world, as he had resolved to leave it out if he ever based a story on his experiences. It was ignoble; it spoiled the glamour of the race.

But he must not let the matter be hushed up. Someone capable of doing that might do something worse later on. (What was worse than blowing up a loaded steamboat? Starting another war?) And it could bring him fame, even glory . . .

His hand was withdrawing the pocket safe. His thumb was flicking open its lid. He heard his voice saying, "Do you know what this is? No? Then I'll tell you. Mica powder! And if it hadn't been for me, there would be a stick of it on the way to the *Atchafalaya's* furnaces. As it is, all you'll be burning is an empty cardboard tube."

"Tell me the story," Barber invited, leaning back and folding his hands.

When the recital was over, he said meditatively, "The man's name is Whitworth, hm? Same who used to be Drew's watchman?"

"Of course! So you must have met him!"

"No, he wasn't aboard the one time I rode the *Atchafalaya* before, which was her maiden voyage. And now I hope to go to my grave without making his acquaintance. But I know *of* him . . . yes. Jones, Cuffy!"

Neither of his bodyguards uttered a word, but they donned identical grins.

"This here Harry Whitworth: you heard what the man said?"

Twin nods; it was as though the black man and the white had grown into brothers during their service.

"He won't make another trip on a riverboat, will he?"

And twin headshakes followed.

"That's settled, then," Barber said, and reached to pour the last of the champagne.

Which he spilled.

At that same instant the *Atchafalaya* went aground, and seconds later the rear door of the cabin flew open and in marched Gaston, furious, carrying a writing board with an inkwell set in the corner that had just slopped half its contents not only over his composition but also his sleeve. Swearing in a fountain of French, he strode by in search of help.

Time stopped in measure with the *Atchafalaya*'s paddle wheels.

Then started up again, with shouts and orders from outside. Barber said glacially, "For a moment I surely would have believed Whitworth's explosive had found its mark. As things are . . ." He heaved himself to his feet. "I shall go and offer a prayer."

"But what happened?" Joel exclaimed.

"I guess you ought to turn around," Barber murmured. He had taken a seat facing the bow; Joel had his back to the rest of the cabin. "See, they just opened the forward door. And what's coming in, if it ain't the densest fog you could wish *not* to meet?"


With an oath Tyburn hit the backing bell rope, then seized the speaking tube that connected with Drew's stateroom, intending to announce what had happened and apologize.

Indeed, it could in no way be termed his fault. It was just late enough into the twilight period for the blurring of landscape that accompanied the march of fog to be mistaken for ordinary dimness. Even if he had had field glasses glued to his eyes, he might well not have realized how thick these traces of evening mist were liable to become around the next bend.

But it was like steaming full tilt into a wall. One moment he had been preparing to swing the *Atchafalaya*'s bow through the necessary few degrees to line her up on his next marks; then the marks had vanished, and in the time it took him to blink, and wipe his eyes, and have second thoughts, she had grounded in what on his last St. Louis trip had been the deep channel.

Maybe Woodley's idea of hiring specialists for the upper river wasn't such a bad one after all . . .

At least no harm would have been done. He was experienced enough to judge when a boat's hull had been strained, and this was soft yielding mud he had hit, and the engineers had been prompt to put their reversing bars over, and already she was striving to free herself. He changed his mind about disturbing Drew, remembering the news he had received tonight. Instead he signaled the texas tender and sent him to rout out Fernand. A council of war was obviously required.

Even before the *Atchafalaya* was floating free again, however, the fog had folded around her like a shroud enveloping a corpse. Just here the channel was narrower than her immense length, which made things worse. Tyburn shuddered to think what could have happened had he been coming down the river, not ascending it. The force of the current on her stern might well have swung her broadside, and left her wedged. In the old days there had been means to get a steamer out of even the worst shallows; for instance there was the technique called grasshoppering, where long poles were erected either side, ropes were passed under the middle of the hull, and the power of the engines was used— very gingerly—to lift the boat as it were by sheerlegs and haul her over a mud-bank into the deep water beyond.

Try that with a boat as long and narrow as the *Atchafalaya*, let alone the *Nonpareil*, and all you'd do would be to break her back.

Still, a drill survived from the past, and the mates were at once ordering their men to carry it out. Chalker and Sexton's voices carried clearly to the pilothouse as they mustered polemen and leadsmen, ready to launch the yawl if need be. One of the speaking tubes whistled and Tyburn answered; it was Gross inquiring whether he should have firebaskets readied.

Before Tyburn had made up his mind, the stairs to the pilothouse creaked and the door was flung open. Here was Fernand dragging on his coat because he had been summoned from bed, and—

Well, it might have been foreseen. No way was Hosea Drew going to remain sequestered when the boat had gone aground.

All the windows were now beset with the gray and baffling mass. It was no longer possible to make out the verge staff.

"That's *bad* out there!" Fernand exclaimed, having sorted out arms and sleeves well enough to attend to his cravat.

"Save your breath!" Tyburn retorted. "Cap'n, Eli's asking about fire baskets."

"Try anything!" was Drew's crisp response. "And launch the yawl!"

"Yeah, I guess we must," Tyburn sighed. The speaking tube was wheezing and complaining; he returned to it and repeated the captain's order.

Shortly there were flaring torches at the bow, and the sound of splashing, which carried clearly now the engines were stopped. Only the faint occasional pulsing of the doctor came up from the engineroom. Everybody aboard, crew and passengers alike, had swarmed to the forward area of the decks, if not otherwise engaged . . . which was going to make her bow-heavy, Tyburn reflected with annoyance. Shouts came from the polemen, wielding their red-and-white bars.

"*One!* . . . And a half! . . . Quarter less *twain!*"

At least she was headed into deeper water. Tyburn gave the order to move ahead slow on both. Whistling once a minute, the *Atchafalaya* made a couple of miles at walking pace. Then:

"'Stern, 'stern!"

And she touched again, just enough to send a shiver from end to end of the hull.

Backed. Swung. Tried anew. But by now there was not a hint or clue or sign to help her pilot.

"It's like plodding through a blanket," Fernand muttered.

"Care to take her, Cap'n?" Tyburn said at last. He pronounced the words with indescribable reluctance; it would be the first time in his career he had ceded the wheel because of fog.

But it was a matter of both courtesy and pride to make the offer.

Drew hesitated a long moment. He wanted so much to keep the *Atchafalaya* moving!

So, however, did they all. And it was cold, dispassionate professional judgment, due to the fact that ahead still lay those traps of the devil—his Island, his Tea-table, his Bake-oven—which made him say gruffly, "Thank you, Mr. Tyburn, but I never saw such fog in twenty years. You may tie up until it lifts."

"I wish we might have raised Cape Girardeau, at least," Fernand sighed, mentioning the next town on the western bank. "Maybe the people there would turn out with lights and skiffs and help us along!"

"We can still hope," I guess," Drew granted. "They should have heard our whistles. But without that . . ." He shook his head heavily. "Our sole consolation is that we're still in the lead, and the fog is moving south, and it's going to handicap the *Nonpareil* after it's blown clear of us."

Dense as the fog, as clammy, as pervasive, a mood of frustrated anger closed over the *Atchafalaya* as she nosed into the bank and men jumped ashore to fix cables around the stoutest trees.

They were a thousand and sixty miles from New Orleans. They had thus far made an average exceeding fourteen miles per hour.

And that average was about to be savagely slashed.

 The arrival aboard the *Nonpareil* of Smith and Tacy had created a council of war of a different kind, because the moment they discovered that Barfoot had been engaged at the going rate, they forgot all intention of simply "looking at the river" and lost their tempers. Up in the pilothouse, with Hogan struggling to concentrate amid the gathering dark, yet unwilling to order everyone else out because he wanted to take his part in the argument along with Trumbull, red-eyed and overdue for his next ration of sleep, there was a shouting match: Woodley, Gordon, Parbury, and the pilots.

Among whom Woodley and Gordon were growing more desperate by the minute. They had seen Whitworth come back aboard, and even greeted him, but it had been in public, and they were eager to sound him out privately, to learn whether his gamble had come off. Fully coaled once again, the *Nonpareil* was making excellent time, drawing so close to her rival that the noise of the *Atchafalaya*'s engines could be heard from the foredeck. Moreover the *Atchafalaya* was in shoal water by this time, whereas the *Nonpareil* was still in a deep channel and would remain so for at least several miles.

Was that regular pounding of pistons going to be replaced abruptly by explosion?

Or—and this was a point that had struck neither of them when authorizing Whitworth to set out by train—might that explosion occur when the *Atchafalaya*, having gone aground, was struggling to break free . . . just as the *Nonpareil* went past?

Those who believed in divine retribution might foresee such an outcome.

Finally Hogan's patience wore out, and he invited the company to adjourn to the office, as more appropriate to money matters. Grumbling, the others perforce complied, leaving only Parbury to scowl and glower on the leather bench.

The countryside around was eerie in the dusk. Darkling, the hills and rocks acquired an aura of menace unknown to those who lived by land, who might look on the surface only and think how much they could draw up to irrigate a farm. Gordon, a foreigner, saw no deeper; Woodley paid as little attention to such matters as any clerk; but the pilots saw, and *knew*.

The shape of the world implied a threat.

Therefore, even before they had reassembled in the office, Barfoot flung up a hand and said, "Did you hear that?"

There was a pause. Then Matthew spoke, who had been excluded as ever from the pilothouse, but now was tagging behind Gordon with all appearance of dutifulness. During the voyage he had been surprised at how much one might learn simply by listening.

He said, "It sounded as though the *Atchafalaya* went aground."

Preparing to announce that revelation himself, Barfoot stared at him, blinking. At last he said, "By God, young fellow, any time you feel like signing on as a pilot's cub, you come see me, d'you hear?"

Flattered to the point of blushing, Matthew muttered some incomprehensible answer.

"Damnation, but he's right," said Tacy. "Hark at her! She's going astern!"

"That's Ketch," Smith said with assurance. "He's bringing her back in the channel neat and prompt."

"You think it's not Drew, do you?" Trumbull offered doubtfully, and corrected himself at once. "No, that's Ketch okay!"

His unlooked-for moment in the limelight over, Matthew withdrew into the background again, leaving Gordon and Woodley to stare at each other.

"Grounded?" the latter said at length. "Nothing more?"

"What the hell else do you want?" Trumbull demanded.

But of course neither could reply.

Not that the rest were paying attention. When the interruption occurred, they had been on the point of entering the office; now they all made for the bows.

The off-duty deckhands already gathered there had reacted likewise. The most athletic of them had swarmed up the verge staff to boiler-deck level for a better view. "Seems to *me*," he announced loudly, "it ain't all jes' reg'lar nightfall up yonder."

"What the hell is that supposed to mean?" Gordon growled. At his side, Matthew supplied the answer.

"Fog, sir. Must be fog that sent the *Atchafalaya* out of the river."

"Think you're smart, don't you, boy?" Gordon rasped.

"I'm sure I don't know what you mean!"

"Och, ye ken it weel!" The shift into Scots was as always a sign of fury. "I saw ye preen when Mr. Barfoot praised ye! An' ye salt what ye speer wi' this 'river talk'! Come tae me for a reference when ye quit, an' ye'll hae nane!"

Matthew felt his cheeks turn fiery-hot, but his voice was perfectly controlled when he said, "Nonetheless, Mr. Gordon, if you bother to look, you will find I'm right about the fog."

And added to himself that that had just doubled the fee he was going to demand of Gordon for keeping his secret.

 At the foremost edge of its advance the mist blew in ragged ribbons, like the curtains of some great house sacked in the war. The breeze was more stirring the air than moving it, and at first those aboard the *Nonpareil* dared to hope it might be coming in waves, as sometimes happened, with wide clear intervals between. Under such circumstances one might keep going, albeit at the risk of grounding now and then.

But the increasing darkness made that less and less likely; it showed too dense for an ordinary summer's night.

Despite which, she kept on for a while. Fire baskets were lighted, leadsmen despatched, the silk banner replaced by a nighthawk, reports shouted up to Hogan at the wheel . . . All else forgotten, the other pilots, plus Gordon and Woodley, returned to the pilothouse, under strict promise of holding their tongues save when they could offer useful information.

Which indeed both Smith and Tacy could, as: "No, lay her a little more to larboard and hold till you come abreast that broken tree. The channel's working down this season." Or, similarly: "That old snag floated free last week and jammed against the eastern bank—you can make a straight run of this reach now."

All the time Hogan was sounding that piercing-sweet whistle, and the *Atchafalaya* was answering, until it seemed they were spending more steam on their whistles than their engines.

And then it was the *Nonpareil's* turn to touch bottom.

She did so with delicacy, almost with politeness, but it was unmistakable: the soft, slushy, not-quite-abrasive sound as the underside of the hull rubbed on mud. The leadsmen had not been quick enough to utter a warning, so as he backed and eased her Hogan muttered curses on them and their progeny unto the third and fourth generation, then sent a message to tell the mates they must look livelier.

Not that there was much hope for it. By now the nighthawk was invisible from the pilothouse, and he was progressing by feel and memory.

Nonetheless all optimism had not fled, for each time the *Atchafalaya* whistled the noise was perceptibly louder, indicating that they were closing on her, and even in fog there were places in this part of the river for two boats to pass abreast. There was no need to fear oncoming or overtaken traffic; none but steamers in a race would still be running under such conditions.

Sometimes with Hogan at the wheel, sometimes with Barfoot—always with counsel from Smith and Tacy, who were far too proud of their profession to let any boat they were aboard run needlessly aground—the *Nonpareil* crept onward, and for a full quarter of an hour followed the channel safely, not so much as hearing mud and gravel scatter under her wheels.

Meantime the whistling from the *Atchafalaya* ceased.

When it had not been heard for two minutes, Hogan said, "She's tied up."

The other pilots nodded confirmation.

"Either she's run into the blindingest fog that ever was," Barfoot pronounced, "or Drew is chicken."

"We can go on," Hogan muttered, and set about proving it.

Three more minutes, four, five, six—as many hundred yards were accomplished. Then there was a sudden break in the fog of the kind they had all been praying for, and they were able to hurry past Thebes up toward Rock Island and make the swing to larboard at mile 1060.

Then a cruel waft of the breeze blocked out the way again and once more the *Nonpareil* grounded.

This was too much for Gordon. He exploded.

"Five pilots we got aboard—*five!* And you still can't keep her in the channel!"

"I'm glad I didn't lay out the money for the lot of you!" Woodley chimed in. "It would have gone to waste!"

His face turning perfectly white, Hogan abandoned his embryo response to the emergency, dropping his hand from the backing bell rope. After a frozen pause he said, "Mr. Woodley, we shall tie up here until the fog clears."

"*No!*"


That cry came from the heart. Parbury was hauling his long gaunt frame upright.

"No," he said again. "Give me that wheel, damn you— *give me that wheel!*"

Striking left and right with his cane, he advanced to precisely the spot he had occupied by invitation on his brainchild's maiden voyage. Dropping the cane, he put a hand accurately to each of the bell ropes, each of the speaking tubes, not missing a single one. He drew himself up to his full height.

"There are some things a man may be fooled by," he declared. "A lone black gunner—a slick-tongued foreigner—a wheedling banker—a fawning girl! In my life they've all deceived or cheated me! But this I swear on whatever grave my parents found when the waters washed them from their farm: I have kept faith with this river and she with me! Of all the fickle females I have loved, this is the one who cannot lie!"

"He's gone out of his mind!" whispered Gordon. Hogan turned to him.

"Oh, no," he said softly. "He's come to himself again."

"You're going to let a blind man steer?"

"In the old days," Trumbull said, "we used to tell our cubs: Miles Parbury could run a reach blindfold better than they could run it in the midday sun. It's our only chance. And blind or not, I—"

He hesitated. Barfoot completed the sentence for him.

"Blind or not, I wouldn't cross him now. He'd kill any man who tried to stop him."

"Mr. Corkran?"—imperiously to the speaking tube that connected with the engineroom.

"Caesar here, suh!" came the faint reply. And after a brief pause: "Say, aint' that Captain Parbury?"

"It is indeed! Advise the engineroom that we are going astern directly; then we shall continue in the channel with leadsmen out, with constant call for backing. Be prepared to jump on my order without notice."

And finished dryly, as he returned the speaking tube to its hook: "You have fire baskets out, I believe. Call them back and douse 'em. I have no need of them, you know."

 By now the fog was so dense, it had begun to gather in the *Atchafalaya*'s cabin. From the bar the painted staterooms near the stern were masked by drifting wisps.

Dispirited, and suddenly realizing how incredibly weary they were after the strain and tension of the past two days, and moreover because those acquainted with the ways of the weather declared the fog might clear in half an hour or at worst a few hours, whereupon the steamer would be able to resume her progress, the passengers one by one retired, and the crew seized their chance to snatch some sleep. Cherouen was last to go, grumbling about his ill fortune and the fate of the Grammont child, but even he finally turned in.

When Fernand entered the cabin, following a debate with Drew and Tyburn concerning their best course of action, there was nobody in view save a snoring tender lying full-length behind the bar.

In the distance the *Nonpareil*'s familiar whistle was continuing . . . but the three pilots had agreed this could only be because thus far the fog had not grown dense enough to halt her, though she had grounded once already and possibly twice. In a while she too would be obliged to tie up, long before she could draw level.

Abruptly a possibility dawned on Fernand, and he found his pulse racing.

He was fresh right now; had been tired enough to drop off after his last watch and sleep deeply, albeit briefly, without dreams. He did not need to return to bed.

At least, not to his *own* bed . . .

Thought turned to action on the instant, and he went striding down the cabin with the lightest paces he could manage, until he arrived at Dorcas's door. He tapped on it.

"Who is it?"

"Fernand!"

"Oh, my love!" she whispered, and the snick of the catch followed. Then, before the door opened: "Are you sure. . . ?"

"No one's about, I swear!"

The door swung, and he slipped inside.

She was wearing nothing but his ring, her skin golden in lamplight; she shone, for she had been washing all over with a cloth dipped in water from the laver; on the bed lay a tumble of her daytime clothes and a nightgown ready to be donned. Dropping the washcloth, taking up a towel as he made to embrace her, she warned, "But I'm all wet!"

"I'll dry you!" he responded, and made a ceremony of it, worshipping each limb in turn and then her torso; most of all, her breasts. At the touch of his hands and lips she moaned and writhed and closed her eyes, and at last pushed away rough cloth and drew him close.

"Beautiful!" she said, as to herself. "Oh, *beautiful!*"

Never in his life had it been like this, not with any of the casual women he had bedded, not even with Dorcas on that first rushed occasion at the Limousin. He felt secure and confident; every thrust he made into her body evoked another sigh of delight, and when she trembled and tautened and exclaimed and relaxed he was able to continue thrusting, like the impersonal efficient piston of a steamer's engine, until he felt his entire being caught up in the rhythm of his muscles.

Beside his ear her moist lips whispered, "Oh, my husband, my lovely husband, my bridegroom, my marvelous man . . . !"

And all the while her hands pressed at him, clawed him, drove her nails deep in the skin of his back. Again she climaxed, and again, and eventually begged, "My love, my lovely one, let go! It's been enough!"

Fernand was smiling so broadly he was afraid he might never loosen his face again. But when the storm within him broke—

A steamboat whistle in the dark, resounding, organ-rich.

Exactly at the instant when he was discharging, he realized what that noise implied: so loud, so close, so unbelievable.

The *Nonpareil* was still running!

"My love, I've disappointed you!"

For a long moment he didn't register the words, being caught up by the terrible knowledge that some pilot, out of those aboard the *Nonpareil*, was working a miracle—or was it merely that he was more patient, or that the fog had temporarily blown aside, or . . . ?

"Never!" he exclaimed and kissed her lips. "But listen! Hear that noise?"

She nodded fearfully, rising on one elbow as he parted from her.

"I don't believe it," he muttered. "But I've got to check it out."

"What?"

"That whistle is the *Nonpareil*'s, and despite the fog she's going to overtake!"

He struggled into his clothes again, cursing as he found them entangled with hers which he had spilled off the bed in the fury of their coupling. And added, "Dorcas, I love you terribly! But if we're to be married—"

"If?"

A single cold word, like a wall between them.

"I mean, if when we're married we're to have a house like I want to give you, and servants, and a nurse to tend our children, and all the luxury I've dreamed of giving my wife—"

No! Wrong! Hastily backtracking again: "Isn't it better to be married to the pilot of a winning boat?"

"I don't care," she said passionately. "I want you here beside me, in my bed! Win or lose, I want *you!*"

"And I love you for it," he said, planting a final kiss on her forehead. "So I want to make you the bride of a winning pilot! Think of it as the best gift I can bring you at our wedding!"

That was the proper note. She smiled, and caught his hand and kissed the palm, and let him go before sinking back with a sigh of vast contentment.

Fernand was barely in time when he stole back into the long, mist-wreathed cabin. He was far from the only person on board to have realized what the sound of the *Nonpareil*'s whistle implied. Fortunately, before anyone appeared who might have observed him emerging from Dorcas's stateroom, he was able to slip out of the rearmost exit as though doing no more than take a short cut.

But the fog was so dense, he could only hear, not see, those who had preceded him. He called out. Eli Gross and David Grant answered.

"Is that Mr. Lamenthe?"

"Yes!" He approached them; they loomed like ghosts in the dimness.

"I was making my last round before turning in," Gross explained. "And what I heard—well, you heard it too! How do you account for it?"

The question was echoed by Joel Siskin: as one might have expected, Fernand reflected sourly, given his reportorial instincts. Here he came, stumbling and fumbling along the deck.

"Either there's a genius aboard," Fernand said positively as he listened to what could now clearly be heard, the plop-plop of the *Nonpareil*'s paddles at something less than dead slow, "or else one of her pilots has gone crazy!"

"Crazy!" a voice barked from somewhere beyond seeing. "Then I wish he'd bite you or Ketch!"

And Drew arrived to join them, still rubbing sleep from his eyes.

"I heard that!" Tyburn rumbled, and he too descended from the texas. "I was dropping off, and that noise woke me, and I thought, 'The fog must have blown away!' What do I find?" He made a gesture eloquent of disgust.

Now Motley and Wills appeared, dressing gowns over their nightwear, slippers on their feet. Stinking still of coal fumes and hot oil, Fonck and O'Dowd turned out also.

The former said in a low tone to Drew, "Cap'n, I'm worried about Walt. I think his burns are going septic. He's running a fever and starting to talk nonsense. Any chance of routing out the Electric Doctor?"—this last with a fine touch of sarcasm.

"Quiet! Ask again in a minute!" Drew replied.

And they obeyed, as did the few passengers who were alert enough to react to the situation. Cherouen and Barber were not among them; judging by the state they had gone to bed in, they would sleep soundly until morning.

The fog remained just as thick. It would have salved the pride and conscience of Fernand, and Tyburn, and Drew as well, had it lifted while the *Atchafalaya* was still tied up. That was not to be. Instead, the cries from the *Nonpareil*'s leadsmen grew perfectly audible, and the plash-plop of those forty-three-foot wheels continued to become more distinct, yet the fog was as impervious as ever.

"For God's sake!" Drew exploded suddenly. "If they can do it, why can't we? Mr. Tyburn, back to the pilothouse! Fernand, you tell the mates to muster their leadsmen again! Get below on the double, Dutch!"

There was a long moment during which nobody moved to comply. Then, against his will, David laughed. Sensing Drew's glare bent on him, he forced out by way of apology, "Double Dutch!"

Tyburn ignored that interruption. He said, "With all respect, Cap'n, I won't attempt to back her off. The *Nonpareil*'s too close. We'd collide!"

Infinitely relieved, Fernand said firmly, "I have to agree with Mr. Tyburn, sir."

"But—" Drew expostulated, and Tyburn cut him short.

"Cap'n, they already pressed their luck too far. They'll be aground before this fog lifts! We'll be in a better position to overtake as soon as that happens!"

And as though to prove him a prophet, there was a sudden interruption in the beat of the *Nonpareil*'s wheels; they had struck mud yet again. The leadsmen's cries had reached fever pitch just before; now they turned to curses.

Drew heaved a vast sigh. Turning away, he said, "Yeah, I guess you have to be right. Nobody but a fool or a madman would have gone on running in this murk. Say, where's Walt? I guess I should have a sight of the poor devil."

"I'll take you to him, sir," Fonck answered, and led the way.

Nonetheless Joel, with Fernand, Tyburn and the other officers, remained on the afterdeck, staring with aching eyes into the fog.

And they were there to hear the *Nonpareil* pull free, and the leadsmen's cries resume, and her wheels turn anew.

Suddenly, Tyburn said, "If I didn't know it was impossible . . ."

"What?" Fernand snapped.

"Once, way back before the war," Tyburn said after a further pause, "I heard the old *Nonpareil* pulling loose after she ran aground. I was on the *Reuben Corner*—a tub if ever there was one. But we thought we could overtake for once, and so we set about trying, but before we caught up, the *Nonpareil* was free and running clear again. That was at night, but not in fog."

"And—?" The question came from David Grant, pushing between his senior colleagues.

"And," Tyburn said with deliberation, "after a while you learn to tell a pilot's style. *That's Parbury's!*"

"A blind man?" Joel burst out. "You're saying a blind man is at the helm of the *Nonpareil?*"

"Listen and I'll tell you a story," Tyburn said, as the *Nonpareil's* sound drew ever closer, and abreast, and then began to fade again—proof of his shrewd judgment in refusing to back the *Atchafalaya* for fear of collision.

Yet never was there any visual sign of her—no glimmer of fire baskets, no torches, no lanterns—only the gray wavering of the fog.

"What need would a blind man have of light?" said Tyburn, and retailed his story to the mix of officers and passengers who had by now gathered on the afterdeck.

"You got to figure you're bringing one of the New Orleans passenger packets down past Helena, and it's a dismal, drizzly night—not foggy, but kind of misty, and the crossing is particularly tangled, which you have to make above the town to meet your wharf boat. Also you have a miserly devil for a captain, and he's hired the one pilot you would most like *not* to be partners with, for he has a reputation. When he's exercised about anything, they say, he walks in his sleep.

"So far this trip, however, you've been convinced it's all foofaraw. This man stays in his bed for his due time, reports to keep his watch, behaves normally in all respects. So when the pilothouse door creeps open without a smidgin of light just as you're on the verge of despair, and this character says, 'I'll take her, for I've seen this crossing since you made it last,' you're overjoyed.

"And all the more when he works into invisible marks and scrapes through in shoal water you'd have avoided like plague, takes her over a reef where you can feel the underside of the hull grinding, delivering her safe and sound into the proper course for Helena. So you say, 'Well done! Amazing! I thought I knew how to steer a steamboat and you showed me I was mistaken! I'll go rout out the texas tender and get him to fix us both some coffee!'

"And then, just as you're coming back from the texas deck with hot coffee and maybe a slice of pie, comes by the watchman, who says, 'Who's at the wheel?'

"'Why,' you say, 'I left it in the charge of Mr.—what's his-name!'

"'Then why,' inquires the watchman, 'is he tightrope-walking on the forward rail?'

"And that was so. Fast asleep, he had quit the pilot house and set about demonstrating his circus act, while this fine steamer went whistling down the middle of the channel at her own sweet will, en route to a collision with the wharf that would have scattered passengers and cargo for a mile each way. And yet the man I had the story from said, 'If he could do such daisy piloting asleep, what couldn't he have done if he were . . . dead?'"

Concluding somberly: "What use is eyesight, anyhow, in fog like this?"

There was a pause, silent save for the noise of the *Nonpareil* receding on a dead-slow bell and the cries of wild birds disturbed from their roosts. It was night now, full night, and the world would have preferred to be asleep, save for nocturnal predators.

And was not one of them the *Nonpareil*, thieving what had looked like certain victory from the *Atchafalaya*?

At last Fernand gave a harsh dry laugh.

"Drew told me that story while we were standing watch together back when I was a cub! I didn't believe it then, and I don't believe it now!"

Joel stepped forward, and the movement fixed all eyes on him. He said, "I heard it too, when I was first covering river news. It was told me by a pilot who felt that outsiders, like reporters, must not be party to the reality of the Mississippi.

"But now I've traveled this amazing river, I *believe*! I'd believe in ghosts and phantoms, and corpses rising from the mud, and haunted barrels and the rest of it! For I know what I've been witnessing, and nobody on earth will make me change my mind! On Mr. Tyburn's say-so, I *believe* a blind pilot overtook us! For if not Parbury, then who?"

"Then nobody," said a chill voice, and Drew stepped back into the limited circle of vision that the fog permitted.

They all shrank back as though he were one of the phantoms Joel had just been talking about.

"How's Walt?" Wills asked, striving to break the tension.

"Oh—sick!" Drew said, and brushed the inquiry aside. "But he's young and fit, and he'll recover. Unlike my dear one who died yesterday . . ."

Embarrassed glances were exchanged. Drew having hidden away immediately he learned the news, none among them except Fernand had yet had a chance to express proper sympathy.

But the captain was in no mood for it anyway.

"No!" Drew continued, striding toward the rail from which, had the air been clear, one might have seen the *Nonpareil* fading into distance. "No, I have been fairly beaten, for who commands the temper of the air? And, lacking sight, he still can move when I'm in fetters—ain't that so?"

The words he was uttering trembled on the verge of poetry; those listening expected him to launch into one of his favorite quotations.

Instead, of a sudden, he checked, as though aware that no quotation could match the event, and when he spoke again it was in a low, intensely personal tone.

"If it hadn't been for the goddamned war, you know, Miles Parbury would have been the greatest pilot ever on the Mississippi! I recall him from way back. He felt the river. Didn't look at it, didn't talk about it, *felt* it. In his guts. In those days he used to stammer. Could scarcely put two sentences together. Stand him up by the wheel, though, and he uttered volumes! It was like reading poetry to watch him as he swung that old broad-beamed boat of his through a tight bend. He could go where no one else would dare. And so long as I live I'll never forget the shock I had when I first set eyes on him after the war, and you told me— didn't you, Ketch?—about the death of his son! That was the one subject he could talk about: his marriage, because he was so amazed any woman would take him with his speech defect, and that kid he sired. Who died at the age of ten."

"I didn't know you knew him!" Joel exclaimed. Tyburn rounded on him.

"Of course we all knew each other! We might not love each other, but we had to band together in the Pilots' Guild and set up standards so we could become a respectable profession, and we did, and Parbury was one of the chief among us! And I'll repeat what Hosea just told you: if it hadn't been for the war, if it hadn't been for the death of his son, if it hadn't been for his wife taking sick and growing foul-tempered to try the patience of the saints, then Miles Parbury would have outdone us all. And maybe he's proving it right now!"

"Could be he's directing another pilot," Drew said heavily. "But if anyone can manage without eyesight, he's the one. And didn't you hear how confidently she went by? You have the use of your eyes; can you walk around your own home with them shut?"

"Takes years to get accustomed," Tyburn said.

"You—you seem almost pleased!" Joel burst out.

"If anyone's to beat me, I'd rather it were Parbury," said Drew, and added half-inaudibly, "Besides, I no longer have any special reason to arrive at St. Louis in a hurry . . ."

*"Even after they tried to blow up your boat?"*

The words escaped Joel before he could cancel them. All eyes fixed on him, full of amazement and horror. He was forced to continue, licking dry lips.

Out poured the whole confused story, including Josephine's vision of a dangerous brown stick, and the disguised log with explosive hidden in it, and Whitworth's contempt for Fernand, and in fact more detail than Joel would have liked, so that in the upshot he told the tale more fully than to Barber.

Afterward there was a drab silence.

"Why, the *devil!*" Motley finally roared. His hands groped in the air as though feeling for Whitworth's throat. "He deserves hanging—no! No, hanging would be too good for him!"

But the others were waiting on Drew. Who said at last, "Mr. Siskin, are you accusing Parbury of being involved in this?"

Surprised, Joel was nonetheless able to say promptly, "Not at all. Nor do I have proof that anybody was, apart from Whitworth. But I do feel that Mr. Parbury is an honorable man, whereas Woodley, and Gordon . . ."

He let the words tail away.

"Why didn't you tell me about this earlier?" Drew demanded.

"I wanted to. With all my heart! But you preferred to be alone with your grief, and I was not prepared to interrupt." Joel shrugged. "So I told Mr. Barber instead, and satisfied him there was no more danger." By way of proof he produced his pocket safe.

"Let me add, sir"—and here came inspiration!—"that I shall forever regret never having had the chance to meet Mrs. Susannah Drew. To have earned your affection in the way she did, she must have been a very remarkable lady."

That was the proper—no, the perfect note. Among the tangled strands of the captain's beard appeared a smile. He said, "Mr. Siskin, I'm sorry too. Because it wasn't legal, we were never able to become, as I'd have wished, husband and wife, and I was thus denied the chance to be a family man. Into the life of everyone enters a meed of sorrow. But I will honor her memory, as in his valiant deed Miles Parbury is honoring his lost son. Cast off, Mr. Tyburn! And we'll try whether a sighted pilot can match a blind one in this fog, although I have to tread like Wenceslas's page in the footprints of a better man!"

Recovered from his mishap with the spilled ink, Gaston reveled in the mood of frustration and despondency engendered by the fog. His pen flew over the pages, setting down line after melancholy line of simple yet grandiose music. As yet he was merely making sketches. Full orchestration—no, once more he was getting ahead of himself—a choral arrangement with solemn organ accompaniment would have to wait.

But this was fine stuff he was marshaling: here a brief quotation from a hymn tune; there a snatch from an anthem he had heard on his only visit to the Cathedral of Notre-Dame in Paris; elsewhere phrases from a richly sonorous, if primitive, melody sung by a bone-weary Negro on the New Orleans waterfront; while eventually he planned to work toward a triumphant section dealing with the resurrection, using a march of the kind beloved by the *Garde Républicaine* in Napoleonic days. And behind it all, on the subconscious level, awareness of the river ran like a susurrus, forecasting that one day this raw material could be reworked into his long-dreamed-of masterwork.

Therefore he was extremely dismayed when he heard the steamer's engines come to life again and felt the deck shift under him as she freed herself from the reluctant grip of mud.

Especially since his pen, newly filled, dropped a great blot, obliging him to make yet *another* fair copy.

Now battle was truly joined between the boats.

Yonder in the murk they could be heard: their audience was freed but workless slaves who had set up in cabins on squatted land; hiders left over from the war, fearful of returning to their old communities, scraping a living by hunting and truck farming; city folk—as cities went in this part of the world—at Cape Girardeau, Hamburg, and even Jackson, who had turned out to witness the great spectacle, thought themselves cheated of it, and now realized they had been doubly deceived; and others who lay abed because their lives were ruled by the sun rather than by clocks, who stirred, half-waking in the night, prompted to ancient dreams of giant lizards bellowing to one another across trackless swamp.

Blind, like monsters from the nethermost gulfs of ocean; sluggish, like cold-blooded creatures not yet rendered active by the enabling sun, but immensely

powerful; the steamers reenacted a duel of dinosaurs in the low and lonely hours
between midnight and dawn.

Yet there was a difference between them and those primordial beasts.

True, in proportion to the colossal size of their carcasses, what drove, governed
and controlled them was minute.

Nonetheless, it was a brain.

A human brain.

 Fierce exultation filled the mind of Miles Parbury as he nego-
tiated the first shoal, the first bend, the next, the next . . .
The *Nonpareil* was moving with painful slowness, as he had
done when first he rose from his sickbed after being blinded, and if she made a
mile per hour between now and the lifting of the fog it would be a miracle. But it
would be enough!

Not merely because it meant the *Atchafalaya* would be far behind—and with
the worst of the fog still to cope with, for what trace of breeze there was was
carrying it south—but, more importantly, because it had given him back to
himself.

How often he had sought in memory to reconstruct that precious moment,
during his darling's trials, when Hogan and Trumbull had invited him to take her
wheel! Then he had felt her latent power, sensed her skittishness, like a young
mare barely broken to the saddle, tried not to suspect how any other pilot but
himself might react to her excessive lightness—oh, yes, even then, though he had
kept it to himself, he had been aware he might have gone too far in slendering her
lines . . .

But it was not something to be talked about. It was to be registered in nerve
and muscle, in the guts, in the sinews and the wordless secret chambers of the
heart.

The tension was terrific. Sweat poured down his face. Unthinking, he pulled
the bandage from his eyes and used it to wipe his forehead, then thrust it in his
pocket. Moments later, he remembered there were those present who might be
alarmed by the sight of his scars, and the reporter who had spoken of them with
such tact had quit the boat, not saying good-bye, as though ashamed to admit he
believed the *Atchafalaya* might win.

And then he realized the pilothouse must be in total darkness, not for his sake
but the sake of those around him, straining for the slightest visual clue: the
shadow of a tree, the glimpse of a star indicative of clear air.

He chuckled throatily. He had no need of that kind of help! He was reacting to
such signals as the rest could not. Oh, like him they could hear the plashing of the
wheels, the dip-and-lift of the yawl's oars beyond the bow and the call warning of
shoal water, and the ting of the engineroom bells and the hiss of steam being

measured into one or other cylinder; he was progressing with such stately slowness, the paddles rarely made more than a single revolution.

But what the others could not know was the pressure of the river and the land surrounding it. Parbury felt it in his head, making a map like the landscape of a dream, impossible to convert into words. (The notion crossed his mind: "If I never speak another word, I shall not care!" For he was back in the days when he stammered, and speech seemed less and less relevant; he was riding a bicycle at his first attempt, he was responding to the twitch of a rudder cable so fast his mentor was complimenting him, he was opening a trade in the spring while others waited for his report before venturing into the new channel, beset with ice floes.) Now and then he sounded the whistle, not by way of warning, but because he could judge by the echoes where there was open water, or bare rock, or tree-clad ground.

And ever and again there was a whisper, which he had strictly forbidden, but could not be repressed, and always the burden of it was along the lines: "Fantastic! Incredible! Nobody in the world could have foreseen it!"

From Gordon, or even Woodley, it was negligible. But from one of the pilots it was manna.

Images from his past came bobbing by, like drift on a spring rise: Adèle, James (though he tried not to recall the sight of the boy in his coffin), his parents, their farm (though, likewise, he wanted to disremember the sight of the flood that drowned it), and finally Dorcas . . .

Even of her he could now think with regret rather than anger. Better she marry a skilled pilot than a wastrel, let him be black, brown or white!

Vast satisfaction was washing through his being now. All hatred and resentment dissolved. He had time to care about nothing except the advance of the *Nonpareil,* driving through fog no other pilot would have defied, with such patience as one might not have dared to ask from saints.

But because this was the boat *he* had created, he was devoted to her . . . more than to his wife, more than to Dorcas, more (should he even think this?) than to his son.

Well, why not? This, and the other two *Nonpareils,* had occupied far more of his existence, and beyond them there were the boats he had trained on, the *Celia G.,* the *Corinth,* the *Pelican,* the *Jackson Lawrence* . . .

No: this was his life and the achievement of his life. To the river he had been a sworn adorer. Now he was proving that what mere men could do to him was as nothing compared to what he had learned in the Mississippi's service. Here the channel swerved so close to a towhead, there were cries of terror from the foredeck and those around him in the pilothouse gasped, hearing the rap-rap of branches on the side of the hull. He continued serenely on his course, knowing, in a way that surpassed language, that beyond lay deep safe water.

He felt fulfilled. He was content.

And then, at the very edge of audibility, he detected a sound that made the hairs rise on the nape of his neck. Sensing his reaction, Barfoot demanded, "Is something wrong?"

Hogan was keener-eared; he caught Barfoot by the sleeve and hissed for utter silence.

There it was: that noise of all which they would have wished never to hear again this trip.

Slow, but implacable, the *Atchafalaya* was on the move.

*Damnation! If he can do it, so can I!*

Shorn of all poetic frills, that slogan beat and beat at Hosea Drew. Trapped between two shoals, the *Atchafalaya* had made it back into the channel by good luck rather than skill, and he knew he wasn't going to get a second helping of that.

Luck was for gamblers. Luck was for the suckers Langston Barber parted from their money. Luck was for fools like Jacob.

Skill was for those like himself, and even more for Fernand and his people, who would need it to make their way in the world, particularly since so many of them—like Dorcas, in Drew's opinion, though he would have died rather than say so to Fernand—were being driven ever so slightly crazy. Well, who could be surprised, given her family had thrown her out? Morality be damned! Religion be damned! All through history they had created more suffering than they had saved, and he was one of the victims! But for the prohibitions against marrying the wife of your deceased half-brother, he would have enjoyed Susannah, nursed and helped and comforted her in those last dark hours, done something to wean away her eldest son from his glib theological jargon, maybe taken her youngest out of the hands of the doctors who confined him to those dark steamy bedrooms and shown him fresh air and wholesome food and an active life, though he must be signed on as a mud clerk!

All the crises and disasters of his life rushed back to awareness as he tracked through the valley of the shadow.

For a while he imitated the sound-patterns of the *Nonpareil* as best he could, with a time index ticking away in his head like a parish clock. Then, just as he thought he had the hang of it, he felt the grind as the *Atchafalaya* went aground once more. Plainly mere copying was not enough.

Striving not to curse, he reached for the backing bell—and was forestalled, because Fonck and O'Dowd, equally wise in the ways of the river, needed no command. Already, despite the fatigue that must be burning their muscles, they were shifting the reversing bars.

A thought struck him. He blew down the speaking tube and waited, holding it in one hand, turning the helm with the other, until finally an explosive voice said, "Yes?"

It was Ealing, furious, using a tone he normally would not have dared to.

"Jim, don't let Walt work on the reversing gear in his condition!"

A short pause. Then: "Beat you to it, Cap'n. But thanks anyhow. He's pretty sick."

As he returned the tube to its hook, Drew felt a hand laid on his shoulder. It was Tyburn's. It said more than words.

Now there was a sand reef close to here, and some rocks. And the safe channel must be—

For a panicky instant he couldn't remember. Then it came clear, and at the cost of a scraping noise he put the bow over to larboard, disregarding the polemen with their dim gray-haloed lantern and their hoarsening voices.

"That's the *Barbarossa*," Fernand said, unthinking. "Went down in '59. Pretty well broken up by now, but some of the upperworks are less than rotten."

"You're quoting me," Drew grunted. "And if you can do it so word-perfect, maybe you should have the wheel!"

"Sorry, I'll hold my tongue," Fernand replied, abashed.

"No, I meant it. But this is between him and me, you know."

"We do. I'm sorry; I'll be quiet."

Inside Drew's head there was now a roaring torrent of mingled words and memories: flashes of poetry, of course, combined with casual recollections of arguments he had had as long ago as his teens, and his confrontations with Barber on the day the old *Atchafalaya* was condemned, and his encounters with Edouard Marocain, and his first meeting with Fernand, and the interviews he had accorded Joel, and his love for Susannah, and the pride he had felt on taking the horns that now swung between his boat's chimneys or ornamented this pilothouse . . .

He looked for the latter from the corner of his eye but darkness hid them, so he had no way of telling that they had not been removed.

Slowly, and with total determination, he quieted the riot. At one point he thought he might do better to close his eyes, imitating Parbury to the last degree; however, running blind was unbearable, even if his sight revealed no more than featureless vapor beyond the windows. There was always the chance of some gap in the mist, and a clue to their whereabouts might make the difference between catching up and running aground again.

But he made his other memories give way to recollections of one single kind: patterns too subtle for speech to describe, relationships, angles, distances . . . Where the men in the yawl reported a rock just after he had turned the helm five degrees larboard, he knew that location, saw it in his mind as clear as sunlight; when they warned of shoal water, he recalled having just made a turn the other way and placed the bend they must be in.

All the time, up ahead, there was the sound of the *Nonpareil*. She was still whistling, as was the *Atchafalaya*, but not at the prescribed minutely intervals— irregularly.

After a while Drew realized why. Once he had met a man blind from birth who, entering a strange room, would clap his hands with his head cocked to one side; after that he could walk around its furniture, or find an empty chair. Next time he himself blew his whistle, Drew did his best to detect the returning sound, but it was no good. His hearing had not been sharpened by years of sightlessness.

The possibility of defeat loomed at the border of awareness. He fought valiantly against it, but with the passage first of minutes, then of hours, in this terrible labyrinth of fog, it grew stronger, fiercer.

He comforted himself with the fact that had the *Atchafalaya* remained tied up the race would certainly have been lost. As things stood, a chance of victory remained.

From the western shore he heard shouts and gunshots. That must be Cape Girardeau. Not daring to consult his own watch—the least hint of light might dazzle him for minutes—he asked the time, and Fernand sounded his repeater.

They were making less than one mile an hour.

 At first those aboard the *Nonpareil* were afraid to believe what was happening; then, as time and distance crept by, they relaxed.

Almost. There was something weighing on three minds.

Woodley whispered suddenly, "Too many people in here! Even breathing could distract him!"

And led the way, walking Agag-fashion, leaving the pilothouse to pilots.

They foregathered again on the boiler deck: he and Gordon—with Matthew yawning in the background—where Whitworth joined them. Woodley said, "Hamish, why don't you let your boy turn in?"

"Hell, he only needed to ask if he felt tired!" Gordon retorted; then he caught the captain's drift, and rounded on Matthew.

"Yes, you've been yawning wide enough to swallow a cow, ha'n't you? *Aff tae yir beid!*"

Matthew muttered a word of thanks and vanished.

Now the three of them could come to the quick of the ulcer, and Woodley did so immediately.

"Who the hell is going to believe in a burst boiler if the *Atchafalaya* blows up on a dead slow bell?"

The words seemed to hang in the clammy air like menacing phantoms. Eventually Whitworth said bluffly, "I made sure I put it well to the front of the coal flat, where it would be loaded first and used for firing last!"

"But now we stand a fair chance of winning," Gordon snapped. "Suppose it stays there until she's in port at St. Louis?"

"So much the better," Whitworth countered.

"How's that?" Woodley demanded. "If she explodes at the wharf it's even less believable than while she's moving!"

"Well, maybe it'll find its way to the furnace on her next trip! Then nobody will connect it with us!"

"If you can't warrant it'll get to the furnace before the trip's over," Gordon hissed, "what the hell was the point of suggesting it in the first place?"

It was as though the enormity of what they had committed themselves to had only now dawned, when their boat had finally gained the lead.

After a long pause Whitworth said, "I did exactly what was agreed! And I expect to be paid whether or not the *Atchafalaya* blows up!"

"Paid?" Woodley repeated. "I never promised to pay you anything."

"Gordon did. Out of his winnings."

"Is that true?" Woodley rounded on the Scotsman.

"If she doesn't explode, I don't see any reason to keep my promise!" was the curt reply.

"You keep talking about exploding—"

"So do you!"

"Yeah, I guess I do." Suddenly Woodley's tone was very cold and distant. "Whitworth, my understanding was that one stick of your explosive would be enough to crack a boiler, at worst, and just put the *Atchafalaya* out of the race for a while."

"That's right!" Whitworth produced one of his panatelas and set it in the gap between his front teeth, cocking it at a defiant angle. "Anyhow, I don't know what you're worried about. It's been known for a charge of blasting powder to misfire and wind up among a pile of coal!"

"Blasting powder can do a sight more than crack a boiler," Gordon said.

"Sure, sure! But this stuff is much less powerful, much less dangerous."

"Less dangerous I'll accept," Woodley said. "Less powerful is another matter. Hamish, what became of that paper Crossall found?"

"I guess he put it back where it came from," Gordon said with a shrug.

"What paper?" Whitworth sounded alarmed.

"The one in the case where you keep your stock of the stuff," Woodley answered.

"What the hell was Crossall doing meddling with my things?"

"Oh, he said something about putting your laundry away! But the devil!" Woodley shook his head. "Let's go find it!"

"No, you don't!" Whitworth stepped back, reaching inside his coat. "I'm not putting up with this any longer! You both knew what I was going to do—you both agreed to my doing it—Gordon promised me fair pay for the job! I'm going to have it! Or I'll blow the gaff on you both!"

"You wouldn't dare!" Gordon said. But his tone was uncertain.

"Why not? I've never had my name in the papers, like you—never had my portrait taken for the press! I can cut loose, change my name, vanish into the crowd. I've been planning to quit the river because I'm sick of it. I could take a job with a railroad and be a thousand miles away before they find out I told the truth, and three people called Woodley and Gordon and Whitworth conspired to blow up a steamer with everybody aboard! You know what I mean, don't you, Gordon?"

The financier's face turned pasty-pale, and he flinched as though to avoid a blow: a far more violent reaction than Whitworth had expected.

Encouraged, he turned back the skirt of his coat to reveal what his hand had flown to moments before: his little pistol. Then, like closing the curtain on a stage performance, he let the coat fall back into its normal position.

"I reckon," he concluded sanctimoniously, "I could do with some shut-eye. Never thought I'd be able to sleep aboard a steamer being piloted by a blind man, but I do feel confidence in Mr. Parbury. Wish I could say the same about you two!"

When he had gone, Gordon exhaled loudly. He said, "I was a fule!"—his Scottish accent briefly conspicuous. "What is't they say o' fire? A guid sarvant an' a puir master? Was't a pistol I saw in yon belt, or a toy?"

"Far as I could judge," Woodley said, swallowing noisily, "halfway between. A two-shot derringer. But to be threatened on my own boat by one of my own officers—!"

"I wad hae slit his weasand wi' ma *sgian dubh!*" Gordon boasted, and from somewhere produced his keen-edged knife, last on display at Mardi Gras.

"I keep my pistol in my stateroom," Woodley said after a while. "It's been a point of honor with me not to carry it. A captain who can't earn respect without resort to arms is a bad commander. I've heard of some who'd shoot a sassy deckhand and laugh as his body was sent to feed the 'gators. But that was long ago."

"Yon Whitworth . . ." Gordon said, and let the words float on the air.

"Aye. I mean yes!" Woodley corrected himself, angry at having unconsciously mimicked the other's usage; seafaring terms had no place aboard a riverboat. "From now on I reckon I'd be best advised to carry it."

"Until we can get rid o' yon chiel."

"Until. . . ?" Woodley checked in mid-word. Eventually he gave a firm nod.

"If he can vanish, as he said," Gordon observed, resuming his customary tone, "being without ties of family or profession, we'd do well to make the arrangements."

"I know someone at St. Louis who . . ."

"Better that he doesn't reach St. Louis."

 All through the small hours the boats crept on at the same snail's pace. By three o'clock the passengers started to rise. When they saw how thick the fog still was, they marveled that any progress at all was being made. Awed, they went about the boat as quietly as though in a cathedral, fixing in their minds the fact—to be retailed on arrival home—that from the bow one could not only not see the stern; one could make out neither the pilothouse nor the wheels. Yet both steamers were still running when visibility was down to less than half their own length.

The sober judgment of those with a claim to know held that there had never been such a race before, and most likely there would never be again.

As for the fact that Parbury was at the helm . . . !

The very muse of history seemed to be brooding on the river, hatching events to nourish memory, creating out of formless chaos the foundation of a legend.

Joel shivered. It was as though he were reading a masterpiece of literature over its author's shoulder, watching the words go down inexorably on the page.

So too did Eulalie and Josephine, convinced that their Lord was widening the boundary of his rule.

Barber kept finding he was crossing himself; each time he tried to prevent the reflex, it recurred.

Cherouen grumpily strove to dream of a day when the power of electricity would abolish not only sickness, but fog; his efforts failed as the interminable journey dragged along.

Arthur begged for sympathy from Hugo and Stella and found his whining had worn out their patience.

Gaston was fighting to keep his sore eyes open. In his head he could hear the fully-harmonized version of his funeral music, but it would be useless until noted down.

Manuel snored; there would be no call for his band until the lifting of the fog. To make music for even the best of reasons could distract the pilot.

Auberon tossed feverishly in his bed, haunted by dreams of burial alive: a just compensation for his act with Josephine? Half-waking as the engines' note changed, he found he was able to think of *The Fall of the House of Usher*, and his fever chills redoubled.

Matthew, between waking and sleeping, thought with relish of the power he now exerted over Gordon, and reached under his pillow to make sure his book about tartans was still safe.

Dorcas was awake, and had been since Fernand left her, though she was terribly tired. She fancied she had felt her baby kicking; what if what they had done together tonight had harmed the child? Eulalie had introduced her to many superstitions on this trip, including the notion that a baby must be affected by what happened when it was in the womb.

Walt Presslie was delirious; his shoulder was as raw as butcher's meat, too tender to be touched. Fonck had ordered him to his bunk, where he lay tossing and turning and bemoaning his inability to go on working.

But those most directly involved in the running of the boats—the other engineers, the pilots, the mates, the clerks even, for their livelihood was at stake and they must stand by helplessly and watch—they had no rest. They bore the most tremendous strain any of them could recall, as the steamers fumbled toward shoal water and shied away and were caught by the current and had to fight back and make crossings that by daylight would have been difficult, at night almost impossible, in fog absolutely unthinkable.

Yet it was happening. In low voices they reminded one another of the fact, as though it would be incredible were there not words to dress it in.

And still the *Nonpareil* retained the lead.

 At last, in the fullness of time, the caldron of the heavens ceased to seethe. Its vapors dissipated with the touch of dawn.

Gasping and sweating, aching in every limb, and yet exalted by what he had endured, Caesar emerged from the engineroom and leaned on the guardrail. He had been through an experience he never imagined he would meet, and found himself. Tomorrow—no, today, when he had slept awhile—he was going to tell Mam'zelle Josephine he would never again have need of her magic. He had discovered his own. The world had done its worst by him; it had made him a slave from birth, it had stolen his wife and children, it had crippled his leg and plagued him with the insolence of white folks. To season the mixture, it had rotted his teeth and made them a constant source of agony.

So what?

He had proved himself aboard this boat, and *to* himself as well as to the others working with him. Running dead slow, the engineers had had the chance to tighten and repack every joint and union that showed signs of strain.

Not, of course, that she could be brought back to her full performance without a full-scale overhaul. Those flimsy pipes, that cut-weight boiler plate, those brick firewalls and furnace-arches constructed to meet the lowest limits the steamboat inspectors would accept—they themselves were a handicap to this sleek vessel. Were she to be fitted with another fifty tons of mass, she would ride smoother in the water, offer her pilot more control, perhaps realize her progenitor's dream in full.

All this he sensed without being able to express it. But it was secondary. What mattered most . . .

Back there in the dark and heat and noise, while four engineers were slaving to improve her on the run, three had forgotten that the fourth was black.

Instead of orders he was given signals, and responded. It was the way Sergeant Tennice would have wished his battery to work their guns. That, though, was war—blind, indiscriminate, destructive. This was the coming together of a team, whose mutual trust transcended words.

His shoulders were bruised. How often he had had to haul the reversing bars from cam to cam, he dared not think—but Corkran, Roy and Steeples had done their share, turn and turn about with him. Each who was free had run to respond when trouble loomed; each had relieved another when weariness interfered with their response to the clamorous bells. Each, given the chance, had carried cups of water to the rest; each had snatched moments of repose, like this, to cleanse his lungs of smoke and smuts. Helpers had been recruited from the firemen, and wound up watching, uninvolved, because it would have taken longer to explain what was needful than to do it.

They reminded Caesar of himself, the first time he was turned out for a gun drill.

Now he wanted to shout aloud for joy. He turned his face toward the sky.

And saw a star.

He blinked, but it was no illusion.

There, in a rift of the mist: a jewel on the black. The fog was broken. Not yet along the river, but above, there was clear air.

All the impulses of childhood came to him and filled his heart with happiness and his throat with music. He could do nothing else but sing, and there was only one choice of song.

"Stars a-shinin' *number*! number one number two, Good Lord!"

The sleepy deckhands cried out to be let alone, but he went on. And after a little there were shouts from the pilothouse, and someone fired a pistol, and the night was over and the *Nonpareil* was still leading as, in the wan light before sunrise, the mist cleared and an anthem rose to greet the day.

 Mile by mile, yard by yard, the Mississippi had grown more real and vivid in Parbury's head. In the days when he had been sighted, he had known color; all his life, though speech had never been of prime importance to him, he had judged people's tone of voice, and sometimes he had enjoyed music; since being blinded, he had learned to use echoes to locate himself, as now with the *Nonpareil*'s whistle.

Never, though, had he known the counterpart of color in the context of movement. It was as though the river had shades of—what to call it? Proportion, direction, bearing?

It didn't matter. He could feel it in his muscles and his guts. He was identifying with this fabulous watercourse. He was building a rainbow of motion. It was marvelous! He trembled with excitement as, automatically, he found he was cross-referring time elapsed against distance covered and sensing the pattern that resulted, as though he were studying a map in uncountable hues representing the river both above and below the surface: here a point and there a reach, here a shoal and there a reef . . .

This was the culmination of everything he had sought when, as a boy, he set out to conquer the Mississippi that had robbed him of home and family. For the first and only time he felt he was mastering the river as a fish might do, unaware of any other environment, using it to survive in.

It felt natural. It felt like home.

But there was one dreadful taint that kept assailing him: like a foul smell.

Whenever he let himself be sufficiently distracted from the functioning of the *Nonpareil*, which by now had become like the beating of his heart and the rhythm of his breathing, there was still the sound of the *Atchafalaya*. Slow those wheel plashes might be; faint and confused the cries of her polemen . . . nonetheless, they were *there*.

A black man had killed the other *Nonpareil*. He had hated him. Then he had met him and invited him aboard to replace that traitorous sot Eb Williams. Issued an order he was not entitled to. But everyone deferred to it. People yielding as the river was yielding to him now—fawning on him, co-operating in the most amazing way!

What had it been like for Caesar, half trained in the borrowed skills of an alien people?

Who had nonetheless survived . . .

How had he eluded the *fuzz*—the men (white, of course) on horseback, whose steeds gave them their nickname, after the slave dealers' pidgin for a horse which, like *okay* and *yam*, had entered English from African dialects? How had he escaped their hounds, who would have bayed on his trail like the *Atchafalaya* on the *Nonpareil's*?

During the hours of fog and darkness this image built in Parbury's mind, matching and sometimes dominating the image he was constructing of the river, as though some striding giant, tall as a steamer's chimney tops, were overlooking the whole course he might follow, baffled only by the mist and ready to outstrip him the second it blew away.

It had been too long since he felt a steamboat integrate herself with him . . .

*Herself.*

All thought of Adèle, or Dorcas, or any other woman, faded. He and his *Nonpareil* had become a partnership, a marriage, and if only it had not been sterile—!

Well, that was past help. All that could be delivered from this union was victory.

He recalled he had been allowed access to the helm by fog. He remembered that other pilots were standing by. But he thought most of all about the runaway slave who had eluded pursuers far worse than the *Atchafalaya* . . . and heard the latter's whistle once again.

And then the voice of the former slave himself, lifted in song.

"*Stars a-shinin'. . . !*"

For a long moment nobody else reacted. Then it dawned on those about him that overhead was a clear sky; the fog was breaking! A paean erupted from the foredeck.

Parbury's heart hammered and slammed and he reviewed their location in both space and time.

After this nightlong ordeal at a mile an hour, they had arrived a trifle above Devil's Island, a thousand and seventy miles from New Orleans, where the channel took a sharp bend to larboard, and from now on a succession of long and straight, though sometimes dangerously shallow, reaches would carry them the remaining hundred and twenty miles to St. Louis. Given that the *Nonpareil* was objectively the faster boat, that meant the race was as good as won.

"All clear!" went up a yell from the foredeck, and the *Nonpareil* slipped into the fresh and fog-free morning.

But of a sudden Parbury was giddy. The toll the night had taken from his reserves of energy was more than he could bear. His mental map of the river grew abruptly blurred. He found himself throbbing to the engines' beat even as he signaled full ahead on both, by reflex rather than by reason.

His grasp on the wheel slackened; he fumbled, finding no purchase, while heavy feet tramped up to the pilothouse and loud excited voices—Woodley's, Gordon's, even Whitworth's—shouted compliments: "We never thought you'd do it, but you did!"

While their arrival distracted Hogan, and Trumbull, and Barfoot, and Smith, and Tacy, the colleagues who had stood this final amazing watch with him and could testify to the miracle he had performed.

But as for himself . . .

He felt and watched it happen: the slide down into dark. All the resources he had retained from his former sufferings were exhausted. His very brain was worn out after his legendary achievement. He could only stand clutching the wheel until his legs weakened and his arms slumped to his sides and a kind of dazzling blackness overwhelmed what had been the incomparable mind of Miles Parbury.

The others were too busy rejoicing for the following ten seconds to realize how terrible was their mistake.

Standing out from the next point, as usual, was an underwater continuation of it, composed of mud and sand. In bank-full conditions, it was possible to run it with a light boat: in other words, cut across the bend. Maybe that was what they thought he planned to do, forgetting he was blind.

Parbury heard Barfoot say, "Oh my God. No! *No!*"

And realized how right he was, and had no more time to think of anything as he fell against the wheel and the *Nonpareil*—whose engines were dutiful and had obeyed his signal—drove at full pressure into the sucking, yielding quagmire of the bar above Devil's Island and below Hamburg which any cub who had paid attention to his lessons could have avoided after his first trip.

A hundred feet of her colossal length slid fast aground and all the speaking tubes whistled with demands to know what was going on.

As senior surviving pilot Hogan was obliged to relay the news after Woodley had knelt over the still, gaunt form and touched his wrist and shaken his head.

He said gruffly, "Captain Parbury is dead."

The morning breeze carried off the remaining fog. And out of it, a scant mile behind, here came the *Atchafalaya* on a full-speed bell.

 To Drew it felt as though he had been holding his breath for ten solid minutes. When the fog cleared, the first thing he saw ahead was the fountain of sparks from the *Nonpareil's* chimneys, but he paid no attention. He was on the verge of collapse; never in his life had he concentrated so hard on any stretch of the river. All his nerves were raw, to the point where he could almost feel the irregularities in the bed of the

channel. But he knew where he was now, and had the confidence to signal full ahead.

Panting, heart pounding, he scarcely dared believe what he had done.

Cheering broke out in the pilothouse. Fernand and Tyburn both clapped him on the shoulder, one each side.

Then the unthinkable happened.

In the midst of showering Drew with compliments, both the other pilots broke off and rushed to the forward window, Fernand remembering to seize the field glasses.

"What the hell are you two doing?" Drew rasped.

"She's grounded!" Tyburn exploded, and snatched the glasses from Fernand, rapidly adjusting the focus. "Yes!" he insisted after a pause. "She's fast aground!"

"Now that's ridiculous—" Drew began, and broke off as the final wisps of mist blew away and he was able to see for himself.

It was too much. A gust of laughter blasted forth, so violent it was painful. Before he had to yield to the second spasm, he was able to beckon someone to relieve him at the helm, and Tyburn was prompt to take over, though he too was chuckling so much that tears threatened to spill down his cheeks, like water over-topping a levee.

Fernand helped the captain to the bench, while from below shouts and cheers greeted the appearance of clear air. In the wan light of dawn Barber and Cherouen and many others turned out to witness the introit of the race's final day.

Amazed, incredulous, they saw the graceful *Nonpareil* stock-still on the mud. Then echoes of the hilarity from above infected them, and as the *Atchafalaya* drove by, passengers and crew alike cheered and hollered insults.

To which, from the *Nonpareil*, shouts were returned. After half a dozen repetitions, at last the message could be made out through the noise of wheels and engines.

"Parbury's dead!"

By now, because Drew kept on being convulsed with laughter, Fernand had grown concerned enough to take him out in the fresh air. Guiding him down the stairs, he encountered Barber and Cherouen.

Just at that time news of the death arrived. They stood for a moment silent, in a formal group like the arrangement of a commemorative painting. Drew's cachinnations ceased. He took his staff in both hands and held it before him as though he meant to break it, and sententiously intoned, "The paths of glory lead but to the grave."

Meantime Tyburn urged the *Atchafalaya* onward at a pace that, were the *Nonpareil* to fail to free herself in at most ten minutes, would assure her of victory.

"Should we cancel all bets?" ventured Barber after crossing himself and muttering a brief prayer. All eyes turned on him.

"Out of the question!" Cherouen roared. "I have a duty to my patients! We must arrive as soon as possible!"

That tune had been heard before. Drew silenced the doctor with a scowl, lowering his staff to the deck and leaning on it.

"Langston," he sighed, "you're not of our kind, are you? With or without a war, we grow used to death. It's a presence haunting us by day and night. We don't accord anybody special obsequies, even our most distinguished captains. Leave such garish nonsense to those who have debased themselves by slaughtering a human enemy. We of the river fight in a nobler cause!"

Abruptly his voice rang out like a steamer's whistle on a dead still night.

"And we're too well acquainted with mortality to bow to it!"

"So am I!" Cherouen said bluffly, when he had gathered his wits after that declaration.

None of the others—and by now they included a whole group of the boat's officers who had been roused on news of the fog's clearance: Motley and Wills, Diamond and Gross and Vehm, Amboy even, elderly and shambling as he now was, all indeed save the weary mates who were ensuring that the men they had sent out in the yawl were safe aboard again—none paid him the least deference. He tried again.

"I have campaigned for years against the Angel of Death with all the means at my command, and—"

"And how often have you tended Walt Presslie without being dragged to the job? Some suffering is beneath your dignity to notice, *ain't that so?*"

It was with pure amazement that Fernand heard those words emerging from his mouth. Once out, however, he found he must continue.

"We'll finish the run at the best speed we can make—not to suit you, but making it a tribute to someone who was worth ten of you!"

"The Grammont child—"

"He had a child! And so shall I, and why don't you?" Passion flamed in Fernand's voice, and his fists folded over as though to strike Cherouen down. He was able to control himself, but his words blasted on like the *Atchafalaya* entering this clear straight reach.

"There's life in everything we build: our boats, our roads, our tools to make life easier for all! Which do you care for more—the miserable child who lies abed of fever or the money and prestige you plan to reap?"

Cherouen's mouth worked, but he could find no answer under the hostile united gaze of all the rest. After a pause, he stormed away.

"Thank you, Fernand," said Drew almost inaudibly, and was himself again, issuing orders for the better conduct of the boat's affairs.

 "Hey!" shouted Whitworth, struck by inspiration as he caught sight of Caesar. "Want to make ten dollars?"

Caesar brushed him aside; he was on an errand for Corkran. But Whitworth came after him, almost fawning.

"Twenty, then!" he offered.

And since it was not wholly politic to disregard a white man, even after what he had been through, Caesar checked and looked at him.

"Rout out Mam'zelle Josephine! Ger her to put a curse on the *Atchafalaya!*"

Which was sliding by in the main channel, her decks alive with mockery.

It was in Whitworth's mind that if she now blew up, a curse could be attributed as the cause.

But Caesar looked him steadily in the eye and said in the most frigid tone he could command, "I guess, sir, you had best address yourself to Mr. Moyne."

And went about his business, which had to do with loosing the *Nonpareil* from her captivity.

Left standing, Whitworth looked at the *Atchafalaya* and marveled that so many people were still aboard. Somehow in the convoluted confines of his head he had concluded that by now the steamer was an entity of itself, stripped of humans, having shed passengers at sundry points along the way. But seeing that there were still—how many?—at least a hundred souls upon her, qualms of conscience struck him.

How could he have been so stupid as to offer to explode her boilers?

But it was done, and there was no help for it. Perhaps if he appealed to Mam'zelle Josephine direct, and paid her well, suspicion might be distracted from him . . .

He set out determinedly on such a mission.

But found, when he reached Josephine's stateroom, no one to answer. For . . .

A little earlier, coincident upon the grounding, Auberon had woken with a curious sense of purpose. Rising, he had drawn on such clothes as might pass for decent, and made his way through the cabin—empty now, since all attention was fixed on the stranding and attempts to back away.

Given his chance, he headed for Josephine's door and found it unfastened. Opening and closing it, he discovered her crying, face in a tear-wet pillow. And inquired: "Because of me . . . ?"

She shook her head. He locked the door and lay down beside her, clumsy-handed pushing away the petticoat she wore for lack of night attire.

Yet when she yielded to his importuning, he made no move to take her, but began to talk.

"Oh, my sister, oh, my bride! Why has the world been cruel to us both? Why am I doomed to spew my life away in bloodred gouts, when I've seen castles, cities, monuments from a thousand years, two thousand, even older? What cursed you that you have to live a life of lies?"

"I was born of a lie," she said stonily. "And beyond that, of a crime."

She could feel the god speaking with her lips, and heard the great echoing of Africa come stress the words.

"I too! I too!" cried Auberon, but whispering. "And my dear Louisette—children of rich and greedy parents who regarded us as little more than slaves, to be married off against another fortune! In that at least I cheated 'em—I'll die before they reap the profit of me!"

"And Louisette?" Josephine inquired, wet lips beside his ear. He gave a horizontal shrug, feeling her stiffen him with a caressing hand.

"I had no news of her at Cairo, and that devil Arthur didn't go ashore . . . If I'd not been so weak, I'd have called him out by now!"

"You think she should have had another husband," she suggested.

"Hell, but for what happened to his family, she'd have married Joel!" he exclaimed. "He's a good friend, and talented. And healthy!"

"And would even that have contented you?" she probed.

"What do you mean?"

"I think you know. That's why you're here." She rose on one elbow, gazing at him though the room was almost lightless.

"You're here because you wanted Louisette," she said in the convinced tone of a doctor making a positive diagnosis. "Not me, but her— Oh, don't run away!" she interrupted herself as he made to get up. "It happened all as was intended. The rite has been consummated."

"I don't understand!" Now he sounded frightened.

"You don't have to. All my life many things have happened to me that I couldn't understand, and patience has been rewarded, because now I do. The making of a magic child is a long and complex process. Between us it has finally occurred. In it there is enough of the new world, enough of the old—"

Her breath was tracing down his chest, his belly; it suffused him with grateful warmth against the chill of horror that pervaded him when he thought about impending death.

He had to yield; he had no more energy to resist. Cast away upon an ocean of delight, he passively awaited doom.

While she, at intervals, wondered about her rival Eulalie.

 Tousle-haired, fresh from bed, her only dress now much crumpled, followed by Dorcas who had at least been able to bring a bagful of clothes with her and looked—albeit sleepy— ravishing, the inheritor of the powers of Athalie Lamenthe frowned at the dawn.

As docile as a well-trained puppy, Dorcas—who had always wanted someone to dominate her and was content when several did, thanks to her upbringing under the rule of multiple aunts—inquired, "*Maman*, what's wrong?"

It seemed correct to address her as Fernand did, since she was so soon to be her daughter-in-law.

"Something very terrible," Eulalie muttered. "I can't make it out. It's as though the fog is hanging on inside my head. But something dreadful, anyhow!"

Belatedly awakened, for he had needed sleep, Joel came out of the cabin just in time to catch that last remark. And bethought himself of the way Josephine had predicted danger from a brown stick. Maybe Eulalie also could pierce the future's veil . . .

"Madame Lamenthe!" he exclaimed, confronting her. "What do you foresee?" And acknowledged Dorcas with a sketchy bow.

"Death."

But the steamer was charging ahead, and the sun was breaking the horizon, and hordes of children were appearing on the banks to wave and shout, and their joy was infectious, and there was not another vessel to be seen on the whole broad bosom of the Mississippi save the *Nonpareil,* and she was fast aground.

Moved by a curious pang of sympathy, Joel put his arm around Eulalie's shoulders.

"You heard the blind captain died aboard the other boat?" he asked. She gave a nod.

"Perhaps that's what you feel: his loss. He was, they say, a great man, who might have held the horns on every run the length of both the rivers! But there's no help for that. Now come with me. I'll get you breakfast; you'll feel better."

*It's more than that!* Dorcas wanted to say. Or, more exactly: *It's other than that!*

But as yet she lacked the skill to put sensations into words. Last night, when Fernand came to her, she had begun to suspect what power she could wield if she were trained. To rule a man who ruled the Mississippi—that was achievement!

Still, it was a great and patient power. Tomorrow would be soon enough.

And when a man was kind to her, or her adoptive kin, especially if the man were white, it behooved her to comply. Such instruction, in Eulalie's calendar, long preceded subtler methods like trickenbags and dolls and herbal brews.

Nonetheless she was disturbed to note that, confronted by coffee and milk and sugar and beignets in a service of shining silver plate, such as Parbury (had he been sighted, and had he been alive) would have commended his Dorcas for producing, Eulalie still spoke of death and the white reporter paid attention.

 The moment the news of Parbury's death was brought to him, Manuel reacted in the best way he knew how. Smartening himself with a wipe of a wet facecloth and a pass of his comb, he tugged on his dark coat, thrust his feet into his boots, and went shouting for the members of his band.

Five minutes, and he had them mustered on the foredeck. Even as they were tuning up he went from group to group, humming parts for them to play, and when he clapped his hands and stomped out the rhythm, they gave forth a lugubrious hymn beloved at funerals in New Orleans: "Flee as a Bird to the Mountain."

Hearing it, everybody except those on essential duty stopped. Men awkwardly removed their hats; some, who had seen military service, came to attention.

By chance that was the moment when Woodley and Hogan emerged from the pilothouse, holding between them, in a clumsy parody of a bearer party, the corpse of Miles Parbury on its way to the cabin, where Bates had cleared the common table and had it spread with his finest tablecloths in lieu of a pall.

From the foot of the pilothouse stairs it was easier to be formal. Hiram Burge had ordered his men to bring a spare door, which served well enough for a bier, and from his own quarters had produced something utterly unexpected: in rags and tatters, burnt along one edge, the Confederate battle flag.

With all the fire and fury of his youth, which had made Parbury select him as his engineer, he defied anybody to prevent him spreading the flag across the captain's body, saying, "That's what the other *Nonpareil* was flying when they sank her, and I've kept it secret until now!"

"Call him the latest casualty of the war," said Hogan grayly, and took his place, along with Woodley, Trumbull and McNab—who insisted—at the corners of the door-turned-bier.

Meantime, up in the pilothouse, Barfoot was holding a discussion via speaking tube with Corkran. It could admit of only one conclusion.

Before Parbury's body had been made decent on the cabin table, the engines were again astir, and the giant wheels had set about their thankless task of dragging the *Nonpareil* free of the sand reef.

Some spoke of sacrilege or insults to the dead; others, who had known the old man better, chided them.

"We can," they said, "honor his memory no better way than taking up the work he has abandoned."

Therefore in minutes, even while the passengers and crew filed past the corpse to pay futile last respects, while McNab intoned quotations from the Psalms, and Auberon and Josephine emerged, shivering, terrified, pretending by mutual agreement that she had once more been tending him in his sickness, so that no one would comment on their having been in the same stateroom (but nobody noticed), and a single thought ran through all their minds: "In the midst of life we are in death!" . . .

Even as all this happened, to the swelling accompaniment of Manuel's band, Woodley and Gordon were arguing furiously about the chance of catching up.

"She's barely ahead of us!" Gordon barked. "It's not yet full daylight! And if the charts are to be trusted, there's a plenty of straight reaches from here to St. Louis, where we'll outstrip her!"

"We have to break free first!" Woodley retorted.

"I'll settle that!" Gordon rasped, and spun on his heel, making for the engine-room. Matthew, who had turned out as much by reflex as by choice, got in his way and almost earned a cuff about the chin, but fell in behind, as usual.

At which moment Tacy appeared to report what the pilots had decided on as a tribute to Parbury: that they would combine, regardless of salary, to ensure the best time to St. Louis, whether they won or lost. Woodley pumped his hand fervently, meantime wondering what had become of Whitworth (but that was all right: he had resumed his duties and was mustering deckhands to help free the bow from the clinging mud).

More to the point, he also wondered what had become of the explosive.

Red-eyed, foul-tempered, with nothing but a cup of black coffee in his belly by way of breakfast, Gaston cursed and struck a line through the last half-dozen bars he had set out, because they were not the least what he intended.

And blinked, and looked again.

True, he had been deceived into noting down what he could hear, at the edge of perception, from the *Nonpareil,* whose band was blasting out banalities as usual.

But the tempo was right. And some of those harmonies, though rough, did convey an impression of grief: as though one were to listen to a whole chorus of mourners, each keening in his or her private key.

It was, on reflection, quite effective.

Chewing the end of his pen, he wondered how to take advantage of this happy accident.

"How long tae pull us free o' yon godfersakit mudpile?"

Gordon barked the question into the dimness of the engine-room, fuller of stench than light because nobody had remembered to raise the canvas awnings used by night to shield stray reflections from the view of the pilot. Matthew stared wildly about him. The tension in the air was so terrific, it minded him to turn and flee. Every time either piston filled and emptied, there was a hiss such as the serpent in the Garden of Eden might have uttered: long, sighing, and seductive.

But under it were the sucking, scraping sounds of the hull fighting loose from the gluey reef.

The four engineers, each turning back from his respective duty—the three whites first, then Caesar—confronted him and let their chief reply.

"About an hour," Corkran said. "If we don't get interrupted!"

The gibe was lost on Gordon. He advanced, clenching his fists.

"By then she'll be miles ahead!"

"I guess she may make ten miles in the next hour, and in the next one twelve." Corkran delivered the words with resignation.

"But the *Nonpareil's* by far the faster boat! We mustnae lose!"

"Objectively," said Corkran after due deliberation, "I reckon that may be so. But fast aground, no boat is fast in the channel."

There was a matching grin on all the engineers' faces: Roy's, Steeple's, even Caesar's, for the latter now felt himself to be a part of this company.

"It willna dae!" hissed Gordon. "Ye're lily-livered, the lot o' ye! Hae ye nae thocht on the answer?"

Before any of them had the chance to speak again, he had taken the two strides necessary to bring him within arm's reach of the device he had insisted on having installed at the time of the *Nonpareil*'s maiden voyage: a seven-foot iron rod to move the weight on the safety-valve lever, which the smith had patterned after a logger's hook, with a wicked curved spike on its end.

"Ye're a' cooards!" he hissed. "I proved tae ye, this boat 'll run wi' twa hunnert tae the inch!"

And twitched the weapon clear of its mount; in his hands, a weapon was what it instantly became. He leveled it like a quarterstaff, defying challenge.

Uncertain, Corkran said, "But the seals—"

"Tae the de'il wi' yir inspectors!" Gordon roared. "Ask wha payit fer this boat! Ask wha was gleddit in his heirt tae see the streinth o' her! Did ye nae hear what Parbury wisht o' his bairn?"

And it was all true. They knew it as well as he did. Steamboat inspectors could be bribed. Her extra power might yet haul the *Nonpareil* into deep water, and the arguments might happen later, and . . .

"And wha' in the de'il's name are ye aboot?" Gordon cried.

For Caesar had turned away. Over his shoulder he said, "She's too light. Everything's too light. She can't properly stand a hundred sixty without we run from joint to joint until we drop. Two hundred will blow her guts out."

"Ye daur bespeak me sae?" exploded Gordon, and raised that vicious iron hook as far as the space between decks would allow, aimed for the back of Caesar's head. "Ye black de'il! Ye son o' Satan! Ye chiel o' Ham! Ye curst o' God!"

Matthew watched all this with a sense of fatality. It did not occur to him that he might alter the course of events until the climactic second when it was plain that Gordon wanted to kill the black engineer.

Who seemed, as far as Matthew could judge, to have more courage and more insight than the others.

And then it struck him how he might intervene.

But at what cost!

Gone, like a blast of spare steam from a riverboat's whistle, would be all hope of funding his future through the secret knowledge he had acquired. Gone, the money with which he planned to return to his uncle and say—dishonestly—how grateful he was.

Gone, all his hopes and dreams, along with the reporter he had intended to enlist as an ally, who had quit the boat and made the wiser choice, and joined the winner.

So what the hell? He, Matthew Rust, was satisfied fate had condemned him to be a loser. Such insight was often denied to men much older than himself.

He did not even need to draw a breath; there was enough in his lungs when the crisis broke. And he learned what was meant by the phrase "making sacrifice."

For he screamed, *"Macrae!"*

The name stopped Gordon in mid-movement, and a second later Steeples had snatched the iron bar from him, and a second later still Matthew felt himself rudely thrust aside as Woodley stormed in, brandishing the pistol he had talked about as a means of quieting Whitworth.

"What the hell is going on?" he barked.

And looked at Gordon, whose face was more like a beast's than a man's. Corkran said, "He was about to murder Caesar!"

"But something Matthew said prevented him," said Roy.

If only Joel might have come rushing in on Woodley's heels . . .

But the chance was lost, for good and all. Matthew said wearily, "His name's not Gordon. It's Macrae. He wore the tartan of the Clan Macrae at Mardi Gras and almost killed someone who insulted it. He's the swindler who sold a forest that didn't belong to him, for making matches, and cheated Mr. Moyne and lots of others."

Dry-mouthed, terrified out of his wits by having so many eyes fixed on him— especially "Gordon's," which were full of hate—he finished, "I didn't know until I bought a book about Scotland, thinking to ingratiate myself, and that was when I realized he's a liar and a fraud!"

"Why, ye—!" Gordon burst out, and would have torn Matthew limb from limb but that the captain thrust the muzzle of his gun into his ribs.

Woodley was very calm. This crisis had concentrated his entire attention. Someone had once said, "The prospect of being hanged in the morning . . ." Something like that. But after the night's false hope of victory, he was resolved he would never again allow anybody to override his judgment or command.

Even though it might mean sacrificing his proud title.

He said coldly to Matthew, "That's a serious charge, and you need evidence."

Pale, lips trembling, Matthew gazed at him in disbelief. He had been so sure that when he broached his secret, it would cause a great scandal; that was how he had planned to extort severance pay from Gordon. And it had struck the financier a body blow . . . hadn't it?

He faltered, "It says in my book—"

"Och! I ken yon wee buik!" Gordon interrupted. "Fakit by twa Polish brithers tae please a Sassenach king! Fu' o' falsities frae first tae last! An' wi' a title in the Latin, no' the honest Gaelic!"

Having thus cavalierly dismissed Matthew's treasure, he rounded on Woodley, shedding his accent in an eyeblink. "Pay no heed to him. He's out of his mind half the time anyhow. Greensickness, in spite of all my efforts to amend it. Just listen to me!"

"I'm disinclined!" Woodley said sharply, though he put up the gun. "Seeing you were set to brain one of my engineers!"

"For that he would not agree to our only sane course!" Gordon's bluster was returning as fast as his burr was vanishing. "I came here to ask how long it will take us to break free! And what answer did I get?"

Corkran made to speak; he was cut short.

"*Too* long!" Gordon roared. "It could leave the *Atchafalaya* with an unbeatable lead! Unless you're prepared to break those seals and use our higher pressure! Don't waste time telling me how the job's best done! I've kept eyes and ears open, and I know you have to set the wheels to churning and let the current they create wash away the mud. But power—power—*power* is the key, and turning at this sluggish rate the wheels will leave us here all day!"

Glaring, he stared from face to face in the group surrounding him and finished, "I proved she'll take two hundred pounds, and that's the answer!"

There was a pause. Then Caesar made for the guards again.

"Where are you going?" Woodley snapped.

"I'll have none of it! Two hundred pounds will open her up like a hog in a slaughterhouse. I said so before you came in. That's why Gordon or whatever his name is took after me—to shut me up. And if he doesn't know what I know, don't believe him! It's too dangerous!"

"Stop him!" Gordon shouted. "He could start a panic!"

As by magic Woodley's gun reappeared. Lent confidence by it, he gestured for Caesar to return.

Limping, furious, terrified, the black man obeyed, driven by conditioning that went back clear to the days before he could talk, when the overseer with his whip and pistol strutted from hut to hut in the slaves' quarters and took his pick of pretty girls and boys.

"There's still a chance!" Woodley declared. "And Mr. Gordon hit on it! Back to your posts! Stand by for higher pressure! Mr. Corkran"—with abrupt formality— "you may break the seals on the safety valves. I'll answer to the steamboat inspectorate."

"I want that on record!" Corkran countered.

"My boy's there!" Gordon rapped, pointing at Matthew. "He'll write it down, I'll witness it!"

"And what's the word of a swindler worth?" Corkran said after a moment's pause.

Gordon purpled and made to rush at him; Woodley clicked the hammer of his pistol so that a full chamber came under it.

"Do as you're told!" he said between clenched teeth. "Or you'll never work this river again! There are laws about disobedience to a captain!"

Waiting only long enough to see his orders being put into effect, he urged Gordon out on deck, where they encountered Whitworth, wearing an uncharacteristic grin.

"Judging by the way she's burning coal," he said in a conspiratorial whisper, tilting his head in the direction of the *Atchafalaya*, "she could blow any minute! And then who's going to have the last laugh, *hm?*"

Gordon first, then Woodley, scowled him down, and he took a step back, surprised. Then he caught sight of the captain's gun as he holstered it. Mouth working, shaping curses, he turned away.

Further talk would anyhow have been pointless. By now the firemen were loading the furnaces as rapidly as muscle and bone could stand. Tossed into the maw of the fire doors, black coal was transformed almost quicker than the eye could follow into brilliant red, then yellow, and then white. The doctor pulsed as hard as it could go. The great wheels started to revolve so fast, they were like potter's hands shaping soft clay as they carved away the sand reef. The water they hurled against the obstacle washed loose the dull inert mass even as it tended to drive the *Nonpareil* astern; the river muddied either side, a puny human counterpart of what nature did every winter, shifting what might one day have been land, committing it to the current, perhaps creating the nucleus of another reef a hundred or five hundred miles below.

But the hull shivered at the pounding it received. In the bar, glasses shook against each other; in the staterooms, ewers knocked against toothmugs; in the kitchens, pans against pots, making a vibration to set teeth on edge. In the pilothouse, the judder was so terrific, Barfoot had to yell for help, and Hogan and Trumbull, weary though they were, took turns with Smith and Tacy at the helm.

While in the hold Hiram Burge was for the first time since he became a carpenter instead of an engineer—happy. He could see the effects; fate had spared him the dull vision of most old men. He could touch a hog chain and shout for men to tighten it; he could lay his hand on a bulwark and order someone to secure a bolt.

Envying, nonetheless, the real engineers . . .

Who would, nonetheless, have traded places with just about anybody at this time.

The shovels clanked and scraped as fuel was moved from the piles in reserve to the piles before the furnaces to the furnaces themselves; the iron frames around the iron doors, set in the high brick arches that also held the boilers, glowed with a dull and sunset red; now and then a thermal shock made something crack and snap—let it be, they prayed, no more than a skim of mortar breaking, not a brick itself or worse yet a rivet in one of those huge iron drums above the fire.

The pistons swept the full ten feet of their stroke with cams set to afford maximum expansion, just as though the *Nonpareil* were hurtling up a straight reach at her highest speed instead of being landlocked by a cruel mishap; whenever the faintest shriek of metal on bare metal was discerned—and the engineers could tell that cry as a mother fast asleep may tell the complaint of her own baby—oil came sluicing down on the bright sliding rods to ease their pain. Here, there, again elsewhere, the thin shrill whistle of escaping steam demanded that they run and tighten joints, bind unions with wire, strap weakened pipes . . .

But she was moving, wasn't she?

She moved! She moved! She *moved*!

And the *Atchafalaya* was in view five miles ahead, and nothing had burst!

"You dirty black coward!" Steeples rasped.

Clenching his fists in impotent fury, Caesar tried to frame necessary words. He knew, as though in his own bones, that there was no way the slender piping, the thin-walled boilers of the *Nonpareil* could take such pressure without damage. He had inspected every inch of her steam system; he had been running a constant list of potential faults in his head, attending to them one by one as time allowed. But there were places unreachable during a voyage, and among them was the most vulnerable of all: the interior of a boiler. Let a flue rupture where it joined the boiler end; let a single rivet pop loose; let the doctor pump fail to pour in enough cool water . . . There were half a dozen dangers there alone, apart from those elsewhere: a split elbow, a ruptured union, a lump of dirt that eluded the mud drum because the water was in such a turmoil . . . !

He cast an agonized glance at the gauges, trembling around two hundred. Then he thought about white men, the bosses, obsessed with greed and glory: the other engineers contemptuous of him as a nigger despite their grudging compliments, whose companionship had seemed so real yet proved so transitory; Gordon denounced just now as a swindler by poor Matthew, who was cowering in a corner because he was afraid to go anywhere else . . . Did no one else realize Matthew had saved his life? Certainly Woodley couldn't, for he was prepared to go on backing the judgment of a fraud and liar, to invoke the law when he was defying reason—

Safely, of course, behind the shelter of his gun.

The *Nonpareil* was back in the channel. The bell rang for full ahead. The engineers responded automatically, except Caesar. He fled from the engineroom, thrusting Woodley aside, and at the risk of drowning—or worse—jumped overboard.

In the blessed moment between full astern and full ahead he was able to swim clear, while Woodley, shouting at the top of his voice, took a shot at him. Startled passengers, who had been cheering, broke off in alarm. But Caesar had swum to freedom before. It was like living part of his life over again.

Nothing of him was to be seen save a little of his head, as hard to hit as any bobbing scrap of drift. And then the great wheels started up anew and their wash swept him toward the land, and he was able to writhe into concealment among stunted brush. By then the range was too great for any pistol.

Soaking, shivering despite the warmth of morning, he lay on his belly and gasped for breath and thought of another steamer called *Nonpareil* and wished with all his heart and soul that on this point he might find another Sergeant Tennice and another battery of cannon.

So tremendous was the excitement as the *Nonpareil* pulled free, with her chimneys barking like a double-barreled gun, that even Josephine and Auberon were caught up in it. Decorously he escorted her on deck, like any brother squiring his sister to view an interesting spectacle.

But between them lay the shadow of terror.

Daylight made Auberon again aware of the consequences of his determination to pack his short life as full of sensation and experience as might be, and caused him to wonder: what next? Am I trapped like Faustus, doomed by lust for knowledge? Doomed by lust?

While as the poison gradually left her system, though it would endure a long time yet in her hair and nails, Josephine was beginning to feel less and less certain about what she had so readily accepted as a magic powerful enough to guarantee her victory over Eulalie.

Yesterday, had she really decided to throw in her lot with the colored people? Had she really made that promise to Caesar and been spurned?

To elude such miserable ideas, she concentrated on her surroundings. How wrong it seemed to think of squalid matters on this clear and lovely morning, in countryside such as she had never seen before! The trees, the landscape, the very water looked different. What few houses were visible were in unfamiliar styles.

Birds she did not recognize were flapping and calling. So few days, a scant thousand miles or so, and a transformation of the world . . .

She was growing uneasy. Beneath their feet the planking vibrated to a thrilling hum. A chance gust brought the stink and fumes back from chimney-top level and made those on deck cough and reach for handkerchiefs. She wanted to think about her family connection with Auberon; she had it in mind to make demands. He was unlikely to survive more than five years—she had seen enough TB cases to be sure of that. His family might pressure him into marriage regardless of what misery it would bring his bride, but they had a daughter and another son, and the name could be carried on . . . As penalty for his use of her, she had thought of insisting that he make a will, an unalterable will, to secure her his share of the Moyne inheritance.

Only—

Did these people truly not know how unlucky it was to sail with a corpse on board? And there was one stiffening on the cabin table under its gaudy shroud! No charm could outweigh the impact of such a curse! The mere fact that he had been struck down at his own helm . . . ! Oh, one would expect the white officers to be ignorant, but she had thought the black fireman and deckhands would mutiny, rather than continue before Parbury's remains had been consigned to the fishes!

How much longer did this boat have to live?

"What's wrong?" Auberon inquired solicitously as she put her hand to her forehead and began to sway, her other fingers clamping painfully on his arm. And she remembered: no, not squiring his sister—merely displaying ordinary courtesy to a helpful nurse. Well, that was something, at least.

But all such thoughts were being snatched from her. A terrible dark cloud had arisen in her mind, reeking of doom, calamity, disaster. Images of a charnel house flooded her brain: ghastly grinning corpses pitched all anyhow, like some engraving of plague victims she had seen as a child. But this was no mere memory. That picture would have been in dull gray-black on yellowing paper. This was in color and in detail, not only offering sight but sound as well, and stink, and actual touch!

"Josephine!"

But she flinched from his attempt to support her, for his hands had the clamminess of flayed meat, and the chimney fumes were the stench of hell, and she knew with preternatural clarity that her Lord had brought her here to be made a sacrifice far, far from home, because she had wanted her powers for her own sake, not in his service, and she had doubted he could reach over such distances, and here he was, great and terrible, speaking with the sound of gongs and thunder while the blood rushed in her ears and created the chanting of his devotees at Congo Square. She could feel the weight of *bram-bram sonnettes* on her wrists and ankles, and they isolated her hands and feet from the rest of her, so she lost all sensation. The numbness crept upward. In a little while it would reach her heart and then she would be dead.

She whimpered, driving the heels of her hands into her eyes, and could not shut out the horror that assailed her. Meantime the *Nonpareil* rushed forward,

beating the best of her former speed by a wide margin, topping—in the view of
those who ought to know—the magic mark of twenty miles per hour.

Caesar had dived overboard by then, from the landward side, invisible. The
first either she or Auberon knew about his escape was when they heard Woodley
shout.

By then it was too late.

"She won't take it!" Barfoot exclaimed, in the pilothouse. "Where's Woodley?"

"Christ knows!" answered Hogan savagely, but reached for the engineroom
speaking tube.

"Shooting at that nigger engineer! He went overside!" Trumbull reported.

"Knows something we don't?" Hogan rasped, and then added to the tube: "Mr.
Corkran! Have you taken leave of your senses? What the hell pressure are you up
to? . . . Holy Mary mother of God! Two hundred?"

He spared a hand from the juddering wheel to cross himself.

"Get it down! Get it down fast! Back to normal working or I'll go the same way
as the black engineer, I swear it! You must be crazy, all of you! And I don't care
how many pistols Woodley has!"

To celebrate their breaking loose, Tacy had ordered the texas tender to come
up and take an order for coffee; they all stood in need of it, especially Hogan and
Trumbull. Unnoticed, he was waiting by the door, and heard and understood the
fateful words, and incontinently spun on his heel and ran clattering back down the
steps.

"What the devil . . . ?" Smith said under his breath, and then exchanged
glances with his colleagues. "Oh my God," he said after a pause. "He'll start a
panic!"

But even that was not entirely necessary. Fear had begun to hover over the
*Nonpareil* like a miasma from a fever swamp, triggered by Caesar's frantic flight.
In this moment of her greatest triumph, when she was running faster upstream
than any steamer had ever managed on the Mississippi, those on board lost their
belief in her and started to cast about for means to get away. The officers were not
immune. Woodley interrupted his cursing of Caesar and looked anxiously toward
the pilothouse, as though seeking inspiration from on high. Gordon seemed not to
notice, save to spot Matthew—fearfully peering from the engineroom—and bran-
dish a fist at him, mouthing oaths. Matthew vanished like a scared rabbit into its
burrow. In a little he began to cry.

Startled, for they too had been out of sight of Caesar, Arthur and the Springs,
who had been cheering the *Nonpareil*'s recovered freedom and admiring the vast
fountain of spray that jetted up from her bows at this terrific speed, fell silent and
gazed around in alarm.

On the foredeck the band continued playing for a little; then, sensing something amiss, Manuel waved them to silence and stared about him for some clue to
what it was.

In the cabin, which had been deserted except by its regular staff and by those
who wished to pray by the body of their old captain, Iliff glanced up in fright. Old

and wise in the ways of the river, McNab reacted similarly; so did Katzmann and Bates.

Out on deck, mustering hands to search for damage to the hull, Burge checked in mid-order and wordlessly consulted with the mates. Whitworth said at once, bluffly, "She's running like a deer! We'll beat the *Atchafalaya* yet!"

At all costs he was determined not to let slip the least hint that the other boat might blow up first.

But Underwood had sensed the same as Burge, and looked grave.

During this time word was spreading among the black crew, thanks to the texas tender. The fearful slogan was abroad: "Two hundred!"

Still working up and down the Mississippi were boats on whose paddleboxes were painted the reassuring words LOW PRESSURE.

Most passengers preferred to get to their destination as fast as possible; many preferred to get there as cheaply as might be, or had no other choice. Some were cautious, and among them were the people who let the US Mail contracts. As often as not, unless there was no alternative, they preferred low-pressure steamers, and the fearful followed this government example.

Some people remembered the explosion of the *Brilliant*, in 1851; some, that the *Pennsylvania* had burst her boilers off Ship Island, seventy miles below Memphis, in 1858, then burned to her waterline; some, the fate of the *Sultana*, which had led to the condemnation of the old *Atchafalaya*, for—as Vanaday had put it to Drew—she had "rained bodies on either bank."

Yet who would have thought it possible, until this moment, that the same doom might strike the smartest and fastest steamer since the war?

Those whispered words, however, were quite terrifying. One had long been accustomed to pressures of over a hundred; even the Act of 1852 had permitted one hundred and fifty. When the *Nonpareil* appeared at a hundred sixty, it had not seemed like any significant jump. One knew people who weighed a hundred and sixty; they were not obese, they were in tolerable health, they led active lives. But at two hundred pounds one was already into the zone of the clumsy, the puffing, the potbellied, who were grateful to slump into an armchair and call for another beer after no more than walking up a flight of stairs.

And the shorter they were, the worse off. Naturally. And since many Negroes were undernourished as children, and by comparison with whites their average height was some two inches less, when "200 pounds" was mentioned they thought in terms of *helpless*, and *brainstorm*, and *apoplexy* . . .

Perhaps that was why the blacks panicked first. Or perhaps it was because Josephine—fighting free of Auberon, who would have restrained her—rushed to the forward rail and shouted warnings in a garbled patois, part English, part French, part Wolof. Most of those who heard her understood, the sole exceptions being the few who had never been either slaves or slave owners.

Auberon understood pretty well, particularly since his ear for French had recently been sharpened. She was saying: "Run, hide, run and hide, for the doom of our black Lord is upon this boat!"

A tremor ran down Auberon's spine. She had spoken of a brown stick, and it turned out there were explosives aboard . . . But it was all nonsense and mumbo-jumbo. *Must* be.

How to calm her before she started a mass desertion?

While on the horizon loomed the trail of the *Atchafalaya*, which had been a pillar of fire by night and now was a pillar of smoke by day.

Some of those who had labored over the *Nonpareil* had loved her: not Parbury alone, but anonymous workers in the yard that brought her into being, paid servants of a firm that built a dozen vessels without caring, then suddenly felt that here was a memorable creation.

Some of those who served aboard her loved her too: it had seeped into the sinews of her pilots that she was tricky but rewarding, that she was due to make her mark on river history; the same held for her engineers, who strove devotedly to cure her faults, convinced that sooner or later she would break such records as had stood a generation.

And some of those who traveled on her felt the like: here was a steamer worthy to join the company of the great.

But over and against them stood the others, who had regarded her entirely as means to an end: chief among them obviously Gordon, who had spent money prodigally which was not his, who if he failed to win his bets was surely faced with worse than what would have befallen him in Britain—so right now was concerned above all with ways to silence Matthew, preferably for good, because the boy had not lied, nor had his book . . . And now and again he was distracted by the possibility that the *Atchafalaya* might yet explode. (And if so, let it be soon!)

The same held for Woodley, more or less: afraid she would not blow up, but his boat might, yet ashamed to go against the single order he had ever given in his own unfettered right. For him the *Nonpareil* had been a path to glory. Now she was rushing onward at a record speed, he dared not think of wiser judgment. He connived.

The pilots knew a little better. But past time. Because her doom was spelt out long ago, by someone without a name working in a hot and noisy assembly shop, following instructions given by a dreamer who had now gone to meet his maker.

One rivet no larger than a little finger was enough.

Sensing that victory might yet be snatched, the firemen were charging the furnaces as though demented. The pressure gauges were steady at a reading nobody had thought could be sustained, so they were cheering as they piled their shovels, heedless of the alarm spreading among the cabin staff and deckhands. Who were these nonentities carrying on a trade which could as well have been ashore? Firing a great steamer, now—that was a challenge!

Moreover, all of them had bet on the *Nonpareil*.

So the fire doors stood permanently open under the eight huge boilers, and the iron that on a normal day felt strong and rigid weakened as it glowed ever brighter, and two hundred pounds of pressure leaned on every softened inch of it, and then at last, before the engineers could obey Hogan's frantic order . . .

The boiler which gave way was number one. A rivet popped, a little shred of metal, like thousands of others: a stem, a mushroom head, a flattened end. The iron plates it held had withstood well; here was the fatal flaw. There was a hole.

And through the hole spurted water more than boiling, and its force drove red-hot embers forth, and unburned fuel, and between eyeblinks the contents of the furnace were washed across the floor where the firemen were at work, scalding some, burning others. Screams greeted this. In vain the men were rallied, ordered to close valves and cut the boiler out of circuit. It was futile.

For the failure of the first rivet caused the second to snap, and then the third, and then others, until the furnace was extinguished, uttering only steam.

But there was other steam, above, and at fantastic pressure.

Moreover seven furnaces were still ablaze, and there was no way in all the world that the single doctor pump Parbury had specified, according to use and custom, could keep up a safe water level in them. Not when most of what it poured in was gushing straight out again through the boiler that had burst . . .

Seeing the water gauge in the engineroom drop, Corkran did his duty, though with a heavy heart. He bawled:

"Get out of here!"

And strode to the speaking tubes to warn the pilot.

It would have been an act of crazy courage. He never reached his goal. For the compulsory fusible plug, set in the wall of the rapidly emptying boiler in accordance with the dictates of the Steamboat Inspectorate, chose that moment to melt and let go a blast of steam. It had not occurred to anyone, not even Parbury, that if and when it did so, it would be deflected across the path that Corkran was taking. A white spear of vapor folded him like a figure made of straw crushed between the casual fingers of a child.

Even as he doubled over, the bravado of the firemen failed them. In face of the stream of hot foul water flooding the boiler room, they dropped their shovels and turned tail.

Thus far the engines pounded on as though nothing were amiss. There was still pressure to drive them despite the leak; indeed, the needles as yet had scarcely quit two hundred.

But flue after flue in the other boilers was being exposed, and the furnaces were still roaring, and it was a matter of seconds only before the end.

Even as people on deck were turning in amazement to see the horde vomiting forth from the engine- and boiler rooms, a flue end melted loose in another boiler. Dry steam—dry because it was so hot—vented directly into the furnace.

This time the embers did not just spill out, or wash out. They were blasted out. They landed on the planking; they lodged on the horizontal stringers of the hull; they found a home on the piles of waiting fuel, which had been supplemented with bacon and rosin and wax . . .

The hissing of the serpent in the Garden of Eden: a message of irrevocable doom.


The lever arm of the steam drum safety valve trembled a little as a local build-up of pressure preceded the ultimate catastrophe. One vain spurt of steam rushed up the escape pipes.

But the valve held back just enough of what remained to complete the pattern.

The main feed pipe to the larboard engine split along its upper side with a noise like an old man's cough, and lifted planking on the boiler deck above.

Two men who had imagined they were making their escape were pitched overboard.

The fire that had begun on the piled-up fuel roared and crackled into furious life.

As though to offer her creator a Viking's funeral, the *Nonpareil* set off down the same course as that last steamer which had borne her name.

 Tyburn was at the wheel of the *Atchafalaya;* Fernand was trying to persuade Drew to rest, but the captain doggedly refused to do so until he had carried out a complete tour of the vessel and complimented everyone on how they had worked during the fog, starting with the men who were enslaved to the engines and the boilers.

That chore completed, they emerged on the guards and were confronted by a beaming Cherouen. A pace or two behind him was Barber, with his bodyguards as always. The latter looked improbably plump and rosy-cheeked, given how long he had spent at the bar and the card table since the start of the trip. It was as though deciding to make plain his racial origin had taken a burden from his heart. Cherouen by contrast, despite his expression, looked haggard and had dark patches under his eyes. Were a prospective patient to compare them, thinking both were doctors, he might well have felt inclined to prefer Barber's medicine.

Yet Cherouen's voice boomed out as resonantly as ever.

"Captain, congratulations!" he exclaimed. "I confess there were times when I doubted your ability to bring me to St. Louis sooner than the *Nonpareil*! But you're certain to do so now, are you not?"

"Lap of the gods," grunted Drew, and made to push past. Barber raised a delaying hand.

"No, don't say that, Hosea! Your skill deserves praise! Miraculous though it may have been for a blind man to pilot the *Nonpareil* in fog, look what's become of her! And here we are leading in the last stage of our journey, thanks to your brilliant steersmanship!"

If he thought to ingratiate himself with Drew by this fulsome compliment, he was wrong. It made the captain bristle.

"It's still in the lap of the gods!" he rapped, giving a nod past Barber's shoulder to acknowledge the arrival of Joel, ever alert to anything that might make news. "But for Mr. Siskin, remember, we'd have been blown to perdition!"

"I know, I know!" Barber made haste to say, and added, "I had it in mind to offer some reward. I'm sure you feel the same, don't you? We can both well afford it when this trip is over: you because you'll have my half of the boat, and your fee from Dr. Cherouen, and me because I bet carefully and with good judgment—"

Drew cut him short with a grimace buried in his salt-and-pepper beard.

"Fee from Dr. Cherouen? I understood it was to be from Mrs. Grammont that I drew my pay. Not that I don't believe you can afford my charges, *Doctor*. I'm sure you can, and double if required. It's just that, having watched you over these past few days, I've arrived at the conclusion that it's a mercy my beloved Susannah did not survive to suffer at your hands. Now let me pass!"

Barber said placatingly, "Hosea, we're all overwrought, you know. Don't say anything you may regret later. We can carry straight on to St. Louis now, and on present showing we can break the record for the run, in spite of being so long held up by the fog, and that's thanks to you, and Fernand"—a dip of his head— "and your other admirable pilot, Mr. Tyburn. And I'm sure the entire river community will wish to show its appreciation of your joint feat. Indeed, I've heard reports of a grand dinner in the Southern Hotel, and preparation of a specially gilded pair of horns. Think how fine the *Atchafalaya* will appear with not one but two between her chimneys!"

He droned on. Fernand, who until a moment ago had been aching for the chance to steer Drew back to his stateroom and lay him down—for only then might he rush in search of Dorcas, whom he had so brusquely abandoned in the midst of fog—was suddenly seized by another preoccupation. It had not occurred to him that they might still break the New Orleans to St. Louis record after such a slow night, but would a gambler say so without evidence?

He hauled out his watch and stared about him, recognizing familiar scenery. Ahead lay Grand Tower and the Devil's Bake-oven and the mouth of the Big Muddy; beyond, Chester and the mouth of the Kaskaskia and Herculaneum where there was a railroad, and—

And one thousand one hundred and ninety-four miles from New Orleans, the city of St. Louis at long last.

He drew a deep breath. Barber was right. If they could shave as little as fifteen minutes off their best previous time from this point to the end, they would set a new overall record. A mere quarter hour! It should be feasible! The boat was running as sweetly as she had ever done; there wasn't a jar or jolt in her piston strokes, and there had been no further trouble in the engineroom, and even the scrapes she had had during the fog had caused no discernible problems, according to Diamond's morning report. She was like—the image came unbidden—his Uncle Edouard in middle age, when he was first a person in his nephew's world: no longer capable of sprinting, but having learned endurance and the sense of timing which could enable one to outdo a younger and less experienced opponent, rushing away from the start at such a rate he grew exhausted.

Fernand shivered. Never before had he had such a sense of a steamer's personality . . . nor of the shortness of her life.

He returned slowly to the here and now. Barber was calming Cherouen, while Drew looked about him for his staff, forgotten somewhere thanks to his fatigue. But for it, doubtless the doctor would have had a wound of his own to heal. There had been words as harsh as vitriol. Fernand remembered their impact, though not what they were, for he had been distracted.

His intervention was needed; Fernand said, "Captain, you really should turn in, you know!"

And hesitated. Drew was paying no attention. All of a sudden he had cocked his head like a dog snuffing the wind.

He was the first, but not the only, one to react in similar fashion. Passing on some errand, Gross—who also looked red-eyed and drawn—turned towards the after rail, staring in the direction of the *Nonpareil*.

Whose engine note had altered. A few minutes ago she had been uttering the powerful, determined panting that logically would accompany her efforts to pull free of the sand reef; then she had been in clear water, then changed from full astern to full ahead and spoken of her newly regained freedom with a vigorous thrusting of her pistons.

But now . . .

Fernand's nails bit deep into his palms. What in the world was her pilot up to? It seemed he could not decide whether to race ahead or dawdle. The noise she was making—

A shout came from above. The after window of the pilothouse was flung open, and there was the texas tender signaling madly with both arms, recruited because Tyburn was alone at the wheel and dared not leave it.

Fernand and Drew exchanged glances, then incontinently ran for the pilot-house. After a second's indecision, Barber and Cherouen followed. So, more enthusiastically, did Joel.

For the message the tender was relaying at the top of his lungs was simple and terrifying:

*"She's afire!"*

Even while they were still on the texas, Drew and Fernand could see there was far too much smoke rising from the *Nonpareil*'s location. But there were binoculars above, and a better vantage point. They rushed up the final flight, almost tripping on one another's heels.

Outside, hindered at the last moment by a pang of conscience, Joel halted, having overtaken Cherouen and Barber on the way. Cherouen's breathing was like an old man's; he had begun to gasp after a dozen strides. Barber had done better, but he was portly, and his weight told.

Uncapping his telescope, Joel trained it . . . and thought of Auberon, and his newly discovered half-sister, and his loathsome brother-in-law Arthur, and poor Louisette, and those friends who had seemed so charming, Hugo and Stella Spring, but had turned out to be so shallow and easily led, and Gordon, and Matthew, and the mad musician Manuel whom Joel found somehow endearing, and the black engineer he had helped to secure a post for—must he answer for that at the day of judgment?—and all the people he had talked to or interviewed, Captain Woodley and his pilots and his engineers and his clerks and chief steward and caterer and mates . . . including Whitworth (and before what court was he to make his plea, who had been prepared to carry murder in a carpetbag?)

Lord! Lord! He could not see through the telescope, for his vision was pre-empted by a panorama of faces. How many were aboard the *Nonpareil*, counting those gamblers and sensation-seekers who had wanted to stick with the boat they had backed until the end? A hundred and twenty—a hundred and fifty?

And as of this moment only Parbury was dead.

The thought of witnessing a calamity that killed them all sickened Joel. He willingly ceded his telescope to Barber, who had now arrived on the platform outside the pilothouse; Cherouen, his chest heaving with effort, was a few steps lower down. As soon as he got his breath, he demanded a share of the telescope, and his tone was greedy, as though he needed the stimulation of seeing the disaster personally to add spice to his existence.

Joel looked at him coldly. It was said this man had been a successful surgeon in the war. Maybe it was war that had corrupted him. Likely enough; it corrupted even the most upright. But it must, in that case, have gone further. It must have brutalized him. For all his machines and electricity, for all his vaunted panaceas, he was a drunkard and a bigot and a swine.

He recalled what Drew had said a few minutes ago, and uttered a private prayer that the surviving Grammont child be too well on their arrival for Cherouen's services to be invoked.

But there was going to be a greater need for them, and sooner. For the plumes of steam and smoke belching up from the *Nonpareil* wrote Indian signals of disaster on the sky.


Preoccupied with the shallow narrow channel, Tyburn said, "I guess they got what was coming to us, hm?"

"What?" Drew glanced around, lowering his field glasses.

"Mr. Siskin said—"

"Forget it! She's afire!" And he gave a captain's leave to the texas tender, who was still standing by the door, eyes wide in his dark face, licking his lips.

When he opened the door, however, he found his way blocked, and shrank back as if he were somehow to blame for what was happening. Fernand saw and made a resolution: no child of his should cringe so, though it be for a king!

And thought of Dorcas, and wished he might be with her.

Through the open door, Cherouen called, "That seals it, Cap'n!"

And Barber echoed him, beaming.

"What?" Drew growled.

They were taken aback for a moment. Barber recovered first.

"Why, that we can win this race *and* beat the record!"

"Right!" chimed in Cherouen. "From now on it's 'plain sailing'—don't they say?"

In that instant Fernand realized he loathed this man. He didn't hate him— hating involved the expenditure of energy, and Cherouen wasn't worth it. No: he loathed him, like a wet gray slug found under a flagstone, not because of any particular fault he had committed, but because of what he was.

The contrast between this humbug and Dr. Malone . . . ! Could one imagine Cherouen stopping his carriage because he had seen a stranger fall fainting on the sidewalk?

As for Barber, though—

Him he could only detest. And that was different again. He wished Barber no harm, but had no least desire to emulate his way of living. To take money from fools who thought they were going to get more without working for it—that was understandable, yet detestable. It was not cleverness; it was mere cunning, and animals could exhibit that. And withal he was an honorable man.

How was it he had started to think in such terms as Edouard Marocain might have used?

The answer dawned on Fernand the next instant. This was his legacy. This was what Edouard had bequeathed him, infinitely more valuable than gold or property, the thing his own sons would not learn: a power of judgment.

He felt his lips tremble as they had when leaving Edouard's requiem mass, and knew in his heart for the first time how much he had loved that crotchety uncle. He had been deprived of a part of himself when the old man was laid to rest. But he had been given more. To recognize that he could love—not like, not lust after, not feel proud of owning—another person: was that not a grand bequest?

And he did. He loved Dorcas, and their child, and—and yes, despite her faults, his mother too, and likewise . . .

Drew?

Yes! Yes, and maybe above all! This man who had stood in a father's role when teaching him the river: sometimes patient, sometimes snappish, always ready with a borrowed phrase from some favorite poet which could fix a lesson in his pupil's mind . . . he was somehow less than likable, but nonetheless transcended that. He was more than honorable.

He was honest.

Within Fernand's head there were shiftings like a winter revision of the Mississippi's course, like landslides, like the legendary earthquake that once caused the river to run *backward*. (Yet it was no myth; he had spoken with people who had spoken with people who had seen it.)

And they were abruptly halted by a sound he recognized, faint though it was, echoing from far below in the engineroom. He came to himself again and realized that Drew, in one decisive step and gesture and in dreadful breach of manners as they held on the river, had reached past Tyburn and rung the bells to stop and back, and laid his hand upon the wheel and said, "I got her!"

*Stop and back?*

Even those ignoramuses outside, Barber and Cherouen and the reporter, recognized the effect, if not the signal, and came shouting into the pilothouse, trying to issue orders of their own.

"You can't do that!"—from raging Cherouen. "I have to cure a sick child in St. Louis!"

"You can't do that!"—from furious Barber. "If we don't break the record I won't win half of what I hoped for!"

Looking at him, seeing the naked greed that marred his face, Fernand realized: it was credible in spite of all denials that this man who had finally admitted his African blood—but to a white man!—should have connived at selling freed slaves back to slavery.

It didn't matter anymore whether he had done so. It was enough to recognize: *he could have done.*

And with that, Fernand's attachment to any stranger on the ground of color vanished. That Dorcas matched him was, from now on and forever, his good fortune. That Drew did not, or Cherouen, was indifferent; that Caesar did, and Josephine, the same.

He wanted Drew to stand godfather to his first-born: not Barber, who had let the room where they conceived it.

All the misery of Drew's existence came together in the next words he uttered.

He had no business reclaiming the wheel, and knew that Tyburn knew it, hovering ready to take over again. What he had done during the night was as amazing as Parbury's navigation without eyes; it had called for total control and total insight.

Well, he had managed it. But his achievement had entailed such fatigue as he had never known.

Yet some last resource, like a runner's second wind, was affording him new energy, and when he spoke he spoke with perfect certainty.

"*I won't!*" he exploded, swinging the wheel as he felt the engineers respond to his commands. And in the simple declaration he felt all his remotest ancestors coming to voice their frenzy through his mouth, from that apelike creature whose bones, even, had been dissolved into the mud of time—yet had been the first to deny what the world in its obsessive monotony offered!—clear to that father whom he scarcely thought about these days, who had sincerely mourned the doom of his elder son and was dead before he had a chance to praise the younger.

All those who wanted the world to be otherwise, *and better*, shared the sound of his shout.

The defiance of his cry created a change in Barber, like the shift from a sand reef to a wind reef. He had loomed in Drew's mind as though he were somehow larger than life, epitome of all those who had ruined Jacob. Now he was suddenly no more than a bugaboo.

Blustering, he roared, "If you don't keep right on going you don't get my half of the boat!"

"Mr. Lamenthe," Drew said with weariness half real, half affected, "this person has no business in my pilothouse. Expel him."

"It will be a perfect pleasure," Fernand said.

"Jones! Cuffy!" Barber bellowed, retreating nervously toward the door, and there were immediate footsteps on the stairs.

For a second Fernand was irresolute; then he felt a tap on his arm. Tyburn was handing him Drew's staff, which had stood forgotten in the corner. He took it with a feral grin and, holding it like a bayoneted rifle, made to drive it into Barber's paunch.

It was almost funny, how smoothly it went: as though it had been rehearsed for the theater.

Behind Barber the door was ajar; a chance motion of the boat was swinging it wide open. Through it his fear of Fernand's onslaught drove him into the arms of his bodyguards, who lost their footing, so the three of them fell shouting and scrabbling to the foot of the stairs. After them Drew hurled a parting message in a voice like Jove announcing thunderstorms: "One more attempt to usurp my authority aboard this boat, and you and your henchmen will wind up in irons!"

It passed through Fernand's mind that he had never before heard—only read—that archaic term.

Trust Old Poetical to come up with it when it was needed . . .

Barber and Jones and Cuffy struggled to their feet, and reached a sensible decision not to return. And that left Cherouen.

Who sniveled, all the bluster leaking out of him: "What about me?"

"Oh, you're a doctor, ain't you?" Drew rasped, setting the *Atchafalaya* into her marks for the southerly course that would shortly bring her back to the stricken *Nonpareil*.

"God damn you, yes! But—"

"I'm giving you more patients than you've ever dreamed of, ain't I? So what are you worried about—who'll pay your fee?"

The words hung rankling in the air for a long moment. At last Cherouen turned blindly and stumbled down the stairs in the wake of Barber, who—recovering his dignity—was holding forth to a cluster of crewmen and astonished passengers about the way he had been treated.

"We're well shut of them," Drew said with satisfaction. "And we should still make it to the *Nonpareil* in time. She's afire, but there should be a chance to ground her before she sinks."

Joel uttered a strangled exclamation. The others looked at him. He had turned ghost-pale.

He said, "But Whitworth must have had more than one stick of mica powder!"

There was a dead pause. Then Drew said with a shrug, "Yes, it's a risk. But I'm not turning back because of it. You, Ketch? Fernand, you?"

Together they shook their heads.

"Then it's decided," Drew said calmly, and tugged the rope for full ahead.

 Loosed from the confines of the furnaces, the fire lay a little while in the belly of the *Nonpareil*, like a menagerie tiger that had found its cage door open, uncertain what to do next.

Above, the engineers and firemen—some so badly scalded, they were afraid to strip off boots and socks in case the skin came with them—had triggered panic. Passengers and crew rushed to the landward rail. The vessel listed dangerously. There was no one left to trim her with the chain wagon.

Gallantly the officers strove to keep order, but they were a handful among a hundred, and Woodley himself was in no state to inspire confidence. His voice cracked when he tried to utter an order; his face was paper-white; his whole body trembled with terror.

Nor was Gordon any better. Matthew's charge had struck home past the shield of his excuses, and he was dashing back and forth muttering oaths, thrusting aside anybody who got in his way. There was no sign of Matthew himself.

Now down the stairs from the pilothouse came the pilots, all bar one: Trumbull had accepted to remain at the wheel. Hogan told whoever would listen that he would have done so, but he was shaking as badly as Woodley—not from fright, but mere fatigue—and Barfoot confirmed that he, Smith and Tacy had tossed for the privilege, and Trumbull won.

Yet the task of running the *Nonpareil* aground, the only sane course of action, was not simple. Here in the upper reaches of the river the current was far more rapid than it had been south of Cairo; the channel was narrower and more beset with every kind of obstacle from snags through sawyers to actual rocks. Moreover there were sunken hulls, relics of war and accident. The river was a cold-hearted god.

The fire below was opposite. The engineroom had been abandoned, so the pilot had no means to control the wheels; as the pressure dropped, so they turned more and more sluggishly and, instead of driving the boat, began to drag her. There remained the rudder . . . but how long until flames ate through the cables?

Using every ounce of strength, Trumbull hauled the wheel about, broadsiding the boat, forcing her toward the eastern shallows where there would be a chance for people to scramble ashore.

As he struggled, he spared time for a glance upriver and was amazed, delighted, and more than a little awed by what he saw.

No doubt of it! The *Atchafalaya* was rounding to and coming back.

"Hallelujah!" he exploded, and drove the wheel around an extra inch, and saw his effort was to be rewarded. At this angle the hull would act like the sail of a yacht; the slant of the current would generate a pull that dragged her sideways, nose toward the sanctuary of the towhead where Caesar hid. After that he had no time for thinking. He did not even manage to curse Gordon.

With the eruption of the scalded men, the band had almost scattered like everybody else. But Manuel had summed up the situation in a flash. Not for nothing had he spent his youth in a poor fishing village, where now and then a boat failed to return even on a calm night because someone had spilled the oil that fueled the lamps they hung over the bows to attract their catch, and it had caught on fire. He looked at the breadth of the water, and the way the wheels were churning randomly, and realized that jumping overside was not yet safe. In a little it would be the only recourse. But not yet!

Therefore he drove his musicians back to their station and ordered them to strike up the liveliest tune he could think of on the spur of the moment. To him it meant nothing else; he did not understand why the blackest of the players lowered their instruments and scowled at him, so he had to take half a threatening pace toward them, whistling the parts they were supposed to play. Someone had once told him how at the end of the war President Lincoln called for it from a band in Washington; if Lincoln asked for it, that was good enough for Manuel Campos.

It was *Dixie*.

Almost as though it had decided to join in the full-throated roar of the music, the fire began its rampage down below.

Licking across planking, it started to char stanchions; it ate wooden cross members like a kid chewing on a stalk of sugarcane, gnawing here, then there, until the juice turned into energy: *whump!* Gas boiled out, mingled with air, reached flash point, and the whole midships section of the *Nonpareil* was one vast blaze.

Patient upon his hasty catafalque, Miles Parbury awaited immolation. The fire spoke through the cabin floor of his impending, honorable, end.

Sight of the men pouring from the boiler room, screaming, desperate, and the gouts of steam and smoke that followed them, transfixed Josephine.

One moment ago this splendid vessel had been careering on against all odds, exceeding her best-ever speed between these high and handsome rocks and banks.

Now the Lord had shown his power beyond a peradventure.

Somewhere, some time, long long ago, she had heard a song about a demon lover, about a woman who had pledged her first-born to the devil, changed her mind, abandoned husband and baby and set sail across the sea with the one she was sworn to, lured by his lies and bribes. And then, in mid-ocean, he stood up taller than the mainmast and dismissed her and the ship to a watery grave.

To her terrified and poisoned vision, those columns of smoke, looming higher than the chimneys as the fire ran wild, took on the shape of Damballah.

When Auberon tried to calm her, she fled, shrieking mad prayers.

"Auberon!"

Turning with the stink of doom in his nostrils, he found himself confronted by the last people he would have wished to see: Hugo and Stella Spring—Stella in tears, with grime on her face—and Arthur Gattry.

Presentiments of horror assailed him; yet in the midst of them, like coal dust sodden with water on the floor of the boiler room, too wet to answer the call of the surrounding blaze, came a dull pang of recollection.

This was the man he hated for taking his sister and making her a bride.

Weariness overcame him. He forced a smile and even made to offer his hand.

"Arthur, have you news of Louisette?"

But the three of them stared as though believing him insane: to ask such a question with the boat alight beneath their feet!

"I have a gun!" roared Hugo, and turned back his coat to display it. "We must make them put us in the yawl and row ashore! I'd be there now with Stella, but that Arthur thought of you!"

He had to shout; the racket was tremendous, and in among it somewhere the band was still blasting away.

Auberon reflected for the space of a heartbeat or two, thinking about the putrefaction of his lungs, his disappointment in Cherouen, the weakness that betrayed him more and more often, the woman he had lain with on this voyage, a hundred others previous, mostly in Europe . . .

And there was so much of this planet still to see!

But it was shut off from him, not in space but time. He drew himself up and looked at Arthur squarely.

"If his solicitude had extended to my sister, I'd have been glad. Now, don't you think it's rather late?"

Contempt rang loud in every syllable. Overcome by fury, Arthur snatched the gun from Hugo's belt and leveled it.

"Come with us, damn you! If I have to go on living with your fucking sister, I daren't tell her I left you to die!"

Auberon smiled. There was something so elegantly theatrical about this resolution of their quarrel, he was no longer sorry to think it might be a final one.

"Gentlemen don't ordinarily use such language, Arthur. Perhaps you learned the word from Louisette? I taught it to her, I recall."

And waited for the answer. And it came, as he expected.

"Stop him!" Stella cried. She had read in Arthur's look what he intended. Too late.

*What trivia to occupy this crucial chunk of time.* Auberon found it amusing to think so.

For Arthur, purpling, had leveled the gun and his knuckle whitened on the trigger. It made a pretty color scheme.

The blood that burst out on his own shirt front, if anything, enhanced it. There was no pain. Just a deafening dullness in his ears, and awareness that the explosion must have outdone the rest of the fierce noise filling the air, for heads were turning on every side.

Of course, being shot to death by a drink-sodden fool was hardly his idea of a perfect end, but . . .

There was a wash of red, then black. Then nothing.

"You son of a bitch!" Hugo roared, snatching back the gun. "That was murder! And at St. Louis I'll make sure you stand your trial!"

"But—!" Arthur was almost whimpering.

"You heard me! Or I'll execute you here and now! Which do you want?"

The answer, if there was one, was drowned out. For at that moment the fire took a fresh grip on the wood below, and a cough of flame spurted up, along with such stifling fumes that speech was impossible. Gasping and groping in a maze of smoke, they fled, not knowing whither.

"We'll never make it!" Fernand exclaimed, staring through field glasses at the smoke pouring from the *Nonpareil*.

"Not if you just stand there!" Drew snarled, all his tiredness apparently forgotten. "Why don't you go rustle up some help from shore—or hurry up the boat astern?"

"What?" Confused, Fernand glanced around. "I didn't see any—"

"The *Lothair*," Tyburn said curtly, swinging the helm into another of what felt like far more bends than there had been on the way up. "Saw the green collars on her chimneys."

For the latest of uncountably many times Fernand realized just how much longer he had to serve before he could truly call himself a pilot. He had known very well that they must be due to meet the *Lothair* about now, given the schedule she was keeping between Alton and Cairo. But the knowledge had been driven from his mind by the excitement.

Perhaps one should offer this definition of a finished pilot: a man who would not allow that to happen . . .

Carrying his binoculars, he fled down the steps, looking for Gross and the mates and whatever guns and flags they might employ to make the *Lothair* hurry.

When he met Dorcas and his mother on the foredeck, he spared them scarcely a glance.

 Now the fire had taken a fatal grip on the *Nonpareil*. There would be a fair chance of retrieving her engines, boilers and piping—never again to work at such high pressure, naturally. But she was as surely doomed as a deer whose entrails had been torn out by a mountain lion.

Such thoughts, proper to clerks and mates, went through the heads of those who retained a degree of calm as Trumbull used the current to ground her in the shallows. Katzmann and Bates and their staff were having trouble with people who wanted to go back for prized possessions, who to regain a jewel would have dared the horizontal chimney of the cabin.

For that was what it had become: a vast flue laid on its side, fed not only by the woodwork of the hull and the fuel stored in the boiler room, but also by paint with a base of linseed oil, that lifted and blistered and uttered flammable vapor, and the prized carpets, and the oilcloth on the gaming tables, and eventually the liquor at the bar and the improvised catafalque.

The sound of the flames was as loud as the band's music, or the screams now swelling up on every side.

And once the clerestory shattered and let in a fresh supply of air . . .

But above, on the texas, a man scarcely more than a boy was disobeying orders and wondering whether his elders were fit to be trusted, if they could have forgotten what he remembered.

For those like Anthony Crossall they said dismissively "mud clerk," in memory of the apprentices sent down by night at swampy landings to check goods loaded or put ashore. Let them come back with their boots full of water, while their seniors joked on the safe dry deck and stood ready to deliver a cuff about the head if there were the least error in a manifest made out with a scratchy pen by the light of a windstruck lantern.

Chance, though, had brought Anthony in touch with great events, when he discovered those brown sticks under Whitworth's bed . . .

Ever since, he had been quaking inwardly. Now he was outright trembling. Captain Woodley had claimed to know all about that explosive; if that were so, why had he not sent somebody to dump it safely overboard? What about Mr. Gordon—though rumour was already rife that his name was something else—who had been equally dismissive?

And what about Mr. Whitworth, come to that? Was he on his way through the veils of smoke to collect his dangerous treasure and pitch it in the river?

But it was useless trying to talk to his superiors. He was brushed aside.

Therefore there was only one thing he could do.

Fetch it himself.

It had been open to Whitworth to dive overboard. He was a capable swimmer and knew he could make it to the bank regardless of the current hereabouts. He had no attachment to the boat or the people who owned her; seeing Gordon's investment going up in smoke informed him that his trip by rail from Memphis to Cairo would go unrewarded, for there would now be no winnings for him to take his percentage of.

But if he quit the river, what else could he earn his living by?

The string he had intended to keep to his bow was in danger of being burnt up. Fire was now greedily snatching toward the officers' quarters.

Best to reclaim the stuff, he decided. Even though the *Atchafalaya* was still intact. By rights she should have exploded long ago. Which implied that what had been sold to him as mica powder must be nothing more than a confidence trick.

Well, that wasn't so surprising when the nationally respected enterprise, Sears Roebuck & Co., could blatantly state in their catalog anent their "Trainmen's Special" that "this is a cheap trading watch, made to look like the most expensive 23-jeweled adjusted railway watch made," and boast to their customers, "If you want a very showy watch for trading purposes, there is nothing that will match this . . ."

He might as well take advantage of the example set him, reclaim what he had laid out good money for, sell it piecemeal to ignorant farmers west of St. Louis and rake together a grubstake to see him right again, taking care to move out of the area before anyone actually tried to use the fake explosive.

But he'd have to hurry. If it were even to get charred, someone with sharp eyes might realize his one remaining asset was as worthless as its failure to destroy the *Atchafalaya* had proved.

Smoke by now was curling up to the texas and all around the officers' state-rooms, and from below the sound of crackling was as loud as the engines at full blast. Anthony's mouth was cotton dry and his guts were tied in a tight knot. But now he was committed he must go on.

Eyes watering, throat smarting, he thrust open the door of Whitworth's room. There was the case with its deadly contents. He seized it with a sense of exhilaration. It wasn't heavy. He could easily pitch it overside.

And a harsh voice said, "What the hell are you doing in my room?"

Anthony gasped and almost dropped the case; a moment later it was snatched from his grasp. Tears blurring his vision, he found himself staring into the muzzle of a tiny gun.

"Thought you could safely steal while the fire distracted the rest of us, did you?" the second mate rasped.

"No, I swear it!" Anthony cried. "I only wanted to make sure that didn't explode!" He pointed at the case with a trembling finger.

"Ah, yes! You went rummaging around my room before, didn't you? And finding this stuff scared the daylights out of your lily-livered carcass, didn't it?" Whitworth's tone was savagely caressing. "Well, get the hell away from me before I plug you for a dirty little thief!"

Anthony fled and shortly could be heard coughing his guts up, having inhaled a lungful of the now dense smoke.

Whitworth, holstering his derringer, followed more slowly, judging his best course of action. He was dismayed to find that the route he had counted on following back to the lower decks was blocked; Anthony had just made it before the fumes became intolerable.

He had planned on leaving the boat by her landward side, where there was already a mass of seething bodies up to waist or chest in water, but where a dozen strides through mud led you to a firm footing and safety. The coolest of the crew, directed by Underwood and the pilots—there was no sign of Woodley right now—were helping the panic-stricken survivors, some rushing down the stages, some jumping from the main or even the boiler deck. Whitworth viewed the scene calmly. He had been present more than once before when steamers caught fire, and this was no great shakes. A burst boiler could have done infinitely more harm and very much more quickly. If worse came to worst, he could still go over the riverward side and swim ashore. It would, though, be a shame to lose what was now bound to be his mainstay for the foreseeable future.

If only it had been the *Atchafalaya* that exploded, as he'd planned—!

But there was no time to curse the man who had sweet-talked him.

He tugged a bandanna from his pocket and wrapped it around his head, bandit-fashion; it helped a little. Then he rushed along the hurricane deck, down the stairs to the boiler deck—where he heard glass shatter as the fire finally broke the clerestory windows from their frames—and was brought to a dead stop at the head of the stairs to the main deck. They themselves were not yet alight, but at their foot the white-painted planking had turned brown.

Beginning to be frightened, Whitworth glanced over his shoulder. There was no retreat to the forward stairs; so thick was the smoke, he could not have seen his way, let alone run full tilt without drawing breath in order to reach them. No, he must descend as far as possible, then jump across the burning area. Near the side there was still a zone of what looked like sound boards, and from there he could simply drop into the water.

But he must be quick. Fumes were winding up from under the guards.

He took six of the steps, two at a time, hesitated fractionally, then vaulted the stair-rail, swinging the case to lend extra momentum. And made it, clearing the patch of charred planking.

But he landed awkwardly. The case burst open. Brown tubes rolled in all directions. Many tumbled off the edge of the deck.

Uttering an oath, Whitworth scrambled to his feet, determined to salvage what he could. The heat was unbearable; gouts of flame were erupting from the cabin windows, whose glass now lay around in jagged shards.

One spike met his groping hand and made him jerk with pain, knocking the stick of mica powder he was reaching for. It rolled like its brethren, but the other way, toward the fire.

Sucking his cut finger, Whitworth—half-blind with smoke—took a step toward it.

The deck was already splitting with the heat; his weight was too much. It gaped. The explosive fell through as he struggled to regain his balance.

Next moment all the claims that Messrs. Mowbray made for their product were proved true.

 Those who were watching from the pilothouse of the *Atchafalaya,* or from elsewhere with telescopes and field glasses— they saw him lifted like a sawdust-stuffed dummy high in the air among a cascade of splintered wood, hurled clear of the *Nonpareil,* dropped with a great splash into the dull brown water.

But it was already long in the past, by the space of half a dozen heartbeats, before the noise arrived.

Under his breath Joel said, "Surely that can't have been . . ."

It was too late for wondering. Now there was crisis.

The explosion ripped away huge sections of the *Nonpareil*'s after planking, tore the side of her hull, cracked wide its bottom. Greedy and implacable, the Mississippi flooded in. As she settled, there was a hissing noise, for everything within her that was hot combined to generate a vast cloud of dirty steam among the smoke of her great burning. The last of the pressure in her boilers vanished with a spurt and a sigh, and she blurred into a shabby wreck stuck in the mud like any rotten hulk mishandled by an ill-taught cub.

Only in the cabin did the flames roar on, enfolding in a shroud of orange glory the cadaver of Miles Parbury, who had fought against such odds as heroes dream of.

Then the superstructure folded down, and the pilothouse collapsed into the cabin, and her boastful silken banner crisped and flared, and the *Nonpareil* was dead as her designer.

Until absolutely the latest possible moment, driven by his suspicion that these gringos did not believe anyone who spoke Spanish—let alone persons of color like his musicians—could act bravely, Manuel had kept the band playing at its loudest, partly by threat, partly by example.

But with the roar of the explosion he broke off in mid-bar and yelled, "*¡Vamos!*"

They tumbled headlong into the water, and he followed.

For a second, as he floundered with his nose below the surface, he imagined he and they were done for. Then he found a slippery footing, and was able to stand up and wade ashore. Still over knees in the river, he crossed himself and muttered a prayer of thanks, then turned and looked at the wreck. It burned so fiercely, he had to shield his face against the heat.

Awe overcame him, who had known of so many lost at sea. The grandeur of death by storm paled beside this, the doom of fire. And what was one fishing boat compared with a great steamer like the *Nonpareil*?

Then, magically, the banks and the water teemed with help. From nowhere appeared ragged men and women with ropes and poles, while from both up- and downstream came rowboats with men leaning frantically on their oars, sailboats with their skippers cursing that there wasn't better wind, and—above all—the *Atchafalaya* at full speed in the deep channel. Those who had damned her yesterday now cheered as she swung broadside and drew close, casting out barrels and crates and anything that might float long enough to save a life. In the distance, too, the *Lothair* loomed.

Awed, Gaston watched from the foredeck. Never in his life had he been present at such a drama! He ached to be of practical assistance, but everything seemed so amazingly organized and controlled, even though there were people screaming in agony. Those more fortunate were coming to the victims' aid as though they had been rehearsed, guiding them step by step toward dry land.

And— Why, that was surely Gordon he could see, knee-deep in mud, half his beard burned away! And wasn't that Captain Woodley, waving like a madman, shouting something that nobody was paying the least attention to? And . . .

A sudden gleam caught his eye. As the *Atchafalaya* rounded to, he spotted an arm upholding something shiny and metallic.

A saxhorn. He would have recognized it anywhere, even though he felt as though he were a million miles from everything he had known in his superficial world of hotels and theaters and dance halls; he might as well have been on a different planet.

Before he could check himself, he was running. They were lowering a swinging stage from the *Atchafalaya*'s bow; he was the first to rush down it, elbowing aside those who would have preceded him, and—forgetful of his clothes and boots and life itself in the heat of the moment—plunged into the filthy water. Discarding his coat as he struggled on toward the gleaming instrument, he felt himself caught by the arm and would have shaken off the grip but that he recognized Manuel, bent on the same errand.

For a long second they stood frozen; then Manuel grinned and clapped him on the shoulder, and they set out together to retrieve what they could of the *Nonpareil*'s band. Thanks to Manuel's promptness, they were all alive, though some were sick from swallowing river water and some half-choked by smoke and some deprived of their instruments; the fiddles and banjoes were ruined.

Nonetheless the brass survived: trumpets, trombone, baritone horn, tuba . . . And there was at least one clarinet that would be playable again.

Assembling the frightened, cursing, miserable musicians on dry land, Gaston felt a surge of triumph.

But when he glanced back, he saw that others had not been so lucky.

Grave, slow-moving, crewmen and anonymous strangers were laying out on the bank corpse, after corpse, after corpse . . .

And who could tell, as yet, how many had been trapped and burned—perhaps alive?

Overwhelmed, Gaston grew aware that beside him Manuel was mechanically moving his hands. At first he thought he might be pantomiming the patterns of an instrument, but then he realized he was holding a nonexistent broad-brimmed hat, turning it around and around.

How often had he seen men stand that way at funerals? And it had been a funeral he was rushing to St. Louis to attend . . .

Inspiration dawned. He spoke in soft but urgent tones. It was a while before his French-English and the Mexican's Spanish-English coincided; when they did, Manuel's eyes lit up, and together they turned back to the musicians.

An hour or so later, they were able to scramble aboard the *Atchafalaya*.

 For Denis Cherouen it all became too much in the moment when he saw Walt Presslie with his shoulder swathed in pus-soaked bandages, halfway to delirium through septicemia, nonetheless struggling out on deck at news of the disaster to see if he could help.

But visions of an endless stream of burned and blighted patients, like a renewal of the war, were already obsessing the Electric Doctor. Why did it have to be this way? Why could not some magic touch from on high make everybody whole and handsome? Why could not his miraculous cures be worked on all mankind, ridding the world of ulcers and cancers and infected wounds and lungs rotten with TB and genitals foul with gonorrhea and eyelids crusted shut with matter and decaying gums and aching teeth and all the rest? And what malevolent deity had doomed the *Nonpareil*, which he could so easily have been aboard?

And which Josephine *had* been on, his right arm since his army days.

It was unbearable. He turned blindly back into the cabin. There was no tender at the bar, nor a waiter or steward to be seen. All had turned out to aid the *Atchafalaya*'s stricken rival.

For a moment he was set to shout with rage; he changed his mind and went behind the bar and found a glass and tipped it full of whiskey. Gulping it down made him feel better. He did it again.

When he was found, much later, he was lying across the bar in a pool of vomit. Those who were ordered to drag him away spat on him before they did so.

They had been expecting him to help the hurt.

\*     \*     \*

Eulalie Lamenthe was in her element. Healing she understood, and desired skill in it more than the power which came with Athalie's inheritance; perhaps, she later reasoned, that was why Damballah spared her the fate he had reserved for Josephine. She confiscated sheets and towels and set the laundresses to tearing bandages; she commandeered grease from the kitchen by way of salve; she found cord to bind the limbs that leaked the lifeblood of the injured. Men gazed on her with astonishment, for she was beautiful: a tyrant on the instant, but such a woman as no man would dare defy.

The sight of her ablaze with energy made Fernand choke on his own emotions, resolving to remeet her when the trip was done and try to preserve this new and admirable version of his mother. But there was someone who must claim his prior attention; where was Dorcas?

He found her at the after end of the cabin, weeping while Cherouen was boozing at the bar.

Regretting the obligation when he was needed on deck, Fernand spared time to comfort her, and shortly forced her to admit why she was so upset.

Eulalie had taught her that a child in the womb could be affected by what its mother saw, and adduced as a case in point the newspaper reports she had seen about some woman in danger of losing her baby being carried ashore from the *Nonpareil*—whose husband, moreover, had cruelly ignored her plight. For such an infant Eulalie predicted a disastrous fate.

So Dorcas was afraid to look at the victims, let alone help them, for fear her offspring might be born deformed.

A chill ran down Fernand's spine. He too had been told that story, ever since childhood, and the way he was currently feeling about his mother, he was inclined to credit it.

But that was for the future; there were present screams ringing in his ears. So he steeled himself and summoned a black laundress who much resented being ordered to keep Dorcas company but obeyed because all the colored people on the river admired and respected the first colored pilot.

And went outside again, to a vision of hell.


Hung over most abominably, so that in paradoxical fashion the cool water in which he was wading up to his waist, and sometimes his shoulders, was comforting, Arthur struggled to drag one victim after another up on shore. He was weeping as he drove himself on. The shock of having the boat blow up had terrified him; his alcohol-dazed conscience, revived yesterday but successfully repressed, had been blasted into full life . . . or at least he had been reminded of mortality.

All the more when the third of the victims he helped to rescue gave a gasp, and a quiver, and was abruptly dead.

He glanced around for someone else to aid, and remembered with horror that at best these efforts of his were only an act of penitence, for he would not find Auberon alive.

At the edge of consciousness a rational idea fought to claim attention: he could slip away into those concealing trees, he could forget himself and his identity, he could adopt an alias and escape the consequences of his deeds—leave behind his wife, and his baby if it had survived, and head westward, never again to see the Springs who had promised they would have him put on trial for murder . . .

There was such chaos around the wreck of the *Nonpareil*, it would not be hard to evade attention. By now the bank resembled a casualty station during the war, and because both the *Atchafalaya* and the *Lothair* were in earshot there was a distracting racket. Like a mutinous slave, he could have cut and run.

But, while he was still struggling in a post-alcoholic fog, he heard his name called. He turned. There was Hugo, soaked from head to foot, bearing a great blue bruise across one cheek. All else forgotten, he shouted, "Have you seen Stella? The blast knocked me over! I don't know what became of her!"

It occurred to Arthur that if he rescued his friend's wife, Hugo might perhaps not bear witness in a court of law about his shooting of Auberon.

He was still sufficiently frightened of him, though, to look away reflexively across the river. The *Atchafalaya* was dealing with those who had managed to read the bank; the *Lothair* had gone past and was now rounding to and dropping a kedge to steady her in the channel without using her wheels, for there was much floating debris and some of it was people. One indistinct object was the same color as the dress Stella had been wearing.

Everything else banished from his mind but the slender chance of evading prosecution, Arthur struck out after it, heedless of the cries that followed him.

But the current was strong, and when he discovered it was only a bale of cloth after all, he looked around, and realized he had swum beyond his power to return, and though he shouted and cursed and shed his clothes and did his utmost, he was exhausted before the *Lothair*'s yawl could reach him, and sank at last to become the newest of the Mississippi's countless human offerings. When his lungs were full with water, it no longer seemed to matter that his bets, which he had banked on to make a fortune and finance his family, had been lost with the *Nonpareil*.

Aboard the *Atchafalaya* Barber, who was also much concerned with winning bets, fumed and fretted and swore vengeance on Drew, until he realized that even Jones and Cuffy were looking askance on him. He forced himself to calm down; then he began to think about the capital to be made out of the publicity which would surely follow the *Atchafalaya*'s errand of mercy. Little by little he began to feel cheerful again.

He said, "Jones, do you think that if I conceded my half of the *Atchafalaya* to Drew anyhow, it might be a gesture people would appreciate?"

And Jones glanced at Cuffy, and the latter said wearily, "Boss, you have to ask?"

Whereupon both turned away to gaze toward the ruin of the *Nonpareil*, and Barber felt the blood rush hot into his cheeks.

In consequence he decided to make his decision about his wagers, especially the one with Drew, public as soon as they arrived at St. Louis . . . and to as many reporters as possible, in the hope that their papers would then offer favorable advertising rates for the Limousin. The *Intelligencer* certainly ought to!

Though he was sorry now he had admitted his touch of Africa to Joel.

It would be impolitic to let, for instance, Cuffy try to treat him as an equal.

 How right Dorcas had been to want to shut herself away from these horrors! They were such as Fernand had only been told about, by veterans of the war: there was a man limping along with a great burnt patch on the left leg of his pants—and on the skin below; there was another retching and moaning for some invisible injury, who clutched his ribs every time he tried to draw breath; yonder was another with his head wrapped in a scarlet mask from a scalp wound, asking weakly whether he was blind, for blood had run down and filled his eyes . . .

But ever and again he found himself glancing toward the saddest victim of this tragedy: the *Nonpareil*.

She smoldered in the shallows like a ghastly parody of some seabeast's skeleton, the frames of her wheels disposed on either side of her carcass-like fin bones, her boilers, piping and engines, ash-encrusted, revealed like that beast's vital organs to a harsh and pitiless sky. Some smoke was still rising, but only where her pilot-house had foundered, adding a last supply of fuel to the blaze.

Fernand looked about him for someone who might share his emotion at the sight of this grand vessel's fate, and recognized Joel gazing toward her and muttering, "Obe! My cousin, my best friend! Obe, where are you?"

Fernand put his arm around the reporter.

"Maybe he'll be among the next batch to come on board," he whispered. "Let's look out for him."

Shiny-eyed, Joel glanced at his comforter. "Yes," he said in a thick voice. "Yes, that's a fine idea. I guess."

Now here came Gordon almost unrecognizable, cursing those who had built the *Nonpareil*, who had done precisely what they were told and paid to do, no more, no less; and after him, bemoaning the fact that because the steamer had been racing there would not even be any payment from the insurers: Woodley. Out of habit other casualties from his steamer made way for him. Out of habit he did not thank them.

At Fernand's side a voice said softly, "The paths of glory lead but to the grave . . . but this is no time for recriminations, is it?"

Having left the pilothouse in care of Tyburn, here was Drew, cap square on head, carriage erect, the conscious victor of a race that now could never be decided. Advancing toward Woodley, he held out his hand.

"Captain!" he exclaimed. "I know and you know—either of us would gladly have lost our match, rather than lose a splendid boat like yours! Come aboard! We'll dress your wounds and put a stateroom at your disposal!"

It was a magnificent gesture, and two or three who stood around began to clap.

But of a sudden Gordon caught at his companion's arm, eyes wide and wild, and whispered something in his ear. Woodley blanched and they both incontinently turned tail, striving to push past those who were wearily dragging up the stage.

"What the hell is biting on those two?" Drew rasped.

"I can tell you," Joel said, pale-faced, producing his pocket safe. Striding after the pair, who were making no headway, he caught Woodley's arm.

"Captain! Why are you so determined to get away from the *Atchafalaya?*"

Visibly in shock, his forehead pearled with sweat, Woodley hesitated, then muttered, "Damned if I'll take the hospitality of a traitor like Drew!"

Gordon was paying no attention; like a maddened beast he was trying to claw his way back to shore. At a nod from Drew, Sexton stepped forward to restrain him.

"I don't believe you!" Joel declared. "It's because you think she's going to explode! Well, she's not! I found Whitworth's stick of mica powder and I emptied it and threw the stuff away except for this bit here, which is enough evidence to hang you, and Gordon too! Stateroom? *Stateroom?*" He rounded on Drew. "You'd do better to put 'em in handcuffs!"

There was a long dead pause. Even the moaning of the injured seemed to recede to a great distance, while Gordon and Woodley stood statue still, guilt eloquent in every line of their posture.

Finally Drew heaved a sigh.

"I would not have wished it to end like this," he muttered. "But you're right, Mr. Siskin. Not for what they tried to do to me, but the threat they posed to my passengers and crew, we must arrest them. Mr. Chalker, bring sufficient rope."

"I don't know what you're talking about!" Woodley cried hysterically. "It was all Whitworth's idea—"

Abruptly and horribly aware of what had escaped him, he bit down on his lower lip so hard he made it bleed.

In a little while they were led away, and Joel said to Fernand privately, "Was it not Whitworth who . . . ?"

"Got blown overboard? I think so. I had my glasses trained, but of course it was so quick. . . . Oh, never mind. We still haven't found your cousin, have we?"

So they resumed their tour of the *Atchafalaya*'s decks, littered now with the injured and the dying. Smoke from the *Nonpareil* was blowing this way, carrying with it sparks like the disease germs Cherouen was so contemptuous of. They were promptly stamped out by people less incredulous about infection. By this time—and Fernand marveled to see it—the river was aswarm, not only with the rowboats and sailboats, which had been quickest on the scene, but with steam launches too, while the *Lothair* must have beaten her own best time by a tremendous margin, to be here already!

Where had so many people, so many vessels, come from so swiftly?

And then it occurred to him to consult his watch, and he realized it was no miracle after all. It was almost two hours since the fire began, and time had melted like ice in sunshine.

With the realization came awareness of how tired he was; he ached in every limb and joint and he could scarcely feel his feet. But the task was not yet over. Following the distraught Joel, he located the *Nonpareil's* pilots: Hogan, with a broken arm; Tacy, with severe burns; Barfoot, with a burned leg and many abrasions; Smith, with a hand that was one great blister, like a boxing glove; and Trumbull who had suffered countless cuts and bruises but was able to grin and say they had got off lightly.

When, a few minutes later, Fernand reported to Drew that all five of them had been on the opposite side of the *Nonpareil* from the explosion, and though all hurt were all alive, the captain heaved a deep sigh.

"You know," he said meditatively, "I have had a family after all—two families, in fact. I guess I'm stuck with those nephews of mine in the regular way of kinship, but there ain't a one among 'em I'd exchange for you, or any goddamned pilot on this river. They're like a bunch of cousins; now and then they—*we* fight, but when push comes to shove . . ."

He clapped Fernand on the shoulder, shaking his head, and concluded: "Ain't it crazy, though, that kinfolk should come most to know each other at funerals?"

"It's the way of the world," said Fernand. "It was at a funeral I first came to know myself."

From the very stern there resounded yet again Joel's despairing cry: "*Where's Auberon?*"

It was the last time. After that, dejectedly, he resumed his professional duties, listing the quick and the dead.

With all her pilots injured and her captain and her co-owner facing criminal charges, seniority among the survivors from the *Nonpareil* devolved on her chief clerk. His deputy Sam Iliff had sprained a knee in jumping overboard; more cautious, McNab had made a decorous descent of the stage and was well clear of the explosion. Relieved, he went about the *Atchafalaya* in search of those he needed to account for and found Anthony, still coughing from the smoke but otherwise intact. From Roy and Steeples, both of whom were scalded but would live, he heard about the death of Corkran, and doffed his hat for a moment before continuing his mission. Katzmann and Bates had been aft, and hurt by the explosion, but survived. There was no sign, though, of Burge, and eventually they were forced to conclude he too had not escaped.

Possibly his body was among the last to be brought on board. McNab headed for the foredeck.

And, as he approached, was amazed to hear music.

The last thing those of Manuel's bandsmen who had salvaged their instruments wanted to do when they were brought aboard, shivering, was start playing again. But Vehm had been prodigal with liquor from the *Atchafalaya's* bar, distributing brandy and whiskey by the cupful. A dose of that made the world seem less detestable.

And Gaston's head was ringing with the solemn strains he had planned for the Grammont funeral. What it had taken to bring them into focus was this tragedy. With half his mind he was appalled at himself for capitalizing on disaster; with the rest, he welcomed the chance to hear what until now had been locked away in his imagination.

It was of course a far cry from the full score he was trying to work out, but he was amazed how quickly these bedraggled, untutored men picked up the parts he hummed over to them. He had never worked like this before, by ear alone, but within minutes he was ready to concede that it was faster than drilling the musicians at the Grand Philharmonic Hall through careful arrangements which half of them could not read anyway. This group seemed actually to be listening to what they were playing, and instead of dropping out when they came to a difficult passage, making the texture thin and sterile, took the trouble to fill out the harmonies—perhaps not always with academic precision, but nonetheless with innate feeling for a proper chordal progression.

Why had it taken a catastrophe to enlighten him concerning the talents of these people? They did not even need a rehearsal! The first time he signaled them to strike up, they played what they had been shown, near to note perfect!

Embarrassed, for he was standing where he knew Manuel had stood before, conducting them, he glanced around. And there was the little Mexican, grinning like a cat under his drooping moustache.

"Needs more trumpet!" he declared, and went to snatch one from the hands of a player who was too overcome by the experience he had undergone to keep his part.

"Yes, but you should be directing your own orchestra—"

A dismissive wave: "Ah, you are *composer,* sir! I'm only man who knows how to blow through here! Can't even read the dots and lines. Maybe one day you teach me, *'stà bueno?* Right now we make grand sad music for the souls that went away."

And, setting the trumpet to his lips, took his place in the front row, waiting for Gaston to premiere what later became the adagio section of his *Mississippi Suite,* a development of the preceding rubato entitled "The Steamboat Explosion."

It emerged somber and majestic, and those in earshot removed their hats and stood to attention, as though listening to a national anthem.

Abruptly Gaston realized he could no longer see, but only hear, because his eyes were brimming full of tears.

"You may pull clear of the shore, Mr. Tyburn," said Drew formally, having surveyed the bank and shallows with his glasses. "There's nothing left for us to do here. Now we must get those poor devils to a hospital, and if they don't make it, to a decent burial. Full speed ahead."

 All this Caesar had witnessed at a distance, hiding among the new saplings where he had found refuge. His face and guts alike twisted by bitterness at the way he had been treated, he thought at first only of how right he had been to run away. He sat, hunkered

down behind a screen of branches, and with grim satisfaction watched as the *Nonpareil* caught fire and finally blew up. The river began to carry down traces of the wreck: first scraps of wood, then human beings. He saw one—two—three go by. They were already dead. He let them be.

Then there was a disturbance among the bushes, and he heard moans. Reluctantly he roused himself, recognizing what he had often heard during the war. Here was somebody lost and panicking, careless of whether it was friend or enemy who found him.

Limping, he made his way to cross the other's blundering path, and discovered it was Matthew.

Who, on being checked in his flight, looked up and all of a sudden shifted from shouting to sobbing.

Hysteria. Caesar had been taught to deal with that, and slapped his face on either cheek.

Startled out of his blind terror, Matthew gulped and said inanely, "If he isn't dead he's bound to kill me."

"What? Who?"

"Gordon! Except he isn't Gordon! Damn it"—this with swelling pride, the pride of a child who has learned an adult term and used it right—"knowing that helped me to save your life, didn't it?"

Caesar said slowly, "I was kind of thinking of other things at the time. Tell me again."

"He isn't Hamish Gordon! He's a swindler from Scotland called Macrae! He tricked hundreds of people into paying for shares in a forest that didn't belong to him, including Mr. Moyne, Mr. Auberon's father! And I wanted him to pay me a thousand dollars to keep my mouth shut, and that was blackmail, and that's why the boat blew up! It was divine retribution, that's what it was!"

*Black . . . mail?*

Suddenly Caesar was sick of this world, especially its rich inhabitants who could do terrible things without worrying about how they affected the less fortunate. He took Matthew's arm, discovering as he did so that the boy was hurt; by the way he cringed, he had a broken collarbone.

"This way," he sighed. "There are enough boats on the river for us to get rescued pretty soon."

But at the water's edge there was a new companion for him.

Bobbing gently in the ripples, her stern and handsome features deformed by a violent blow, her short black hair burned off, kept afloat by air trapped in her dress, was the maker of his trickenbag, the devotee of Damballah whom her master had not intervened to save despite her performance of a grand and dreadful ritual in his service. Had her charm still hung around his neck, at that moment Caesar would have cast it in the river, because that was far fitter to be worshiped: the wide, the long, the awesome Mississippi.

To whom even unbelievers must make sacrifice.

He said eventually to Matthew, "We'll go find that reporter guy, tell him the whole story about Gordon. Tell about how they skimped on the boilers and the piping for the *Nonpareil*, how that son of a bitch ordered engineers who should have known better to raise the pressure past what she could stand. We'll see him put on trial and sent to jail. Now you wait here; I'll go find somebody to take us off."

He hobbled into the shallows, doffing his shirt to wave it like a flag. On the way he spurned the body of Josephine Var, and it came loose from the tree root it was snagged on and drifted back toward midstream. Caesar paid it no more mind.

For it had come to him what everybody must rely on. No charms, no tricken-bags, no church services or conjuration—nothing but commitment to oneself.

In a little while an old man in a rowboat came to collect them, but by then the *Atchafalaya* was under way, and it was too late to catch her, or the *Lothair*.

Never mind.

## 4TH JULY 1870

# NO BAD SYMBOL

~~~~

"In *Evangeline* Caroline Norton read
the strange-sounding Atchafalaya, the
river where the lovers failed in their
meeting. She had it cut upon a seal,
and later found that the King of the
Belgians had been equally impressed
by the same word. Neither knew the
meaning, but for once the romantic
instinct was right; 'long river' is no
bad symbol for destiny."
—George R. Stewart,
*Names on the Land*

This therefore was the manner of the coming of the steamer *Atchafalaya* to St. Louis half a day past what all expected to be the time of her great triumph: dead bodies on her decks and those who cried for death as merciful release from pain; shaken and shattered victims of disaster, and others who, though far more fortunate, had vowed they would not so tempt fate again; and a scratch band playing elegiac music.

And while they canceled the dinners and receptions and the firework shows, and those who had thought to win huge sums by backing her subsided into petty argument about whether or not their bets must stand, and all the flags in sight were lowered to half-mast . . .

Drew sobered Denis Cherouen with coffee and sent him and his machines ashore posthaste; the younger Grammont child died shortly after.

Whereat the captain felt profoundly grateful that his dear one had escaped such ministrations.

And also that his protégé Fernand was tough and vital and had proved his fitness with a pretty girl he planned to marry. Such matters smacked of the reality of the river: not barred and circumscribed by human law, but natural. Had he been so free in his mind, then with Susannah . . .

Too late. All his life he felt he'd been too late. And now most of all. For he would have given anything—the share of his own boat which Barber now so *generously* conceded him, before an audience of reporters and businessmen, or a limb, or as much of his heart as Susannah had left him—to have made friends with that stern, solitary, and amazing man who had outrun him without eyesight through the fog.

Too late. Too late. Too late . . .

Wearily, once the casualties had been borne ashore, those who had endured this voyage descended the stage, Fernand with his wife and mother on either arm, the captain last despite the conspicuous impatience of Elphin who waited on the wharf. What need was there for hurry now? Meantime the band repeated the most stirring strain of that music which tomorrow would be heard in the cathedral.

There were not as many steamers at this wharf as last year; half as many as ten years ago. Next year there would be fewer still. Not only this last race, but a whole epoch, was at its close.

Out of sight, save for its plume of smoke and steam, a railroad locomotive uttered the shriek that warned of the departure of a train.

# AFTERWORD & ACKNOWLEDGMENTS

Strictly, you know, this is not a historical novel. It's an example of what science fiction people call a retrospective parallel world. There were of course no such steamers as the *Atchafalaya* and the *Nonpareil,* any more than there were real captains called Parbury, Drew, and Woodley, or pilots called Tyburn or Lamenthe . . .

Nor is the river up which my race is run the Mississippi of 1870. It's rather that of ten years earlier, for no better reason than that in 1861 Schönberg & Company, New York, published a chart of its colossal length "as seen from the hurricane deck," and I laid hands on a copy of it.

But there was a race, and a memorable one, over just that Independence Day weekend in 1870 which I chose for my book. It was between the *Natchez* and the *Robert E. Lee.*

The problem was—to my mind—that that race started over nothing nobler than a quarrel about freight charges; the opposing captains had come to blows in a bar. Worse still, from a dramatic standpoint, the boat that seized the lead on departure held it all the way, and for the last two days the rivals were not even in sight of one another.

Something obviously had to be done about *that.*

During the five years of my struggle with this project, I received help from too many sources for me to be able to list them all. But I must express my particular gratitude to the staff of The New York Public Library at Fifth Avenue and Forty-second Street; to Bob Carr of International House, New Orleans, thanks to whose good offices I spent the Bicentennial weekend, 1976, riding the towboat *John D. Geary* from New Orleans to Memphis, Tennessee; to Captain Loyd Arnold and pilot Bill Lanier and the rest of the *Geary's* officers and crew, and to her owners, who granted permission for me to travel on her; to Captain Tate of Memphis, one of the few remaining pilots to hold a paddlewheeler license; to Norbury L. Wayman of St. Louis; and to David Drake, now of Chapel Hill, North Carolina, but formerly of the riverside cities Clinton and Dubuque, Iowa, whose counsel and assistance proved invaluable.

# REFERENCES AND BIBLIOGRAPHY

Among the publications I drew on most were the following:

Asher and Adams. *Pictorial Album of American Industry 1876*. New York: Rutledge Books (facsimile reprint), 1976.
My Dr. Cherouen is largely modeled on the Dr. Blood who advertised herein his panacea, oxygenated air.

Barkhau, Roy L. *The Great Steamboat Race Between the Natchez and the Rob't E. Lee*. Cincinnati: Steamship Historical Society of America, 1972.
A brief popular account.

Benét, Stephen Vincent. *John Brown's Body*. Garden City, NY: Doubleday, Doran, 1928.
Arguably the finest long narrative poem published this century; certainly the best Civil War novel in verse or prose.

Blassingame, John W. *Black New Orleans 1860–1880*. University of Chicago Press: Phoenix Books, 1976.
Immensely useful, not only for first-hand reactions to the Civil War and the "alternative religion" centering on, for example, Dr. John and Marie Laveau, but in particular for details of black and Creole economic enterprise.

Corps of Engineers, US Army. *Flood Control and Navigation Maps of the Mississippi River, Cairo, Illinois, to the Gulf of Mexico*. (Forty-third edition, 1975).

*Delta Queen Cruise Handbook*. New Orleans, 1976.
An exercise book for students aboard "the last packet boat on the western rivers" (Norbury L. Wayman).

Evans, I.O. *Flags*. London: Hamlyn, 1970.

Gardners Directory for 1863. *New Plan of the City and Environs of New Orleans* (photographic copy). New Orleans: Louisiana State Museum, 1976.

*Harper's Atlas of American History with Map Studies by Dixon Ryan Fox, Ph.D.* New York and London: Harper, 1920.

Harris, Joel Chandler. *Uncle Remus or Mr. Fox, Mr. Rabbit and Mr. Terrapin*. London: George Routledge, n.d.
This is my childhood copy, which I was given when I was about seven. I have of course made no attempt to imitate the dialects Harris transcribed from firsthand experience; some of the attitudes reflected in his ancillary matter, however, I found especially enlightening.

Hechtlinger, Adelaide. *The Great Patent Medicine Era or Without Benefit of Doctor*. New York: Galahad Books, by arrangement with Grosset & Dunlap, 1970.
A scrapbook that confirmed my impression that, if most of the people I was

going to write about were by our standards half-crazy, it was largely owing to the drugs prescribed for them by professional as well as amateur doctors.

Huber, Leonard V. *Advertisements of Lower Mississippi River Steamboats 1812–1920*. West Barrington, Rhode Island: Steamship Historical Society of America, 1959.
Includes a few contemporary descriptions of steamboats and reports of steamboat disasters.

Hunter, Louis C., with Beatrice Jones Hunter. *Steamboats on the Western Rivers, an Economic and Technological History*. New York: Octagon Books, 1969.
A monumental academic study of the subject, a basic text for anybody investigating the field.

Jones, Maldwyn A. *Destination America*. London: Weidenfeld & Nicolson, 1976.
A comprehensive survey of "the immigrant experience."

Jones, Michael Wynn. *The World 100 Years Ago*. Book Club Associates, by arrangement with Macmillan London Ltd., 1976.
A useful general work including a picture of Canal Street, New Orleans, in 1870 and many contemporary descriptions of the city.

Levine, Lawrence W. *Black Culture and Black Consciousness, Afro-American Folk Thought from Slavery to Freedom*. New York: Oxford University Press, 1977.
Especially good on contemporary black attitudes, beliefs and behavior; also useful for folk religion and folk medicine.

Life Nature Library. *The Land and Wild Life of North America*. Time-Life International (Nederland) NV, 1968.
Details of flora and fauna along the Mississippi.

*Life Pictorial Atlas of the World*. New York: Time, Inc., 1961.

Lomax, Alan. *Mister Jelly Roll*. London: Cassell, 1952.
Biography of the jazz pianist after whom I named Fernand Lamenthe, and after whose godmother I named Eulalie; right up to his death in the 1940's he believed in the power of the alternative religion, as some still do today.

*Muir's Historical Atlas, Ancient, Medieval and Modern*. Book Club Associates by arrangement with George Philip & Son Ltd., London, 1973.

*New Orleans Magazine*. Bicentennial issue, July 1976.
Includes a history of local architecture and some details of paved and unpaved streets around 1870.

*Punch*, vols. LVI–LIX (1869–70).
Source, *inter alia*, of the datum that in 1869 fashionable New York ladies were eating arsenic to lighten the complexion . . . a habit that, incredible though it may seem, was also vouched for in a BBC television play on 3rd July 1980!

Queensbury Group, The. *The Book of Key Facts*. New York: Ballantine, 1979.

*Robert Bain's The Clans and Tartans of Scotland, Enlarged and Re-edited by Margaret O. MacDougall*. London & Glasgow: William Collins, 1964.

Robertson, Patrick. *The Shell Book of Firsts*. Book Club Associates by arrangement with Ebury Press and Michael Joseph Ltd., 1975.

Saved me, on more than one occasion, from including something that hadn't been invented yet. . . .

Sabin, Edwin L. *Wild Men of the Wild West*. New York: Thomas Y. Crowell, 1929.
A somewhat sensational work that nonetheless enabled me to correct a few suspect statements in other books I was referring to.

Sandburg, Carl. *The American Songbag*. New York: Harcourt, Brace, 1927.
"Stars a-Shining" *(By'm By)* is in this collection.

Schönberg & Co. *The Mississippi (Alton to the Gulf of Mexico) As Seen from the Hurricane Deck*. New York, 1861; photostat copy, NY Public Library, 1976.
It claims "Constructed from Reliable Sources," but I found it contradicted by a lot of my other authorities, most notably Mark Twain.

Schroeder Jr., Joseph J., ed. *Sears, Roebuck & Co. 1908 Catalogue No. 117, The Great Price Maker*. Northfield, Illinois: DBI Books, 1971.
A facsimile selection that gives chapter and verse for the reprehensible trading practices Harry Whitworth imagined he had fallen foul of but intended to emulate—a little out of time, but never mind.

Shenton, James, ed. *Free Enterprise Forever! Scientific American in the 19th Century*. New York: Images Graphiques, 1977.

Stampp, Kenneth M. *The Era of Reconstruction, 1865–1877*. New York: Vintage Books, by arrangement with Alfred A. Knopf, 1965.
A wholesome corrective to the common view of the postbellum period as an epoch of nothing but corruption and carpetbaggers.

Stewart, George R. *Names on the Land*. New York: Armed Services Edition by arrangement with Random House, 1945.
A history of American place-naming by the author of that greatest of all science fiction novels, *Earth Abides*.

*Times Atlas of World History, The*. London: Book Club Associates, by arrangement with Times Books Ltd., 1978.

Twain, Mark (Samuel Langhorne Clemens). *Life on the Mississippi*. New York: Signet, 1961.
*The* indispensable source for information concerning the training of a Mississippi pilot's cub, from which I confess I stole by wholesale.

Vries, Leonard de, with Ilonka van Amstel. *Victorian Inventions*. London: John Murray, 1971.
As corrective on the technical side as Stampp's on the social and political, though mistitled, since it begins its coverage in 1865, not 1837.

Ward, Ralph T. *Steamboats, a History of the Early Adventure*. Indianapolis and New York: Bobbs-Merrill, 1973.
Kindly sent to me by my editor at Ballantine Books, Judy-Lynn del Rey.

Wayman, Norbury L. *Life on the River, a Pictorial History of the Mississippi, the Missouri, and the Western River System*. New York: Bonanza Books, by arrangement with Crown Publishers, 1971.
Uniquely useful for details of boatyards and wharves, although its alleged picture of the pioneering *New Orleans* of 1812 does lead one to wonder how many

more of its 900-odd illustrations may be wrongly captioned.

Wellman, Manly Wade. *Fastest on the River*. New York: Holt, 1957.
The definitive account of the race between the *Natchez* and the *Lee,* but wrong by two full hours at Baton Rouge.

Wilson, Everett B. *Early America at Work, a Pictorial Guide to our Vanishing Occupations*. Cranbury, New Jersey: A. S. Barnes, 1963.
A superficial and trivial book whose numerous illustrations somewhat redeem its puerile text.

Wykes, Alan. *Gambling*. London: Spring Books/Aldus Books, 1964.
Extensive data on the gambling fever that swept the United States after the Civil War.

## ABOUT THE AUTHOR

John Brunner was born in England in 1934 and educated at Cheltenham College. He sold his first novel in 1951 and has been publishing sf steadily since then. His books have won him international acclaim from both mainstream and genre audiences. His most famous novel, the classic *Stand On Zanzibar*, won the Hugo Award for Best Novel in 1969, the British Science Fiction Award, and the Prix Apollo in France. Mr. Brunner lives in Somerset, England.